ALSO BY THOMAS TRYON

In the Fire of Spring

In the Fire of Spring

THOMAS TRYON

Alfred A. Knopf

NEW YORK

1992

THIS IS A BORZOI BOOK
PUBLISHED BY ALFRED A. KNOPF, INC.

Copyright © 1992 by The Estate of Thomas Tryon
Endpaper map copyright © 1992 by Philip Lohman

Library of Congress Cataloging-in-Publication Data

Tryon, Thomas.
In the fire of spring / Thomas Tryon. — 1st ed.
p.   cm.
ISBN 0-394-58588-7
I. Title.
PS3570.R9B9   1992
813'.54—dc20   91-414
CIP

Manufactured in the United States of America

First Edition

For my family

Everywhere man blames nature and fate, yet his fate is mostly but the echo of his character and passions, his mistakes and weaknesses.

—DEMOCRITUS

Contents

Principal Characters

For the two families were implacable enemies, they clashed like brazen cymbals; the Wars of the Roses had not set York against Lancaster with more futile hatred than Grimes warred on Talcott and Talcott on Grimes.

> —*From the prologue to* The Wings of the Morning

The Talcotts

Old Bobby, family patriarch
Appleton, his eldest son; proprietor of Kingdom Come
Mabel ("Mab," née Riley), Appleton's wife
Appleton's children:
    Electra, abolitionist; wife of Lloyd Warburton
    Priam, head of the Talcott, Lane Assurance Company; married to Peggy;
        father of Lane, Robert, Katie, Susan
    Agrippina, spinster
    Aurora, Lady Henry Sheffield; mother of Caroline (Caro)
    Minerva, wife of Leland Peckham; mother of Appleton, Guilford, John
        Quincy, Elizabeth (Betsy), Sophy
    Hector, army officer
    Achilles, Hector's twin; also an army officer
    Persephone ("Posie")
Jack, Appleton's "lawyer" brother
James, youngest of Old Bobby's sons; manages Talcott homestead,
    Follybrook Farm; married to Susie; father of James, Jr.
Great-Aunt Blanche (née Poindexter), Old Bobby's sister-in-law
Aunt Matilda and Aunt Bettina, Old Bobby's sisters

The Grimeses

Abednego, family patriarch
Rachel (née Saxe), his wife
Zion, his eldest son, by an earlier marriage
Bushrod, Zion's son
Helen, Zion's daughter; married to Dr. Lucas Haverstraw; mother of
    Georgie, Darby, Chloe, and Phoebe
Sinjin, Zion's stepson; sea captain

The Priests

Judah, manservant to Old Bobby Talcott; freed slave

Hallelujah ("Halley"), his wife; freed slave

Trubey, their daughter; maidservant to Mab Talcott

Alabaster, Trubey's son; major domo at Kingdom Come; father of Jeffrey-Amherst

Sylvester, Trubey's second son; gardener at Kingdom Come

Reuben, Trubey's youngest son; Talcott coachman

Burdy, Trubey's daughter; married to Lockry Tando; mother of Ella, Cleola, Snowy

Others, on one side of the quarrel or the other

Georgiana Ross, mistress of the Free School

Rose, an escaped slave

Abbé Margeaux, Roman Catholic priest

Mehatibel (Aunt Hat) Duckworth, former schoolteacher

Hermie Light, formerly Sinjin Grimes's first mate

Cinnamon Comorra, the Indian princess Suneemon; witch

Ambo Buck, Cinnamon's half-breed grandson (adopted); head clerk at Burdin's seed store

Warren Burdin, proprietor of the seed store

Milehigh and Sallie Jenckes, tavernkeepers

Valentine ("Val") Morgan, constable

Pastor Weeks, minister at First Church

Willie Wandsworth, deacon

Mat Kindu, Sinjin Grimes's Malay manservant

PART ONE

The Painted Fan

I

Four-and-Twenty Blackbirds

ON A SPLENDID October morning in the year 1841, a custom-built coach of the Concord design was to be seen heading north along the Boston Post Road, oldest thoroughfare in the United States. Yellow as Cinderella's pumpkin, its robust steel springs providing it as smooth and silky a ride as was to be managed in that day and age, Old Bobby Talcott's celebrated vehicle breezily covered the forty miles between New Haven and Hartford, Connecticut, for its occupants were anxious to reach home in Pequot Landing by midafternoon. The Talcotts' Negro coachman, Reuben Priest, the many capes of his driving coat fluttering in the brisk autumn wind, sat erect on the box, as always in easy control of the double span of horses, while his brother Alabaster's eldest son, ten-year-old Jeffrey-Amherst, rode postilion athwart the broad back of the near leader. Jeff was muffled against the chill in a second-hand coat, a good blue melton, a little moth-eaten, but boasting a natty brace of felt-covered buttons at the small of the back. A striped scarf knit by Jeff's mother encircled his throat, and a smaller version of Reuben's top hat tugged securely down about his ears gave him a droll look despite the intense gravity of the expression on his dark face.

"Hey, Frieda, keep to yer own side!" he bawled at the horse, whose flank slapped against the heavy leather boot protecting his foot and leg. Though the morning was well begun and the day superlative, Jeffrey found the landscape monotonous, and his mind was already on lunch and a happy conclusion to his journey. Still, it wasn't every day a Pequot boy got to horseback it clear down to New York City and home again with six exciting days between. What a time he'd had seeing the sights with his uncle Reuben—the harbor bustling with ships, the wharves, the busy streets, the fancy restaurants, all the folks got up in their fine dress. Hartford was nothing by comparison—was there another place that was? Jeff couldn't wait to get home to tell everybody all about it.

Some six days previous, Appleton Talcott, accompanied by his youngest daughter, Posie, had met his eldest daughter, Electra Warburton, just arrived in the metropolis from Washington. After four giddy days of shopping, sightseeing, dining, and play going, the trio was returning to Pequot Landing. They had spent last night in comfortable accommodations at New Haven's best hotel, the evening being given over to an address presented by Electra before the local chapter of the Connecticut Anti-Slavery Society, and after a delayed start this morning—Appleton having conducted an important transaction with several scientific gentlemen at Yale concerning a new inventions patent—they were now making good time, with Posie entertaining her father and sister by pointing out the sights as they sped past and engaging her elders by turns in amusing and enlightening conversation.

In her fashionable new bonnet, with its cluster of shiny red gutta-percha cherries at the brim and bright red ribbons fluttering behind, with her somewhat Quakerish cloak and dress, its neckline modest and devoid of ornament, with her large, shining blue eyes that gazed out so honestly and beguilingly at everything they saw, Posie Talcott was the very picture of a well-brought-up young New England miss. At sixteen, she existed secure in the knowledge that she was loved, was in fact the darling of the family, that indeed she occupied the favored place once belonging to her sister Aurora, who had relinquished it upon her marriage and departure abroad. Still, though acutely aware of her gentle powers, Posie knew better than to trespass on her father's affections or generosity. A little less beautiful than Aurora, a trifle less gay than Minnie, decidedly less excitable than Agrippina, less modish than the elegant Electra who sat beside her, Posie Talcott nonetheless seemed to embrace in her own person the best traits of all of them. In her the total was greater than the sum of the parts, and although she had no beaux yet to speak of, she radiated a charm and warmth that irresistibly drew people to her. Decorous and ladylike beyond her years, affectionate and loyal and full of sympathy, she possessed a valuable gift: this lay in giving and in making people love her, a priceless endowment indeed.

Now she smiled up at her father, who beamed back at her and gave her arm an affectionate squeeze. Appleton knew how thrilling it was for her to have traveled all the way to New York to fetch home her sister Electra. Her *famous* sister Electra. Cool, poised, sophisticated, now one of the country's most distinguished female lecturers and authors, whose published work, *The Path of the American Woman,* had attracted the attention of the nation, Electra Talcott Warburton currently served as a model for many women of her time, not the least of whom was her adoring youngest sister. To hear Posie tell it, Lecky knew practically everyone everywhere, crowds simply flocked to her banner or to hear her speak. And, for a fact, she did keep a busy schedule of lectures, her near-perfect likeness appeared frequently in antislavery broadsides, and in prominent cities—Boston and New York—abolitionist groups clamored for and applauded her speeches and espoused her as their champion. Now she had been accorded the rare honor of being invited to address the state assembly of the Connecticut Anti-Slavery Society.

All these public affairs and a life of crowded and sometimes turbulent activity were agreeably managed with her husband's full approval, for Lloyd Warburton was justifiably proud of Electra's extraordinary success. And if she was meanly labeled a lunatic-in-skirts by some, a dangerous incendiary by others, it mattered little, since (in Posie's view, and, indeed, in Appleton's) these hostile critics and character assassins were mainly misguided members of the opposite sex, drawn from among the lower element, or persons whose political and moral stands were radically opposed to her own, and by association, Lloyd's. For where her name was mentioned, as it was so often, his was likewise bound to appear, even if only parenthesized as (spouse) or, worse, abbreviated to (husb.), the requisite male appendage to an attractive, assertive, and forthright female.

By and large, however, Lloyd seemed content with his career at the State Department, in its United States Patent Office. Here he worked closely under the commissioner of patents, a taskmaster who encouraged his staff to keep their noses to the grindstone. Many was the night when the commissioner's assistant was called upon to work late, while his wife's guests in their house by the Chesapeake and Ohio Canal went in to dinner without their host. Married to so famous a person as Electra Warburton, Lloyd lived life at the edge of a whirlwind, and though he was proud of her and took it all with good grace, he sometimes found Electra's agenda hard to keep up with, and her striving ways inconvenient. For he was ambitious himself, and hopeful of promotion wherever such might come; nor did he disdain the idea that a home life meant children—something Electra was either reluctant or unable to provide him—and the cozy atmosphere that engendered solid contentment in a man who has done a hard day's work, stock loosened, pipe filled, slippers under his chair.

Somewhat inclined to stuffiness as he grew older, Lloyd was nonetheless goodhearted and well-meaning; Posie liked her brother-in-law and felt sorry for him, too. Still, while he would suffer his wife's absence, it would be grand fun to have Lecky returned to the bosom of her family for several weeks. Taking in her appearance in her smart traveling outfit of French gray and burgundy, her spotted veil thrown back from her smooth ivory face, Posie admired the way the fluffy ostrich plume in Lecky's Paris bonnet curled its cunning tips along her cheek, the way her lively blue eyes flashed with controlled animation, the way her well-modulated voice compelled even her father to attend to her when she spoke. So far as Posie was concerned, the several days in New York had by no means exhausted the novelty of having close by an older, wiser, and more experienced sister in whom she might confide, and she looked forward to the kind of intimate talks she could never have with her second-oldest sister, Agrippina, who still lived at home.

Under crisp blue skies the day continued fine and fair as the red wheels spun their spokes, and in all directions the view was bright and compelling in the way of the New England countryside in autumn, when the leaves have turned after the first frosts. The coach had already passed through North Haven and Wallingford; next were to come Meriden, then Still, and finally New France, Wangum Lodge, Two Stone, and at last Pequot Landing itself. Home. It was always good to come home, wasn't it?

Posie angled her glance up at her father. For the past quarter of an hour or so, Appleton had been deep in thought, and now she touched his arm to claim his attention. "Father dear, you oughtn't to be so worried," she said earnestly. It was only lately that she had taken to addressing "Papa" as "Father," and she did it in emulation of Electra.

"Eh? How's that, my dear?" Appleton started, coming out of his reverie.

"Posie's right, Father. You were simply drowning in thought," Electra said, smiling, her gloved hands folded serenely in her lap. "She thinks you look worried."

Appleton rummaged for his bandanna and mopped his brow. "Perhaps I was being unduly reflective," he said apologetically. Though he was disinclined to admit it, for the last three or four miles his thoughts had dwelt with his daughter Aurora, his Beauty, whose face he had not been permitted to look upon in these past ten years, since she had left Pequot Landing with her husband, Lord Henry Sheffield, and their daughter. There were some things in life that were unbearable, yet were to be borne, as Appleton knew to his sorrow. But that she should remain abroad—*why* had she never come home again, or allowed him and Mab to visit her and little Caroline? Caroline, not so little anymore, whom her grandparents doted on, but whom they were now acquainted with by nothing more than the miniature portrait that Mab kept on her dresser and Caro's charming childish letters.

With the passage of the years Appleton had been provided ample time to reflect on the circumstances that had produced this intolerable situation, and even now he could make nothing of it, except that it had all been of a piece with the arrant madness that had first shown itself when his Beauty had been stolen from him by that scoundrel and knave Sinjin Grimes. For, not content to have once attempted to make off with her, the man had gone to chasing after Aurora again with the insane notion of tearing her from the arms of her husband. All that he'd got for his pains, however, was a crack on the head; served him right, what he deserved. Now he was in China, where he could do little harm to any Talcott, and for this Appleton was profoundly grateful. Let the rascal go to the dogs among the Canton hongs.

Such thoughts he could not voice, however, to his youngest child, who had evinced a regrettable if forgivable affection for Captain Grimes ever since he had saved her from drowning on that June day so long ago when John Quincy Adams had come for supper—and Aurora had first been lost. Now Posie reached up with a finger and traced the creases in his brow. "Father, dear, you have frown lines, there and there. Before you know it you'll turn gray and be keeping to your fireside with pipe and slippers. And you're far too young for that—yet, dear Father. You really mustn't worry you know. We're so much better off than many other folk, and life has brought us many blessings, I think."

Appleton exchanged an amused smile with his older daughter. The elevated tenor of Posie's remarks was the result of three years at the Hartford Female Seminary, where she had excelled in her studies.

"So you say, my dear, and so I must agree, as must we all. Still, things have not been so easy these past several years; our resources have not been as abundant as they once were."

Both his daughters knew he was thinking of the bank panic back in '37, a catastrophe that had wiped out several individuals among his acquaintance-ship and had diminished the family fortunes due to some outstanding obligations his banker was unable to meet. This of course had been the fault of that rascally Tennessean, then the White House incumbent, Old Hickory.

"But Father dearest, you really oughtn't to worry about money. Rora has lots, and Priam's doing quite nicely, isn't he? And Granddaddy's still got a great deal, after all. I don't think we're in danger of ending up paupers, do you?"

"Posie, my dear, generally speaking it's not considered proper form to discuss money so freely," her father said, giving her knee a cautionary rap.

"I don't see why not, when it's just us three. No one can hear. I suppose you're right, though—money shouldn't be talked of, it's really not impor-tant. Except I do think that we ought to try to do good with it and allow those less fortunate to profit from it."

Appleton's bushy brows shot up. "Do you indeed? And has Mr. Brace been teaching you high finance at the seminary?"

"No, Father, but it only stands to reason, don't you think? The rich ought to help the poor, the strong should help the weak, and every man should love his neighbor—if he can, anyway. Heaven forbid that we should have to go without, as so many others do, but I think it behooves one to help out where one can."

"Bravo, Posie darling!" exclaimed her sister.

"Yes indeed," said Appleton. "But, tell me, just how would you go about such an undertaking, my dear?"

"I'm not sure. It would have to be studied and thought out, of course, but I think it's a matter of education. Doors must be opened to let the light in." She turned her earnest eyes on her sister. "Don't you agree, Lecky?"

"I most certainly do, Posie dear," Electra declared in her clear, crisp voice, adding, "and you express yourself quite admirably."

Appleton craned to peer more closely into Posie's face. "What you suggest is highly commendable," he said, "but I fear it would be no easy matter."

"Oh, goodness, nothing's easy in this life!" Posie exclaimed, mildly indignant. "It's a vale of tears we must all get through as best we are able. Isn't that so?"

"Is it, my little Po-Po?"

Posie lifted a sober face. "Dearest Father, if I may ask it, would you please not call me 'Po-Po'? It sounds awfully babyish, don't you agree?"

Appleton sighed and ran his hand across his eyes. "And 'Persephone' sounds much too grown-up, I think. What must I call you, then? Miss Rose or Lily or Chrysanthemum? Zeus knows I have a wide choice there."

"Won't plain Posie do?" She dimpled and tucked her small hand in his pocket. Though the charcoal braziers were lighted underfoot and she carried a pretty beaver muff with a satin bow on it, the air inside the coach was chilly.

While pondering how it was that his youngest daughter, that guileless and innocent creature, had come to look upon life on earth as a vale of tears, Appleton took comfort in the certain knowledge that in that same offspring he had raised a truly remarkable child. What a sweet, fragrant bloom for some lucky devil to come along and pluck from his hands, he considered, then instantly regretted the dread thought. Child she no longer was, and as a parent he was not eager to lose this priceless treasure to some hearty, bold-faced male he hardly knew. But it was inevitable. Life intervened, and always at the wrong time; soon . . . *too* soon . . . she would be a married woman with children of her own. Recoiling inwardly at the prospect, he drew her closer within the circle of his arm, feeling the good, solid, human warmth of her. Time was his enemy, he knew. It had crept upon him like some painted savage in one of Fenimore Cooper's tales. Great Zeus, where had they gone to, the years? So swift, so few. More, he wanted more! Oh, he was not alone; what man in his middle years with the silver creeping into his hair does not crave more, does not know fear at finding his later life rushing by him pell-mell, as fast as the team pulling the coach, rattling him blindly into his dotage? Ah me, he thought, such was the way of the world. His heart grew heavier as his mind now revolved again to that other matter that troubled him vastly more than losing one of his daughters: the current state of his wife, Mabel. Something was amiss there or Appleton didn't know his apples. In their thirty-five years of married life—true wedded bliss this was—he had never known her to keep a secret from him; yet over the past weeks he had been increasingly prey to the idea that she was indeed hiding something.

Not so foolish as to imagine there was Another Man somewhere in the picture, some thief come into Appleton's orchard to steal his sweetest fruits from him, he nonetheless was convinced that he was being kept in the dark about matters, and it troubled him deeply. It was frustrating, too; he did not enjoy being confronted by situations he was helpless to do anything about. He must hold himself in patience and watch carefully to see what might develop. Ill: was she ill? No, he didn't think so, he would have detected the signs if this were true.

On rolled the coach past smoking fields where stumps were smoldering and being torn from the earth by teams in chains; past barren fields being planted to winter rye; past corn-stooked fields with Byzantine heaps of pumpkins; past piles of stacked cordwood, neat and even as matches, the woodcutter's humble art; past last summer's scarecrows brooding on their tatters; past an old tree on an upland reach.

"Goodness—look at that!" exclaimed Electra suddenly. "Just see them—there must be millions!" She had lowered the window on its leather strap and was leaning out. Over the tawny, low-lying meadows and the fiery hills to the east the sky began to darken, the light to fade, as though an enormous black cloud were being drawn across the heavens. By no means an unusual sight to the three travelers, it remained nonetheless an impressive one—a monster flock of passenger pigeons heading toward them, comprising unbelievable numbers of birds, birds in the millions, birds by the hundredweight. Their passage overhead was always keenly awaited by hunters across the land, who with their guns and nets would scurry out to shoot and trap them by the hundreds of thousands until, falling out of the sky like hailstones, they lay heaped knee-deep in the fields, filling for a thousand thousand pigeon pies, or common fodder for pigs.

"How many, how many?" cried Posie. "How many birds, Papa?" she asked, slipping into their old childhood game.

"Skatey-eight and four-and-twenty for a pie." Appleton volunteered the customary answer. On they came, casting a broad, almost sinister, shadow across the whole countryside, their clustered forms blotting out the sun's rays; they came and still came, and came more and more, until with a clatter they veered sharply in their course, then, as if at some invisible signal, swooped suddenly downward and with a tumultuous clamor dropped into a dense wood on the far edge of an empty plowed field.

As they settled among the trees, their gabble all but deafened the travelers, a hideous sound, as if some biblical scourge were being visited upon the neighborhood. The sharp sound of branches cracking could be heard as the sheer weight of the birds snapped the boughs on which they roosted. Reuben

had slowed his wheels, the better to view the phenomenon, and was about
to touch up the team again when at the edge of the wood a young woman
appeared fleeing frantically from among the trees, hands pressed over ears,
her dark hair streaming wildly behind her. As she dashed across the field
toward the coach she screamed, casting fearful looks over her shoulder as
if she expected the whole mad avian multitude to swoop down on her at
any moment and peck her to death.

"*He'p! He'p!* God *he'p* us all!" she cried, heedlessly stumbling across the
uneven furrows. She was no more than halfway to the road when the frayed
hem of her yellow dress caused her to trip, and she sprawled headlong on
the hard ground, where she lay, her hands still clutching her head, screeching
in terror. At Appleton's direction, Reuben pulled up in the roadway.
Electra, who had already thrown open the coach door, leaped down.

"Don't just sit there, Jeff," she called to the postilion. "Can't you see help
is needed? Come along."

Appleton and Posie also got down, watching as Electra and Jeffrey-
Amherst made their way to the stricken girl and helped her to her feet. There
was a brief exchange, after which Jeffrey ran off toward the bird-infested
wood, while Electra aided the girl in straightening her hair and dress, then
supported her as she limped painfully toward the waiting coach.

"I'm afraid she's hurt her ankle," Electra said as the exhausted and terrified
creature sank onto the step, clutching her ragged shawl around her, her teeth
chattering audibly.

"Permit me, miss," Appleton said, stooping to examine the affected ankle,
which had already begun to swell. He had no more than lightly pressed the
puffy flesh when the distraught girl cried out in pain.

"I beg your pardon," he said kindly. "I meant no harm. We must see to
this at once."

Electra bent to tuck a pillow under the injured foot, while Posie slipped
off the disreputable-looking shoe. "Try to relax now," she said gently. "No
one's going to hurt you. You're among friends."

"Them birds, them horr'bul birds, they near scairt me half t' death." The
girl's prominent, hysterical eyes bulged under her brow, and her voice came
in husky bleats, her teeth clicking miserably. No wonder, Posie thought: the
tattered dress of yellow calico sprigged with tiny red flowers, the pathetic
remnants of a black fringe shawl, and a pair of worn shoes were all the
protection she had against the autumn chill that raised gooseflesh along her
pale arms. Looking at her, Posie decided she had never seen anyone in a more
pitiable state. Surely something must be done to help her.

Electra and Appleton by turns attempted to assure the girl that she had
no further cause for alarm, but their words fell on deaf ears. Nothing seemed
able to placate or reassure her, and when Jeffrey had come running back
from the wood with a pathetic bundle of personal effects, evidently all she

had in the world, she snatched it from his hands and clutched it to her bosom as if she were in danger of being robbed. In her dark eyes Appleton and Electra had already perceived the telltale signs of the fugitive, signs that neither was unfamiliar with.

"Where are you going, miss?" Appleton asked, offering a reassuring smile.

"Har'ferd. Then—" She stopped, as if uncertain of her destination or her path to it.

"Hartford, is it," Appleton said. "Do you seek employment there?"

She shrugged her narrow shoulders and groaned a little. "Dunno. Guess maybe, if—" She stopped again, clawing at the riot of tangled hair that partially obscured her pallid features. "One place be good as 'nother, Ah reckon," she added finally, as if to disguise with indifference the despair she was feeling. Her lids blinked rapidly as she spoke, fighting back the tears.

"Are you traveling alone, miss?" Posie asked, wrapping around her a blanket she had brought from the coach.

"Reckon Ah is. Ah was with frens, they—we done got parted. Ah was gettin' me a drink from a stream yonder when those birds come. Ah ain't et since yestiddy mawnin' an' Ah is plumb down-winded." She stopped, her eyes again filled with tears, and reached out to pluck a burr from her skirt. "Never gonna see Knoxie no more."

"Who's Knoxie?" Posie asked gently.

"M'grammaw. She be all Ah got in the whole wide world, Knoxie, an'—an'—"

Electra poured some brandy from a traveling flask into a cup and held it to the girl's lips. She peered up from behind her tangle of hair and gulped eagerly, downing the liquor in a wink, then as eagerly accepted more.

"You mustn't cry, no one's going to hurt you," said Electra, once more trying to reassure her.

"They's hu't me an' hu't me," she declared tearfully. "That's all they got t'do is hu't po' folks lak me. If they cotches me they's gonna hu't me bad." She trembled at the thought.

"Who is going to hurt you?" Electra asked. When no response was forthcoming she signaled to the others that she wished to speak with the girl alone. After Posie and Appleton had tactfully drawn a few yards off, she gently brushed the hair back from the girl's face and began talking earnestly to her.

Four or five minutes passed while the horses flicked their tails and twitched their ears nervously. Finally, impatient with waiting, Appleton checked his watch, then glanced up at the sky. He shrugged and called out, "Come along, Lecky, we don't want to be late. Your mother will worry." After another brief exchange with the girl, Electra joined her father and sister for a brief parley.

"What have you discovered, my dear?" Appleton asked.

"You can see it, Father, I'm sure. Can't you? There are all the usual signs."

"She's a runaway, you mean?"

Electra nodded. "She's lost, and absolutely terrified, poor thing. Some men have already captured her companions and taken them away and she's afraid slave catchers are on her trail. I've promised we'll help her."

"Of course we'll help her!" Appleton declared resolutely. "We can't abandon her in this desolate place. Let's be quick about it, though, before anyone sees us." He looked up and down the road as though the slave catchers were likely to appear at any moment. "We can turn her over to Aunt Tilda and Aunt Betts, they'll soon have her on the way to Canada."

"Bravo, darling. I told her you'd champion her. The poor thing's been beaten and starved—even branded. But she's got spunk. She's already chosen a name for herself. 'Miss Rose Mary Mills,' she said right out when I asked. If we don't help her I doubt I'll sleep another night of my life."

"Me either, not a wink," said Posie.

Still nursing her injured ankle, the girl was now seated on the coach step gnawing on a cold leg of chicken (meant for Appleton's lunch) given her by Reuben. Her eyes swiveled apprehensively between the group engaged in conversation and the coachman, who stood to one side eyeing her impassively.

"Whatchou lookin' at, big man?" she demanded in an accusing tone. "Ain'tchou never seen no nigger gal before?"

"Never seen a white nigger before," Reuben conceded dubiously. "You look just like a white girl."

"Wisht Ah was," she drawled wistfully. "Was Ah white, wouldn't be settin' here in the cole with mah laig half broke."

As Reuben moved off to see to his horses, Appleton again approached the fugitive. "Well, miss," he began, "it appears you are a runaway from your legal master, is that not the case?" The girl jerked her head once, grown fearful again. "And your name is Rose? Rose Mills?"

She scowled and threw her hair back from her face. "Is you gon' t'pack me back? Hand Rose over to the paterollers?"

"Good gracious no, we're not so cruel," he returned.

"We're going to take you along with us," Electra said, coming up and grasping her hand. "We're going to see that you are put back on the road to Canada."

"Lord above! Freedom in Canady! May the good Gawd bless you," Rose cried, and heedless of her injury fell on her knees and tearfully embraced Electra's skirts.

Appleton cleared his throat. "Come then, be quick aboard. Reuben, don't hesitate to use your whip. This delay may cause worry to your mistress at home, and we don't want that."

"Sure don't, Mist' App," Reuben said, flourishing his lash. When all his passengers were installed inside, he sprang nimbly onto the coach box, Jeffrey-Amherst slammed the door, then leaped to the back of the near leader, and without a second's pause the coach lurched forward on its way again. With the sudden movement of the horses and the grating of the wheels, the offending flock of pigeons rose up from the wood in even more brazen clamor than before, clattering into the air high above the trees, re-forming their enormous cloud and heading westward, numberless like the fishes in the sea.

When Posie placed a cushion behind Rose's head and steadied the injured ankle as best she could, Rose smiled; an attractive smile this was, rendering her thin, pinched face surprisingly pretty. Though her dress was torn, her hair unkempt, though her hands were dirty and her nails broken, nevertheless it was apparent to all that this was no ordinary runaway slave. Appleton judged her to be not much more than seventeen or eighteen, not much older than Posie, and her pale face and slender figure set her apart from most of the unfortunate escapees who in these desperate times were continually making their way north across the Mason-Dixon line in search of freedom. Appleton thought her a plucky soul, even bold, and imagined how her story might read in the papers after she had reached safety. As quickly as could be managed she must be put into the hands of his aunts, who would see to her further progress.

Like the squares of a patchwork quilt, the fallow, dun-colored New England farmland continued to unroll outside the open windows of the coach, and the girl began to doze, the warmth of the brazier, the effects of the brandy, and the monotonous motion having made her drowsy. Her fellow passengers exchanged sympathetic glances and curbed their conversation as the iron tires of the four wheels rolled over the well-laid road, now and then flaring up whirling comets of sparks as they struck the flinty rock embedded in it. Before long, Rose had fallen fully asleep and Posie reached out to extract the chicken bone from her closed fist; it had been picked clean as though a cat had been at it. The others might now conveniently partake of the contents of their hamper, and, signaling Reuben to adopt a somewhat more leisurely pace, Appleton allowed his daughters to provide him with lunch on his lap, and a foaming bottle of cider to wash it down.

Though the miles flew quickly by, the sun was already well past its zenith when the coach pulled into Meriden, and with each passing quarter of an hour the road became filled with more traffic. At Meriden a brief rest stop was undertaken and then they were on their way again, but they had gone barely two or three miles when Reuben's brisk tattoo from overhead threw the travelers into confusion. Leaning out, Appleton saw at once the cause for the alarm: a pair of horses galloping after them, the riders straining forward in their saddles. Realizing that if they were slave catchers to try and outrun them would be impossible, he ordered Reuben to pull up as quickly as he could and issued hurried instructions to his daughters, while Rose began to moan and clutch her hands in a frenzy of fear at being taken.

"Lord Gawd, they's gon' t'cotch me!"

Electra and Posie both turned to allay her fears, and when the coach stopped, Appleton got hurriedly down and held parley with Jeffrey-Amherst as the pair of horses came cantering up. He tipped his hat and greeted the two riders amiably. "Good morning, gentlemen. Or I should say afternoon, since it appears to be past twelve, does it not?" He ostentatiously consulted his watch. "Seems one of our horses may have picked up a stone," he added.

The men made no response to this. One of them, wearing an iron black suit, a shirt with no collar, and a broad flat hat of sooty felt, made an impatient gesture. "Seen anyone passin' along here afoot?" he asked. "Maybe a female on her own?"

Appleton smiled in friendly fashion. "We were only just remarking on the large number of travelers along this road. Were you seeking anyone in particular, Mr.——?"

"Marth, m'name's Franklin Marth, this here's Swayne." He jabbed a thumb toward his companion. "We're lookin' fer a gal. Nigger runaway. Wearin' a yeller dress," the man added, "yeller spotted red. Carryin' a bag of gear."

"Is that a fact? Black girl, yellow dress. Bag of gear." Appleton seemed to fix the description in his mind for future reference. "And what makes you think she might be along here?"

"Confedruts. We caught 'em, they told us what we wanted to know—a nigger'd forswear his mother for a soup bone. Left Noo Haven yestiddy, she's bound to be along this here road somewheres."

"Passes for white, she does," Swayne volunteered. "But yeller dress fer sure, couldn't miss it. You folks ain't seen any such a varmint along the way?"

"I thought you said it was a human, not a varmint,' " Electra said sharply.

"Same thing, ain't it? Her bein' a nigger. Niggers is all varmints. Now I ast you, did you folks catch sight of her?"

Appleton gave his lip a thoughtful tug. "Well-l—I—hard to say, so many we've passed."

"Where you stopped, back at Meriden, they said a gal in a yeller dress was seen gettin' out of your coach and back in again." Marth nodded at the coach. "Now, sir, if you're harborin' a fugitive in there, the law's ag'in you. I got a warrant here and we want a look inside your vee-hickle."

"I don't see why we should be obliged to allow strangers to investigate the inside of our coach, sir."

"Oh for goodness' sake, Papa, tell the man the truth," Posie exclaimed, in accordance with Appleton's hastily contrived plan. "We don't want to be lawbreakers, do we? Tell him how we *did* see that girl, gave her a ride to the crossing, that was all. She led us to believe she was going to Farmington to visit her aunt who's sick. Gracious, whoever would've thought she wasn't white?"

"Where is she now, then?" demanded Marth.

Before Appleton could reply, Posie spoke up again, deftly embroidering her tale. "A farmer came along with a hay wagon and said he'd take her straight to Farmington Common."

The man grunted. "Gave her a ride, did he? *Hmp.* He'll have his ass in a clamp before he's done." He consulted the sun and his colleague in that order. Then, evidently still suspicious, he wheeled his horse and reined in closer to the coach, and began ducking and bending in his saddle, trying to peer inside. "Who's that you got in there?" he asked.

"See here, gentlemen," Appleton protested. "You've no business stopping people along this road and—"

Just then Electra leaned forward and the coach door sprang open. "It's only Martha-Sue, gentlemen. See for yourself. The poor thing's been feeling ill ever since we left New Haven." When the men put their heads inside for a closer look, "Martha Sue" emitted a feeble moan and exhibited a pale, sickly visage.

"Our sister's been terribly ill," Posie added. "Vapors, I'll be bound; I do hope she'll be recovered by the time we get home."

"Where's home?" demanded Marth.

As Posie replied, the slave catcher peered more closely at Rose. Snuggled in a corner, the telltale yellow dress hidden under Electra's shawl, her features partially obscured by the curling plume of a fashionable bonnet, Rose Mills continued to feign the illness that had been dreamed up for her.

"Martha-Sue does not travel well, I fear," Electra said.

"She don't look so sick to me. Let's have her out and take a look."

Appleton spoke up quickly. "I wouldn't do that if I were you, gentlemen. You are ill advised to disturb Martha-Sue, or to further detain this coach. Since you obviously are unaware of the situation, let me apprise you of the fact that this lady here is none other than Mrs. Electra Warburton."

"Who's she?" demanded Marth.

"Mrs. Warburton is an extremely well-known personage. Here is a copy of the work she has authored; there—you see her name clearly printed. Now, if you'll kindly excuse us . . . Drive on, please, Reuben, there's a good fellow."

Appleton got into the coach and, settling himself by the window, bid the slave catchers adieu. "I trust you will find your fugitive. Gentlemen, allow me to relieve you of the book." He repossessed himself of Electra's essays and watched the disgruntled pair wheel their horses and speed off.

As their hoofbeats retreated, the coach passengers drew a relieved breath, then broke headlong into a fit of merriment. Even the runaway relaxed a little. Among them they had richly bested the slave catchers, and soon Rose Mills would be on her way to freedom across the northern border, for what was to prevent it now? Wouldn't Knoxie be pleased to know!

2

The Queen in Her Domain

ON THE ANNIVERSARY of the first night they had spent under the roof of their new house, Appleton Talcott had made his wife Mab a thoughtful and affectionate gift, a handsomely wrapped box containing gilt-edged writing paper of the best quality, with the words "Kingdom Come" engraved at the top of half the pages and the address, 17 High Street, Pequot Landing, below. Above the legend was a formation of clouds through which shone the brilliant rays of the sun, illuminating a bird in flight. As Appleton explained it, the sun emblem was designed to signify bright hopes and happy days to come, fair weather for all who dwelled under the roof of Kingdom Come, as the house had come to be known, while the bird represented the Dove of Peace.

A year later, much to Appleton's chagrin, the name of the street on which his house had been built was, by vote of the Board of Selectmen—at the time presided over by his enemy Zion Grimes—officially changed to Main Street. Mab, however, never troubled to strike out the "High" and write "Main" over it, and indeed she was prepared to uphold the status quo while breath remained or until her stationery ran out. But since the paper had been printed in substantial supply (Appleton could never stint where Queen Mab was concerned), it had of recent date seemed to her that the box was decidedly promising to outlast its owner.

Mab had arisen later than her usual hour today, as she did increasingly often these days, for she was gravely ill and knew she must conserve her strength. This morning the doctor had paid her a third visit in as many weeks, surreptitious visits, to be sure, for she and he were in league and no one must know. At all costs the truth must be kept from Appleton, who would be devastated by such news. She had lain on her bed in her morning gown, waiting as Terry Standish silently put away his instruments. He had looked across his open bag and given her a silent nod. There had been no need for words, they understood each other perfectly.

When the doctor's chaise had pulled away from the house, Mab reflected on her situation. She did not relish admitting that she was alarmed, when she had seldom been frightened by anything ever. She must be brave, she told herself, if it must come, then let it come. She would endure all. If only the awful truth could be kept from her Jake, as she called her spouse—she was his Molly; not indefinitely, surely, that was impossible, but for some while yet, until she herself could accept the fact of her situation.

Trubey Priest had come up to assist her with her morning toilette. In the mirror their glances met; Trubey was a sensible woman, she too would say nothing of the doctor's visit.

While Mab dressed, covering her graying hair with one of Trubey's freshly ironed caps, she asked for news, first of her father-in-law, Old Bobby, who, she was informed, was hard at work in the study—his "Pequaug: A Villager's History of Pequot Landing" had been aborning for more than ten years now; then of Agrippina, who Mab was told had driven to Hartford for a sketching class.

"Can't I get you something, Miss Mab?" Trubey asked. "Momma says you didn't eat but a bird's breakfast."

Mab's laugh made the room ring. "Don't give it a thought, dearie; if I'm hungry you'll hear about it, I promise."

With a deceptively gay salute she left her bedroom and proceeded carefully downstairs to the back parlor, where she drew up a chair and sat gazing out through the panes of the glass doors at the garden that lay beyond the terrace where Sylvester Priest was busy raking leaves. She placed a hand over her breast and felt the faint beating of her heart, distantly, as if from a long way off.

From the kitchen came the sounds of the voices of the Priests—Halley and Judah, now two ancients, the soft-spoken Trubey, and the more insistent tones of Burdy Priest Tando, Trubey's daughter, who had married Lockry Tando back in 1834 and now had three children of her own. Alabaster's deep consonants could be heard as he fetched a fresh pot of coffee for Old Bobby. What would she do without them; and what they without her? Halley and Judah had been at Follybrook Farm when Mab came to Pequot a bride thirty-five years ago, and Trubey had returned there with her children when her husband deserted her. And now . . . no, better not to think of it. She had lived here in this house for twelve years, and she still missed the farm; nostalgic thoughts of Follybrook lingered yet. There, only half a mile away, she had been safely removed from life's insistent sway; here at Kingdom Come she lived at the hub of the village, which truthfully she didn't much care for. She preferred the green fields and pastures, the sounds and smell of livestock, the simpler mode of life she'd known around the old farmhouse. Here, all day long the roadway outside echoed to the sounds of hooves and wheels, the shouts of men and boys, the barking of dogs, as life's busy traffic thronged past the gates. For no one traveling

Greenshadow Road from Two Stone to North Pequot Landing could avoid
passing Number 17 Main Street, remarking how well pointed the brickwork
remained after a decade of wear, admiring the entrance with its fanlight and
paired Ionic columns and the gilded weathervane flashing in the sun. The
house remained by far the most elegant dwelling along the entire street, a
house built to last—"till Kingdom Come," as President John Quincy Adams
had once put it. And, as they formerly had done at Follybrook Farm, so
the famous and the near famous now came here to partake of the particular
brand of conviviality, good food, and conversation that was the touchstone
of the Talcotts. John Quincy had presented himself more than once, stopping
there on his way to and from the Congress in Washington; Mr. Garrison,
the fiery editor of the *Liberator,* had been a guest on several occasions; the
eminent French writer Alexis de Tocqueville had made a call after having
visited the penitentiary; Fanny Kemble had dined. And one must not forget
Bob's boyhood friend Noah Webster, he of spelling fame, or Cent Dunnoult, Hartford's foremost trial lawyer and another crony of Bob's, or
Horace Bushnell, also from Hartford, and a strong ally in the abolitionist
struggle—only a few among a long list of outspoken, liberal-thinking men
and women of a kidney to please both Appleton and Old Bobby, who were
made welcome in Kingdom Come's best parlor amid its fine English and
American furnishings, and the gilded French harp in the corner.

Presently Mab opened a door and, taking along her old sealskin coat,
ventured out onto the terrace of handsome herringbone brickwork and sat
in her favorite chair breathing in the brisk October air and taking in the
tawny lawns that rolled away on both sides of the stepped garden planted
in the English fashion, apparently helter-skelter but with its own rhyme and
reason, and the meadow beyond unfurling itself clear to the riverside, where
the weeping willow boughs dripped at the water's edge.

Idly she glanced down at her callused hands lying in her lap. Like the
rest of her they were getting older, wrinkled now, though still tough; she
had a gardener's hands, she would die with a gardener's hands. Her potting
shed, hidden away in a corner near the pheasant coop, was yet another of
the pleasures Appleton had contrived for her; there she kept all her tools
and implements, her work aprons, her seeds and bulbs and cuttings, and the
gloves he had bought her but that she never wore. And not far from the
shed stood that most perfect of all her delights to the eye, the summerhouse,
that cunningly constructed piece of Chinese caprice, which had been
uprooted from the Follybrook garden and transplanted to this place. She had
left the structure behind when she moved, then found she could not bear
to be without it, and Old Bobby had insisted it be moved here to Kingdom
Come.

At the risk of feeling an ingrate, lovely as it all was, Mab still mourned
her former garden at the farm, and the years it had taken to create it, and

despite Appleton's thoughtful labors over her potting shed, lately she'd occasionally wished it were a chapel instead. Try as she might, she had never become used to the notion of living in the new house. Now that the children were grown, it had proved not only too large but too grand as well—not at all the homey place she believed a house ought to be. The ceilings were too lofty, too ornate, the floors were too shiny, the wallpapers too fancy, the carpets too rich, and there was an excess of chandeliers. How had it happened, she wondered, that she, Mabel Riley, a brewer's daughter, would die in such grandeur? Appleton's folly, she thought, and then scolded herself. Few women had been blessed with such a generous and loving mate, no matter the cost of his indulgences. Merciful God, how was she ever going to confess to him what she now knew, that soon she would be leaving him, that their life together was over?

These morbid thoughts were interrupted as a sturdy farm wagon rattled up the drive. Mab waved to her nephew, son and namesake of Appleton's youngest brother, James, who hopped down from the seat and began unloading a small harvest of pumpkins.

"Punkin time, Aunt," he called cheerily. "I've brought farm to city. How do you like them?"

"Well, James, there's a deal of punkins, I'd say. Planning to enter the jack-o'-lantern trade, are you?"

"Posie ordered these up, Aunt Mab. No idea what she plans for them. Pie, maybe?"

"Possibly. She certainly knows my weakness. My mouth's simply watering for punkin pie."

When he had set the pumpkins in a line along the drive, James clumped his way up the stairs, a strapping fellow with the winning charm shared by all the Talcotts. "Give us a kiss then," she said, putting up her cheek to be bussed. She liked her nephew; at twenty, James, Jr. was canny and had a wry, down-home humor that sorted well with her own. Like his father, he had forgone a college education the sooner to take up farming, and though he owned a good suit, you seldom saw it except at weddings and funerals.

"Mother said Uncle App's gone to New York."

"Indeed he has, he's bringing Lecky home, you know she's to address the Anti-Slavery Society. Posie went along as well."

"What a feather in your cap; Cousin Lecky appearing before the whole damn Society. 'Scuse it, Aunt."

"That's all right, dearie, I've heard the word. Yes, we're all set up to see our girl again. Too bad your mother and father can't be dining with us. Well, you'll see her anyway, she'll be around for a nice stay. How is everything at the farm?" James reported that things went well. Harvest had been good; next spring the elder James would be adding to the property by plowing up land that had lain fallow for over twenty years. Soon more onions would be on their way around the world. One of Granddaddy's two-year-olds had foaled two days ago; Great-Aunt Blanche, likewise a horse fancier, had named the colt Eastwind.

"Oh, I like that!" Mab exclaimed. She admired horses but never liked to ride and seldom bothered with the local racing, leaving all that to Blanche and Old Bobby.

"Say—somebody sick around here?" James asked suddenly, catching Mab off guard.

Feigning surprise, she answered glibly, "Not to my knowledge. Why?"

"I thought I saw Doc Standish's rig coming out of your drive earlier."

"Oh, that." Mab laughed and flashed her handkerchief negligently. "Halley had a bit of rheumatism this morning, Terry came to leave her some medicine, that's all. But you're sweet to ask. And thanks for the punkins. Your father was most generous, please tell him. I'll have to give some of those beauties away before they spoil."

"As you like, Aunt; there's plenty more," James responded. He whipped his head around as a noisy bell sounded from over at the Center.

"Uh-oh, there's a fire," he said, bending to kiss Mab's cheek before rushing off. He was a member of the volunteer fire company, and as he scrambled to answer his call to join the brigade wherever the conflagration might be, she reflected on how often Old Bobby had plumped at town meeting for an investment of village monies in one of the modern pieces of fire-fighting equipment such as the Hartford companies were now using, and on how skinflinted some Yankees could be. Rather than spend a little now they would prefer to wait until a major holocaust set off half the town and think they'd done well to hoard their money in a sock.

"Give my love to your mother," Mab called after him. "Tell her we must visit soon."

She watched her nephew climb into his wagon and gee his horses up. James was a good boy, independent and forthright, qualities she admired; one of these days he'd be marrying, and the family cradle would be sent round for a new occupant. She really must invite his mother for a visit; as sisters-in-law she and Susie saw all too little of each other, and Mab was ever conscious of her family obligations. She didn't want any noses out of joint because of neglect on her part.

With James and his wagon gone, the scene fell silent again, and for a time Mab sat watching the passing show of water traffic out on the river, thinking hard and trying not to think, incapable of preventing her mind from drifting to the unpleasant topic, then attempting to force it away again in confusion. Though the warming sun was cozy feeling, she mustn't stay outdoors too long; it wouldn't do to take cold. Nearly the end of October already; how fast the time passed. Nineteen weeks since her trouble had first begun, last spring, in fact. Soon it would be Thanksgiving, and before you knew it, Christmas. Another Christmas. It would be her last, she was convinced.

Plans were already being laid. As was customary, the family would gather for the holidays—except for Rora, of course. Mab closed her eyes, inwardly wincing at the thought of her errant daughter, absent from home these many years and living abroad . . . Since the single visit she and Lord Henry had made to Pequot Landing had been cut short by the old earl's death there had been only her daughter's all too sketchy and infrequent letters to bring her close. Time after time, Rora had put off any suggestion of the family coming to see her in Italy, where she spent a good part of the year, now at Naples, now at Leghorn, now at Pisa, for since the death of his father and the ascension to the earldom of his elder brother, Lord Henry had taken an apparent aversion to English society; nor had Aurora seen fit to cross the sea again herself. Four letters had Mab written in as many months, merely suggesting at first, finally entreating her daughter to return home this year; yet each summons had been dealt with in a hurried note saying soon . . . soon. It was always soon; but "soon" might not be soon enough for Mabel Talcott.

She sighed and gazed off down to the water, where in the last few years the flow of river activity had thinned out more and more. How nice it would be to be sitting here having a loving mother-and-daughter conversation with Rora, to hold Caro on her lap. No, she must try and remember that Caroline was much too old now for such babyish things. But, Mab reminded herself, if Aurora wouldn't come to see her ailing mother, Minnie-Minerva surely would. What a joy, what happiness was that darling girl, now grown to womanhood and marriage, mother of five of the happiest babies anyone ever set eyes on. Like Aurora, Minnie had met her husband, Lee, on one of the family's annual excursions to Saratoga Springs, but there the similarities of circumstance decidedly ended. Leland Peckham, editor and publisher of the *Battlecry,* a frankly inflammatory abolitionist publication, was a serious, hardworking newspaperman, a worthy provider, a man of courage and conviction. Though far from what might be called good-looking, and unlikely ever to be rich, Lee was a son-in-law to esteem, for Minnie would always have a loving husband whom she adored in return, and a good father for her children.

In truth, putting aside the disappointment of Aurora's behavior, Mab considered herself blessed in all her children, her two eldest in particular, though Electra's barrenness was a disappointment for her mother, who, having raised three sons and five daughters found it hard to imagine a woman without her own to love. Yet Lecky seemed happy enough, and Mab would not pry. She had brought her children up to go their own ways in life; to be "mama-ish" was the cardinal sin so far as she was concerned.

As the eldest son of Appleton Talcott, Priam maintained a deep sense of the serious responsibilities he would one day naturally assume as head of the family, to whom many would look for guidance and support. Not merely in her own maternal eyes, but in many others' as well, he ranked as a blooded prince, the prime inheritor of the Talcott name.

And whether he would or no, he had for years come in for the lion's share of attention; it remained a question of time only until the mantle would descend to his shoulders. Already he was one of Hartford's leading business-men, having become head of the Talcott, Lane Assurance Company, upon the death of old Arthur Lane. Together with his college friend Asher Ingolls, he had swept the cobwebs from the musty old firm, located on Hartford's Mulberry Street, putting several octogenarians out to pasture and adding a department specializing in marine assurance and contracts of bottomry. By now the company had attracted a large clientele and both Priam and Asher were living on adjacent properties on Hartford's fashionable Farmington Avenue and looking forward to ever more prosperous and distinguished futures.

Only Priam's continuing detestation of all members of the house of Grimes caused Mab any concern, seeming as it did to separate him from other successful men his age, all of whom had better things to do than fan the flames of a hundred-and-fifty-year-old quarrel that most people would rather forget. Though the feud had for several years past been put to simmer on the hob and there was little reason to continue manifesting what many were convinced were now obsolete feelings, foolish and even ridiculous, Priam was still occasionally inclined to pump the bellows that kept the coals aflame, that the fire should not die out altogether. Still, more than ten years of marriage to an adoring wife had done its work in seeing him become a loving husband and a good father to his children, whom he doted on. And besides, these days he had more admirable undertakings to think about than any Grimes's head being served up on a platter.

As for her other boys, Hector and Achilles, they, too, were young men to be proud of: twins with budding military careers. Now both first lieuten-ants aspiring to their captaincies, they were well embarked on the course they had anticipated since childhood days, and unless some unlooked-for conflict suddenly broke out, which mercifully seemed unlikely at present, they gave their doting mother little reason for anxiety—though Mab knew how hard her death would fall on both of them, Achilles especially. Despite his more sensitive and sentimental nature, Hector was far better armored against the loss of the mother he adored, and she prayed he would help Killy through the dark times she knew must inevitably come.

Agrippina, sad to say, was proving a cause for worry; alas for poor Pina with her nerves and her vapors, her humors and her rashes, her twinges and headaches and sundry other indispositions—and, above all, her lack of a suitor. And if by now Mab had more or less resigned herself to the daunting prospect of her second daughter's being an old maid, this hardly made things easier, for, unlike her great-aunts, Old Bobby's maiden sisters, Matilda and Bettina, Pina lacked the facility for making the best of what life had to offer "a lady of singular virtue." Among the family it was generally felt that her precarious hold on life and mercurial nature had much to do with the intermittent series of lingering maladies she had contracted from infancy through late childhood, ranging from the commonplaces of measles and mumps and whooping cough to a dangerous bout of rheumatic fever. Even as a child prone to outbreaks of hives and similar skin irritations, and to headaches, which she called her "megrims," in her more mature years she had fallen victim to a variety of nervous disorders, her main complaint being recurring attacks of erysipelas, a fiery inflammation of the skin, and had taken recently to carrying smelling salts and dosing herself with laudanum. Time and again she had been sent to a new doctor, only to discover that after another series of expensive treatments there was no appreciable change in her condition. Hot baths, long walks, excursions and diversions—the cures came and went in cycles, to little avail. Pale, thin, excitable, seldom tactful in her speech, she cut through life with a sharpness that required constant dressing and kept those closest to her on the anxious edge, worried for fear that something yet unthought of should come along to debilitate her further. Though she had not yet begun in earnest any notable series of annual progressions in the royal fashion of Good Queen Bess, moving from one house and set of relations to another, she was entirely parochial in her outlook and nature. She cared about little that did not directly concern herself or those close to her; she kept herself martyr to a hundred woes, a thousand pettish, ill-disguised jealousies; and the outer limits of her pallid interests were prescribed by her prejudices. As she was a fervent abolitionist, so was she outspoken for temperance, and she frowned mightily on her father's unstinting liquid hospitality. What would happen when her mother was no longer there time alone would tell, but Mab feared that Pina would leap at the chance to take over the running of the house and the caring for her father, an unhappy fate for them both. What was to be done? Why wasn't Mab cleverer, wiser, better equipped to handle these matters, now, when it was so terribly important?

Mercifully, she and Appleton had fared far better with Posie. Always so sensible where her children were concerned, even Mab found herself utterly helpless before her youngest daughter's unaffected and beguiling manner, the ebullient charm, the entrancing grace that made her beloved of everyone. To see Persephone Talcott grown into young womanhood had been one of the sublime joys of her mother's life; to hold Posie's little ones on her lap a cherished dream, alas, one not now to be realized, she knew. Yet how could she consign her precious darling to her father's care alone, or to

Agrippina's? Who would see the girl properly wed and embarked upon her married life as was most fitting?

Mab sighed again and drew the lace border of her handkerchief through her fingers. How was a dying woman to control the sundry destinies of her children; let go, let go . . . She had to force her mind to dwell on other things, to stop brooding on what lay ahead. "Thy will be done, Lord," she murmured. "Only let me die quietly," she added, "and in these last months get on with the business of the rest of my life. And let Rora come home again before I die, please God." Oh Lord, she thought, how was such a thing ever to be arranged without the truth being told?

She felt a breath of cold, and drew the collar of her coat tighter at the neck. She had not been to mass in several days, and sadly felt the need, but Pina had taken the trap to Hartford, the Yellow Pumpkin was gone to New York, and a wheel was off the barouche. Of all days! When she heard the steeple bell ring the noon hour, it occurred to her that she could easily negotiate the brief distance down the street to First Church. Though a devout Catholic, could she still not pray for her soul in the bastion of local Protestantism, Ruth amid the alien Congregationalists? Or would people misunderstand? Would a Church-of-Rome intruder in those Puritan precincts risk being struck by lightning? The Ancient Burying Ground was packed cheek by jowl with a lineage of Talcotts going back over two centuries. Would their shades rise up to drive Mab Talcott from the place? And what of herself? Would this be disloyal to her own faith? Nonsense. A church was a church; surely God's spirit inhabited one as well as another! She rose, her mind made up. She would go to the First Church to pray, devil take the hindmost. She sent Burdy upstairs to fetch a linen fichu, her good one, and a better pair of shoes and, still wearing her sealskin, she proceeded down the front walk of her house and out through the gate.

The First Congregational Church of Pequot Landing, one of the oldest churches in that region, was a building worthy of note. Though a Catholic through and through, with her own dead infants laid to rest in a bit of consecrated ground set apart from the orchard at Follybrook, Mab had always admired it for its style and venerability. She didn't mind that her daughters had frequently raised their voices in song among the choir up in the loft. A church such as this lent a town distinction; many villages throughout the New England states had their pretty white steeples poking up among the trees, but with the exception of Boston, where was there so handsome and vivifying a manifestation of a simple man's faith in God?

As Mab rounded the corner across the little green where the flag spanked at its white mast, she found the church doors open, and her ear quickly picked up the soft rumble of the new organ, toward whose purchase she and Jake had contributed a goodly sum in his mother's name. Climbing the steps, she nodded to the sexton, Giles Corry, who as was his habit sat in his straight-backed chair beside the door, knitting a woolen sock. Inside, she sought the nearest pew, where she quickly lowered her bulk and peered about her. A lovely place, surely, so unadorned yet so spacious, so filled with light and the spirit of the Divinity. Her eye could not discern what individual was lightly fingering the keys of the organ, but the melodious, almost random chords touched her, and she felt within herself a momentary sense of peace and well-being. She knelt and crossed herself with reverence, and after she had murmured a Hail Mary, she took out her rosary and, letting the beads of pink coral slip through her worn fingers, began her decades.

Some moments later she heard the side door open and felt a presence as someone entered the church, but she kept her eyes closed while she continued her prayers. When she opened them again she saw the back of a woman who was arranging a vase of flowers on the refectory table before the altar: Patience Weeks, the minister's wife. Mab coughed and Mrs. Weeks turned. "Why, Mabel Talcott, for mercy sakes, I *thought* that must be you. What a surprise!" She gave a little laugh, her eye on the rosary.

"Yes, it's me all right," Mab replied in her forthright manner. She sat up and settled into the pew again, grateful to be off her knees. "How are you, Patience?"

"Guston and I are both well, thank you. But what a shock you gave me; fancy seeing you at prayers in our little church."

"I admire your church," Mab returned briskly. "I hope you don't mind admitting me within your portals. It's very restful, conducive to—whatever churches are meant to be conducive to. In fact, I may come again—if I'm allowed."

"Oh, my *dear* Mabel, of course—use it any time you like. You might even consider a—a conversion?"

"I don't think I'd go so far as that," Mab said, "though it is a very lovely and restful spot."

"I was just saying to Guston yesterday, haven't we the prettiest church! You might enjoy to hear tomorrow's sermon—Guston's taking as his text 'And a little child shall lead them.' " Then, smiling as she somehow always managed to do, Patience snatched another glance at Mab's rosary, and disappeared behind the altar. As Mab left, she could see her brushing down the pastor's robes for Sunday service.

Those who might have observed Mabel Talcott enter the church were not likely to have seen her depart, for she slipped out the side door and made her way into the Ancient Burying Ground, where she moved slowly among the tombstones, reading the inscriptions, noting names and dates. Not a collector of epitaphs, she nonetheless spent a good three-quarters of an hour leisurely skirting her way around the briar patch separating the church property from her own. She came out a hundred or so yards from the boathouse and proceeded up through the meadow, slowing her step as she reached the garden path past the summerhouse, then passed Jake's workshop, and the pheasant coop, where nary a bird was to be seen. When she reached the terrace she found a frowning Halley Priest waiting for her.

"Miz Talca, whut you mean stayin' outdoors so long? Is you tryin' to drive this ole woman early into her grave?"

"Not a bit of it, Halley, though I've just been looking at some lovely ones. Graves, I mean."

"If you's gwine t'go runnin' all 'bout the neighborhood, you best tell someone 'fo' you goes wanderin' off. Ah done sent Burdy to look fo' you."

"Well, here I am."

"An' here you stays. You jes come on inside now an' eat yo' lunch whut Ah ben keepin' hot fo' you. How you gwine keep yo' strent' 'ceptin' you eat good? An' you ain't buntle' up 'nuff agin the cole. Doctuh he say—"

Mab knew the end of that one. "I'm sure you're right, Halley," she concurred meekly. "I'm sorry if I worried you. Perhaps I'll have a bite and sip right here, it's so nice and sunny. I'll look over my garden." She sank into her chair and eased her feet in their shoes.

"Now you jes set an' Halley she gwine t'serve you yo' lunch husseff!"

Five minutes later Mab's chair had been moved into the lee of the terrace, and, with a tray across her lap, she sat nibbling the chicken Halley had fricasseed. Still, she had little appetite, and she wished for once that there was a dog about to lick the bowl so Halley wouldn't scold.

When Halley reappeared to take the tray she came right out with it. "Miz Talca, the doctuh—"

"Oh, Halley dear, please, not now." Mab lowered her eyes, unable to look at that anxious face, the dark forehead corrugated with worry.

"Ah ain't gwine ter say nuthin t' Mist' App, but if you thinks you is foolin' this one, you's got t'think agin. Whut kin Ah do ter he'p?"

"Nothing, dearie, I'm fine, truly. Only—*please,* just don't say anything."

"No'm, Ah ain't tellin' nuthin' to nobody roun' hyere," she solemnly intoned, "an' ef anyone goes roun' blabbin' Ah is gon' t'shut they mouth good. Ress you'seff, now, nap a bit." She unfolded the robe she had brought out, tucked it around Mab's lap and knees, then went away with the tray. Mab dozed fitfully. She awoke at the sound of wheels in the driveway. She heard a door open, then close; voices conferred, and presently the Abbé Margeaux presented himself to view.

She had been hoping he would stop by. Since he had ceased being her family priest and gone to work among the half-breeds at Lamentation Mountain, she had learned to do without his daily counsel. Now she needed it.

"Ah, Léon," she said, running her hands over her cap and hair. "What a nice thing—you must have read my thoughts, I was hoping I'd have a chance for a word with you."

"*Chère madame,*" he said as he approached her, "are you not feeling well? The doctor has been, has he?"

"Oh yes, come and gone, there's a mercy. It never does to have doctors underfoot for too long. Come and sit, tell me the news." As he drew up another chair she spread her hands on her lap and eyed them ruefully. "Disgraceful, aren't they? But I simply cannot wear gloves. How can anyone ever really *garden* without having her fingers feel the dirt that things grow in? You've got to *feel,* no matter who might be coming to tea."

He smiled, glancing down at his own roughened hands—hands that had once been as meticulously manicured as any woman's, and but one mark of the transformation that had been wrought in his appearance since he left the service of the Talcott family. Thinner, but a good deal more fit than he had been in those days, he had about him an aura of vigorous health and well-being, though the heels of his shoes were serviceably worn down, his usually immaculate cassock was missing a button on its front, and the biretta he had laid by was frayed in spots. His personal jewelry had been sold to help fund his mission; he closed his shirtcuffs now with sets of acorns, his hair was home-trimmed, and he traveled about the countryside in the same old dilapidated rig he'd driven for years. "The Italians have a saying," he said, " '*Gatta guantata non piglia sorce.*' That is: 'The gloved cat catches no mice.' "

Mab laughed appreciatively. "The Italians aren't to be outdone when it comes to gardening—always grandiose, like their operas. I've my English garden here and Rora has her Italian garden there, and English ones too, I suppose. Not that *she* would ever soil her hands with such humble labors."

It was the abbé's turn to be amused. "Speaking of which," he added, "I mean of course our *chère* Aurora—I am this day a wingéd Mercury and I bring you a letter." He drew from one of his copious pockets an envelope, which he placed in Mab's hand. "I think she has been feeling guilty in not having written in so long."

"Ah yes, but she will take time to write to you, to nearly anyone excepting her own mother. And haven't I been sitting here this quarter of an hour past with my thoughts flying across the ocean to her?"

"Then see the results," returned the abbé generously. "Here is the loving response to those same thoughts. You must read it in a like spirit as if it had been penned to you, and you shall be comforted."

Leaning back in his chair and folding his hands across his stomach he watched as Mab extracted the pages of Aurora's letter.

"Read it to me, then, Léon, my eyes are troubling me a little."

She returned the pages to him and, with a smile, he adjusted his spectacles and began to read aloud.

" '*Mon cher abbé,* words fail! You cannot imagine my chagrin at realizing how terribly long it's been since I have taken up my pen in your behalf.

An age, surely, and I am a naughty creature to be such a poke! And you always so good at keeping me informed of home doings, too. I cannot think why I cannot manage writing oftener, unless it's that I never seem able to plan my time properly.

" 'I still adore my lovely Italy, it reminds me of so many things and'—something seems to be scratched out there, I can't make it out," the abbé interpolated, then went on. " 'Naples is always amusing. Henry insists on taking a charming villa at Porto d'Ischia, to which he can sneak away in the hot weather and have the salt sea baths he so enjoys. Presently we travel to Switzerland, where we place our darling Caro in school at Vevey. She won't care for the idea of being from home, but such things are necessary if she is to be a properly brought up young lady and if we are to find her a match befitting the granddaughter of an earl. Perish the Swiss, they are a dull lot in the main, not a bad thing though when it comes to young ladies of her age, and she will be carefully schooled. Though not, I trust, too sternly disciplined. Use the rod and spoil the child, I say. Vevey is lovely, even the winters; nearby there is Coppet, the pretty château of Madame de Staël, who of course was far too smart for her own good. A woman must decide if she is to gleam or to glitter. Frankly for Caro I prefer the gleam—she'll have no Byron sitting at her feet, as that lady did.

" 'Mon père, she has become the sweetest-natured child, and so terribly bright. (Whence does this come? Surely not her mother.) She speaks four languages, imagine. And her mother able to speak but one. No, not true, my Italian's fairly smooth now, and I do rather well in French. But Caro speaks German as well. It is the governess, you see, Fräulein Bleinstuber, such a formidable creature—a Düsseldorfer (I shan't miss the woman, she's such a marionette).' "

The abbé paused over this last phrase. "I wonder if she doesn't mean 'martinet'?" he murmured.

Mab giggled. "Never could spell. Go on, go on."

"Let me see . . ." The priest searched for his place. "Alors. 'Just think, she will be thirteen next March—how time flies! At Christmas we will go to London for the holidays, but will not stay long, as Henry dislikes the cold. In the spring we will go to Paris for the races. Sometimes I think Henry would rather be married to a horse than your poor Rora.

" 'Have I gone on long enough? I daren't read back to see what I have said for fear of discovering I've said nothing. Mon père, though many a year has passed since we last saw each other, yet I hope always that I am in your prayers—I and my darling Caro, and her father too. What a long time it has been since we were all together. Little did we think that—' "

Père Margeaux broke off abruptly and looked up. "Mais—c'est tout," he said.

"What? Are we to be left dangling by our heels, then?" demanded Mab. "Surely she didn't just end like that?"

"I fear that's all there is," the abbé said again, apologizing, as though the fault were his. "She simply stops, as if—"

"As if what, dearie?"

"I don't know. But it's most peculiar, is it not? Perhaps there was a page omitted."

"And what is one to conclude from that, I wonder?" Mab wanted to know; Père Margeaux had no answer. He refolded the pages with care and slipped them back into their envelope. When he looked up again he saw Mab stiffening against the back of her chair, her eyes filled with sadness.

"Madame?"

"No, no, it's all right, it's only that she's so far away and I—it would be so nice to see her again—" She ducked her head and dabbed at the tears that had started.

The abbé was anxious. "But what is it? My most *chère* madame Maybelle, I entreat you to tell me," he pleaded. "If only you would permit that I should help sometimes."

Mab smiled through her tears at her Christian name, for he had not used it for many years, not since he had left Kingdom Come.

"I'm only being mama-ish and acting foolish. Think no more of it." Putting on a smile, she waved the matter away, though her eye strayed back to Aurora's letter which the abbé had laid on the table. "What have you been doing today, Léon?" she asked before he could question her further.

"Ah, madame, I have been visiting my friends at the settlement. On the Mount of Lament there are many tears shed everyday, and alas, much, much to be done. We are to have a new baby—Camp Willott's wife. Her name is Bessie, you may have heard us mention her. Any time now. The midwife is already with her."

One more child, thought Mab, quickly setting aside her own sorrows, one more unlucky infant to be brought into that bleak and inhospitable world. Lamentation Mountain was aptly named, and no member of the Talcott family was ignorant of the suffering among its inhabitants since the priest had taken up his work in that place.

No more than anyone else did Mab know the reason for the abbé's startling transformation, only that some years ago he had with no warning relinquished his comfortable bed here at Kingdom Come and gone about disseminating the Roman faith among the indigents and bringing those lost souls such comfort and heart's ease as he was able. At the start of this new and surprising phase of his life he had attempted to church his charges at New France, at Father Rupprecht's chapel, but the rival priest had refused to allow his small fiefdom to be sullied by that unsavory, woebegone, and often drunken lot, and he had shut his doors against them. His Grace the bishop of Boston, not seeing much use in increasing his flock with Lamenters, had supported Father Rupprecht. The Congregational pastor had been equally unaccommodating. Guston Weeks had not taken kindly to the notion of Mab Talcott's priest proselytizing among the half-breeds, though neither was he himself inclined to do so. In the end, the abbé had sought permission from Old Bobby to use the mill house at Grimes Mill for services. Here the abbé, having expelled, with bell, book, and candle, the feverish ghosts said to haunt the place since the bloody tragedy that had occurred there some dozen years before, when the miller Tom Ross had slaughtered his wife and all his children except for the eldest, Georgiana, and then blown out his own brains, regularly said mass and offered both the sacrament and confession.

Père Margeaux slipped a yawn into the end of his ragged sleeve, and the sharp-eyed Mab saw that though it was not yet four, plainly the man was fatigued, but when she suggested ringing for tea, he declined. He could not stay, he must go on to Two Stone and Lamentation, for Bessie's baby might be born at any moment.

"The child will be in need of things," she said, and the priest beamed.

"Now it is you who have read my thoughts. It is precisely this that I have come for. If you could provide—"

"Yes, of course, nothing easier. A blanket and some warm clothing, to be sure. Pina will see to it when she returns from Hartford."

"*Mille remercîments, madame.* But you haven't yet said—what is it you wished to tell me?"

Mab cast her eyes to her lap, at a loss how to bring out the difficult words. "Nothing. Merely the pleasure of your company. We see so little of you these days, you're always so busy."

"I am always happy to offer you my company; for you I can always find time. It is little enough. But you have not said, how may I serve you?"

Mab took out her handkerchief and thought hard as she thoroughly blew her nose. "As it happens, there *is* a matter of some importance," she committed herself to declaring.

"Yes, Madame, you have only to speak." He waited patiently and presently Mab began talking again, finally persuading herself to entrust to him her dread knowledge. Père Margeaux listened until she fell silent, then he raised his anguished eyes to hers.

"Ahh—madame—*ma très chère* madame May-belle—*Je suis desolé.* What can one say? God's will be done."

"I only needed to confess it," Mab returned lightly. "They say it's good for the soul."

"Such a kind and gentle soul," said the abbé, anxiously searching his benefactor's face. "I am grieved to hear it. But can one be sure? Such matters are not always without hope."

"There's always that possibility. But what I want you to do is—I wish you to write to Rora. You must not tell her what I have told you—this knowledge must be suppressed, of course—but if you should still have any influence with her, urge her to come home, let me see her. I must see her once before—"

"Certainly, rely on me, it shall be done," said Father Margeaux. "Ah, dear madame," he went on mournfully, "such news, such unhappy news . . ."

Mab put out a restraining hand. "No, no, that will not be the way, Father," she declared emphatically. "We will have no unhappiness here."

He nodded. They had known each other so long; they were kindred spirits. "Shall we pray?" he asked.

"I have already been to church once today. Not at New France, though." She related her noontime experience.

"Wrong?" he repeated in response to her question. "I trust not, since God is everywhere. M'sieu' Appleton does not attend the church of his fathers, yet I know him for a godly man, not the pagan people like to call him." He leaned toward her. "Is it your intention that he should be told?"

Mab's reply was firm. "To the contrary, I wish him not to know until— until he divines the situation for himself. Then there will no longer be any point in discretion. The cat will be out of the bag."

"But would it not be better if you were to take him into your confidence, gradually, to be sure . . .?"

"No, this is how I wish it." She grew severe, anxious to conclude what was obviously a painful exchange. "I've kept you from your duties long enough, *mon père.* I'll be sure to remember about the baby things." She walked with him to the door where she said good-bye and accepted his blessing. "Don't forget Lecky's homecoming," she reminded him. "Seven o'clock."

The abbé smiled and shrugged. "God in His time, *ma chère madame.*"

She watched him go down the walk to his waiting rig, then went inside.

In the back parlor she found that 'Baster had laid a fire in the stove, and she dozed in its comforting warmth until she heard Agrippina's voice in the front hallway. She forced herself upright as her daughter closed her parasol, set it down with her reticule and sketching kit, then slipped off her gloves— Agrippina Talcott would as soon march naked through the streets as go anywhere without her gloves. When she had divested herself of these items, she came in to greet her mother.

Mab kissed her. "How did the sketching go? I hope they're teaching you something useful, the time you spend at your easel."

"Mama, you'll never guess—next month we're going to sketch 'Apollo.'"

"That's nice, dear," Mab said absently, her mind somewhere along the Boston Post Road.

"But Mama, he's Greek!"

"Does that make a difference?"

"You don't understand, the statue is unclad. Not a stitch does the man wear! What must we think when innocents like Posie may gaze upon such excess of form?"

Mab could not restrain her mirth. "Oh dear, I hope it's not too excessive. In any case I doubt that Posie's morals would be seriously impaired by the sight. She's not too far off from a husband, anyway, she'll most likely catch a glimpse or two then, I shouldn't wonder. Now run along and have your nap, dearie, you want to look your freshest when Lecky arrives."

Agrippina glanced anxiously at the clock. "I do hope they're not going to be late. I'll just have a word with Halley about not overcooking the roast. Papa must have his beef rare, and I do so want everything to go smoothly tonight."

"Perhaps we'd better put dinner back an hour," Mab suggested helpfully. Agrippina was in accord; the beef roast would be held so as to go on the table at half past eight.

She swished through the door and in a moment Mab could hear them talking—Pina, Halley, Trubey, and Burdy—going over tonight's menu. It was on occasions like this that the mother felt most grateful for her daughter's willingness—nay, eagerness—to assist with the household duties. A moment later, Trubey entered. Over her arm was a shawl, which she laid across her mistress's shoulders. Mab smiled gratefully, allowing herself to be cosseted, then got up and went to the front window. "They're late, aren't they?" she said, peering out.

"Yes, but you mustn't worry. They probably stopped for a bite, or Mist' App might want a pint. Momma says—"

Mab nodded. "Momma says." How many times had she heard that phrase in the last thirty-five years? "Momma says . . ." Men and women, whole families lived their lives by "Momma says." She smiled and sent Trubey away to fetch tea. Old Bobby would be joining her for the afternoon repast, as was his habit.

Again she reminded herself how lucky she was to have Appleton's father, Bob Talcott, for a father-in-law. Though at the outset he had been dead set against her marriage to his son, he had soon relented, and for more than thirty years they had been the warmest of friends and companions. It was not difficult for Mab, or anyone else, to recognize his great worth. He was mint gold, beyond assaying.

The steady passage of time had only served to enlarge Old Bobby's preeminence among his fellow townsfolk, always excepting the house of Grimes, and by now he had assumed the stature of both village treasure and historical personage. The passing years seemed merely to have touched him with light, graceful strokes, and while he had reached the not inconsiderable age of seventy-six, he was as dapper and debonair, as sunny and courtly as ever, so that people often declared the man must have discovered the Fountain of Youth.

Presently she saw him coming up the terrace steps clutching a small bouquet of flowers in one hand, a knobby, soiled burlap sack in the other. Crooking a friendly finger at her beyond the pane, he opened the door and came into the warm room, bringing the chill of the autumn afternoon with him. He doffed his wide-brimmed farmer's straw hat and set the sack down by the door, then bowed as he presented the flowers and took the chair next to her.

"From Hattie's garden," he explained. "The last of them, I'm afraid."

Mab smelled the chrysanthemums. "Lovely. Thank you, Granddaddy. I must thank Hattie too." Hattie's garden was more sheltered than her own.

"Hattie sends you her love," he told her. "I didn't go in—it's Penelope's Hour over there," he added wryly. "Indeed, I fled in fear of my life."

Mab laughed. "Penelope's Hour" was Bobby's phrase for those afternoons when her old friend Hattie Duckworth entertained the ladies from the Brick Farm, as the town's almshouse was called, at a sewing bee in her parlor. "You mean in fear of Mary-Martha Grisby bringing you to wed and you coming home with a new wife," she said acerbically as she passed the cups.

"I fear that in Mary-Martha's case it would scarcely be anything like a 'new' wife, my dear." He chuckled. "In the case of Mary-Martha I would find myself teamed with a yoke mate far older than most men would care to keep."

Mab's laugh was merry as ever. "And so you would, dearie. Besides," she added, glancing up at him, "I don't know that you require another spouse. Although that's not to say *all* men don't—being widowed, I mean." As he blew on and sipped his tea she gazed into the sparkling blue eyes that belonged to him and no one else, then found her look faltering, as if those same eyes were seeking answers to questions she would prefer not to have voiced. She turned her wedding band on her finger, looser now than in former times, and daintily smoothed down the bosom of her dress.

"How are you feeling, my dear?" he asked casually, yet she could tell the query was a probe. "I met Terry Standish in the hall this morning," he went on, as if he'd only just remembered. "He said you had a bit of a stomach, hey?"

Mab nodded; she and the doctor were in a tacit state of collusion. "Touch of indigestion. Might have been the fish last night. Were you affected?"

"Not I."

"I'm glad. And of course I'm perfectly fine now, nothing to worry about. We needn't mention it to anyone," she troubled to add.

Though far from satisfied, Bobby leaned over to pat her hand and give her his warmest smile. Certainly she didn't look ill. Her cheeks were in high color, her eyes clear, her skin showed a healthy tone. Handsome, still; he'd always liked Mabel's good country-fed looks—the open face grown to plumpness, the hair graying into stateliness, in the large round eyes the twinkle that had been inherited by Minnie-Minerva.

She faced him now with the same equable candor and warmth it had been her grace to bestow on him these many years. "Now, Granddaddy, you've set that disreputable-looking sack there by the door knowing full well I'm bursting with curiosity to know what's in it. Are you going to tell me? Or is it to be a secret?"

"By no means, my dear, by no means. That sack contains a gift to you—from Warren Burdin. Can you guess?"

"Not an idea."

"Some of those new lily bulbs he's been talking about all summer. He thought you might like to see how they do. I told him I'd dig them in around the walkway and see what we get."

Mab's eyes sparkled. "Oh yes, do. How thoughtful of Warren. What color will they be?"

"A pale lemony shade with very delicate markings. Who knows, they might win a prize one year. And do you know, I shouldn't be at all surprised if Warren doesn't come and ask to name the lily after you. What do you think of that?"

Mab bristled. "I think it's disgraceful! The very idea, naming a flower after me, as if I were dead and buried! You tell Warren Burdin, in case he hasn't noticed, I haven't turned my toes to the daisies yet."

"My dear—" Bobby was taken aback by her vehemence. "Warren thought it would bring you pleasure. I'm sure his intentions were of the best. How could they not be, when he admires you so greatly?"

"That's all right, dearie, I'm sure he meant well."

"Ayah, I judge so." He set his cup aside and stood. "Well, suppose I get my trusty trowel and dig these in, hey?" He opened the neck of the sack and let her peek inside: half a dozen fleshy bulbs with papery skins.

"I've another idea, Granddaddy. Instead of along the walkway, you might think of planting them under the window of Jake's laboratory, where he'll have the good of them while he's working. You know how he loves lilies."

"The very thing," he said. "You do have the eye, my dear." He reached for the door but before he could open it Judah Priest appeared with a message: Mist' Bob was wanted immediately over at the Center.

"Reuben, he come to tell us. You're to go to the jail and meet Mist' App. And—" He whispered in Bobby's ear, then stood back as Mab interrupted him.

"Jail? What's occurring? Granddaddy—"

"Nothing, Mabel, nothing to worry you, not a bit. You just wait here while I see about this little matter." So saying, he hurried upstairs, then as quickly came back down and joined Reuben, waiting at the gate. In another moment they had disappeared in the direction of the Center, leaving Mab in wondering silence. What could have happened? And what could her husband be doing at the local jail? She sat down and tried to keep herself from fretting until the answers to her questions should be made known to her.

3

To Jail or Not to Jail

A GOOD HOUR EARLIER the Talcotts' yellow coach had rolled off the turnpike and onto the southernmost extremity of the Old Two Stone Road. Within minutes it was rounding the foot of Lamentation Mountain and then, as Reuben slackened his reins and let his team stretch out, they made Burning Bush Hill in record time and presently were rolling along Greenshadow Road toward the center of Pequot Landing. Soon the roofs and chimneys of the small country village themselves came into view, and Reuben was drawing back on his reins, following his master's order to slow as they rumbled onto the Old Middletown Road and approached the Broad Street Common from the south. Discretion and no little care were what was called for now, plus a bit of luck into the bargain, if their illegal charge was to reach safety.

As they drew nearer to the large homestead known as Lilacs, where his aunts lived, Appleton leaned out the window, shrewdly assessing the situation. Old Beebo, the Negro man of all work, sat on a chair under a maple tree, shucking a basket of late corn, and as the coach slowed, Matilda Talcott appeared in the front doorway. Appleton got down while the coach was still moving and hurried to meet her. She listened to him attentively before calling her sister outside. The three spoke briefly, then Appleton signaled Reuben to turn into the drive with his coach and horses.

Meanwhile, Rose Mills cowered inside the coach, nervously gnawing her knuckles. It seemed to her that all eyes in the village must have been attracted by their arrival, and she attempted to hide her face again behind the plume of Electra's bonnet as the two spinster sisters approached the window and peered in. After greeting their nieces they turned their attention to the runaway. "Don't be alarmed, my dear," Aunt Tilda said, "we will help you if we can." She signaled Rose to get out, but the girl cringed against the upholstery, afraid to make the slightest move.

"Come along, then, Rose, be sensible and step down," said Appleton. "It's perfectly all right, you'll see."

Aunt Bettina, who had been catching all the words to be managed through her ear trumpet, attempted to soothe her. "Truly, you'll soon be safe. Wouldn't you like a drink of water?"

"I'll bring it." Posie jumped out and hurried toward the well at the side of the house where she filled the dipper and carried it back to the coach. Rose drank thirstily, and Posie was returning the empty dipper to the well when she saw two men on horses beating their way up Broad Street toward the Common—the two slave catchers! Her heart froze as they pulled up, and she began waving her handkerchief to warn Electra, but it was too late. The far door of the coach had swung open and Rose was attempting to get out. The shawl had slipped from her shoulders and the dress of yellow calico stood out like a beacon.

"There she is! That's the one fer sure! Grab her!" shouted the men. "She's a runaway. We claim runaway!"

Marth sprang from his saddle to capture Rose by the arm. "This woman is slave property! I have a writ for her arrest." He waved some documents, clutched in one hand. "It's all legal, so we need have no discussion on that subject!" He brought out a set of hand irons, which he proceeded to lock onto Rose's thin wrists, while Rose, terrified to speechlessness, looked desperately around for someone to help her.

"You let go of that girl!" commanded Aunt Matilda, smacking the man's hands away as he prepared to lead Rose off. "What proof have you that she's the one you want?"

"Proof enough. She's branded on the shoulder, if you care to look, just like the warrant says. I'd suggest you hand her over, lady, unless you want some trouble."

"How dare you speak so to a lady!" Appleton stepped up and, seizing the man's wrist, jerked him around and stood panting face-to-face.

"Here now, not so fast, friend, you're interfering with our lawful dooty—you can go to jail for that." Marth turned to his partner. "Swayne, ride on up the place and catch holt'a the constable, we'll bring the law in on this thing." Swayne ducked his horse and rode off in the direction of the church steeple, which poked up above the trees.

"There!" said Marth with some satisfaction. "You'll soon be seeing the inside of your own jail, mister."

"We'll just see who among us is going to jail," Appleton retorted heatedly, while Electra and Posie came to stand on either side of the terrified slave girl.

She fell to her knees, her face contorted with fear. "Doan let them mens take Rose, folks, Ah begs you, doan let 'em take me. If they takes me back they'll have kilt po' Rose fo' sure. This be mah third time Ah done run off."

"Now, now, Rose," said Aunt Bettina, hurrying to her side and helping her to her feet. "They haven't got you yet. And sir," she went on, addressing the slave catcher, "you are trespassing on private property! Your horse is cropping our lilacs!"

Marth was undismayed. "Lady, that horse ain't et since mornin' and neither have I," he retorted. "But let me tell you folks one thing. If you persist in meddling in this business, you're asking for trouble. I'll have the law on you for sure! Will you hand her over, sir?" he demanded of Appleton.

"I will do nothing of the kind. Not without a good fight, I promise you that. And if you're smart, you'll turn around and ride off straight away before you find yourself in trouble for kidnapping."

Meanwhile Posie had been quietly speaking into Aunt Tilda's ear, and when she was done, Tilda marched up to the slave catcher. "See here, my man, if you'd care for us to make it worth your while, I have fifty dollars cash you and your partner may divide between you."

Marth's jaw dropped. "Fifty dollars? Thank'ee, no. The girl's worth three-four hundred bottom!" He eyed Rose menacingly, as if picturing the stern punishment that would be inflicted on her when he had her home again.

Heads turned as hoofbeats sounded farther up the street: it was Swayne returning, and with him was Valentine Morgan, the constable. Ignoring the others, Marth strode forward, waving his documents. "I'm glad you're here," he said, addressing himself to the constable. "I have a complaint. I am Franklin Marth, an officer of the law, and I charge these people with the obstruction of justice."

Surveying the scene, the constable greeted Appleton. "Afternoon, App. You obstructing justice again?" He winked.

"I am, Val," Appleton said.

"This ain't no joke, damn it!" Marth shouted. "This here female's an excaped slave."

"That so?" Val said again. "You feel the need of those irons on her, do you? A dangerous criminal, is she, in need of restraint?"

"By God she is! She's the bounden property of Mr. Joseph Lacey, Junior of Hunt's River Point near Laceyville, South Ca'lina, and me an' Swayne here've been sent to catch her and fetch her back!"

"From all appearances I'd say you've caught her," Val said coolly. "Whether you'll be fetching her back's another thing," he added. "I'd have to have a fair amount of proof of your statements."

"You think I don't have it?" Marth retorted, again brandishing the warrants. "If you are the legally constituted arm of the law in this place,

I call on you to do your dooty. As for this high-toned fellow here—it's all his fault. Him and those two females, they led us a pretty dance, I promise you. But we won't be hoodwinked again."

Val dismounted and took the proffered documents, which he perused carefully. "Is this you, miss?" he asked, approaching Rose, who was trying to hide behind Electra.

"She's badly frightened, Val," Electra said quietly. "Can't something be done to—to—?"

"Well, Lecky, welcome home," said Val, giving her an admiring look. He glanced from her to Rose, as though putting the pieces together for himself, then to the slave catchers again and back to Appleton and his aunts. "I think we might do well to move these concerns over to my office, if you wouldn't mind, App," he said.

" 'If he wouldn't mind!' " scoffed Marth. "'Course he minds, but he'll come if he knows what's good for him!"

"See here, fellow—"

"That's all right, App," Val said soothingly, "it's only a step or two out of your way. Will you accompany me and talk this thing over?"

"Of course he will," Electra said. "Father, you go with Val; Posie and I will bring Rose along in the coach."

"Yes, yes, by all means," Appleton said impatiently, giving the two slave catchers another hard glare. "There's no sense standing about arguing like this."

Guiding Marth by an elbow, Val shepherded the party along toward the Center, where, predictably, there was a goodly Saturday afternoon crowd about. Patrons smoking cigars lined the porch of the Old Hundred tavern, in the yard the hired girl was pinning a sheet to the wash line, and over by the trough the ostler waited, bucket in hand, to water the horses. Along the wooden sidewalk, familiar faces passed by, villagers on their Saturday errands, toting baskets or parcels, disappearing into the butcher's, the cobbler's, while the whittling fraternity sat lined up in front of Archibald's store like so many crows on a fence rail.

As the coach drew up outside the jail, Marth was quick to yank the door open and order the occupants out. When Rose appeared he grabbed her arm and roughly hauled her down. Realizing that this was Old Bobby Talcott's coach, the more curious of the passersby paused, then gathered round to ogle the action.

"What's happening?" someone asked, and Marth was quick to explain the situation.

"Darky slave, is she? Looks pearly white t'me," said one onlooker; his companions agreed.

"That's the thing! She's been passin', the hussy! Thinks she's white folks."

Marth gave Rose a push toward the jail. "Come along then, nigger gal," he said. "Let's get this over and we'll be on our way afore dark. I know somebody down home's gonna be mighty glad t'see you." But his rough treatment of the dazed slave drew angry looks, and several voices rang out. "Leave the girl alone!" "Pick on a man, coward!" "Low down slave catcher!" "Cur!"

"All right, let's everyone just quiet down," said Val, but even as he spoke, another group of citizens appeared in the doorway of Archibald's store and pressed forward.

"One moment, Constable, what's the trouble here?" It was the nasal voice of Zion Grimes; beside his tall, morose figure stood his crony and fellow deacon in the First Church, Willie Wandsworth. They sported black beaver hats of notable dimension; Willie carried a blackthorn walking stick.

"No trouble, Deacon," Val returned easily.

"And no affair of yours, sir," Appleton added pointedly.

Evidently inspired by the sudden appearance of his detested enemy, Appleton began energetically addressing the crowd of spectators on the girl's behalf, citing some of the facts of her case and appealing to them to take pity on her and save her from her tormentors. Instantly the crowd began to divide itself in its sympathies, a dozen or so enthusiastically backing Appleton, an approximately equal number, especially those who had come from Archibald's with Zion Grimes, taking sullen exception to them.

As though by some previously arranged signal, when Appleton finished his remarks Zion Grimes took up the theme, addressing his lifelong foe. "It appears, sir, that you are the party who is meddling in matters that are no concern of yours," he stated flatly. "Exactly what is this runaway slave to you, if one may ask?"

"Ask what you like," Appleton countered. "I am merely an interested bystander who has this person's welfare at heart."

Zion sniffed through his long nose. "Interested bystander, I doubt, since it appears you are abetting her in an illicit flight from her master. Interested in circumventing the duly constituted laws of this state and nation, I believe you mean. I suggest that in so doing, you are liable to prosecution under those same laws."

At this point, Posie, after a word with Electra, ducked around her father and made her way through the crowd, heading toward the law office of her uncle Jack Talcott across the street, while the terrified Rose Mills, the center of the controversy, helplessly wrung her hands. Who was this dreadful-looking man with the angry, bulging eyes, the long nose, the hard, hollow voice that was like a shovel dragged on sand? And the nasty little ratlike man who hopped about beside him? She could perceive that the quarrel between them and the Talcotts went considerably beyond her own case, but for what reason she had no idea, nor did she care. Only let her be saved. Make a miracle, God, she earnestly implored, make a miracle for Rose, don't send her back to Laceyville and the whip!

"Well, do you intend just to stand there, Constable, or will you do something?" demanded Deacon Grimes. "It's plain what's going on here. Appleton Talcott is taken bold-faced trying to abet this girl in escaping from her legal master. Arrest them and lock them up and let the law take its course!"

"Don't you worry none about the law, Deacon," Val temporized, but though he was a friend of the Talcotts as well as an abolitionist sympathizer, he could hardly fail in the performance of his duty. Buying time, he turned to the crowd. "Now, why don't you folks all move along before there's any trouble? The show's about over anyways."

"They will most certainly *not* disperse!" declared Willie Wandsworth, scurrying up to Val. "They'll all stay right where they are, if you please. They want to see justice done just as much as we do!"

"Willie, do be silent," said Zion Grimes grimly. "These people have been assisting a miscreant, a point on which the law is perfectly clear. As an apprehended runaway she must be returned to her master and whatever unhappy fate awaits her at home, while her confederates shall go to jail in this place so that the law may take its prescribed course!"

"Yes, yes!" Deacon Willie darted to Zion's side. "There's no use your soft-soaping this matter, Constable," he whined. "It's the law—the law must be served—"

"Stick a cork in it, Willie!" boomed Jack Talcott. "Afternoon, App—Val—Deacon Grimes. What seems to be going on?"

"Gentleman Jack," as he was known thereabouts, directed his look at Zion, who stared balefully back and said, "No need for you to mix in this, Jack Talcott, the matter is perfectly in hand. Your brother is attempting to break the law in the matter of this escaped slave. These two men have ridden all the way from South Carolina in pursuit of their property."

"That a fact? Well, well, they've had a long hard run, I'd say." Jack turned to his brother again and with his handsome smile said, "Glad to see you home, App. Lecky, I vow, you're a sight for sore eyes." Doffing his hat, he gallantly kissed his niece's cheek, then stood back to admire her handsome figure. "Very becoming, my dear, very becoming."

"Are we to stand here in the street while he appraises this lady's attire?" cried Willie Wandsworth. "Apple Talcott has broken the law. So have your own nieces, *and* your aunts, Jack Talcott—!"

Jack cast his sunny smile down on Willie-the-rat, barely half his size. "Whether the law has been broken shall of necessity be determined elsewhere," he replied, and stepping over to his aunts, he doffed his hat again. "Afternoon, Aunt Betts—Aunt Tilda. It seems we have a bit of commotion."

"Glad you came, Johnny, it's all nonsense!" declared Tilda, tossing the pair of deacons a scornful look. "The poor girl was thirsty, the coach stopped to water the horses, she was taking a drink from our well, nothing more. We've done nothing wrong except to offer a bit of Christian charity, as any decent folk would do." She gave Deacon Grimes one of his own sniffs. *"There's* the troublemaker, there's the true culprit—Zi Grimes, and his kiss-up, Willie Wandsworth!"

"Be careful of your words, madam." Zion's puffy lids blinked rapidly.

"It's a fact," put in an indignant Bettina, lending support to her sister's accusation. If there was going to be trouble, both ladies were prepared to stand up to it. "Why, the poor creature ought to be fed and cared for, 'stead of being taken to jail, anyone can see that!"

"I do not see it," countered Zion Grimes. "If the laws of this land are being traduced, the traducers must pay the penalty for their malfeasance, while the slave—the slave goes back to her rightful owner to receive her just deserts!" He turned to glare at Appleton. *"Property,* sir, *property*—men must learn not to tamper with the legal chattels of decent, law-abiding American citizens. God's order is based on law, sir, and we poor humans must bow before it as wheat before the wind."

Appleton faced his adversary squarely. "You sanctimonious hypocrite, what do you know of God's order? I do not scorn the law but I do scorn you. And if you don't like it, then, sir, you may lump it."

"Steady, Jake," his brother muttered.

"Mind your words, Pagan Talcott!" replied Zion, using the sobriquet for Appleton that had attached to him since his college days, in consequence (among his friends) of his avid study of the classics and (among his enemies) of his abjuration of formal religion. "How dare you prate to me of God, you who haven't set foot in church anytime these last twenty years. Say more and I'll have an action for slander against you!"

"Have away, then. I scorn you as I scorn all men who would brutally and unfeelingly send a poor, half-starved human being such as that young girl back to a wicked master who has used her as you, sir, use your dog." Raising his voice once more, Appleton again addressed the crowd at large. "And I call on all good people in this place to stand up, to *rise* up if necessary, and to resist such laws to the last ounce of their strength!"

"Sedition!" cried Willie, dancing about. "The man's preaching rebellion!"

Zion Grimes's long pale hand came up in a hortatory gesture, and he loudly addressed the gathering crowd. "I call on all of you to witness before God, your Maker, that you have seen this man, Appleton Talcott of this place, stand in the streets and preach against the laws of this nation. I say the laws are being broken!"

Appleton pursed his lips thoughtfully. "Then in reference to the *law*, Deacon Grimes," he said, "I suggest you give some thought to cleaning your own house."

"Eh? What's that? How dare you, sir!"

Appleton spoke out clearly for all to hear. "I dare. And why not? It's a fact known by everyone here. That villainous son of yours who tried to run my daughter off to China with him has for years been sitting in lofty estate smuggling opium past the Chinese emperor's conservator for the profit of Grimes & Company, all the while cohabiting with a Chinese concubine, and committing no man knows what kind of outrages where he thinks none but himself can smell his filthy garbage."

"See here, Sinjin Grimes is no son of mine!—he is a rogue, sir, a rogue and a rascal, and none of my blood. I'm surprised you don't know that, since it was upon your precious Aurora the fellow's eye fell."

At this, Appleton flushed, lowering his large head as if to butt Zion's belly with it. Between clenched teeth he said, "My daughter's name is befouled on your lying lips, sir."

"Listen to the man, as if the girl were alabaster pure!" exclaimed Willie Wandsworth.

"Don't act a bigger fool than you have to, Willie," Appleton retorted, reaching out and giving the deacon's nose a businesslike tweak.

"Look! See—he's assaulted me!" cried Willie. "Everyone bear witness! You there, Constable, arrest the fellow—"

But no one was paying the deacon any attention as Val escorted the principals in the affair toward the jail door. "You, too," he said, nodding toward the slave catchers. "We don't require your presence, Willie," he added, slamming the door in the deacon's face.

No sooner had Willie put an ear to it than the door sprang open again. As he leapt backwards Jack Talcott stuck his head out. "You, there, Reuben," he called to Appleton's coachman. "Step lively, I want a word with you."

Jostling Willie aside, Reuben Priest made his way into the jail. But he was not out of sight for long. "What's happening in there?" demanded Willie when Reuben reappeared.

"That's fer me to know and you to find out," he replied without so much as a glance.

"The day is coming," Willie shouted after him. "You'll see!"

"So's Christmas, Deacon," replied the Negro, and made his way past the crowd, then broke into a trot, heading up the street toward Kingdom Come.

4

The Gates to Kingdom Come

HAVING FAILED TO extract any further details from Judah in the matter of Old Bobby's abrupt departure, Mab could not help her concern. What possible business had Appleton at the jail, unless there had been some difficulty? She pressed her hand to her breast. No, she reminded herself, I mustn't do that. Such telltale gestures were an invitation to questions she preferred not to answer.

For another quarter of an hour she waited, fretful and agitated. She sent Trubey running for a fresh cap and set it on her head, then fiddled nervously with the ribbons, the crown, the ruffles. She repinned her fichu with her coral brooch, then frolicked the lace tips of her handkerchief all across her front. She sighed, the clock ticked. Judah waited in the hall, a statue.

At last rousing hoofbeats sounded in the roadway; Judah opened the front door. "It's them, mistress." Reuben was swinging his team into the drive.

"Praise God, it's all right, then," Mab said, crossing herself. Judah disappeared and she could hear the servants all hurrying to the side door to meet the coach as it pulled into the drive, and, straightening her cap once more, she wrapped herself in her shawl and went out to greet the truants.

Jake, thank heaven, wore a broad smile that told her nothing too serious had befallen, and Lecky was smiling too. And there was Posie, with a new bonnet.

"Posie—your hat, I love it!" she exclaimed gaily. "What elegance!"

"From Lecky, Mama," Posie said, rushing up the steps to kiss her mother. "A present."

"Very stylish, dearie. Cherries are scrumptious. Lecky!" she called. "Come give your poor mama a kiss. Gray suits you, dearie, I always said it. The color of doves, soft and cool." She threw open her arms to hug and be hugged.

"Mother dear, how nice you look," Electra said, running up to Mab and kissing both her cheeks.

"Nonsense—I look a fright, but let's not speak of that. Tell me what's kept you all—?" Just then she realized that Old Bobby was in their midst. "Granddaddy—Jake! Will someone please tell me what's been going on? What were you doing at the jail? Is that—?"

"How now, pretty Kate, sweet Kate, loving Kate," said her husband, interrupting her flood of questions as he came up to buss her roundly. "Eftsoons, wench, hast thou no welcome for this, thy faithful loving husband? Wish you not, thy Jakie hast returned now?"

"Oh, Jake—!" Despite her pleasure at having him home safe and sound,

Mab ducked her head and pushed at his chest, for now she noticed the unfamiliar figure of a girl standing at the foot of the coach steps. "Who is that?" she whispered.

"Ah, indeed, you may well ask, my dear," began Appleton, carefully feeling his way with her. "That is a young woman of our acquaintance who—who—"

Electra hastened to her father's rescue. "Her name is Rose Mills, Mother; she's had a bit of difficulty and we were able to help her. We've brought her along here now and we—we—"

"We happened across her on the Post Road, Mama," Posie put in. "She had a slight accident."

"What sort of accident?"

"She turned her ankle. It really ought to be looked at, now we're home. I'm afraid it's badly swollen."

"Rose is a runaway, Mother," Electra said. "Some slave catchers were chasing her. We chanced across her and—"

Mab's expression was changing by degrees. "A runaway slave? Jake? Is it true?"

"It's true, Molly," Appleton said. "I'm afraid she's had quite a bad time of it, but she's on safe ground now and there's no further need for worry."

"Aren't the slave catchers still after her?"

"Not a bit, Mother. Rose is free."

"It's true! Granddaddy freed her!" Posie proclaimed. "He's bought and paid for her."

Bewildered, Mab turned to her father-in-law. "You've bought a slave? Is this why you were summoned to the jail?"

"Correct on both counts, my dear," said Old Bobby, smiling broadly. "For all of six minutes this young person was my bounden property."

"Six minutes?"

"I *told* you, Mother, Granddaddy freed her! The slave catchers took the money and went away and now Rose is with us."

Mab looked more closely at the silent girl. "But what are we to do with her?"

"I think she needs a warm bath and some fresh clothes," Posie said. "Don't you?"

Mab agreed. "I expect a bath might be a good beginning," she said. "Trubey, take the girl along to the kitchen and give her something to eat. And send Jeff to fetch Dr. Standish to look at that ankle. She can be put to bed over the carriage house."

While Trubey and Electra assisted Rose inside and along the kitchen passage, Mab took her husband's hand again. "No sense standing here; come in where it's warm, all of you. I want to know more about this business. What do you plan to do with the girl?"

When they were in the parlor it was Posie who took the matter up. "Mother, we thought you might find a place for Rose here. You could use another pair of hands."

"Nonsense, there are far too many hands—and mouths—as it is." Mab sat down by the fire and looked up at her husband. "Go on."

"See here, Molly, the girl's unfortunate, she's been starved and whipped—"

"And branded!" Posie put in.

"Yes, branded, too," Appleton concurred. "We thought—that is, *Lecky* thought—well . . . you haven't had anyone to rub up lately—"

"Oh no, dearie, thank you kindly!" Mab said sharply. "You're not bringing another waif home for rubbing up, Jake Talcott. I'm not in a rubbing-up mood, thank you all the same."

"Mother, don't upset yourself," Posie said, composing herself on the arm of Mab's chair. "Anyway, we don't have to decide anything just now. When Rose has had her bath and rested and Dr. Terry has seen to her ankle—"

"Oh Papa! You're home!" Pina came tripping down the staircase to kiss her father. "Why did no one wake me? I ought to have been down. Po, Posie, darling—and where's Lecky?"

"In the kitchen," Posie said, giving her sister a kiss. "We have a visitor," she added. "Come along and I'll tell you all about it."

"Wait—Papa, dear, did you remember to bring me my Schubert?"

"My dear, if you'll just run up and look in my morocco portmanteau. And you might come across a tin of peppermint drops as well . . ."

"Oh dearest Papa, thank you!" cried Pina, running to kiss him again. The bell of her skirts swung as she wheeled and started out, then turned back the other way. "First I must examine this mysterious visitor you've brought home with you. Whoever can it be?"

When she and Posie had gone and Old Bobby had excused himself, Mab sighed and laid her head against the back of the chair, glancing up to meet Appleton's gaze.

"So, my dear, all well at home?" he inquired.

"Ducky," she replied, putting out a hand. He took it and pressed it to his lips.

"Glad to see your old Jake, are you?"

"What a question! Do you suppose you can go off for a week without my missing you?"

"I have something for you. I . . ." His manner was tentative, as if he feared she might not like it.

"Ahh, Jake, how many times—you're not to spend your money on me," she scolded. Still, she had known he would; he never went away without bringing something back to give her. He felt in his pockets and produced a small box, which he placed in her hand.

"Open it, Molly dear," he said. Inside was a ring, its violet-colored stone sparkling in the light.

"Why, Jake," she said with mock severity, "what's a wife to think when her husband brings her home jewelry after he's been off to the big city?"

"She's to think he loves her very much, I expect. Certainly no other reason. Does it fit? Try it on and see."

"It's beautiful, Jake," she said, slipping it on and holding out her hand to admire it. "An amethyst, too—my favorite! Count on you to remember. Saints above, you'll spoil me dreadfully. Where'd you get it?"

"I bought it off a Chinaman on the docks."

"The very idea! Buying gems from heathens amid the sinks of New York. Next you'll be telling me you've been at the Five Points, dancing and consorting with who knows what hussies."

"No, my love, the only female I've happened upon is this unhappy Miss Mills."

Mab made a rueful face. "Oh, Jake, honestly. You have such a tender heart, you *had* to bring her home. What *am* I to do with you?"

"Not my idea. Lecky's the one. And Posie. And I have to say Dad snapped to when it came to the ante. He never blinked."

"He wouldn't," Mab said. "But I still don't want—"

Her words were cut off by a violent screech from the kitchen quarters and in a moment Agrippina rushed through the doorway. "Papa! Mama! Well, I never—!"

"What is it, what's happened?" cried Mab, getting to her feet in alarm.

"That girl—that wretched little—"

"It's all right, everyone," said Electra, hurrying in after her sister.

"Pina dear, calm yourself for pity's sake."

"But what's happened?" Appleton demanded. "Is someone hurt?"

"No, Father, there's no cause for alarm," Electra said. "It was merely a discussion that went a bit too far."

"She called me a nasty name, the wicked creature!" Pina cried, her expression a tragic mask.

"Pina—Pina, dear, it's all *right*," Electra insisted gently. "You're overwrought."

"I don't care! I won't stay another minute in this house while that wretched girl is under our roof! Mama—Papa—you must tell her to go, this very instant! Or I shall pack and take flight to Glens Falls."

"Pina dear, your sister's right, you're overwrought," said her father. "Calm yourself, do. Go along upstairs and find your music; we can speak of this later."

"Very well, Papa. I'm going." She sniffed and dabbed at her eyes. "But I won't come down again until that interloper is gone."

She struck one of her melodramatic poses in the doorway until Electra coaxed her from the room; as soon as she was gone Posie flew in.

"Father?"

"Yes, dearest?"

"It really wasn't Rose's fault. Pina provoked her. She kept asking her questions, and Rose is extremely tired, truly."

"What is she doing now?"

"We've fed her, she's having a bath, then she's going to lie down. They're warming the room and fixing a bed."

"Good. After dinner I would like her to come into the parlor and meet everyone. We'll hear her story then. Now, why don't you go up and help Lecky calm Pina."

When Posie had gone, Appleton persuaded his wife to sit beside him again, and taking her hand, he turned the ring on her finger.

"Do you truly like it? Does it please you?"

"Of course it pleases me. But this girl, Jake—certainly you can see that taking her in will prove a serious mistake."

"You know how excitable Pina is. She'll soon come around."

"So you may believe," Mab returned. "But it seems to me there's trouble written right across that girl's forehead, trouble with a capital T. I'm surprised you don't see it for yourself. You want to do the right thing, I know, but we don't need any discord in this house. Please, I entreat you."

"I'm sure you're right, my dear." He leaned down and kissed her. "Well, we'll allow her to stay the night, shall we?"

"Yes, to be sure." But despite Appleton's assurances, Mab feared Miss Rose Mills was very much like that camel one had heard of, which being allowed to put its head in at the window for a peek, very quickly had not only head but neck, four feet, tail, and hump in as well. And Mabel Talcott was not just now in the market for camels.

5

The Universal Aunt

Since the bitter loss of her cherished Captain Barnaby, whose ship, the *Hattie D.,* had gone to Davy Jones's locker at Havana harbor a dozen years before, it had become Mehatibel Duckworth's frequent custom to entertain an elite group of guests culled from among the female complement of the almshouse on the opposite side of March Street. Hattie endeavored to arrange these gatherings with the occupants of the Brick Farm several times a month during the summers, more frequently to help pass the long New England winters, encouraging the ladies to bring along their piecework, to sit in her cozy parlor with their teacups and their cakes, after which modest repast they thriftily pecked at whatever crumbs of gossip chanced to be lying about while their needles sang their sewing songs.

Hattie's invitations were her way of showing her profound gratitude, for unlike these other widows, she had been able to retain her own house and hearth, and in her nightly prayers she thanked the Almighty and her Barnaby for keeping her out of the almshouse. "I hope to die afore I ever see the day they catch me on the Brick Farm," she would vow. "I hate the very notion, and m' Barn'd be ashamed t'know I was left to end up in such a place."

Going "across the way" to Snug Harbor gave the almshouse ladies something to look forward to besides sitting in the window to watch what little there was to be watched, or carding tow or cutting shoe soles from saddle slabs, which tedious labors provided them a portion of their keep. Reduced in circumstances, they had been obliged to surrender what little independence had remained to them and sleep in a charity bed, eat charity food, and hope for charity clothes to cover their naked backs. Still, they were stalwart souls who met their fate with admirable stoicism, knitting and sewing and tatting their separate ways to the boneyard down the road.

On the day that Rose Mills arrived in Pequot Landing, half a dozen of these ladies were gathered in Aunt Hat's cluttered front room, the patchwork of bright calicoes and ginghams spread across their laps as neatly and deftly they drew their needles in and out, their gold thimbles poised daintily above the patches. Like so many silver-haired Dorcases, they stitched and cross-stitched, their petite, aged feet shod in darned cotton stockings and worn strap shoes resting on little footstools or on piled volumes—*Pilgrim's Progress, Plutarch's Lives,* the *Aeneid*—the murmur of their conversation like the gentle cooing of doves.

Presently the clock sounded four solemn notes, and Aunt Hat rested her needle.

"Georgie late today?" asked Mrs. Dinshaw.

"Oh, Georgianner'll be along, don't you fret. She'll stay at that store till the last cock crows if things aren't just right to her eye. Warren Burdin was sayin' just t'other day he don't know what he ever did afore she come to work for him."

"Wel-l, I don't know that anyone else would have took Georgie Ross," said a doubtful Mary-Martha Grisby, drawing her needle through and pausing with it immobile in the air. "Folks don't always care to have a queer type around them, do they?"

"Shame on you, Mary-Martha!" declared Hat with asperity. "Sure Georgie had a bad spell after seein' her family dead, who wouldn't? But that were ten years ago, an' now she's no more queer than your own silly self! If you're goin' t'live in a glass house, dear, best keep your thoughts to yourself lest a body lob a stone through your pane."

"Poor thing," said Adah Coverly, shaking her head. "Such a tragedy. I just hope that strain don't run in the family."

Hat bristled again. "Oh, do hush, Adah, I'm not partial to that sort o' talk either," she said. "Georgie Ross don't need the likes of us old ladies cluckin' over her. Leave her t'be."

"Can I help it if I feel sorry for the poor thing?" asked Mrs. Coverly. "We're just afraid she'll still end up with addled brains, like that poor Alice Acres who drowned herself in the well."

"Alice Acres, my foot," Hat snorted. "Alice Acres wasn't sound in the beezer from the time she was weaned."

Aunt Hat's tone had turned slightly contrary, and Mrs. May endeavored to pour oil on troubled waters. "I know she's a comfort to you, Hattie, just having her here in the house."

"Aye, she is," Hat agreed. "Georgie'd be a comfort to the Archangel Gabriel himself."

"But she's been so often heard to say she won't marry." Mary-Martha took up the argument again. "I guess she's afraid to pass the craziness along to her offspring. Enid Multree married her cousin Bill; Bill, he was a crazy coot, and between the two of 'em, they passed the bats on through that family like a case of warts."

"Warts yourself!" Aunt Hat scoffed. "Not a one of you knows Georgian-ner Ross like I do, and I tell you she's right as rain! If a girl don't choose to marry, whose applesauce is that, after all? Spinsterdom's a honorable state, ask Tilda and Bettina Talcott, ask Rowena Gildersleeve." The latter name produced a titter: Rowena Gildersleeve was the village's oldest old maid.

"Pray tell, what have they to do with anything, Mehatibel?" Mary-Martha was not to be silenced. "I guess if *my* father was a madman and a murderer five times over, I'd think twice afore bringin' any spawn into this world."

Hat's gold thimble rapped sharply on the arm of her chair, a rattlesnake sounding its warning. "Mary-Martha Grisby, I'm surprised at you, I truly am!" she snapped.

"I ain't," put in Mrs. Dinshaw. "Mary-Martha, you never did have the care of your words. Where's the brain the Almighty gave you? How can you talk 'bout Georgiana Ross like that, an old parcel like you? Wasn't your ma in an Irish fit when them Mohawks scalped your granddad over at the Cherry Valley massacre? Didn't they have to put her in a tight bag to quiet her some? Every cupboard's got its skeleton, y'know."

Aunt Hat smiled with grim satisfaction. Let Mary-Martha fill her pipe with that. She always had been an addlepated fool!

Heads turned toward the door as the gate latch was heard to lift and fall and a wagon pulled alongside the house. "That'll be Hermie Light with m'load of firewood," Hat said, "and he's got Ambo along with him," she added, peering out the window. She watched as Ambo Buck pulled an axe from the woodpile and zestfully began chopping kindling.

"Well, Hermie, have you brought me m'cord o' stove fuel?" Hat asked, opening the door for him. "Step in, it's chilly, don't cool off m'house."

Hermie trooped in with a heavy tread, his burly figure filling the narrow doorway, removed his cap, and bobbed to the circle. "What a lot of seamstresses you have here, Aunt Hat. How do, ladies, you're all looking pert this afternoon." Red-faced and hearty, with Atlas shoulders, he seemed to take up the whole room. "Phew, it's gettin' frosty out there."

"Present your backside to the flames, Herm, why don'tcha?" Hat suggested, shutting the door behind him. "And give us the news from abroad."

"I guess there's news aplenty all right. Haven't you heard, you bide-at-homes?"

"Nary a word. What's about?"

"Some doin's up t'the Center a bit ago. Appleton Talcott bought himself a darky gal. A bounden slave."

"Surely not a human one!" cried a scandalized Mary-Martha.

"Don't talk nonsense, Mary-Martha, what other kind is there!" Hat snapped. "Explain yourself, son, and don't leave out a word."

Hermie assured the gathering that he had never spoken truer words and he went on to describe how the Talcott coach had rolled into town hiding a runaway slave, how the slave catchers had found them and were going to take the girl back until Old Bobby Talcott put his cash on the barrel head to buy her up.

"Mercy!" "He didn't!" "Think of that!" came the startled reactions.

"There's bold work for Jake!" said Hat. "What else?"

"Deacon Grimes threatened App with the law."

"Yes? And then what?" the ladies cried.

"Then Jack Talcott arranged a settlement, and that was when Apple paid up on the runaway. Only he didn't have the wherewithal, so Old Bobby was called in to answer the need. 'Twas his cash that clinched the deal."

"But what's a Talcott doin', buyin' a slave, for pity's sakes?" Hat asked, incredulous. "Talcotts is abolition, every last one of 'em."

Hermie shook his head. " 'Twas only for the moment, Aunt Hat. No sooner paid for than she got manumitted. All done official."

"Mean to say Bob paid good money for her, then freed her on the spot?"

"That he did."

"There's a good Christian sperrit," declared Hat with considerable satisfaction. "What happened then?"

"They took her off to Kingdom Come."

"For Mabel to rub up, I'll bet!" cried Hat, clapping her hands. "And you say Zion Grimes didn't like it? I'm not surprised. He'd go to lengths to see every darky weighed down in fetters or chased outta town."

Just then the back door banged open and the dark-faced, thickset figure of Cinnamon Comorra appeared, lugging a bucket of water from the well.

Toothless and wrinkled, her copper brow ribbed with perpetual reproach of the world, Ambo Buck's "grandmother," the Princess Suneemon, who had raised him, had been part of Hattie Duckworth's pint-sized menage for more than a decade now. Having abandoned her former digs in the tavern cellar to chore for Georgiana after her illness, she had simply stayed, making herself at home in Hat's toolshed. It was her way of repaying Georgiana for what she had done for Ambo, who, having begun as a wild half-breed boy chained up in the tavern yard, now held down the job of chief clerk at Burdin's seed store, where Georgiana kept the accounts and, if truth be told, pretty much managed the day-to-day operation of the business.

Now, seeing Cinnamon enter, Hat said, "Cinnermin, set down your bucket there an' come on in here quick. Tell us if you seen Appleton Talcott facing down the deacon!"

Cinnamon stood in the kitchen doorway, her expression as close as it could manage to a grin. "Dat Mist' Apple Tackett, he han' it some smart to dat Zi' Gri', plenny sass, you bet. Suneemon hear ev' word. Dat scrawny li'l Deacon Willie, he go runnin' all 'bout like a long-tailed rat. Him make plenny mischeff, you bet. Apple Tackett, him get de las' laugh. Shee-*yut!*"

"*Eek!*" Mary-Martha Grisby cheeped, fluttering a birdlike hand to her withered lips. The rest were equally agog.

When half an hour later a rig pulled up outside and a bright-cheeked Georgiana Ross came in with her office satchel, she found Hat putting the kettle on and blowing up the fire.

"Who was't brought you home, dear?" Hat inquired with interest. "Not the Rev'rend?"

Georgiana said it was the man from the printing office, with whom she'd been going over copy for Burdin's spring catalogue. "Cinnamon," she added, "put on a sadiron to heat, please. I'll just give my dress a lick. Agrippina sent word dinner's been called for half past eight, so I don't have to rush as usual."

"If you was at the printin' office, I 'spect you missed the fa-fa-ra at the jail," Hat said. "Set down, while I fix you a nice cup o' tea and I'll tell all."

For the next quarter hour, along with the tea, Georgiana Ross was served up the details of the surprising event as related by Hermie Light to the ladies of Hat's sewing circle. "It's a fact as I'm standin' here, George. A real live slave—what d'ya think of that?"

Georgiana didn't know what to think of it, but she wasn't surprised by Old Bobby's generosity. As long as she had known him, Grandaddy Talcott had been guilty of all manner of humane acts; seeing a runaway slave set free, even at the not inconsiderable price of three hundred and twenty-five dollars, was but one more. And as far as Georgiana was concerned, it was money well spent, for she was as devoted and eager an abolitionist as any of the Talcotts.

"I-ron hot," Cinnamon grunted from the kitchen. Georgiana excused herself, and, taking her tea, went to press out her dress for the party.

Minutes later, Ambo Buck was rapping at the kitchen door, asking to speak with her. Ambo was a demon at splitting kindling, and he came by Snug Harbor regularly to oblige Georgiana and Hat with whatever yard chores needed seeing to. His once long lank hair had been cut into a close-cropped poll, and as he came in, his hands were hidden in the roomy pockets of a heavy belted jacket Georgiana's shears and needle had fashioned for him.

Was it possible, she wondered, looking at him, that this astonishing transformation had actually been accomplished? There were some who denied that the two beings could possibly be the same, the stinking near-savage brutally chained in the tavern yard and the dark giant, soft-spoken, well-mannered, and well-read, who was now third in command at Burdin's Best Seeds. Of the boys who had lorded it over him when he had first slowly and methodically measured seeds into paper packets, three now were hired hands on other men's farms, two had small spreads of their own but could scarcely write their names, while two more had disappeared altogether, swallowed up out on the Ohio Reserve. To none of them could a person point with pride; Ambo alone stood out, Ambo of all of them was worth notice or the time of day. Ambo was Georgiana's pride and joy.

He was accompanied by Mavra, the red dog he kept always by him, a descendant of the dog named Red that had been hers when she was a girl, and now Georgiana and her former pupil laughed together as the setter bitch and the cat, Murray Hill, warily renewed their acquaintanceship. Refusing the chair she offered him, Ambo accepted a steaming cup of broth and a square of johnnycake.

"Now *you* tell me," Georgiana began. "What about this runaway slave— did you see her? What does she look like?"

"She was a sorry sight, Miss Ross. If it wasn't for the Talcotts, she'd be on her way south again, that's for sure. I feel sorry for her, all right, but they ought to just let her go on her way, now she's freed."

"Why do you say that?"

"She's got a way about her. Grammaw says she'll be trouble for the Talcotts if they keep her around."

"Is Cinnamon foretelling again? Well, we'll just have to see, won't we?"

"Yes, ma'am. Branded, too, I heard, on her shoulder. She must have run away before."

"Then I'm glad she finally succeeded. And if she's going to stay around these parts we must try and help her."

Ambo shook his head gravely. "Dunno, Miss Ross, some folks are past helping."

"Why, Ambo Buck, I'm surprised at you! After what you and I have been through together! Perhaps Mabel Talcott means to rub her up."

"She'll take a deal of that, I reckon. There's sows and silk purses, but the one's not the other." He set down his empty cup and licked some crumbs from his lips while Georgiana wielded the iron. "Miss Ross," he began again, "I've heightened the kindling pile, tomorrow Hermie and I'll unload the rest of the cordwood. I want to get out to the Mountain before dark, if you don't mind. Bessie's baby's due."

The seriousness of his tone picked Georgiana up sharp. "What is it, is something wrong?"

Ambo shook his head. "No more than usual. Things just aren't much good out there. Mr. Burdin sent them plenty of seed this year, but you can't raise any kind of respectable crop on that land—there's hardly enough water to drink. You know what it's like. Most of the men don't have much to do but sit around and swill the whiskey Deacon Willie sells in that grogshop of his, while the women go hungry. Père Margeaux does what he can, but they need—I don't know—something—someone . . ." He shifted his boots, seeking expression.

What he said was certainly true. While Pequot housewives had begun employing some of the older Lamentation girls as domestics, in recent years a village subscription had kept most of the indigents on the dole, paying them to stay out of town, confined to Two Stone and points west and liable to a fine if they were found within the purlieus of Pequot. Since most of the dole money was recouped through the deacon's hard spirits enterprise, only the Abbé Margeaux's indefatigable efforts on behalf of his "children" had prevented outright disaster.

"Anyhow," Ambo went on, heading for the door, "thank you for the soup. And the corn cake." He stopped at the door. "Oh, by the bye, I found three more shingles on the ground. I think Mrs. Duckworth ought to give some thought to laying on a new roof."

Georgiana's look was doubtful. "Hm. How much do you think such a thing might cost?"

"I'll see to it, don't you worry."

"We couldn't let you do it gratis, Ambo. Besides, Mr. Burdin needs all your time."

"I've got Sundays. Foote Crowe and some other fellows could probably help me out."

"All right, but I insist we pay for the shingles. You know Aunt Hat never likes to be beholden."

"It's a small thing compared to what you've done for me all these years. I couldn't ever repay you for that."

She put a hand on his arm. "That's very kind, Ambo, but you already have—there's nothing to repay, truly. You know how I feel about it."

Both of them were experiencing a distinct embarrassment at the turn the conversation had taken. Neither enjoyed recalling certain episodes of the long-ago past, but after Ambo had said good evening, turning to give her one of his rare smiles as he slipped out the door, Georgiana could not keep her mind from harking back, while she put the finishing touches on the dress Miss Simms had sewn for her last summer.

More than a decade had passed and still she felt cold as the tomb recalling that snowy Christmas Day when Old Bobby had appeared here in this very room with the awful news. Dead. All dead. She could think now of Momma and Peter, of Little Tom and Mary Ann and Dottie, as they had been in life, not as horribly mutilated bodies, the ghastliness of which had filled her mind at first; but the sharp, wrenching sense of guilt would never entirely leave her. Her fault, hers alone—she ought to have seen what was coming and prevented it. But for her, Momma would still be alive. And *she herself had lived,* she alone had been spared. Had she really gone mad? She thought perhaps she must have done, but her memory remained cloudy. Certainly her behavior had been odd, and the strange paradox was that although she had feared madness because of Tom Ross, it was the certain knowledge that she was not his issue that had temporarily deprived her of her reason.

Over the years, she had managed to make a little life for herself: useful employment at Burdin's seed store; a home at Snug Harbor with Hattie Duckworth, an aged cat called Murray Hill, and Cinnamon Comorra, who lived at the bottom of the sunflower patch in Hat's toolshed, keeping chickens and brewing up her herbal decoctions, which she bottled and sold around town. And she had good friends: the Talcotts, of course, and the Quoiles, Hermie Light, and above all, Helen Haverstraw, bless her soul. Thanks to God for Helen. Out of the horror and tragedy that had blighted Georgiana's life and left her alone in the world, there had come this single blessing. Helen, who in so short a time had become her friend, and then was discovered to be her sister as well. And if the mere thought of Zion Grimes made her inwardly cringe, and the sight of him filled her with detestation and the profoundest feelings of antipathy—fortunately for her peace of mind the man went to lengths to shun her, even going so far as to cross the street at her approach—his daughter (for such Georgiana had learned she was, and as such half-sister to Helen) was not the same girl who had sat lazy summer evenings teaching Ambo his ABC's, who had felt the urgency of growing up, eager to be about her life's business, to unfurl and fly bright lily banners before the world, determined to make something not only of the wretched Indian boy but of herself into the bargain.

Looking back, she often reflected on the bold rashness of the girl she had once been, that foolish, headstrong girl who had hoped to right all the wrongs and cure all the ills of the planet. She found a certain ironic amusement in contemplating that other person, so brash and idealistic, so crammed with notions of how the world ought to be, and disdain for those who did not agree with her. But she no longer was that naive person. She was "Miss Ross," the old maid who ran the seed store office, fond of children, the "universal aunt" to all the small fry, happy in her friends, keeping to her door stoop and hearthside. If she looked prim and severe, this was part of her design, for despite the dismaying truth of her parentage as it had been revealed to her by Rachel Grimes, and despite Cinnamon's prediction of not one marriage but three, she had determined never to take a husband. The narrow confines of spinsterdom had been mapped out for females like her, and she believed there was a perfectly good reason why this should be so: God intended to spare her from further pain and horror, but spare her only if she would slip quietly and unobtrusively through her allotted span of years, never disturbing the calm surface of things, no wind upon the water making ripples. No matter that the guest minister at Sunday service found her alto solo charming, or the widower abolitionist Dr. Parker declared her delightfully forthright and sincere, no matter that Hermie Light seldom hid his hopes of making her his wife: marriages were made in heaven and heaven was not for her, not anymore.

But then, what *was* for her? What could the future hold for Miss Ross, keeper of the keys and seals and cabinets at Burdin's Best Seeds of Pequot Landing, Connecticut, with her kneehole desk in the back corner lit by its Argand lamp, with her hair pinned in a neat bun, broadcloth sleeves pulled over her own, a tidy smock over her dress—making no more of looking glasses than she had as a girl, when Tom Ross was alive and watching her? Was this what became of dreams, to have life grind them in the dust?

"You've seen the worst God's got in store for you, George," Aunt Hat had once said to her. "There's nothin's ever goin' t'happen in your life bad as what's been. You've taken the measure of your stren'th and you know what you're capable of. You've been heated up in the flames, like Shadrach in the fiery furnace, and you didn't melt, you're whole again. That hot furnace made good steel of you. God annealed you and that's His blessin' on you. You're a late bloomer, Georgianner Ross. You're goin' t'bloom late but hardy. See if your Aunt Hat's not right."

At the time Georgiana had refused to acknowledge any possibility of truth in Hat's words, but of late they had been sounding again in her ears, buzzing like a swarm of wasps. Foolish ever to imagine that she would flaunt her banners, foolish to think that she, a simple village girl, could change the world, or alter fate one whit. For her the die was cast, cast in hard pig-iron, nothing to be done about that. Best to hide herself away, let the world spin as it would, and stay well out of the wind, and yet . . .

As she heard the church bell's solemn ring, she came quickly back to herself, to who and where she was, and she thanked her stars she was no more than who she was, and was glad as well she was no less.

6

Under the Bust of Walter Scott

SHORTLY BEFORE SEVEN o'clock that evening, wearing her modish dress of dark blue barrège, with her mother's brooch pinned where the tips of her lace collar joined, and her best bonnet and cloak, and carrying her reticule and flute case—there was usually music at Talcott "evenings"—Georgiana walked up March Street toward Main. The chilly evening was thick with the pungent smell of burning leaves and as she passed the church she could hear the strains of Aunt Hat's organ playing—Friday evening choir practice.

Holy, holy, holy, Lord God Almighty . . . the notes of the hymn followed her as she rounded the church and proceeded along Main Street.

"Hullo, Georgie Ross!" A familiar voice interrupted her thoughts and she looked to see Bushrod Grimes's rig circle the church green and pull up beside her. "Well, say there, what're you all dressed up for?"

"Oh, Rod, don't be such a stuffed duck," Georgiana returned smartly. "I'm going in to dinner at Kingdom Come. Lecky's home."

"Tell me something I don't know, lady. Everywhere you go that's all you hear, 'Lecky Lecky Lecky.' Sounds like someone's callin' the hens to feed. I hear she's going to shoot off her mouth in front of the Anti-Slavery Society, that'll be a treat."

"I'm sure they'll think it is. Will you be attending?"

"Hell, you know better than that, Georgie Ross. The only time you'll see me at one of your abolition meetin's is when I'll be breakin' it up."

"Oh, but I forgot, you're the town know-it-all, aren't you? Well, just read the papers, I'm sure they'll be giving it full coverage."

"Yeah, I'll be sure and do that. Well, I gotta gee up, Isobel can't stand bein' kept waitin'."

He rolled away without tipping his hat, a form of manners he seldom observed with her.

Georgiana had little trouble imagining how much Isobel enjoyed being kept waiting. Bushrod Grimes and Isobel Shaylor had become engaged, and it was Georgiana's wager that Rod would be toeing the line the minute the ring was on Isobel's finger. Though why the daughter of Syd Shaylor, scion of one of the old "River God" families, would want Bushrod Grimes for a husband was beyond Georgiana's understanding. Still she had to admit that in the last few years Rod had undergone a considerable transformation. Though he was the son and heir of Zion Grimes, as a youth he had affected the manners of a farmhand. Now there were few hints of the farm about him. Perhaps it was reading law with Judge Palfrey that had changed him, or the power his position at Grimes & Company gave him over his step-brother Sinjin, who, as sea captain, toiled for the house of Grimes in the China Seas. Whatever the cause, Rod had taken on the appearance and attitudes of a man whose eye was on large goals, who looked forward to a successful future, a large bank account, and his name in all the papers. His clumsy gait had become a citified pace, he no longer guffawed over bawdy jokes but favored a more sophisticated style of humor, and he wore not a hunting cap but a tall beaver hat with a curling brim. He had learn to say "please" and "thank you," and he was a pious churchgoer, the youngest deacon in the congregation.

How he would react if he ever learned that he was also her half-brother was something Georgiana had often thought about. He was turning into a shrewd man, no doubt, but suddenly to find out that Georgie Ross, the miller's girl, the butt of so much of his humor, was actually his sister would surely pull him up short. Nor would such a shocking piece of news sit well with his intended wife.

Brother mine, Georgiana reflected as Rod's shiny trap drove out of sight, go and live your life and leave me to live mine, and with this thought she went briskly on her way. She had better things to do than worry over the heir to the house of Grimes. The bill of fare at Kingdom Come was always exemplary, and she had a good appetite.

Arriving at Number 17, she opened the gate and turned in, filled with a sudden pleasure and anticipation as she hurried up the walk. Though very nearly a member of the family, she never entered the house after four without ringing; Trubey would come, or Judah. She heard a familiar, merry laugh in the hallway and when the door was opened it was Posie Talcott herself who greeted her. They rushed into each other's arms as if they hadn't seen each other for a month, with kisses, exclamations, and words of welcome.

"How cold your cheek is, Georgie," Posie said, drawing her in and shutting the door. "Give me your things. I see you brought your flute, but I don't think there's to be any music this evening."

As Georgiana untied her cloak and bonnet she looked around her. This was the way she loved the house, bright and warm, replete with that festive sense of fun and family that had made Kingdom Come so talked about. After hanging up her things, she took Posie's hands and spun her around. "Posie, dear, how pretty you look! A new frock—and your hair, captivating—I love those little curls. Tell me everything, I can see you're bursting to talk. How was your trip?"

"It was wonderful, I'll tell you all about it later. Of course you've heard about Rose—what excitement! After dinner, she's going to describe to us what it was like being a slave. Lecky wants her to speak to the Anti-Slavery Society here in Pequot at the next meeting, too. It's all going to be in the papers! Think of it—she'll soon be famous." She put a finger to her lips: from the parlor there emanated Great-Aunt Blanche Talcott's vigorous complaint against the Deacons Grimes and Wandsworth. "Come meet Rose first," Posie whispered, slipping an arm through Georgiana's and conducting her along the kitchen passageway. "I don't think she's in a terribly good mood. She's already had one quarrel with Pina, and another with Halley. We don't want Mama to know about that one—she's bound to send her packing. And I want us to keep her. She'll like it here when she gets to feeling at home. We're bound to help her."

The kitchen was bustling, with Halley and her helpers engaged in getting dinner ready for the table. In the corner, her bandaged ankle propped on a stool, sat the girl Rose Mills. Instead of the well-advertised dress of yellow calico, she now wore a dark gown whose austerity somehow suited her, bringing out her olive skin and lending her a decorous air. Georgiana recognized the garment as an old one of Pina's that her practical-minded mother had undoubtedly dispossessed her of.

"Hello. I'm Georgiana Ross," she said to the girl, who glanced up warily, then dropped her eyes. "You must be Rose. Posie's been telling me about you. How is your ankle? Did Dr. Standish take care of it for you?"

Rose's look narrowed. "Folks round here sure ask a heap o' questions."

Georgiana laughed. "You're perfectly right, I do. I'm sorry, I didn't mean to pry."

Rose turned toward Posie. "Who she?" she asked behind her hand.

"I told you about her, Rose," Posie replied. "Georgie used to work for us."

"Doan look like no hired gal t'me."

Georgiana laughed again. "It was quite a few years ago, I'm afraid. I must have been just about your age, I imagine."

Rose darted her a look, almost rude. "How come you knows how old Ah is?"

"I'm just guessing—but you don't look twenty yet. What a lucky escape you've had. Aren't you fortunate the Talcotts happened along."

Rose shrugged, as if such things hardly mattered.

"How does it feel to be a free woman?" Georgiana asked.

"Feel the same. 'Cept Ah done been fed good fo' a change. An' Ah got me a nice downy bed."

"Posie tells me you're from South Carolina. She also says that you can read and write."

"Ah reads from the Bible some. 'Bout Solomon an' Sheba, 'bout Sampson jerkin' down the temple, 'bout Rebecca takes her bucket to the well."

"You must do very nicely, Rose." Georgiana half-turned to speak over her shoulder. "Halley, did you hear that?" she asked.

"Ah hears." From the scowl on Halley's face it was plain that she did not care to have Rose in her kitchen even if she was familiar with the Scriptures.

"And what will you do, now that you're here?" Georgiana inquired of Rose.

"How should Ah know? Rose ain't no forchune-teller. Ah 'specks they's gon' t'put me t'work. An' Ah cain't but hobble aroun' some, Ah done spraint m' ankle an' the doctuh say Ah done pull two tennins. White folks allus 'specks a heap o' work outta a darky. Ah doan see that Rose'll be settin' aroun' much."

"You needn't worry, Rose," Georgiana said. "I'm sure the Talcotts won't expect too much of you. Would you like some books to read?"

Rose tossed her head. "Ah ain't studyin' t'read no books."

"Well, if you change your mind, Posie can lend you some, I'm sure." She smiled warmly and touched Rose's hand. "I'm glad you're here. You'll soon fit right in, you'll see. If I can help, let me know, won't you?"

Rose jerked her hand away and glowered. "Rose don't need nothin' from nobody. Ah ain't axin' no favors."

"Georgie Ross, y'all get inside with the white folks," interposed Halley with a disapproving glare. "That ungrateful gal plumb full up with meanness, she need a switch took to huh backside, thass all." She pushed Georgiana toward the door, then turned on Rose with another frown. "For shame, gal. You don't know how t'talk to yo' bettahs. You ain't down home in no 'gator swamp, you's in Pequot Lannin' now an' you gots t'learn to ack lak a lady."

Rose's reply was cut off by the swinging door as Posie ushered Georgiana back down the passageway.

"I was right, wasn't I?" Posie said.

"She is a bit unfriendly. I expect you've got to give her time."

The doors between the parlors had been thrown open to accommodate the sizable gathering. Georgiana was greeted by cheery fires burning in both grates, extra lamps had been lighted, and in the best parlor the familiar portrait of Aurora Sheffield gazed down from its gilt frame. It was always the breath of yesterday to Georgiana, that exquisitely modeled face, the milky flesh of the shoulders showing above the yellow dress, the sweet smile on those rosy lips, the golden hair.

Slowly Georgiana made her way through the room, greeting first her hostess, then Old Bobby, then the aunts, Bettina and Tilda, and finally moving on to present herself before Aunt Blanche, who, as she invariably did, inspected her as if she were still the Follybrook hired girl about to pass around the soup. "Good evening, Aunt Blanche," she said politely, but withholding the curtsy the dowager obviously expected.

"You are looking thin, Georgiana," Aunt Blanche noted. "You're letting Burdin work you too hard. Have you heard the news? Appleton's bought himself a slave. And put the quietus to Zion Grimes. *There's* news!"

Georgiana nodded. "Yes, Aunt. I've just met Rose. I'm sure she'll get on fine."

"She's a plucky creature," Matilda Talcott put in, while Betts wielded her ear trumpet to catch every word. "You have to look twice to see she's a darky, too."

"Has Jake decided what to do with her yet?" Betts asked loudly.

"Lower your voice, Bettina," said her sister. *"We're* not deaf—*you* are."

"Apple wants to keep her—Mabel says no," Blanche put in, turning her rings on wrinkled fingers. "Who'll win that battle, I wonder?" Abruptly she changed the subject. "Georgie, can't you find me something amusing from the lending library next time you're there?"

"Yes, of course, Aunt, I'll be happy to see what I can find."

"And can you spare me some time to write one or two brief letters for me?" Blanche had arthritis in her fingers, and Georgiana occasionally acted as her amanuensis. It was tedious and often tiring work, yet she could hardly say no.

She was freed from having to respond to any more of Aunt Blanche's importunings by Jack Talcott, who came across the room to rescue her. Like so many others, Georgiana enjoyed a warm relationship with Pequot's favorite bachelor. At fifty-three, Appleton's younger brother was as charming and insouciant as ever. Still the town's gayest bon vivant and wit, possessed of a masterful cook and a comfortable house and invitations everywhere, "Gentleman Jack" enjoyed a rare social status, in addition to being regarded as one of the finest trial lawyers in the state of Connecticut, unsurpassed in the courtroom unless by that wily septuagenarian Cent Dunnoult.

"Georgie, my dear, here you are." Appleton Talcott, excusing himself from a discussion of a colt Priam had just bought, came to greet her. "And how nice you look tonight—have I seen this dress?" He kissed both her cheeks and she knew that he was in the finest of fettles, even after the fatiguing journey and the day's adventures. To have him returned safely made her feel safe; his was always a presence she could trust and had come to rely on. "And, of course, you've heard about the prize our Posie has brought home," he said finally.

"I've already had the pleasure of meeting Rose."

"Hers is quite a story. You shall hear it in due course. And now," he added, "if you would be so good as to go look on the sideboard between the tea caddies you are likely to discover an item to interest you." He nodded to where a small package lay. She could tell from its shape that it was probably a book, and when she undid the wrapping she discovered a copy of Scott's *Redgauntlet,* a handsomely bound edition with gilt edges.

"How thoughtful," she said with a smile. "But you shouldn't have . . ." Her protest was useless. They had often discussed Scott's novels together; it was so like him to have brought this one especially for her.

As she murmured her thanks, Agrippina joined them, making her way to Georgiana and taking the book from her hands. Pina glanced at the words her father had inscribed on the flyleaf. "Gracious, you and Papa and your Walter Scott. It looks a terribly expensive volume to me. You'll be sure to take care of it, won't you?" With this remark she wafted to the punch bowl while Georgiana went to greet Priam and his wife, Peggy, who was expecting a child in a few weeks.

"Hello, Georgie!" said Priam, taking her hand and kissing her cheek, playing the gallant.

"How are the boys, Pri?" she asked. "Did you buy them the pony?"

"Two," Peggy put in. "They each got one."

Georgie laughed. "And how have *you* been keeping, Peggy?"

"We're all fine," she replied. "Buried in Hartford, you might say. And Katie's started schooling this year."

Georgiana was fond of Peggy's offspring, although her feelings for that branch of the family were never so affectionate as those she held for the other Talcotts, or indeed for Helen and Lucas Haverstraw and their brood. Though Priam never showed it, she was certain he had not forgiven her for her friendship with Sinjin Grimes, nor ceased blaming her for Sinjin's behavior toward Aurora.

Priam soon excused himself to go speak with Aunt Bettina, while Peggy continued to engage Georgiana in conversation, as was her style.

"Isn't it grand, having Lecky home again?" she was saying. "And tell me—is it true what Pina says? That the runaway is going to come in after dinner and tell us about her adventures? That *will* be enlightening."

"I expect it will," Georgiana agreed. "Apparently Lecky plans to write an account of it for the *Courant*—ah, here she is now, she can tell you all about it herself."

As Georgiana spoke, the guest of honor appeared in the doorway on her grandfather's arm. No one was more adept at making an assured entrance than Electra Warburton, yet it was done with such guileless charm that one was aware only of the effect of a fresh "presence."

She greeted her aunts, her brother, and after a lively exchange of remarks she hurried to Georgiana and hugged her warmly.

"Georgie dear, how good it is to see you. And how wonderfully well you look! Mother tells me you're still performing prodigies at the seed store."

Georgiana offered a modest reply, warming, as she always did, to Electra's company. With her arrival, the party had already become more animated. She accepted a glass of sherry from Old Bobby, who tendered a jolly toast of welcome to Electra, for his oldest granddaughter returned home so seldom that the current occasion was judged an extraordinary event.

Five minutes later, Judah's solemn appearance in the doorway heralded the start of dinner. Rising together, the company proceeded across the hall into the handsome dining room, one of whose notable classical features was the oval niche that housed Appleton's copy of the famous Smith bust of Sir Walter Scott.

Glancing among the faces of the family members, Georgiana marveled at how she never tired of seeing them, even—she smiled to herself—shrill, nervous Agrippina and the redoubtable Aunt Blanche, sunny Peggy and solemn Priam. As the years rolled by some persons might be succeeded by others around the family board, but the general tenor of more formal Talcott gatherings seldom altered: the discreet clatter of old silverware against fine china, the chink of costly crystal, the soft flicker of dozens of candles, the congenial babble of many voices, the energetic explosions of humor, the beaming, ebullient host dealing handily with the standing seven-rib roast of beef on its silver platter, and the steaming, nicely browned Yorkshire pudding Halley had learned to make from Old Bobby's wife, Miss Vicky Talcott.

"Evenin', Miss Georgie, you're looking mighty purty t'night."

"Thank you, Judah." Georgiana greeted him cordially as he came around with the buttered brussels sprouts. His dark forehead glistened as he moved from place to place, careful to carry the platter low and at the most convenient angle for service.

"Before we eat a bite I want to propose a toast!" Priam announced, rising to his feet. His damp hair made ringlets across his forehead and around his ears, giving him the air of an antique Roman, Georgiana thought. He should have a toga, and vine leaves in that golden hair. His smile was charming as he raised his glass and spoke movingly. "I want to drink to *us*, to each and every *one* of us, to all the Talcotts, no matter where they may be. I give you our family, two hundred years in this town. Right or wrong, we'll always be here, won't we? The Talcotts of

Pequot Landing." He held out his glass, then tossed down his wine with gusto while the toast was echoed around the table, though Georgiana did not consider such a self-congratulatory salute quite the proper thing. Aunt Blanche apparently thought the same.

"Isn't it bad luck to drink to oneself?" she inquired, but no one minded her. Blanche had always been crammed with private notions that rubbed against the common grain of things.

"Georgiana, you give us a health, do," urged Bobby from his place at Mab's right hand.

"With all my heart!" Rising, Georgiana lifted her glass and clinked it with Bobby's. "To all the Talcotts, first to last. Long may they thrive. And may Pequot Landing thrive as well."

"Hear hear, hear hear," came the response from all sides.

Next Appleton rose in his place, beaming his pleasure in the return of his famous daughter. "I give you my beloved Lecky, the pride of all our family, and never was a man more blessed in his issue than I."

Another chorus of ayes followed this generous remark, and then Old Bobby, as was traditional with him, rose and offered his toast to Mab, bringing tears to Appleton's eyes. He in turn refilled his glass and in a voice filled with emotion saluted the missing Aurora—"My Beauty, far away over the seas, may she be kept ever safe from harm, may she return to us again soon, for, I confess it, where she is, there is her own papa's heart." As he resumed his seat, Electra used her linen napkin to dry his eyes.

"Now it's my turn," declared Pina, and offered a toast to Posie, taking pains to remind the gathering of John Quincy Adams's long-ago prediction that her little sister would be the torchbearer into the coming century, after which Posie herself toasted—not Pina, as Pina had anticipated, but the newest arrival in the family circle, Rose Mills. "Mother—Father—all—I say welcome to Rose, may our roof shelter her and keep her safe from harm." Her happy smile went round the table while the glasses rang.

Shortly thereafter Père Margeaux came bustling in. Deeply apologetic for being late, he slipped into his chair without fuss, and began modestly partaking of the plate Judah had kept hot for him.

"Was it a boy or a girl, Father?" Mab asked, having explained to the assembly the reason for the abbé's tardiness.

"A boy, God bless us," he replied. "He is to be called Adam George Washington Willotts."

For a time, while the priest ate, the conversation focused on the current health and progress of Minnie-Minerva's infant, Appleton's latest grandchild, but when Père Margeaux had finished, Electra inquired further about the new arrival on Lamentation Mountain, and he did not hide the truth, for beyond what Mab had already promised in aid of the child he was counting heavily on the family's assistance.

To the abbé's hopeful remarks, Georgiana contributed those observations made earlier by Ambo Buck, whose concern for the Lamenters was equal to that of the priest.

"What's to be done, then?" asked Peggy.

"We must take up a collection," Electra said. "Don't you agree?" she asked Appleton, who nodded. "You shall tell us exactly what is needed, Père Margeaux; we and our friends shall provide."

The priest complied enthusiastically. He knew that, when it came to opening their purses, the Talcotts would not be outdone. It was their nature to be generous; even Aunt Blanche, who still had little use for Catholic priests, would ransack her attic once again for wearables and slip in a liberal cash gift besides.

When arrangements for collecting and distributing this largess had been agreed upon, the conversation turned to the brusque manner in which Zion Grimes had had several Lamenters up for poaching small game within the boundaries of his Two Stone demesne. If found guilty, the accused could be made to do a month's time over the matter of a few squirrels or rabbits.

"Rod'll see they're meted out a stiff sentence," Priam observed, "if he can get the case up before Louis Palfrey or one of that crowd."

"Oh, he's a dreadful man, Louis Palfrey," Aunt Tilda put in. "Hard as nails."

"Pity the poachers," added Aunt Bettina. "They'll surely get a jail sentence."

Uncle Jack used his knife blade in a grisly pantomime across the back of his wrist. "In China, Betts dear, the yellow heathens simply chop off the hands of anyone caught poaching on the imperial preserves."

"Oh dear, Jack, not at table, please, I'm eating my pudding!" exclaimed Matilda.

"What is the latest news of the Chinese conflict?" asked Père Margeaux, blotting his lips with one of the company drawn-linen napkins embroidered with Vicky Talcott's monogram.

For more than a year now, angry hostilities had been waged between China and Great Britain, and though it was the British who were most actively engaged in the notorious opium trade, that being the basic cause of the conflict, American vessels were also involved in the nasty business—including, astonishingly, ships belonging to such venerable New England trading firms as Russell & Co., trading out of Macao and Canton, and Grimes & Co. The result was that everyone was eager to render a personal disquisition on that far-off, exotic land, which had become, whether they willed or not, a part of all their lives, and Uncle Jack was no exception as he began to expound on the subject. "It appears that the blasted John Bulls have got themselves into a peck of trouble this time," he declared, "but I'm blessed if I can see where it'll do 'em much good. Think of it, fighting over the seizure of a few chests of opium."

"What's that?" asked Aunt Bettina, shifting her trumpet to her other ear. "What, did he say?"

"Opium, Aunt Betts," Jack explained. "British ships smuggle the drug from India into China. The populace dotes on it, but their government doesn't want it. Lecky, you and Lloyd must be getting some wind of this business in Washington. What have you to tell us?"

Everyone at the table listened avidly as Electra related what she had recently learned. The Chinese emperor had called for a civil commission to investigate all the traders at every hong in Canton and to get rid of the foreign mud, however this might be seen to. "If he has his way," she concluded, "every smuggler caught will be forced to pay the penalty."

"Yes?" Aunt Blanche questioned sharply. "What penalty?"

"They'll be put to death, I shouldn't wonder. And in a not very nice manner, Aunt. The Oriental mind is singularly inventive when it comes to the execution of criminals."

"I should think if they don't want the terrible stuff they shouldn't be obliged to accept it," Aunt Matilda declared forcefully. "Why don't they simply put a stop to it? Have a—what is the word?—embargo!"

"That's just what they're trying to do, Aunt," Electra explained. "But it's an insidious trafficking. You've no idea how intricate it all is. Or how far-reaching."

"I should say it is!" Priam put in, his tone sharp. "And can there be any doubt of who among the traffickers is the most pernicious?"

"Well, now, Pri, I don't think we need to discuss that here," murmured Old Bobby, glancing toward Georgiana, who had lowered her head in embarrassment.

"Why not, Granddad?" Priam demanded. "It's certainly no secret. Everyone here knows who commands the queen of vessels, the *ne plus ultra* among the smuggling ships."

"Who, Pri, dear?" inquired Aunt Bettina, shifting her trumpet again.

"Why, that blackguard Sinjin Grimes, Aunt, that's who. Captain Sinjin Grimes of the *Lord Byron.*" Priam's words sounded sternly in the crowded room and brought the conversation to a momentary halt, though this announcement revealed nothing heretofore unknown. Indeed, the whole-hearted participation of Captain Grimes in the infamous Chinese drug trade was a local scandal, for accounts of his doings were reported almost weekly by returning ships and brought upriver quite as regularly as the evening post.

It had been more than ten years since Sinjin Grimes's last departure from Pequot Landing, and for almost as long the stories had been carried back, not only concerning the sinister vessel that regularly plied the waters be-

tween the South China Sea and the Bay of Bengal, her hold crammed with
contraband, but of vicious barroom brawls and sinful debauches, exotic
Oriental orgies that decent folk stopped their ears against, as well as hazard-
ous feats of derringdo that made men's eyes widen with disbelief. Gossip
had it that the flamboyant captain had shot a Portuguese *lazzarone* between
the eyes in a duel, merely because the fellow had made a few uncalled-for
remarks about Sinjin's female companion. And was it really true that in a
drunken set-to he had wrestled a man twice his size to the floor, knocked
him senseless, then one by one had broken the fingers of his right hand,
effectively incapacitating him?

Oh, he was a scandal, all right; Sinjin Grimes had gone quite beyond
the pale. As for the "women in his life"—creatures of the sort no decent
female dared talk about, but did—there appeared to be several of these at
present. The favorite was the so-called Canton princess, a heathen creature
with the disgraceful "golden-lily feet," the bound, mutilated extremities
of high-born Chinese females; the lesser favorite was a notoriously loose-
living courtesan of the new European aristocracy whose impecunious Portuguese husband had widowed her with a list of debts as long as a prison
sentence, and who had in turn been exiled as a result of her licentious and
extravagant mode of living, first from Lisbon, then Rio, finally Lima,
whence she had fled to the Orient.

Laying aside her napkin, Georgiana sat quietly listening as the discussion
continued. It wasn't the first time she had heard such gossip, nor, she
supposed, would it be the last. More than ever here in Pequot Landing
Sinjin's name was de trop, not least in the Talcott enclave, and indeed, but
for his sister Helen and herself, and his grandmother, Rachel Grimes, there
was hardly anyone to say a good word for the man anywhere. In her talks
with Miss Rachel, whose bidding Sinjin continued to do on behalf of the
family firm, Georgiana had learned far more of the captain's foolhardy
escapades than she wished to know; now, rather than hear more, she would
gladly have diverted the dinner conversation into less conflicting channels,
but she was forced to sit by and submit to the latest round of gossip and
wharfside hearsay. How could she stand up to the whole family, when it
was a case of the Talcotts against the Grimeses?

"The *on dit* is that this so-called *princess* of his is as yellow as a topaz,"
Pina was saying, "and that she came out of the Willow Lane in Canton."

"Pina, dear . . ." her mother started to caution her, only to be interrupted
by Aunt Bettina.

"Eh? What's that?" she asked, cupping her ear. "Willow what?"

Agrippina had the grace to blush. That Willow Lane was the infamous
thoroughfare housing Canton's prostitutes was not an explanation easily
made at the family table.

"And he has had a host of other women as well," Pina hastened on. "You know they say that one poor misguided female actually killed herself for love of that blackguard. After he'd had his way with her, he simply tossed her over for another light-o'-love. I shudder to think what sort of life Rora would have led had she ever married the man. Thank God Priam stopped him before he stole Rora clean away."

"Pina dear," said her mother gently but firmly, "I believe your point has been made. I want to hear from Electra how things are in the capital."

"To be sure, Molly dear, but in a moment," Appleton put in. "First I want to tell you an interesting tidbit I picked up during our New York stay. *Very* interesting, if I do say so. May I proceed, my dear?"

"Why does he trouble to ask, when he'll do it anyway?" Mab demanded of the assembly at large. "Have at it, dearie, lay on with a will."

Appleton sat back in his chair, thumbs tucked in his vest pockets. "I have gleaned noteworthy tidings about the very vessel Priam was speaking of. I allude to the *Lord Byron*. My New York informant tells me that this same ship was recently involved in a stirring coastal engagement with half a dozen Chinese war junks, and was totally disabled, her crew taken prisoner."

"There's one for virtue!" Priam's pleasure at this intelligence was evident as he grabbed up his half-empty wineglass, filled it, and held it high. "So the Chinese have got him at last! Here's death to Dick Grimes!"

"Nothing of the sort," said Appleton. "No sooner was he incarcerated than the wily fellow bribed his way to freedom and escaped with his men from the jail where they were being held."

"All? *All* escaped?"

"So I am told."

"What a pity," Agrippina said archly. "If it were up to me, I would gladly see him and all his cutthroats at the bottom of the sea! He's nothing but a pirate—and a bloodthirsty one, too!"

"Pina, dear—" Electra began, glancing at Georgiana, but Pina was not to be silenced.

"It's true, it's not to be denied!" she rushed on recklessly. "Lecky, you haven't been around Pequot, you don't hear the things we do. Tell her, Papa!"

"Indeed, we hear many tales. And there's more to this one, Lecky."

"About that Grimes fellow, do you mean?" asked Aunt Blanche.

Appleton nodded. "I was told that he last put into Batavia Roads aboard a Chinese junk, one of the same war junks that was said to have crippled his ship."

"But what was he doing at Batavia?" asked Old Bobby. Appleton folded his napkin and laid it aside. His Oriental informant had had no idea. The vessel was now completely rerigged and refitted, and her black hull was repainted in a brilliant vermilion, with eyes of white and black either side of the prow.

"Like the Greek ships, you know," said Bobby, "so she can see to come home. But what's he up to? With so spectacular a ship surely he won't be smuggling opium anymore."

"The coolie trade, maybe," Priam suggested. "Maybe he's gone into the yellow slave trade—he's despicable enough."

"The coolie trade!" cried Aunt Blanche, nearly sputtering. Everyone had heard of this newest business, in which whole shiploads of hapless Chinese coolies were illegally transported east across the Pacific to the Chilean salt and copper mines, where the unfortunates were engaged in forced labor until death ended their term. And there were none at table who, as feeling Christians and abolitionists, would not lift their voices against the vicious traffic. Yellow slavery, it was agreed, was every bit as bad as the black variety.

"Just who is your informant, Jake?" asked brother Jack.

Appleton wriggled his brows and pointed to the other end of the table. "You have all been admiring the ring Molly is newly sporting on her finger." His present to his wife had earlier come in for its share of comment and he recapitulated its novel provenance, describing the stranger he had encountered along the Manhattan waterfront, the sailor who had provided him with the news. "I am obliged to tell you, as it now appears, that our estimable Captain Grimes has been proscribed at both Canton and Macao, as well as any other local ports. If the viceroy gets his hands on him, I doubt things will go easy for him."

"I'll wager it'll be the garrote!" Priam exclaimed. "By God, I hope so! A rope'd be a fitting end to him!"

"And good riddance, too, I say." Aunt Blanche added fuel to the flames. "I always said the boy would come to a bad end, like his father before him."

At these remarks from the distaff side there commenced another lively surge in the talk, of the nature that the family enjoyed, the shrill, resentful tones of Agrippina carrying well above the rest.

"If I didn't say only the other day how that monster would get his just deserts," she asserted. "Haven't I been saying so all along? I do hope the Chinese execute him, truly. Lord knows he's assassinated enough men himself!"

At these words, Georgiana, who had borne all she could in this impromptu trial and sentencing of the man she still regarded as a friend, spoke up firmly. "Pina, perhaps it hasn't occurred to you that most of what you are repeating is merely hearsay—gossip, if you like—and that your victim is nowhere at hand to defend his name."

Pina's eyes narrowed, but before she could respond Posie had entered the fray.

"Georgie's right," she said. "Why must everybody speak of him in that dreadful way? Can you have forgotten how he saved my life when I fell in the river?" Georgiana smiled at her gratefully. "Besides," Posie went on, "must we spoil Lecky's party with this bickering?"

The Abbé Margeaux now interposed his mild voice. "Perhaps we might also try not to find the captain guilty of crimes of which he may very well be innocent."

"Innocent!" Again Priam leaped to the attack. "How can he be innocent? He's a Grimes, isn't he?"

"No, he isn't," Georgiana countered forcefully. "How many times must it be repeated that he is *not* a Grimes? Zion Grimes adopted him when he married Sinjin's mother." As she said these words she reminded herself that while *Sinjin* might not be of Grimes blood, *she* certainly was, and unable to control herself any longer, she pressed her napkin to her lips and stood up.

But Priam would not take heed. "I wonder at you, Georgie, that you can be our friend and *his* champion and defender."

"I am that. He has ever been my friend, and despite his peccadilloes I still regard him as such," she replied.

"Perhaps, but only think how disloyal to us, Georgie." Pina drilled her with a gimlet eye. "How unkind. And if it hadn't been for you—"

"Pina . . ." her mother interjected in a warning tone.

"But it's true, Mama, everybody knows how Georgie helped Rora elope with that—that—"

"That will be enough, Pina," said her father, his voice stern. "I suggest we discover another, less unpleasant topic for our dinner conversation." He was mortified to see tears sparkling in Georgiana's eyes as, visibly trembling, she once again pressed her napkin to her lips and made a hasty move to leave the room.

"I'm sorry—if I may be excused for a moment, please, I'll just see if I can help Trubey in the—" Breaking off, she quickly disappeared through the kitchen doorway. "Trubey," they heard her announce, "I think the table's ready to be cleared."

The door swung shut, and there was a silent exchange of looks.

"Well I never!" exclaimed Agrippina and threw down her napkin. "What do you make of that! If she's not the limit! Taking up for that scoundrel!"

"We've gone too far," Bobby lamented. "Haven't I said these matters ought not to be discussed at table—or in front of Georgie, since she is loyal to a friend, as anyone should be. Posie dear, run and bring her back. And let us say no more of matters that are none of our concern."

Appleton agreed. "Dad's right. Our conversation is upsetting to Georgie, and Lecky, too, I've no doubt." Imprudent of him to have thought to entertain with more talk of the *Lord Byron* and the misadventures of her master. His fault, too, for allowing Pina's rancor and Priam's hatred to gain sway over the evening. Though Appleton himself could do little other than agree with his offsprings' opinion of the man, it behooved him to keep things tamped down, before they boiled over and people got blistered, as had poor Georgie tonight, and his own Rora so many years ago.

Realizing how close they had come to a real quarrel, everyone now shunned the sore topic, with Uncle Jack asking Electra what the content of her speech to the Anti-Slavery Society would be, and Lecky readily availing herself of the opportunity to divert the overheated discussion into calmer channels until the hall clock struck and Judah came in to announce that coffee and dessert would be served in the parlor, where Rose Mills was to relate her story.

7

What Slavery Was Like

THE COFFEE TRAY and service rested on the Pembroke table in the best parlor, with Mab's Crown Derby heirloom cups and the silver Apostle coffee spoons that had been one of Appleton's wedding anniversary presents to her, and as the ritual consumption of after-dinner coffee began, the family settled themselves and the room grew silent. The sight of the unwelcome female intruder in Halley's kitchen being borne away by her brawny grandsons did her humor little good; but Sylvester and Alabaster made easy work of Appleton's bidding and carefully deposited their human burden in the large chair he indicated. Rose's bandaged ankle was arranged to rest on a downy pillow, then the gathering waited for the girl to begin her story. The Priest family had been invited in, and they stood grouped together, all seven of them, watching wordlessly as Rose, obviously intimidated by the circle of faces about her, at first sat silent in her place, her thin hands nervously gripping its arms. Even when Electra drew up a footstool and sat close by, encouraging her to speak, Rose ducked her head.

"Don't rightly know where to start," she said hoarsely.

"First tell everyone your name, won't you?" Electra suggested.

"Mah name be Rose, Rose Mary Mills."

"And where are you from, Rose?"

"Ah be from Laceyville, South Ca'lina. Ah ben baptize' in the Baptiss Church. Ah done run'd off three time. Third time Ah gits clean away. They done roped in mah frens, though. Ah ain't the least sorry Ah done it. Ah'd do it again if Ah had to." Her prominent eyes swerved from side to side. "You folks ain't fixin' t'send me back, is you?"

"Certainly not!" Appleton declared. "You have been paid for and freed."

"There's a mercy," said Aunt Bettina, brandishing her trumpet. "Don't you fear a thing, child, you're safe as day in this house. You'll be looked after."

"Mother, perhaps you'd like to ask Rose one or two questions," Electra suggested.

"Very well, I shall." Mab leaned over the arm of her chair. "Tell us, Rose, how old are you?"

"Eighteen, missus. Ah be nineteen in Jan'wary."

"And have you any brothers or sisters?"

"Yes'm. Got me two of each."

"Where are they now?"

Rose shook her head. "Reckon Ah doan know, missus. They ben sold. Ah ain't seen 'em in a coon's age."

"And your mother? Father?"

Rose dropped her head and twisted her fingers. "Momma, she be daid, bit by a cottonmouth pullin' indigo in the swamp. Mah pap—he ol' Mist' Lacey."

A ripple of shock ran among her auditors, though it was a common enough circumstance, and Rose's white heritage was clearly evident in the paleness of her skin.

"How are such things possible?" asked Aunt Blanche.

"Ah doan know, missus, but they is. Mist' Lacey, mah pap—he a cussed man, he all the time drinkin' an' cussin' an' shootin' up the works. He done shot at Rose, make her behave. Them Lacey boys, they all hollerin', 'Hit her twixt the eyes, Pap!' Think they's funny. Mist' Lacey, he get it good, though. Pretty soon, Pap, he done for."

"How was this, Rose?" asked Mab.

"He got took bad with the fever, they pick him up an' cart him off to Bentin's Island. Now he stone dead. Doan matter, got plenny other Laceys bad as he be. Them Laceys breed lak stoats. They's Laceys to fill the whole pit o' hell, one en' t'other."

"And who raised you?" At her mother's signal, Electra had taken up the interrogation again.

"Knoxie done raise me. She mah grammaw. Momma's momma. She done look out fo' me till she couldn't do no mo'. Then Ah wuz in the hands o' them wicked folks."

"Which wicked folk?" Priam wanted to know.

"All them Laceyville white mens what treat Rose so bad. They's nothin' but a pack o' Philistines, chasin' Rose, plaguin' her, forcin' theyselves on her. God give 'em good punishment, the lot."

More looks passed among her listeners. "Tell us about it, Rose," Electra said. "We want to hear. You can start anywhere, just pretend we're not even here, and say whatever you think of, just talk right out."

"Yes'm, Miz' Wahbutton," Rose said, more at ease now, pleased to be the focus of attention. The obvious sympathy of the older ladies, the grim interest of the men were unfamiliar to her, and she urged herself to take advantage of them.

Rose's story was not one calculated to delight or amuse, involving as it did a life of servitude under the most degrading circumstances: a cruel master, a crueler, spiteful mistress, and an ignorant swamp family indifferent to the plight of the miserable souls it held in bondage.

The reason for Rose's light complexion was simple: both of her grandfathers and her father had been white, one of her grandmothers as well. After her mother had succumbed to fever, it was with her black grandmother, Knoxie, that she had lived. The mistress of the house, Lacey's widow and a harsh-tempered woman, had despised the girl and done everything she could to make her life miserable, for Rose was the living proof of her husband's infidelity. From childhood on, Rose had been obliged to harvest rice in the paddies or to pull indigo, knee-deep in swamp water, onerous labor that had kept her rail-thin and in a constant state of exhaustion. From the time she was eleven, her master's sons—her brothers—had used her to satisfy their lust, though they knew she was their father's get.

The single ray of hope in such an existence had been the fact that Rose could read and write a little. One Mrs. Frain, wife of the Baptist preacher, had taught her secretly, and between lessons, Knoxie, who also could read a little, went on teaching her by means of a dog-eared almanac and a Bible, both of which she kept hidden from her master in a teakettle left on the stove shelf.

"They takes it bad down there, teachin' us'ns. As soon kill a nigger whut's learned t'read as look at him. One boy, Utica, he learn t'write some, they chop off his thumb an' finger both. But that doan stop Utica none, he jes use t'other han'. Some folks is stubborn. Mo' you say 'em no, mo' they thinks yes. Nigger folks be mighty stubborn if they's pushed. Ol' Mist' Lacey, he think we ain't got feelin's, ain't got brains. An' Miz Lacey, she think so too, an' she get out her horsewhip. Ah didn't want to leave Knoxie, but Knoxie, she make me go. 'No matter whut, chile,' she say, 'you git no'th. You show them Lacey's yo' dust—so that's whut Ah done. But all them others, they's caught, they be sent back, Miz Lacey get to use her whip plenny when they comes."

"Don't think about it, child," said Aunt Tilda kindly.

Electra leaned forward on the footstool. "No, Rose, you mustn't. It's never good to look back. You're going to have a new life here, far different from what you've been used to, and who knows—" She broke off, glancing first at her father, then her grandfather, who sat back to await further words.

"Since you tell us this kind Mrs. Frain has taught you some reading, perhaps you'd allow us to hear how you've come along. I'm sure we'd all enjoy that."

Rose's eyes swerved about the group of faces. "Ah only reads the leas' bit."

"That's all right. We'd be much obliged if you would. Just a few lines."

"Yes, do, by all means," urged Aunt Tilda, while Betts gave an encouraging nod.

Rose opened the book Electra handed her from a nearby table and stared at the page. "Ah cain't rightly read that," she said, closed the book and handed it back. "Ah kin read some Bible, though, if'n you has one."

"Bring the Bible, please, someone."

Georgiana, who was standing closest to the Talcott family Bible, lifted it from its place on the table and handed it over to Jack, who in turn passed it to Electra. Rose cradled the heavy volume on her lap, remarking that it was "the biggest book Ah ever did see," and opened the cover, turning several pages to the first verses of Genesis.

"In—the—beginning—God—created—" she began in a halting voice, her finger underscoring each syllable as her eyes spied it, "the heaven—and the—earth. And the—earth—"

She managed a number of verses creditably, with only occasional mistakes. At last Electra took the book back and, after some prompting, Rose resumed her story. Her tired voice grew resonant as she gained confidence, and Georgiana noted its timbre, soft and husky, almost like a boy's the way Jeffrey-Amherst sometimes sounded in his less exuberant moments. Her heart went out to the unfortunate girl as she took in each of Rose's features: the face, thin to gauntness after her recent deprivations, was so pale that in the lamplight she could easily be taken for white; only the prominent eyes might give her away. She had good bones, and her head sat on her slender neck like a blossom on a stem. Her hands, however, were a worker's hands; slave hands, bondage hands.

The room was silent as Rose described the first two times she had attempted escape, once by dugout into the deep, reptile- and fever-infested swamps, where terror and sickness had driven her back to accept her punishment; the second time hidden in the wagonbed of an itinerant peddler who, in exchange for her sexual favors, had promised to get her safely out of the state, but who, when he tired of her, had turned her over to the "paterollers" instead.

"Fus' time, when they cotch me they whip me plenny," Rose said. "Secon' time, they brings me back an' they sticks the bran' on me, makes a L on Rose's shoulder. L for Lacey, lak Ah was they butterchurn, like Ah was they set o' drawers."

Pausing in her narrative, and with no apparent embarrassment, she unhooked the top of her bodice and slipped it down from her shoulder sufficiently to reveal the L-shaped scar that marred her smooth skin. The aunts gasped in unison, and everyone's eyes remained fixed on the brand. "My *goodness!*" exclaimed Old Bobby as he stared at the livid cicatrice. Peggy moaned sympathetically, while Pina drew out her handkerchief and pressed the tears from the corners of her eyes.

"Oh my dear, how you must have suffered," said Aunt Betts in her tenderest voice.

"A man did that to you?" demanded Aunt Tilda suspiciously; she was ever distrustful of the opposite sex.

Rose nodded energetically. "Two of 'em held me, they wuz big bucks, too," she went on. "Young Lacey, he got the arn all hotted up in the coals an' he stuck it to me. Jesus, Ah hollers. Lawd, it hurt somethin' fierce. That mist'ess, she jes laugh right out. She say, 'That'll teach you not to run off.' Knoxie, they fetched Knoxie an' made her watch, but Knoxie, she wouldn't cry or say nothin'. The mist'ess, she say, 'Nex' time you take it into you head t'run off we gon' t'mark you cheek.' They'd've done it, too, Ah reckon." Rose shrugged, her face impassive as she drew her bodice up and neatened her attire. "Folks kin do anythin' when they owns you body an' soul."

Plainly her story had touched all hearts. "Poor thing." "Poor, poor creature." "What must we do?" whispered the sympathetic ladies, while the men exchanged grave looks. Old Bobby cleared his throat, pressed his lips with the corners of his handkerchief, and spoke.

"Please go on, young woman. As Mrs. Warburton has told you, there's nothing to fear here. You are among friends. I want you to tell us everything you have to say, if you're not too tired."

Rose gave him a grateful look. "Rose ain't tired, Mist', she'll do it if it kill her. Ah says to myself, Rose, you is gonna get out of here one way or the other, an' if anyone stick the arn on you 'gain, you kill 'em daid."

"You wouldn't have done so, surely, child," said Aunt Tilda.

"Yes ma'am, Ah would," Rose affirmed. "But when Miz Frain, she seen what them Laceys done, she say, 'Rose, hit ain't to be borne. Hit mo' than human flesh kin stan'. I'se gonna see you free or die.' An' that's whut Miz Frain done."

"It was she who helped you run away?" Mab asked.

Rose nodded. "Yes'm. She sen' Dodie Cruthers. Dodie, he runned away years before, he comed back an' back, ever' time leadin' some out, jes lak Moses leadin' his people into the Promise' Lan'. He come the night o' Mist' Lacey Junior's burfday, when they's all drinkin' an' dancin' an' carryin' on, an' we done slip off in the spring wagon, Rose 'n' three others."

Rose's story now became one of even greater terror, of trudging by night along lonely roads, hiding by day in the fields, of men with guns on the lookout for her and her companions. Finally they had reached Roanoke, where Dodie had arranged for them to be smuggled aboard a ship bound for New York.

"That be mah first-time ride in a real boat," Rose confessed with a little laugh.

As the recital continued, Georgiana's gaze came to rest on Peggy Talcott, who sat with wet eyes, hardly stirring on the bench beside Posie. Priam had not stayed beside her as he usually did, but stood with Jack and Appleton, as though to align the family males on this all-important matter. When Georgiana returned her attention to Rose, the long narrative was winding to its end, the part most of them knew by now.

"Ah thanks you all kinely fo' whut you done," Rose said in conclusion, "savin' po' Rose from the paterollers. Is Ah really free, Mist'?" she asked, turning to Old Bobby.

"Yes, young woman, you are indeed free," he said. "Not a man can touch you—you have that writ. And now you must be very tired. I suggest you say good night and find your bed."

"Yessuh, thank you—only what's goin' t'happen t'Rose in the mawnin'? What you folks plannin' t'do with her?"

"Sleep, Rose," Appleton said. "There's plenty of time for making plans tomorrow. Good night, good night . . ." He beckoned to Alabaster and Sylvester and bade them carry Rose along to her lodgings above the carriage house.

No sooner had she been taken from the room than a heated discussion arose among her listeners, for everyone had something to say, an opinion to offer concerning the unfortunate girl and what was to become of her. In the end, Appleton restated his view that nothing need be decided that night.

"But I feel quite sure," he added, with a covert glance at Mab, "that no one here imagines a young woman with that sort of upbringing can just go out into the world and survive on her own."

"I'm sure not, App." Old Bobby was most concerned. "And obviously she is too infirm to travel anywhere just now. I do believe it incumbent on us to keep her here, at least until such time as she can leave of her own accord."

On that note, Priam, who had been stifling yawns for an hour, suggested that it had been a tiring day and he and Peggy still had to drive home to Hartford.

"Good-bye, my dear," he said, kissing his mother's cheek.

"It was a wonderful dinner," Peggy added, going out, "a real Talcott evening."

It was the signal for the others to leave as well, and while good-byes continued on the threshold, Georgiana collected her things. Hat would be waiting up to hear about the party, and tomorrow was Sunday. As she was trying her bonnet strings, she paused for a word with Electra.

"I think it was very kind of you all to come to her rescue. And very generous of Granddaddy to buy her freedom."

"I feel sure it's money well spent, my dear," Old Bobby put in.

"I'm so glad you're home, Lecky." Georgiana kissed her friend's cheek, thanked Appleton again for the book, and Judah saw her to the gate, which he closed behind her.

When he came in and shut and locked the front door, he bid Appleton and Bob good night and withdrew to the kitchen. In the study, the Talcotts, father and son, made themselves comfortable over a brandy.

"Well, Dad," Appleton began a bit tentatively, "what have we here, do you think?"

Old Bobby returned a smile. "Interesting situation, Jake, is it not?"

"I hope you don't think we've done the wrong thing, bringing this young woman here."

"Not a bit, son, not a bit. If we won't help her, who will?"

"By Zeus, they made me angry, that damnable pair of scoundrels," Appleton declared, speaking of the slave catchers. "And then for Zion Grimes and Willie Wandsworth to try and make capital of the situation."

Bob gave his mild chuckle. "You did right, you absolutely did. And I think Mabel will have her in the end. I do believe she will."

"I suppose she may—though she's dead set against it now. Not like her, though." He hesitated, then went on. "Dad?"

"Yes, son?"

"Does she—Molly, that is—does she strike you as in any way different?"

Bobby answered carefully, with another question. "Why—does she seem different to you?"

"Yes, she does, by Zeus! She's hiding something, I do believe she is."

"Not like her to hide things from you, is it?" Old Bobby asked.

"No, it isn't. You don't suppose she's ailing, do you? She hardly ate a thing tonight."

"Nothing to worry about, I trust," Old Bobby replied easily.

After one or two further reassuring comments, the older gentleman began making his way up the stairs, leaving his son beside the newel post, plucking at his brows and frowning. Come, come, Appleton told himself, no need for morbid thinking. He was inclined to worry too much over trifles. Certainly Molly was all right; why, just think how splendid she'd looked this evening. Idiotic to imagine anything happening to her. And yet, he thought, as he went to pour himself just one drop more, what if—? His worried glance found its way to the ceiling with its plaster medallion and frieze. Were his Molly to leave him, why, that selfsame ceiling would collapse, the whole house would fall in on him, burying him under its great oaken beams. And why not? Surely he would not want to live, with Queen Mab gone on without him.

8

In Which a Seed Is Planted

THE WIND BLEW GUSTS of leaves across the doorway as the house settled down for the night. On the lower floor Judah tiptoed around, blowing out the lamps, then lighting his way to bed, where Halley had preceded him. Appleton sat alone in the study, while upstairs in his cozy back room Old Bobby was comfortably propped against two immaculate bolsters, his spectacles perched on the bridge of his nose, an open volume on his lap. "Angling may be said to be so like the mathematics that it can never be fully learnt," he read. His well-worn volume was *The Compleat Angler,* and he had perused Izaak Walton's lines so many times that he scarcely needed now to look at the pages before him. "As no man is born an artist, so no man is born an angler . . ."

At the front of the house, Mab sat at her dressing table, brushing out her hair, thinking about Rose Mills. Poor homeless thing, Mab's heart went out to her, but as an experienced hand in such matters she didn't see much chance of success in the matter of her rubbing up—*if* she decided to let her stay.

She glanced toward the door as it opened, and Posie, her cheeks pink with excitement, her eyes glowing, hurried in. She shut the door quietly and came up behind her mother, relieved her of the brush, and began brushing her hair down her back.

"Mama darling, it was a lovely dinner party, truly. I know how much Lecky appreciated all your work. And you looked simply ravishing."

Mab made a face. "There's quite enough of your blarney, dearie. It's the Irish in you coming out and truthfully I'm in no mood—after all the mischief you've caused me this day."

"But Mother! It's true! Blue always brings out your eyes, and they're one of your best features. And the Chinese wallpaper behind you, it made the most attractive background. As though you were on a stage. Really! And Papa looked so pleased and proud. Didn't you notice? It was written all over him."

"Persephone, dear, I'm sure you're very sweet to say these things to your poor mother," Mab said, pleased in spite of herself, but wondering what was coming next. "Still, I'm glad the party's over and I can have a little peace."

"Oh Mama—I haven't come to disturb you, truly."

Mab gave her a hug, then, drawing away from the brush, began plaiting her hair with expert fingers. "Of course you haven't. I'm so glad you're back. I missed you dreadfully. Did you enjoy New York?"

"Oh, yes, Mother, I did. You were darling to let me go. And Mama dear, you're simply not to worry about anything . . . not even Rose," she appended, cautiously broaching the delicate subject. "Wait, don't say it—I know you don't want her to stay here, but you'll see, if we keep her—just for a *little* while—she's bound to settle in and before you know it you'll be ever so glad to have her."

Mab pursed her lips. "I'd love it if someone would please explain to me exactly when and where it has been decided that this unfortunate is to stay on here after she's well enough to walk? I honestly don't know what gets into you sometimes, dearie. First to persuade your poor grandfather to pay out good money for some runaway, then to pack her along home for me to look after!"

"But we could help her, couldn't we? With a little of your rubbing up—"

Mab got to her feet, a bit unsteadily. "Listen to the girl! Haven't I said I don't want to hear those words again? Your mother's rubbing-up days are over, it's time everybody realized that." She popped on her ruffled nightcap, did up the strings under her round chin, then mounted the bed steps to sink gratefully back against the down pillows heaped high to receive her.

Posie climbed onto the corner of the bed, taking care not to jostle her mother. "I know, Mama, it's all right," she said comfortingly. "We're not going to let anything distress you or upset you, we promise. You will have everything exactly as you please. And Rose will grow less wild, you'll see. You should have heard her ohs and ahs about her room—and that quilt Electra found for her. You'd think she was living in the lap of luxury."

With a sigh of weariness, Mab closed her eyes and made her head more comfortable. She would, she thought, have to give in at last. How could she refuse, without rousing suspicion?

A brief silence ensued, during which the French clock between the tea caddies on the mantel struck eleven. Mab felt Posie change position.

"Mother—?"

"Yes, dear."

"What they were saying tonight—about Sinjin Grimes—"

Mab's eyes widened and her mouth turned down. "You've read my mind, dearie. I felt sorry for Georgie, she's fond of the fellow. Allow me to say, however, that I for one have already heard considerably more than I would like tonight on the subject of Captain Grimes."

"Of course, Mother dear," Posie said calmly. "It does makes me wonder, though."

"What does?"

"Well—as you say, Georgie's quite fond of him, Captain Grimes, she says he's got many good qualities, and if she feels that way, then—I'm just wondering if maybe he isn't so bad after all—what do you think?"

"I do not think! I don't care to think about that—that reprobate. Georgie's the darling of the world, but not always prudent, perhaps. Really, to think that but for the grace of God your own sister might have been living out there in China with him. He's a devout womanizer *and* a drunkard, *not* to mention a smuggler of opium. And now yellow slaves? What can the man be thinking of?"

"But, Mama, surely you can see what it is that makes him do those things. What makes him drink so much and . . . debauch—if he *does* debauch—and one may safely suppose he does, a little."

"I haven't a notion, and I don't want to know," Mab said, pushing with the back of her head to make herself more comfortable against the pillows. "Some men can't help it, they're born to—to make trouble. And a sweeter mother a boy never had than Louisa Wilson."

"I'm sure it's because he's still in love with Rora," Posie went on, undeterred by her mother's remarks.

Mab drew back in indignation. "Persephone Talcott, how *can* you make such a ridiculous statement? I'm glad your father isn't in this room to hear such words. Why, your sister's been married for thirteen years, she's a peeress of the realm and a mother to boot! Think of your niece Caroline. Where on earth could you have got such a farfetched notion?"

"It's just something I feel, Mother. Whenever I see Hermie Light he always asks me how Rora's doing. I'm sure it's because Sinjin asks Hermie about her in his letters. I think he still loves her, and that's why he acts the way he does."

"Oh, you think, do you? That's absurdly romantic, my little one. If you ask me, you're flying south on your imagination."

"I'm not, Mother, it's true, you said so yourself once. It was a long time ago, but you *did* say it. Here's Lecky, support me, won't you, Lecky?" Posie jumped down as her eldest sister came in and swept to the bed with a feminine rustle of taffeta and silk.

"Mother, dear, in bed at last, and looking so comfy." She kissed Mab's brow. "I'm sure you deserve it. And wasn't it a lovely gathering? You're very sweet to have gone to all that trouble just for me. What a shame Lloyd couldn't have been here, he loves our family gatherings so." She leaned down to give Posie a kiss. "And you, my angel, looked simply delicious tonight—didn't she, Mother? So grown-up, I hardly recognized my baby sister. Before we know it you'll be married and have flown from the nest too."

"Never mind about Posie flying from the nest, dearie," Mab said. "At sixteen there's plenty of time for flying. And you ought to hear the silliness she's been spouting. I think the child must be moon-mad or something."

"What have you been saying, Po, tell me," Electra asked, settling into the chair while Posie leaned against the bedpost.

"We were talking about Sinjin," Posie began, only to be interrupted.

"About *Captain Grimes,* if you please," Mab said.

"Very well, Captain Grimes, if you so wish, Mama." Smiling she turned to her sister. "I don't think he's as much an Algonquian as he's painted, really. He has a good heart, and I *know* he adored Rora; it simply broke his heart to lose her. That's why he went to Bolivia the way he did."

"Bolivia?" Mab's eyes widened. "I thought he went to China."

Posie laughed merrily and wagged Mab's toes under the covers. "It's my joke, Mama." She turned to her sister. "Lecky, do you remember that time we were all at Home Island, the summer Rora eloped with Henry? We were sitting on the porch of Blue Shutters one evening and you thought I was fast asleep in the scrap basket, only I wasn't, I was listening—"

"*Aha!*" Mab croaked triumphantly, shaking her finger. "Little pitchers have big ears! It's a congenital affliction in this family."

"What did you hear, Po?" Electra prompted.

Posie giggled. "I heard Mother say that the reason Sinjin Grimes drank himself into oblivion every night was because he was in love with Aurora. Only *I* thought she said he drank himself into Bolivia!"

Electra threw back her head and laughed. "Posie, you are the limit. Mother, do you recall that night?"

"I do; Bolivia, indeed! That foolish man was well on the way to ruin even then. Now, Lecky, as to this Rose Mills, whom you all have seen fit to drop on my doorstep as if I were the proprietress of a hotel. I know you think your mother's being insensitive, but tell me—what *is* to be done with the girl?"

"She's intelligent, Mother, and with a bit of furbishing to bring out the best in her—"

"Good heavens, not you too!" Mab expostulated. "No, I say, and again no! I've done all the furbishing I care to do. I have no time to break in a new girl. Besides, we don't need another servant."

"Yes, you do," Electra said, a shade too quickly. "With Burdy going home nights, and Halley's rheumatism troubling her, someone like Rose could be very useful to you, Mother. She can look after personal things for you."

"Are you saying I can't look after myself? Well, I never—!"

"I have an idea, Mama," Posie said tactfully. "Perhaps if Rose stayed on we could put her to school. She's already had a start at books with that minister's wife."

"She has, indeed," Electra agreed. "And you're absolutely right, Po, she *should* be put to school. Aren't you clever!"

"But school—here in this place?" Mab protested. Negro children attending local schools were few and far between in Connecticut, and Pequot was no exception.

There was a footstep at the doorway. "Hey-o, my dears," Old Bobby said, standing on the threshold and peering about at the occupants of the room. "It looks like a Turkish seraglio in here. Fortunate the pasha who could take his pick of these odalisques. May I say a quick good night, Mabel?"

"No, no, Granddaddy, come in and sit a moment, won't you?" Electra said. "We want your opinion." She drew him into the room and sat him in the chair she'd vacated.

"My opinion of what?" he asked.

"Of what's to be done with your protégée," Mab said. "To keep the girl out of my hair—to say nothing of Halley's. Posie and Lecky suggest she be sent to school, but the question is, where?"

"The Academy will never take her, nor will Center School," Posie pointed out.

Electra nodded. "The plain fact is that a school for Rose simply doesn't exist around here."

Posie, who had grown thoughtful, said pointedly, "Perhaps we should see what Georgie thinks. After all, she's the one who taught Ambo. Maybe she could help Rose, too."

"And pray, *what* could Georgie help *Rose* with?" Agrippina appeared on the threshold and gave Posie a sharp look. "Surely no one is thinking of keeping this unruly creature under our roof once she's able to walk again. Truly, she has the most fearful temper—and such language—" She covered her ears to demonstrate.

Electra interrupted. "Pina, I honestly don't think we should pursue this subject any further tonight. Mother's tired, we must let her rest."

"Then you *are* going to keep her! I can tell! Mama, how could you? I suppose you're going to try to rub her up, aren't you, like Georgie and all the others? And everyone's going to fuss over her and—I vow, I shall simply shrivel and die if she stays—"

"Pina, stop it this instant!" Mab cried, clapping her hands as if at a flock of birds. "We've heard quite enough of your complaints this evening. I should think you'd be ashamed, the way you treated Georgiana at table—and at Lecky's welcome-home too. As for Rose Mills, I guarantee you this—it shan't be yours truly who decides her fate, but your father. This is still his house and his word is law, always. Frankly, I hope he sends her on to Canada, but if he says stay, stay she shall. Now kiss your mama good night and go straight along to bed, it's late and you'll be getting those smudges under your eyes."

About to make further protest, Agrippina was forestalled by Old Bobby, who, playing the cavalier, kissed her cheek, chucked her chin, and gallantly escorted her to the door. "Good night, dear Pina, sweet dreams to you!" Pina offered Mab a chastened if tearful good night, then Bobby waved her out, and when her footsteps were heard no more, Electra took up the thread of the conversation.

"In any case, it appears certain that what we've just mentioned isn't going to do the job by half, I don't think—one person teaching one other person, I mean, be it Rose, or any other girl."

"Lecky's right," Posie said. "What it needs is one person teaching many. A whole classroom of pupils."

Bobby stirred in his chair. "I do believe you've hit upon a good idea, you two," he said thoughtfully. "A special school, a place where young Negro women like Rose might be taught a fuller curriculum than plain meat-and-potatoes reading and writing. A place where they would get the chance to study history and geography and arithmetic as well, even languages."

"Certainly a school of such liberality wouldn't be regarded favorably," Mab pointed out.

"Why not regarded favorably?" Posie asked.

"Because most white people don't want darkies learning those things," Bobby put in. "I'm sure reading and writing and training them to be well-mannered and do domestic work would be acceptable, but such limited schooling isn't what we had in mind, is it, my dears?"

"No, indeed!" Electra clapped her hands together. "What is wanted is a school offering a liberal curriculum of studies for colored misses!"

"But who would teach it?" Mab asked.

"*Georgie could.*"

It was not Electra but Posie who had spoken. In the silence everyone stared at her. "I wonder if she wouldn't—if the idea were put to her in the best way. What do you think, Lecky?"

Before Lecky could reply, Mab's "No!" rang out. "Oh my dears," she cried from her mountain of pillows, "you're mad, the lot of you. I won't hear of it, not when everything's going so well for Georgie at last! People around here won't stand for it, I tell you, they'll throw bricks at her. And don't you give me your innocent looks, either. I know what you're up to, Granddaddy—you too, Lecky. You're not fooling me. This is just the neat ticket you've been looking for, isn't it? You'll have your precious Mr. Garrison writing about it, the whole world will be talking, and there'll be poor Georgiana Ross, smack in the middle of it all. No, I say, I won't have it!"

"Mabel, my dear," Bobby put in mildly, "we've no wish to upset you. But I believe if you were to sleep on this notion you'd agree it's not such a bad one. It certainly would spare you the care of Rose. And of course, if Georgie didn't wish to participate in the enterprise, we would look elsewhere for a teacher."

As if her outburst had utterly exhausted her, Mab yawned without reserve or apology and drew the covers to her firm little chin. "Very well, I can see you've got a bee in your bonnet, the lot of you. Plan Rose's future if you will, only leave me out of it."

"But Mother," said Posie, "Georgie's the helping type. Look how patient she was with Ambo—and see how well he's done. Imagine Rose coming up in the world the same way, making something of herself—"

"I'm afraid such an elevation is beyond my powers to conjure," Mab said wearily. "But I've no doubt you'll all do exactly as you wish, no matter what your mother says. I only want some peace and quiet."

"I'll just step along, then," said Old Bobby, taking the hint. "Good night, my dear." He kissed Mab's brow with affection; then each of his grand-daughters in turn. "Not too late, now, girls," he said. "Your mama has had a long day. So glad you're home, Lecky. Tomorrow we must put our heads together." He withdrew with a smile and a nod.

"Yes, Mother, dear, that's quite enough for one day," Electra said. "But would you like us to stay and pray with you?"

Mab nodded. "Very well—if I don't have to get out of bed again and kneel. I am quite fussed, I confess it. Hand me my beads, child."

Posie picked up the rosary from the night table and handed it to her mother, then knelt beside Electra at the prie-dieu, covertly watching her mother's face through half-opened lids.

When they had finished, Mab seemed more tranquil, and Electra and Posie kissed her a loving good night. Then hand in hand they slipped out, while Mab waited for Appleton to come up to her. Jake would know what best to do, she thought, forgetting how upset she'd been with him when Rose first stepped from the coach. She dimmed the lamp, and with her rosary clasped in her hand recommenced her decades.

While Mab continued her orisons Old Bobby had returned to bed and his book was again propped upon his knee. He was scarcely aware of what he read, however, since his mind was just now engaged very much elsewhere, to wit, with the suggestion that had been made a quarter of an hour before. So revolutionary an idea gave Bobby pause, as it would many others if he judged the matter rightly. Playing with fire, that's what it amounted to. While such an enterprise would certainly find its supporters in the village, it would find its critics as well, critics who were likely to be decidedly vocal.

But if it could be arranged, this plan for a school might start a brush fire that would catch on in other parts of the country. The danger of course was that such a small fire might become a holocaust and then where would they be? It did not do to think one's way too far into so problematic a thing, so fraught with obstacles and hurdles to be overcome. In such a case Bob subscribed to the theory that where ignorance was bliss surely it was folly to be wise. If a man was happier in his ignorance, what use wisdom?

Or so determined Old Bobby, who was not only giving considerable thought to the proposition, but was fully willing to contribute considerable cash into the bargain.

9

"...And So to Bed"

MEANWHILE, GEORGIANA MADE her way home, her thoughts dwelling on Rose Mills and the strange sequence of events that had brought the girl under the roof of Kingdom Come. Georgiana thought she would do well, despite her unseemly truculence. After all, anyone connected to the Talcotts could look forward to life on a higher plane than might otherwise be expected.

As she opened the gate at Snug Harbor, the wind tossed something at her feet; a shingle. Ambo was right; if something wasn't done Hat's little house would have leaks next spring. In the parlor, Hat was in the fireside chair, head back, snoring. She came awake with a fitful start, then insisted she'd only been grabbing forty winks and wanted to hear all about the party.

Georgiana hesitated. Though she seldom kept things from Hattie, there were various threads of the evening that she preferred to sort out on her own, so she characterized it as having been enjoyable and enlivening, rendered especially pleasurable because of Electra's presence, and edifying in the opportunity it afforded to hear Rose's story. Then, since Hat sat discreetly stifling a series of surreptitious yawns through most of the narrative, there was little difficulty in getting her packed off to bed, leaving Georgiana alone. Though she was tired after her long day she didn't feel sleepy, and her thoughts continued to circle and flurry around her as she climbed the loft stairs and went about her bedtime ritual. Murray Hill padded softly in, and when Georgiana's clothes were hung away, her nightgown donned, she lay down on the bed and let the cat stretch out across her middle, while her mind drifted back over what had happened, in particular the talk of Sinjin Grimes.

The unguarded remarks of both Priam and Agrippina had wounded her, and, sad to say, her temper had gotten the better of her and she had risen to the bait. Whatever the truth of Sinjin's present situation, no matter what the gossip that seemed always to erupt at the mere mention of his name, she could usually ignore it by the simple expedient of not hearing it. Tonight, however, this had proved impossible, and she was angry with herself for having allowed her resentment to be witnessed by everyone at table. It wasn't easy being a friend to both the Talcott family and Captain Grimes.

"I just couldn't help myself," she said to Murray Hill, briefly interrupting the cat's purr. At least Posie had come to Sinjin's defense, and she blessed the girl for her belief in his fundamental worth.

In her heart of hearts, Georgiana could not doubt for a minute that to a large extent the lurid reports about the captain in China were true, or at least had some basis in fact. One might try to disregard them or rate them the product of malicious and spiteful tongues, but the fact remained that "the elements in him were so mixed," the good and bad so continuously warring, that even Georgiana sometimes wondered if the bad might not attain mastery. And, truthfully, most of the time she didn't know what to make of her feelings for the man, or even what those feelings might be.

Certainly "out of sight, out of mind" did not apply. She thought of him too often for that, recalling much of what had passed between them over the years, trying to sift through the anomalies, to solve the baffling puzzle of his paradoxical character. The dark, wild, romantic spirit that was the Byronic hero, possessed by violent excesses of thwarted love and blind passion, failing utterly to come to terms with life, was this Sinjin Grimes? Or was he more truly the affectionate friend of her childhood, the sweet-natured boy who stuck up for her and took her part, who acted gentlemanly, was caring of her feelings, who sought her out for conversation, who brought his questions to her for answers, who had impressed her as the kind of startling and unique young man who could do anything he set his mind to? Or the opium smuggler, engaged in every sort of sin and vice, a buccaneer with a price on his head? Or the slaver . . .? But surely, that could not be true—could it?

The fact was, what sort of man he had become, she did not know and could not tell. How could she, with only hearsay and his infrequent letters to go by? For never once since he had left town ten years before in pursuit of Aurora and Henry and little Caroline had he returned to his native heath. Nor was there any evidence that he intended ever to come home again.

Over the years she had learned of him through Hermie and through his sister, Helen, as well as through his letters to her. He made sure one reached her each year, usually around the time of her birthday. And although none had come as yet this year, these communications always brought her a special pleasure, and nights, when Hat was asleep, she liked to bring them out and reread them by the fire, finding their contents at once revealing and perplexing, both for what they did not say and for what they did.

Sometimes his lines spoke of how pleasant and relaxing life could be in the colony of Macao, with its "lemon-scented gardens" and its porcelain observatory tower whose telescope would "easily pick out even the most distant planets, and all the mountains of the moon." Another time he wrote, "Fancy how some thrill-seeking American ladies at Macao have been smuggled up the Pearl River, into the environs of Canton where imperial edict forbids white women to set foot and where they spent some three or four weeks of leisure and amusement before the mandarins sent them down to Macao again. My friend Twinqua who's the big bug in these parts does no more than giggle and say 'No lookee, no see.' "

But just as frequently she read melancholy remarks betokening the darkness that provoked his dissipations and foolhardy exploits. Such comments as "Tedium is the surest path to death, I find," and "Lord, how ruinously dull it is out here, and what is one to do with the smells?" Or "I now find myself truly at the end of a badly frayed rope. I would gladly hang from it if someone would but kick the stool for me." Or, from a number of years ago, "I have recently lost a lovely island friend whose passionate but ungoverned nature has convinced her that a life in the next world is preferable to one in this. Since she struck me as a reasonably balanced creature I am forced to wonder at the preponderance of emotion in her that has caused her to do away with herself. Alas, she was very pretty and did much to enliven my lonely existence." Of that unfortunate lady, no further word, but of his own "youthful mad mistake," he wrote, in an absurdly slanting hand, "God (or whoever) protect all innocent males from the sweetly singing Circe who wraps the poor blind idiot about her finger, then blithely unwinds the thread and uses it to darn her linen." Once—and only once—had he made mention of his last unhappy encounter with Aurora, "when like some lovesick Romeo I hoisted myself onto her balcony. This at the city of Naples. Sadly, 'twas *not* the east and Juliet was *not* the sun—but there I laid my humble offering and the letter in which I so ridiculously poured out my heart, imagining—yes, *daring* ever to imagine that she would give up that nincompoop she had married and come away with me, the admitted father of her child, she, and I, and Caro together, to China, whose exotic scents and sights I had briefly wafted past her nostrils. The fellow actually set the servants on me, six muscled *ragazzi* who relished cudgeling a poor deluded *straniero.*"

In letter after letter she saw how his thoughts so often dwelled on the child Caroline, expressing his longing to see this daughter of his again. It was the expression of these deepest feelings that so often caused Georgiana's heart to go out to him, and she in turn answered with every scrap of news that reached her from Aurora. In none of his letters in recent years, however—and she felt this sorely—had he mentioned his writing, and she wondered if he'd forsaken it entirely, and whether she herself had had any hand in its abandonment. Despite all that had happened since, nowadays she often found herself recalling the foolish quarrel she'd provoked with him over his youthful epic work, "Al Qadar." How he must have labored over those cantos, how sternly he must have disciplined himself to write at such length, and she had attacked it and torn it to shreds. "Drivel on camelback," she'd called it. No wonder he'd been furious at her. No mention since, not ever; not a word. His pages lay in Hat's attic, tucked away in that old tea chest, and from time to time she took them out and read them through again. Her opinion had not changed, but as she and he grew older, she saw in it a promise unfulfilled, and it saddened her to think all his work was unavailing.

Georgiana had spent a good deal of time trying to equate the man she used to know with the picaresque and unscrupulous adventurer he was rumored to have become, and now, thinking of him and his lost love, Aurora, and their child, Caroline, who called Lord Henry father, she opened the table drawer again and slipped out the letter that had arrived some ten years before, and which, according to its author, had been written by oil lamp at a tavern in the Plaka quarter of Athens, at a table where Byron had putatively sat—same table, same chair. There were infuriatingly few details regarding the captain's personal circumstances at the time; instead he described night on the Acropolis, the ghostly marble columns of the Parthenon silhouetted against the climbing moon, the familiar constellations overhead. He exerted his considerable powers of description in evoking the ancient temple as he had viewed it, rambling on in a Byronic vein. His rhapsodizing continued for several paragraphs as among the fluted columns he presumed to have met and spoken with the shades of Pericles, Demosthenes, Socrates, and their ilk. His mind seemed occupied with the massing of the Greek forces to sail for Troy to capture the purloined Helen, while she, the Beauty, became by turns Calypso, Nausicaa, Circe, the Sirens three, and eventually the faithful Penelope, waiting by her hearthside, picking out the threads of her day's weaving.

"Some things I have decided" the letter went on, "to wit: life is the greatest gift we are offered, wrong to waste it, foolish to wish it away, as I have done so often. I am presently resolved to put all that behind me, and with it, cities and men and corruption, the dung heap with its buzzing flies and crawling beetles. I am resolved now to live a life of monastic chastity, mental as well as physical. I have renounced forever all thoughts of marriage, I will remain a solitary soul, for I am convinced that such is my destiny. Tonight the stars are singing, I heard them clear, they ring out like the bells of Babylon. The music of the spheres, it plays about in my head in a most curious manner, remote and otherworldly as the stars themselves.

"From the distance, over the dark hills and vales, I could hear as well the melancholy winding of pipes of Pan, so potent in their dolor, such sweetly sad notes. Played by some simple shepherd lad, no doubt, they stirred yearnings in me—for what I cannot say, but surely such things as I will never have, and no doubt do not deserve. Self-knowledge, or the elevation of my paltry spirit? Belief in *something*? Success in love? (That, surely!) Love of my fellow man? (I love no one, thyself always excepted, Miss Mouse, oh most faithful mouse.) All remains confused in my reeling mind, it is the spell of glorious Greece, a gorgeous Attic whiff, and I am thrilled to the marrow.

"I shall soon embark on a journey over somewhat familiar territory, and take *Paulina's Fancy* and her crew to China, where I intend bearding the Dragon Emperor in the Forbidden City. Now, if that strikes you as an outlandish thing to attempt, I must agree, yet less bizarre an undertaking than others I have engaged in at various points in my life. The East is ever the siren's song to me, and this seems as good a time as any to heed its call. In any case, I place my wholehearted trust in the words of the wise Hafiz: 'Woe betide the man who allows himself to be trapped by fate.' No such snares for this, your faithful correspondent. Rather, I shall make my own fate, I shall journey to the Flowery Kingdom, there I shall be crowned with laurels and comforted with apples, I shall one day return a rich and famous man—see if I do not.

"If I remark at this point that I have successfully executed a deed of some undertaking, you shall know it is not my *amour-propre* that leads me to place the mention of it before you, but merely the fact of my knowing which budget of news is of primary interest to you. I, like George Gordon Lord B. before me—to say nothing of the no less heroic Leander—have presumed to swim that infamous body of water that the geog. books call the Hellespont. You will hoot at the idea, of course, but you will learn better hereafter. You will know, of course, that I am a wizard and, like Simon Magus of old, can perform certain sleight-of-hands to confuse and astonish the local populace. Without flying through the air or turning base metals into precious ore, I now find my audacious impromptu exploit to have consternated and confabulated all of the Ottoman's realm, to say nothing of one or two foreign parties as well. I refer in major part to that eminent booby, Lord Henry.

"In the meantime, my pet, do not believe everything you may hear of me, or of my current modus operandi. It is of course merely a comedy, and I shall doubtless be punished for my sins, it cannot help but come. The gods on high Olympus look down and wink, and flail their whips. Well, well, we live our lives however we may. To some it is given to fly on a broom, others to ride the camel's hump, while I myself am destined to fare forth in seven league boots. More anon if I live to hold pen again. Thine, S"

The first time she read it, Georgiana had found the letter astonishing in its content, while Aunt Hat had loudly expostulated.

"I tell you the man's gone plumb daft!" she cried, unable to take it all in. "Read it again, Georgianner, and don't leave out a word!"

This Georgiana had proceeded to do, and with care, she likewise having experienced difficulty in embracing the full substance of Sinjin's lines. Did he really expect anybody to believe such a tale? Who better than she knew that he did not swim, *couldn't* swim? It must be nonsense; he'd been drinking ouzo in the Plaka and courting delusions of grandeur.

There had, however, been a sequel of sorts to Sinjin's report of the curious episode. Even while Georgiana was dismissing the thing from her mind Lloyd Warburton had arrived at Pequot in possession of a dispatch from the Turkish correspondent to a Washington newspaper, giving indications of what had taken place in Asia Minor:

> On Tuesday last, an American seaman successfully negotiated the waters of the world-famous Hellespont, duplicating the earlier exploit of George Gordon, Lord Byron, the noted English poet, and that of Leander, hero of Greek mythology. Refusing to give his name, the unidentified American entered the waters of the Hellespont at Abydus, on the identical site where the British peer had commenced his daring swim some ten years previous, and was fetched up at Sestos after three and one half hours in near-freezing waters, seemingly little the worse for his death-defying ordeal. Having accomplished this extraordinary feat, the protagonist took a meal at a fish shop, after which he went off, shod in wooden shoes and wearing an eplidrikas (a Greek costume), his destination as unknown as his identity.

Pequot Landing had been dumbfounded. Who else could the anonymous American seaman be but Sinjin Grimes? And how exactly like him to undertake something so foolhardy—and at such a risk to his own life! How could he have managed it when, insofar as anyone knew, he still hadn't learned to swim? Was he able, after all, to walk on water, as Billy Albuquerque and others of his devoted crew were convinced he could do? And why this outrageous act? What point had he been trying to prove? Moreover, how long would the man go on tempting fate, and what would happen when that same fate, tired at being toyed with, decided to call in all bets, including the life of Sinjin Grimes?

Within months he was in China again, having made the slow passage in *Paulina's Fancy* down the coast of Africa and around the Cape, thence into the Indian Ocean, and on to the Far East, trading from port to port as he went. At Macao, he had met the remarkable Parsee merchant-trader called Jamset Satidjee, whose humble mien and modest character successfully disguised one of the shrewdest minds in the whole of the China trade, a character who, along with the great Twinqua, was thereafter destined to enjoy a sizable role in Sinjin's China career.

With neither desk nor office, but only an oilskin-covered traveling trunk, with a portable etui of pens and bister inks in identical small bottles, the trunk tucked away in an unused corner of the Red Tiger Hong overlooking Macao's Praya Grande, for which space he paid the nominal rent of six taels every four months; with but one suit of clothes to his back, two dhoti, a turban, and the most elegant and legible Spencerian script in the eastern hemisphere, Satidjee or "Mr. Saturday," as he was called, was one of the richest of the hong merchants, a frog-who-was-a-prince, since his own kind shunned him for the betrayal of his race, while the Westerners resented him for his shrewdness in out trading them. It was thanks to the help and support of this modest gentleman that Captain Grimes had risen to be called Lord Koxinga. Pleased by what he saw, the Parsee, who had much to teach, had taken the American captain, who had much to learn, under his wing, and little by little made known to him the niceties of a profitable trade along the South China Coast, the highly rewarding but illegal and dangerous business of opium smuggling.

As Georgiana knew, such illicit traffic was nothing new in that part of the world, while the British economy rose and fell according to its profits and losses, causing the unwitting Queen Victoria to wonder to Lord Palmerston why the emperor was interfering in the established workings of British trade. And if other companies were profiting, why not Grimes & Co. as well? Why not indeed?

Sinjin Grimes had caught on quickly, absorbing a quantity of knowledge about the so-called black mud, its manufacture and sale; that though the Turkish opium was of an inferior grade compared with the more refined Indian Malwa or Patna of Benares, there was nonetheless an active market for the stuff; how the sinister cargoes were ceaselessly smuggled into the Flowery Kingdom, sixty katties to one mango-wood chest, thousands of chests to every cargo, in exchange for the emperor's precious mint of Spanish silver. Much was returned for squeeze, the huge sums called cumshaw, paid out to the Hoppo and the intricate levels of the gluttonous and corrupt Chinese hierarchy, yet as much remained, and so the trade went on.

As a professional smuggler of contraband Captain Grimes was soon without peer, for few Westerners knew more than he concerning the endless maze of creek mouths and watery debouchments along the dangerous China coastline. Why should he not, with the wily Mat Kindu to guide him? A hundred times over he had slipped the keel of his vessel, which he had rechristened the *Lord Byron,* aboard which he both worked and lived, in and out of these hidden places without detection, and on every occasion he had lined with silver not only the pockets of Grimes & Co., but his own as well, and those of his Parsee mentor, and of any others who stood with him and behind him, for he was not a greedy man and enjoyed sharing the fruits of his daring career.

Such savvy, linked to such uncommon largess, had before long come to the attention of the single most influential individual, the man whose patronage was worth a hundredfold all the gold of Midas, the renowned Chinese merchant Twinqua—head of the mercantile trading group termed the co-hong and reputed to be the richest man in the eastern hemisphere. Corrupt but amiable, Twinqua made no bones about the fact that he had taken a fancy to the freebooting American sea captain, who, unlike others of his brotherhood, had striven to learn the Chinese language that was spoken thereabouts, who was partial to the exotic taste of sea cucumbers and pickled eel, who didn't drop his eyes when he stood before the great man, who, as Twinqua liked to say, wore the habiliments if not the crown of a monarch. So it was with the help of Twinqua as well as the friendly Parsee that Sinjin rose, and rose, and rose—and in this elevated state was living as well and loftily as was possible for a Yankee to do in that place at that time. He had in fact become a legend in China whose likes not even that wondrous realm had seen of late.

The true legends of this world are almost always exhausting in their creation, and usually woven with long threads; Sinjin's was made of short ends, and quickly too. China was his natural element and he appeared to revel in it. The buccaneers who had plied the Caribbean a century earlier from Port au Prince to Maracaibo were not greater pirates than he, and as the wild fictions gained currency and were exaggerated for effect, another part of the legend grew: the captain's prowess with the fair sex, and in a decade he had done nothing to arrest the tide of gossip. To the contrary, he seemed to glory in the unlikeliest bit of scandal, and before long the name given to his ship was understandably being applied to himself by the titillated colonials at Macao, English and Portuguese alike.

But while the wives of the traders and East India Company officials might whisper and snipe behind the back of this latter-day Byron, to his face they simpered and scraped, even presumed to plump him as a suitor for their unwed daughters, though without success, and the exotic aspects of his character seemed to attract every kind of eye, until even the unlikeliest tradesman, the demurest of that tradesman's daughters, felt the draw of the enterprising Yankee freebooter.

None of this had remained undisclosed to Georgiana; Hermie had let her read the letters from Billy Albuquerque, Sinjin's first mate ever since Hermie himself had been forced by the loss of his leg to give up the sea. What she did not know, however, was the truth of what she had heard at the Talcotts' dinner party. She was aware, of course, that toward the end of 1836 the newly appointed imperial viceroy, Teng T'ing Chen, had indicted nine smugglers of the foreign mud: seven British, including the well-known

trader Jardine; one American, Sinjin Grimes; and the Parsee trader. While
Satidjee was able to disappear like a bee in a busy hive, seldom viewed but
capable of keeping his affairs in smooth running order, the captain, given
to a much higher level of visibility, had been forced to pull up stakes at
Macao. He had surrendered command of his *Lord Byron,* left the affairs of
Grimes & Co. in Satidjee's capable hands, and dropped down to Sarawak,
where he offered his services in whatever capacity to the raja and spent a
satisfying interval studying a number of arcane subjects at the college at
Penang. Two years later, however, having got word from his Parsee partner
that too few of their vessels were getting through to sustain profits, he had
returned to China despite the indictment against him. There he had taken
command of an armed schooner, also christened the *Lord Byron,* and become
a valiant sea warrior, something he had never been before. Foolhardy and
irrepressible, he had distinguished himself in a series of daring engagements
against the imperial war junks that came wallowing out of their hiding
places like so many big-bottomed water buffalo to do battle with the
smugglers, with the result that he had achieved even greater celebrity, and
had seen his name placed once again at the head of the list of the proscribed
drawn up by the viceroy for the emperor's perusal.

"Koxinga!" scoffed the emperor, Tao Kuang; the epithet had enraged
him, the real Koxinga having been one of China's greatest and most noble
rulers. To hear the name so debased had thrown his imperial majesty into
a fury, and the viceroy had his order: capture this Koxinga and drag him
in chains to the Imperial City for public execution, the Death of a Thousand
Cuts. And apparently they had captured him at last, but before the emperor's
order could be finally executed, the offender had decamped—which was
what Georgiana had learned tonight.

Now, to her mind, there came a chilling image of Sinjin's latest vessel,
with her hull of bright scarlet and white-painted eyes, her huge lateen sail
of bamboo aslant the horizon, and she recalled, as she frequently did, the
prophecy Cinnamon had whispered in the tent at Follybrook on the night
of John Quincy Adams's visit, and the sheep's bones that had foretold that
he would join his father at the bottom of the sea.

Would he return, ever? Would he set his foot on Town Wharf once
more? She did not know. Something in her bones told her that the destiny
of Sinjin Grimes lay in the East, not in a sleepy river town at the mercy
of village tongues. If you dug a hole deep enough you'd come out in China;
that was what they'd often said as children. If she dug and looked down into
the hole would she see him again? And would she recognize him if she did?

Dear Lord in heaven, she prayed, keep him safe and let him see the light
before he goes deep-fathom. Turning over, she drew Murray Hill closer for
warmth, then blew out her candle, and hoped for happy dreams that, despite
such hope, failed to materialize.

PART TWO

To Book and Slate!

10

The Breakfast Patriot

NEXT MORNING, WHILE Mab and her daughters were attending Mass and Appleton was off on one of his early riverside rambles, Old Bobby Talcott breakfasted alone in the dining room, where over his first cup of coffee he was devoting strictest consideration to the introductory remarks he had agreed to make at Hartford before the meeting of the Anti-Slavery Society, an honor indeed, since his words would serve as preamble to Electra's own address. From being fixed on the yellow chrysanthemums filling a blue Amoy bowl in the center of the glossy table his eye roved beyond the windows to the terrace, to the gardens below it, the meadow beyond that rolled to the river. Ah, the river, that tranquil, serenely flowing artery, birthed in Vermont and dropping in lazy serpentines through the center of the Land of Steady Habits, on down to Long Island Sound at the Saybrook Estuary, its banks dotted with those modest, circumspect New England towns: Green River, Deeping, Middletown, Cromwell, neighboring Stepney Parish, and Pequot Landing; white houses, green shutters, red chimneys all caught as if under a spell, all knitted under cobwebs and gossamer, drowsing in the sun.

As he continued to observe the outdoor scene the dining room door swung to, and Trubey Priest entered to serve his meal, bearing from the Sheraton sideboard silver dishes that gave off the most savory of odors.

"Trubey—?" began Old Bobby in a somewhat tentative tone.

"Yes, Mist' Bob," returned the servant.

"Trubey, tell me something. If you had the chance to send your granddaughters to a school and get them a proper education, would you do it?"

"Lord, yes, Mist' Bob, I'd do it in a snap. Nothing like a education to see folks get on in the world."

"Amen to that, Trubey. So you would approve and support a small institution of learning dedicated to the education of young colored misses? Right here in Pequot?"

Trubey's face grew somber. "A school for coloreds, right here in the village?" She shook her head and lowered her voice to a confidential level. "Mist' Bob, there's a lot of mean folks around. Folks who wouldn't take kindly to my grandchildren being taught much more than to read and write. Such a thing might cause a mighty lot of trouble. A whole store of trouble."

"There are bad people everywhere, Trubey, people who disdain the kind of thinking that drives the world, but must we be thwarted by their likes? Shall we be deterred by their narrowness and bigotry?"

Trubey sighed. "I dunno, Mist' Bob, I just don't know. Is that what they're planning to do, start up a school?"

"There has been some discussion of such an undertaking," Bobby returned tactfully.

"Well, they'll get my support," Trubey said staunchly, "and they'll get my grandkids into the bargain, if I have anything to say about it."

"Bravo, Trubey," returned Bob. "I'm glad you see things in such a light."

"Who's the teacher to be?"

The color in Bob's cheeks deepened slightly. "We'll have to see about that," he said, and buttered a bun.

When Trubey had left the room he went on eating leisurely and well, drinking another cup of steaming coffee from his large Amoy cup while attempting without notable success to concentrate his thoughts on the matter of his address. Oh, to be a Thucydides, a Patrick Henry, a Tom Paine; oh, to have the gift of the silver tongue, to stir people with ideas, profoundly felt words of the sort that came so facilely to other men. Why must he labor so hard to bring off a good turn of phrase, a likely thought?

As if seeking inspiration, his eye traveled upward to the renowned portrait of his adored, long-deceased sister, the oft-spoken-of Great-Aunt Susan Lane, whose rosy countenance and alert blue eyes (eyes of Talcott blue) gazed warmly down from a gilt frame in all its eighteenth-century glory, her hair powdered white and bedizened with diamonds, her rounded bosom shockingly décolleté in that earlier, less prudish time, the well-modeled head crowned by a toque the size of a tallish plum pudding and feathered with two ostrich plumes dyed to match the eyes. It occurred to Bob that a notable Stuart work such as this would fetch a pretty penny these days—not that he would ever sell the picture.

"Well, Sue, you were always of a liberal leaning. What would *you* say to a little school for the darky girls?" Bob asked, addressing the likeness. Susan gazed back at him with that candid expression, as if asking what *he* thought and what he intended doing to push forward such a worthy and engrossing enterprise.

"Hey ho," Bobby said softly, "we must see about this; we must see." Such a school might make the planet a better place, or at least this one small corner of it. And anything anyone might do to improve a world that was so badly in need of improvement was decidedly a step in the right direction. Casting his look across the windowsill, mentally assessing the temperature, he tested his freshly reaped chin and reflected soberly. How was it possible on so glorious an autumn morning that the world should be so topsy-turvy? How could it be that in the mere sixty-odd years since the signing of the Declaration of Independence matters should be set so rudely askew? With the birth of the new nation, that shining young republic, had come Bob's own deep-seated belief in her glorious future and he had lived to garner the rewards of her free society, but now he had cause to wonder at her present course. People said the country was going to the dogs, and Bob wasn't sure but they were right. More than half a century had passed since the redcoats had been licked, and America's precious independence was no longer challenged; but, alas, now the golden luster of the flourishing republic was dimmed, that fine, shining model of nationhood she had presented to the world was tarnished and cracked, and what or who was to repair or polish it? Oh, she had settled down to the business of growing and expanding, right enough, these United States; indeed, God's great and glorious sun had not shone more brightly upon the youthful Greece or suckling Rome than on the land now being broadly settled and populated by this new breed called Americans. As a people, they were of a genus hitherto unseen among the nations of the world. They had said, those soft and bag-fat, narrow-thinking Europeans, that no ordinary men, certainly no so-called *Americans,* could be trusted to rule themselves or to fashion suitable tablets of governance. Yet, surprising as it might seem, that was precisely what the new American had done. His industriousness and probity, his innate simplicity of nature, his considerable store of useful, homely knowledge, his hardihood and manly hope, his fearlessness of good, hard, dawn-to-dusk labor, his unquestioning trust in the God that had made him—his plain *common sense*—had seen him through to the realization of a bright dream unknown since the Age of Pericles.

And, as Bob saw it, there was a useful and attractive product that the men of America had to sell to their country's fellow nations: more than cotton or indigo, more than pipe staves and onions, more than fish and peltry, they had this single national commodity scarcely to be found anywhere else in the world—liberty. Let that precious product be shipped away from the American shores to all the ports of the world, let it burgeon and ripen and produce its happy yield in every land. Let *them* taste that sweetest of fruits, the old countries, let *them* copy this new American, let such a man be emulated and respected for that which his hopes and dreams had brought forth at Boston and Concord, Philadelphia and Hartford, in Virginia. Let the seller charge not one nickel for the sale, make a gift of it, and he would be repaid a thousandfold.

But—and this was a very large but—but this was easier said than done. True, the world had given admiration, some willingly, some grudgingly, for who could foretell if the noble experiment would work, if it was really true that men were capable of governing themselves? In sixty years such had been proved, and the world had stood amazed. But during those same years who was there who could count how many men's souls had been sold for gold, how many women and children had been raised for no other reason than to pick the cotton, hoe the rows of tobacco, to die, not like men, but like so many head of cattle. Surely God's light must shine not just on some, those favored few, but on all men, all members of the human family, regardless of the color of their skin. Wrong; slavery was wrong, and men like Bob Talcott were convinced that nothing would ever make it right. There was only one thing to do: to abhor, to shun, to reject, and ultimately to abolish it, to tread it into the dust like the venomous serpent it was. It was shameful that this bold new being who cut so fair a figure, this fine American, should come onto the world's stage lugging with him the ignoble baggage of slavery, the slave pen, the auction block, the fetters, and the burning brand. Defiance was what was called for now, contempt and civil disobedience and ten thousand, nay, a million men to rise up and shout, "It shall not happen here, *not from this day forth, not here, not in America!*"

True, in 1797 the State of Connecticut had passed a law manumitting all Negros born into slavery when they should reach the age of twenty-one. Yet, even in such a liberal state, slavery was still legal, and there were altogether too many citizens who saw nothing wrong with that "peculiar institution," citizens who stubbornly refused to acknowledge the abuses inherent in it or that God had intended all men, regardless of race or color, to be free.

What a travesty. What a corrupt notion. What a dismal end for the glorious dream. How had it happened? How was it that the Declaration of Independence, that astonishing instrument of man's noble will, having stated in writing that all men were created equal, should have meant freedom for some but not for all? There was the flaw, and as Bobby saw it, such a flaw was a crucial and perilous one. No nation could pretend to be one thing and in fact be another, it was the worst form of hypocrisy, inviting censure and mockery. And what was to come of it? Surely there would be violence and bloodshed.

Something must be done, and soon. But how? And by whom? By men, Bob told himself. By men like those who had built the country originally and hewn it out of the wilderness. By right-thinking human beings whose keen foresight and sympathetic hearts raised them above their fellows. By men *and women*—here he amended his thought—liberal-thinking women such as his own granddaughter, Electra Talcott Warburton, and his sisters, Tilda and Bettina, who in the last few years had undertaken to open a station on the Underground Railroad and were every day of their lives breaking the laws of their country, a matter of concern to even such a firm abolitionist as Old Bobby, who well knew the serious penalty they could be made to pay if exposed.

Any account of these activities, of course, he must omit from his speech, as he must hold back any mention of the village blacksmith, Sid Smyth, formerly a runaway himself, or Andy Cleves, the barber, also an escapee, who had upon more than one occasion journeyed below the Mason-Dixon line, placing himself at risk in order to guide more of his brethren north to freedom. There were other liberty-loving folk in Pequot as well—the Ashleys, the Burdins, Milehigh and Sallie Jenckes, Hermie Light, Izz and Erna Quoile—all willing to break the country's laws on behalf of true justice. None could Bob publicly name, but he could still speak out for them, focus attention on the festering situation.

For festering it was, and right here in Pequot Landing. Why, this very Thursday evening, a notice in the newspaper had stated, the Right Reverend Simon Honeycutt of Harrisburg, Pennsylvania, would be addressing the local Hickory Club at a meeting in the Academy Hall of Pequot Landing. While in town, the clergyman would be the honored guest of Deacon Zion Grimes of Burning Bush Farm. The uninformed reader might regard this tidbit as mere social tattle, but Old Bobby was able to read between its lines. The so-called Right Reverend was a notorious antiabolitionist speaker, little more than a bigoted rabble-rouser, who because of his fanatical support of slavery was greatly admired by Zion Grimes and those of his ilk who comprised the Hickory Club, an antiabolitionist organization thinly disguised as a congenial social group.

Bobby had been forced to smile at the coincidental juxtaposition of this news item with the formal announcement of Electra's visit. It seemed highly fitting that the Talcott family and their traditional rivals, the Grimeses, should sit as solidly opposed in the press as in their principles—though in truth it could not be said that Zion Grimes acted from conviction, unless it was hatred for the Talcotts, whose stand against slavery was well-known, and an unshakable faith in mercantile profits: it was the business of the New England mills—and Grimes & Co. owned more than one—to spin southern cotton into cloth, straw into gold. And, thought Bobby, ancient family enmities might also play a role. Certainly one of the sources of the rancor existing between Talcott and Grimes was the fact that Zion's father, Abednego, and his father, Cyprian, before him, had each flown the company flag on vessels engaged in the Triangle Trade. Though they were no longer actively involved in the abominable slave barter, a Grimes was not one to change his sentiments readily, especially where profit was concerned.

Principled or not, however, Zion Grimes was ever a dangerous adversary, a vehement leader among the proslavery forces whose attacks against free thinkers and abolitionists had begun to coax a less educated element to make serious mischief in the streets. Not so long ago a loutish crowd had hanged a Hartford Negro from a lamppost in broad daylight, while even so celebrated a figure as Mr. Garrison himself had felt the rope about his neck.

And more trouble was coming, Bobby was sure, a dark time of violent upheaval and national convulsion when brother would rise up against brother and the whole country would be bloodied and laid waste. Nor was he alone in foreseeing this, for though the law as it existed was evil, such men as Zion Grimes would fight to enforce it.

He straightened at the sound of coach wheels, laid aside his pen and paper, and rose as the returning distaff members of the household came in through the door. Then, Electra and Posie each slipping an arm through his, out they sailed to board the coach once more and be about the important business of the day, a hegira to the nearby community of Brooklyn, Connecticut. But first, one all-important stop along the way, for their enterprise could not hope for success without the participation of Georgiana Ross.

II

The Birth of the Free School

CHURCH HAD BEEN out for less than half an hour when the natural curiosity of certain among the almshouse company was given a healthy prod by the sight of Old Bobby's Yellow Pumpkin pulling up at the picket gate of Snug Harbor across the way. Those curiosity-filled faces gathered at the various windows witnessed first Electra Warburton, then Posie Talcott, then Old Bobby himself descend from the coach and march up to the threshold of Hat's house, where they were admitted and the door shut behind them. What, the Brick Farm watchdogs asked one another, did such unexpected doings signify? Social call, merely, or was something afoot?

In Hat's parlor, Old Bobby declined his hostess's hospitable offers of early refreshment; he and his granddaughters were embarked upon a journey of some thirty miles, he explained, but before starting on their way they had come to sound Georgiana Ross out concerning a matter of uncommon importance.

"What matter is that, Granddaddy?" Georgiana asked. For assistance Old Bobby turned his blue eyes to Electra, who spoke without preamble.

"Georgie dear, I've been thinking—that is, we've all been thinking—and we wondered, since you are so knowledgeable in such matters, what you might have to say about the idea of starting up a little school here in Pequot? A sort of special school for our Pequot girls who don't get to attend the regular classes—I am speaking of the darkies—someone like our newfound Rose Mills, say, and Burdy Tando's daughters."

"What a capital idea!" Georgiana smiled warmly at Electra. "Yours, isn't it?"

"No, it was Posie's, actually—"

"Bravo, Po," said Georgiana warmly.

Electra hurried on. "Then you *do* agree it's a good one?"

"Yes I do! One hundred percent."

"I'm so glad," Posie said happily. "I told them you'd do it."

"You—I'd do what?"

Electra went to touch Georgiana's hand. "Why, that you'd be our schoolmistress."

"Well, I swan!" exclaimed Aunt Hat, smacking her hands together. "There's a tomahawk for ye, Georgie!"

Georgiana's bewilderment was plain to see. "But you can't be serious. I gave up teaching years ago. Besides, I already have a position. And a happy one, I promise. What would Warren Burdin do—he depends on me—"

"Warren has Ambo to help him. We need you, Georgie," Electra said. "You believe in the idea, you've had experience in such things, you could make it work, couldn't she, Granddaddy?"

Old Bobby smiled. "It's true, my dear," he said. "It won't be an easy matter, but if anyone could take the bit in her teeth and *make* the thing go, I do believe you are the one. And of course it would be your school, your very own, however you weigh it. You'd be free to teach all the subjects you deemed proper, exactly the way you wanted, and right here in Pequot. Doesn't that sound like a good opportunity?"

Georgiana felt her cheeks growing warm and she twisted her handkerchief around her fingers. "It's very kind but I couldn't possibly. Really I can't—it's simply not realistic. I haven't any interest in teaching anymore. Besides, who would want me? You know how people are around here—they think I'm crazy as a loon."

"Georgie, that's not true!" Posie exclaimed.

"Yes it is. I don't care for myself, it doesn't bother me, but how could I be expected to teach a class of students when their folks would fear I'd suddenly take to bringing a cow to school or going around wearing men's trousers?"

Now they all rushed to present their arguments, Old Bobby with the wisdom of his years, Electra with her passionate depth of feeling, and Posie with her earnest appeal, while Hat blinked at one or the other in bewilderment.

The discussion went on for some time, until Electra suggested that, rather than make up her mind then and there, Georgiana should postpone any decision until they had driven over to Brooklyn, where they could talk with William Lloyd Garrison, the famous abolitionist newspaperman.

But no, Georgiana protested, she had no wish to talk to Mr. Garrison when her mind was already made up. It was out of the question. Let this be her last word on the subject.

Nonetheless, her friends prevailed. The same trio who had entered an
hour earlier took their leave of Snug Harbor accompanied by a fourth: Miss
Georgiana Ross, wearing her go-to-meeting bonnet and wrapped in the
cashmere shawl Mab had given her for her birthday.

It was considerably later, close on four, in fact, when the yellow coach
reappeared to deposit Georgiana back at her door, then rattled off along
March Street and, so it was generally assumed, home. Curiosity was jacked
to new levels as inquiring faces popped up at the almshouse windows, and
several of the ladies even presumed to venture forth in search of clues,
trotting across the way to discover what they could. This proved blessed
little, however, neither Hat nor Georgiana being in a discursive mood, and
the inquisitors retired to their abode none the wiser.

Yet, the term spent at Brooklyn had not been uneventful. To the contrary: William Lloyd Garrison, coincidentally courting a young lady of that
neighborhood, had been most eager to hear more concerning the proposed
school, had, indeed, been eloquent on the subject of what such an establishment could mean to the waxing abolition movement. Georgiana had been
flattered by his attention and was impressed by the support the fiery editor
was willing to pledge through his paper, the justly famous Boston *Liberator*.
He had even promised that in the event the school should be established,
he would present himself in person to tender his congratulations and would
not only provide ample *Liberator* space to publicize the undertaking but
would offer free advertising columns as well in order to attract suitable
pupils.

What could be better? Electra was elated. She and Mr. Garrison would
map out a working strategy and enlist the support of organized abolition
societies, and with so formidable a backer as the eloquent firebrand and
number one abolitionist, the project could not help but get off to a flying
start. As a result, by the time the gathering had broken up, Georgiana found
herself wondering what she was going to say to Warren Burdin.

After her return to Snug Harbor, she discussed the matter at length with
Aunt Hat. A school for colored girls? With Georgiana its teacher? Though
Hat was not averse to the notion, she nevertheless harbored reservations. She
attended closely, rocking all the while as her fingers busied themselves with
another square in the counterpane she was currently working, then suggested
that Georgiana stroll over to Gaunt House and discuss these important
matters with her dear friend Helen Haverstraw. Readily agreeing, Georgiana clapped on her bonnet to walk the short distance to the Broad Street
Common to see what Helen and Luke might think of the idea.

IN THE minds of Pequotters there were two sides to the oval-shaped Broad
Street Common, the fashionable side and the unfashionable side. Lilacs, the

handsome old house belonging to the Talcott sisters, Matilda and Bettina, stood on the fashionable or west side, while Dr. Lucas Haverstraw and his family had spread themselves among the rooms of the rambling, ramshackle house on the east or unfashionable side. Built some sixty years earlier by old Cyrus Gaunt, who had gone mad and tried to set fire to the place, the clapboard structure had stood vacant for more than twenty years until the Haverstraws, returning to Pequot after five years as missionaries in Hawaii, had bought it of the current owner, a grandson of old Cyrus.

Despite the wealth of Helen's father, Zion Grimes, it was the best they could afford, for Helen had married against Zion's will. All but estranged from him not only for his harsh treatment of her husband but for his implacable vindictiveness toward her stepbrother, Sinjin, whom she adored, she could expect little help from her parent, except as affected her children, and even that was sadly begrudging. She saw Zion at infrequent intervals; he would never set foot in Gaunt House and seldom was she invited to cross the threshold at Burning Bush, in consequence of which Rachel Grimes was required to drive into the village to visit with her great-grandchildren. Zion never alluded to having disinherited his only daughter, so it remained to be seen if he really meant to go to such lengths; meanwhile, there was little enough to live on. Still the family at least had a roof over their heads, and the rundown place was now a real home to a sizable number of Haverstraws. Besides Helen and Luke, there were the two boys, George, named for Georgiana Ross, and Darcy, eleven and ten respectively, as well as the three girls, Chloe, nine; Phoebe, five; and the baby, Rachel-Ada. The hired man, Foote Crowe, who came over daily from Lamentation Mountain, was also an active part of the family circle.

Though Georgiana had often heard Helen remark that she had nothing to do but sit back and relax and let the house run itself, it was a fact of life that houses seldom did so; indeed, this particular dwelling had something of the appearance of a stage depot. The drafty rooms were sparsely furnished: bits and pieces randomly accumulated since the Haverstraws' return from Hawaii, interspersed with the few exotic treasures they had brought back with them, souvenirs of five years of missionary work set out for little "corners of interest." In the barn out back, Plymouth hens were being raised, and behind it a family of Poland swine rooted in the pig pen, while a small herd of Devons grazed in the Great South Meadow that stretched a quarter mile to the river. In May a family of swallows returned yearly to nests among the rafters of the barn, the descendants of last year's frogs reestablished themselves in the chinks in the well, canines of dubious pedigrees came and went, and "Aunt Georgie" chalked the children's heights as they made their way up the kitchen doorjamb.

Georgiana had splendid friends: among the Talcotts (aside from Mab and Appleton and Old Bobby), Electra, whom she admired extravagantly;

Aurora, with whom she had shared such intimate secrets but who remained, alas, on the opposite side of the Atlantic; Posie, of whom she was deeply fond; even such older women friends outside the family as Aunt Hat and Rachel Grimes. Still, in terms of warmth and constancy and intimacy, none could measure up to Helen Haverstraw, and in Georgiana's mind it remained a miracle that she and Helen were friends, in addition to being, secretly, half-sisters. Moreover, if ever two people had been meant for each other, they were Helen and Luke Haverstraw. Luke had been unexpected bounty; together he and Helen had become Georgiana's refuge, her bulwark and her anchor.

Sometimes after she'd closed up the seed store (she was always the last to leave) Georgiana would walk the short distance to the Broad Street Common, not to pay a social visit but merely to pass by, or to stand under the tall pine tree that grew in front of the old homestead and gaze at the warmly lighted windows and take heart from what went on inside, where Helen performed her housewifely tasks, cleaning, cooking, sewing, bathing, putting to bed, and otherwise doing what she believed was her duty, to make a happy home for a loving family. It was a challenge willingly met and Georgiana stood in warmest admiration at the seeming ease and grace with which all was accomplished.

Then, too, there was the simple fact that Helen was not only Georgiana's sister, but Sinjin's as well. For many years, Sinjin Grimes had stood as common cause between the two women, theirs was a defiant and loyal, if unspoken, alliance to uphold his good name, so often besmirched, to let the rest of the world know that whoever else might condemn the man, here at least were two who loved and cared for him.

It was only natural, then, that Georgiana should advise Helen and Luke of the latest turn in her fortunes, for everything that came her way, good or bad, she faithfully confided to her sister, offering up the subject for comment around the Haverstraws' kitchen table. When she arrived on this occasion she found Luke and Helen holding hands by the parlor fire. The Sunday dinner hour was well past, George and Darcy hadn't come in from squirrel hunting, the girls were gathered around the table, cutting out and waxing paper flowers, leaving the adults to converse uninterrupted.

"Would you quit Burdin's, then?" Helen asked after Georgiana had disclosed her news. "I suppose you'd have to, wouldn't you?" She looked at her husband, who had said nothing till now. "What do you think, dear?"

Luke thought it was a splendid idea—if it could be managed without arousing the ire of the less liberal-minded villagers. "You may just be biting off a good size chunk, though," he warned, unwinding his stock and loosening his collar in the fire's warmth. "I daresay you'll find yourself with your hands full and then some. But we'll be with you, Helen and I, count on us."

"Am I up to it, though?" This was Georgiana's primary concern. "Do you think I can do it?"

"Georgie, I guess you can do anything you make up your mind to, but that doesn't mean it's going to be easy." He glanced at his spouse, who withheld comment. "If you mean are you up to it physically, I'd say you're strong as an ox, at least as far as teaching a handful of youngsters goes. As for dealing with any opposition to such an idea, that's another story. Some of these Brobdingnags and Yahoos hereabouts are bound to come down hard against it."

"But with a little persistence the opposition can be overcome, surely," Georgiana returned. "I know there's bound to be those who'll object, and we're prepared for that. Lecky says that in the end it may even help, since controversy will cause talk, and that's what we want. Lots of talk. We want people in other parts of the country to hear about our school—and they will, thanks to Mr. Garrison. The way he'll write about it, well, you can imagine, can't you?"

Luke ran his fingers through his bushy mop and shook his head gloomily. "Folks aren't going to want to see darkies learning more than their ABC's. They're bound to say it places them above their natural station and makes them unmanageable, even hostile."

Georgiana's chin came up and she drew back in her chair. "Who cares what people say? It's not against the law, is it?"

"I shouldn't think so," Luke said. "Where do you plan to open this school of yours?"

"Aunt Hat says we can hold classes in her parlor."

"Lord knows you can't squeeze much human flesh into that place. Why not use our barn? It's a sight bigger."

Touched by the offer, Georgiana leaned over to pat Luke's hand. But a space as large as the barn would be too difficult to heat. Besides, there probably wouldn't be so many pupils that they couldn't all fit in at Snug Harbor. Winter was on the way, Hat's little parlor would be nice and cozy.

"Who's going to help you?" Helen wanted to know.

Georgiana laughed. "Helen, I don't need any help. We'll go forward very quickly, I know it."

"Who's going to pay your salary? What about supplies—books?" asked Luke. Georgiana explained that it was Old Bobby's proposal that a subscription be taken up among those villagers sympathetic to the plan, and he himself had already advanced the generous sum of one hundred dollars. Luke quickly dipped into his pocket and made a donation which, at Helen's stern urging, Georgiana reluctantly accepted, knowing it was money they could ill afford to give.

"And if there's anything else we can do," Helen said, "you know we're always here, close by."

Georgiana kissed and thanked them both, and before leaving went to visit with the girls, still busy with their paper flowers in the parlor. Helen remained talking with Luke in the kitchen, and after a while they, too, came into the parlor, where he made Georgiana a startling proposition.

"Georgie, Helen has an idea. We thought we'd discuss it with you—and the girls." Georgiana was puzzled as the doctor turned to his two older daughters.

"Girls, Aunt Georgie plans on starting up a little school here in Pequot. And your mother and I were wondering if you two would like to attend?"

"Oh, but Luke, I don't think—" Georgiana began, but the girls' excited clamor silenced her. Yes! Yes! they chorused, they would love to go to Aunt Georgie's school.

Luke held up a hand. "There's just one thing. The rest of Aunt Georgie's pupils will be colored girls. How would you feel about that?"

"We don't care," Chloe said, going to Georgiana's side.

"Don't you want us, Aunt Georgie?" asked the smaller Phoebe, noting Georgiana's hesitation.

Georgiana gave her a hug. "Goodness, I don't really see how I could keep school without you girls!" she declared, laughing, and turned back to Helen and Luke. "I'm just not sure that—Helen, perhaps they'd be better off remaining at Center School, especially if—"

"Don't say it—don't even think it!" Helen declared. "In our view it's important there should be white girls as well as Negroes. And I'm going to start around collecting money."

"Aunt Georgie," Phoebe said suddenly, "why are you so unhappy?"

"Oh I'm not, darling! I'm not unhappy in the least!" she cried, hugging the child to her. Then, bursting into tears, she snatched up her bonnet and rushed from the house, leaving the children to wonder why grown-ups always cried when they were "happy."

LATER Georgiana's eyes sparkled as she sat in the parlor with Hat, describing the support she'd found at the Haverstraws'. It was doubly welcome because it meant that a Grimes—Zion's very own daughter—was offering the proposed school her approval. Hat rocked energetically while she absorbed this news and gave it her deepest consideration. Yes, she agreed, Helen's approval was certainly welcome. But wouldn't it as certainly put a bee in Deacon Grimes's bonnet? When that bee and a lot of other bees began to swarm, someone was bound to get stung. And what would Zion say when he learned that his grandchildren planned to attend a school for colored girls?

Georgiana, while not unconcerned, put such daunting thoughts from her. In this school she would be making a contribution of the sort she had long ago hoped to make to the sum total of human good, and her whole being was excited by the prospect. It would be the education of Ambo Buck all over again, but this time no one would be able to say no, don't, stop, wrong. True, she was being made use of for the cause of abolition, but who better than she, who mattered so little to so few, and in what better cause? How eloquently Mr. Garrison had spoken to her, how staunch and determined had been Electra, how dearly hopeful Old Bobby in offering her this commission, how generous Posie in her enthusiasm and support.

And yet—Hat was right, and Luke. A school of the nature they had in mind would surely bait the growly bear. Was she so foolhardy as to encourage the wrath of Zion Grimes and all his tribe? Even with the Talcotts behind her, and Helen and Luke too, would she have the stamina and conviction to stand up to them? And what of that pleasant little life that she had so carefully worked out for herself? Her decision, her *wish,* not to draw attention to herself? Was she once again to walk into the lion's den? This was unfurling banners with a vengeance.

Yes, she thought, yes, I will be a Daniel, and suddenly everything seemed perfectly clear. A girl like Rose Mills should not be denied an education, nor should others like her be denied. Teaching them was the right and fitting thing to do, something she was meant to try: to use the methods she had formerly devised in teaching Ambo Buck to help others. Her mind was made up.

The following morning, with some trepidation, she went to face her employer and resign her position. Kind soul that he was, Warren Burdin accepted the news almost as if he had been expecting something of the sort. "I never kidded myself I could hold on to you forever, Georgie, though I confess I'm that sorry to see you go. Burdin's won't be the same without you."

"Think, you have Ambo, Mr. Burdin. He's well trained now, he's bright, and he's hardworking, you've said so yourself. And if he needs any help, I'll be just around the corner, he'll find me readily enough."

"Sure, we're lucky to have Ambo—if he don't take it into his head to run off someplace, too. But say, how you goin' to fit a whole school into Snug Harbor? There won't be room to shoot ducks in that little parlor of Mehatibel's. You'd better be on the lookout for a more convenient schoolroom."

And, indeed, in the space of a week Georgiana was confronted by nearly a dozen girls from around the village. First to be enrolled was the runaway ex-slave Rose Mills, who didn't care "if I does or not," but she would try it. Mab Talcott had had a private talk with her new hired girl; as far as Mab was concerned it was "school or nothing," with regular attendance at Sunday worship tossed in as part of the deal, and Rose had prudently chosen school. Such as they were, her household duties would for the present come second to her classwork, and she pictured herself stretched out on her bed, nibbling cookies while reading a book.

Then came Sooky Smyth, the blacksmith's daughter; Maria and Jessie Cleves were next, two of the barber's girls.

The Tando tribe, into which Burdy Priest had married, was another matter. Since time immemorial Tandos had occupied a congeries of broken-down shacks at the end of Middletown Avenue, near Gypsy Woods, where Beaver Brook rounded and the gypsies camped on their annual pilgrimages between Canada and points south. Most of the male Tandos scratched a precarious existence trapping small animals for their furs and doing some fishing, and through the years they had managed to produce a considerable progeny, some of whose forebears had been members of the original Won-gunk stock and were distantly related to Cinnamon Comorra.

Burdy was pleased at the prospect of her female offspring receiving a free education, but Dake Tando, the wrinkled, grizzled patriarch with the sad eyes of a bloodhound, whose word was law with all his descendants, was doubtful about the venture. He hooted when Georgiana explained what she wanted. "S'cuse me, missy, but that's the foolingest idear I heard in a long time. Folks round hyere ain't gonter cotton to no Tandos gettin' book larnin'. You might as well try teachin' 'em their dancin' steps fer Friday night 'semblies."

Georgiana didn't bother to argue with Dake. Instead, she sent Old Bobby as her ambassador, and as a result of his powers of persuasion, not only Burdy's two daughters, Ella and Cleola, but three other Tando cousins were soon enrolled.

The first class of "young misses" convened in orderly fashion in Hat's parlor, Georgiana's students distributed primly about the room, listening attentively while Rose Mills read aloud, haltingly, though not without some display of pride, the account in Genesis of Nimrod and the Tower of Babel. Thus did Snug Harbor take on a certain distinction as the place where the famous "darky school" of Pequot Landing had begun. However, with a baker's dozen making up the original complement of students—not a notable number, to be sure, but sufficient to occupy every bit of available space—from the outset the inadequacies of Hat's small house were all too apparent. But if not Snug Harbor, where? During fair weather Sunday-school teachers often conducted alfresco classes in the Ancient Burying Ground, but in wintertime this was hardly feasible. If only it were spring, Georgiana thought, and they could spread outdoors into the garden. Teaching under the blossoming apple boughs, what a nice thing that would be!

But springtime was still a good way off. Meanwhile, at least there were chalk slates enough to go around, and these were all the teacher required for the moment, for she had inaugurated her former methods of teaching: telling stories and having the girls associate objects with sounds. Lessons at

Center School were often dull; at Snug Harbor the schoolmistress was determined they would not be, that they would, in fact, be amusing.

On the school's opening day, Old Bobby, Appleton, and Electra were on hand, along with Judge Perry and Maude and Merrill Ashley, and Milehigh and Sally Jenckes from the Old Hundred tavern. Though certain invitees like Pastor Weeks and his wife were conspicuous by their absence, Izz and Erna Quoile were present to lend support—Erna had baked ginger snaps for the girls, Izzard had brought a tall can of milk; though they had exchanged a rural existence for life in town as proprietors of the Heavenly Bakery on Chemical Lane, they still kept a cow, a pig, and a mule in their barn.

Most important, also present for the opening day ceremonies, as promised, was William Lloyd Garrison, who had made a special trip down from Boston to write up the event for the *Liberator*. Asking which of the pupils had been the first to enroll, he was presented with the Talcotts' new hired girl. Looking pert in her well-starched cap and apron, with her slate in hand and the primer by which she was going to improve her reading skills, Rose Mills bobbed a proper curtsy to the newspaperman and promised to work hard at her studies and be a credit to her race.

Then each of Georgiana's special guests shook hands with all the girls and pronounced their names, and Electra even took the time to describe the city of Washington and the president, Mr. Tyler, whom she had seen in person and spoken with on several occasions, after which, declaring the school would make history, she went away with Mr. Garrison in his coach.

Excited by the prospect of learning more than their letters, a thing most of them had never imagined possible, from the first the girls (with one exception) went about their studies with an earnestness and modest diligence that gratified their teacher, or teachers, for Hattie Duckworth was only too willing to spell Georgiana at the easel she used in place of a blackboard, and at intervals throughout the day either Ambo Buck or Hermie Light, coming by to check up on the fuel supply and give the fire a hot-up with the bellows, could usually be persuaded to offer the girls a short discourse, Ambo on some topic of natural science, or the history of the local Indians, Hermie describing the exotic ports he had visited when he sailed as Sinjin Grimes's mate. In the late afternoons a formal tea was served, with real china cups and saucers and a napkin for each lap, and the girls were instructed in matters of proper deportment and etiquette, sometimes by Helen Haverstraw, who would stop over, bringing a loaf warm from her oven, or some useful reading material she'd come across up-attic. Helen paid no more special attention to her own offspring than she did to Sooky Smyth or the Tando girls, and when the neighborhood boys stood out on the walk making japes or noisily rattling sticks along the pickets, she would spring out at them and chase them away.

Then there was Posie Talcott, who, from the beginning, when her own regular classes at the Female Seminary in Hartford were done with, had insisted on reporting to Snug Harbor to undertake whatever available tasks might be assigned her. She fitted right in. She excelled at telling stories that made Georgiana's students all laugh, especially the younger ones, who adored her, and presently they and she had formed their own little story-telling group in the corner.

The single fly in the ointment—besides the "silly boys," as Miss Ross called them—was Rose, the hired girl from Kingdom Come, who though she might look white was really colored too. Oldest of the pupils and first to come among them, she often put on fancy airs, and frequently intimidated the younger girls with her abrasive ways. She pinched Sooky Smyth to force her to give up her place, and when she spattered her pinafore with her tea she used naughty words. Sometimes, while Auntie Hat was talking, Georgiana would invite Rose into the kitchen, where they would sit at the table speaking privately. On one occasion there was a noisy ruction between Rose and Cinnamon, the Injun witch. There was another ruction between Rose and the witch's grandson, Ambo Buck, who had accidentally trod on her foot, and Rose loudly claimed he'd done it on purpose. No, Rose did not make it easy for anyone.

It was as the school was moving into its third week that Warren Burdin came to Georgiana and, loosening his collar as if getting down to business, asked her to spare a minute and hear out a proposition he had to make.

"Georgie, how would it be if you used one of the empty attic rooms over at the seed store? We've a deal of space up there, and there's an old Shaker stove that'll throw a sight of heat."

Georgiana looked up into his earnest, leathery face. "Warren," she said firmly, "there's a lot of folks around here who aren't going to take kindly to our school. You're a businessman, people buy your seeds, they won't like your renting us space."

"Oh, the space ain't for rent," Warren replied, scratching his spade beard. "It's for free. Free of charge, yessir. See here, Georgiana Ross, I aim to give some slavers a black eye if I can. It's time we abolitionists took a stand, 'pears this is a good way to do it. Alice and I want to help, so there it is, yours for the taking."

Georgiana's protests were unavailing. Volunteering his attic was Warren Burdin's way of shaking a fist at the antiabolitionists. Thus the business was decided, and a sign was painted to be hung above the door; Warren also stretched a ribbon across the doorway, and Georgiana was offered a new pair of shears to cut it and lead the way upstairs, where a small army of the school's supporters was enlisted to sweep and dust and white wash, as well as to construct the requisite desks and benches.

In the matter of the sign, there had been some discussion. Georgiana's original idea had been to name the school the Electra Warburton School, after its leading female patron. Electra, however, had declined the honor.

"I'm enormously flattered," she said, "but it's your school, Georgie. It should be called the Georgiana Ross School."

This wouldn't do at all, Georgiana decided. Having her name emblazoned on a sign would unnecessarily inflame those townsfolk who were already ill disposed toward her venture. Thus, when the new sign went up, on the last day of November, it read:

The Free School of Pequot Landing
Est. 1841

The hanging of the sign for the new school fortuitously coincided with Electra Warburton's purpose in having come to Pequot in the first place: her address before the special gathering of the Connecticut Anti-Slavery Society, and with the obvious exception of the Grimes faction, many among the Pequot Old Guard drove the five miles up to Hartford to fill the galleries of the State House, where the meeting was being held. There the assembled abolitionists from the near and far reaches of the state were first treated to a few words from the former squire of Follybrook Farm, who rose to warm applause and delivered himself of his chosen remarks—well chosen, his auditors later said, for they in no way infringed on Electra's finest moment. Then it was Electra's turn, and the hearts of her partisans swelled with pride as she assumed the rostrum and spoke out ringingly on that most serious matter besetting not only Connecticut, but all of New England: the fact that the cotton woven into cloth here in New England mills was grown and picked by black slave labor in the south.

Her remarks excited repeated applause, in particular near their conclusion, when she made a formal declaration of the existence of the Free School of Pequot Landing, identifying the new schoolmistress and supplying the names of its board of directors, among whom, she was happy to state, was herself. Then, putting on her glasses, she undertook to read a clipping from the *Liberator:*

WANTED

Young ladies and little Misses of color desirous of attending school. Special curriculum offered, including the following branches of study:

Reading, Writing, Arithmetic, English Grammar, Geography, History, Natural and Moral Philosophy, Chemistry, Astronomy, Drawing and Painting, Music of the Piano and Flute, together with the French and Italian languages as well as Latin.

Also included are instruction for females in Deportment and proper Social Etiquette and correlated subjects. Tuition, Books, and Stationery furnished gratis.

Applicants may address themselves to the schoolmistress, Miss Georgiana Ross of Pequot Landing, at the Offices of Burdin's Best Seeds, Main Street of that place.

As the loudly shouted *ayes!* rose to ring the chandelier, Electra, stepping down, turned to smile and wave to Georgiana in the gallery, seated between Aunt Hat and Mab. It had been a neatly accomplished business. At a stroke, the school was given status and considerable notoriety, and it became obvious to many that the enterprise was to be the opening wedge in a far-reaching abolitionist scheme, one the opposition was immediately resolved to prevent.

Further evidence for this, if such were wanted, was the meeting on the following Sunday of the local Pequot chapter of the Anti-Slavery Society, which was addressed by none other than the school's "model pupil," Rose Mills. The girl was introduced by her employer, Appleton Talcott, at his eloquent best that evening, and by Lloyd Garrison himself, who was sojourning at Kingdom Come for several days, and whose presence created considerable stir in the village. Subsequently, Rose's remarks were printed to considerable acclaim, especially by that same Mr. Garrison, whose personal reaction to the evening appeared in the *Liberator* amid a torrent of hortatory rhetoric. At the same time, an account, also from Mr. Garrison's pen, was published concerning the recent inauguration of the Free School, praising its teacher, Miss Ross, underscoring her "revolutionary" teaching methods and eulogizing her efforts on behalf of her colored students, who in this remarkable institution were permitted to sit side by side with white girls, offspring of a local doctor.

THINGS moved quickly now. In a matter of weeks the Free School of Pequot Landing became an enterprise to be reckoned with. As a consequence of the advertisement, several out-of-town colored girls were soon enrolled: the Gilbert sisters, Hazel and Hannah, from Pawtucket, who were accepted as boarders by the Talcott sisters, and Mary Feebs from Providence, Rhode Island, who rented a room from Izz and Erna Quoile, where they lived next door to the bakery in Chemical Lane. And there were a number of letters of inquiry, though many seemed inclined to caution, to wait and see how matters would work out before committing their children to the school.

Then, following Ambo Buck's reiterated suggestion that Georgiana give further consideration to the young women of Lamentation Mountain, she in turn, having discussed matters with Père Margeaux, wondered why not: if the Free School was going to profit colored girls, why not those indigenous Indian or part-Indian girls as well? To this end, she persuaded Hermie Light to drive her out to the Mountain, where she would personally propose to Chief Waikoit and the tribal elders that some few of their likeliest daughters be sent to her for instruction.

Georgiana was reckoning heavily on the chief's willingness to accommodate not only her but the Talcotts, who over the years had been so generous to the Lamenters, but to her surprise her earnest appeal met with Waikoit's curt refusal. He solemnly declared he could not be responsible for allowing any of his charges to be made part of such a farfetched scheme. Weren't there difficulties and dangers enough? Deliberately exposing innocent young women to the contempt and scorn of the villagers would only increase the chances of their being degraded, ridiculed, shamed.

But the chief's blunt refusal had only fueled Georgiana's desire to get her hands on a few of his girls, and the next day she undertook to bring both the Abbé Margeaux and Old Bobby into the argument, with the result that little by little Waikoit was worn down, until a handful of girls and young women, consisting of the new mother, Bessie Willotts, her friends Easter Dawn, Hutta Teal, and Maria Coleman, along with Culla Bryant and a crippled girl, Loney Bass, was offered up. They would be permitted to leave the Mountain between the hours of seven and four, Mondays through Fridays, until planting season in the spring.

Georgiana eagerly agreed, vowing in an aside to Hermie that eventually Waikoit would turn over ten or a dozen additional girls to the Free School. And, happily, before long, such indeed was the case, with the chief well pleased not only by the rapid advancement of the first token few, but by the fact that they took their midday meal in town, courtesy of Sallie Jenckes, and thereby more food was made available for those left at home.

Thus it was with a deep sense of gratification that, on the first school day of the New Year, Georgiana assumed the direction of a class in the school's expanded quarters over Burdin's seed store, the spacious room with its neat rows of desks and benches, a sizable blackboard hung up behind her desk, and a well-drawing Shaker stove to keep things warm. Thanks to the generosity of the Free School's supporters, there were enough schoolroom supplies with which to progress beyond the stage when mere slates would be sufficient—and thanks to Warren Burdin's kindness there was plenty of room to employ them in. In addition to a hand-painted world globe of papier-mâché, Appleton's thoughtful gift, there were new primers and Webster's spellers, purchased with a check from Priam Talcott's partner, Asher Ingolls, to be used, he had written, in the interest of scholarly endeavor. Ambo had cut handfuls of quills from goosefeathers; a generous sum had been anonymously donated for pens, pen wipers, and bottles of good bister ink.

And as she led the morning prayer, followed by the singing of a spirited hymn, which would henceforth begin each school day's efforts, Georgiana reflected on how different most of these girls were from the lackadaisical and haphazardly educated white boys and girls she had tried to teach so many years before at Center School; how eager and determined, how calmly serious and well-mannered they were, expressing their gratitude for the opportunity that was being offered them. At noon she found it hard to believe the morning was over, the time had passed so quickly. Suddenly she felt confident, brimful of hope and feelings of worthwhileness and effort rewarded. It was all so simple, really. Sometimes you had to take the bull by the horns, but just look what could be done! Certainly she recognized the difficulties and obstacles that lay ahead. Having cloaked herself in Quakerish meekness, a little brown chameleon on a piece of brown bark, she was now once again making herself vulnerable, offering herself up to the narrowest scrutiny, knowing that her every action would be observed and commented on, her every word open to criticism. But one need only look at Ambo Buck to see what could be achieved! What he had accomplished, these girls could and would also; Georgiana was certain of it. During a painful period in her life she had sworn never to attempt it again—the anguish, the humiliation, the ignominy had been too overwhelming. She had not thought to endure it another time. Now she was equally determined that nothing on earth should prevent her from succeeding when she had so miserably failed before.

12

One Foot in the Enemy Camp

THERE WAS NO DOUBT in anyone's mind that once aroused Zion Grimes would bend his best efforts to oppose the Free School of Pequot Landing, thus setting himself at loggerheads with his traditional adversaries, Appleton and Old Bobby Talcott. Indeed, privately it pleased him to have the entire Talcott clan so zealous in their support of abolition, for he was thereby provided with the ideal vehicle to freight his heavy load of hatred against them. By damning abolition and the furtherance of such liberal aims as were manifested by Georgiana Ross's newly opened school, he could at the same time publicly vilify his opponents as anarchists and revolutionaries, enemies of the Constitution and of private property, while presenting himself as wisely possessed of strictly antithetical principles. Almshouses were for the aged—this was Zion's eleemosynary posture; workhouses for the indigent; orphanages for the motherless; and the slave pens for every woolly-headed nigger whether or not he could dine with a fork.

Talcotts aside, it was perhaps inevitable that the house of Grimes should have elected to stand not on the side of the angels but against, for it was considerably to their advantage that in the matter of slavery the status quo should be rigidly upheld. The all-important reason was this: a goodly share of the considerable fortune that had accrued to Grimes & Co. in the last twenty years came from several cotton mills on the upper Quinnebaug River, and the cotton spun and woven there came in turn from deep in the South, handpicked in the Mississippi Delta fields by half a million black hands and transported in Grimes bottoms from southern ports to Yankee ones. Moreover, a number of Grimeses had considerable sums invested in small manufactories that turned out the machine fittings that made up the intricate workings of New England's spinning jennies. The brass foundry tucked behind the Shad Run down at Talcotts Ferry was Grimes-owned and -operated, and Grimes-owned were more than half the shares in several manufacturing enterprises over in New Britain, some fifteen miles away, and farther down state at Bridgeport. The Talcotts owned no cotton mills, no looms, no foundries, and therefore could afford to adopt a high-toned moral stance. But just let them try to produce a yard of muslin at five cents the ell, with wage earners who received seven cents an hour, if the cotton was likewise grown by paid labor!

So declared Zion, loudly and often, at meetings of the Hickory Club, as the number of Georgiana Ross's pupils was enlarged by the addition of girls from out of state and from among those dwelling at Lamentation Mountain, who daily were driven into the village past Burning Bush itself. But in the end, when all was said and done, it was neither the outsiders nor the ragtail half-breed Lamenters who set the pot to boiling, it was the Free School's primary enrolled scholar, Miss Rose Mary Mills, and the astonishing incident that occurred in, of all places, the Congregational church. On a Sunday morning toward the end of January, those worshipers attending service were treated to an episode of such rare description that it was to stamp itself indelibly on the memory of all those present, at the same time providing considerable fuel for the smoldering fire of opposition Georgiana's school had already ignited.

Bound by the solemn compact entered into with Mab Talcott, Rose had been in the habit of accompanying the Priest family to Sunday worship. On the day in question, the former slave, who was in the forefront of the little group, looked around her as they passed through the church vestibule, then set out down the center aisle. Her progress was interrupted only when the sexton, Giles Corry, placed his hickory staff across her path and enjoined her to follow Trubey and the others to the gallery, where people of her race were long accustomed to sit.

"Why does we have to set way up here?" Rose complained as she plunked down on the hard bench provided overhead. "It's fearful cole. An' they got cushions to sit on down yonder."

"Hush, girl, it's where you belong," Trubey told her.

"Ah be damned if it is," said Rose and jerked away. "They's plenty of room below."

Hattie Duckworth, softly sketching in some simplified Bach at the organ, heard and saw what was happening. "Set down there, girl, you'll rock the boat," she muttered, wishing Georgiana were on hand to intervene. Rose, however, paid no attention. With a saucy toss of her head she disappeared down the little stairway behind the organ, and moments later the incoming churchgoers witnessed the shocking sight of Mabel Talcott's hired girl, having eluded Mr. Corry, slipping down the center aisle to accommodate herself with a place in the front pew to the right of the offertory table.

No sooner had she settled herself than the minister's wife, who was putting the finishing touches on some decorative boughs of greens, noticed the intruder and informed her that she was forbidden to sit in that pew.

Rose glared at her, then looked around at the congregation. "Nobody else settin' here," she said shortly.

"It makes no difference," said Mrs. Weeks. "That pew is reserved for our head deacon."

"Ah kin make room if needs be," said Rose, idly toying with her bonnet strings.

"But you don't belong down here!" Mrs. Weeks did not enjoy being defied by saucy darkies. "You belong up *there!*"

"It's a sight too cole up there. Ah'll cotch me a plurr'sy if Ah ain't keerful," retorted Rose.

"Surely that's not my affair," Mrs. Weeks pointed out.

"Jes you go try settin' up there, lady."

"My *name* is Mrs. *Weeks.* I am the pastor's *wife.*"

"Mah name is Rose Mary Mills. *Ah* ain't *nobody's* wife. But Ah doan aim t'freeze mah backside neither."

There was a titter among those who overheard this brisk exchange. Paling, Mrs. Weeks urgently summoned the sexton, who trundled down the aisle as fast as his bandy legs would carry him.

"Mr. Corry, this person is being intractable. I have explained to her that she doesn't belong in this pew. However did she get in here, anyway?"

"What're you doing, then?" demanded Giles of Rose. "Weren't you told to go upstairs?"

"You ain't mah boss," Rose said defiantly. "Ah is a free darky, you cain't make me go. Ah gots mah papers to prove it."

By this time several congregants were making their way down the aisle. One, having only just arrived in the church, surveyed the situation, then demanded peremptorily to know the meaning of the disturbance.

"Good morning, Deacon Wandsworth," began the pastor's wife. "We are having difficulty ejecting this bold young creature from the Grimes pew."

"Why, I'll be buzzed if that ain't the Talcotts' darky," said Willie, peering more closely at her. "How does it happen that she is seated there, where she has no business being seated?"

"She says," averred Mrs. Weeks sarcastically, "that it is too cold for her up in the gallery, which is utter nonsense. I would be much obliged if you could persuade her to vacate the pew before the rightful occupants arrive."

"Get up, get up!" snapped the deacon, who had not forgotten Rose Mills's shameful arrival in Pequot, nor her well-publicized connection with the school now disturbing the town's peace. "This is not your place. You belong in the gallery with the rest of your ilk. Come along now, hussy, step out of there." As he reached to apprehend Rose, she slid to the farther end of the bench, where she maintained herself with a defiant expression on her pale face.

"Why, what an obstinate mule the baggage is!" exclaimed the indignant deacon. "Very well, here is the owner of this box, perhaps you'll see fit to make way for him."

"What seems to be the difficulty?" the new arrival inquired, taking in the contretemps. It was Deacon Grimes himself, accompanied by his stepmother, father, and son.

"You can see how it is," Mrs. Weeks began. "This young woman—"

"Is occupying your pew, Deacon," declared Willie, "and refuses to vacate it."

Zion's eyes bulged. "Does she indeed?" he said, keeping his voice low in deference to his surroundings. "Why . . . it's the Talcotts' runaway, I'll be bound. Who does she think she is, the foolish upstart?"

Rose felt intimidated, for this was the same choleric man who upon her arrival in the village had threatened to send her back to her master, yet she refused to budge.

"This is abominable," Zion expostulated, his brow black with outrage. "Young woman, have a care in how you provoke me." Glancing around, he saw that he was the object of every eye in the vicinity.

"Rose ain't provokin' no one, she jes settin', is all."

"Not here you won't set. There are laws governing such behavior. Do you know I can have you whipped for this?"

Rose blanched. "Whupped?" she whispered fearfully. Then her defiance flared. "You cain't whup me, no suh—Rose be a free darky now. Gotta paper t'prove it."

"Paper be deuced! We are decent upstanding citizens of this community, while you are—are no better than you should be, obviously. And unless you want to feel the lash across your back—"

The deacon had unwittingly raised his voice, and worshipers were whispering behind their hands. A bristling Rachel Grimes moved to interpose herself between Zion and the girl. "Oh, for pity's sake, let the poor thing sit," she said with a sniff. "Where's the difference in sharing our pew, if we share the Almighty?" So saying, she sat down in the place next to Rose.

"Come on, Abed," she told her husband. "She won't bite you."

"I should hope not!" retorted the indignant Abednego. "But I wasn't brought up to set for service with no nigger girls, thank you. I'll set elsewhere." With this he jerked his way back up the aisle, to be followed by his son and, somewhat reluctantly by his grandson, Bushrod, who, with his hands shoved in his pockets, had been observing the confrontation with some relish. Though his sentiments when it came to abolition mirrored his sire's, he admired spunk, especially the spunk of a pretty woman, no matter her antecedents.

In the meantime Rachel had settled herself more thoroughly into her place, running a pair of sharp eyes over the girl who for better or worse had carried the day over her stepson. "So. You're Apple Talcott's runaway, are you," Rachel said. "It takes a sight of gumption to defy Deacon Grimes." She cast an eye to the gallery. "Why aren't you sitting up there where you belong?"

"It be cole." Rose yawned widely, making no effort to cover her open mouth.

Rachel looked her starchiest. "You want manners, miss. Don't they give you enough rest over there?"

"Ah works roun' the house *an'* goes t' school. Ah sleeps all right, but—" She yawned again to demonstrate just how fatigued she was.

Rachel sniffed and turned away as Reverend Weeks proceeded down the aisle and assumed the pulpit, then, lifting his arms, invited the congregation to rise. The organ sounded.

> *Praise God from whom all blessings flow,*
> *Praise Him all creatures here below,*
> *Praise Him above, ye heavenly host,*
> *Praise Father, Son and Holy Ghost.*
> *Amen-n-n-n-n . . .*

The echoes of the final notes died reverently away. As the pastor, clad in his black ecclesiastical robes with their white tabs, rattled his papers and coughed once or twice, necks craned and heads turned, not to Reverend Weeks, but to this nervy darky who had dared to plunk herself down in the Grimeses' pew, and who, while the rest had sung out lustily, had dozed off before the doxology had ended.

It made a pretty tale around the village dinner tables that day. Some had a good laugh about it, especially certain of those members of the Noontide Club, the weekly Tuesday luncheon convocation of the town's business elite, who gathered in the Long Room at the Old Hundred. Members of the opposite persuasion, however, like Zion Grimes's brother-in-law Piper Lamb, declared it a social outrage and speedily denounced the manners of both the Talcotts *and* their hired girl, who was so ignorant she didn't know where colored folk were supposed to sit in church and then had the effrontery to fall asleep during the service. Naturally an account of the provoking incident was carried back to Kingdom Come. Though Appleton was inclined to ignore the episode, and Mab as well, Old Bobby, while amused, did suggest to Rose in passing that she should better mind her manners and not be so candid in her remarks. Halley Priest, on the other hand, was so put out over the business that she refused even to speak to Rose, and henceforth issued her commands through Trubey.

Rose, however, endured the aftermath with aplomb, seeming to take pleasure in the disturbance she had caused among the congregation, and declaring herself quite unafraid of the formidable Deacon Grimes. Indeed, for a week afterwards she went about with a secret feeling of pride at having got the better of the man who had wanted to throw her to the slave catchers and see her shipped back to the Laceys.

As for the deacon himself, the incident, while of no great account in the overall design of things, had put him greatly out of countenance, and because of it his opposition to the Free School, already publicly declared, became a profoundly personal quarrel against the institution, its mistress, and its score of pupils—in particular Miss Rose Mills.

On the face of things, it seemed both petty and silly that so insignificant a matter should cause a deacon of First Church to take such violent exception to a mere chit of a girl, an ignorant darky at that, and undoubtedly the fact that she was the Talcotts' protégée had much to do with Zion's rancor. But there was more to it than that, a sequel of sorts in which the newly freed slave tried once again to fit herself into the unfamiliar patterns of life in Pequot Landing.

On the snowy Saturday afternoon that followed her contretemps with Zion Grimes, Rose was sitting by the kitchen window watching the large white flakes fall from the sky. From time to time they struck the glass and her eye took in their lacy shapes; she'd heard Georgie Ross say that no matter how many snowflakes there might be, no two were alike, each one was of a different design. Though she disliked the cold winter temperatures, snow was still a new experience for Rose, and she delighted in the feel of it against her cheeks. She sighed, and Trubey, seated with her mother at the table paring turnips, took pity on her and suggested that she go out and enjoy herself for a spell. This Rose did at once without a word of thanks to Trubey for her thoughtfulness, leaving Halley to grumble over that no-'count chile.

As she got to the end of March Street Rose turned toward the river, to watch the skaters, who were out in numbers. The ice had reached a thickness of over half a foot and Rose was captivated by the idea that a river could actually be walked upon, like Jesus walking on the Sea of Galilee. The skaters all looked so zestful and carefree as they went whizzing by, scarves fluttering behind them; she longed to join them, but even if she could skate, she thought they would not want her.

Turning up the collar of her coat she retraced her steps. As she came along the River Road, head down against the snow, she heard the jingle of sleigh bells. A befurred driver in a cutter hove into view along the roadway, the horse's footfalls muffled on the hard-packed snow. The sleigh passed her, then slowed, and a voice called, "Get in." Staring, Rose recognized the broad face of Bushrod Grimes, red from the cold.

"No thanks," she said and hurried her step.

The cutter kept on behind her. "Get in, darn it," Rod repeated impatiently. "No one's going to hurt you."

She darted him a look, then, throwing away caution, clambered onto the seat beside him. For moments the scene blurred. Was this possible, the son of Zion Grimes giving the Talcotts' hired darky a sleigh ride? His nearness made her nervous, it was the closest she'd been to any man since the slave catchers had let go of her. From time to time as they slipped along, the steel runners singing under them, she stole glances at her escort. He looked like quite a man, this Bushrod Grimes, a regular bear of a fellow. Something of the father's power made itself felt in the son's girth and robustness, intimidating her in a similar if not so distasteful way. She'd heard them talking about this Bushrod Grimes, how he'd not been of much account as a boy but had settled down to lawyering and business and was slated to wed the daughter of a rich man.

Rod didn't continue along the River Road, but cut west before reaching the Broad Street Common, between snowy fields already turning blue in the late afternoon light. As Rose sat fingering flakes from her lashes she felt obliged to recall the untoward scene at church and the way she had spoken up to Zion.

"Your paw, he ain't nothin' but a lousy polecat," she declared boldly. "Smells like one, too."

Rod guffawed. "I won't gainsay that. But you had better not let him hear *you* say it."

"Huh! He'd rather this po' darky still be a slave, see me get whupped.

Ah tole him, cain't whup Rose, Rose got a paper. Ain't no one can whup her ass no more."

Rod laughed again and dropped his hand on her knee. "Good for you." He gave her a friendly pat, then snaked his reins over the horse's flanks. The panting mare was game, and never slackened her smart trot. Under the blanket it was warm and cozy, and Rose could feel the pressure of Rod's strong thigh against hers. After a while he removed his glove and slid one bare hand in under the robe and stroked her side. Though this intimate act induced a pleasant, even exciting, feeling in her, she pushed his hand away, saying, prim as Georgiana Ross:

"You oughtn't t'do that."

"Why not?"

"It ain't—it's not—right."

"How come?"

"Just because." She thought hard. Why was it wrong? "You's a Grimes, Ah'm a Talcott," she said, as if this were reason enough for propriety. Her rationale made him chuckle.

"That doesn't mean a person can't be friendly," he said.

"Yes it do."

Rod laughed again, then grew expansive, and as he went on talking about this and that Rose knew he was trying to impress her; knew why, too.

Huh, men; they were all alike. At least he was keeping his hands to himself now—no, he wasn't either; but this time she didn't edge away. She listened attentively as he spoke about his future and what he intended to do to be successful. "Hell, before I'm done I'm going to be one of the most important men in the whole damn state," he bragged. Rose decided he was probably full of beans; but on second thought, she wondered if perhaps he wasn't right. Something in his forceful words and manner told her that someday Bushrod Grimes might just turn out to be a big frog in Pequot's little pond, and she allowed him her most winsome smile; as they headed back toward town she coyly tucked her hand into his side pocket.

They passed the Common at a fair clip until, rounding the corner from Broad Street onto March Street, Rod slowed his horse to allow a female figure to cross in front of them.

"Good af-ter-*noon*, Rod," came a faintly reproachful voice.

"Good afternoon, Mrs. Weeks," said Rod, abruptly sobersided. They rushed by in a fan of wet snow.

"That's the preacher's wife and she done seen us!" Rose exclaimed, frantically yanking on his arm. "Pull up—Ah bes' get out right here."

Even before Rod could stop she jumped out and hurried off toward Main Street.

"Nice to have met you, Miss Mills," he called after her, unmindful of others' ears or eyes.

"Oh, hush yourself, big man," Rose muttered to herself. She might be flattered by his attentions, but she was fearful of the consequences should word of her escapade be spread among Talcotts—or Grimeses.

It was almost dark when she returned to the kitchen; Halley was on hand to give her what-for. "Gal, where was you? What was you up to? We needs kindlin' fetched."

"Ah was out ice walkin'," came Rose's blithe return.

"You and who?"

"Me an' ol' Jack Frost, that's who."

She tossed her coat and scarf on a peg, then stuck her pink tongue out at Halley's stiffened back. At the wood stove, stirring the soup, Trubey frowned. She'd tried to be nice earlier, letting Rose off work for a little, but sometimes being nice to people just didn't pay.

THAT evening the old house atop Burning Bush Hill seemed to draw in its shrunken eaves against the cold, the random gusts beat helter-skelter upon the clapboards and rattled the loose shutters that no one ever bothered to secure. The tall Burning Bush tree, so fiery in November, was in late January bare as a beggar, its thousand sharp branches scarifying the slate-colored sky like the pointed tines of a farmer's pitchfork. Though the length of Greenshadow Road was kept well tamped by the town snow rollers, and ordinarily the runners of casual travelers were seldom turned in at the snowbound drive of Burning Bush, tonight numbers of vehicles were pulled up in clusters around the base of the old tree. Inside, in the front parlor, the lamps burned brightly—something they rarely did, for the closefisted Abednego Grimes was a bear when it came to the wasteful burning of oil. A meeting of some size and importance was taking place, one that seemed likely to have serious repercussions not only for the unlucky Rose Mills but for Georgiana Ross and all those who had so eagerly flocked to her banner.

In the kitchen Rachel sat knitting at the table, while the grim and silent Oriental servant, Joseph, polished the silver tea service and his wife, Mary, turned a roast of mutton, which sizzled and splattered on the spit. As Rachel plied her needles she harkened with a keen ear, trying to catch snatches of the discussion coming from the parlor where Abednego, Rod, Zion, his brothers Cephas and Gilead, and brother-in-law Piper Lamb, were sitting with a dozen of their cronies, Willie Wandsworth, and Guston Weeks included, as well as two or three male members of the cross-river Grimes families.

Such glum assemblies were nothing new at Burning Bush; the buzz had been going round for weeks, and Rachel kept her ears cocked for any revelatory tidbits: though she might be a Grimes herself, it was not her intention to see Georgiana's brave efforts thwarted by any Grimes deviltry if she could help it. Since the contretemps at First Church, Rachel had been sure that some twisty plot was being hatched like a vulture's egg, but such was the secretiveness of the deliberations that the men kept their voices low. Unable to divine anything of consequence, she endured the pangs of frustration. What the general tone of their conversation expressed, however, was resentment and outrage, as if these strong-minded, important men of affairs had had something put over on them by a mere female. It made Rachel flush with resentment. Thank heaven Helen had offered her personal support to the school as she had. And enrolling her daughters had taken real courage.

Exactly what Rachel herself could do to help was another matter. Her grasp of life was not so firm as it once had been, and these days a good deal of her time was spent in poor health. It was her heart, for which she took regular doses of laudanum—twenty drops in half a glass of water administered upon the slightest flutter or let-down. "Bring me my court bottle!" she would bark at Joseph. "I want my med'cine!" Still, she thought, if these days her gingery snap was a bit less snappy, she was not so derelict that she couldn't administer a smart word where and when she felt it was called for. And, with her foot firmly entrenched in the enemy camp, curse her for a Pharisee if she wouldn't tip into the beam any stray remark she chanced across, and when the time came, ill health or no, she would run her own colors up the mast.

When Joseph put down the sugar bowl, Rachel picked it up and looked it over. Merciful heavens, what a face! she thought, catching sight of her distorted reflection in the rotund bulges. About her head the straight lines and planes of the room bent and curved, recapitulating themselves into novel forms, as if the rules of geometry and logical perspective failed to apply in this dwelling where it seemed even the slightest canons of courtesy and breeding no longer made themselves felt.

On the underside of the bowl, the silversmith's hallmarks indicated the silver had been worked in China rather than in London. Abednego's doing: obtaining on the cheap what the Talcotts had spent roundly for at the hands of Paul Revere. Still, the service *was* lovely, she had to admit. And if its acquisition some ten years before had been less in honor of the twenty-fifth anniversary of their nuptials, as Abednego claimed, and more to spite Old Bobby Talcott, she was nonetheless glad to have it, and vowed to see it go to Helen in due course, however much Zion might protest.

From the parlor the voices rose and fell; through the monotonic babel two stood out: Zion's declared he was decidedly vexed this evening; Rod's was purposeful, the voice of a man whose words would be heeded by others older and richer than he. Rod had turned out to be a young man of parts, a change Rachel was grateful for.

Her thoughts were interrupted as, hearing the scrape of chairs in the parlor, she was quickly alert. In the other room the visitors were preparing to leave. She signaled to Joseph to distribute cloaks and hats, then she herself stood at the door to see them out, with a word for each. All of the Grimes males had remained behind, however, talking over the evening's proceedings, and Rachel whispered to Mary to hold the roast, then stole back along the hallway to the parlor.

Glancing inside, she saw Abednego in the fireside chair, and grouped around him as in a formal tableau, three of his sons. All the men were attending, stern-faced and smug, as Rod spoke.

"Well, then we're agreed—it's time to put a stop to all such nonsense and tighten the screws," she heard him declare.

"Tighten the screws on what?" she asked innocently, stepping into the room, though she knew well enough what Rod was referring to.

"We are discussing certain civic problems, Rachel," said Zion sententiously. "Please, do not interrupt."

Uninvited, she moved to occupy an empty chair, sat down, as if she truly expected an explanation, rather than the crumbs that might come her way as the others assiduously avoided enlightening her.

"Politics, we're talking politics," Cephas Grimes put in. "What woman cares for politics?"

"True," said brother Gilead. "Why, a woman never knows what's good for her until she's been properly told by a man."

"That a fact, Gil? And nary a brain in a wagonload, I expect. I wonder what Sarah Jane has to say about that?" Sarah Jane was Gilead's wife, and not overly known for keeping her opinions to herself.

"We are not discussing anything that would interest you, Rachel," said Zion, with his usual punctilio in addressing his father's spouse.

She observed his dour, mottled face closely from under her hooded lids. These days Zion Grimes had taken on the flint-eyed, heavy-larded look of a Roman senator of the decadent period, his beetling brow a grim frown, the corners of his lips fallen into lines of perpetual disagreeableness.

"It'd certainly interest me to learn what it is you conspirators are bent on putting a stop to," Rachel said. "Do you intend stabbing great Caesar in the senate house?"

"We're not discussing homicide here," Zion returned caustically. "We *are* speaking of a crime, however, one being committed right in the middle of this pretty town of ours."

Rachel was at her most sarcastic. "You don't say. Right here in Pequot!"

Darting her an offended look, Zion turned to his brothers and picked up the conversation where it had been interrupted. "Gil is right, our talk does not concern the distaff side. As I was saying before we were intruded upon, our jurist friend Louis Palfrey has always shown the good sense to look upon these matters for what they are. Rod has assured me that we can count on the judge's full cooperation in the business."

Aha, thought Rachel, all ears; Louis Palfrey, was it? Now there was a poltroon of the first water.

"Georgie Ross is a stubborn creature, Dad," Rod said. "She's like a rock where this school business is concerned—"

Zion gazed down the considerable length of his nose. "I am not interested in hearing what this person is or isn't like, and I will thank you to omit her name from our present discussion," he intoned.

"I'm just telling you, Dad, that's all," Rod said.

"Hee hee hee." Abednego cackled in grim mirth. "Like a rock, is she? The miller's girl? Bah! You don't know what you're talking about! Are you such a fool you can't see who's put her up to this deviltry? It's a plot, I tell you, a damnable conspiracy!"

"If we're talking plots, Abed, let's just see who's doing the plotting," Rachel said.

Zion gave her a stern glare, then turned back to Rod. "What your grandfather means is that they've cooked up this dirty school business just so's to create a public issue. They are choosing to bait us deliberately. Do you imagine it was an accident, what transpired last Sunday, the Talcotts' nigger girl perched down front in our pew? Someone put her up to that knavery. To make fools of us. Spectacle, that's all it was."

"Hear, hear," murmured Cephas and Gilead in unison.

Sparing Rod the necessity of responding to Zion's statement, Abednego resumed his tirade. "The damn school's for free, too. What's the matter, can't they work, those lazy indigents? Didn't their mommas teach them to do a washing or iron a rag? They have it too soft, there's your trouble."

"My stars, 'Bednego, how you do rant on," chided his wife. "Haven't you a shard of Christian charity in that cast-iron heart of yours? Those unfortunates are human beings, they have rights."

"Rights!" Abednego hunched lower in his chair. "Next thing you'll hear them sayin' they're every bit as good as you an' me. Why, by the time they're done, there'll be nigger brats spouting their Sunday verses in every pew an' they'll be livin' all up and down Greenshadder Road. Mayhap you can't tell a book by its cover but you sure can tell a man by his skin. Bible says so, Bible says—"

"Bible says, Bible says," snapped Rachel. "As though *you* ever did much reading of *that* work! If you're smart, the lot of you, you'll just shut up about this school and allow matters to take their natural course."

Cephas was quick upon her. "Educatin' niggers and Injuns ain't natural."

Rachel hiked her chin. "Is that a fact?"

"Yes it is! And them that does the educatin' is got a little surprise coming their way, don't they though! 'Twas young Bushrod there who thought it up."

Rachel was on the alert. "What's he talking about, Rod?"

Rod's smile was, for him, enigmatic. "You'll see, Grammaw, you'll see," was all the answer she got.

"Don't go playing Sphinx with me, I want to know what you're up to."

"And have you go running to Georgie Ross with the news? No thanks. She'll find out when the time's ripe."

Abednego cackled again. "And that snot-nosed Bob Talcott, too, he'll get tumbled off his high horse. Livin' so fine and grand in that fancy house. Didn't I say 'twould be a pagan temple? Colyums and pillars and pediments, you'd think you was a Greek on the Acropolis just to drive past."

"Oh, how the man talks!" Rachel exclaimed. "Joseph—" she called past the portières, "tell Mary not to let the roast dry out! I'm coming. Besides," she added as she left the room, "I believe it was a noble gesture on Helen's part, allowing her own girls to attend the school." In the hall she stopped and listened.

"Only hear the foolish thing!" croaked Abednego, turning livid, gripping the arms of his chair. "Noble gesture! My gre't-grandchildren settin' down cheek by jowl with a bunch of niggers to get their ABC's? *There's* more mischief of your blasted Georgianner Ross! 'Tis she that's turned Helen's head, put her up to the doin' of it. Why, they're laughin' from one end of town t'other—black an' white, white an' black, like 'twas a checkerboard. Next thing you know some black buck'll be beddin' your own kin an' see how you'll like it then!"

"No!" Zion shook an angry first. "By God, there'll be an end to it! I'll not sit by idly while the female descendants of an ancient line are obliged to sit on the same puncheon as a clutch of goggle-eyed darkies!"

"No, nor I!" declared the indignant Cephas. He consulted his watch, then, along with Gilead, prepared to quit the house, for his stomach had been complaining at the cooking odors from Rachel's kitchen. "Zi, we'll leave all this in your hands, trusting you and Rod will know best how to proceed uptown." He and his brother went out, taking the garments proffered by Joseph and tipping their hats to Rachel as they left.

When they had gone, Rachel went back down the hall to the parlor door, hopeful of gleaning further information, but more was not immediately forthcoming.

"Well," Rod said, getting up with a stretch and a yawn, "I'm going to run uptown and tell the boys what's afoot."

"You'll do nothing of the sort," snapped his father. "You'll wait for further instructions."

"But it's my idea, Dad."

Zion's voice cleaved the air. "I said you will wait. I don't want this job botched by any city blockheads. Our plan calls for finesse. You just hold your horses, boy."

Rod's look grew sullen. "Damn it, I'm not a boy, I'm a man!"

"Then start acting like one!" Zion exclaimed. "And as we're addressing the subject, let me point out that you are bringing no honor on either our family or these plans of yours by being seen sleighing about with Apple Talcott's black doxy. Do you want to cause a scandal? Isn't it bad enough that your stepbrother's penchant for serving wenches has caused years of talk, do you have to flaunt your proclivities at the populace? What would Sydney Shaylor say were he to learn of your behavior?"

"I wasn't doing anything, I just gave the wench a ride is all."

Zion's voice trembled with suppressed rage. "Yes, and I'll wager you'd like to give her another kind of ride."

Rod's features assumed the sort of sneer his parent was known for. "I wouldn't talk if I were you, Dad."

"Eh? What? How's that?" Zion's eyes began to bulge.

"You know what I'm talking about. You and that Gold Street female. That hussy—"

"Silence! Not a word will I hear on that subject. The name is taboo in this house and while you are in it you will not dare to utter it."

"Murray! Her name's Murray and she's a whore. Or proprietress of a whorehouse, whichever you like. Obviously she's not above turning tricks with her customers. Of which you seem to be primary."

"*Silence!*" thundered Zion. "I will not listen to such talk! Go—begone to your room."

Rod stared at his father, then laughed insolently. "Are you crazy? You can't send me to my room as if I were a child." He jumped up and marched toward the door. "I'm going, by God, and one of these days I'll go and I won't be back. Just you remember that—you old fool!"

He flung himself from the room, taking no notice of Rachel lingering in the hall, and when he had furiously slammed his way out of the house she hurried back into the parlor. "I hope you're satisfied," she said, shaking her head at Zion. "One of these days he'll make good that threat and you'll wind up with neither son *nor* daughter."

Zion turned on her furiously. "Since you've brought *her* up, and since you visit her, please inform her that if she persists in her folly, if she won't take Chloe and Phoebe out of that damnable seed-store attic, she must accept what comes. I shall consult my attorney and have any mention of her or her family extirpated from my will. So I say, so shall I do. Be warned."

Rachel lowered her voice and spoke with fierce intensity. "You've a hard head, Zion Grimes, but be careful, one of these days you'll get it cracked. What a cruel man to attack his own flesh and blood! No, don't bother to deny it. You know it's not Helen I'm speaking of now, but Georgiana Ross. *That* daughter, whom you seek to bring down however you can!"

Zion stared at her, aghast that his own stepmother would dare to bring the wretched subject into the open. "Be silent!" he commanded. He scowled at his father. "Really, can't you control her, or must I go on listening to this sort of blather?"

Abednego smacked his gums and his watery eyes swiveled from one to the other; he relished a quarrel and never cared who won, as long as the words were sharp, the recriminations bitter, the noise shrill.

"You'll listen quick enough if I choose to speak of it," Rachel went on impatiently. "I vow I'd shrivel like a scorpion if I'd ever whelped the likes of you. A vale of tears you'd make of the world, Zion Grimes. Where you set your foot the sod turns brown."

She watched him wave his hands in that sanctimonious way of his and piously lift his eyes to heaven. "A night's mistake," he groaned, hand over heart. "Must I pay for it all of my life?"

Just then Joseph appeared to announce dinner. The air was rife with the smell of mutton. Rachel despaired at the thought of having to spend the dinner hour with the likes of her stepson. Such did not become necessary, however, when Zion informed her that he intended dining elsewhere. She accepted the announcement with relief, and eschewing further words, marched stiffly from the room, dark skirts crackling like autumn leaves.

In the kitchen she sank into the closest chair, trying to control the trembling that had suddenly overcome her, and knocked over a dish. The crash brought Joseph and Mary hurrying to her side. She put out a quaking hand.

"My med'cine, quick—"

The laudanum bottle was brought and uncorked, Rachel was dosed, and when she was able they helped her to bed. After she lay resting, the servants went downstairs again. In the hall the master was putting on his things. Off he went to the city and the house lay nighttime quiet as Joseph and Mary sat at the kitchen table whispering in Chinese over the latest domestic upheaval.

I3

"Sticks and Stones"

ON A MONDAY MORNING while being driven in to school from her miserable abode on Lamentation Mountain, Culla Bryant was struck on the head by a rock thrown by one of the village boys. Several stitches were needed to close the wound. A day later the sides of the wagon that carried Georgiana's pupils to and fro were emblazoned with the words:

NIGGER HAULER

and with that blow and with those words trouble came to Pequot Landing, trouble of a sort heretofore unknown in that place. In the space of a few days rock throwing became an active pastime, and boys took to chasing after the wagon whenever it passed, shouting taunts and derogatory epithets. The pleasure derived by Chief Waikoit from his girls' success at the Free School turned to alarm and he stirred uneasily in his malodorous hut, threatening to revoke the permission he had so grudgingly granted. Once again, Georgiana drove out to the settlement, where she smoothed the chief's ruffled feathers, assuring him that these unfortunate episodes were evidence of the resentments of only a small segment of the population (and as such would soon die down), and in any case, henceforth the wagon would be guarded: While Foote Crowe drove, Stix Bailey and Kneebone Apperbee would give up their places among the whittling fraternity that daily occupied the sidewalk in front of Archibald's store to spell each other riding guard.

It was not long after these initial sinister stirrings, however, that the first "incident" at the school itself took place. Georgiana had been conducting her class for no more than ten minutes after the end of noon recess when an alarming crash sounded at one of the windows. A stone smashed a pane and struck the floor; there was a note attached. "I see that we have been sent a message, girls," she said laughing. "Let us hope it is one of congratulation on our current efforts." While the pupils regarded her solemnly, she picked up the stone and looked at the note. *"Go and live! Stay and die!"* it read, and it was decorated with a crudely drawn skull and crossbones.

Making light of the business, Georgiana crumpled the screed and dropped it into the stove. "As we might have guessed, it is definitely *not* a message of encouragement. Easter, would you be good enough to sweep up the glass before anyone cuts herself? And since this may be only the first of many such communications," she added, addressing the class, "I suggest we all learn to ignore them, whatever their content. Chloe, would you care to read a little for us?"

Chloe Haverstraw, who had learned her ABC's at Center School, read, and nicely so, and when at the end of class Georgiana reported to Hattie Duckworth and Maude Ashley, who had passed by, she merely mentioned the rock through the window to explain the broken panes, and said nothing of the note.

"Is it an augury, George?" asked Aunt Hat, her homely face screwed up into a map of anxiety.

"Certainly not," Georgiana replied stoutly. "It's only some mischief-makers trying to frighten us."

"It's more than that," Maude declared. "Georgiana, have you really thought about what you're doing here? What it may cost in the end?"

Georgiana replied that yes, she had given it much thought. But the odds were with them. Hadn't the school been Electra's idea? Didn't it have the backing of the Talcotts and other right-thinking folks? Didn't Mr. Garrison support it? Were any laws being broken?

Maude was not reassured. "That's all well and good, I suppose, but if my guess is right, stones thrown through the window or at the Lamenters' wagon are just the opening salvo of a long battle. The gauntlet's been hurled. If they're of a mind, those benighted slaveryites'll tar and feather you before they're done."

"Maudie, cut your buzz," cautioned Aunt Hat. "You're scarin' the poor thing to death."

"No she's not!" Georgiana retorted forcefully. "She's just whetting my appetite. I'm hungry for a scrap."

Maude's laugh rang out. "If that's the case, then you can count on Merrill and me. Put me to book and slate, too."

Georgiana was elated. With the likes of Maude Ashley frequenting the classroom, what reckless objectors would dare to interfere. Still, for every day that Georgiana stood in front of her pupils with her pointer and maps, for every stack of corrected papers, for every spelling list and exercise in deportment, for every hour of grinding work and its small but steadily burgeoning rewards, she became more and more aware of the growing rancor among a swelling number of the local populace. An uncommon vein of bigotry was being mined by the antiabolitionists, and it required no Merlin, nor even a Cinnamon Comorra, to forecast that trouble lay ahead.

Most daunting to Georgiana was the realization that even the church had aligned itself against her school, that same Protestant church she'd been baptized in, at whose services she had sung, *her* church. Yet it was so. Over the course of the past month Pastor Weeks had addressed a series of highly critical remarks to his congregation regarding the foolishness of a radical-minded young woman who had taken it into her head to seek to raise certain lowborn people above their heaven-assigned station. So virulent were the pastor's feelings in this matter that he had also allowed himself to be elected chairman of a newly formed organization designed to combat the spread of such iniquities, the so-called Committee of Fair-Mindedness, whose roster of passionate adherents rapidly ballooned; nor was it long before Georgiana heard from the group face to face.

One afternoon in February, when her pupils had gone home and she was waiting for Maude Ashley to drop off some useful mineral specimens gathering dust in her attic, she heard the street door open, followed by the sound of footsteps coming up the stairs. She rose politely as in the doorway there appeared a "delegation," which seemed to be a useful term for the sextet of men and women that now invaded the schoolroom and arrayed themselves before her desk. They were Pastor Guston Weeks and his diminutive wife, Patience; Deacon Wandsworth and his larger-than-he wife, Lily;

and the Ritchies, the dread Flora and her husband, George—that same pompous Master George who had been instrumental in having Georgiana dismissed from her position at Center School for having tried to teach Ambo Buck there so many years ago.

"Good afternoon, everyone," Georgiana said cheerfully. "Welcome to our school. Have you come to contribute to our cause?"

Flora Ritchie stepped forward. "Certainly not!" she responded. "I confess, Georgie Ross, I am deeply surprised at you, yes, surprised and shocked. Are you deliberately trying to astonish the world and shame yourself into the bargain?"

Georgiana maintained her poise. "How do I surprise you?" she asked equably.

The parrot-faced Flora Ritchie had been an outspoken foe of the Free School, to the point that as a leading light of the newly organized committee, she had already talked to the newspaper stating her objections.

His suety cheeks trembling, Master George spoke up. "Mrs. Ritchie is right," he proclaimed. "It's scarcely to be believed, that you are teaching these darkies a lot more than their ABC's and the other things they *ought* to be learning."

"What things are those?"

"I mean solid, practical things, such as how to clean a gentleman's house and cook proper meals, so they can find suitable employment as domestics."

"But it isn't at all our intention to turn out girls to be common domestics or hired girls," Georgiana replied in a reasonable tone. "We're hoping for far more rewarding ends."

Flora was ready with a sharp retort. "Georgie Ross, you're a fool if you think you can do that," she countered. "People around here are getting riled. This is why we have formed this committee, to make our wishes known. We don't want you teaching these ne'er-do-wells the things you're teaching them and as a delegation we are here to inform you that we do not intend that you go on with this . . . this farce."

"I assure you, it is no farce," replied Georgiana, carefully controlling her words. "We are quite serious here, I promise it."

"Have you lost your wits completely, Georgie Ross? If you go on acting this way people will wonder why you're not in the madhouse your father ought to have been locked up in."

When the schoolmistress refused to dignify these remarks with a response, Deacon Willie pointed an accusing finger at her and took up the attack. "Georgie Ross, as surely as you hope one day to meet the Maker of us all, so surely you are committing a sin in the eyes of that same Deity."

"What sin is that, Deacon?"

"You are encouraging these pupils of yours to think they can rise above their ordained station. You are deliberately subverting the ways and customs of this place and stirring up a pot of trouble without thought or governance."

"Those are lofty words, Deacon. But I beg you, consider: if we wish to help a few young women whose lot in life is far worse than ours, isn't that the spirit of the church where you are a vested deacon?"

"Have a care, young woman," put in Pastor Weeks sternly. "Are you saying that you believe God *intends* that you should spend your time attempting to educate young women of color who ought better to be taught to know their place in the world and not hope for vain rewards?"

"Not at all," Georgiana replied, still taking a reasonable tack. "We merely believe that nobody should be obliged to go without learning, particularly young ladies of color who have almost no other chance of betterment. Surely intelligent people such as yourselves must agree."

"We most assuredly do not!" asserted the deacon angrily. "Not only have you enrolled the Talcotts' hired girl, that shameless darky Apple Talcott all but stole from her rightful owners"—suffering from a winter cold, he touched his reddened nose gingerly—"but you have boldly taken on a ragged assortment of girls from that slag heap at Lament. *And* you and your friends, that high-and-mighty Talcott tribe and that ink-stained rabble-rouser Garrison, have actually invited out-of-town darkies to move into our village and be made part of this ridiculous enterprise you've concocted. Now, Georgie Ross, hear me," he went on, his voice twanging through pinched nasal passages. "There can be no doubt that that unfortunate episode at church last month was a direct consequence of your own radical activities. I wish to know, Are we to expect further examples of such insolence?"

Before Georgiana could reply, Master Ritchie took up the refrain. "Yes, indeed. How can we expect otherwise when these days we hear of little but what *they* need, these mongrel ne'er-do-wells you have collected like so much garbage and dragged into the very heart of our village? Next their lazy, thieving, drunken brothers will be boldly crowding decent people off our sidewalks, causing all sorts of mischief, when we have so carefully sought to keep them confined outside the town's boundaries."

"It's true," seconded the deacon. "Why, only the other day I saw one of those stinkwater Lamenters so drunk he couldn't stand up, and it wasn't yet noon."

"Did you?" Georgiana inquired calmly. "But how did he acquire the liquor when there are laws governing the sale of alcoholic beverages to Indians? Is it not a fact that you yourself, Deacon, are the proprietor of a grogshop that dispenses intoxicating drink—"

"Enough!" declared Willy, incensed. "My spirits shop is a perfectly legal enterprise in this community and I see nothing to prohibit its continuance nor any reason to alter its status. I shall thank you kindly to mind your own affairs, Georgie Ross, and not to meddle in mine!"

He shook his fist at her, while another voice was heard desperately trying to get a word in. "Georgie—Georgie dear—" It was Mrs. Weeks in her Saturday bonnet with the strings blowing about her pink face, speaking in breathless bursts in her prim, babyish voice. "I can hardly believe—your dear mother—such a lovely person—so clever with her needle—what *would* she think if she were alive today, to see you—such a dear sweet child you were—I shudder to think what the poor soul must be thinking of—lying there in yonder graveyard, that her little girl has grown up to be a political agitator—trying to pull down about our ears the temple of dignity we have worked so hard to erect here in our little Utopia. Truthfully, Georgiana—I think Flora may be right: I sometimes wonder if your experiences *haven't* unhinged your mind."

"My mind is neatly hinged—and oiled—thank you, Mrs. Weeks," Georgiana returned without rancor. "I thank you, moreover, for voicing your concern about my mother's feelings, but it is needless. And I really don't see what trying to outfit some disadvantaged young women for a hard life has to do with political agitation or creating unrest in the village." She turned to George Ritchie and her eyes flashed. "I truly hope there isn't going to be any more trouble—and of course there won't be if we are left to go about our business unmolested."

Master Ritchie fixed her with his most forbidding look. "Georgiana Ross, I have only these words for you. Heed them: Such a foolhardy and disgraceful enterprise as this must not be allowed to go forward, and we are dedicated, we members of the Fair-Mindedness Committee, to seeing that it does not, no matter what the Talcotts and their softhearted and soft-brained adherents may intend to the contrary. We have sundry weapons in our hands, so you will do well to mark what I say."

"I do, sir, I mark you well," Georgiana returned calmly. "But if you have come here to persuade me to close the doors to my school, I can tell you that you're wasting your time, for I have no intention of doing anything of the sort. I think you all should pass along now. I hope you have a pleasant evening."

"If you are the wise young woman I believe you to be," Pastor Weeks cautioned, "you will think on what has been said here. As a Christian and as a human being I tell you you are wrong. You and all those who back this insidious folly of yours. In the meantime, the doors of our church are ever open to you, should you feel the need of spiritual comfort." He gazed at Georgiana with his most pious expression, then, taking his wife by the elbow, prepared to escort her down. As he made for the staircase Willie-the-rat couldn't resist a Parthian shot.

"Heed us well, Georgie Ross!" he cried in his shrill voice. "You have set your foot upon a stony path and you cannot help but stumble. Take our words for what they are worth: send those damnable half-breeds and darkies back where they came from and restore Warren Burdin's warehouse attic to the purpose for which it was originally constructed."

"And if I do not?"

"If you do not, we promise you'll live to regret the day you ever thought to open this insidious hotbed of unrest and revolution. Don't forget, we know you, young woman! We know all about *you,* descended as you are from a madman and a murderer who is this very moment surely burning in the fires of hell—"

"Stop it!" The blood rushed to Georgiana's cheeks. "I won't hear it— stop—whatever else you have to say, I won't hear it!"

"You will hear it, and from other lips than ours before you're done if you go on with the course you've set. In case you may have forgotten, *we* have the law on our side, ask anybody. We'll see you incarcerated before we're done! You and Hattie Duckworth—*and* Maude Ashley, if it comes to that!"

"Just a minute before you talk of jailing anyone, Willie Wandsworth!" This was the lady herself, Maude, who had appeared in the doorway with Ambo Buck, each carrying a box heaped with mineral chunks.

"There you are, Maude Ashley!" trumpeted Flora. The two women were ancient rivals in the social order of the village. "I'm surprised at you, encouraging this poor misguided creature to stir up such mischief."

"Mischief, is it? To school some innocent youngsters? I'd watch my tongue, if I were you, Flora dear," Maude returned in sugary tones. "People in glass houses, you know . . ."

Affronted, Flora drew herself up and her voice cracked as she spoke. "Just what is that supposed to mean, Maude Ashley, if one may ask?"

"One may, indeed," said Maude. "It means that if anyone is going to make remarks about the misfortunes of another"—here she looked hard at the deacon—"he might do well to remember that his own grandfather once hanged himself just there at the tavern stable."

"How spiteful of you to bring that up! Anyone who would do that should be horsewhipped!"

Maude showed her teeth. "If the cap fits, dear . . . As for horsewhipping, I'll be glad to oblige you at any time. It might help you to adjust your sights. Now, I suggest you just march along, all of you. We've work to do. Willie Wandsworth, do you hear me? March!" Crossing her arms over her breast, Maude presented a singularly formidable aspect.

"This is outrageous!" cried the deacon, his frantic eyes swerving from face to face. "We represent a duly constituted organization, we have a say in things around here. People listen to us—*decent* people do. And I warn you,

Maude Ashley, you won't be so high and mighty when we're done with you, either."

"Really, Willie? That sounds suspiciously like a threat."

"Take my meaning any which way you like."

Having delivered himself of these words, he shoved aside a chair and marched down the stairs, quickly followed by his companions.

"That's all right, Georgiana," Maude said when they had gone, "don't let that flock of gabbling geese unsettle you. Now tell me what they said before I got here, and don't leave out a word!" Setting down her carton of specimens she drew up a chair. "Ambo, you come sit too, don't look so ferocious, those animals have teeth but they won't bite; not yet they won't."

DURING the cold winter days that followed, Georgiana gave considerable thought to this unpromising visit and all it might mean for the school. She had expected opposition, to be sure, and was prepared to meet it head on, but now, for the first time, she began seriously to consider just what might happen if her school did persist as planned, and if it mightn't be better to close things up now before some real trouble came her way. But no, she told herself again, go on it shall; in the end she must prevail, the right would win. And if there were those who would try and thwart her plans—well, *her* allies had not yet begun to fight. But the fight—neighbor against neighbor, friend against friend, villager against villager? What would it all lead to?

She did not know. What she did shortly discover, however, was that she had a staunch supporter in the very heart of the enemy camp. A scant twenty-four hours after the schoolroom imbroglio, an unexpected visitor appeared at the seed store. Upon completion of grading some promising penmanship exercises, among them that of Miss Rose Mills, Georgiana glanced down at the street in time to see the Grimes coach approaching, with the tall-hatted Hogarth seated on the box. For a moment she feared that Zion Grimes had come himself to confront her; instead it was Miss Rachel who emerged from the conveyance, helped down by Helen, who was trying to keep her bonnet on in the stiff wind.

Hastily setting her work aside, Georgiana sped about the room, making a few random (and unnecessary) adjustments, then hurried to greet her visitors.

"Well, Georgie Ross," Rachel began, proceeding up the narrow, enclosed staircase, "I decided I'd poke my nose in and see what's to be seen." When she reached the top of the stairs she clutched the railing and pressed her hand to her side. Helen quickly helped her into a chair, where the old lady sat trying to control her erratic breathing.

"There, there, I'm quite all right," she said after a moment, "a stitch, no more."

"You ought not to have climbed all those stairs, Grammaw," Helen said. Georgiana agreed. "I could have come down."

"Nonsense! I climb as many every night of my life. And how else should I see your classroom, which is what I've come to do?" She peered about, taking in the further details of the attic room. "Well, it all looks fine to me, just as Helen described it. Though she tells me you have some wants—do you? Maps—maps would be nice, though I see you've a model of the globe."

"Yes, indeed," Georgiana said. "A fine one. Appleton Talcott gave it to us. But maps will have to wait, I'm afraid, there are so many other things we need."

Rachel nodded. "Helen says you've had some disagreeable callers. Gave you some lip, did they?"

"They tried, but Maude Ashley gave it right back to them."

Rachel's eyes sparked brightly and she clapped her hands. "Good for Maude! If I were they I shouldn't go about incurring the wrath of Maude Ashley, not if I valued my hide."

"Grammaw's right," Helen said. "Maude's a good one to have on your side."

"And—you have *other* backing as well, do you not?" Rachel said pointedly. "*Influential* backing. A corner with Bob Talcott in it can't be a pinched one."

Georgiana nodded. "We're grateful for everyone's help," she said. "People have been very generous—many people."

"Hah! *Many,* to be sure!" She leaned forward in her chair and lowered her voice. "Though, Georgie, let me say betwixt you, me, and the bedpost, Burning Bush is a prickly patch these days. There are plots afoot, I warrant it. The clan connives, and not to your advantage." She turned for confirmation to Helen, who nodded.

"Georgiana, Grammaw's been listening to my father and Rod and my uncles talking."

"Is it a cabal, then? Do they really think they can shut us down?"

"They do indeed! They're definitely out to bring you grief if they can." Rachel shook a woeful head. "Georgiana, I hate it that it's my own kin, when I do so long to see you succeed. I can't fight the lot of them. But there *is* something I can do." She began tugging on the string attached to her little purse. Several jerks were required to coax the "sow's ear" from her reticule. She unfastened the clasp and a fistful of coins sprang into view. "There's some cash," she declared, handing them over, "so buy your maps or whatever you've a mind to have. Now, now, I don't want your thanks, just you use the money for those girls of yours. In the meanwhile I'll be on the lookout for any homegrown mischief, try to find out exactly what they're up to, those miserable plotters."

Helen smiled grimly. "I'd like to see the look on Father's face when he finds out you've given Georgiana that money for the school."

"It's nothing to sound trumpets over, it's just a little tuck is all."

Though Rachel viewed her contribution modestly, it was a goodly sum. Georgiana was touched and thanked her with all her heart. "Maybe it should be our secret, though," she added. "I wouldn't want to poke the hornet's nest."

"Nonsense. It'll let the old vultures know where they stand—and where *we* stand, too! All right, Helen, let's go down before I get chilblains, this place is no oven up here." She began looking about for her things. As she stood Helen and Georgiana each took an arm to assist her.

"I'm not a cripple, I can walk!" she snapped, shaking off their hands. "Well, do I get a kiss—from my granddaughter?" she asked tartly.

Georgiana kissed her warmly. "Thank you," she said, "thank you for coming, and thank you again for your generous gift. We'll put it to useful ends, never fear. It—it's very nice to visit with you," she added, holding out her hand.

Rachel pressed it in both of hers. "Ah, Georgie, if you don't think I've missed you. It has been too long, and I thought we'd become friends, you and I. I told Helen—a body of my advanced years needs friends, good young folks like yourself. Well, well, we must see to rectifying matters. Helen, we must meet more often at your house. It won't do for Georgie to come to the farm, you know——"

She fell to biting her lip and it was clear to both Georgiana and Helen that she was embarrassed by her position: wife to Abednego Grimes, step-mother to Zion, grandmother to Bushrod, all of whom were now trying to prevent the school from proceeding. But the fact that Helen was involved in the work, coming every day to help out with the girls, to let others know where she stood—squarely against her family—seemed to inspirit the old lady. It was as if it had become necessary for her also to take a firm stand in the quarrel, irrespective of her name and her position at Burning Bush Farm—to fling down a gauntlet of her own.

Georgiana was leading Rachel to the stairs when she heard a voice call out, and going to the window, she discovered Hermie Light down in the street waving an envelope.

"Hullo, Georgie—see what I got? A letter from Sinjin."

"For you?"

"No, for *you!*"

"Eh? How's that?" demanded Rachel, cupping her ear to the glass. "What's that peg-legged mushmouth saying? A letter from Dick, is it?" Her impatient rap on the pane instructed Hermie to come up as fast as his infirmity would allow, and in no time he was in the room, holding the letter before him. He'd picked it up downriver while at Saybrookport, he explained. A schooner bound for New Bedford had brought it along from Cape Verde, where Captain Goodnaught of the *Grace & Favour* had left it, his vessel having obtained an unexpected commission and being bound for Maracaibo, not home.

Georgiana accepted the missive gratefully. "I never got my birthday letter," she said. "Thank you for bringing it to me, Hermie. Wait, you don't have to go, I'm sure you'll want to know what it says, too."

"Letter's private," said Rachel. "He can hear later." She gave his bulky shoulder a push. "Stump along out of here, I say, you can find out later if it's any of your affair!"

She dispatched him imperiously; Hermie did not protest being ousted; rather he seemed relieved to be banned from the old woman's testy society. After he'd gone, Rachel sat down again, Helen beside her, while Georgiana went around to her own chair and used the blade of her scissors to slit open the envelope.

As she quickly perused the script she gave a little gasp of surprise.

"What's wrong, Georgie?" Helen asked.

"This letter is months old, it's my birthday letter!" She flushed with pleasure, then her expression sobered as her eye traveled the broadly slanting lines.

"Don't keep me in suspense, my heart won't stand it!" said Rachel. "Read it out, girl."

Georgiana blinked her eyes and began.

" 'My dear birthday girl, how are you there in Yankeeland? Having counted on my fingers I mark your natal day to be your thirty-second. Can such be possible?' "

"Why, he's mad, you were but thirty-one last October!" cried Rachel. "What can he be thinking of?"

"Go on, Georgie," Helen said. Georgiana continued. " 'Felicitous greetings from your old admirer, he who used to read Cicero and Tacitus to you in that haystack at Izz Quoile's farm. I trust these pages find you in good health as you go about laying out your catalogue of seeds for next spring.' "

"Hmp, shows how much *he* knows!" Rachel grumbled. "Seeds are a thing of the past for Georgie Ross," she said, speaking as if Sinjin were there in the room. "Her school's the thing now, Sonny."

"Please let Georgie read on, Grammaw," Helen said.

" 'Our adventures in this fifth corner of the world have been myriad and extravagant, and I sometimes marvel that I am still alive to write of them. Though I am at present at Macao, I do not linger long, for, let me tell you, my mouse, there are Big Events in the offing, yes. Because of the many niceties involved, concerning as they do a raft of other principals—one party in particular, details of whom I shall shortly progress to—' "

"Oh, hear the man, why doesn't he get to the point!" exclaimed Rachel.

" 'In the meantime,' " Georgiana read, " 'let me tell you I am soon to embark on a voyage of unimaginable prospects and, let me be immodest and say brilliance, which if successful will surely bring me the fame I have so long hankered after, and recoup my personal fortune, which has been sadly depleted as a result of some recent difficulties, of which you may have heard.' "

"Yes indeed we have," said Rachel a bit grimly. "But if anyone can recoup, I warrant Sonny's the man to do it. Go on, Georgie."

" 'I have recently taken command of a new vessel, and now, thanks to a consortium of Macaoans, local figures of some note including my friends Satidjee and Arthur Fair, as well as Lord Bristol, one of the colony's big shareholders in the East India Company—' "

"Eh? Who's this Fair person?"

"Grammaw, it's that painter friend of Sinjin's, the one who does the miniatures."

"Well, what's a painter doing mixed up in this great scheme for? Let him stick to his easel and leave financial matters to those who understand them. Go on, Georgie, do," she commanded. Georgiana did so.

" '—with the major share held by that particular individual of whom I have made earlier mention, and of whom I now hesitate to write, fearing some of the local gossip may have reached you there, unflattering in the extreme, but isn't gossip always? I have no need to point out to one wise as you, my mouse, that things are seldom what they appear, and while I admit that where smoke is, there fire must also be, I promise you that the tales are thoroughly hairy ones and quite untrue.' "

"Now who is he talking about, do you suppose?" Rachel wondered.

Who, indeed? There was no answer, and she frowned at the possibilities that crossed her mind as Georgiana went on:

" 'We have gathered together a shipload—*such a cargo!* You may believe me when I say few cargoes are equal to this one; I cannot here report of what it consists, you shall know of this hereafter—it has been purchased and is now stowed for our immediate departure. A rare set of commodities, too, the rarest, I could say, which when put to proper use I am convinced will fill all our coffers many times over. About the ship herself, as it happens she is a Chinese junk (of a gorgeous and thoroughly terrifying shade of vermilion), and in herself of no large intrinsic value; what I *intend doing with her,* however, is of enormous value. Now, George, read carefully and harken to my words. This is important. What I *need, must have,* is for both vessel and cargo to be insured for their full value, and as you are there in Pequot, a stone's throw away from all those Hartford insurance companies, I entreat you to accept the important commission I hereby lay upon you, knowing that your enviable acumen for business and your innate prudence in such things will assist you in dealing with matters whose delicacy you will quickly detect. I have no doubt that I can rely on your discretion. You may wonder that I do not undertake to deal with such affairs myself here at Macao; truth is, what I intend to do must be done in secret, for there are those in this place, jealous greedy parties, who would gladly see me lose All.

" 'Now, let me proceed further. Even out here one hears interesting things about the Talcott, Lane Assurance Company—I have recently dined with Hiram Goodnaught aboard the *Grace & Favour* (he is to carry these pages to you) and he has spoken highly of the things those two fellows Priam Talcott and Asher Ingolls—friends of yours, I know—are doing in matters of bottomry, how they guarantee to insure the riskiest ventures, the ones no one else will touch—for a suitably high premium, of course. And as you and Priam Talcott were once so thick—I trust you remain so—is it possible that you might privately consult with him on my behalf? I would have been happy to write him myself, and indeed shall certainly do so in future, but for the moment, and because our personal relationship has suffered such a strain, I deem such overtures better and more politic as originating with you. As to our former differences, for my own part I bear him no rancor and trust that on his side he is as much a man to say he too holds no grudge over old animosities far better forgotten.' "

Lifting her eyes from the page, Georgiana looked over at Helen, who shrugged; Rachel coughed. Georgiana began again:

" 'I can hear Talcott's response—"I cannot in all conscience insure a cargo worth tens of thousands without knowing what it is!" But yes, he can, he can indeed, dear George. Let him write me a policy to cover any and all purchased items aboard my vessel, as well as the ship itself, in the amount of a quarter of a million dollars. Since I am temporarily short of funds, the sum required to meet the premium for these assurances must of necessity be borne by my grandmother—' "

Rachel thumped the desktop. "Aha, now there it is!" she crowed. "There's the crux. I knew it. Wants my money, the scoundrel. Hurry on, Georgie, let me hear the rest."

" 'I would of course repay her with interest out of profits, once the enterprise is successfully concluded according to plan. (I repeat, this is a risky affair and must be kept quiet, we don't want others to get wind of it, deceitful parties who might attempt a similar scheme and steal my thunder.) But—a large but here—since it's such a chancy deal all round, if you should not succeed in the commission I have set you, in the event I should fail in this enterprise—I mean should I be relegated to Davy Jones's locker, and if by some chance Grammaw herself has predeceased me—' "

Rachel started in her chair. "What's that? 'Predeceased' him? But I haven't died; what can the man mean? Has he lost his mind?"

Blushing furiously, Georgiana stammered out an excuse. "I think—

maybe—I guess he must mean if the letter should have been delayed or gone astray—"

"Yes," said Helen, corroborating Georgiana's thought. But such weak excuses did no good. Rachel was beside herself with indignation. "It would have to have been delayed a goodly time, I promise you," she said tartly, "since I don't plan on dying soon. Well, go on, then, Georgiana."

Georgiana did as she was bid. " '—if Grammaw herself has predeceased me and has remembered me in her last will and testament as she has so often indicated she would, in the name of old affections between us I beg you to be good enough to speak to Mr. Winthrop Ellsworth, Esq., attorney of Pearl Street at Hartford, and instruct him to collect at the earliest opportunity said monies from my deceased grandmother's estate, be the sum however large or small, and write a bank draft to the Portuguese Republican Banco de Macao, said draft to be deposited to the account of an individual to whom I am vastly obliged for reasons far too numerous to be set down in detail here.' "

"Eh? What's he talking about now? Another mysterious man?"

Georgiana blushed. "It's not a man. Listen: 'Though she does not employ it for commercial ends, the lady in question is known by this title: *Denyse, Sua Alteza a Condessa da Silva e Duarte Doyogas Estriguerras, resident of the city of Macao, formerly of São Paolo and Rio de Janeiro, legal widow of Sua Alteza o Conde da ditto.*

" 'Should any doubts arise as to this individual's legitimacy, Ellsworth may wish to consult the Almanac de Gotha in which the da Silva family rates one full page. Be so advised.' "

Again Rachel interrupted with a flash of indignation.

"Well, of all the nerve!" she gasped. "Imagine! Taking money from a creature of that sort. He shall hear from me, I vow it. Not a penny of mine shall he ever have! This glorious adventure is twaddle, nothing but twaddle. He's knee-deep in romance again! But go on, go on, I want to hear every last word."

" 'I trust this is not too much of a task for you, my dear mouse. Should you be able to conclude the matter happily, I am more in your gentle debt than ever. Believe me grateful. You are well, I know, for my mind will permit of no other estate where you are concerned. I have your letters, for which much thanks. Ever thine . . . Sinjin.' "

Georgiana looked up. "That is all. There isn't any more," she said, and handed the pages to Helen to peruse.

"*All!* I should think that was enough!" Rachel retorted. "No post scriptum, no addendum? No word for his grammaw, his loving sister? *Faugh!* I'll see him at the bottom of the sea yet!" She snatched the pages from Helen's hands and put them under her own hawk's eye for more intimate scrutiny.

"The idea! 'Deceased' indeed!" she muttered. "Won't I just give that rascal a good piece of my mind when I get my hands on him! Oh yes, that's the scarlet creature—lending him money to keep him in her snare, the hussy. Circe didn't die with Ulysses, sad to relate. Well, I don't care, I hope he does go beneath the waves, *she'll* never put her fingers on my money, not a penny shall the wretched woman see!"

Rachel's words alarmed Helen. "Oh, Grammaw, don't hope he drowns," she said.

"Yes, please, Helen's right," Georgiana put in. "Pray God he comes home safely, do."

"You've both good Christian souls in your bodies. The monster doesn't deserve such charity. The world's far too good a place for the likes of him. He belongs in the fiery pit, shoveling coals with a hot pitchfork!" She pulled on her furred mittens. "I promise you one thing, it's as well that he's on the other side of the globe, for I'll give him a good shaking if he comes yawing around here trying to get his hooks into my accounts. Write him, both of you, tell him his grammaw died and left every cent she has to an orphan named Little Johnny Jump-up! Tell him there's no reason to show that guilty face of his around here. Tell him—oh, bother the man, don't tell him a thing! Let him rot in heathen China for all of me!"

Refusing all offers of help, she got up and made her way down into the street where her coachman attended her. Helen grabbed her cloak and followed after, with Georgiana behind her.

"I meant every word I said!" the old lady declared as she clambered into the coach. When Hogarth had seen her safely tucked under the throw, he drove away. Georgiana and Helen turned to each other helplessly.

"I'm so sorry she learned of this," Georgiana began.

"I think it's better she knows," Helen said. "Maybe—oh, what's the use, he's bound to hurt her feelings no matter what he does."

They returned to the schoolroom where they talked matters over. The upshot of their discussion was that Georgiana agreed to go and speak to Priam concerning Sinjin's mysterious enterprise, while Helen would attempt to smooth Rachel's ruffled feathers on Sinjin's behalf. On the whole, they thought, Georgiana would have the easier task.

14

Outside Looking In

AND WHAT OF THE Talcotts' new hired girl and the Free School's model pupil? How was she faring during these long winter months since her arrival in Pequot Landing? Rose, whose appearance in the village had started all the fireworks, however inadvertently. Truth to tell, the ex-slave was a knotty proposition if ever there was one, giving rise to speculation on Mab's part as to how such a misfortune had befallen her and inducing Appleton to ask himself whatever had possessed him to give heed to little Miss Posie's proposition. For one thing, Rose's fellow servants, led by Halley, were forever in a stew; either Rose would be banished from the kitchen for some infraction, or Burdy would be seen fleeing the place in tears after one of Rose's cutting remarks. All the while, the latecomer, armed with her turkey duster, emblem of her new estate, dusted her way upstairs and down on Saturdays, which was Burdy's day off, ate well and heartily, and in general passed the time in far greater comfort than she had ever known. Despite the fact that when winter fell upon her her feet never seemed to get warm, the weeks nonetheless sped quickly by.

From the outset, however, Rose was aware of an undercurrent of distress, a feeling of anxiety at Kingdom Come; it stole into the rooms, under the doors, as it were, around the edges. Before very many weeks had passed, she came up with the reason: like everyone else in the household, except the master, she had learned that her mistress was ill unto death. No one said so in just that many words, but Rose didn't need to be told; she had eyes, she was sharp, and she saw and heard things.

It was hard to believe that the master was ignorant of the truth of the situation; but there it was. This was the mistress's wish and will, and must be obeyed. So Rose answered the side door for the doctor to slip in and out of at odd times when Appleton was busy elsewhere or altogether absent, giving abolition speeches in New Haven or Springfield, and medicine bottles were kept out of sight; people tiptoed around, thinking things, maybe, but never a word anywhere, anytime. The Queen would have it so. You had to admire a woman like that. She was rich and she was white, but she had courage, a thing Rose could appreciate. It couldn't be easy, trying to carry off an act like that right under her husband's nose. But women had been succeeding in fooling their menfolk for ages, and Rose commonly operated on the theory that what a man didn't know would never hurt him.

Still, she felt bad. Death had never been a stranger to her; she was used to having folks up and die all around her—fever carried them off in cartloads, or they got bit by a cottonmouth or drowned or burnt up in a fire; God had all kinds of ways for people to die—but with the Queen it was different. And, Rose wondered, what would happen when Mab did die? With the mistress in the graveyard, mean Agrippina would be in charge, and if Rose wasn't careful she was liable to find herself tossed out in the snow.

She had other causes for complaint—primarily her education. She hated school. Every day of the week she had to drag her feet the short distance from Kingdom Come to the seed store, climb the stairs to the attic store-room, and take her place among that pack of village ninnies and half-breeds off the Mountain at the desk assigned to her. Lessons? *Shit.* Though it came easily to her, she was frankly bored, bored to the rafters with the whole notion of book learning.

As for the schoolteacher, Rose had severe misgivings, primarily because she knew that Georgiana Ross had also once been the Talcotts' hired girl—that she had managed to rise above her previous station. Georgiana might be prim and starchy, but she was kind and considerate of others, and almost against her will Rose admired her. She was deep, Georgie Ross was, she had spirit. When Rose really thought about it—aside from the prissy, spinsterish mannerisms and Quakerish willingness to turn the other cheek— she wished in some ways she were more like her. But there was something about her Rose couldn't fathom, something to do with the Talcotts and a certain Captain Grimes she kept hearing talk of. Take the day that Georgiana had been in the study with Priam Talcott—this was last Saturday. They'd been together behind the closed door, and Rose, tickling her feather duster around the chair rail had put her ear to the keyhole. Heard things, too, mostly 'bout this Captain Grimes, out there in China, he had this ship, a "junk"—she didn't know what was meant by "junk." The captain wanted his junk insured—whatever that meant—and Miss Ross was asking Priam to do it. Priam had been real put out—he had a fierce temper sometimes.

"Are you saying to me that you want me to do this for the ravisher of my own sister," Rose heard him demand, "the blackhearted ravisher who tried to run off with her when she was still a child?"

Georgiana, she said to keep his voice down before the Queen hears him, and she said that that bad stuff was way back there in the past and couldn't they just forget it, but no, he said, he'd never forget, not as long as he lived, he'd remember always. And how Rora had took poison and near died of it and how it took the Injun witch to cure her. (Sure, thought Rose, Ah could've done that, Ah knows what to do 'bout them things.)

Then Priam, he was ranting on again; besides, he said, the junk scheme was harebrained and what was this mysterious cargo, anyway? Probably coolie slaves bound for the tin mines in Peru, was what Priam said. Geor-giana was all aghast. "He'd never do such a thing," she said to him, and he said right back, "Why not, when his own grandfather was a slaver in the

Caribbean," which got Georgiana's goat and she said was he in business like he said or wasn't he. He said he'd have to consult his partner 'bout the rates and such and Georgiana said okay, that would be fine, but not to wait too long and then they started talking about the Queen—Priam, he said he knew all about the sickness that was killing his mother and there wasn't anything anyone could do for her except try to keep it from his father and then the door opened and Rose had to move fast to hide behind it and not get caught eavesdropping. When Rose looked over her shoulder, there was Miss Pina at the end of the passage, staring straight at her. Had she seen? Rose couldn't tell, but she hurried her duster along, her feet too. Later she watched Priam drive away, then Georgiana came and said she wanted a word. They sat in the kitchen, Halley scowling in the corner by the stove, and talked about schoolwork. School, always school, and where was it going to get her, anyway?

There were rewards. In such a house, so filled with literary pursuits, crammed with books and all kinds of reading matter, Rose felt herself exposed to forces she had known nothing of, and she had a creeping notion that it would be good to improve her reading skills. Pina had numerous volumes. They bore different titles but were all the same in content, filled with wimpled demozels, castle battlements, dark tarns, crofters' cottages, flagged courtyards ringing to iron-shod hooves striking sparks, foresworn lovers, ruined chapels moonlight drenched, heroes in doublet and scarlet hose, cruel princesses, hunchbacks clad in motley, haughty prioresses, wicked viziers with turbans and black forked beards to be stroked—none of which Rose had ever heard of but which fascinated her all the same. It was not infrequently that some family member would stray across the hired girl tucked away in some corner with a book in her hands, pouring over its pages, trying to extract with her limited learning what secrets the printed lines hid.

So THE winter passed, if slowly, and as called for by the almanacs, March came on in leonine state and went out lambishly. Due to the March thaw the river had seen huge blocks of ice come sliding downstream from Enfield Falls on their way into the Sound, and as occasionally happened, this year the shad began to run early. The ferryman at Talcotts Ferry made up for the freezing winter by selling pounds of shad roe, and Hattie Duckworth, who doted on that native delicacy fried up with bacon and a bit of onion, feasted herself and all comers. Mab Talcott's garden began to pop into bloom before the end of the month, with crocuses around the foot of the twin beech trees, the broad swaths of white narcissus and yellow jonquils, and the pussywillows and bright clumps of spicebush.

On a particularly fine Saturday morning in April, freed of school business, Rose was busy with neglected house chores, under Halley's watchful eye. Through the open window the bright *snip-snip* of Sylvester's gardening shears could be heard as he trimmed the shrubbery, and from down the street came the familiar creak of the ice wagon and the yapping of dogs. As she went about her duties, Rose wondered what was wrong with her, so fluttery was her heart, so passionately did she yearn to be outdoors where the air was honeyed and folks could see her switching her skirts and showing the ruffle on the petticoat Mrs. Warburton had bestowed on her.

In the front hall the case clock announced the hour of ten. The sound startled Rose, who had been rearranging the dust on its finials, and when she had given them the quick going over she felt they were due, she paused before the gilt mirror where she observed her reflection in the shiny glass— her uniform of black alpaca, the freshly starched and ironed apron that crackled when she walked, the ruffled mob cap setting off her pale skin— giving her chin a little jerk in order to set her earbobs swaying, the cheap bobs she had bought off the Jew peddler with her first spending money. What, she wondered, would Knoxie say if she could only see Rose and the way she'd come up in the world?

She passed the tips of her duster over the newel post. Lilting chords, plucked from Agrippina's harp strings, sounded through the open door of the best parlor. Goodness, but Miss Pina surely liked to practice on that harp! Forgoing her labors, Rose sat down on the bottom step to listen. While Miss Pina might make pretty melodies, her words were something else entirely. Pina Talcott had the tongue of a snake; its fangs, too. Of all the family she seemed most to delight in plaguing Rose, in ordering her about and criticizing her. "Rose do this, Rose do that"—and worse—"Rose don't do this and *don't* do that!" But Pina wasn't nothin' but a dried-up old maid, with a face like a prune, sour and sharp, and a voice to match.

Rose got up again and waggled the turkey feathers negligently about various surfaces as she idly made her way into the dining room. This was one of her favorite rooms in the house; she was fascinated with its extravagant wallpaper, a brightly hued scene of funny-looking boats and misty mountains and feathery trees, with humpbacked bridges and people in silken robes wandering about. One lady with long needles stuck into her hair wafted a pretty bamboo fan; she looked proud and sad all at once; Rose knew just how she felt.

Turning to look through the opposite doorway, she gazed across the interval at the portrait of Aurora Talcott—Lady Sheffle, if you please—that graced the fireplace mantel, the smiling features in that lovely face, the sweet lips and violet eyes that regarded the world with such a disarming expression, the very image of the fine lady Rose wished herself to be. She could imagine such a dazzling creature going out to gala affairs dripping with diamonds and feathers in her hair, a great lady in the great world.

As she continued to gaze at the portrait, she began to hum a ditty, whose sound was sure to irritate the musician in the next room.

Sure enough. "Stop that screeching this instant!" Agrippina cried, having plucked a sheaf of discordant notes from her strings. She leaped up from her instrument and came rushing into the hall to confront her tormentor. "Exactly what do you think you're doing?" she demanded.

"Dustin'," came the laconic reply.

"Need you sing while I am practicing?"

"Wasn't singin', jes hummin'. Keep Rose from gettin' homesick."

Agrippina gave a good sniff. "You'll be a lot more than homesick if I catch you making noises like that around here again, do you understand me?"

"Yes'm." Rose took a step, then turned back to face Agrippina. "Ah was lookin' at the pitcher of Lady Sheffle hangin' there an' Ah was wond'rin'—" She paused.

"Well?"

"Ah was askin' mahse'f, 'Rose, where was Miss Pina the day the Lord done give out all the good looks?' "

Agrippina paled and her eyes widened. "What a nasty thing to say!"

"Ah didn't *say,* missus, Ah was jes askin' myself, that's all."

"You'll soon be asking why you got fetched a good slap if you don't get on about your work. And don't you dare to smirk at me, you're not so favored around here that you can't get dismissed the same way you were hired."

Agrippina spun away, skirts flying, and presently more chords floated from the parlor as she resumed her attempts at coaxing a melody from her strings. Halfheartedly continuing her dusting, Rose wondered if she'd gone too far. Maybe. Still, tormenting Miss Pina was certainly one of the un-looked-for joys of her new existence.

Moments later the back door slammed, and Rose was gone, her apron carelessly flung across the seat of a chair. From her kitchen window Halley could see down the drive to where the girl lingered by the dripping ice cart, gabbing with the iceman. The Talcotts did not take ice because they had their own year-round reservoir warehoused at the Cove, but when that local purveyor serviced the neighboring houses Rose could always find some excuse for a tête-à-tête with him. Today it was the iceman, tomorrow it would be the man who supplied the cordwood and replenished last winter's coal supply, after that Meyer Mandelbaum, the peddler who every month or so came pushing his cart through town, hawking his secondhand wares.

"You, Rosa," Halley called through the window as Rose switched her hips up the walk, "how many times Ah gots ter tell you not to hang roun' gabbin' with no iceman, nobody. You talk a horse's hind leg off."

Rose tilted her nose. "How many time Ah gots to tell you mah name

Rose, ain't *Rosa.* An' Ah guess Ah can talk to the iceman if Ah wants to."

"You feels like it too many times; next time Ah's gwine tell Miz Talca."

"You ain't gonna tell Miz Talca nuthin'," Rose said, storming into the kitchen. "You's gon' t'keep yo' mouth shet tight."

"Hush yo' noise, gal, Ah done palaverin' with you." Halley's fierce, monkeylike scowl failed to intimidate the girl.

"If that's a promise, ol' lady, Rose accepts." She gave Halley her haughtiest look. "An' lemme tell you somethin' if nobody done tole you befo', you is *one mean ol' cannibal.* You got a sharp bite to them yeller monkey-teeth of yours. But that's all right, you don't scare Rose none." Snapping her fingers under Halley's nose, she went out again and slammed the door, privately vowing to put a curse on the old crone so her rheumatism would worsen.

There were two things Rose could be perfectly certain of: one, that Mab Talcott must have her nap every afternoon, at the same hour, and, two, that Hallelujah was likewise indulged. Then, as though part of a conjurer's trick, as often as not, when Rose was supposed to be at her housework, her apron would lie crumpled on a chair, her duster would be tossed into a corner, and she would absent herself from her duties. In no time she would pop up at the Center, where she would cast a covetous eye over the latest of Liza Eales's dress findings, or linger about at the fringes of both taverns to catch the latest river news, or stop to chat with the wharf rats at the steamboat landing.

Sometimes she would pause outside the Quoiles' bakery—the Heavenly Bakery, as the sign with the gilded angel on it said—where she would eye the array of delectable treats filling the window.

"Mawnin', Miz Coil," Rose would begin as she entered the little shop. "They's mighty temptin' lookin' cakes you got today."

"Thank you, Rose," Erna Quoile would reply, her round arms floury to the elbows.

"Ah ain't been give mah wages this week, but . . ." Rose would murmur hopefully, standing before Izz and switching her skirt, "maybe you kin lemme have a sweet bun on account."

"On account of what?"

"On account of Ah likes 'em."

Izz would laugh good-naturedly. "Say, that's a good one, Rose."

"But you haven't paid for the last two buns," Erna would remind her.

Nevertheless, neither Izzard nor Erna could say no to Rose's request for a free treat. As to past accounts one day being rendered, they both knew such a thing would never happen, not with Mabel Talcott's new hired girl. And so Rose would go off, taking nibbles out of her bun and daintily licking the sugar from the corners of her mouth.

Watching her go, people would shake their heads in wonder at her nonchalance and brazenness. With her narrow-waisted figure, her disdainful expression, the smoldering gaze in her velvet eyes, Rose seldom went unnoticed around Pequot, but when the male patrons of the Headless Anne, devouring her with their oglings, ventured to make insinuating proposals, she only hooted and switched away to meet the packet at the steamboat landing, where she could display her person to strangers in the best light, which is to say not only free as a bird, but white as the driven snow.

This was Saturdays. But any day, once spring had come, when soirées or assemblies were being given, when the village belles, escorted by their eager and attentive beaux, danced the evening away at the Academy Hall, Rose might slip away from Kingdom Come to peer out of the purple shadows as pretty ivory-skinned girls in pale-colored dresses with bell-like skirts and giant puffed sleeves, wearing combs and flowers in their hair, their faces bright and smiling, went whirling by the open doorway in the arms of handsome young gallants. She would hear the infectious strumming of banjos and guitars, and the lively sawing of fiddles, and she'd burn to pick up her skirts and fly to the music, it excited her so, to dash pell-mell and fling herself straight into its beat and feel her feet skipping and sliding too. This was how she had always imagined life to be, and in Pequot, so it was; where girls and boys met and kissed and fell in love in the deepening dusk, where fantasy and flesh met and joined together. But not for Rose Mills of Laceyville, South Carolina; she could only stand outside looking in, dreaming dreams that in her heart of hearts she knew would never come true, for, like those nasty winking coachmen who nudged one another as they looked over her slender form, she too was black.

One thing Rose counted on, however: Pequot Landing was only a stopping-off place. She was merely paying the town a visit. As soon as she had enough money saved she would pack up and move on, to some place where she could freely pass for white, and the devil with anyone who tried to stop her. That precious legal document that she kept in her bureau drawer declared her to be free, but week after week it was borne home to her what those people who went to the Academy dances and lived behind their prim white picket fences thought of her, the Talcotts' hired girl who had been the cause of so much fuss, the prize monkey in Georgiana Ross's menagerie of darky girls.

No, although she was smart enough to realize the extent of her good fortune and presented herself as the soul of meekness to the Talcotts, Agrippina excepted, demurely bobbing her curtsies, smiling winsomely, and hastening her step, Rose didn't plan on running around the rest of her life wafting a feather duster for the white folks. She planned on being a mistress herself one day, and having her own hired girl to do the dusting. She wanted a picket fence and a grass lawn of her own, she wanted a carriage and a pair of high-stepping horses and a coachman on the box. And she knew that no

matter how much she might learn in school, no matter how much "property" she might acquire and store away under the bed, beneath her pillow,
in the backs of her bureau drawers, in this town she would never be the lady
she wanted to be.

But if patience was not Rose's greatest virtue, biding her time had become
more or less habitual; if she could not have the whole bolt, an ell would
do—for now. And she did have one friend among the Talcotts: Posie, who
enjoyed listening to Rose's magpie chatter and was determined to see that
things went well for her; after all, hadn't it been her idea in the first place
to buy Rose from the slave catchers and give her her freedom? Hadn't she
talked her mother into keeping her? Wasn't she Rose's staunchest defender,
taking her part as often and as affirmatively as she could? Didn't she help
her with her lessons, encourage her reading, show her how to improve her
grammar, neaten her stitches? It was hard to imagine how Rose would have
gotten on without Posie's astute help and gently guiding hand.

Certainly Posie Talcott was an ideal model when it came to matters
ladylike and genteel. Rose was amused to watch her conduct in the classroom, where, in the late afternoon, she took charge of the younger set (Jessie
Cleves and Phoebe Haverstraw, Ella and Cleola Tando, several others).
Everyone said the same thing, to view Posie in the role of teacher was to
look upon a little aunt with a dozen nieces sitting on low chairs around her
knees, listening with their angels' faces to the salmagundi of invented stories
that spilled like running water from her lips, her young mind busily fashioning yards of fictional lace, enthralling her wide-eyed auditors and in the
evenings Rose as well, who profited by hearing the "Children's Corner"
stories.

In turn Rose confided to Posie her trove of "back-home" tales, tales of
fat Aunt Sagmo, who had the evil eye and could halt a thieving tinker dead
in his tracks; of the Widow Ulf, who'd been twice struck by lightning on
the exact same spot and lived to tell the tale, then choked to death on a
chicken wing; of sulphur-green salamanders the girls bought at fairs and
wore on little chains between their titties; of swamps where 'gators the size
of tree trunks lay in wait to pull you under and gobble you up at a bite.
She gave amazing accounts of people like Sue-Jennie Dee, who'd hid in the
flour barrel and got smothered; of Nonna Munroe, who'd committed suicide
by eating poisoned toadstools; of 'Lalie, who'd had her throat cut by her
big brown lover and afterward covered the scar with a vermilion ribbon;
and of Callo Picker, who'd borne seventeen children, all girls, every one
of whom had gone to her grave unwed because some nigger put a curse on
her. She described green snaking rivers abuzz with clouds of insects and
glaucous sumps where silver ghosts hung like the morning mists moaning
for recognition among the flags and reeds, and talked of hollow trees where
unwanted babies were left so the gypsies would come and take them.

"Ah is partial gypsy," she confided to Posie. "My great-grandmother, that'd be Knoxie's ma, she was a gypsy queen."

"Truly, Rose? Where?" Miss Posie, Rose was happy to see, would believe any story at all.

She was most fascinated by Rose's account of the old Geechee woman, a snuff-dipping witch who raised collards and made love charms and hate charms, who saved bulls' pizzles and snakes' fangs and lizard skins, who could scrape green poison off a log, enough to kill ten men.

"We have Cinnamon," Posie said, not without pride. Rose snorted contemptuously. Pshaw! When it came to spells and charms and moonlight witching, that stupid ol' redskin couldn't hold a candle to the Geechee woman.

But while Posie may have reveled in private over such gothic fancies, Georgiana took a less benign view of Rose's careless tongue when it was wagged in public, especially around the younger students. Helen, having overheard Rose tittering with a group one day, among them her own Chloe, confided to Georgiana that the girl was talking about sexual relations with them, graphically describing the men's "pushies" being inserted into the women's "placies."

The next day after school, Georgiana asked Rose to accompany her to Snug Harbor "for a little chat."

"Rose," she began as they walked, "I do wish you would try to be more careful what you say around the younger girls. You're far more experienced, you know. They're innocent, they don't comprehend the relation between the sexes."

Rose laughed. "That's a funny one. Ah guess you mean like gettin' the jitters."

"Jitters?"

"You know, when a gal meets a fellah they gets the jitters for each other, so they just wrap they arms around 'em an' they *jitters.* An' that's how babies are borned."

"Rose, you know that, and I know that," Georgiana said primly, "but we have little girls at school. We must safeguard their innocence until— until the time when—"

"Why, Miss Geo'giana, you be blushin', jes look at you. Ah ain't never seen nobody—"

"*I* haven't *ever* seen *anybody,*" Georgiana corrected her.

"*I* haven't *ever* seen *anybody*—my God, it's hard talkin' like you talks."

"Never mind, one day you'll be glad you learned to speak properly."

"The way *I* see it, them young-uns got to learn 'bout the mens, 'fo' they gets caught in the briar patch. They bes' fine out what a passel of scoundrels mens kin be. They all thinks babies is brung by the stork or come by in the cabbage patch. They gonna have a heap of trouble if they don't watch out."

For all Rose's apparent nonchalance in such matters, Georgiana had noticed before that she had nothing good to say about the opposite sex, except the kindly Negro man who'd brought her north, and it was apparent that she'd suffered much anguish at the hands of males. "Well," Rose said now, as they reached the gate to Snug Harbor, "Ah gots t'git home, 'fo' that scrawny ol' witch come lookin' fo' me on her broomstick."

"Whom do you mean, Rose? Surely not Mrs. Talcott?"

"Ah means Halley, that's who. She hates to leave me outta her sight more'n a second. She got eyes in the back of her head, she surely do."

Georgiana smiled in an attempt to disarm Rose. "I'm sure Halley can spare you so we can visit a while longer. Come sit a moment or two in Aunt Hat's garden. You might even let me try my hand at sketching you."

Rose finally agreed to present herself as a subject for Georgiana's sketchbook, and while the artist assumed a position on an upturned peach basket in the corner of the grape arbor, her sitter arranged herself on the grass nearby. She posed with her head held in regal calm on its long stalk of neck, her hands folded in her lap. Only the purplish tint of her nails revealed her blood, Georgie thought, and something about her skin, the color of ripe plums, perhaps, in her thin cheeks. Her large, pansy-petal eyes strayed nervously, with something at once pitiful and wary in their expression.

"Well, Rose, now that spring has come, how do you like it here?"

Rose shrugged. "It's all right, *I* guess, if you lives here."

"But you live here now, don't you?"

"Reckon. Sort of . . ."

There was a wistful, pathetic quality in the girl's reply that Georgiana couldn't fail to note, and she spoke gently. "Rose, you know, if you want people to like you, you've got to start by liking them. That wasn't very nice, what you said to Easter about her drawing this afternoon."

Rose shrugged. "She asked me, *I* done tole her."

"That's what's known as being brutally frank, and it's seldom the kindest thing to do." Rose seemed to be paying attention, and Georgie ventured further with her little talk. "Rose, has it occurred to you that you have already begun attracting a good deal of attention hereabouts, that you might even become a well-known young woman? You and the school are both celebrated. Mr. Garrison has written your story in the newspaper."

Rose, who had been toying with her skirt, sat up attentively. "Mean 'cause I was a runaway and Granddaddy Talcott bought me up from the paterollers?"

"Yes, that. But mostly I mean because you were the first pupil to be enrolled in the Free School. You are in the vanguard."

Rose frowned; those big words again. "That means at the forefront," Georgiana explained, "the place where you'll be noticed, that will cause people to talk about you."

Rose's eyes narrowed slyly. "The iceman says you is a agitator, Miss Georgiana. You is fermentin' trouble hereabouts."

Georgiana smiled. "I believe he meant 'fomenting' trouble. And what if I am? I'm proud if something I do, no matter how unattractive it may be to some minds, stirs things up and keeps them on the boil. It's what's needed if ever there is to be an end to slavery. And an end must come, it must. These aren't easy times for us here in Pequot just now, and I fear they will get worse before they get better. That's our cross to bear if we want to have our school, so young women like yourself can be educated. And you must be enthusiastic about your schooling, and set an example."

"What zample?"

"An example for others to follow and look up to. Not just here, but other places as well. So people will get used to the idea of colored people learning their lessons just like white people."

Rose's eyes flashed. "I ain't colored people, I is white folks," she said resentfully.

Georgiana spoke with patient logic. "Rose, nothing can change the circumstances of our births. You were born with Negro blood, which makes you—"

"Don't you go tellin' me what nuthin' makes me!" Rose glowered and her eyes smoldered. "Rose know what she is, an' she ain't no nigger. Rose, she goin' t'marry a white man, she goin' t'have white babies, an' ain't nobody goin' t'tell her she born a darky!"

"Well, if that's the case, I hope things may eventuate as you say. In the meantime, however, it's important that you keep your eyes and ears open; you'll pick up all sorts of useful things at Kingdom Come. *I* did, you know."

"Did what?"

"Learn from the Talcotts, I mean. After all, I was once Mrs. Talcott's hired girl, just like you."

Rose frowned and licked her thumb. "Not jes like *me*. I ben burnt. *My* flesh—here." She touched the place on her shoulder where the Lacey brand had marked her.

Georgiana smiled sympathetically. "Of course that's true. But that doesn't mean that if you do the best work you are capable of, you won't progress. Look at Ambo Buck—he's practically the boss at Burdin's."

Rose made a face. "That Ambo. He a pure 'n' simple ape. Honest, the way he goes around, behavin' as if he knows everything. Jes 'cause he can read and write and do sums."

Georgiana was miffed. "Really, there's no need to go on that way, Rose," she said severely. "Ambo's never done anything to make you so resentful of him. He's getting on in the world, don't you agree?"

"If that's your notion of gettin' on." She yawned elaborately. "*My* notion's a little different. *I'm* goin' to get on outta here first chance comes along."

"I see. And where do you plan to go?"

"Someplace where I can have some fun! New York, maybe. I likes the big city, lots of things to do. I'd like to wear purty clothes and a big bonnet with a bow. I'd like to wave my fan and be a lady. And I'd like to find me a real good-lookin' man—Miss Georgiana, how come you don't have no man? You a lady." She peered closely at Georgiana's blushing cheeks. "You is blushin' again. Why, I b'lieve you never had no man ever. Is it true? You a sally, Miss Georgie?"

"I don't believe I know what a 'sally' is," Georgiana returned stiffly.

"A sally's a girl who ain't never had a man. I don't think a woman's a woman less she's got a man to do her up proper. That's how the Lord meant it to be. Otherwise, you jes go on settin' an' a-rockin'. You like the lilies o' the field, you neither a toiler nor a spinner be."

"I'm glad to see you're so well acquainted with your Scripture," Georgiana replied, a touch tart. "It's nothing I'm prepared to discuss, however."

A notable silence ensued, and as Georgiana went on with her sketching, Rose, bored, began to pluck idly at the blades of spear grass around her. Georgiana observed as her slender fingers worked, deftly shucking the outer coat to free the more supple hearts of each shaft, then haphazardly weaving trios of strands into delicate plaits. These in turn she braided into a still wider plait, until they formed a band, which she braceleted around her thin bony wrist.

"Where did you learn to do that?" Georgiana asked.

Rose shrugged. "Knoxie showed me when Ah was jes a little thing. That's nothin'—lots of girls down home can plait." She shook her head. "But ain't nuthin' goin' to come of plaitin' no grass, Ah reckon."

She had lapsed into her "down-home" talk, the speech Georgiana was trying so hard to discourage through education. She knew Rose often did it just to irk her, but she refused to be baited. "Come, Rose," she said. "Come and see your portrait." There was a sharp intake of breath as Rose contemplated her own likeness on the page.

"Is that what Rose looks like?"

"To me, yes. More or less. Do you like it?"

Rose stared at the sketch some more, angling her head with a critical air. "Maybe," she said. "Maybe not." She peered closer, then backed away a step or two. "But maybe."

"Maybe" was as much of a compliment as Georgiana was likely to get today courtesy of Rose Mills. The steamboat whistle sounded from over at the landing. Rose stretched and sauntered out into the sunshine, shading her eyes toward the river.

"I'd surely like to be on that boat," she said wistfully, and Georgiana knew she had lost her subject for good. She wiped the charcoal smudges from her fingers and began packing up her things. Indicating the grass plaits, which had slipped from Rose's lap when she got up, she asked, "May I keep those?"

"Why?" Rose was immediately suspicious.

"I'd like to show them to someone. In fact I'd like to learn how they're made. Do you think you could show me sometime?"

"Reckon, sometime," Rose replied, not inclined to make commitments. She tossed her hair back, then, picking up her skirts like a lady, she traipsed off without saying good-bye, disappearing behind Cinnamon's shed.

Georgiana wondered if her words had reached the girl at all. Plainly, Mab's housemaid was clever and bright, but if she ever did learn some manners, what then for her? Watching her sashay away, her hips lost among the nodding meadow flowers, Georgiana was briefly reminded of another person. Though Rose had dark hair and was unmistakably the Talcotts' houseworker, for a moment Georgiana had thought of Aurora. Of course, Aurora Talcott was as unlike Rose Mills as a swan was to a goose, yet the impression remained, something in the walk and carriage, the proud lift of the head.

With a sigh she finished putting her sketching things away, and when she looked again she found Cinnamon standing in the doorway of the shed, silently watching her. This was nothing new; Georgiana often felt the witch's eye on her, and she told herself it was pure coincidence that she had been thinking of prophecies only moments before.

Pretending to ignore her now, Cinnamon chewed some, spat into the sunflowers, then took up her bucket and trudged over to the pump. Georgiana helped her and between them they lugged the bucket into the kitchen.

"Dat girrul, she be some mizzabul critter," Cinnamon muttered, squeezing the words around the stem of her corncob.

"Who, Cinnamon?" Georgiana asked, knowing full well.

"Dat Rose, das who. She gonter mek big trouble roun' hyere, Geo'ge, you lissen ol' Cinnamon, she tell you truff."

"What kind of trouble?"

"Dunno. Whist I did. But she won' jus' be no leetle trouble, pretty soon she make beeg trouble. You see, Geo'ge, some day soon—you see."

THE following Saturday Halley was rattling the pans in the kitchen sink, always a dangerous sign, and her ominous pronouncements were every bit as tympanic. She thanked the Lord that He hadn't thought to bestow such a hindrance as Rose Mills on her, for she was sure she could not have borne it. Next to that she-devil her own child was a saint and her grandchildren and great-grandchildren were paragons, and she blessed God for having given them to her. She'd like to take a switch to Rose's backside, that was the truth. It infuriated her to see the girl making up to Posie, teaching that innocent child her nasty tricks. But Halley would say nothing, for at all costs the Queen must be protected from unnecessary trouble or disturbance, and Halley and all her kin would go to any lengths short of murder to ensure this.

Peering across her sink through the checked gingham curtains, Halley regarded her mistress out in her garden with a worried brow and a heavy feeling in her breast. During the past months Mab had continued to maintain the strict schedule that had been her life, going over the household accounts and the menus that were tempting to Appleton's palate, never forgetting Old Bobby's tastes and hankerings, writing a letter or two to keep up with old friends, arranging the early blooms from the flower beds. But nothing in the Queen's behavior had fooled anyone but the master into believing what they knew in their hearts to be the truth.

If Mab was aware of the fears and presentiments of her servants and her family, she gave no sign, treating this year exactly like last year, pretending next year would be the same. She had made a mental list of things requiring attention, things she worried about without seeming to show concern, matters she wished to be assured of being attended to before the end came, and she still found that her moments of rarest solace came while working in her potting shed, where she could hide herself away and observe minutely the methodical and satisfying rites of gardening.

This morning, however, it appeared she had attacked things much too energetically, and now, forced to call a halt, she breathlessly worked her way up through the garden, hoping to reach her rocking chair before anyone noticed her state of fatigue. She had a bit of difficulty negotiating the steps, and she had no more than got to the top of the terrace and sunk gratefully into the chair when she heard Halley's voice importuning her through the kitchen window.

"Miz Talca, you's wukkin' too hard! You bettah git some ress."

"I am, Halley. See?" Mab exhibited herself in her current state of repose.

"Well, you jes set youseff there an' rock a spell," Halley insisted, and her head disappeared again.

Mab's quiet was soon interrupted by a crash from the kitchen as something smashed, followed by Trubey's alarmed cry, then a loud expletive from Rose. Next came Hallelujah's brimstone declaration and the shrillings of Agrippina, who had evidently been called away from her harp practice by one of the household matters she made it her business to oversee.

"Pina, dear, what is happening in our kitchen?" Mab called out. "It sounds like a troop of Russians in there."

"It's Rose, Mama!" cried Agrippina, hurrying out to her. "She dropped a skillet and broke the porcelain turkey platter. It's a scandal the way that creature carries on."

"Don't fret about it, dearie. Rose isn't your cross to bear. Come and sit with me," said her mother soothingly. "But—oh, calamity, there they go again!" From inside came another resounding crash and Trubey's wail rose like the keening of a mourner in County Cork.

"Just hear!" cried Pina, flying into the house and slamming the door behind her.

Presently the obstreperous voices were stilled, and when Rose appeared on the terrace minus her apron, Mab inquired, "Are you having some difficulty this morning, Rose?"

"No, *ma'am,*" Rose said innocently. " 'Cept that Trubey, she get me so nervous she make me drop everything like I got butterfingers. She think she Queen of Sheba 'roun' this place. You the Queen, Missus Talcott, you the one ought t'squash her like a bug."

"I don't think Trubey needs any squashing." Mab found it hard to ignore these squabbles. "Rose, why must you say such things? We're all trying, truly we are. Mr. Talcott paid over a good deal of money for your freedom, you go to school to better your lot in life, you seem to be coming along, you have a nice house to work in, nice clothes, some money to put by, you're not worked to death, surely. You have your room, it's clean, and a lovely view of the river . . ."

"That's all right, ma'am, a featherbed's a sight better than a sack filled with huskin's, but it don't make no never mine to me when it comes to folks bein' nice. Folks roun' this place is plain mean, that's all. Mean as a Rickett County sheriff."

"Why do you say that?"

" 'Cause it true. They's all high and mighty with all they fine houses an' clothes and cah'iges, but when it come down to treatin' folks kinely they don't know how t'do it."

Mab found a certain injustice in the girl's words and was quick to say so. "I'm surprised to hear you talk that way when so many have done their utmost to be kind to you. I think it would be far more true to say that you go out of the way to stir up trouble around here. And *here* is a place where we don't *need* extra trouble." Taking in Rose's pouting look she was inclined to dismiss the girl on the spot, but again bit her tongue before she said something she'd be sorry for. "Rose, I want you to think over what I've said. Now go along and put on a clean apron, please. Père Margeaux will be bringing the bishop. I want you looking proper for him."

Butter wouldn't have melted in Rose's mouth as she served coffee to the bishop in the best parlor. She was at her most mannerly, so much so that his Grace complimented her on her dispatch. Rose bridled and smiled, delighted that Trubey had received no such praise, and she repeated the bishop's words in the kitchen so Halley and Judah would be sure to hear.

That night, unable to sleep, Mab thought about the girl as she reposed in the window seat of her room. Rose's main difficulty, she surmised, was that she wasn't black and she wasn't white; yet she wanted to be accepted as a white person, which was to say she wanted to be just like everyone else, and such a thing simply wasn't possible.

After another moment she heard a sound—not the mockingbird that nested in the tree, whose lyrical notes she was used to, but the puzzling sound of weeping. Alarmed, she leaned toward the window to peer out into the darkness.

It was Rose. Mab could just make out her slender form as she moved slowly among the flower beds. The girl had plucked a flower and was holding it listlessly in one hand while she went on softly crying. Then, after a few moments, the sounds ceased, she sniffed, then another sound replaced it, a gentle crooning, mixed with intermittent humming. She was singing. So, there *was* a soft side to her. A pretty voice, too. Though low, it was surprisingly sweet; too sweet, thought Mab, for a girl of such unbridled temper.

Out in the garden, in the warm spring night, hushed and still, Rose gave herself up to the dull feelings of melancholic longing that had stolen over her. She broke a flower from its stem and fastened it in her hair, then, drawing a long, still breath, she raised her face to the sky. Her lips began to move and words escaped them, strange words, unintelligible to Mab, though carried clearly on the soft breeze. But that they were deeply felt there could be no doubt. She did not know that there, under the magnolia tree, in the African tongue of her grandmother Knoxie, Rose Mills had vowed that no matter what it took, no matter who might suffer, or what the cost, she would succeed. It would not be she who fell by the wayside— not Rose Mills. She would not rest an instant until she had jacked herself up, risen like bread into the kind of life she could just now only envy and despair of.

15

How Abednego Got to Ride in Bob's Coach, and Rose Did Well in the Cemetery

ABEDNEGO GRIMES BREATHED his last on the Saturday following the annual town meeting during the second week in May, and if he did not die a happy man he surely died a rich one. Though to many the play hardly seemed worth the candle—since to all intents and purposes his passing went unmourned—the manner of it was yet noteworthy, as violent as unexpected, and the obituary printed in the *Courant* was fulsome in its praise of the deceased.

Rest in peace, ancient warrior! Come gently lay thy bald head upon earth's soothing breast and close thine eyes, oh weary son, thou zealous collector of land parcels and debentures and reclaimed bonds. Sleep and be thou now the worm's repast, let flights of angels sing thee to thy rest, and let others rejoice, those multitudes no longer plagued by the breathing in of the same airs and humors with thee. For those unlucky parties still owing thee, gentle usurer (a score or more of these there were), exultation shall all be wasted effort, as that outstanding paper still held against them must assuredly be passed along by legal testament to the horny hand and dusty pocket of thy legal son and heir, Zion.

Given the quirky temperament of the man, and the untoward, nearly peculiar circumstances governing his bizarre demise, Abednego's final utterances were more or less as might have been expected, though it could with truth be said that, had he known he was but a wheel's turn away from that undiscovered bourn from which no coach traveler returns, he might have chosen something less colloquial than "God damn the dirty bastard for a turd-winding fartcatcher!" Needless to say, no mention of these sentiments appeared in the *Courant,* for they were addressed merely to the thin air into which they were ejaculated.

The subject, or rather object, of Abednego's ire may be guessed at: it was none other than his archenemy and ancient rival, Bob Talcott himself, and the motive for Abednego's rancorous words was twofold. First, he had earlier taken exception to certain remarks made by Old Bobby at town meeting, remarks in favor of the Free School, and, second, having spurred his coachman, the haughty Hogarth, into chancing an illegal trial of wheeled vehicles, he had silently vowed that one time before he died his coach was going to whip Old Bobby's to a fare-thee-well.

Now it must be remembered that in the village there were two coaches of similar hue and construction, both of the widely known and vastly admired Concord, New Hampshire design. Most celebrated of these vehicles was the conveyance of the Talcotts, which had for years been looked upon by the local populace as a symbol of success and achievement, conferring status not only on its owner but on the entire community as well. Only let the rousing thunder of those sixteen iron-shod hooves be heard galloping along the village thoroughfare and heads must turn to view the Yellow Pumpkin go speeding past. The second, duplicate of the first in each minute detail, was not so all-fired shiny, not quite so well cared for. Its door panels were often mud-spattered where someone had neglected to sponge them down after the last rain, its isinglass shades were fogged and in need of replacement, nor was this twin chariot ever drawn by steeds as bravely blooded as those of the first coach, as if big-bellied hayburners were all its poor owner could afford. This was the Grimes coach, its owner, Abednego of Burning Bush.

It remained, however illogically, one of the bitter pills of Bob Talcott's life that his vanity had been irksomely trodden upon in the matter of Abednego's facsimile. The insult had lodged deep in his breast and would not let him go. For Bobby was certain beyond the faintest doubt that he had been the first purchaser of a Concord coach in Pequot Landing, the first to have his conveyance painted a bright yellow, while the Grimeses' coach, appearing more than a year later, had originally been lacquered Lincoln green—until repainted according to Abednego's instructions. When this happened it had occurred to Bobby to sell his Yellow Pumpkin, as the children had dubbed it, or at the very least in his turn to repaint it, but he had found that he could not bring himself to do so. What he had done, and probably prudently so, was bide his time. Year after year he had waited it out, biting his tongue whenever the detested Grimes coach chanced to cross his vision, with its coachman, Hogarth, puffed up like a toad on the box. Nor had Bob commented when he learned that Reuben had been contesting against Hogarth, coach vying against coach, Grimes against Talcott, though, as was well-known, such trials of speed were strictly condemned as a peril to the civil peace, to say nothing of life, limb, and property. Indeed, Bob had been known to slip Reuben a five-dollar gold piece upon the occasion of his first having emerged victorious in such a tournament.

But a match between mere hired coachmen driving empty coaches—of what avail was that? Before he shook off this mortal coil, Abednego was bound to try to prove once and for all who the best man was, which the swiftest coach. This, Bobby well knew and was prepared for: a Last Race, one that Abednego Grimes was determined he would win, but one that Bob himself had no intention of losing.

On the fatal morning, Old Bobby set out on a potentially pleasant excursion of some eight or so miles, the distance from Pequot Landing to the nearby community of Still, where he planned to inspect a pair of yearling Narragansett pacers, from all accounts two beauties that he already had made up his mind to have in his stable at Follybrook. The coach horses were not even straining as the Yellow Pumpkin topped Burning Bush Hill, and Reuben was shaking out his reins across their broad rumps, whistling a tune as he prepared to negotiate the leisurely descent into Two Stone, when suddenly and without warning from out of the Grimeses' drive flashed the Grimeses' coach. A collision was only narrowly averted as Reuben swung wide, and Bobby looked out just in time to catch Hogarth's supercilious look and the triumphant smile on the yellow parchment face of Abednego, who gleefully shook his cane out the window as he hurtled past.

"Don't let that son-of-a-buck get ahead of us!" Bobby shouted at his driver. "Overtake, overtake!"

Several moments were necessary before Reuben could apply himself properly to the task. Then, employing his long whip to advantage, he let his team full out, and the Yellow Pumpkin shot down the hill behind the other coach as Bobby, refusing to roll up his window, choked in the rising cloud of dust.

Though Hogarth had a crucial lead, before long the Talcott coach had closed the distance, and as the horses stretched out on the flat and tore past the branch road, from time to time Bobby glimpsed again through the dust that wizened little mug squinting furiously out of the coach window ahead, the crabbed hand furiously shaking the silver-headed cane.

Toilers in the field stopped their hoes mid-stroke to watch the twin coaches careering along the road, the wheel spokes a blur of red as the coachmen further urged their teams. Roiling up a thick, nearly impenetrable balloon of dust behind him, the Grimes driver sped on, while aboard the Talcott coach Reuben was obliged to slow as he tried to navigate the pumice-colored cloud now enveloping him. Under the sky of flawless blue, between the green fields, crows flew up at the racket as, reckless as boys on a jag, the rival drivers vied in the contest, straining from the waist over the buckboard to give full play to their whips, the horses pricking up their ears, stretching their necks to their utmost, their manes and tails flying behind like so many black plumes. Up hill and down dale, on they went, rushing past house and barn, bouncing over rock and rill, Talcott gaining again, Grimes fearful of losing the lead, the horses and vehicles, desperate passengers and more desperate drivers all making a fearful din as they plunged on.

Ahead lay Lamentation Mountain, where the roadway curved, hugging its rocky base. Though the way was normally wide enough for one vehicle to pass another, on this occasion the lead coach continued greedily to steer the middle course, so that when the Talcott coach at last overtook, just rounding the foot of the hill, it was forced to lag behind, and Reuben had to pull hard on his reins. It was well he did so at that precise moment, for Hogarth was so bent on preventing his opponent from passing that he failed utterly to see the immediate danger.

A force of some half dozen workmen, recruited from among the indigent Lamenters, was hard at work with picks and shovels, filling a large cavity in the road produced by a healthy spring freshet. Catching sight of the two coaches bearing down on them helter-skelter, the men tossed their equipment and scattered like chaff in a high wind. On thundered the Grimes horses, their dark nostrils flaring, their ebony manes streaming back from their necks, tails flourishing in the breeze as, with a maniacal scowl on his brow, Hogarth lowered his whip against their sweating backs.

Now, all at once perceiving the peril that lay ahead, the coachman flung away his whip to secure a better purchase on his reins and viciously swung the horses to the loosely graveled roadside so that his wheels might avoid the looming gap in the road. Nor did he for an instant slacken his speed, but with some adroit handling negotiated the difficult turn, a maneuver his master, alas, failed to complete.

As chance would have it, Abednego happened at the same instant to be leaning out of his window, a posture that quickly became untenable when, at the crucial moment, the off-wheel struck a large rock destined for the hole, causing the body of the coach to bounce upward in a sudden violent spasm. On the box, Hogarth was precipitated vertically into the air by some ten inches. Simultaneously, the heavy jolt caused the coach door to fly open and Abednego Grimes to shoot sideways out of the coach, heading toward the earthen bank on his right, where he struck a rock and broke his neck.

Hogarth the invincible failed to register his not inconsiderable loss. Since his ear told him the Talcott coach was bearing down hard on his tail, he calmly resumed the race, letting out his team and rolling onward to the turnpike that lay in view to the west, while Reuben, having observed the tragedy, pulled up, allowing Old Bobby to descend and join the handful of laborers who had gathered around the inert form of Squire Grimes. Since Abednego had obviously given up the ghost, there seemed little to be done except to inform the next-of-kin and see that the earthly remains were deposited into the proper hands. Giving over thought of any further travel that day, Old Bobby saw the corpse of his ancient enemy placed within the Yellow Pumpkin and set out to convey it to Burning Bush Farm, where he undertook the task of consoling the newly made widow of his erstwhile enemy.

"I do regret it, Rachel," Bob confessed when she met him on the porch and his carriage was relieved of its untidy burden, "I do regret it mightily. We have never been friends, your husband and I, but I had rather almost anything else untoward had occurred than it should be I who must approach you on such an errand." He glanced through the porch window to where the stiffening corpse had been laid out on the horsehair sofa.

"You are kind, Robert," replied Rachel, "kinder than you have any reason to be. It's the man's own fault, Abed's, and none of yours. I saw from my window how he frothed to get the lead of you as you came along. Well, well, he'll not race his coach again in this life, and there's mercy. And he'll be buried with small pomp, I warrant you! His passing won't draw so large a crowd as the Sermon on the Mount."

"Is there aught further I can do?" asked Bobby, obliged to admire her candor.

"Why, bless the man, just hear him! You are the soul of Christian charity, as I've reason to know." Her smile was almost winsome. "But I can think of nothing—other than that you should forgive the man his trespasses, which I reckon as being numerous. You have held yourself in check for many a year and brooked many an insult from the members of this long-nosed family. We all must pay for our follies—not the least Abednego himself." She wagged her head forlornly. "Thank you, Bobby, there is nothing you can do. It's spilt milk, all of it, and I'll ne'er shed a tear, for what's spilt is spilt and quickly run off between the stones. And there's always a deal more milk in the cow than was ever squeezed out of her."

"I'm glad to hear you say so, for I would not sleep if I thought that Bob Talcott had been the means of bringing distress to Rachel Grimes."

"How good of you," she responded warmly. "And, tell me, Bob"—and her voice softened—"when you go away now, will it be another coon's age before we speak again?"

Chuckling mildly, Bobby ducked his head and with a schoolboy air rubbed the side of his nose with his finger. "We must hope not, dear lady, for I haven't that long to live, alas."

"Pshaw—you'll go on like Methuselah!" returned Rachel. "Indeed, it's I who must make the most of my time. I won't say I've wasted what's gone, but I will say if I had it to do over I'd do it a good deal differently."

"How—differently?"

"Well, I'd never have married into this tribe in the first place. Sitting up here for nigh onto thirty-five years, as if Burning Bush Hill were the Mount of Olives, and Moses and his ten tablets were out there in the dooryard garden amongst the cabbages. Better to have remained a spinster, though I would have missed having Zion's children to call me grammaw. Still, some things are better left undisturbed, Bob. I'll bide my time as is meet, and then they'll put me down and sod me over—where I should have been put long ago."

Though she spoke in her usual brisk fashion, there was in her manner a nicety and a deep feminine regard for the man who stood but a step below her on the porch, yet would not cross the threshold and take a chair as people generally do in such circumstances.

"'Sleeping dogs,' hey?" said Old Bobby. "Well, perhaps you're right."

"I believe I am. Sleeping dogs are usually safest."

Bobby straightened his spine and raised his hat with conscious ceremony. "Then I'll take my leave. I must explain matters to the constable. Are you all right? Is there aught one can do for you?"

Rachel was touched by this show of sympathy. "No, I'm pleased to say, I retain all my faculties. Please not to worry about me."

"Not a likely prospect, with you a scant four miles from my own doorstoop," declared Bobby with some force. "Rachel, I've seen many a worthy woman in my day, pretty ones, too, but there's none alive to hold a candle to you when the sun sets. I doubt my presence at the obsequies of the deceased will be welcomed, so I shall absent myself. But please know my thoughts are with you."

"And my thanks go with you. Ah, well—go along then, Bob. And you had better not come again, or people'll start to talk—just as they did when we were young, before you went away to war and married your Miss Vicky."

They smiled at each other, and she stood on the porch, waving him off in the Yellow Pumpkin, then dispatched the boy for the minister. Abednego Grimes was dead of a coach race, and a hole would have to be dug to receive him, a marker would have to be cut, nothing fancy. *Sic transit gloria mundi.* The sweating Hogarth got clear to this side of New Britain before he ever missed his master.

THE death of Abednego Grimes produced one unexpected result. The grave-site that was destined to receive the body lay at the foot of the Fathers' Rise, and as they set about digging a hole in which to put the corpse to rest, the sexton and his two assistants stumbled upon some far older bones than Abednego Grimes's. Tibiae, fibulae, scapulae, and clavicles, as well as choice sections of crania came unexpectedly to light and were subsequently dis-closed to be parts of the skeletons of certain Wongunk tribesmen who during some earlier era had employed that same burial mound. But though Appleton Talcott, Judge Perry, and others of a scientific turn attempted to halt further excavation, which they termed a desecration against the sum total of man's knowledge, the fact remained that this hallowed ground was the time-honored Grimes family plot, bought and paid for, and Zion Grimes could not be persuaded that the funeral plans should in any way be affected. So the hole was completed according to normal specifications, three feet by six by six, and by dusk it gapingly awaited the remains of the dead Abednego.

Imagine this scene: Moonrise. The evening, when ordinary folk are in their front parlors, reading in Leviticus or Deuteronomy, and the swollen orange moon hangs over the river like a medallion struck in the blue-green sky. In the air the plaintive sound of doves, the *skeet* of partridges running in the low grass, the snuffling of swine escaped again to Hog Meadow. Onto the placid breast of the river slides a flock of scaup, quacking in moon lunacy, while downstream the fishing skiffs hang in the water with their night watches set, the boys strung up in hammocks in the stern lee. Lights flicker in the windows of the taverns where the peddlers and drummers sit, feet up in the taproom, venturing an exchange of information. At the Academy Hall—no matter that the shade of Abednego Grimes hovers in the nearby church—the monthly Assembly is under way, fiddlers sawing, heads bobbing, feet skipping. It is a night of purple shadows and moon-gilt corners, ideal for an adventure of an amatory sort. Nature's stage is set. Enter the actors on cue:

As Rose Mills strolled along the street, past the budding lilac bushes, she could hear the sound of dancing feet. She drew a despairing breath through her teeth and bit her lip till it throbbed, while her nails curled into her palms and dug in frustration. Turning away she felt the folds of her dress drag, then catch on something along a fence. Impatiently she jerked at the material and heard it tear. She could have cried for having been so careless. She thrust out her chin as she passed the loitering coachmen along Main Street, and coldly stared them out of countenance, daring one of them to speak a syllable to her. The lilting music soon died away as she abandoned the warm glow of lamplight to be engulfed by loneliness and some nameless feeling of loss.

She wanted a man. That was it. She wanted to have a man's arms around her, to feel his closeness; wanted to be loved for a little while. She thought of Priam Talcott and the adoring way his wife always looked at him; Priam *was* handsome, no doubt, the kind of man any woman would hanker for, but what kind of man could a girl like Rose expect to find? Who but a wharf rat or traveling man would set his cap for her, and then for what? A moment, that was all. But tonight—a man, really any man, would satisfy. And if no man would circle her waist with his arm and dance with her, surely some man would kiss her, would take her and ease the longings that were warmly stirring in her. Thoughts of Bushrod Grimes came to her, memories of that cold snowy day, she and he under the robe, her body close to his. Yes, Bushrod Grimes would do tonight and do nicely.

But Bushrod was nowhere to be seen, and she worked to blot the thought from her mind. As she idled along the sidewalk, the loneliness seeped through her flesh deep into her heart, heavily weighing it, like a boat filled with stones. Slowly she continued along Main Street, past the church green, and proceeded east on March Street, gazing at the brightly lighted windows of the Old Hundred. The windows and doors of the public rooms stood wide open, and muffled conversation was to be heard, punctuated by bursts of burly laughter. The voices and the laughter, the lamplight, the evident conviviality and camaraderie swamped her. Where do I belong, she wondered? Where's the place for Rose? Somewhere, please, let me come inside.

As she started off again she saw a figure appear on the side porch of the tavern. It was actually the cigar she saw first, the red tip glowing in the darkness. A man stood stock-still, and she had the eerie feeling he was watching her. Presently his hand came up and took the cigar from his mouth and holding it before him, he employed the tip to describe slow circles in the air. A signal? Immediately she grew indignant: one of Sallie's dry-goods men, looking for some way of spending the rest of his evening. But not with Rose, she told herself, and walked on. Still she managed to drag her step a little, and glancing over her shoulder, she saw him crossing the street toward her.

Now she began to feel a mounting excitement in the pit of her stomach, and the impulse overcame her to stand close to him, just to see what he might do. She remained where she was, absently rubbing a hand against her arm, waiting, nervous and expectant, anticipating she knew not what. What should she do? Would he harm her? Ought she to run away? Or was he—the one she was seeking? His arm moved and she watched the lighted cigar describe a fiery arc through the darkness, throwing off tiny sparks as it spun away among the bushes.

She drew in a breath, then took several steps farther along the walk, bringing her before the stone portal to the Ancient Burying Ground. With a furtive look over her shoulder, she entered the cemetery. When she had gone a little farther she darted another glance behind her: he was following along the gravel roadway, leisurely but with purpose. She could hear the stones crunch under his heel. Raising her skirts several inches, she proceeded vaguely in the direction of the Fathers' Rise, where the stark silhouettes of table stones and cracked grave markers could be made out beneath the sheltering trees. A strange excitement engulfed her and she felt out of breath as she climbed the slope. The tall, slender church spire rose beyond her left shoulder, and from the tavern across the way could still be heard the scrape of fiddles, the noisy clapping of hands.

Almost at the top of the Rise she paused and glanced back once again. Slowly she untied her scarf and let her hair fall loosely about her shoulders, then drew the fabric through her fingers and stretched it taut. She nonchalantly hummed a few bars of music and sang some of the words. Where was he? What was he doing there in the dark? She wanted to look again but was afraid to. She heard a sound somewhere behind her, and she lowered herself so she was half-seated on the nearest table stone. She heard him footing it up the slope toward her and then, suddenly, he was there, she had only to reach out. There. *Just* there.

He stepped around the corner of the table stone and with scarcely a pause acknowledged her. She felt his hand lightly graze her arm, then begin casually to slide upward along its length toward her shoulder, and was only a little surprised when he bent above her and softly kissed her on the lips, raising her up to him and pressing her body hard against his. Oh, Rose thought, this is good. This is very good. She wondered whether she ought to say something—ask his name or tell him hers, exchange certain token phrases of salute or social intercourse. He, however, did not seem in a conversational mood; nor in actuality was Rose. Talk could come later; now other pursuits were in hand, other intercourse.

Between the two there began a silent but intensive straining and murmuring, a muffled yearning, a panting, and the avid process of mutual investigation that with time and physical arousal saw hasty, accommodating movements, with garments loosened or altogether unfastened for convenience' sake. It all seemed, in the velvety dark, a perfectly uncomplicated and realistic undertaking, requiring neither illumination nor foreknowledge of each other's person or identity, the parlor maid and the stranger.

Permitting her posture to be rearranged, Rose lay back atop the table stone (as it happened, the table stone of that worthy ancient Eben Grimes) with her shoes sticking straight in the air, their past buckles occasionally glinting, while her partner took and gave, alternately coaxing and assaulting her with the various portions of his anatomy, now soothingly tender, now impatiently violent, now sweetly kissing her, now fiercely working her, energetically bouncing her on the stone surface. Panting, she encouraged him, gnawing on the back of her hand to muffle her cries. A fresh tune from the Academy Hall drifted disjointedly among the tree branches and the stars pitched about as though loosened from their moorings in the firmament.

Have a care, Rose thought, but did not voice her words, and he sank his incisors into the soft swell of her breast and drove at her below, forcing her legs farther apart, gripping her ankles with his strong hands, enclosing her in a vise, relentlessly and indifferently banging her body against the unyielding stone until both flesh and bone were sore.

Oh! she moaned aloud as he plunged and reared and plunged again. Sweet Jesus, how I love this, she thought, while to her lips came only the ancient litanies of need and desire, the two prescribed words that were the single certainty in an uncertain world. As he plunged on—oh!—head tossed back, riding her like some noble but untamed steed and glorying in his journey—*oh!—oh!*—she knew they could never stop now, surely, not until they were done, and she—*OH!*—she imagined what it would be like to have a man like this one each and every night, for her sheer pleasure, a man for whom she could cook and wash and sew and keep house, and do any sort of womanly task at all, only so he would come home nights and do this— oh!—and this—*oh!*—and *this*—*ohh* . . .

Then, while he performed manfully—spectacularly—in the final stages of this boneyard congress, cursing and muttering and crying out, with sweat running from his head onto her naked breasts, spilling into her open eyes and stinging, all at once the Fathers' Rise heaved upwards, rockets began exploding, the stars went mad, and they were falling together, tilting, sliding, helplessly. There followed an ominous grinding sound, a wobbling sensation that had nothing to do with their roistering, an almost sickening sense of disorientation, and in another moment she and he and the gravestone and the cemetery and the world itself were collapsing. In a masterpiece of unfortunate timing, the heavy table stone rocked off its legs, struck the ground, and broke under them, even as the abrupt change in position obliged their two bodies to part, however reluctantly, and the seed that was destined for her corridor went spurting through the air in a futile arc. He cried out, *Ah!* cursing loudly, then *oh!* again in a whisper as a stern, inquiring voice was heard from the darkness.

"What's that, then? Who's there? Make yourselves known," the voice demanded, inducing in Rose the hideous panic of discovery and exposure. She felt her partner's warm fingers cover her mouth, as if he thought she might betray their whereabouts, then the clamor of barking dogs reached her ears and struck the old terror in her heart, the deathly fear of the hunted. Unable to restrain herself, she shoved him from her and staggered to her feet, and leaving him with his pale bent knees sticking out above his lowered trousers, she bounded down the far side of the mound and disappeared behind a dark clump of mallows.

Apparently the intruder with the ravening dogs (it was the sexton, Giles; the dogs were his pets and wouldn't hurt a fly) hadn't seen fit to pursue his investigation, for nothing further was heard from that party, and after a while the abandoned lover struggled to gather himself together and find his way back the same way he had come. The muscles and sinews of his body had performed admirably, given the impromptu circumstances, but he felt dismally cheated in the matter of the episode's conclusion—or rather its lack of a satisfactory conclusion, and when he had but half yanked up his trousers he found himself tottering away into the dark. The heavy pull of gravity when he began descending from the top of the mound forced him into a heedless state of locomotion far speedier than he would have liked. Everything about him seemed awry, as, cursing, he stumbled down the Fathers' Rise until, sighting between the upright markers the semblance of a path toward the darkened street, he next found himself stepping off the planet altogether. To say that he saw his entire life in an instant was to say nothing, for not only his life but those of countless others whose existences were somehow fatefully intertwined with his seemed to pass before him as, falling, he tried to examine their intricacies and tangled complications; but, falling, every answer seemed to elude him and, still falling—it seemed to him he was falling a terribly long distance, Newton's natural force had him in its clutch and would not let him go, he must have been falling miles by now, and for hours, aeons, too—still falling, he struck something hard and, deciding he had been deposited at the center of the earth, but having merely preempted his grandfather's grave pit, he promptly passed out.

Once again Sinjin Grimes had drunk himself into Bolivia . . .

PART THREE

Rose by
Any Other Name

16

The Bad Penny Turns Up

THUS IT WAS THAT old Abednego Grimes departed a world too mean to acknowledge his truer parts and honest virtues; and thus it was that his grandson Sinjin returned at last to his native heath, each in so ignoble a manner. It was a stroke of luck that Rachel Grimes failed to learn until well after the fact that upon the very morning of Abednego's funeral the deceased's freshly dug grave had served to cradle, however uncomfortably, the whiskey-sodden person of the prodigal son.

Shortly after dark of the previous evening, a lone horseman had come trotting into the village via the River Road and without causing undue notice had reined up at the door of Gaunt House, where he turned his steed over to Foote Crowe and slipped inside, hardly anyone the wiser. After a surprise reunion with his sister and her family, already attired in sternest black from respect for the dead patriarch, "Uncle Sinjin" had left Helen's house en route to the Hundred, where he bent a sturdy elbow with Milehigh Jenckes and other tavern regulars. Later, much the worse for drink, the newly returned mariner had slipped outside for a breath of air, at which point the hired girl from Kingdom Come had discerned the glowing tip of his cigar describing congenial circles on the tavern porch.

The following morning, having been hoisted from his grandfather's gaping grave, he again repaired to his sister's house, where he bathed and dressed and prepared to enact the role of dutiful grandson and solemn mourner, pale and shaken but game. It was a fact that Sinjin Grimes always looked well in black: the burning coallike eyes, the raven's wing hair, the air of bitterness betokening imminent shatterability. And while the village-at-large erupted in an effulgence of excitement and speculation at his unexpected return, astonished that the truant adventurer had so auspiciously reappeared and was displaying admirable punctilio by offering his attendance at his grandfather's funeral rites, fortunately there were none alive save old Giles Corry to attest to the fact that the captain had just spent four hours sleeping off a drunk at the bottom of Abednego Grimes's freshly dug grave.

Following the formal obsequies, his further attendance upon the family being called for, Sinjin repaired to Burning Bush Farm, where Miss Rachel received him in a private audience. Not given to tears, she nonetheless wept copiously as she put her withered arms around him and felt his body close to hers, forgetting in her joy her ire at the contents of his last letter to Georgiana, ire that even the pleadings of Helen and Georgiana over so many weeks had not assuaged, so that she had continued to refuse to pay the premium of twenty-five thousand dollars demanded, not without reason considering the risk, by the Talcott, Lane Assurance Company. That she had failed him in this she regretted profoundly, for though, given the circumstances of his return, he had perforce said little about the voyage, even to Helen and Luke, the whole town was by now aware that once again he had lost his ship. Now, to put off for a little the necessity of informing him of her dereliction, she sat opposite him and demanded to be told every detail of the history of the voyage of the red junk.

Having of necessity given over his smuggling activities, and on the run from the emperor's minions, his personal fortune confiscated or windblown, he had concocted what he and others believed to be a highly novel venture, one he had hoped would be profitable in the extreme.

As indicated in his letter to Georgiana, he had formed a syndicate with himself as president and principal stockholder; the subscribed funds went toward the complete overhauling of the structure, hull, masts, and rigging of a seagoing war junk, with the purpose of turning her into a floating museum.

"A museum!" Rachel had trouble absorbing this startling piece of information. But it was true. The plan had been to sail the junk filled with Chinese furnishings and articles of interest to American viewers, from Macao to New York, where after her daring transocean voyage she was to be displayed as a dockside public attraction at a South Street pier, opening her decks and hold and exhibiting at a nominal fee the trove of rare and costly Oriental artifacts she carried for the inspection and edification of the curious.

His voyage had been Ulysses-like, with no Penelope or Telemachus, no friendly hound to greet him upon his return, only the bitter knowledge that again he had failed, again fate had tricked him. When the valuables had been safely stowed on board, Sinjin and his crew, including his mate Billy Albuquerque and his manservant Mat Kindu, had embarked for home, driving down the South China Sea on the flank of the autumn monsoon, through the Straits of Sunda, picking up the southerly trades, lugging slowly across the Indian Ocean to the tip of Africa, and around the Cape of Good Hope.

Then he had sailed her north along the coast, making for Brava in the Cape Verde Islands, thence west across the Atlantic to Key West at the southernmost tip of Florida. From there, by gradual degrees, the hardy vessel was scheduled to work her way northward to the port of New York, there to become famous, along with her master and crew, whose courage and extraordinary seamanship had brought a vessel built only for coastal voyaging across a full twelve thousand miles of open water. Unfortunately, the junk had been caught in a hard blow off Nassau, and only the quick thinking and adroit seamanship of her master had seen all hands safely brought ashore, while the *Koxinga* had slipped beneath the waves, and lay now athwart a coral reef, full fathom five.

Rachel wrung her hands at the dismal picture he painted for her. "Lost, lost," she moaned. "What a shame, after all your hard work. Never mind, you may be poor again, but I'll make it up to you."

"But Grammaw, the insurance—the things are gone but they're covered, aren't they? You *did* take out the policy I wrote Georgie about?"

"Oh pshaw." Her look was sorrowful as she told him how she had refused to do so. "I ought to've done it somehow," she said. "But you vexed me so—oh, what a dreadful thing to have set down on paper for others to read—" She could not refrain from painfully calling up the matter of the letter whose contents referring to the likelihood of her death and the bequests as set forth in her last will and testament still rankled her.

Dazed and daunted by the news that the luckless voyage had been a complete loss, not only to himself but to his backers, Sinjin stammered out as earnest an apology as he had ever given voice to, imploring the old lady to believe that he had never wished for her death, and as for her money—

Indulgent as ever, Rachel stopped the words on his lips with a loving kiss, vowing that she would make good his debts—even, she declared in her happiness at having him safe home, the sum owed to that brazen creature the Condessa da Silva. Moreover, she would see him aboard a new ship, one that would carry him anywhere he chose to go. And when she *did* breathe her last, he would not be disappointed. Then she sent him down to intercept the callers who had begun arriving to offer their condolences.

While approximate expressions of grief were being tendered around the Brussels carpet laid in the front parlor, for his grandmother's sake Sinjin attempted a halfhearted reconciliation with his stepfather, toward whom he bore the same rancor he had felt since boyhood. His commendable effort went by the board, however, for, after each male guest had had recourse to as much whiskey as there was to be found on the premises, tempers flared, not about the sinking of the red junk, but as the result of a discussion of Georgiana Ross and her school.

Forgetting his pledge to Rachel not to stir the pot and consigning his stepfather straight to hell—Bushrod along with him—Sinjin stormed out and headed back to the tavern, there to take up his old rooms. The matter of his lodging having been dealt with by Sallie Jenckes, her number one boarder quickly summoned Hermie Light, who joined him in the taproom to retail all the news of Pequot Landing that had not yet reached his ears.

Not far behind their skipper had come his two familiars, his valet, the yellow shadow, Mat Kindu, and his mate, Billy Albuquerque, sporting a dark beard close-cropped in the Moorish style. On the morrow Billy would proceed to Cape Cod and his family hearth, while Matty would remain close at hand to do his master's bidding, the all-important morning shave, the curling irons on his hair, the buffing of his boots. Though Sallie held no brief for the murderous-looking Malay, for the sake of Sinjin's goodwill she tolerated his presence, nonetheless declaring her conviction that the day would arrive when they'd all wake up with their throats cut.

Sinjin had no more than put in his initial appearance than half the room of curious topers was eagerly grouped around the corner table to welcome him home and to lend an ear to the tale of his latest, fantastic voyage. As might be expected, the papers made capital of the story, and though the venture was regarded by many as foolhardy on the face of it (shades of the Hellespont swim), Sinjin Grimes once again found himself the man of the hour, albeit with blessed little other than his grandmother's largess to show for his pains. He had the good sense, however, to congratulate himself for having once again outwitted the sea and his long-charted destiny. Despite all of Cinnamon's prophesying, by now he had lived enough and thought enough and read books enough to have convinced himself that he and he alone was the master of his fate, and that the ocean wave had not been seen that could take him. No reef would claim the bones of Sinjin Grimes as the shoals off Gay Head had claimed those of his father, Dick Wilson.

SINJIN's initial encounter with the schoolmistress of the Free School on the evening of his second day in town got off to an unfortunate start. Since he and Mat had taken on some bully fellows at the Headless Anne only half an hour before, it was not his best foot that the captain put forward when he interrupted Hattie Duckworth by noisily banging on her front door as she went about her ritual preparations for bed.

"Hold your rumpus, blockhead!" she snapped, making her way carefully across the rag rug to find him swaying on her stoop with a cut lip and a nasty bump on his head. A beribboned hatbox dangled from one slack hand.

"Ahoy, Snug Harbor," he said in a voice slightly slurred, tipping his cap. "What o'clock, matey?"

"The Lord in His time!" Hat exclaimed, snatching him by his lapels and dragging him in quickly before Mrs. Grisby across the street could make out the identity and inebriated state of her visitor.

"Well, I swan, if you ain't a sight," Hat began, "and I don't mean for sore eyes, neither. Look at him, please, Lord. No sooner back than he's brawlin' like a bargeman."

She clucked over him like a mother hen as she maneuvered him to the settee and brought the lamp nearer.

"Sit and never stir, consarn ye," she ordered, snatching away the hatbox, and hanging his cap on the peg next to where one of Captain Barnaby's old caps still hung.

She came back with the arnica, a swab, and some bandage, and Sinjin offered himself meekly up to her fussings as she dabbed at his injuries, yanking his head back again as quickly as he would yank it away.

"Plague take it, don't fidget, you big dummox—worse than a schoolgirl, y'are. I won't ask where you've been or who you been travelin' with, 'cause I don't give a spit to know. What I would like to hear is, how it's taken you two whole days t'come and say hello to your Aunt Hat."

He dropped his gaze, unable to face her snapping blue eyes, and mumbled a feeble excuse about having been kept occupied by his grandmother.

"I'm an old lady, don't matter t'me," Hat vowed, "but you could give a thought to Georgie, couldn'tcha? Well, *couldn't*cha?" She paused, gave him a frown, then went on. "Durn yer seagoin' hide, Singe, you haven't changed a lick s'far as I can see, for all you're a decade older." Finished with her bandaging, she put aside her medicaments. "That cut wants stitches, Singe."

"No, no, Matty'll see to it. He can baste it up well enough."

"He's had practice aplenty, I'll wager."

"You haven't said—how *is* Georgie?"

"She's well—how should she be?" She stopped as the latch clicked on the gate outside.

"Hush, here she is," she said as Georgiana's firm step sounded on the slates.

"Lordy! It's you!" Georgiana exclaimed as she came through the door. Her face lighted with pleasure, then quickly clouded. The sight of him, smugly lolling on Hat's settee, with his bandaged wounds, his cocky devil-may-care demeanor, set Georgiana's eyes to blazing, and she felt a sudden sense of injustice that after more than ten years away he should have so unceremoniously deposited himself on her doorstep. "Well, Aunt Hat, I see the bad penny has turned up again," she said starchily.

"I expect I better go put the kettle on," said Hat, displaying a rare instance of tact.

"Hullo, George," Sinjin said, sheepishly rising to stand in the glare of her anger. "Did you miss me?"

"I can't say that I did." Turning away from him she asked, "Did you collect your wounds here or did you bring them back with you?"

"Got 'em at the Headless. I was provoked."

"You are easily provoked, Captain."

"Not for my own part, permit me to say. We were busy defending a lady's name."

"How gallant of you. I hope she merits it."

Sinjin cocked an amused brow. "Oh, I'd say she does. A female of no small repute."

She resisted the temptation to lash out at him again, to accuse him of she knew not which crimes against mankind and herself in particular, but the captain was not so far gone as not to perceive the fact that she was peeved, and he made no further attempts at humor. Instead he picked up the hatbox and grinned as he tendered his peace offering. When she refused to accept his gift he put her hands around the box and urged her to look inside. "Go on, George, open it, it won't bite you."

Sitting again, he watched as she undid the ribbon and slipped off the paperboard lid. From amid folds of crushed paper she extricated an elegant bonnet, a genuine leghorn straw of the finest Italian manufacture.

"Oh my, isn't it pretty!" she exclaimed, flushing with embarrassment at such unlooked-for attention. "But I don't see how I could ever wear it—it's much too nice."

"So it is. But not too nice for you." Hearing his words she glanced abruptly at him. His voice had lost its raillery, it was soft and gentle, and against her will it pleased her to hear it.

"Well, put it on, for pity's sakes," said Aunt Hat as she carried in the tea tray. "Let's see how you look."

"Oh, not like this," Georgiana protested. "I need my best go-to-meeting dress."

"Nonsense." Sinjin got up and settled the bonnet on her head and did up the purple ribbons. "Wear that on Sunday and set the town agog."

"He's right, Georgie," Hat agreed. "Well—there's two cups for ye. Looks like the captain could use a spot o' tea, so I'll just say good night and steal to m'bed. Two's comp'ny, three's the many-headed Hydra." She drew up in front of Sinjin and gave him a stiff glare from behind her spectacles.

"Welcome home, Dick. I only hope you brought home more horse sense than you made off with," she said, and bobbed away.

"Good night, Mehatibel, my darling," Sinjin replied, "and flights of angels sing thee to thy rest." With elaborate ceremony he ushered her to her door, where he seized her around the waist and bussed her cheek.

"Unhand me, you great ape!" she shrieked, batting at him but enjoying the attention all the same. Despite her resentment, Georgiana was forced to smile. Hat looked so small and helpless, with her bare toes sticking out from under the hem of her night dress, and the stray wisps of white hair protruding from beneath her nightcap. When Hat had shut her door, Georgiana returned the bonnet to its box and began putting away the bandages and ointments. Drawing in his cheeks, Sinjin watched her, but remained silent.

When she sat down on the settee, he placed the hatbox on her lap, as if bargaining for no further criticism, then lowered himself beside her, hooking a boot over one knee and folding his arms across his chest.

"We heard you lost your ship. I'm sorry," she said, taking up the teapot and filling the cups. "Bad luck, wasn't it?"

"Oh yes—very bad luck."

"Imagine, trying to close-haul a Chinese junk all that distance. Who but you?"

"Mm. Who but me indeed?" He tasted his tea, then angled a glance over his shoulder.

"If you're looking for something more muscular, Captain, we're fresh out, I'm afraid. Drink the tea, it's good for you."

A small silence fell between them, until Sinjin set down his cup and took her hand in his. "Are you happy, George? Are you?"

"Yes, quite, thank you."

He touched her chin. "Truth? You can't draw the wool over this old ram's eyes, you know."

In spite of her annoyance with him she found herself smiling at the familiar glint she saw in his eyes. The look between them held for a beat, then fractured. He jammed his fists into his pockets and pushed out his lower lip pensively.

"George?"

"Yes?"

"Do you ever hear anything? Any news of—?"

"You're speaking of Aurora, I imagine."

He nodded.

"Yes, an occasional letter. She and Henry are in Italy just now, I think. They enjoy that country."

"Do 'they,' for a fact?" His tone was tart as alum. For another moment neither spoke. Then, sighing, he lit a cigar and engineered a change in subject matter.

"Tell me something about this school you've started," he said. "By the yellow god, George, you do relish hard work."

"I'm not complaining."

"They're not going to let you get away with it, you know; my esteemed relations and their friends. They'll stop you one way or the other, or they'll dish up your pretty head on a silver platter with an apple in your mouth."

"I've been expecting some new maneuver. In fact it's overdue. But if they think I'm going to bang my head, they're mistaken, and you can tell them I said so. I'll show the lot of them!"

His voice was soft and thoughtful as he regarded her. "George . . ." he murmured. "Georgie . . . Georgiana . . ."

She gave him a cross look. "Yes? What is it? And don't you *dare* to patronize me, Sinjin Grimes!"

"Is that the reason you're doing this thing? To show them? Because if you are—I don't care if Electra Warburton put you up to it or not, I don't care if Bobby Talcott's giving you the money—"

"It's not only Granddaddy, many people have been generous," she protested, "including your own grandmother—to say nothing of your wonderful brother-in-law, Luke, who, may I remind you, can hardly afford to donate funds. So I propose we end this discussion right now. I'm sorry you don't approve, but we'll just have to try to struggle along without you."

His eyes were sad, his voice husky. "Georgie, don't go on with it. Don't."

"Why not?"

"It's not a sound idea."

"And I suppose sailing a wallow-bottomed junk halfway round the world was?"

"Obviously it wasn't. But that's different. Anyway, I hoped you'd be pleased to see me, maybe even proud that I survived another wreck."

"Proud! The day you do anything to make *me* proud of you is the day I'll—oh, I don't know what I'll do!" When he laid a hand on her shoulder she sprang up and began pacing nervously. "More than ten years gone by, ten blessed years, and you haven't changed a whit! You're still the same foolish, stargazing boy mooning over—over things you can't have!"

"Don't say it, George." The pain in his voice pulled her up short. "I just swung my hammock and stowed my locker, so let's not have that sort of talk again."

"Why not, it's written all over your face. You still think life's dealt you a cheap hand, and you're determined to suffer as much as you can manage. You come here and almost the first words out of your mouth are 'What's the latest of Aurora?' I hoped by this time you'd have returned to your senses, but if you could have her sitting in that chair this very minute you'd darn well do it. You and your palpitant heart! Can't you get it through your head that all that's done and gone and is best forgot? Remembering's not going to help. You've got to forget! You can't continually look back, no one can!" He stretched his legs out but she merely stepped over them and continued pacing. "What a waste you are," she went on. "Haven't you learned anything?"

"Not so's you'd notice, I guess."

"Don't be impudent. Everyone says the wickedest things about you. You're a smuggler and a drunk, and there was talk about the yellow trade, too."

"Oh yes, off to the tin mines by the hundred head. Surely you don't believe that. Do you? Do you really think so ill of me?" He looked into her eyes. "Ah yes, you do, I can see it in your face. Well, I'm a villain, there you have it."

"Oh you!"

She started away but he drew her back on the settee beside him. "George, George," he said coaxingly, "after all this time, with you here and me half a world away, have I come home only to quarrel with you?" He reached out and took her hands and held them, and again, suddenly, his voice was soft and husky. "Come, this isn't for us—is it? We're too good friends, you and I. And surely you know that all the time I was away you were never far out of my thoughts. It's true—I think of you so often, especially when I'm at sea. It's funny but—the thought of you, it always soothes me, sometimes it even seems to calm the waves. I mean it, George, no joke." He spoke with such a genuine earnestness that she was touched. She was like his grandmother—he could always get around her; yet the somberness in his eyes told her he meant what he was saying. He leaned over and pecked her cheek. "Friends?" he asked soberly.

She looked at him for a moment, then smiled. "Yes, I suppose . . . yes, friends, always," she said, as if against her better judgment.

"I'd hate it if we weren't, you know. After all these years." Suddenly he grinned at her. "And still some jammoke hasn't come along and snatched you up for a wife. My god, don't these dolts know a good thing when they see it?"

She flushed again. "I really don't think that's any of your business."

"You ought to, you know," he insisted. "You're made for marriage and a home, children, some good fellow who loves you. Who's got a good job and who could support you, keep you happy."

"Well, thank you for your concern, Captain Grimes. I'm beholden. I really don't know how I've managed without you all these years."

"Don't mock me, George. I *am* concerned."

"I'm sure you are." Her softness hardened to scorn again. "You're concerned with so many things that don't concern you, Captain—you always have been. Learning that I'm experiencing certain difficulties in my work—minor ones, and all thanks to the Grimeses at that—you now feel it incumbent on you to offer a dose of that sage Oriental wisdom of yours, which is that I must close the doors to my school, as if the whole business were simply the silly whim of some foolish and improvident spinster, and get married. Well, Captain Grimes, you needn't be concerned over me, and I don't need anyone—you or anyone else—to tell me what to do in life!"

"Georgie, will you listen one damn minute?"

"No, I will *not* listen! I'm done listening to you. Now will you kindly just leave?" Her eyes sparked and she tossed her chin in defiance of him. "And you can take *that* with you," she added, indicating the bonnet. "I don't want it."

"Oh for Christ's sake, Georgiana. Will you stop this nonsense and behave yourself?"

"I said *I don't—want—it!*" Her arm swung out and she swept hat and box from the table, and when they struck the floor she gave each in turn a lusty kick. He looked from them to her, then shrugged.

"Give it to your hired girl, then."

"*I'm* my hired girl, darn you! And now, Captain Grimes, just go!"

"All right, I will, damn it. But not before I tell you who I was fighting over tonight. It was *you!*"

"Me?"

"Yes, you and your damn school. Because some jackass opened his big fat word-hole to say your students were nothing but a bunch of dummies— and you were the greatest dummy of all for even trying to teach them."

"Thank you kindly, Captain Grimes, that was very gallant, I'm sure, but you needn't leap so readily to my defense—I'm perfectly capable of looking after myself. Such people don't scare me."

"That's all very well, but a word to the wise—"

"Is sufficient. I've read *Poor Richard* too. And now, if you'll excuse me, I believe I have had more than sufficient of your brilliant conversation. I long for my bed, so let me say good night."

"Very well. I hope I won't have to say I told you so."

"You won't. I wish you good night." She marched to the door, threw it open, and stood back. As he brushed past her, he dared her wrath by giving her cheek a friendly peck, then danced out the door before she could strike him. Since he merely closed it behind him, she hastened to open it again and give it a good slam. On the windowsill Murray Hill raised a sleepy head and gazed on her with sphinxlike yellow eyes, twitching his long whiskers and silently wondering how the race of humans could behave in such ridiculous ways.

17

Among the Groves Of Academe

IN NO TIME AT ALL it had been made abundantly clear to the people of Pequot Landing that the Sinjin Grimes who had come up out of China aboard the red junk was not the man who had fled the place over ten years before fast upon the heels of a woman married to another man. And indeed, how should he have been, when he was that many years older and when the windward forces that had worked on him in the interim included every sort of debauchery and vice?

These days the sun seldom shone upon the captain's countenance much before noon, until which hour he kept to his room and even to his bed. Usually the social disrepair from the night before took far longer to put to rights than in a more youthful period, and when he had set foot to floor, a hair-of-the-dog (usually one of Sallie's Flips) was not long in reaching his gullet. One good turn deserving another, it wanted several friendly libations more before he could stomach the thought of solid sustenance. He had also become an habitual user of opium—in this, at least, the rumors seemed true. Taken at first to ease the violent headaches that had afflicted him ever since the night so long ago when he and Priam Talcott had tangled in the Hundred, and Cinnamon Comorra had felled him with the cuspidor, the stuff had become almost as necessary to him as drink.

The sunny, lighthearted humor once so characteristic of him now was dimmed, and in its place lowered a kind of sardonic wit, a biting cynicism and honed sarcasm. The bright, flashing grin was seldom seen, a definite cleft had formed between his dark brows, inducing an almost perpetual scowl, while the dandyish mustache he had grown barely disguised the disdainful downward curve of his lips.

But if it was impossible for the captain to take up the raveled threads of a previous existence in Pequot, if these days he avoided Burning Bush, swearing he would sooner sleep in jail than under Zion Grimes's roof, he did well enough. His bed at the Hundred was soft and warm, the grub from Sallie's kitchen highly palatable, her wines decidedly potable, and as he explained, he could come and go by the back stairs without attracting attention. Not a bad notion, given his profligate habits, thought Miss Rachel, saddened to see the apple of her eye spoiled, yet not entirely ready to believe it rotten to the core.

However he might deny it, to himself or to others, this period of general laxity and sluggishness was to him a welcome respite from the complexities and paradoxes, the exotic brilliance and corruption of life in the Far East. From these, Pequot, where existence was measured in fence rails and sabbaths, in fresh-baked cherry tarts and blueberry pies, was a refuge, though he scorned its humble conventions and, in the evenings, sorely mocked them, holding court at his old corner table at the tavern, spinning yarns of the South China Coast to whoever lingered to listen.

In one respect, however, Sinjin resembled his old self: having failed to persuade Georgiana to renounce the Free School for her own good, he now plunged wholeheartedly into the fray on her behalf. Damning the antiabolitionists for a pack of milksops and philistines, he embarked on a personal crusade, standing up at the tavern and daring anyone who took exception to the school to come and invite him out. And one morning, nearly two weeks after his return to Pequot Landing, Georgiana looked up from First Kings—she was in the middle of Bible-reading class—to find the captain standing at the head of the stairs. She blinked in surprise, so spanking-fresh and neatly turned out did he look, with combed hair, polished boots, a pressed set of blues, and a boiled shirt, his mien sober and sheepish, even contrite.

"Good morning, Mistress Ross," he began, adopting a mock-serious attitude. "I do believe you said visitors were welcome to your schoolroom." He looked around, noticing but not recognizing Posie Talcott, who, now that the spring term at the Seminary had ended, had taken full charge of the youngest pupils.

"We had not heard that you were given to early rising, Captain," Georgiana said. "Nevertheless, we're pleased to welcome you," she added, comprehending that this visit was by way of appeasement after their recent differences at Snug Harbor. "Do come in."

"Thank you, Mistress Ross," Sinjin returned, humorously echoing her formality. "I have been meaning to call round for some time."

"Indeed?" She indicated an empty chair. "I pray you—please be seated, Captain Grimes. Girls, say good morning to Captain."

"Good morning Captain Grimes," they chorused obediently, dazzled by his smile and courtly air.

At her desk toward the back of the room Rose Mills sat as though transfixed, her eyes taking in every inch of this piratical-looking Captain Grimes of whom she'd heard so much. Yet, what *was* it about him . . . ? Something plucked the chord of remembrance in her mind, and she frowned, trying to fix it in her thoughts. It was almost as if she'd already met him, as if she knew him . . .

Like the polite fellow he was playing today, Sinjin sat with his hands neatly folded at one of the empty desks. With a nonchalant wave to his nieces, Chloe and Phoebe Haverstraw, he directed his look from one face to another, as if searching for the familiar ones. As his eye moved among Georgiana's sober-looking pupils, Rose, through whose busily clicking brain a sharp white light of recognition had suddenly blazed, clutched her handkerchief and hastily dropped her gaze, then put her slate up to her nose. Frozen in her place, she felt the worst kind of creeping horror. Lord Godamighty! She prayed, don't let him see me, don't let him remember. But *she* had suddenly remembered—this visitor of Miss Georgiana's was none other than the dark stranger who'd been her lover in the graveyard that night, the man whose lips and hands and other anatomical portions she'd known if only briefly. She felt herself grow hot and cold by turns as his dark, piercing eyes lingered on her. After another minute he unfolded himself from his chair and slowly approached her.

"And whom have we here?" he drawled, cocking his eyebrow as he looked down at her. She trembled and nibbled her lip.

"Tell the captain your name, please, Rose," Georgiana said kindly, moving up the aisle to her. Rose opened her mouth but no sound issued forth.

"Captain Grimes, allow me to present to you our very first student at the Free School," Georgiana said, taking Rose's hand to reassure her. "Her name is Rose Mills. She is also the freedwoman you may have heard about—the young person Old Bobby Talcott purchased from the slave catchers. Stand up, Rose, and offer your hand to Captain Grimes."

Like some poor dazed thing Rose managed to struggle to her feet and stuck out her hand as instructed. At the instant Sinjin's flesh made contact with her own, she began to tremble and in a moment her eyes rolled up into her head and she swooned.

"Ooh!" whispered the other girls. "She fainted. Rose done fainted!"

Georgiana moved Sinjin aside and knelt beside the prostrate girl, fanning her and calling for water. Hutta, who was closest to the bucket, came with the dipper and held it to Rose's lips. When she'd sipped a bit and could sit up again she averted her face and asked to be excused.

Taking no chances, Georgiana called for Bessie Willotts and Candelmass Goff to see Rose safely back to Kingdom Come. When order had been restored in the classroom, the schoolmistress apologized to their visitor, then invited him to return to his chair before resuming the day's lesson.

As Sinjin sat, his eye again lit on the girl in the corner with her golden curls and her freshly pressed embroidered apron falling over her knees.

He looked questioningly to Georgiana. "And this young lady?—I don't believe we've met."

The girl's dimpled smile seemed familiar. "You may not know me, Captain, but I most assuredly know you. I'm Posie. Posie Talcott."

"Good lord—*Posie? You* are that little child?"

Posie dimpled winningly. "I *was* that little child, Captain," she said with mock gravity. *"Now* I am the grown-up person you see before you."

"By the yellow god, you certainly are!" he exclaimed in amazed recognition.

"Posie teaches our littlest ones," Georgiana put in. "Including Phoebe."

Sinjin stepped to his niece and picked her up and gave her a kiss, then set her down again.

The other girls exchanged looks that said they were jealous of Phoebe and that they wished they too had an "Uncle Sinjin" to make a fuss over them.

Sinjin generously spread his grin around the room. "I'll be uncle to you all, if you like," he said bravely.

"Oh, but they must not say Uncle Sinjin to you," Georgiana declared. "It wouldn't be fitting."

"Why not? To tell the truth, I rather like the idea of having so many nieces. But please don't let me interrupt the class. What are you all learning today?"

"We were engaged in reading from the Bible. Though I doubt such matters would interest you overmuch." In her smile was the hint of the gauntlet flung, a tinge of defiance, but he refused to take it up.

"I'm sure you're right there, ma'am," he replied meekly enough. He turned to the class and quickly quoted: " 'For the lips of a strange woman drop as an honeycomb, and her mouth is smoother than oil: But her end is bitter as wormwood, sharp as a two-edged sword.' Proverbs, young ladies, chapter five, verses three and four."

An admiring murmur stirred among the older girls. He crinkled his brows and smiled somewhat more broadly.

His mischievous expression was not lost on Georgiana. "I think, young ladies," she said, "that Captain Grimes may have been doing a bit of biblical brushing-up before he came among us."

Sinjin shot her an easy grin. "To the contrary, Mistress Ross. I have it all here." He laid a hand solemnly over his heart.

"Then, Captain Grimes, for an avowed nonbeliever, you have an astonishing grasp of Scripture," she allowed. "How pleased Deacon Wandsworth would be to have you in his Sunday-school class."

"Ah yes. A stalwart little rodent, our Deacon Willie, but I had much rather be enrolled in *your* class, Miss Ross." At this sally, the girls tittered and one of them whispered to her companion.

"Speak up, Loftie Tando," Georgiana said. "What did you say?"

"I was askin', is that the sailor what's ship sunk that he be sailin' clear from China?"

"The very one, Loftie," Sinjin confessed, giving his cap a jaunty twirl. "Now which Tando would you be? Not one of Acre Tando's? By the flaming pitchfork, I guess you are. Your father and I used to scrap like the devil. You tell him Wing-o Grimes sends regards."

Drowning in shyness, the girl murmured something and ducked her head.

Once again Sinjin addressed the class. "I must confess, however, I fear I would not do well in this school of yours. I would soon be wearing the dunce cap." He looked around with a comic leer, making the girls titter again. "And, pray, where *is* your dunce cap, Teacher?"

"We do not have a dunce cap in our classes. If a pupil does not know her lessons, she is the loser, which she will discover quickly enough without having donned some foolish article of headgear. But since our next subject is to be geography, Captain Grimes, and since you are well traveled, possibly you could stay long enough to instruct us in some exotic or enlightening circumstance you may have stumbled across."

He looked closely at her to assess the seriousness of her suggestion, then his teeth flashed under his black mustache. "Ah, Miss Ross, have you not heard that my life has been a wayward one and none too tidy? I fear that the um . . . circumstances I may have 'stumbled across'—as you put it—

along the way might prove somewhat too vivid for such tender buds as these—if you catch my drift."

"Indeed I do, Captain," she replied, smiling now with undisguised amusement. "Yet I can't help wondering if there is not something suitable, some unobjectionable topic on which you could reasonably expound. That is, unless you feel that *all* your exploits are of such character that they do not bear elucidation," she added.

"Not at all," he said expansively. "Perhaps *you* might suggest a topic for discussion, something you yourself may have been curious about. The females of Samoa, for example? Their methods of weaving grass skirts? Their mating dances at the full of the moon? Their . . . love calls . . .?"

"This is a seat of learning, Captain, not a tavern ordinary." Fearing to blush again, Georgiana clung fast to her prim schoolmistress's demeanor. "As you've doubtless heard, young ladies, Captain Grimes has been nearly everywhere and done—nearly everything. Come, Captain, what shall it be? May I suggest Morocco? Stony Arabia? The pirates of Malay, perhaps? A gun battle with the emperor's junks?"

An eager murmur rose among the girls at the words "gun battle," and they turned their faces toward him as he again unfolded himself from his seat and approached Georgiana's desk. "As you wish, Mistress Ross," he said, relishing the moment. "As you wish." Moving aside a stack of papers, he sat on the corner of the desk and took the papier-mâché globe onto his lap.

"Young ladies," he began, "your schoolmistress and I are old friends, so you must take no notice if we enjoy a bit of badinage with each other. Miss Ross and I attended school together many years ago, right up the street here, although I'm afraid she got all the learning while I received only the dunce cap." As he spoke, easily and with good humor, he made a pass at the globe, which rotated only under protest, and, covering his eyes, he let his fingertip stop it at a random spot. With another comical grimace that caused the girls to giggle again, he peeked under his finger to see what place he had captured.

"Constantinople," he announced, widening his eyes and causing further mirth. "Well, well, good old Constantinople. Of course, we say Istanbul these days. The Golden Crescent. It sits astride the western world and the eastern. Now, teacher, I wonder, what can I tell your gentle young ladies about Constantinople? First, let me assure you all, that city is hardly the sort of place a voyager travels to merely for the fun of it. It is a goodly distance from Pequot Landing, as you can see. What is it like? Well, it has one of the most famous mosques in the world, which used to be the Church of Santa Sophia, built by the Emperor Constantine in 537 A.D. It is the crossroads of the world, for many civilizations and cultures meet there, Christian and Moslem, East and West, is that not so, Miss Ross?"

"Indeed it is. You might even expound a bit further." She smiled at her class. "Captain Grimes is well acquainted with the Golden Crescent. In fact, he has had adventures there, some very wet adventures. What do you think of that, girls?"

"Tell! Tell," came the enthusiastic chorus.

"Yes, by all means, Captain, tell the girls how it was that you swam the famous Hellespont."

Sinjin fiddled with his collar. "I really must demur, teacher."

"But no, we long to hear, don't we, girls?"

"Yes! Yes. The Hella—the Hella!"

"The Hellespont," Georgiana pronounced again. "A very dangerous body of water, rushing from here to here"—she pointed out the Black Sea and the Aegean on the globe—"whose current is—"

"Very swift, very fast. It can easily carry a man to his doom—"

"Just as his tongue may do," Georgiana put in, "if he fails to guard it with prudence. But I feel sure the story of the captain's swim must be most interesting. He was duplicating the accomplishment of Lord Byron, who also performed the feat."

"Not to mention Leander. For love of Hero—and, please recall, Leander drowned."

"Yes, I do recall that fact."

Sinjin related Leander's story, then quickly went on to the anecdote about King Xerxes, who watched his troops build a bridge of boats, then had the waters flogged with chains when they destroyed it.

"Most interesting, Captain," said the schoolmistress, "but why not tell the class your own story?"

"Some other time," he said, setting aside the globe. He tugged at his tie so the ends hung down, then loosened his stock. "I declare, Schoolmistress," he added, tilting his head toward Georgiana, "Mr. Burdin's attic is a touch warm today. I wonder if . . ." Again he cocked that sardonic brow, hinting at some unorthodox action. "Since it *is* so lumpish under these eaves, may I herewith suggest that we move the Free School of Pequot Landing out of doors—just for a little while? Fresh air is always so salubrious anyway, I'm sure you will agree. So why don't we just . . . um? Come along, girls, all of you, and let's continue our talk yonder in the boneyard. A bit of alfresco never hurt anyone."

Before Georgiana could protest, he was coaxing the pupils from their desks, leading them out of the schoolroom, down the stairs and across the street, past the church and into the Ancient Burying Ground, where he invited them to take their ease in the shade of the spreading elm trees, and there on the Fathers' Rise, the hallowed burial mound beneath which lay the ancient bones of Shumackpock, Prince Naqui, and the others of the long defunct Wongunk tribe—as well as those of Abednego Grimes—he began regaling the girls with amusing, offhand, yet consistently stimulating and informative anecdotes on various subjects.

Seated among her fascinated pupils, Georgiana couldn't help marveling at him as he held his audience spellbound with an account of how a murderous horde of Malay pirates had once appeared in their praus, slipping out of the evening mists to attack his nearly undefended vessel as it beat downwind for the Malacca Straits.

Being a thoroughly good actor, Sinjin knew exactly when to get offstage, leaving his audience eager for more, so that Georgiana was obliged to inquire when the captain might again be persuaded to address her pupils in a similar fashion. Having discovered to his surprise how much he had enjoyed his little lecture, he proceeded to offer his services any time in the future, weather permitting.

Thus commenced the famous "cemetery lectures" of Sinjin Grimes, which were to make those first weeks of the summer of 1842 in Pequot Landing so memorable. Inaugurating yet another new era in local education, on several afternoons a week Georgiana's pupils would convene in the grave-yard, where the lecturer would informally address them on such diverse topics as the Pacific sea slug—bêche-de-mer they were called—a favored delicacy of the Chinese; English romantic poetry, including Byron; Mother Goose; the nautical phenomenon known as St. Elmo's fire; the man-eating appetites of the Bengal tiger; the sea passage flying fish and dolphins; the discovery of Antarctica by Nat Palmer, who hailed from Stonington, sixty miles away; and even slavery as practiced in ancient Rome.

Before long, these informed talks began attracting a loose-knit gathering of other folk, curious villagers who quickly became devotees of the ad hoc lectures, forgoing whatever tasks they might have in hand to slip into the cemetery to hear what Captain Grimes had to tell of today. Milehigh Jenckes would wander over from the tavern, Warren Burdin would leave his seed store safely in the hands of Ambo Buck, Izz Quoile would hightail it hot and floury from the bakery, Maude Ashley was there, never to miss a word; the same applied to Hattie Duckworth, and through Hat's urgings, some of the almshouse ladies were soon in regular attendance. Helen Haverstraw came equipped with paper and pencil, making copious notes, and Luke when he was able. More came. The blacksmith and the barber, Syd Smyth and Andy Cleves, hung WILL RETURN IN AN HOUR signs on their doors and stepped around, and even Kneebone Apperbee and Stix Bailey, learning that on a particular day Sinjin was going to discourse on navigating a ship around Cape Horn, abandoned their posts in front of Archibald's store to ankle over and grab some turf.

Why, Captain Grimes was better than a lyceum speaker, old Adah Coverly from the Brick Farm declared as, perched atop a flat table stone cross-legged, like a tailor at his basting, the captain described for his audience the marvels of the Great Sphinx at Giza, relived his trials and experiences as an Arab slave in North Africa, and retraced his steps along the old Silk

Road, across the deserts of Arabia and the Hindu Kush, through Afghanistan and Tartary, down through Outer Mongolia into the heart of old Cathay. All eyes were on him, all ears attentive. He demonstrated to his auditors the remarkable capabilities of the Bactrian camel and the sportive habits of the Antarctic penguin, provided an Oriental recipe for concocting a savory dish from baked dog, dwelled on the homeopathic uses of sassafras and camphor, the arcana of botanizing and collecting nature specimens (with interesting notes regarding the person of Pliny the Elder, who'd uncovered the tenderest crocus blooms amid the Alpine snows), and was sometimes inclined to recite at length from the prose of Thomas Carlyle, the verse of Virgil, the plays of Shakespeare. John Milton was often at hand; John Whittier, too. Through these and similar orations boys like Jeffrey-Amherst Priest first learned of Michelangelo; it was the salt's rousing words that caused Josh Tillforth to make up his mind to run away to sea, and Hutta Teal and Easter Dawn to take up botanizing with an utter seriousness of purpose.

Each time, close by Sinjin sat his adoring niece Phoebe. "He's my own darling uncle" her rapt expression seemed to say, and when he finished and hopped down from his place the child would be the first to reach him, and he would pick her up and perch her on his shoulder like a trophy while he spoke with the older members of his enthusiastic audience, which by now included even the Abbé Margeaux, who, whenever someone alerted him, would drive his shay into town to hear the captain speak, and a good many members of the Noontide Club, not the least of these being Old Bobby Talcott himself.

"Why d'you give the rascal the time of day?" demanded Great-Aunt Blanche, outraged to think any Talcott would pay the slightest attention to a Grimes, especially to a renegade like this leading light of the Macao smuggling trade.

With his usual mildness Bobby replied, "My dear, you'd be surprised the clever and inventive notions that young man's got. I vow, the Porch of Athens was nothing to our Burying Ground, and I count myself fortunate that I am on hand to learn something of our friend the gray ottsterwaddy."

"I beg your pardon?"

"Never mind, it's very rare. But the captain once saw one. He's even better than the Talking Head. Hey-ho." With a chuckle of amusement, off he went to find his place among Miss Ross's pupils and be instructed by the grandson of his old adversary, Abednego Grimes.

"He has a head on his shoulders," Bob said to Georgiana one day. "Unless he's just weaving up whole cloth. Sailors are notorious yarn spinners, as we know. They have their own warp and woof."

Georgiana regarded Bob suspiciously, until she saw the humorous light in his eyes. "He does speak well, doesn't he?"

"He's got a silver tongue, all right, but it's of some interest how he piques the attention of those girls and young women. Mesmer himself could do no better. Here's a thought, my dear," he added. "After the captain is done speaking, why not send round the hat on behalf of the school?"

Georgiana clapped her hands.

"Why, Granddaddy, what a splendid idea! I'm surprised I didn't think of it myself."

Hattie cackled when she heard. "Leave it to Old Bobby to come up with an idea like that!" she exclaimed when Mat Kindu's first circulating of the hat netted the school fund four whole dollars. Having Mat collect contributions was a masterstroke, his sinister appearance leading some to remark—in jest, of course—that if they did not ante up they might be murdered in their beds.

THERE was one of Georgiana's pupils, however, who was in a constant state of distress, her poor brain all in a swirl, her body all atremble with ungovernable—and unmentionable—yearnings. After fainting dead away in Georgiana's class, the Talcotts' hired girl could sleep hardly a wink. She was too nervous, too full of tempestuous and ungovernable thoughts. Having recognized *him,* she was left to wonder if *he* in turn had recognized *her.* Surely he must have, he had eyes to see with, didn't he? And what sport he would be making of that, what shame and calumny was even now being heaped upon the innocent name of Rose Mills! Worse, what would the Talcotts do when the story of the disgraceful activities in the graveyard reached Mab's delicate ears, as it seemed likely to?

During several days following the humiliating encounter in the classroom Rose had feigned illness, giving her complexion a spurious pallor with a dusting of flour swiped from the pantry bin, eating next to nothing, and in general offering as miserable and pathetic a picture of a helpless invalid as she could concoct. "How are you today?" Mab would ask, only to have the girl croak at her, "Mighty po'ly, ma'am." So sly was her counterfeit that she managed to elicit the sympathy of Dr. Standish himself, who prescribed gruel, thin broths, and plenty of bed rest, saying the patient was plainly overwrought. Rose took full advantage. It afforded her profound satisfaction when, in consequence of the doctor's visit, she was instructed to remain in her room, where she was waited on hand and foot by Burdy Tando. But when Burdy had gone, Rose, amorously clutching her pillow to her breast, recalled details of that nocturnal skirmish in the graveyard with the celebrated captain, and she longed to see him again, to gaze on his dark lean face, to hear the voice whose heady resonances had sent such a thrill through her. Yet still she quailed at the thought of actually facing him again, afraid of what he might do or say to embarrass her.

On the second day of Rose's "illness," Posie had come in to visit with her and talk over the captain's lecture, describing for her the sensation he had created, and how there were further enchantments to be unveiled. "You really must try to get well quickly so you don't miss any more," she urged. "Why—what's the matter, Rose, you're not worse, are you? Your hands are trembling ever so much."

Rose's heart thudded under her nightdress, since she feared it would be her dark secret that was to be unveiled, and after Posie had gone she even went so far as to map out an escape from her misery, planning to run away in the dead of night rather than be shamed by the terrible truth. She strayed not a foot. Where would she go, whom could she run to? So she threw herself on fate's mercy and resolved to stay, praying that some miracle would summon the captain out of town before he stumbled across her again—or that the earth might open up and swallow him whole.

And meanwhile she would eke out her truancy, making sure that the dreaded encounter should not occur under Georgiana's prying nose. But of course the day came when the word "malingerer," previously unknown to Rose, was uttered, and as a result, on Mab's order she was returned to the classroom, and forthwith found herself being guided by Posie toward the Ancient Burying Ground.

As they came upon the graveyard and the congregation, already comfortably reposing about the green slopes of the Fathers' Rise, Posie pointed to a place. "Come, Rose, we'll sit over there." Presently the Haverstraw girls came up to throw themselves into Posie's arms and give her hugs and kisses, and they acknowledged Rose with friendly greetings, and inquiries concerning her health. The captain was not yet in evidence, but a glance around told her that the lectures had become momentous events: the scene was such a gay one, just like a holiday outing, with nothing of school or studiousness about it. Then Phoebe cried, "Here comes Uncle Sinjin!" and, daring a glance, Rose was awed by the glamorous figure of the great Captain Grimes threading his way through the crowd, in company with his yellow-skinned henchman and Hermie Light. Spying Posie and his nieces, he tossed a jaunty wave, then, to Rose's consternation, headed straight toward them. He swooped Phoebe up and kissed her, Chloe as well, and greeted Posie warmly. Then his eyes fell on Rose.

"Well, see who's here. Quite recovered, I trust, Miss Mills?" he said in a slightly mocking tone that both excited and alarmed her. Her reply choked in her throat.

"Say good morning, Rose," Posie prompted, and put Rose's hand out to the captain, who took it and gave it a formal shake. "A very warm hand, young lady, we must hope you haven't a cold heart to go with it."

The others giggled while the mortified Rose, aware of dozens of eyes on her, ducked her head.

Sinjin's laugh rang out as, carrying Phoebe on his shoulder, he strode to the top of the Rise, where he waited for his "class" to quiet itself and began to address them—not in a pretentious sort of way, not at all like a school-teacher, but merely as a person welcoming his guests at a party. He made a joke or two, then amid the laughter tilted his cap back on his head, flung his jacket aside, and hopped onto the table stone. He had not got far with his remarks, however, before he suffered an unexpected interruption. A group of late arrivals, females all, made their way noisily into the graveyard, chattering away and feigning total ignorance of the disturbance they were deliberately causing. Among them were the redoubtable Flora Ritchie and her ally Mrs. Wandsworth, and they proceeded up the Rise until they came abreast of Sinjin seated on the table stone. All eyes followed the progress of the intruders, who gradually fell silent. Flora Ritchie tossed her head in defiance. "I s'pose a body can talk, if she cares to," she proclaimed for everyone to hear. "We're not in church, after all. This burying ground's free to all."

Her declaration caused Sinjin to flash his grin. "As we all know, fair lady," he said. "Come and join us, do, and your companions as well."

"That'll be the day!" snapped Flora. "We have no wish to associate with the likes of you, *Captain* Grimes. Frankly, I'd rather die!"

"Oh please, dear and kind madam—not here," he murmured with a humorous twitch of the lip. "Yet—if you were to do so, only think of the happy convenience—" He motioned toward a nearby headstone.

His joke flattened Flora like a pancake, and in short order she and her companions retired from the field.

When the intruders were gone Sinjin resumed his lecture amid nods of approval, and Rose struggled valiantly to follow the thread of his discourse. But, over the next three-quarters of an hour, as he continued speaking—what was he talking about? Something to do with icebergs?—with the sun shining and the tall white church steeple piercing the sky, with familiar faces picked out among the crowd (there was Aunt Hat, there Milehigh Jenckes, there the doctor, there the constable, there Helen Haverstraw briskly scrib-bling on a tablet on her knees), with her whole being suffused with the same languid, molasses-y feeling she'd felt before, with a growing awareness of a tingling that rippled clear to her fingertips, with a roaring in her ears as of a cataract plunging through some rocky gorge, with acute terror and unbearable pleasure, and a rapturous ecstasy she was not experienced enough to recognize for what it was, during a little talk on the aborigines of New Guinea, Rose Mills fell headlong in love.

By the time the captain had concluded his lecture, when he tipped his cap onto his brow and the applause rained from the crowd of listeners, she felt squarely trapped. Posie and her friends jumped up, but as Rose tried to stand her legs went soft; she felt she was going to be sick, that at any moment her breakfast must come up.

"What is it, Rose? Are you ill again?" she heard Posie asking.

She shook her head and forced herself to remain upright, her eye drawn like a magnet toward the captain, now surrounded by admirers who chivvied to get close to him.

"I'm not sick," Rose said, and turned away. As she made her way through the crowd, a hand reached out and halted her.

"Hello, Rose," said Bushrod Grimes. He had his coat over his shoulder and wore a pearl-buttoned shirt of the finest Chinese pongee and a ribbon tie. His hat was silk and he had a thick cheroot in his hand. "How've you been?" he inquired, looking her up and down. "Say, you've gained a few pounds—you're a lot solider. They must be feeding you up at Kingdom Come."

Embarrassed by this unexpected but obvious attention, Rose lowered her eyes and spoke in a husky murmur.

"What'd you say? Can't hear you, girl," Rod said.

"It's okay," she managed.

Rod guffawed, and people turned to look. " 'Okay,' she says, living in that big house. I told you, Rose, didn't I? Last winter when we were sleighing I said you'd like it 'round here. But you never sent me a message. And here I've been hankering to see you." When she remained silent he put his face close to hers. " 'S'matter, cat got your tongue?"

"No."

"Maybe you forgot me since that little snowstorm. I been patient all winter, Rosie. Now the roses are in bloom and you haven't come for another ride with me. Must I wait for the next snowfall?"

"I'm late, I have to go," she said, stepping around a gravestone. Rod was quick after her, taking her hand and preventing her from leaving. When she tried to free herself he squeezed her wrist till she winced.

"Don't, that hurts," she said, stifling a cry.

"Let her go."

Rod jumped at the sound of the voice. The captain stood facing his brother, his fingers gently loosening Rod's grip.

"Now then, brother mine, step along lightly for your dinner and leave Georgiana's pupil alone. Hands off."

Rod smirked. "So that's how it is, eh? Hands off for me, hands on for you?"

Sinjin ignored him in favor of the girl. "Pay him no attention, Rose. This sometime relative of mine sometimes harbors bizarre notions." He tipped his hat and grinned. "Glad you could come, Rod, feel free to join us at any time. You might learn a thing or two."

"No chance. You won't be giving your talks much longer," Rod said.

"Say you so? Why is that?"

"You'll see." He stuck his cigar between his teeth and showed his teeth at Rose. "Rosie, my girl, be warned, this fellow's a sizzler with the girls. He'll singe the fuzz right off you. He hasn't been around long enough for you to get a fix on, but you're a smart one, you'll find out. Poor fellow, he can't even sail a ship home without hitting a reef. Two times now—that Chinese junk's in Davy Jones's locker and the *Adele* sits high on the Nag's Head at Saltaire. Well, that's as good a place as any for that jinxed hulk. And I guess we know who jinxed her, too."

"Rod, put a pipe in it."

Rod ignored him. "Women and ships, ships and women, he loses them all. I guess the lady jinxed *him* too. I'm talking about your mistress's daughter, Rose, the eminent Lady Sheffield—"

He got no further. Sinjin's fist shot out, catching Rod on the chin. "*Oww!*" shouted Rod, and the two closed on each other. They tussled, grappling clumsily and landing no blows, until Val Morgan came striding among the graves and elbowed the assailants apart.

"Someone's got to teach you to watch what you say, Rod," Sinjin said, straightening his cravat.

"By hell, I didn't know you were still bewitched by the Talcott wench." Rod rubbed his jaw, then, chuckling, marched off in one direction, while Sinjin left in the other.

For Rose a dark cloud seemed to have scudded across the sun, dimming its light and warmth, leaving her in a cold, gray world, and as she watched the captain's departing back she felt a desperate pang of loneliness. She looked around for Posie, who was nowhere to be seen, and rather than leaving the graveyard by the regular route, she hurried down the far side of the Fathers' Rise, to disappear behind the blackberry bushes and return by the shortcut to Halley's kitchen. But the incident with the captain and his stepbrother had done its work, promoting gossip around the Center that, as if they didn't have enough to argue over, Bushrod and Sinjin Grimes had fallen to quarreling over the Talcotts' hired girl.

THE next episode to take place in the Ancient Burying Ground was even more exciting and provoked even greater comment. Present on this occasion was William Lloyd Garrison, who had driven over from nearby Brooklyn with a party of interested observers from the Anti-Slavery Society, among them the editor's fiancée, a Miss Benson, as well as her father, and the minister from the Baptist church at Jericho, the Reverend Jocelyn. They had joined the influx of villagers who had for thirty minutes been making their way into the cemetery, to arrange themselves among the gravestones, waiting for Captain Grimes to arrive.

Heads craned to see Georgiana Ross, marching primly at the head of her line of pupils as they tripped along the walk in graduated rows, the smallest

and youngest in front, tallest and oldest behind: Bessie Willotts carrying her
baby in a willow-weave basket, and the pale, slender figure of Rose Mills
in a sprig-muslin dress that had once been Posie's.

Since the captain's lectures were being offered for their benefit, they got
to sit closest to the table stone that had become Sinjin's stage, and presently
here he came, striding across from the tavern in company with Mat Kindu
and Milehigh Jenckes, who joined the gathering on the hillside, while Sinjin
moved among his audience, amiably shaking hands and pausing for a word
of greeting here and there.

Georgiana watched him as he spoke with Mr. Garrison and his group.
And though she was pleased and grateful that the editor had again taken time
to visit Pequot on her behalf and focus further attention on the school, she
knew, as did many among the gathering, that the real attraction today was
not the noted abolitionist but Sinjin Grimes. Sinjin's support of the Free
School was not, however, thoroughly positive in its effects, for not only did
the success of his lectures give him a leg up on the proslaveryites, it was
a direct insult to the members of his own family who were such violent
opponents of both abolition and the Free School, and increasingly their
faction had moved to disrupt the proceedings.

Today, however, the crowd seemed to be entirely enthusiastic as the
speaker seated himself atop his table stone and held forth on the subject of
the ancient Greek polis. The greater share of his auditors had never heard
the names Pericles or Xenophon, or knew or even cared until now that
Demosthenes had put pebbles under his tongue to facilitate public orating,
or that Themistocles had kept two wives. But so persuasive were the
captain's words, so engaging his manner, so lively and vivid his vocabulary,
so witty his asides and sallies, so modest yet earnest his entire demeanor, that
all listened attentively, while the little birds sang in the trees and the arcing
sun used the church spire as a sundial, its slender shadow moving by the
quarter hour across the grave-dotted grass.

When he had finished his formal talk, Sinjin changed the subject, and for
the benefit of the out-of-town visitors began to speak about the Free School
of Pequot Landing itself. "Look around you, my friends," he said, raising
his voice as he addressed them. "If you would, be pleased to regard this bevy
of hardworking pupils from Miss Ross's school. Who are they, these scholarly young ladies, you may ask. I shall tell you. Though some are village
girls, my own two nieces, Chloe and Phoebe Haverstraw included, and some
have come from farther afield"—he nodded at the Gilbert sisters and Mary
Feebs—"the larger share of them are the spawn of Mount Lament, of those
unfortunate indigents we Pequotters so readily turn our backs on. These are
their daughters, and yet see how the light of learning has been lit in their
faces. Yes, look at them—No, girls, don't hang your heads, there's no shame
in it, you know. I want these good people all to see what is happening here

with this Free School you are so lucky to be attending, a school provided by the generous contributions of many of the men and women—and children—gathered here today. Now, if you please, let us give our guests one or two examples of the sort of thing you have learned at your book and slate. I want to remind our visitors that with few exceptions, until little more than six months ago not one of these young ladies had had a moment's formal instruction in letters, numbers, history, or language. Now, where shall we begin? Candelmass Goff, let's start with you. Tell the people, if you please, when did Columbus discover America?"

"Fourteen hundred and ninety-two."

Sinjin nodded encouragingly. "And, tell us, please, Loftie Tando, for whose crown and country did he sail?"

"For King Ferdinand and Queen Isabella of Spain."

"And, tell us, Maria Coleman, he voyaged in search of what?"

"A short route to the Indies."

"Indeed he did. And did he find it?"

"No."

"And, Carrie Poole, where did he fetch up?"

"In Hispaniola."

"And, Candelmass, you can answer this, too—how did Columbus fare?"

"He was made Admiral of the Ocean."

"And afterward, Sarah Cleves, what did the king and queen do to him?"

"They put him in chains."

"Thus suffer all gallant explorers, thus does the dog bite the hand that feeds it. Thus we learn: 'Put not your trust in princes.' And where is that written, Hutta Teal?"

"In Psalms. Number one hundred forty-six."

"Well, there we have history, Bible study, and morals each touched upon in turn. Now tell us, Bessie Willotts, you who as I have seen are so quick with your numbers, what's two hundred seventy-five divided by twenty-five?"

Bessie, whose hand was in the basket, keeping her baby quiet, responded quickly enough: "Eleven, Cap'n."

"Very good. Now, Maria, where is the Ultima Thule?"

"In the Arctic."

"What sorts of things are to be found there?"

"Whales."

"What else? come on, everyone together."

"Eskimos!" the girls said, lifting their voices in unison. There was a scattering of applause.

"And in what do they live, these Eskimos?"

"In igloos."

"And of what are igloos made?"

"Ice and snow, ice and snow!"

The girls' faces were alight, and the listeners were filled with a kind of astonished excitement no one would have thought possible.

Now Sinjin rose up on the table stone and spread his arms, embracing the pupils and the gathering at large. "And is the Free School a good thing?" he shouted.

"*Yes!*" they clamored.

"Shall we keep our school?"

"*Yes!*"

"And what will we do with the slaveryites?"

"Run 'em out of town!"

There were cheers and shouts, a general rejoicing in the idea of Georgiana's school, and then a man pushed his way through the crowd and stood angrily facing Sinjin, his wet lip curled in a sneer. "Why don't you all shut up and get out of here?" demanded Ike Bleezer, the village gravedigger.

"What did you say?" returned Sinjin Grimes, staring down at him.

"You heard me!" Ike shoved his red raw mug out at Georgiana, standing close by.

"Welcome, Ike." She greeted him calmly. "It's kind of you to join us."

Ike, who had obviously been sleeping himself sober in the little gardener's hut dug into the side of the Fathers' Rise, belched loudly and shifted bleary eyes. He was somewhat unsteady on his feet as he boldly surveyed what he obviously took to be invaders of his own personal domain.

"This is a pack of whores and niggers you got here," he rasped, his eye fixing the solemn faces of the girls. "Get 'em outta this place. This is my graveyard an' I want 'em gone pronto."

Sinjin hopped down from his stone perch and addressed the objector in a reasonable tone. "It's a public place, Ike, not a private cemetery." He sniffed the air. "Mmn . . . Ike," he murmured, "I do believe you've had a nip at the keg, hm? Or is that just your natural aroma?"

"You better button your lip, sailor, we don't need you here." He staggered around, darting sullen glances at Sinjin, Georgiana, her girls. "Yer just askin' fer trouble, the whole lot of you," he growled fiercely.

"Oh, go dig yourself a hole, Ike Bleezer, and crawl in it." This from Hattie Duckworth, who had jumped up to give him what-for, earning hearty applause.

"You'll all be sorry one of these days. This school business is a lot of foolishness. Ain't no use t'teach these brown-skin darky sluts." Ike's voice was so loud that Bessie's baby began to wail; the mother picked it up from the basket and held it against her breast, where it groped for the nipple and began to suckle.

"As for you, Cap'n," Bleezer went on, "whyn't you just take up yer sailin' again."

Then, as if he felt he was obligated to do so, he swung a clumsy fist at Sinjin, who made an adroit sidestep, parried, and Bleezer tumbled backward, striking his head against a stone. He lay there dazed and no one made an effort to help him up until another figure made an unexpected appearance in the cemetery: Priam Talcott, who for some weeks had been away from Hartford on business, traveling to several southern ports, and who had therefore missed the advent of the cemetery lectures, was seen making his way among the gravestones. Striding up to the fallen Ike, he thrust out a hand and helped him to his feet.

"Are you hurt?" he asked.

"I got me a bump on my head."

"Well, go soak it!" shouted a raucous voice. Laughter and guffaws followed.

"You'd best go tend it, then," Priam said in a stern voice. Bleezer blinked stupidly and gingerly felt his injury. "Who're you?" he demanded.

"I'm Priam Talcott. You know me."

"Then get all these damn nigger lovers off my property, won't you? They got no business here."

"Yes they have. This is village property, and they are listening to a speaker, and you're interrupting. So you just come along with me and we'll let Captain Grimes continue his talk."

Without more ado he led Ike down the slope to the hut under the hill. The men, women, and children on the rise above broke out in an animated babble. No one could imagine a more unexpected happenstance than to have Priam Talcott bow to Sinjin Grimes. Moreover, no sooner had Sinjin resumed his remarks atop the table stone than Priam emerged from the hut and sat down on the grass where he too gave ear to the speaker's closing remarks, and this was a thing no villager had ever thought to see in this lifetime. Then, while the gathering was breaking up and Sinjin was accepting the congratulations of William Garrison and his party, John Perry, president pro tem of the Noontide Club, stepped up to invite Captain Grimes to join the members across the street for a pint, and so, while Georgiana took Miss Benson to visit the schoolroom, the men regrouped, with the judge and Mr. Garrison leading the way, in Milehigh's ordinary, where under the low-raftered ceiling, on the rail side of the bar, together with the cream of Pequot male society, Sinjin Grimes and Priam Talcott performed the astonishing act of actually raising a glass of beer to salute a common cause.

18

Charms to Soothe the Savage

THOUGH SHE HAD good reason to be so, Rose Mills was not a happy hired girl. Though she had struggled through her bouts of spring fever, though she had pined to trip the light fantastic at a Friday night assembly along with the village belles, had idly yearned for some masculine arm encircling her narrow waist, had even hungered to be made love to, and even though her wildest dreams of passion had been made reality by her phantom graveyard lover—now, having given herself willingly, eagerly, having shared the fruits of passion, she was feeling painfully bereft. Night after night she sat by her solitary window, the fragrance of roses in her nostrils, the sweet breath of the night breeze on her cheek, as alone as she had been back in January when the winter winds howled about the eaves. And day by day, as the captain filled the cemetery with his lectures, most rapt among his audience was the erstwhile truant Rose Mills, who, far from trying to concoct excuses for absenting herself from the classes her mistress had insisted on, now advanced her step eagerly to take her place on the chance that she would get to see and hear her hero. For what better way to display her charms before the man she worshiped and adored than in her fresh-pressed frock, her hair neatly arranged, and smelling of lemon verbena purloined from Pina's blue-glass scent bottle?

But if she had thought to see Sinjin Grimes trotting after her like some breathless village swain, sweating to take her in his embrace, she was sadly disappointed. She took hard the offhanded looks he slipped her, his mocking tone, the sardonic cocking of his dark brow, the wry sucking in of his cheeks, the wicked twinkle in his eye. Never had she felt so profoundly the gap between herself and white people, and never had she desired more desperately to be white herself, to be like them in every respect. Fortunately, she had the wit to realize that the gulf separating her from others was widened by her lack of experience, and it was this awareness of her own ignorance that made her decide to study the harder how to be a lady. Those tedious hours she spent cooped up in the stifling schoolroom, while still tedious, now were seen to serve a purpose, and she went to work with a will, all for the love of Sinjin Grimes. This was a new Rose, and with her new feelings came an earnestness of purpose that drew notice from the household, though Halley muttered that "that devil be up to no good." But little did she or Posie or Queen Mab or anyone else comprehend that the former slave had set her ruffled cap for the notorious seafarer, for who could possibly imagine such a thing? Who could believe that in her mind and heart she had already surrendered her lips and body to him a hundred times over, as she had once in fact upon a table stone on the Fathers' Rise, had heard those breathless love words soft in her ear, felt her flesh heat up with anticipated passion and the profoundest stirrings of lust she had ever known or tried to imagine?

Whenever she could manage it now she stalked him, observing his every move, lying in wait for him, ready for ambush, loitering outside the Old Hundred, the Headless, the boatyard, the bakery, any place she thought him likely to appear, praying for a glimpse; more, a word, a look, anything. Just to be noticed, the paltriest acknowledgment. She longed to fling herself into his arms and bleat out all the secret dreams hidden in her breast. But how was this to be managed, especially when the man was hardly ever alone, never out of sight of the Yellow Shadow? And if they could not meet, how was she to get him to acknowledge her and, ultimately, enter into the sort of intimate relationship she had in mind? How?

Then it came to her. Something Posie had said put the idea in her head. Cinnamon Comorra! What Rose must do was get a charm from the old Injun witch! Something to wear close to her body, something with the power to fire his heart for her. She disliked the notion of going to Cinnamon for anything, even a witch's charm (much as Rose looked down on the creature for her base position in the world, she also perceived that the old woman was to be feared), and it took her some few days to get up the nerve to approach her on the matter. But one Saturday, while Mab and Halley napped, she slipped away from Kingdom Come and crept through Hat's vegetable patch to find the object of her quest dozing in the sunny dooryard of her shed, a handful of chickens pecking around the drooping hem of her long, mud-colored skirts bright with random calico patches. As Rose emerged from behind the stand of sunflowers and straddled a row of pale cabbages, Cinnamon opened her wrinkled lids, instantly alert.

"Whatchou want, gurrl?" she drawled. "Get you's feet outta my Savvy cabbages 'fore I takes a hoe to you's black ass."

"Rose come on business," she explained, reverting somewhat to her earlier mode of speech, which she felt the witch would better apprehend. "I wants a charm."

Cinnamon grunted and shut her eyes.

"Can't you hear me, woman? I says Rose wants a charm." Keeping her voice low, she tossed one or two looks toward Hat's house, though neither Hat nor Georgiana was to be seen.

Cinnamon grunted again. "What kine charm?" she demanded, opening her eyes a second time. "Wrong charm make plenny mizry." She wheezed and coughed, then spat.

"A love charm." Rose leaned down, whispering. "I wants me a true love charm. For to get me a man. I wants one man. You can get him for me, can't you?"

Though the question was put with urgency, Cinnamon seemed only slightly interested. "Which man?"

Rose became impatient. "The cap'n. You know, cap'n Grimes."

"Shee-yut." Cinnamon spat again. "I guess I knows dat cap'n. Whatchou want wid dat one?"

"I loves him."

Cinnamon wheezed, mirthfully rocking back and forth in her chair and wiping the back of her hand across her eyes. She shook her head. "You one sad bitch, girrul. You cain' git no Cap'n Grimes."

"Who says?"

Cinnamon was more scornful. "What a banty rooster like him want wid a scrawny hen de likes ob you? You jus' a ole nigger slabe. You is bought 'n' paid for. You's ben on de block. You is ruint goods. I bet de whole county ben spreadin' you gams."

"That's a lie! I never was on no block!" Rose tossed her head proudly. "Anyways, I is free now. You make me a proper charm I'll catch him, you'll see."

The fold of skin above Cinnamon's eye quivered and the fatty pockets underneath narrowed as she thoughtfully assessed the slender figure, the thin, pale face, the long neck and tempting ripe breasts of Rose Mills. She chewed and spat and chewed some more, thinking, then asked, "How much dolluh you pay?"

"How much you figure to want?"

"Fifty dollar."

Rose's eyes blazed. "Hoo-ee! You is outta yo' mine, woman! Where Rose s'pose t' get fifty dollar?" Then, in a more reasonable tone, she proposed a lesser sum. "I maybe could give you five. Or—ten?"

Cinnamon was adamant; she restated her price.

But Rose was equally stubborn. "Ah ain't got no fifty dollars. Ain't I done tole you?" Cinnamon shut her eyes and appeared to doze off. When she opened them Rose was still there.

"—But I kin he'p you get it," Rose said.

"Mmmn?" Cinnamon eyed her doubtfully. "Whatchou say, girrul?"

"Sell you hair." Cinnamon's agate eyes began to glitter and as she gnawed the insides of her cheeks, Rose knew she had piqued her interest. "I knows a fellow hereabouts what'll buy you hair, pay good fo' it, too. What you say to that?"

"What feller?"

"Never mind, Rose knows," she said mysteriously. She was thinking of the peddler Mandelbaum, who had once offered to buy her own hair.

Cinnamon's eyes gleamed brighter, as if she were actually seeing the cash falling into her hands. As it was for Mab, time was running out for the Princess Suneemon, and there remained important matters to be seen to.

More than anything she yearned to be buried in the Ancient Burying Ground, to rest among the bones of her forebears.

"You tell me if Suneemon kin git burit dere," she had once asked Georgiana.

"We'd have to ask the selectmen," Georgiana had replied, knowing that the property did not belong to the church but to the citizenry of the village. Since that year Jack Talcott had been First Selectman, and the majority of the Board his allies, the selectmen had agreed—but on one condition: to placate the villagers they had stipulated that the princess might join her ancestors only after paying a fifty-dollar fee. Now, thanks to Rose Mills, Cinnamon knew how to come by the money she required. (The tariff, however, had not been enough to calm ruffled feathers, and it was partly as a result of this liberal-minded but impolitic vote that the Board of Selectmen had fallen into the hands of the Grimes faction, where it yet remained.)

She nodded, lit her pipe, puffed, made smoke. Then she beckoned Rose close and provided her with certain instructions. She was to seek out and bring to the witch something personal belonging to Captain Grimes, either something that had been close to his body, or some actual part of his body. When Rose had seen to this task Cinnamon would give her the hair to sell, and work her magic on the item in question, handing over the charm only when the cash was safely in her hands. Rose nodded and slipped away, and before another five minutes had elapsed, Cinnamon had undone her pins, taken up the sewing shears and cut off her long black hair.

"Lordamercy Cinnermin! What have ye done, woman?" cried Aunt Hat, gazing upon the shorn head. "Why, you're nigh on to bald!"

Cinnamon muttered that some folks could "mine dey bidness" and went out and chopped off a chicken's head. The chicken was for the pot, the head for more occult purposes.

At the end of the week, there was a bizarre sequel to Cinnamon's shearing. A meeting of the Hickory Club was held at the Academy Hall, to which Zion Grimes was driven by Hogarth. Once he had seen his master enter the building, the coachman drew his vehicle up at the head of the rank and went across the street to the May Fly Tavern for a glass of porter and a bit of social intercourse. He was absent for perhaps an hour, during which time the coach stood unattended. Then, shortly before eleven, coming from the tavern, he discovered that one of the matched pair of bays purchased by Zion since Abednego's death had been tampered with. In fear and trembling he awaited his master, whose truculent mood upon emerging from the meeting did little to dispel the servant's qualms. Believing that the best way out of the situation was the speediest way in, Hogarth seized Zion's arm and led him to the horse which, in the rays of the lamp the coachman held aloft, was discovered to have been deprived of the larger portion of its tail.

"Who has committed this act of vandalism?" roared the outraged owner. "Who has dared to meddle with this horse's tail?" he demanded of startled passersby who stopped to examine the brutally lopped-off tail, all that remained of what had formerly been a proud and flourishing growth. None had a reply, nor was Zion ever able to discover more regarding the sacrilege. He saw readily, however, how they all smirked behind his back at the ruin of his horse's beauty of line; in fact the beast became such a local joke that Zion was forced to sell it if only to rid himself of an irritating source of embarrassment.

The morning after Zion Grimes suffered the loss of his horse's tail, Hat had occasion to go out to the shed to ask something of Cinnamon. There sat the old woman, her head restored to its former glory, her coil of gleaming black hair sleekly plaited and pinned in a topknot with the familiar ivory and silver pins.

"Why, Cinnermin," said Hat in some surprise, "I thought you sold off your hair."

"Um. Did," replied the Indian, touching the piece that had been fashioned from Zion Grimes's property. "Got new. Much nice," she said, patting it with coy satisfaction.

"Will wonders never cease," murmured Hat, forgetting what she had come for. She and Georgiana laughed about it over supper: it wasn't often a body bested Zion Grimes, especially an old Indian woman off the Mountain.

Meanwhile, Rose had gone about securing those items Cinnamon required for her sorceries. On Thursday, as soon as class was dismissed, instead of reporting back to Halley for kitchen duties, and having ascertained that the captain had ridden up to Hartford on his grandmother's affairs, taking Mat Kindu with him, Rose approached the tavern unobserved and crept up the back stairs and into Sinjin's quarters. Her heart knocking in her bosom, hands trembling, she scanned the room and its scattering of masculine accoutrements.

"Sinjin, Sinjin Grimes . . ." she murmured softly, as if by verbalizing she might conjure him up. It was hot, the air stultifying, and she raised the sash, then was forced to duck from sight as a passerby glanced up. She peered around as a sound from the back stairs startled her. She must hurry. She rushed headlong at the clothespress, one half of whose interior was devoted to drawers, the other half to clothing hung on pegs. Yanking open one of the drawers, she discovered a neatly laundered stack of articles, and taking out a pair of the captain's smallclothes she stroked the fabric with her hand, then laid it against her cheek. Her reverie lasted only a moment. She must be quick. Tucking the garment into her pocket, she went to the bureau and located his hairbrushes, a matched set with monogrammed silver backs. She ran the comb through the bristles, harvesting the dark hairs with care, then looked around for something to wrap them in, settling on a scrap of paper she appropriated from the tabletop.

She was reaching for the door latch when the sound of Sinjin's voice reached her. Returned from Hartford already? She heard him talking to the chambermaid, Annie Skaats, and in another moment there were his footsteps at the door. What was she to do? She glanced around, frantically seeking a place in which to hide. Finally, desperately, she whirled and plunged headlong into the depths of the wardrobe, yanking the door closed just as the bedroom door opened and the captain strode in, the fall of his boot heels causing the floor to shake. He called to Annie for a pail of suds and a bowl of hot water, and from her hiding place Rose could hear him as he kicked off his boots and flung himself on the bed. She bit her fingers, facing the fact of her predicament and wondering how long she must stay cooped up in this damnable box whose stuffiness was already oppressing her. Why had she allowed herself to be trapped like this, and how was she going to extricate herself? Who knew how soon he might be leaving so she could make her escape. She felt her legs getting tired, for she could hardly move; certainly she couldn't sit, but must remain upright. She fingered the pair of smallclothes she had in her hand, wondering if she should return them before she was found out. But how could she replace them when there was no room to open the drawer?

TEN minutes later the captain had roused himself and was sitting at his table quaffing the salted beer Annie had served him, waiting for his shaving water to cool, when a breathless sigh followed by a thud issued from the wardrobe. Sinjin laid down his pen and, leaping at the furniture, he threw open the panels—to discover the motionless form of Rose Mills sprawled at his feet.

He picked her up and carried her to his bed, laying her down where he himself had stretched out only moments ago. He spread a wet cloth across her brow, introduced a few drops of water between her parted lips, and presently she stirred. She moaned faintly, her lids fluttered, her gaze swam into focus, then expressed alarm, and she would have cried out if he had not put his hand over her lips.

"Have you come to rob me, then?" he asked as he took his hand away.

She glared, her eyes showing their whites, her lips drawn back from her small, even teeth, and for a moment he thought she was a human bewitched into a beast. Then he laughed as with a muffled cry she began to squirm in his arms, writhing like a cat, spitting like one too. When he exerted greater force, trying to subdue her, she raked his bare forearms with her nails, and as he fell to shaking her she sank her teeth into his flesh.

He cursed her, and when she raised her head he snapped his hand back and struck her hard with the palm. "Cat, are you? I'll teach you to claw and bite, my pretty pussy!" Picking her up, he tossed her halfway across the room, then stood over her while she gazed woozily up at him, her spasm of energy now spent and replaced with something far different. He looked down at her breast, rapidly rising and falling, and into her eyes, where a message could easily be read.

"Cat?" he repeated, offering his hand.

"No cat," she said.

He helped her to her feet. She stood close to him, the same anticipatory light in her eyes. "Did I hurt you?" she asked.

He examined his hand. She'd drawn blood and he licked it with his tongue, sucked the wound and spat into the ironstone basin, then poured rum over the red marks.

"No," was all he said. He blew on the marks, which still stung, then faced her. "Well, have you come to rob me?" he asked again.

"No."

"Then what?"

She ducked her head and he drew her chin up with his fingers, forcing her to look at him. "Then what, little pussycat?" he repeated softly. In her dark flashing eyes he saw his own image reflected as if in a mirror and he thought he had never seen such large eyes in a human face. Suspicion, wariness, fear, all these were there—and something else as well; the look he had seen before in women's eyes, a look that thrilled him: the look of a fox at bay.

"It doesn't matter, I suppose," he said, giving her a comforting pat. "Not much to steal around here, anyway." He glanced at his desk. Had she meddled with his things? No, he thought not. Yet, why had she come? Why was she in his room at all, hiding in his wardrobe? He allowed his *amour propre* to whisper that she had come, not to steal from his pockets—for indeed, what was there of his to steal?—but rather because he had bewitched her. That first day he'd come to school, she'd fainted dead away, had to be helped home, and all because of him—his overpowering presence had crushed her. Now it had happened again. This was nothing new to him, this effect he often had on the fair sex: one look and they were lost.

With a swift, sudden movement he leaned down, drew her head to his and kissed her hard, hard and long and lovingly, eliciting murmurs of assent from her lips as he moved his expert hands over her contours, making her shiver. "That's more like it," he whispered. She stirred slightly, still looking at him, half frightened, half intrepid.

"Well now, my little vixen, are you going to tell me why you're here? Or should I call the constable?"

"*No—don't!*"

"Very well. See here, I'm not going to hurt you, providing you tell me what you're up to. What were you doing there in the wardrobe?"

"Was hidin'," she said.

"From me?"

"Mm hm."

"Certainly you're not afraid of me?"

She scowled and stared at him defiantly. "Rose ain't afraid of no man—*isn't* afraid," she corrected herself.

"Indeed, and why should you be?" He brought his lips close to her ear. "But you *are* afraid of me, aren't you? Just a little?"

"Maybe just a bit." She pushed away. "I got to get back. Lemme go," she said as he took hold of her again.

"Not just yet," he whispered. "Stay with me awhile."

She began to struggle. "I said I got to go. You want me to holler?"

"Holler away, my dark jewel. You'll quickly find yourself a resident of our local jail. But such a pedestrian solution strikes me as sheer waste when it's so obvious to me whom you came to see. Come, confess it, Rose, isn't it true? You did come to be with me." He sank into the pillows on his bed and drew her down with him, his mouth covering hers, his hands palpating her breasts. "Would you like me to make love to you? Hm? Would that suit you? Love you in ways no other man has loved you—or is likely to?"

Rose giggled. "You already loved me the way nobody else ever done. Guess you plumb forgot the gravestone."

"What's that?"

"I says—"

"I heard what you said, but what does it mean?"

"It means you damn near broke po' Rose's back, the way you was coming at me on that tabletop. When it split I like to bust from laughin'. I thought it was the end of the world come at last."

There followed a pause, during which he stared hard at her, frowning slightly and biting his lip. Then:

"Unholy Christ!" he burst out. "Don't tell me *you're* the one—that night—in the cemetery? By the hairy tail of the yellow god! Here I thought you'd walked into my life, then you were gone forever, and now I find you've been under my nose all this time." He gave her a sound hug. "Well, well, it's a small world after all. I must say, I'm very glad to see you." He kissed her again, lightly. "Ah, Rose, sweet girl that you are, my very sweet *sweet* girl," he whispered, drawing her closer. "Rose, as long as you're here and the circumstances seem so—propitious—come, admit they are—don't you feel we ought to commemorate our earlier meeting in some suitable fashion?"

"Com—"

"Com-*mem*-orate."

She had never heard the word and because she didn't understand it he made her feel stupid. He let his warm fingertips stray along her forearm to her elbow, causing her blood to race even more.

"That is to say, as long as *you* are here and *I* too am here—*we* are here together—oughtn't we to formally recall our first meeting?"

"Oh, I recalls that all right," she said, brightening. "I never forgot for one minute."

"I'm glad to hear you say so. I, too, have . . . reflected on the details of our all too brief rendezvous . . . hmm . . .?" His fingers moved to her shoulders and again he advanced his lips to hers. Her kiss was sweet and faintly spicy; it made him think of nutmeg and cloves. He slid his palms downward, feeling the heat of her.

"Is *that* what you's fixin' t'do right now?" she whispered huskily. He nodded gravely. "Oh," she said, a light dawning. At last she understood what "to commemorate" meant, and she was quick to add the new word to her growing vocabulary. It had been a long time since he'd spent a more enjoyable fifty minutes. Rose left with a smile on her lips.

In her room again she thanked the good Lord she hadn't been missed; moreover, that she'd got clean away with his smallclothes and the packet of hairs from his head. She counted them; there were seventeen in all, and at the first opportunity she bore them triumphantly to the Princess Suneemon. What the witch intended to do with such personal items was no business of Rose's, but unleashed, her imagination proved vivid, and not too long thereafter the Talcotts' hired girl had become possessed of a small bag sewn from a patch of red cotton, filled with the sort of magic she hankered after. She was instructed to wear the bag on a string hanging between her legs, at just the spot where it should manifest its greatest power, and not to remove it for any reason except to bathe; and regarding these instructions Rose was utterly scrupulous, following Cinnamon's orders to the letter while she waited for the magic to begin its work.

19

Vox Populi

FOR THE TIME BEING the undeclared truce between Sinjin Grimes and Priam Talcott continued to stand in place. Tacit as it was, unarranged and undiscussed by either party, it was considered by one and all to be a remarkable state of affairs. Forgotten now—or so it seemed—was that near fatal occasion when the captain had intruded at the party for John Quincy

Adams and attempted to elope with Priam's adored sister, Aurora, and Priam had cracked Sinjin's skull for his pains; even forgotten was the captain's later, disgraceful pursuit of Lady Sheffield, his debauchery and opium smuggling. When the two happened to meet in Milehigh's ordinary, they might mull over the latest item in the *Liberator* or the abolitionist Hartford press, or discuss the need for additional protection for Georgiana's pupils. They were unlikely ever to have their hands in each other's pockets, or an arm flung carelessly over each other's shoulders, the way Priam did with Asher Ingolls, or Sinjin with Hermie Light; they were not friends, never would be, the tavern patrons opined, watching the smoke curl from Sinjin's cigar, while Priam's golden hair gleamed in the lamplight before he paid for the drinks and marched out, to make the drive to Hartford and the dinner Peggy would have waiting for him.

But neither were they at each other's throat, as they had formerly been, and as the days went by one by one such was their continuing rapprochement that it told friend and foe alike how much greater were the issues at stake here than the ancient and weary conflict between Talcott and Grimes. If Sinjin Grimes and Priam Talcott could throw down their weapons and beat their swords into plowshares to join in common cause against the forces working to bring down the Free School, did this not signal to the world that the cause was worthwhile and of value to the greater good? With no planning or forethought the two adversaries were now united, to some extent at least, in the desire to further Georgiana Ross's personal interests, those of the Free School, and in the broader view, the cause of abolition itself—united in a battle that could go either way, but one that Abednego Grimes's son Zion and Zion's son Bushrod were determined to win at any cost, a fight that Priam and Sinjin, who loathed them almost as much as did his erstwhile enemy, would despise themselves for losing.

HAVING been exasperated beyond endurance by the accounts of the continued gatherings in the Ancient Burying Ground, Zion Grimes had gone so far as to interrupt his schedule of work and one afternoon to sneak over undetected for a look at this public desecration. Predictably, he had been outraged by the sight, and as Rod had promised, he took steps to silence his outspoken stepson. On a midweek evening another family council was held around the board at Burning Bush. Various reports were tendered— across his soup by Willie Wandsworth, by Rod during the roast, and over dessert by brothers Seaborne, Cephas and Gilead, along with brother-in-law Piper—while over coffee Zion himself held forth at length on the painful subject. Finally a decision was arrived at: a special town meeting would be contrived, at which assembly Rod would state the objections of the antiabolition party, which had now become the "protect and sanctify the graves of our loving dead" party as well, to any further talks or speeches among the tombstones.

The public assemblies known as town meetings held in the First Church were among Pequot Landing's most venerated traditions, reaching back two hundred years into village history. As British colonists, the settlers who had followed the original Ten Adventurers into the Connecticut Valley had been long used to being present at these open forums, where any citizen currently on the tax rolls and possessed of village property, and also a member in good standing of the Congregational church, was permitted to get up and have his say. Since it seldom behooved a man to act with modest restraint in support of or opposition to any pending action, the gatherings were more often than not outspoken and boisterous, and on a few occasions even violent.

In these latter times it was frequently said that folk attended town meetings just to hear men like Pagan Talcott speak out on one or another crucial issue of the day. Among his many other accomplishments Appleton had a lively way with words, and few things pleased his fellow citizens more than to hear him debate one or another of the village sages; and few were those speakers who in their turn had contrived to best him when he took to the floor of the meeting house, as First Church was still known to Pequotters.

Thus it was that Zion Grimes was enjoined to exercise due caution in selecting a date for the planned meeting, lest the argument go against him. He had not long to wait, however. Old Bobby, Appleton, and Jack Talcott had all accepted the invitation of the Reverend Joel Hawes to address the Anti-Slavery Society in Hartford, and an announcement of the major speakers appeared in the paper. The very next day, an "emergency" town meeting was called for that same evening, to discuss a "vitally important matter bearing upon the village at large." The Talcotts readily perceived that some sort of plot was being hatched, but there was no help for it; they could hardly snub the Reverend Hawes, and so, shortly before six in the evening, the small party left for Hartford to take supper with Priam prior to the meeting.

Sharp on the hour of seven, Mabel Talcott appeared below stairs with the announcement that she intended venturing forth to the Meeting House, where she would occupy her husband's place and try to discover what mischief was afoot. She asked that Posie accompany her.

"But Mother, you'll find it tedious. You stay, I'll attend and tell you what was said when I get home."

Mab was adamant. "I shall go," she declared.

"But Mama," Agrippina objected, "Posie's right—you really oughtn't. Stay at home with me, do." For three days Pina had been entertaining one of her maladies; an unattractive scarlet rash covered her extremities, and as a result she was in one of her testier moods. "Papa won't like it, your going out alone," she added.

"That's beside the point in this case, dearie," her mother returned shortly. "Besides, Posie can come with me; Rose too." Without waiting for further objections she called briskly for Trubey to help her exchange her afternoon dress for something more suitable, and bade Posie and Rose to do the same. Her suggestion rejected, Pina retired to her room where Burdy's little boy Snowy had been snared to cool her with the peacock fan, for the evening was humid.

"Why must Mama be so stubborn?" Agrippina wondered aloud, climbing onto her bed and stretching out.

"Must run in the family, mistress," Snowy suggested in his piping treble. "Momma say all you Talcotts is stubborn folks from way back."

Agrippina displayed indignation. "I'll thank your momma to keep such remarks to herself! Go down and tell her I want another mint tea. Tell her to be sure to put the lemon in. And tell her if she *wants* stubborn she'll *get* stubborn."

"I don't think she does," drawled the boy soberly as he skipped off on his errand. Pina got down from the bed to peer out the window as Posie and their mother, primly followed by Rose, stepped through the front gate and turned toward the Center.

"Posie Talcott, you come right in this house and put Mama in the shay and have Reuben drive you round like proper folk!" Agrippina screeched, leaning out the window. But all she got for her trouble was a dismissive wave of Mab's hand as the trio of pedestrians continued on their way.

Pina shrugged her shoulders and decided to have another bath. "Tell 'Baster to bring up the water," she said when Snowy came in with the mint tea. "And inform him he can bring some ice as well."

Snowy hurried away again to do her bidding. "Gramma," he said to Halley, who was fanning herself in the corner, "Miss Pina sure does a heap of tub-settin'."

It was to be Agrippina's third bath that day.

MABEL Talcott had not been often seen in public during recent weeks, and many heads, curious and surprised, turned for a closer inspection as she entered the church. A substantial gathering was already seated along the pews—the proslavery faction on the right, she noted, the abolition party on the left—and by now the galleries were filling up as well. Quickly sensing an air of tension in the place, Mab told herself it was a good thing she had come, no matter the inconvenience. Entering through the vestibule, the women passed the figures of Captain Grimes and Hermie Light conferring with Val Morgan and several other faces familiar to Mab. As the men inclined their heads and removed their hats, Mab took comfort in the fact that they were all staunch supporters of Georgiana and the school. Clearing the way, the gentlemen allowed the three women to move inside.

"Don't dally, Rose!" commanded her mistress before the girl could have a furtive word with Captain Grimes.

"Good evening, Captain," said Posie, smiling as she took her mother's arm.

"No, no, dearie, let me walk by myself," Mab protested, and while heads craned, she tipped her chin up and marched resolutely down the aisle to the Talcott pew. Making room for Rose, Posie sat beside her mother, nodding to friends and acquaintances. In a few moments they saw Bushrod Grimes enter, escorting Miss Rachel to the pew directly opposite, where Rod solicitously disposed of her person before hurrying back to confer behind hand with his uncles, as well as with the ubiquitous Deacon Willie and other figures familiar among the antiabolition gang who were gathered in a malignant-looking cluster among the central pews. In the pulpit, ready to call the meeting to order, stood the First Selectman of Pequot Landing, Zion Grimes.

The room was hot and stuffy. All afternoon the sun had streamed in through the tall windows, and worse, following the deacon's orders, the sexton had quietly closed the three sets of doors, whereupon Zion began rapping his gavel on the pulpit, calling for order.

In a flash Deacon Willie shot to his feet and, moving into the aisle, began demanding the passage of an ordinance forbidding further "lectures presented in a falsely educational vein, designed to inflame or radicalize the speaker's auditors." Further, no educational groups would be permitted to forgather in the Ancient Burying Ground for any reason whatever; both Giles Corry and Ike Bleezer would be charged with keeping the aisles between the tombstones clear of congestion so that those desirous of placing wreaths on the graves of their dear departed could do so in peace.

No sooner had Willie shut his mouth than Zion called for a vote. The motion was seconded and in the wink of an eye carried, and the Cemetery Resolution went on the books. But the work of Zion Grimes was not done with this new ordinance, no indeed. There was other dirt to be shoveled, other pits to be dug. No sooner had Zion declared the statute passed than he turned the pulpit over to his son, saying Rod had some words of importance to divulge to the community, " . . . words I am sure will be welcomed by all those caring citizens who wish to see an end to the pernicious establishment of bogus educational institutions for misses of color within our village boundaries."

With a good deal of bustling about and shifting of papers and adjusting of cravat, collar, and the silver spectacles he set on the end of his nose, Bushrod Grimes rose from his pew and took the pulpit, and, displaying the sort of oratorical bombast for which he was becoming known, and which farmers looked upon as words from the lips of a latter-day Demosthenes, announced that as he had recently learned, he was to be appointed to the state legislature to fill out the term of the late lamented incumbent Eliphalet Jasper.

Though rumored for weeks, this announcement was greeted with the anticipated cheers and disapprobation, according to which side of the church his listeners happened to be seated on, whereupon Rod grandly dropped a second bombshell by declaring that it was the firm intention of all the forces now marshaled in opposition to the school to see to it that a special session of the General Assembly was called in September to consider what was to be done about the grave threat to respectable property owners posed by the Free School and its ilk. At that time, he vowed, he would take it upon himself to introduce into law a bill to prohibit the education of the children of men who were proscribed from becoming full voting citizens of the state of Connecticut in such matters as might encourage them to attempt to rise above their natural station.

"No, by God!" shouted one of his auditors, jumping to his feet. "What grounds have you for such 'law' as you call it?"

"The simple and logical and most reasonable grounds, Cent Dunnoult, that persons of color being an obviously inferior race are not entitled to the education of their superiors. Why, the very notion is preposterous!"

"Then I hereby put the case that any such statute would perforce be held unconstitutional," stated Cent Dunnoult, canny lawyer and a town elder, for the challenger was indeed he. Shifting his straw hat back on his head, Cent squinted up at the pulpit. "Rod Grimes, better you should give clear thought to what you're proposing."

"I have," came Rod's sour reply. "Cent, I'd appreciate your sitting down and keeping quiet until I surrender this rostrum."

"Stand there long as you like, young fellow," returned Cent, "talk till you're blue in the face, but neither you nor your friends will ever convince me you're out to protect the Constitution. And if you should sufficiently connive to get any such statute passed by the legislature, I'll warrant it'll be slid in on rails neatly greased with coin of the realm."

Several voices rang out in support of these comments: "You tell him, Cent!" But such shouts of approval were opposed by angry boos and catcalls.

For and against, the clamor engulfed the auditorium, and Cent waited calmly for it to abate, then with placating hands upraised, he spoke again. " 'Course, I'm just a country lawyer hereabouts, but I wonder if you'll be so good, young Bushrod Grimes, as to answer one question: Will you be so kind to inform me, sir, is it the intention of this statute of yours to disbar all people of color from entering the higher circles of society?"

"It is, and I warrant most here agree that they should not do so," replied Bushrod. "If we cannot rid our village of this accursed school any other way, then we are resolved to seek succor in the state governing body."

Cent wafted a hand in the air, a negligent, even apologetic gesture. "Mr. Grimes, pardon my interruption, but I'm wondering now—are you completely aware that if this act were to find favor among our more exalted brethren at the capitol, if in fact such legislation were to be passed into law, that the children of the colored servants of at least two score of our most upstanding village households would be prohibited from aspiring to any higher education?"

"Maybe so," said Rod, "and I'm sorry for that. But the fact is, Pequot is being overrun by halfbreed females off the Mountain, not to mention out-of-town darkies. Pretty soon who'll want to buy property here in Pequot, I ask?"

"Darkytown! Darkytown's what they'll call it!" shouted Deacon Wandsworth, scrambling to his feet. "It don't take much to see whose side you're on, Cent Dunnoult! But you'll have your work cut out for you, I promise. If it takes every breath in our bodies we intend to see that pernicious schoolroom closed down. It stands like a blight on the landscape, and if you don't care what happens to this town of ours, it just so happens we do! And when such an invidious thing is sanctioned by some of this town's oldest and most esteemed families—you all know who I mean: Old Bobby Talcott, his son Apple, that freethinking woman Electra—idiotic appellation—and their creature, that infernal bluestocking miller's girl who doesn't know enough to keep her nose out of matters not concerning her—it's beyond countenancing. Bob Talcott's a rich man, yessirree, and he thinks to buy anything or anyone he has a mind to buy. Same with Pagan—given his way he'd incite the Lamenters to riot till they march over here in a body and rob us of our land, our houses, and our women! And what'll be next? I'll be happy to tell you. Marrying! Yes sir, they'll be wanting to marry with our daughters, every man jack of 'em. *That's* what Pagan Talcott wants to see happen around here, that's what Old Bobby hopes to see, and I tell you no good'll ever come of such a monstrous thing! A half-nigger baby in every household!"

A hearty cheer went up from the right side of the church. "Hooray! You tell 'em, Willie!" came the cries, while hats were tossed in the air. "To hell with Jake Talcott—to hell with Old Bobby too! To hell with the whole lot of 'em! Down with the high and mighty Talcotts, down with anarchy, down with—!"

"One moment, if you please!"

This voice rang out clear as a bell on a winter's day. Heads jerked backward and forward, and the owner's name buzzed about the rows. Unable to contain herself any longer, Mab Talcott had been propelled to her feet, quivering with indignation.

"My name is Mabel Talcott. You all know me, I've lived long enough among you. I'm not born-and-bred hereabouts, some of you still regard me as a foreigner, coming from downriver as I did thirty-six years ago. And I know that to have a female upon her feet at town meeting and speaking out to boot, is unheard of. But, gents, you'll pardon me for a word or two, since it seems to me there's a good deal of maligning being done here tonight."

Standing in her place and speaking out in a trembling voice filled with resentment, she faced her family's detractors. "Since neither my husband nor his father is present to defend himself, maybe I'll be permitted to say a word or two in their behalf. As for you, Willie Wandsworth, you're an uncharitable soul, furthermore you don't know what you're talking about. The fact is, if you care to hear it, I'm ashamed to know you! You talk as if Jake and Bob had some nasty motive in supporting a small school whose aim is to teach a few unfortunate young women their ABC's, and, yes, a bit more. So tell me, Deacon, if you will, since when aren't the children of this village—don't bother mentioning the color of their skins—since when aren't they to be taught their reading and writing? And who's to say where the line's to be drawn between those who shall be taught and those who shan't? I've lived among you folk ever since I was married, I came here still a young woman, now I'm an older one, but I never thought to hear a Pequotter say a little girl shouldn't get a slate and learn to write on it."

"Sit down, Irish lady—sit down," a contemptuous voice boomed, "you haven't got the floor!"

"What'd you expect from a bogtrotting Irisher?" shouted another. "She probably brought her pig in tonight."

"Get her a broom and fly her out of here!"

"Get me a broom, Ike Bleezer, and I'll sweep you out with the rest of the trash!" Mab loudly proclaimed. "And don't you go interrupting me or I'll march over there and settle your hash." She was not to be intimidated, not if every bruiser in the place stood up against her. Defiantly she faced the pulpit and, gripping the back of the pew, continued to speak out.

"Rod Grimes, you've known me since you were whelped and you've never seen me on my feet at town meeting before. That's because I don't like standing, and *that's* because my feet hurt." She waited for her laugh, and after it came she went on. "I usually speak through my husband. Yes, that's right, my husband, Apple Talcott, the man Deacon Wandsworth here's been spouting about. But I'll not sit by and have him sharp-bit behind his back. If he were here himself you can bet he'd tell the lot of you slave-owner sympathizers the brand of gutless windbags you are. You're all potatoes out of the same pot and I guess we know well enough whose pot I'm talking about. There! *There's* the culprit!" She pointed an accusing finger at Rod, who stared unbelievingly at the turn the meeting had taken. "Bushrod Grimes—*and* his father! Yes—I mean you, Zion Grimes! And you, Willie Wandsworth, and your conniving minions, you're all in cahoots. If it weren't for you not a soul would have raised a peep if we'd started up a school for a pack of trained monkeys picking nits. So I am standing here to say in front of God and everybody that the kind of talk I'm hearing tonight is fool's talk, and trouble talk, too. You're not talking about letting people get to the graves to put flowers on them, or abandoning their picnic lunches, or even stopping Captain Grimes from addressing Georgiana Ross's pupils. And it's not that one little school you're against, it's worry for your own property, worry for your bedsteads and stoves and chimney corners. You think others covet them and they'll snatch them from you if they get the chance. You're talking about lectures in the cemetery and schools for the children of voters or prospective voters only, but what you're meaning is support of slavery pure and simple! You want to go on keeping dark-skinned people slaves, you want to deny them their rights as human beings! As to such orneriness as throwing rocks at innocent girls, let me say this: We none of us knows when the good Lord'll call us to judgment, but before He lays claim to my soul I'm here to say I'm ashamed to be a citizen of this place. Now if there's some noodle hereabouts who doesn't understand why that should be, then let him just come by my gate, I'll be glad to step out and give him the good word, anytime, day or night. You're nothing but a pack of sheep following a goat—the goat in this case is that apple-cheeked darling standing there, Bushrod Grimes."

"See here!" Rod bawled out. "This has gone far enough! Madam, how can you say such things?"

"I say them because they're true, and anybody who listens to your balderdash is a fool!" She paused, glaring all around her. Rod was silent. Then she raised her face to the pulpit once again. "That's all I have to say, Rod Grimes. I've done and I'll sit again. But you had better think twice, the lot of you, before you stand up tonight and try to besmirch Apple Talcott's good reputation—in this place or any other! I thank you one and all for your forbearance." So saying, she stepped out of the pew and, looking neither right nor left, firmly marched up the aisle. Ignoring the sexton, she advanced to the door beside which lounged an admiring Captain Grimes. Administering him a severe look, she tried to deal with the knob, but the door had stuck. Then, as she impatiently jerked at it, a moan escaped her lips and she slipped to the floor, her head striking the boards with a loud sound.

Sinjin immediately dropped to his knees beside her, listened to her heart, then felt for her pulse. "She banged her head pretty hard, but I think she's all right," he said to Posie, who had pushed her way through the circle of curious onlookers that had gathered around.

"We told her she oughtn't try to come, but she insisted. Mama? Mama, dear? Are you all right?"

As she patted her mother's cheek, Mab's eyes opened and she stared up at the ring of faces. "What's happened, dearie?" she asked weakly.

"You fell, Mama. Do you think if we help you, you could get up?" Mab nodded and Posie motioned for Rose to assist her. Mab attempted it, without success; she slumped once more to the floor.

Posie turned to Sinjin, who, before she could speak, was brushing past Rose and with little effort lifting Mab into his arms. Kicking the door wide, he carried her through, followed by the two girls. On the street he looked for the Talcott coach.

"We walked," Posie explained, coming up behind him. "Is it too far to carry her, do you suppose?"

Sinjin shook his head and with his burden struck out in the direction of Kingdom Come. As he strode rapidly along, Mab stirred and her eyes blinked open. "It's all right, ma'am," he assured her. "Another moment and we'll be at your door."

"Put me down at once," she said, weakly struggling.

"It's all right, Mama, let Captain Grimes carry you," said Posie, obliged to quick-step in order to keep up with Sinjin's leggy stride, which soon brought him to the gate. Rose lifted the latch, then, as he started up the walk, she darted ahead to open the front door. It was locked and she began ringing frantically while Sinjin held Mab calmly in his arms.

"I say put me down, Captain," she repeated. "I am quite capable of standing."

"Yes, ma'am, I'll do that—soon as you're safely inside."

The door opened and an openmouthed 'Baster stood in the doorway. "Jesus help us!" he exclaimed. "Is she all right?"

"Yes, 'Baster. Please bring Mother into the parlor, Captain."

The passageway door sprang open suddenly and the birdlike figure of Halley Priest scurried toward them. "Whut's goin' on? Whut them folks is done to the missus?" she cried, running to Mab and peering closely at her pale face. "Miz Talca, ain't Ah done tole you? An' whut that scoun'rel doin' in this house?"

"It's all right, Halley, the captain has been kind enough to bring Mama home," Posie explained.

As Sinjin crossed the front hall with his burden he glimpsed a grim, white-clad figure rushing down the staircase and heard Agrippina's hysterical wail.

"Mama! What's happened? Are you hurt?"

"No, I am not hurt and nothing has happened," returned her mother. "I had a spell and this gentleman was kind enough to bring me home. Captain, perhaps you can put me down now."

Sinjin carefully deposited Mab in the Pilgrim Carver chair that stood against the wall, then tipped his cap and made a slight bow. "At your service, ma'am."

"Thank you very much," she said, panting a little. "Now if you will just be good enough to go along."

"Mother!" Posie cried. "The captain was only being helpful."

Halley scowled her fiercest. "Bad man, got no bizness in this house. You git 'long, man."

"That will be enough, Halley," Posie said severely.

But now Agrippina spoke up. "Halley's right. He ought not to be here. It isn't fitting—"

"Perfectly all right, Miss Talcott," Sinjin said with a debonair tilt of his head. "I have only done as your sister requested. I bid you good night, Mrs. Talcott. I trust you've suffered no serious injury and will soon recover your spirits."

Agrippina did not fail to note his mocking expression as he bowed, then was gone, his heels clicking on the gravel as he sauntered down the walk. "Posie Talcott, how could you!" she exclaimed. "Allowing that terrible man to put his hands on Mama that way."

But Pina's objection went ignored. Mab was already being assisted up the stairs by Trubey and Posie, where she was put to bed, refusing to so much as consider summoning the doctor. Moments later Agrippina hurried into her mother's room, her unbound locks flying behind.

"Oh Mama, dearest, whatever can have possessed you? To go over there, with no one to protect you, and address the town meeting? What will people say?"

"I haven't a notion, dearie. I was thinking of your dear father, and of the way he was being talked about. And him ten miles away. If a bunch of country bumpkins think I'm going to sit around on my derriere while some red-nosed Yahoo like Ike Bleezer assaults your papa's good name, they've another think coming. I'm just sorry I didn't say more." She laughed.

Agrippina spoke up again. "I don't care, I think it's wrong. Papa will be upset when he hears."

"Pina, dear," said her weary mother from the high bed.

"Yes, Mama?"

"Be silent."

"Mama!"

"I don't care to hear another word tonight, not one word. Pass me my cap, dearie," she said to Posie, who settled the nightcap on her mother's head and tied up the strings, then, taking Agrippina's elbow, firmly escorted her out, leaving Mab panting against her pillow.

Through the partially raised window a pleasant night breeze strayed, and among the boughs of the trees in the backyard the birds made their subdued melodies. The air was soft and drowsy and sweet to the nostrils. Mab smiled to herself as she lowered her lids, unable to keep awake until Jake came home. What *would* he say upon learning of the evening's misadventure? Despite Pina's complaint, Mab believed she had done the proper thing. If she was ever to speak out, she'd best do it now. Time was running out, and her lips would be a long time silent. She'd already had more time than she'd thought possible. How much longer?

20

Hats

THE TOWN MEETING had sundry annoying ramifications besides the summary ending of the cemetery lectures, among them being that Mab became the victim of sharp village tongues; she was accused of having been sent to the meeting by her husband and father-in-law deliberately to break up the proceedings, or at any rate to throw a hitch into them so that the lectures might continue. Though proud of what his spouse had done in his absence, Appleton had been aghast at learning how Mab had been spoken to by Ike Bleezer and, worse, by Rod Grimes. Lapsing into one of the violent fits of temper for which he was known, he threatened to wait on the church steps on Sunday morning with a whip in his hand, ready to flay the hide off the young deacon's back. Luckily, prudence was made to prevail, and Rod had gone unchastised, the whip remaining on its tackroom peg, leaving Appleton to brood on a world that allowed such cravens to exist in it, and on the shocking fact that it was Zion's stepson who had carried Mab home. Who did the upstart think he was to come marching into the house with the wife of Apple Talcott in his brawny arms! Appleton wanted no Grimes feet crossing the threshold of Kingdom Come. True, Priam had drunk healths with this particular Grimes at the Hundred, true as well that the captain was generously giving of his time and efforts on behalf of Georgiana and the Free School. But Priam was so busy these days hurrying from place to place either in the cause of abolition or on his private business that he really didn't know what had been happening for ten days past, activities that had put Appleton badly out of countenance.

And what *was* happening that was causing Appleton such anxiety? Merely that Priam's little sister Posie and the captain were seeing each other on occasions far too frequent and too public to be ignored, especially by her adoring and concerned parent. It was scarcely surprising that Appleton should take marked exception to his daughter's interest in Sinjin Grimes, nor was it likely that he would simply allow the matter to pass without critical comment. But what was to be said? Surely words were called for. Though he had assiduously raised all his children to function as independent and resourceful individuals beholden only to the law of the land and their own well-honed consciences, the drift of the talk that had reached his ears— wherein some were heard to declare that if Sinjin Grimes couldn't get the one daughter by stealth, he was bound to get the other—was too alarming to ignore.

Over the years a quantity of loving "dialogues" had taken place between parent and offspring; in fact, Appleton often congratulated himself on having established warmer, more intimate links with his youngest daughter than with any other member of his family, his wife excepted. He relished their personal conversations, and it never ceased to amaze him how adult in her attitudes Posie was even as a child, how prudent and commonsensical in her views. During these warming weeks of summer, however, the ticklish matter—and it *was* undeniably ticklish—distressing her father was of such gravity that he had hesitated several times before broaching it. Now, he felt compelled to state his case, no matter how cautiously, and on Saturday morning, when from the river-side window of his laboratory he spied Posie down in the boathouse, executing one of her watercolor sketches, he decided this was the perfect time to "happen upon her" for a "little chat." Pushing aside his work, he removed his eye shade and spectacles and walked out into the sunshine to make his way along the garden flagging and across the meadow, coming upon the watercolorist unawares as she bent over what he judged to be a commendable composition of some canoers out on the river.

"Posie, my dear," he began, entering the boathouse, "do I interrupt you at your work?"

"No, Father, come in and talk to me. I was just feeling lonesome and here you are. Come sit." She indicated a chair and when he had taken it she turned to him expectantly. "Is there anything in particular you wished to discuss?"

"No, nothing, really. Only—that is—I confess a certain thought had crossed my mind, a little something worth a trifling bit discussion, if you can spare me a moment from your work?"

"Yes, Father, of course."

How like Lecky she sounded—how grown-up, how much the master of herself. By way of preamble he cleared his throat, feeling his way into the touchy subject. "My dear, I am reliably informed that you were recently seen leaving the ordinary of the Old Hundred. Is this true?"

A faint crease marred that perfect brow and she drew in her ripe underlip. "Yes, Father, I'm afraid it is. Who told you, I wonder?"

"It's of no consequence. A remark made in passing, no more. But I am interested in knowing to what end you found yourself in those purlieus. It occurs to me that saloons ought not to be your bailiwick, what do you think?"

Turning back to her work, Posie rinsed her brush, then deepened her blue a bit. "Oh no, Father, I'm hardly a frequenter of saloons. I was merely procuring something from Sallie Jenckes."

"I see. May I know what this something was?"

"Pickles, Father."

"Pickles. I see. To what end, if one may make so bold?"

"I have a friend who has a liking for pickles. I was merely taking them to him."

"To him where?"

"In the Ancient Burying Ground."

"Is one to deduce from this that your friend takes his lunch in the cemetery, then?" Posie agreed that this was so.

Appleton thought the matter over. "To my way of thinking, eating in consecrated grounds smacks of a certain lack of reverence, don't you agree?" he inquired.

Posie had the nerve to giggle. "Oh Father, dear, and you an atheist, as if that mattered. And it's so pretty and restful there. Food digests better in such tranquil places, even pickles."

"Tranquil. Yes, I'm sure it is, being a cemetery. And we all must worry about our digestion. But, not to put too fine a point on the matter, is it likewise a fact that the individual in question is Captain Grimes?"

"Of course it is, Father dear, otherwise we would not now be having this conversation, isn't that so?"

Normally the candor of her reply would have caused Appleton to smile indulgently, but now he frowned. This sort of badinage was not appropriate to the circumstances. "Now see here, my *very* dear young lady," he expostulated, "do you comprehend the character of this—this—reprobate you appear to have taken up with? Why, most fathers wouldn't hear of your exchanging a single word with him, yet I—"

"Yes, Father dear, I know; yet you allow me the privilege of holding open converse and the free exchange of ideas with other members of the opposite sex and with individuals of all ages, beliefs, and colors. Must I then draw the line at Captain Grimes, who has been so helpful to the school?"

Yes, Appleton had to agree, the captain had been helpful. The lectures had been a triumph. And even in the face of the ordinance that had been passed at the town meeting, the captain had not been deterred, simply moving his "classes" over to Gaunt House, where Luke had offered the use of his barn.

"And he knows so much lovely poetry, Father," Posie went on, dimpling. "You know—'Byron and Sheats and Kelley.' "

This was an old joke with Georgiana, and Appleton smiled in spite of himself. But he was not content to let matters lie. "You know the captain's reputation, surely. And, sweetling, please don't call me 'Father,' call me 'Papa' as you used to do."

"Very well, Papa. But Papa, dear, the captain is rated a most courageous man and one of the best skippers to helm a ship. The rest is just bits of gossip and you know how *you* feel about gossip. Besides, he's really very nice, truly—I know that Pina says unflattering things about him, but he's not that way at all. He's kind and thoughtful and actually quite shy. I'm sure if you'd get to know him you'd find him most amusing and intelligent. Sissie certainly did."

"To her sorrow, I'm afraid. In any case I think we would do well to leave your sister out of this discussion."

"Yes, of course, Papa, but we have to remember, he loves her."

"What?" Appleton's cheeks became suffused with a roseate hue. "What's that you say? Are you telling me that that bounder thinks he's still in love with Aurora?"

"There are some loves that never die, that can't be stamped out. He hasn't said so in so many words, but I can tell. He sorrows for Sissie. He's devoted to her memory."

"I'll see him devoted to Old Nick is what I'll do! It's preposterous, after all these years—and all the women he's had in the course of them! The idea of him mooning over my Beauty to every Tom, Dick, and Harry in this town. I'll have him ridden out on a rail!"

"No, you won't Papa. And please do remember what you said about giving people the benefit of the doubt? That's really all I'm doing, you know. It has to do with character analysis and the governing logic of personality."

Appleton's eyes sought the rafters overhead. "By Zeus, how the child talks! She's been reading again, there's the trouble!" He put his head in his hands.

"But Papa, dearest," returned Posie sweetly, "how am I to make up my mind about people without knowing them?"

"You, my darling girl, are of so sweet and innocent a nature that a man could be the devil incarnate and you'd have no notion."

"But we only walk and talk together. He's a perfect gentleman and simply crammed with thrilling stories; you've no idea. And besides, he likes me."

"Everyone likes you, my dear, that is not a very hard thing to do. Soon the world will be at your feet, and fittingly so. But when it comes to the gentleman in question, I'm afraid that if you cannot better choose your company you will force me to choose it for you. I think you would do far better to pick friends nearer to your own age." He paused and drew on the end of his nose. "A word to the wise, my dear, eh?"

Posie gave him her most angelic look. "Oh Papa, I'm sure that would be very dull, truly. Nor would I learn as much, Papa, would I? Of *course* I wouldn't! Don't you agree?"

His spirit contracted in the face of her damnable logic—logic he himself had taught her! Was this to be his reward for the education he had given her? Fearful of defeat in his purpose, and of looking foolish, he decided to withdraw from the field as tactfully as he could. Gently he took her brush and paper block away, then drew her close and laid her cheek against his own, feeling the sweetness of her. Let me keep her, he prayed, don't take her from me as you took my Beauty. Leave me this one, at least.

She smiled at him, and kissed his cheek and patted it. "Papa, you mustn't worry, you know. I'll be here, truly I shall. Don't be afraid."

He drew back in amazement. How had she read his thoughts?

"Yes, my dear, I know," he said. "You won't leave your old dad. What would happen *then,* if you were to go away?"

"You mustn't even think of such a thing," she said, patting his shoulder. "Trust me, Papa, please do. Now there's Halley calling—Pina's gone up-street, I'd better see what she wants."

With another kiss she stood up. Somberly he watched her drift away, like a spring zephyr in her lightly fluttering dress; then, rousing himself, he returned to his experiments.

THAT evening the subject of this dialogue was hunched over the corner table in the Old Hundred taproom, doing his resolute best to induce in his bloodstream a reasonable state of inebriation, and in this endeavor he was succeeding admirably. Moreover, as his intake of spirits became more liberal, likewise did his lugubriousness, that streak of sentimentality that had betrayed him so often. He was not so far gone that he couldn't remember the song being played, that tune he'd first heard as a baby, when his sailor-father Dick Wilson had come bowling along the walk, the blue-and-yellow parrot on his shoulder, a gold ring in his ear, that carefree young tar in his duck trousers and black varnished hat with yellow ribbons who was never coming home again.

> *Full fathom five thy father lies,*
> *Of coral all his bones are made . . .*
> *Ding dong bell . . .*

He knocked off the dregs of his drink and when the girl had refreshed his glass he leaned back on the legs of his chair, one boot crossed over the other. Today had not been one of his better days; he was behind in his rent and had run a heavy bar tab, which made facing Milehigh hard on a fellow. He'd had to nudge Grammaw for another little tuck to settle accounts. But Grammaw was mad at her Sonny; she'd made a special trip to Gaunt House to beard him in the barn, telling him she would tolerate no more talk about him and "that colored girl." Grammaw was right, probably; he ought to be more careful where Rose was concerned: Sallie had eyes and ears and someone or other had evidently alerted Miss Rachel. Still, he found Rose's charms so appetizing that it was difficult to say no when she wanted to sneak up the back stairs and jump into the featherbed with him. But that was the trouble with women like Rose; no matter how remarkable their perform-ance, no matter the promises you made them, there always came that day of reckoning, the day he'd had with so many others like her. The piper must be paid.

His mother had said that once, referring to herself. What would she think now, seeing how her boy had turned out in what was fast becoming an encroaching middle age? What disapproving words would she have had for him? As for his father, there'd have been no criticism from that quarter; Dick Wilson would have cheered him. "Go to it, lad!" he would have said. "Have one, have all!"

As though to consult more directly with these two ghostly forebears he slipped the fingers of one hand into his jacket pocket and extracted dual hinged portraits in miniature. He cupped one in his hand, regarding it somberly by the light of the candle on the tabletop. He was his father's son all right, no doubt of it, there were the same dark eyes, the same high cheekbones, the lank black hair, even the complexion was swarthy, the look that informed of his Indian ancestry. In the eyes glimmered a light, a trifle mocking, which these days was to be found in Sinjin's own, and which the miniaturist had observed and cleverly recorded, as he had the lips with their trace of humor; there was apparent in the expression a jaunty, devil-may-care attitude, as if the mariner dared the world to say him nay.

A devilish looker with the ladies, sailor Dick had happened along one day swinging his seabag over his shoulder, tipping his hat to the young girl who had been Louisa St. John, one of the Begger–St. Johns of Green River. The modest daughter of a profit-turning ships chandler, through the years of her growing up her father had put by a handy dowry against the day when his only child would be safely bestowed on a man of promise and fair substance. But Louisa had fallen head over ears in love with a jack of a sailor boy, who had stolen her heart as a weasel steals hens' eggs. The father had said he was the devil incarnated, come to mulct him of his only child, but through a long summer Dick hung about, and the time came when Louisa confided to her mother that she ought to be married. Then Dick, whistling a wedding tune, took her down to New London, where they were joined in matrimony by a ship's captain, and after a three-day honeymoon, gone was Dick to the Bering Sea with the whaling fleet.

The baby was a full six months old before Dick turned up again, delighted to feast his eyes upon his bouncing son. He stuck it for all of a month, playing daddy, then was off again, back to sea, and thus the pattern was set. Cut off by her unforgiving father, barred from communication with her mother, Louisa was left to the charity of a tavern keeper, a friend of the sometime-husband, who gave her a room and board in exchange for scullery chores. Then one day Dashing Dick did not come home at all. His ship had dropped from sight off Gay Head making for the Grand Banks, and Louisa became the Widow Wilson.

From the time he was old enough to understand his native tongue, Sinjin had heard from his mother of the nobility of his father. She would relate fanciful tales of his exploits, feats that always ended in the same place, at the bottom of the sea, a place that grew to terrify the young boy's nights and haunt his dreams. No, he decided early on, he would never be a sailor, not he. But the lad had reckoned without his new stepfather.

Sinjin's eyes now turned to the matching miniature, the face of the pretty, gay, smiling creature with roses in her hair, the girl who had been his young mother. Large, dark eyes gazed out at him from the ebony oval with an expressive luminosity, the lips held a smile of ineffable sweetness and calm, and the pale ivory skin seemed to him like the cool fragrant flesh of a camellia petal. Shortly after the death of his father, that poor and not-quite-honest adventurer, crammed with romantic notions, with impossible dreams and promises that would never be kept, she had been forced to sell herself to the flinty widower Zion Grimes, making a loveless bargain in order to provide her darling son the advantages she had always hoped for him. And then her pretty face had changed, her gaiety had melted like ice in August, until one day, she, too, left him. A bout of fevernager carried her off, and the boy, now named Grimes, was left to face life alone, with the malignant Zion for a father, Bushrod for a brother, and, more happily, a sister Helen who adored him.

In the summers after, when school was out, Sinjin labored hard, planting, hoeing, and harvesting, until the more miserable day arrived when he could be articled aboard the *Nonpareil*. Before he knew it, he himself was in turn "sailor Dick," ordered to sea by Zion Grimes as a grummet aboard a leaky vessel with a cruel master. Hating his stepfather with ample reason and little trouble, in all things Sinjin struck out to copy his natural parent as a ne'er-do-well and a rip. The sweet memory of Louisa St. John burned in him, and God help the man who made remarks about a sailor who kept the pictures of his mother and father close to hand in his pocket. For her sake he hated Zion Grimes, for her sake he touted his own antecedents, making sure that everyone knew that he "was not really that old bastard's son," and prayed for the day when divine vengeance would be his to enjoy.

With an inaudible sigh Sinjin snapped the little gold latch on the two faces, pocketed them, then, his glass being empty, he signalled the girl, who brought another one. After a healthy draught, he licked his lips and tossed the hair back from his eyes. The girl was lingering at his shoulder, hoping for a bit of chat, maybe an invitation to his room; she got short shrift. As they did so often these summer days and evenings his thoughts strayed across the Atlantic, to Italy, where Aurora was. There she stood, in an Italian garden, her hand resting on the stone balustrade, where peacocks strolled and the moon dripped its honey. Her face danced tantalizingly before him, those blue eyes framed by a cloud of golden hair. He became suffused with the essence of her, the beauty that burned in her like an incandescent flame in whose bright glow he knelt and worshiped.

Ah, my lost love, he thought, becoming not only morose but maudlin. He might stretch out his arms to embrace her phantom, but in the end he clutched only empty air.

Sensing his mood, Sallie gave him wide berth, along with those others who knew better than to intrude on his solitude. Ah, why did he not have a miniature of *her,* his dearly beloved, to keep in his pocket, along with his mother's and father's pictures? Why was she not here beside him where she belonged?

The finished, polished way in which she turned herself out, the silken hose, the shoes with rosettes or ribbons, the slender gold bangle encircling her wrist, the cross hung at her neck, the ruffles at her bosom—very enticing those ruffles—her soft gloves with their small pearl buttons, her fan—oh yes, the yellow fan he'd given to her in the cabin of the *Adele,* the fan he'd last seen in Agrippina Talcott's hatbox two years later, when he'd learned he had a daughter—and, as it turned out, had lost Aurora forever.

In a burst of carnal feeling he owned to the allure of her feet, for him one of her greatest charms, those petite extremities whose line and form he had memorized, that he longed to admire, to touch, to fondle. But wait, there was more to his erotic tally. Add to those slender and alluring feet equally slender ankles, a dainty waist whose heavenly circumference was less than the span of his two hands, a rounded bosom that drew into it the breath of life itself, and that porcelain tinted flesh that tempted the eye and never satisfied a man's hunger. He burned, he blistered, he sizzled like a chop in a skillet. Oh what bliss, oh what sorrow. He yearned for her with all his being, to touch and hold, caress and kiss. Oh, to lie beside her, naked, on the grass, in a field, a bed . . .

But no, these maunderings were the coinage of a diseased brain, fantasies that would never come true. He was alone, would be alone like this for the rest of his life, nothing would ever change it, he knew that now. Still, she loved him. He knew she did. She'd admitted it, hadn't she? And the child—*their* child—little Caro, his own sweet darling daughter. The child life had robbed him of, just as it had robbed him of his beloved. Who gave a damn for anything without the two of them? He raged to remember the beating he'd suffered at the filthy hands of those louts employed by Henry Sheffield, who'd left him bloodied in the square outside the villa, when Sinjin had tried to slip a gift for Aurora into the house without Henry's knowing. But he'd got caught, and who knew where those beads were now, that had cost him so dearly.

Through the open window at his elbow the locusts loudly thrummed amid the sultry dark, the crickets chirped, walkers passed the tavern grounds, afoot or in carriages, dogs barked, spirited boys and girls ran by laughing with torches held aloft. The sky beyond the silhouetted elms was star spangled, the heat oppressive. He longed for a cooling swim in a pond somewhere, some cooling, relaxing diversion—but not in the arms of Rose Mills. Somehow the idea of her warm embrace felt equal to the heat, oppressive and unpromising. He was wrong to have got mixed up with the wench in the first place. He must do something about that before their activities made a real scandal . . .

He caught sight of the Indian woman's sharp dark eyes on him. What was Cinnamon thinking? Had she read his thoughts? Surely she knew what was going on; she never missed a trick. Maybe he should invite her over to his table, have her tell his fortune. No, not tonight, not that one. Just the sight of her made him nervous.

A part of him felt dead; another part of him seethed and throbbed, leaving him no peace of mind, no pleasure or contentment. What had happened to him? Another ship sunk beneath his boot soles, a fortune in art and antiquities relegated to Davy Jones, and he without a vessel, landlocked and filled with gloom. What had brought him to such a pass, a life so filled with emptiness? The oxymoron piqued his drollery and he grinned to himself.

Again he drained his glass, and was on the point of ordering yet another when a far more gratifying idea occurred to him: he would have that drink at Snug Harbor instead. Having thus made up his mind, and abandoning his table, he mockingly saluted Milehigh as he went, gave Sal a peck on the cheek, and tipped his cap to the room.

The night air felt fresh and clean as he walked somewhat unsteadily across the road, passing the church and cemetery. Arriving at the gate of Hat's cottage, he vaulted the pickets and made his way up the walk. He entered without knocking, to hear voices from the kitchen, and when he popped his head through the doorway he found Georgiana and Helen seated at the oilcloth-covered table engaged in some project. As he came in, Georgiana looked up, eyeing him with faint disfavor, and it was Helen who answered his question as to their endeavor.

"We're trying to weave a bonnet." On the table sat a pile of grass, alongside the leghorn bonnet Sinjin had brought Georgiana as a present. To his amazement he saw that the women were actually attempting to copy it, a feeble piece of work at best.

"What's that you're using? Horse hay?"

"It's marsh grass," Helen replied. Though their industrious fingers were nowhere near as deft as Rose's, between them Georgiana and Helen's primitive efforts had produced several halfhearted replicas of the famous leghorn braid.

Sinjin snorted, earning Georgiana's sharpest look. "What d'you hope to get with making hats out of marsh grass?" he asked.

"Money!" she snapped caustically. Plainly, Mistress Ross was in one of her bad moods this evening.

"Sorry I asked," he drawled airily. "To tell the truth, I hadn't known that ladies' millinery—the fashionable kind, I mean, the leghorn sort— could be made from the humble marsh grass. You'll be at it till next year."

"Who says?" Georgiana demanded, reddening.

"Look at it, it's tough and hard; and the color's all wrong."

"That's how much *you* know," Georgiana retorted at her most crisp. "Perhaps you'd do better, Captain Grimes, to keep your comments to yourself."

"Sinjin, never mind," Helen said in a warning tone. He selected a finished plait from the table and held it up for examination.

"Not bad, this one. Who made it?"

"Rose Mills did," Helen said.

Georgiana showed a frosty smile. "I believe you and Miss Mills are somewhat acquainted, Captain, are you not?"

He stared at her; her intention was clear: tonight she was out for blood. Wishing he'd heeded Helen's mute warning, he did so now when she suggested he go in and say hello to Aunt Hat. He excused himself and moved back into the passageway, where he came across the old lady, who had just stepped out of her little bedroom. Presently the two were sitting in her cozy parlor, Hat sharing her chair with Murray Hill, who seductively waved his long, fat tail at the newcomer. Sinjin threw himself onto the settee.

Hat clicked her teeth and wagged her head. "By dad, you're a clod sometimes, Sinjin Grimes, the way you go bargin' through life, makin' tracks in a body's parlor. Don't you ever stop t'wipe yer feet?" Her look was fierce and she ground out her words through her clicking teeth. "If a goose came and sat on your dumb thick skull you wouldn't know it."

"What're you getting so riled up over, Aunt Hattie?" Sinjin demanded.

"What's happening around here anyway? First I get an Arctic freeze from the local schoolmarm, now you're flaying me to the bone. A gentleman comes to pay a friendly call and see what he gets."

"Hah! Gentleman, is it? That word ain't in yer lexicon, Skeebo, you don't know the meanin' of the word. Why, you big—" She stopped suddenly, clamping her lips shut and folding her arms over her chest.

"Go on, Hat, say what's on your mind."

She shook her head. "No sir, I ain't, I said I won't and I won't."

"Never knew the cat to get your tongue. And I never thought to see the day when you wouldn't speak what was on your mind, either."

Hat glanced over her shoulder and drew her chair closer. She lowered her voice, saying, "some folks got nothing t'do but talk, Singe, partic'larly in a little town like this one." He stretched his legs out to their full length and contemplated the toes of his boots.

"I have an idea this is a prelude to something, so why don't you just plow right on through. I'm causing talk and I'm not a gentleman, is that it?"

"Yer right on both counts so far as it goes, but it ain't all, not by a durn sight."

"Then suppose you stop beating around the bush and come right out with it. What am I doing that's causing you ladies such concern?"

"Sakes alive, lower your voice, you ain't a-sail in a high wind, y'know." She lowered her own to a whisper. "No one ought t'have t'tell you, but you're playin' with fire, if you don't know it."

"So was Prometheus."

"And look where it got him. Why the idear, of all the fish you could hook, you have to take off after Mabel Talcott's hired girl. There, I've said it and I'm glad, don'tcha think I ain't!" She jerked her chin in defiance and dared him to come back at her.

"Aha, so that's it." He whistled softly through his teeth. "Well, well, I had no idea my activities were of such moment to you ladies, truly I had not. So, you disapprove of my interesting myself in one poor, sad creature not another decent man in this town will have a thing to do with."

"Decent! I guess! My lord, Sinjin, she's a *darky,* as if you didn't know it, and there's poor Mab tryin' to make somethin' worthwhile out of her, not to mention Georgianner, and you're invitin' her up to yer room for a bit of pillow fun any chance you get. Lord, if Georgie don't have troubles enough with that school and you have t'come around and light a blaze under her. Can't yer grandmother find something for you t'do, keep you out of mischief? You must be itchin' t'return to sea."

"Return to sea?" His laugh was sardonic. "Not likely." He leaped up as if he'd been pinched and stepped to the mantel, where he picked up one of Barnaby Duckworth's pipes from the rack. "Let me tell you something, Hat, the only things worse than the horrors on land are the horrors a-swim in the deep, dark sea." He sniffed the pipe, returned it to the rack, and took up a second. "I wonder," he went on, "how many sailors have drowned in the sea, all told, how many millions, from the days of Sidon and Tyre till now. Hat, did you ever see a typhoon?" he asked, suddenly turning back to her.

"Barely missed one in the Chiner Sea once. Barn outran it though, good sailor that he was."

"Damned if I know who or what makes a storm like that, except to send good ships and cargo and men to the bottom. The deep bottom. Oh Christ, it's so deep down there, deep and green. I'd rather be hanged than drown; God help the poor bastard awash in the sea that's going to claim him."

Hat blinked behind her glasses. "Was't like that for Barn, d'ye guess?"

"Don't think of it, Hat."

"But you'll be returnin', one of these days, won't you? To Chiner, I mean."

"I guess."

"Do you like it much, Singe? Livin' out there and all? Chiner's a mighty strange place if you ask me."

She put the question in such an emphatic way that he realized she was interested and had never thought about it before.

"I like it. It suits me. They leave a fellow alone over there, providing he comes up with enough cumshaw."

Aunt Hat hooted, "Cumshaw! Greasin' all those yellow palms, I guess. Cumshaw! Barn always said the Chinese were wilier than any Injun born and I b'lieve him. A wonder you've come home with your skin on, though I heard tell you manage quite well with the yellow heathen, for a fact."

"If I do I still haven't a dollar to my name. Though there's good money to be made, believe me."

"Ayuh, I believe you, son. If you like selling that poppy stuff to those poor demented people. Sooner starve, m'self."

"If your Barn were alive today, he'd tell you otherwise, Aunt Hat," he explained. "I was China-side a good long time and I know."

"What d'ye know?"

"I know there wasn't a cannier trader on the whole China coast than Barnaby Duckworth."

"Or a better mate. I was lucky enough to get him, I s'pose." She darted him a quick look. "But, you know, I didn't want him, Singe, I had m'heart set elsewhere." She nodded soberly. "Ayuh, it's true, for a fact. Set on a man I never could've marrit, never ought t'have. But things have their way of siftin' scum. I settled on Barnaby as second best, thinking I'd maybe rue the day, but 'twas the smartest thing I ever done. And all those years I waited for him to say, 'Well, that's torn it, I'm home t'stay and I'll never go sailin' n'more.' He never did. He sailed right till the last, tiller in his hand, quarterdeck underfoot, and then the sea took him. I think you'd be smart t'give it up, Singe. You've had one too many ships wash under you. Fancy a man tryin' t'skipper one o' them wallowy junks clear 'cross the sea. Sorry you didn't make it, you'd be a rich man now."

"I would at that, Hat, I promise you."

"Oh, I know you would! You've got your flaws, you're as cracked as a Dutch plate in lots o' ways, but you're generous to a fault. I hear things."

"What things?"

"I know how you ben slippin' money to"—she jerked her head kitchen-wards—"yer sis t'give t'Georgianner for her school fund. That's why your carryin' on the way you do makes no sense, Singe, helpin' her with one hand and cuttin' the ground from under her feet with the other."

"I wish Sal had kept her lip buttoned. She didn't have call to go blabbing about that money."

"No matter; it shows your heart's in the right place even if your brain ain't." Her expression was anxious as she strained toward him. "But Singe, you've got to stop wranglin' with Georgie, she's plumb tuckered out. That school's li'bul t'be the end o' her. Oh, the savagin' she's taken all year. And what for? Because she wants to teach some darky girls to read and write. 'Tain't fair, it just ain't fair."

"Whoever said life was fair, Auntie?" Sinjin drawled, pulling out a cigar from his breast pocket. "Life is never fair, and it's filled with the most fearful things imaginable." He rolled the cigar between his fingers but did not immediately light up.

"Tell me something, Singe," Hat said after a while. "Since you was talkin' 'bout typhoons and sich like, and your fear of the aqua natura, how do you fit up that hairy tale 'bout havin' swum the Hellespont? Or is it just that, a hairy tale?"

"Not at all, Auntie. I crossed that body of water just as I wrote Georgiana, all in one piece."

Hat shifted her spectacles and squinted hard at him. "Mebbe, but you didn't say *how* you done it."

"Would you care to hear about it now?"

"I would that and then some. And let's invite in the ladies from their hatmaking, they've a notion to hear as well—Georgianner, Helen, leave off your braidin' and come in and set a spell. The captain's goin' t' tell how he swam the Hellespont."

Georgiana's reproachful features appeared in the doorway. "I don't think I want to hear it," she said.

But by means of one or two adroit remarks Sinjin soon had his adversary in a receptive mood and she and Helen, easing their tired fingers, took up places.

"It's been quite a few years, remember," he cautioned, "so if I don't get all the facts straight, you'll forgive me, I'm sure."

"We'll know you're making them up, you mean," Helen laughed. "But start, by all means."

And so he began, taking up his narrative at the point where he had sailed the *Paulina's Fancy* from Naples. "It was off to Greece then," he said, "for whatever cargo I might get. We put in at Pireus, and from there went on to Mytilene and after that to Gallipoli, and all the while I was feeling the spell of—" he broke off and glanced at Georgiana, "—of Lord Byron," he finished.

He fell silent for a moment, then resumed. "By the time I reached Gallipoli, I knew in my bones that I had to do it, had to swim the Hellespont just as Byron did."

Helen leaned forward in her chair. "But how?" she asked. "How could you hope to do such a thing when you couldn't swim?"

"I'd concocted this plan," he said. The tip of his cigar glowed. "In Mytilene I'd met a Turkish sailor who knew all about the Hellespont, how the current ran fast, and I reasoned that if I could manage to stay afloat that same current would carry me downstream at an angle and with a certain amount of splashing around I could get from the west side to the east safe enough. The Turk told me I was crazy, but by that time I wouldn't have listened to anybody, I was so dead set on doing it.

"I made my way down from Gallipoli to a village called Abydus where I laid my final plans. First I designed a sort of life-saving device, a shirt lined with slabs of cork to support me during the crossing. I'd already written a letter to a newspaper at Constantinople saying what I was going to do, I wanted the whole world to know . . ."

Again he glanced at Georgiana before resuming. "Everything went off according to plan, without a hitch. The water was freezing, and to fight off the cold and to give myself some Dutch courage, I'd brought along a bottle of ouzo, which is a kind of local white lightnin', with a mule's kick guaranteed to warm the cockles of your heart. I drank off half of it before I got into the water. The villagers were all standing along the shore, shaking their heads at this crazy foreigner who surely was going to drown, and the mayor kept kissing my hand and pleading with me not to do it, and I admitted confidentially to being Byron's son and telling him I must do as my father had done before me, and so off I went, carrying the half-drunk bottle of ouzo. The current snatched me up and there I was, bobbing along famously. I forgot all about Byron and—and all my troubles. I even started singing some fool song. Then it dawned on me that the current really was terrifically strong, and it would probably carry me right past Sestos and out to sea where I was bound to drown, cork-lined shirt or no."

"What didja do, Singe?" inquired Hat.

"I didn't have to do anything, it was done for me. Along about then I came athwart a fishing boat, and when they saw me waving and heard my shouts they yanked down a net from the mast and tossed it. Quite a catch they hauled in that morning! They kept me with them till they got close ashore, by which time I'd sobered up. Then they put me over the side again, and I floated into Sestos in fine style. But you know something, George? When I was afraid I was going to drown, all I could think about was you. Isn't that odd?"

Georgiana bridled. "Don't be silly. Why would you be thinking of me at that point?" she demanded.

"I haven't any idea. My mind was pretty fuzzy, don't forget, but I remember it occurred to me that the whole business was silly and childish, me floating down the Hellespont in Byron's wet shoes, and that's when I began thinking of you. I thought that what I was doing was bound to get back to you and embarrass you or disappoint you or—or that you'd even laugh at me for being such a fool. Would you have?"

"Would I have laughed if you'd drowned, do you mean?"

"Yes. Well, in that way, drunk in the Hellespont with the cork-lined shirt and the ouzo."

"I doubt that I'd have laughed very much," she said and stood up from her chair, massaging the small of her back. "But that you should die because of such foolishness—" She stopped, and clamped her lips shut as though to prevent the escape of words she would later regret. There was another short silence, broken only by the rustling sound made by Murray Hill, playing with Hat's newspaper. Then Georgiana turned abruptly and headed toward the kitchen. "Come on, Helen. We have work to do."

"Coming," Helen said, and, standing on tiptoes, gave Sinjin a kiss. "None of us would have laughed," she said, and left the room.

Hat took off her spectacles and squeezed the bridge of her nose. "Go on now," she told Sinjin, "you get out of here. That was a fine story, right enough, but I reckon Georgiana's right, too. Now, I'm tired of talkin', an' I want t'read m'paper, the week's near done." She shooed the cat from the newspaper and Sinjin from the room and made a great business of arranging the pages of newsprint to her satisfaction. Sinjin scooped up Murray Hill and, cat in arms, followed Georgiana and Helen into the kitchen. Curling braids of grass lay about on the tabletop. Catching Helen's pleading expression, he made no further comment concerning the feeble attempts at bonnet manufacture, and was wary of Georgiana's rigid back as she sat and fitted one piece against the other. Clearly the business wasn't going well, and he wondered how she and Helen alone expected to turn out sufficient work to bring any notable profit, even if they should get the knack of it. Didn't they have enough to do just handling the school? When he casually mentioned this, instead of replying Georgiana brusquely relieved him of Murray

Hill and marched with the animal out through the back entryway. When she didn't return immediately he sat at the table with Helen. "Seems to me you ladies'll be needing some help if—"

"We'll have help," Georgiana said, cutting him off as she reappeared, Murray Hill slipping in past her skirts. "Murray Hill—scat!" She stamped her feet as the cat leaped through the open window.

"Chief Waikoit promised his girls would do the work," Helen explained.

"And how many hats do you figure to make in, say, a week or so?"

"We don't know that yet," Helen replied, her look entreating him to guard his words.

"Well, how much d'you figure to charge for one? That is, how much do you calculate you'd earn in, say, a month?"

"We haven't figured that yet either," Helen said. "How could we?"

He laughed outright. "Looks like you ladies haven't done much figuring at all. You really ought to learn more about the hat business before you start up an operation like this. Oh, Georgie, I almost forgot—here's something my grammaw sent along. She asked me to slip it to you and not say anything."

"Please thank her for me." Georgiana pushed the envelope across to Helen. "Helen, would you put the kettle on again? Never mind, I'll do it."

"No, let me." Helen jumped up and took the teakettle from the hob, filled it at the pump, and set it on the stove.

"Where'd you get such an idea as this hat business, anyway?"

"Rose was plaiting some braids one day," Helen put in quickly. "Georgie thought—"

"Helen, I'm sure your brother isn't really interested in anything to do with our feeble attempts at handiwork."

"You mean to say Rose gave you the idea? Why, the wench—"

"Oh, *will* you please just hush up!" Georgiana sprang up, slamming down her work. "I don't know why you bothered coming here, anyway. Just who do you think you are, coming around, making cutting remarks? It's not appreciated, I can tell you that. Now get out of here. And don't bother turning up for any more lectures either! Keep your Eskimos and polar bears and hula dancers to yourself, and stay away from my girls!"

Sinjin cocked a brow. "Am I to understand, good teacher, that you do not wish me to continue my little talks before that score and more of honest maidens whose earnest faces I am so used to looking upon?"

"That's exactly what I mean. You can cease your talks as of right now. I won't have our girls associating with you!"

Helen was stunned. "Georgiana, surely you're not serious," she remonstrated.

"I was never more serious in my life! I've enough problems, I need no more; I won't have him shaming us and the school—"

She stopped suddenly, and Sinjin raised a placating hand. "Say no more, fair damsel, I shall not present myself again before your young ladies. Instead, I shall leave them to their weaving and plaiting, industrious creatures all, earning dimes on dollar headgear."

He got no further. Unable to control herself, Georgiana flew at him like a fighting cock, her flailing arms and fists striking him so he was forced to avert his face and duck away, overturning the chair in the process. Using considerable strength, she knocked and pummeled at him, muttering oaths as she drove him back against the door, where he could do no more than try feebly to defend himself. Then, breathless and near collapse, she fell back into Helen's arms while Sinjin wrestled the door open.

"Much obliged for the drink, ladies, I must stop round again sometime." He ducked as a plate came crashing against the lintel, broken bits flying in all directions, and went out, closing the door behind. A moment later, his face appeared among the geraniums on the sill. "Farewell, sweet creatures." Then he disappeared and they could hear him singing as he went away. "Sin and gin, gin and sin . . . that's the state the world is in . . ."

The room remained silent for a moment, then Helen bent down and began picking up the fragments of shattered chinaware. She watched, stricken, as Georgiana tried to hold back her tears. "Don't, dear, he doesn't mean it, truly he doesn't. It's just his way. Besides, before we're done he'll be laughing out the other side of his mouth."

"No." Georgiana looked pathetic as she held up a piece of their evening's efforts. "He was right. It *is* a foolish idea. Who will buy them? Nobody will want our work if this is any example. It's nothing like a leghorn at all."

Too upset to continue, she kissed Helen and sent her home, then sank down at the table and, taking a tuft of marsh grass, crushed it in her fist. As much as she hated to admit it, Sinjin had spoken the truth: the grass was too coarse and brittle and the color was all wrong. She flung it away, not bothering to watch where it landed. When Hat came in moments later she found Georgiana at the table, her head on her arms; the old woman watched her for a moment, pitying her, but knowing pity was the worst thing she could show.

"C'mon, George, bedtime," she said at last, shaking her shoulder. "School day t'morrer."

Georgiana struggled wearily to her feet. "Is it worth it?" she asked. The desperation in her voice made Hat stiffen her back.

"Get along, 'course 'tis. And you'll go on with it too. You're a good strong girl, and when the time comes to heave to and stand full into the wind, you'll do it. And Hat'll be right alongside o' you." She stood tiptoe to kiss Georgiana's cheek, then, giving her a gentle pat, sent her topside. Murray Hill wrapped his furry tail around Hat's ankles and purred in lusty accord as she blew out the lamp and went to her room, closing the door.

In the soap kettle the bunch of marsh grass, so petulantly tossed away by Georgiana, soaked through the night, and early next morning she heard Hat calling.

"Who's been throwin' spear grass in m'soft soap?" she demanded, blinking at the tufts lying amid the froth. Georgiana rebuked herself for her carelessness and used a long-handled spoon to fish the grass out. The first thing she noticed was how supple and pliable the blades had become from their overnight soaking; the second thing was that they were several shades lighter in tone. Carrying them dripping to the table under the arbor, she laid them out one by one and cooled them. Then she picked up a single blade and examined it. A night in the soap vat had softened the tough, resistant sheath, which now slid easily away from the inner core. She peeled two more shafts, then braided them into a plait. The material felt entirely different. The grass was easily worked into a strip, to which she soon had added a second, then a third, until she had created a handsome, uniform band.

After class that afternoon, with Helen standing by holding a basket containing the braided strips of softened grass and the partially completed bonnet, Georgiana asked Rose to wait for her. "Rose, be good enough to look at these pieces and tell us what you think."

"We know it's not very good," Helen said, displaying the unfinished bonnet.

As expected, Rose sniffed at that crude effort, but after examining the latest braids, grudgingly admitted that it might be possible to fashion a satisfactory bonnet of that material.

" 'Course, you got to know how to do it," she said, stating the obvious. "To tell the truth, you ladies ain't—*aren't*—so deft with your fingers. It's easy enough if you know how, though."

"Exactly, Rose. And *you* know how. We want you to help us. We want you to teach us. And the girls." She eagerly explained the idea she and Helen had come up with, and how, with the older girls doing the work, they could make money to help support the school.

Rose laughed outright. "You can't teach them dumb Injun girls nothin' like this."

Georgiana disliked appearing to seek Rose's favor, but the success of the infant hat enterprise might stand or fall on her willingness to offer her expertise. Georgiana exerted all her powers of persuasion.

"Rose, you must say yes, truly you must. You're clever, you're really very talented. and you'd be helping us out, honestly you would."

"I got lots of work to keep me busy. Missus Talca won't want me settin' round making hats out of grass. 'Sides, like I said, them Lament girls is—are—too stupid."

Georgiana replied that she intended speaking to Mab and securing her permission, at least until the other girls had learned the work. With evident reluctance, but actually grasping the additional opportunity to escape from Halley's tyranny, and deciding that in view of Helen Haverstraw's being Sinjin's sister, a nicer propinquity might be an advantage, Rose agreed.

Once involved, she set to willingly enough. During their first work session in Hat's kitchen, she pointed out that the grass required further lightening. "It wants bleaching," she said.

Georgiana and Helen were already aware of this. Despite the soap treatment, the grass was still a dun shade, not at all the gleaming silver-and-cream tone of the leghorn bonnet. "Pearl ash," Rose decreed, and went in search of some. Using Cinnamon's large cook pot, they put handfuls of the hulled marsh grass to steep in the dissolved pearl ash; next day they discovered that after being rinsed and spread in the sun the grass had bleached out to a handsome wheat color. The plaits woven from them shone almost golden. They were on their way.

That evening after supper, Georgiana and Rose, aided by Helen, began work in earnest. Again setting the leghorn bonnet up for a model, they started braiding. As their fingers worked, the bands grew in length and breadth as they assembled the plaits, moving outward from the crown, around and around, their efforts initially fumbling and uncertain, then increasingly adept. Next afternoon, no sooner was class dismissed than they were in the kitchen again completing their first bonnet. Georgiana produced several yards of royal purple ribbon for trimming it, and when she finished tacking the velvet she placed the bonnet on Rose's head, then took her to view the results in a mirror.

Rose was impressed. "That's good. You could sell it in a shop."

"Exactly," Georgiana said; Helen agreed. The bonnet was somewhat smaller than the leghorn, but it was definitely stylish, it set well and had a professional look to it. Georgiana retrieved the bandbox that had held Sinjin's leghorn, placed the hat inside, clapped on the lid, did up the strings, and started out the door. "Come along, Rose," she said, and Hat was surprised to see with what meekness the girl followed her down the walk. Together they proceeded up March Street to talk with Liza Eales in her hat shop.

Liza Eales, the milliner, had been in business in Pequot Landing for nearly twenty years, and both men and women paused to regard her attractive display of goods set out in the single window fronting Main Street. As the shop was small and the proprietress large, there was little enough room for Liza's customers, not more than three or four could be accommodated at one time to look over the array of millinery or the boxes and trays of sewing findings, buttons, silver hooks-and-eyes, elegant braid, gimp, and silk ribbons. Liza had long maintained her chair in the window corner, from which she decreed the fashions of the day, as they were made known to her, and at the same time kept an eye on street doings.

"Now where'd you get this?" she asked Georgiana, taking the bonnet from its box. "I've never seen one quite like it."

"We made it, Mrs. Eales. Will you put it in your window?"

Into the window went the bonnet, which made its public debut the following Sunday at church, atop the head of no less a figure than Judge John Perry's wife, and created an enthusiastic stir among the congregation. Meanwhile Georgiana already had Rose instructing the girls after school above the seed store. Contrary to Rose's prediction, they took to the work with alacrity. Between other duties, Cinnamon Comorra was set to the task of watching the boiling cook pot in which the grass was softened before being hulled, bleached, then set out to sun-dry. Each individual took to her task with diligence, and by the end of the next week three more bonnets had been created; these likewise subsequently appeared in Mrs. Eales's window.

These likewise did well. Two sold that very day, the third was gone by the following afternoon, and Sunday's church congregation saw new bonnets on an entire quartet of heads. Georgiana's active imagination inspired dreams of a hat factory, lines of nimble-fingered girls in rows, working like the famous factory girls of Lowell, turning out two score of headgear each week, the Pequot Landing bonnet becoming every bit as famous as the Pequot Landing Red Onion. The next day she began to investigate markets for the bonnets beyond the village boundaries. In no time, hats of Connecticut River marsh grass were the latest thing (Old Bobby had bought one and sent it off to John Quincy's wife, Louisa), and soon the Free School was ordering new primers for its classes and a new harness for Ned, the school horse.

21

Good-bye My Lover

BLESS CINNAMON COMORRA for a good witch! That cunning little charm that now swung between Rose's legs was doing the trick. After having despaired of ever catching the captain's eye and believing she must forever suffer his contempt, or, worse, his indifference, Rose had crept, not only into his room, but into his thoughts as well. As dark of mood as he might be, as scornful and impatient with her, she was convinced the charm's power was working as well as ever the old Geechee woman's could and that she might look forward to further "commemorations" as often as she was able to sneak away to meet him. No matter that he sometimes ridiculed her and threatened to turn her out; soon he would be hers, exactly as she had prayed so hard and long for.

In the evenings, when her supper chores were seen to, she would go strolling in the garden. Waves of desire would sweep over her as she conjured up his image. She loved him. She loved him and it frightened her, making her thoughts rush helter-skelter through her head. No other man had ever stirred her the way he did. No man had ever made her hunger for things she'd formerly had no appetite for, and these days was starved for.

Still, now that they were lovers, there were additional concerns. Could she hope to hold such a man just because she now secretly shared his bed? Would that alone bind him to her? Would it change the fact that she was after all only a lowly hired girl, an ex-slave bought and paid for? She *might* aspire to wed the iceman, but the noble sea captain?—that was something else again. Where to find the power to make him altogether hers, to cause him to forget the porcelain face in the portrait hanging in the front parlor? Certainly, Rose had good looks; she knew this, and the captain was after all only a man, and men she knew about. She was therefore resolved that if he had been so readily susceptible to the blond beauty of Aurora Talcott, he could just as easily be made captive to her own darker form of entice-ment. Besides, hadn't Cinnamon promised it?

And so, with the household fast abed and all quiet, she would slip from under her covers and sneak down the carriage house stairs, out into the darkness. Cloaked in dark garments, she would hasten along the walk and cut through the snowball bushes to the Ancient Burying Ground, then slip across March Street and, avoiding the lights from the tavern windows, dart like a bat up the back stairs. Once she had impressed the captain with her day's sum of accrued knowledge, she would begin impatiently tugging at his clothes, then, unlacing and unhooking, she would wriggle out of her own things and slide eagerly into his warm bed . . .

Naked in his arms she was in her glory, triumphant. A ruffled, gartered Paris courtesan, a slippered China concubine, a Venetian *putana* with henna-dyed hair—she was all of these together. The sly, fine arts practiced between the sheets of those sinful arenas were not so different from those of other places, and Rose Mills had soft lips and a tongue that had more than its incidental employments. She made it her business to afford him every drop of pleasure she was capable of producing, while he lay back against the bolster watching her busy herself about his body.

She liked to put the fish skin on him herself, performing that particular ritual with a ladylike gentility that roused him the more, until before long she was kneeling atop him and settling herself comfortably. With her delicious moans of delight he went softly and sweetly to work, and before long he would be ramming her deep, sending her bouncing upwards, wedging his hand in her mouth when her passionate cries rose from deep in her throat, until he shot like a rocket inside her. Then, drained of passion, empty of desire, she would collapse on him as he collapsed within her, and they would sink into spent and sweating apathy, marveling together at what they had accomplished.

Afterward she would snuggle against him and they would converse in subdued tones of inconsequentials until he was ready to respond again, and after that it was time for her to go, no matter how reluctantly, still feeling fugitive tremors of latent ecstasy and the hot sanding of his stubble on her cheeks, while he indolently stretched out atop the rumpled bedcovers, drowsy and yawning in her face, not troubling to disguise his willingness for her to be gone. She would dress and kiss kiss kiss good-bye, prolonging the minutes to make them last, then finally flee down the stairs and hurry her step over the Fathers' Rise, praying no one saw her returning from her rendezvous, breathless and discreet now, until she had gained the seclusion of her room, where she would collapse on the rope bed, relieved that she was safely home again and no one the wiser for her escapade.

Yet, not every rendezvous under the eaves of the Hundred saw so safe or rewarding a denouement. One night the pair were lying in his bed sipping warm beer and talking. He yawned, then reached across her for a cigar. She loved to watch him smoke after they'd made love, enjoying the masculine aroma of the tobacco, the languid curl of the smoke.

"Let me have a puff," she said. She took the smoke into her lungs and blew it out, choking.

"How many times do I have to tell you? You're not supposed to inhale it." This was a Cuban cigar, a good Havana, he said, though nowhere as fine and aromatic as the Manila cigars he found in Macao, a generous supply of which had gone down aboard the hapless red junk. But never mind, he said, puffing, others would be waiting for him when he returned to China.

"When you go to China—you take Rose with you?" she asked with winsome guile.

"Christ, girl, are you crazy?" he snorted. "Why would you want to leave here and go out to China?" He made an O of his lips and blew a volley of blue rings that normally would have distracted her.

"Why not? Rose, she be good for you. She be good *to* you. You like Rose, don't you? Don't you?"

"Not enough to take you with me."

His callous reply cut through her like a knife. "But don't you want me, don't you want me with you? Close like this? All the time? You don't have to marry with me."

He laughed. "Good God, woman, what gives you the crazy notion I'd ever marry a darky?"

She sat up as though struck. "I ain't, damn your eyes, I ain't no darky! Don't you call me that!" Her voice rose and she raised her fist to strike him. "I'm white! My pap was a purely white man. I got his blood. I'm white as anybody. Ain't nobody can tell no different!"

"I thought you weren't going to say 'ain't' anymore. In any case, your pap may have been white as Christmas but that doesn't change the facts. Besides, I never allow females aboard my vessels. They're a jinx, they make ships do weird things."

Rose's laugh was harsh, derisive. "Ooh! You is such a liar. Ain't—aren't no females on your ships, you say? You think Rose don't know how you kidnapped that poor chile from right under her daddy's nose and tried to sail off for China?" She laughed again. "I guess she did pretty good without you, all right. Folks say now she got herself a big house, got a gold-plated husband, too, she got ever'thing she need, and here you is—*are*—livin' over a tavern. Hell, you ain't even got no *ship!*" She had squelched him; he lay as if stunned by her words, and for a while neither spoke. Then she said softly, "She wasn't for you. I know it."

"How do you know?"

"I can tell just from looking at her pitcher in the parlor. Every day I dust, I sees her with her blue dress and her fan and her gloves. Some day Rose is going to be just like that."

He laughed every bit as derisively as she had moments before. "That's a fine idea, Rosie. You be just like Lady Sheffield and wear a silk gown and flutter a fan." He got up and threw on his robe, then went to the mirror and began energetically brushing his hair. "Perhaps you're right," he went on. "Perhaps some fancy Dan will come along one day and provide you a nice little nest in return for your considerable favors. *If* you learn not to expect too much and not be too greedy."

"Rose ain't greedy, she just want what's comin' to her."

"Oh dear, not that, I hope," he murmured, setting his brush down. He bent and picked up her shoe, which he held up before him, examining it critically. "Do you know, you have rather large feet for such a thin girl."

She snatched the shoe from him and clutched it between her naked breasts. "You leave my shoe alone. What's wrong with it? Can I help it if I got big feet?"

"I suppose not. I just happen to prefer small ones, that's all." Yawning, he picked up a roll of coins from the dresser and tendered them to her. "Buy yourself another pretty to hang upon your dazzling person, Rose. Be happy."

She flung the coins to the carpet. "Rose don't want your damn money."

"Poor Rose." He gathered up the scattered money, then straightened to face her. "Or 'rich' Rose, perhaps I should say. What is it you do want?"

"I wants you to love me!" she cried. "I wants you to think about me an' care for me. You son-of-a-bitch, nothin's ever good enough for you!" She began striking him and calling him names, and he grappled with her, clutching her narrow wrists, surprised by the supple force she had summoned as she tried to get at his cheeks to scratch them. She was sobbing loudly now and he felt her suddenly go weak against him, but no sooner did he release her than she jerked up, striking his chin with the crown of her skull, knocking him backward two or three steps. Quickly her nails flashed and she drew blood along his jaw.

"Ow! God damn you!" In return he fetched her a smart crack. At that moment there began a loud banging on the door. "What's going on in there?" It was the voice of Sallie Jenckes.

In a frantic scramble Rose snatched her clothes from furniture and hooks and sped to the far side of the wardrobe, flinging open a door and hiding behind it while she wrestled her way into her things.

"Sinjin? You hear me?" Sallie called. "Open up in there before I break this door down."

Sinjin crept to the door and, feigning sleepy confusion, said, "Huh? Wha'? Who's there? Wha's the hour?"

"I'll tell you the hour all right, when you open this damn door."

Rose was still struggling with her buttons when Sinjin turned the key in the lock and did as he was ordered. In marched Sallie, breathing fire.

"What's going on around here?" she demanded. "For God's sakes, Sinjin, close your robe. If you're not a sight. All right, Rose, you can come out, I see your feet."

Rose appeared from behind the open door, a sheepish, disheveled, bruised-looking creature.

"Well, Rosie my girl," Sallie said, "just passing through, thought you'd stop and press a call? Pardon me for noticing, but you look like last week's laundry. Now will you kindly collect the rest of your clothes and get out of here so decent folks can catch some shuteye? As for you, Captain, you're lucky I didn't get Val Morgan over here to pinch you as a public nuisance. Rose, you're not going to cry—stop it. Stop it, I say!"

Rose had crumpled on the bed, her head hanging, trying between now muffled sobs to tie her shoe latches. When her attire was more or less assembled, Sallie took her by the hand and they went out, leaving Sinjin lighting a cigar and trying not to look a fool.

When Sallie returned, she came in and shut the door. "Jesus, the poor thing's half scared out of her wits."

"I'm not surprised," Sinjin observed dryly, "the way you came busting in here like the whole fire brigade on a call."

"Well, you made me mad. Singe, have you lost your wits entirely? Don't you know what this will do to the Free School, not to mention the reputation of my place if people find out?" She sniffed to and fro. "What's that scent she wears? This whole place smells like a whore's convention."

"Dunno," he answered meekly, sniffing. "Quite a trail, at that." He staggered back to the bed where he flopped, hugging the bolster over his loins.

"And just look at those sheets!" Sallie exclaimed. "Fresh on today." She shook her head. "My God, Sinjin Grimes, haven't you had enough to do with women to know how they are? Before long that one'll be hung around your neck like a millstone, that or she'll pop up one day saying she's going to present your brat to a lucky world."

Sinjin chuckled into his pillow. "Not mine, Sal. These days I'm Cautious Charlie. You know me."

"Sure, I know you. You'd marry the girl just to prove that the age of chivalry isn't gone. Well, don't say I didn't warn you, sailor." She started for the door.

"I won't," he said to her back; she whirled.

"And just remember, Captain, no more females in the dormitories, if you please, else I'll have to have Ed saw off the back stairs."

He cocked a brow. "Does that particular ukase apply to the proprietress of this establishment as well?"

Sallie shook her head in astonishment. "You know, the poor wench is right. You *are* a son-of-a-bitch. G'night, Cap."

"Night, Sal. Pleasant dreams."

"Oh, sure—sleeping with Milehigh Jenckes?"

She went away laughing while Sinjin fell instantly asleep and dreamed of slender feet and yellow hair.

IT HAD in no wise augmented Sinjin's general peace of mind to have had Rose bring up the anguishing subject of Aurora Talcott, and to his everlasting regret he had discovered the tantalizing way in which her alluring image would materialize before his eyes at odd and inconvenient intervals, only to dissolve again, causing him in time to become irritable, his black moods to rush in on him with greater frequency. As described by Rose, the portrait in oils displayed in the best parlor intrigued him, and he yearned to see it for himself, to gaze again on the bewitching face: the Beauty captured on a canvas rectangle when she was young and at her golden fairest, and had been lost to him forever as surely as that sweet and saucy brig, the *Adele* of Pequot Landing. And if he did not sigh with woe, he was wracked with resentment and cursed what he termed his "luck." Romeo did not play fortune's fool half so well as the ex-captain of the drowned *Koxinga*.

In consequence of such melancholy thoughts and, with the abrupt ending
to his school teaching, there were few days that saw him sober at high noon,
or after that very far from the local gaming tables; neither of these activities
was calculated to sit well on Miss Rachel, who, almost always willing to
have a hank of wool pulled over her eyes where Sinjin was concerned, had
begun to wax exceedingly wroth. It irked her especially that he'd stopped
giving his lectures to Georgiana's pupils, which had offered her some reason
to be proud, though she knew all too well the reason why Georgiana had
called them off, and she had begun to think that the likeliest solution to the
problem was to spirit him out of town—even pack him off somewhere on
another sea voyage, however brief or inconsequential.

To this end, having dreamed up a loosely formulated plan of action that
might serve both to remove Sinjin from Pequot Landing and yet keep him
from running off to China again, one afternoon she paid an unannounced
call on him in his rooms at the tavern, resolved to hammer out matters, no
matter how delicate or objectionable. She found him stretched out on his
bed with a book, while Mat Kindu hunkered down by the hearth polishing
a sizable heap of his master's footgear. Dispatching the Malay with one of
her curt gestures, Rachel undid her bonnet strings and tugged off her lace
mitts, while Sinjin eyed her glumly from his pillow.

She gave him an impatient glare, saying, "Now just you take that
hangdog look from off your face, Dick, and attend to what I have to say."
She sat down abruptly and tapped the ferrule of her cane on the planking,
then beckoned him into the chair opposite her. "Now see here, Sonny boy,"
she began.

Sinjin shrank inwardly; here it came, the lecture he feared would be his
lot today. Nothing new there, however; he'd heard it all before. These were
hard times, and who knew what lay ahead? A dollar wouldn't buy what
it used to, help was hard to find.

"Shipping isn't onions and barrelstaves anymore," she went on, as if he
needed reminding. "A large vessel with a decent cargo can't get upriver, and
it costs too much to barge it. Oh, Dick," she added sorrowfully, "with the
railroad come through to Hartford, who knows what the future holds?" She
shifted her waist as if her stays were laced too tightly, then suddenly her
face went dead white and she began to choke. "You'll see—I—can—oh—
oh—Sonny—"

The attack was on her before he realized it. Her head lolled back, her eyes
enlarged, and she made violent, gagging sounds in her throat. In panic he
felt around in her reticule for her laudanum bottle. Not bothering with a
spoon, he placed the open bottleneck to her lips and dribbled a good dose
between her teeth. Gasping, she accepted it gratefully, clutching his hand
as though to hold onto life. He waited, feeling a gradual relief as the drug
went to work.

The attack ended as suddenly as it had begun; a minute and a half had passed, no more. He picked the cork up from the floor and was stopping the bottle when she motioned him with one hand.

"Give me another, do," she gasped with the sly look he knew well; "it's pleasant, makes everything so nice."

He poured another dose into the glass, diluting it with water from the jug. Soon she seemed recovered, though fatigued. She made no pretense of hiding a yawn, not caring that he could see her missing teeth. When he thought her sufficiently revived he got up to summon her coachman.

"No, you don't," she said, a hand gripping his arm. "Draw up your chair again, I haven't had all my say yet." He was relieved to see that the color had returned to her cheeks, and there was a glimmer in the hooded eyes as she leaned across her cane and began her proposal. "See here, Sonny—"

What now? he thought. She fixed him with her gimlet eye. "It's time you shipped out again," she said. "I'll find you a vessel."

Since it was useless to protest, he agreed, for what else could he do? "What hulk had you in mind?"

"Haven't a notion. I'll have to look around, see what's available. Now give me a kiss and I'm off." She put her withered cheek up to him. "It's not the face that launched a thousand ships, but it's the one the Almighty gave me, so make the most of it." As she slipped on her mitts and straightened her bonnet she sighed again. "Ah, Dick, you're such a trial to those who love you most, I vow you are. And when I'm gone, who'll have the care of you? Whoever she is, I pity the poor creature."

Sinjin stretched expansively and wriggled his stocking toes. "That's all right, Grammaw. I don't need a woman looking after me."

"Well, you need someone, and that's a fact if you don't know it." She eyed him through narrowed lids. "And I don't mean that pennywhistle darky of Mabel Talcott's, either. Why you couldn't leave well enough alone—"

He frowned. "If it's all the same to you, Grammaw, I really don't care for any more discussion of my private affairs."

"Private! You're lucky the whole town doesn't know!" She shook her head sadly at him. "Ah, Dick, if you only knew the hopes your dear dead mother had for you. Why, she'd never have married that weaselly malefactor except to make a home for you, never had her heart broken as it was. Oh yes, he'd make a proper lady of the creature, he said, and a gentleman of you, he said, and sent her to an early grave instead, and packed you off to sea, just a lad. Well, he'll get his own reward one day, the monster." She tightened her lips and gave a grim nod to underscore her words.

"In the meantime, Sonny, my advice is for you to lie low for a bit. It'll want some time to land you a suitable vessel. I'll pay your gambling debts and give you a clear board again. But no more playing fast and loose with Mab Talcott's parlor maid, is that understood?"

"Yes, milady, understood."

"Fresh! I'll hold you to your word on that."

He exhibited a bogus humility as she kissed him again and marched out the door, refusing his offer of assistance down the stairs. Through the window he saw her giving orders to Hogarth, so irked that she took a swipe at his tall hat before entering the coach.

THERE was a sequel of sorts in the matter of Rose's clandestine visits to Sinjin's quarters. Having been forbidden entry to his rooms, she prudently avoided the tavern premises. Sinjin, however, continued to manifest a hankering after her charms, for which he maintained a keen appreciation, and despite his promise to his grandmother, scratching his amorous itch he found himself late one evening stealing onto the grounds of Kingdom Come, to stand like an overheated schoolboy, tossing pebbles up at Rose's window. When she put her head out he beckoned her down—he "wanted to apologize to her for their last meeting."

Once down, Rose found, not entirely to her displeasure, that there was little apology called for but in its stead all manner of serious action. To this end Sinjin persuaded her, not to admit him up to her quarters, but to join him in an intimate tryst in, of all places, Old Bobby's coach. Thus, making their way into the carriage house proper, they proceeded to enter the Yellow Pumpkin, in whose handsomely appointed interior they undertook to enjoy themselves in yet another act of "commemoration," one that was for several reasons to remain etched in both participants' memories. So carried away did Sinjin become that his athleticism set the coach to rocking and bucking—perhaps serving to recall for him another occasion many years before when he had found himself inside a similar vehicle with a member of the opposite sex, a night of frantic fulfillment, which in retrospect he had come to regard as his "honeymoon," and of which his daughter Caroline had been the result. The current rendezvous had quite a different conclusion to it, however, for, as luck would have it, at the crucial moment, with his bare knees on the scrap of Turkey carpet covering the coach's floor, his elbows resting on the tufted seat, with Rose's ankles crossed behind his neck, her head flung back, her red lips gurgling her pleasure, the captain found himself staring into the shocked features of Hallelujah Priest. The fuzzy wool of her old gray head done up in straightening papers, her eyes popping in disbelief, her head wagged back and forth in horror at what she looked upon. But even as Sinjin attempted to decide if, given the untoward circumstances, he should continue his labors or grind to a halt, the apparition—for such he judged it to be—evaporated, whereupon he brought matters to their logical pass with as much finesse as he could manage and dispatched his light-o'-love back to her bed with a kiss and a lame excuse for his mistimed performance. Then he scurried back the way he had come, congratulating himself on having got out of another scrape and sternly reminding himself that toying with Rose was playing with fire, and that, since he was not a fireman, good at extinguishing conflagrations once they got started, he must desist. Rose's charms must be saved for the iceman.

HE NEEDN'T have worried over what to do about his *amour,* however, at least for the present, since less than twenty-four hours saw him gone from the village entirely, and for reasons not at all having to do with Rose, but with the Free School. That afternoon, in place of Stix and Kneebone— Warren Burdin had engaged them to drive a wagonload of seeds over to New Britain—Ambo Buck had been enlisted to ride with Foote Crowe on the wagon that carried the Lamentation girls home from school, and, to be safe, Sinjin had suggested that Mat Kindu go along as well. Another irregular was Jeffrey-Amherst, who accompanied the older men "for the ride."

The wagon had left at its regular hour of half past three and should have returned by six, but six o'clock came and went with no sign of it. "I'm sure something's happened," an anxious Georgiana said, putting a stack of school-work aside. She and Hat were in the front room of Snug Harbor, watching the light fade as dusk came on. "If Jeff gets hurt I'll never forgive myself."

As usual, Hat was reassuring. "Nothin's likely t'happen to Jeff when he's with Ambo and the Yeller Shadder. One of those wheels was turnin' sluggish, y'know, the wagon might have broken down along the way."

This much was true at any rate: the left front wheel had been giving Foote trouble after hitting a gulley. Georgiana told herself Hat was right; there was no cause for alarm.

But another hour passed, still with no sign of the missing wagon. Cinna-mon was rattling the supper dishes in the dishpan, Hat was in her fireside chair, sewing on a piece, and Georgiana was again attacking her schoolwork, when a dark form appeared at the side window nearest the fruit tree grove. She started as Sinjin's face flashed behind the pane. He rapped and signaled to undo the latch.

"Use the door, you big ox!" Hat called out.

"Oh, don't let him in," Georgiana whispered behind her hand. "He's probably drunk."

Sinjin rapped harder on the glass. "Open up, damn it!" His voice was hoarse and he panted from some heavy exertion.

Hat undid the latch and raised the sash partway. "What're you doin' in my bushes, Singe?" she demanded.

"I ain't pickin' huckleberries, Auntie." He threw a leg over the sill and tumbled into the room.

"What's amiss, then? Don't wait to tell us. We've been worried about Ambo and Jeffie." Aunt Hat's face was furrowed with apprehension.

"That's what I'm—" He caught his boot heel in the braided rug and grabbed the chair back to keep himself from falling.

Georgiana made a scornful sound. "I was right! He's drunk, I'll be bound, and it's only just past suppertime. See here, Captain Grimes, if you've come here—"

Sinjin frowned. "Squeeze it, George," he said grimly. "I'm not drunk, not really. Hold on a sec—"

He put his head out the window and gave a low whistle. In a moment footsteps were heard among the quince trees and another figure appeared at the window.

"Jeff!" Georgiana cried. "Why are you here? Where's Ambo? Oh lordy, he's hurt!"

"Only a little. Jeff's the hero of the day." Sinjin put an arm out and drew Jeff into the room. He was bleeding from a gash at the temple; the blood was running down the side of his head.

Georgiana took the boy's hand. "I was right, there *was* trouble. Are any of the girls injured? Tell me, please tell me."

"The girls are okay. You don't have to worry about them. Right, Jeff?"

Jeffrey-Amherst nodded.

Hat was clucking like a mother hen as she looked over the boy's wound. "That's a bad gash. I'd best send Cinnermin for the doctor."

"No, we don't want any meddlers around. We'll probably have some visitors before long, and I've got to saddle up and ride to Grimes Mill."

"The mill? What's at the mill?"

"Ambo is, and Mat, they're hiding out there, trying to keep from getting strung up on the Burning Bush tree." Sinjin dropped his cap on the top of Hat's sewing basket, then yanked out his bandanna and wiped his forehead. "Lower the lamp a bit and let me have a shot of that sherry you keep in the cupboard. Give Jeff one, too. He's done yeoman service this day."

"Cinnermin! Bring two sherry glasses!" Hat called out loudly.

"*Sssshhh!* Do you want to wake the dead?" He stepped to the front windows and peered out past the curtains to the street.

Cinnamon's lumbering tread was heard as she came in with the bottle and glasses rattling in her knotty fingers. She set them down, then, grunting, turned Jeff's head into the light and examined the cut.

Sinjin dropped the curtain and put a comforting hand on Jeff's shoulder.

"Well, son, our friends haven't got here yet, but they will, so we'd better not waste any time. Get his head fixed up, Cinnamon, then we'll slip him out of sight."

Dabbing arnica, Hat was at the end of her patience. "What are you talking about? Who'll get here?"

"Our pal Ike Bleezer and his band of Merrie Men. They've been actively employed in the greenwood this afternoon. Tell Aunt Hattie, Jeff."

"Yes, Jeff, tell us, we want to hear," urged Georgiana. The boy stirred in his chair, sipping the sherry Hat had poured for him. Then, while Cinnamon finished tending his wound, he rendered up his account of the afternoon's macabre adventures. They had been driving along past Gypsy Woods, when some men on horseback—eight of them, by Jeff's count—had ridden out from among the trees and intercepted the wagon close beside Beaver Brook. Obviously they were out for no good. When Foote geed up his horses in an attempt to get away, one of the men—this was Tyler Gatchell—had grabbed the bridle and stopped them.

"They made Ambo 'n' Mat 'n' me get down," Jeff said, "and they took Ambo's gun away. One of them socked Ambo and called him a dirty redskin bas— you know."

Georgiana nodded. "Go on, Jeff, what happened then?"

"Foote, he was still up on the wagon with all the girls. The men, they were talkin' 'bout takin' the girls into the woods and—and—"

He stopped. The two women looked questioningly at Sinjin, who nodded grimly. "Ambo came to the rescue. Tell what Ambo did, Jeff."

Jeff wiped his lips and went on with his story. "Ambo, he sort of dropped his hat accidental-like, and when he bent down to pick it up he picked up a stone, too. He shied it at the horses, and before the men knew what was happening, the wagon took off, and the men couldn't catch it. They was so mad at Ambo they said they was going to string him up on the spot. I guess they meant it, too, 'cause one of 'em went to fetch a rope. Another— that was Tyler Gatchell again—he started hittin' Ambo and kickin' him. Then's when Mat Kindu went into action."

"What did Mat do?" Georgiana asked.

"He slipped out a knife from his sleeve and threw it. He got Gatchell. Right here"—he touched his fingers to the front part of his shoulder, at the joint—"and when Gatchell fell we all started runnin', all three of us ducked into the woods where they couldn't find us."

Then, Jeff said, Ambo had made a quick plan. Ambo would take Matty to Grimes Mill, where they would hide out while Jeff sneaked back to the village in search of the captain.

They'd split up then, the two men heading west to Two Stone, Jeff east to Pequot.

"But how'd you get hurt, Jeff?" asked Hat.

Jeff said that when Ike Bleezer had pulled him off the wagon he'd hit his head on the wheel hub.

"And you're sure the girls are all safe?"

So far as Jeff knew they were. As for Foote Crowe, he was probably keeping out of the way at Lamentation, fearing to return along Greenshadow Road again.

When Jeff got to town, having traveled shank's mare all the way and avoided the roads, he headed straight for the tavern to alert Sinjin, whom he found in the taproom. They were just going to saddle up a horse when they saw Bleezer and his gang dismounting at the stables. Sinjin and Jeff had ducked back inside, but thought they'd been seen. The men were helping along the wounded Gatchell, and while they attended to his needs Sinjin and Jeff had slipped from the tavern through the Long Room and hurried here to Snug Harbor. Sinjin was sure the gang must be looking for them now; if Jeff were found it would likely go hard with him.

"Hat," Sinjin said, "find Jeff some place to hide. Don't let him leave until it's safe. I'm heading for the Hundred for a word with Sal and Milehigh and then to the mill. I want to get Mat and Ambo out of town before there's real trouble."

"Where d'ye mean to take them, Singe?" Hat asked. "You'll have a peck o' trouble hidin' that vivid a pair of fellers. They're not your average village folk, y'know."

"I'm going to put them some place where no one'll care if they're Yankees or Hottentots."

"Where, Sinjin?" This was Georgiana's question.

He raised an eyebrow. "You can guess, can't you?"

Georgiana's brows contracted in thought, then her expression lighted up. "Yes! I *can* guess. Shall I say?"

"Maybe not just yet. You can tell Auntie as soon as I get out of here."

"When will you return?"

"When you send Jeff after us, saying the coast is clear."

"Yes, all right."

"Listen!" Hat turned to the window. From outside came the sound of horses' hooves in the roadway. Men were gathered beyond the gate, some of them were running up to the almshouse door, asking questions of the inmates.

"They'll be over here next," Georgiana said, pushing Sinjin toward the kitchen. "Hat, you hide Jeff. Don't open the door till I return."

In the kitchen Georgiana cracked the back door. Sinjin grabbed a piece of cheese off the table and a crust of bread. "I'm starved. Georgie, you can handle this all right, can't you?"

She looked at him; his concern for her was obvious. Despite everything—even his disastrous *affaire de coeur* with Rose Mills—he was her friend. "Yes. Now hurry." She urged him toward the door. "And Sinjin—"

"Yes?"

"Thank you."

He immediately assumed his pose of mockery. Cocking his brow, he said,

"Always glad to oblige you, Miss Mouse. I'll think about you when I'm gone." He gave her cheek a peck and disappeared into the darkness. As she shut the door, the warm feeling of his lips on her cheek, from beyond the parlor came the sound of banging. She hurried into the room and looked around. Hat was in her chair, Cinnamon on the settle. Jeff was nowhere to be seen. Georgiana picked up Hat's sewing and set it in her lap, then went to open the door.

"Took ya long enough," growled Ike Bleezer, standing on the threshold peering in. "All right, where is he?"

Hat dropped her sewing and stood. "He? Who d'ye mean, 'he'? This is a house full o' women. And I'll thank ye kindly to wipe your big hooves before you come traipsing through my parlor."

"Never mind that, Aunt Hat. This here's business. We're huntin' a murderer." The speaker was Newt Gill, head of the fire volunteers and like Ike Bleezer an outspoken opponent of the Free School.

"Murderer? Then look among your cronies, we have no murderers here."

"Of whom are you speaking?" Georgiana demanded.

"That Injun of yours, that's who. And that yellow bastard with the big knife. He damn near kilt Ty Gatchell. We seen that nigger kid Jeff Priest fetch Cap'n Grimes at the Hundred, figured they'd lead us to 'em. We want to look around."

"Not in here you don't. Go get a warrant."

"We don't need no warrant to pay you a little visit." His eye fell on Cinnamon, who sat stolidly smoking on the settle.

"Why in God's name is she here?"

"She is attending us, as she has done anytime these past ten years."

"Get her outta here. I don't like the way that redskin's lookin' at me. She's givin' me the evil eye."

Then his glance fell on the settle itself; Georgiana felt a pang of apprehension. Suddenly she realized that Hat had put Jeff inside the hollow seat.

"Don't you move, Princess," Hat said, according Cinnamon her due title.

"Princess!" Ike spat. "If she's a princess I'm a goat."

"You sure behave like a goat," Hat retorted, eyeing his spittle on the floor. "And smell like one, too." She marched into the kitchen and returned with the rag mop. "Now you and the rest of these bravos get out of my house."

She brandished her mop; Newt stepped back, but Ike Bleezer, feet astride, arms defiantly folded across his burly chest, stood his ground. He flicked his eye around the room. Hat and Georgiana saw it at the same instant; Sinjin's cap atop the sewing basket. Hat reached to shut the lid but Ike stayed her move.

"All right, now, what's this, then? Looks to be Singe's cap. So he has been here."

"You know he has, many times."

"I mean tonight."

"No."

"You're lying, all of you. Maybe you don't know it, but you're interfering with the law."

Georgiana's eyes flashed and she spoke contemptuously. "Since when are you the law hereabouts, you drunken sot? Go climb a rope."

"You've got a loose tongue, woman, one day you'll wag it once too often."

Outside, the gate latch was heard to lift and fall, and the sound of uneven steps along the flagging. Newt checked the window. "Here comes Pegleg Light."

In a moment a knock came at the door; Georgiana opened it and found Hermie on the threshold.

"Hullo, Georgie," he said, pushing back his hat. "Sal said—"

He noted the grim assortment of intruders and quickly interrupted his own sentence. "I brought you these collards fer your and Hat's supper." He held up a sack of greens. "What's happenin', Ike?"

"We're lookin' fer some people, that's what. Fugitives from the law."

Hermie glanced around the room.

"Don't look as if there's any here," Hermie said easily. He opened the door again. "Maybe you boys ought to just go along."

Ike blew his cheeks. His eye fell again on Cinnamon, calmly puffing on her pipe as she spread her considerable girth on the settle seat.

"What's in there?" he demanded. "Redskin witch, what d'you think you're hiding under you?"

"She's not hiding anything," Georgiana said quickly. Hermie, who saw the look of alarm on her face, pivoted on his good leg and, raising its fellow, used its wooden stump as a weapon. Holding it straight out before him, he lightly pushed the walnut tip against Bleezer's overhanging belly.

"Out, Ike. And be quick about it before I get Val Morgan over here. He'll jail you and yer gang for the night for trespassin'. Hear me?"

Ike looked at the leg protruding into his soft belly, then shrugged. "All right, fellers," he said, "let's go over t'the tavern. Cap'n and that nigger kid haven't gone far, we'll find 'em yet."

He backed away from Hermie, who lowered his peg leg and, using his body to encourage them to leave the room, followed them out.

When they had all gone, Hat grabbed the mop and broom and swept both carpet and floor where their feet had trod, as if by so doing she could rid the place of the memory of their unwelcome presence, while Georgiana raised the settle lid and brought Jeffrey-Amherst out, checked his wound again, then sent him off via the shortcut through the Ancient Burying Ground to Kingdom Come, where he would be safe.

When the small house was restored to peace and order again, Georgiana and Hat sat down at the kitchen table, whispering together.

"Lordy, what a mess," Georgiana sighed.

"Oh, let's not worry about it. Singe has Ambo and the Malay, they'll fare all right. Now tell, Georgie, where'd they go?"

Georgiana glanced out the window to the deserted street.

"To Bible Rock. That's what he went back to the Hundred for, to arrange to borrow Milehigh's big canoe."

Hat's face lighted. "You don't say! Now there's a sovereign idea."

Georgiana agreed. Bible Rock lay some twenty-five miles downriver, and years ago Sinjin had kept a ramshackle cabin there, from which he ventured forth on hunting and fishing expeditions. No one would ever think of looking for the fugitives there; they could hide out until the coast was clear.

22

Straws in the Wind

ON THE FOLLOWING morning, Georgiana asked Hermie to drive to Two Stone to ascertain if Sinjin had managed to spirit Ambo and Mat safely away, and when he reported back that there were no signs of the fugitives and that the mill was indeed deserted, she took heart. Fugitives they were, however; Bleezer had finagled a warrant for their arrest, Ambo and Mat on a charge of aggravated assault and attempted murder, Sinjin for aiding and abetting their escape. But since no one but Georgiana, Hat, and the Jenckses knew their whereabouts, and with Val Morgan out of sympathy with the whole business, though obliged by law to serve the warrant if he found the missing men, for the moment they were safe. Even with Tyler Gatchell going about with his arm in a sling, telling all comers that he'd been viciously attacked by Sinjin Grimes's murderous body servant, and bragging that when caught both Mat and Ambo would go to jail, Jack Talcott, with whom Georgiana consulted during the noon recess, felt sure he could prevent such an outcome.

"Tyler's got a mouth on him and he likes to flap it in the breeze," Jack said. "Ike Bleezer, too, they're a pair of mischief-makers. But warrants can be quashed. I'll talk with Johnny Perry and see what's to be done."

The news of the debacle at Gypsy Woods traveled round the Center in no time and everyone was soon made privy to the situation. One person, however, had not got the details correctly sorted out. In the kitchen of

Kingdom Come, Rose Mills heard from Halley Priest's own lips that Captain Grimes had left town on the previous evening, taking with him Ambo Buck and Mat Kindu, and wouldn't be returning.

"Gone t'China, Ah 'speck," Halley Priest said, "an' good riddance."

When this declaration struck her ears Rose had flung off her apron, caught up her skirts, and fled to the tavern to assess the situation for herself.

Having climbed the back stairs two at a time, she burst into his room, tripped over his bootjack, and fell, slumped at the foot of his bed, whereupon, taking in the empty room, she began to wail.

"Sweet Magee, what's goin' on in here?" demanded Sallie, choosing this moment to come in with a stack of fresh linen in her husky arms. Her suspicious eyes took in the miserable creature sprawled on the rug.

"God damn him for a blackhearted bastard!" Rose hollered at Sallie. "I curse the night I done met him, and I feels sorry for any woman what gets caught in his beartrap, the miserable lowdown skunk!"

"Here now, Rose, cease your caterwaulin', they'll be hearin' you clear to Stepney Parish."

"I don't care, I'd kill him, could I get my hands on him." Rose's face was deathly pale and her breath came in short, animal pants. Then, before Sallie's eyes, she collapsed in tears on the bed.

"You love him, I guess," Sallie said, slipping off a wrinkled pillowcase. Rose nodded. "Well, there's a line about a mile long in front of you, honey, so you might as well just hook on with the rest of the ladies. I'm surprised, though; a smart gal like you ought to know better'n to get attached to the likes of him."

"Whatchamean, a smart girl like me?" Rose demanded, flinging her black hair out of her face.

"Don't try to fool with me, Rosie, I know what goes on," Sallie said, hiding the sympathy she felt.

"Reckon you do. Won't nothing catch him now, will it?" She paced frantically up and down before her. "What boat's he done gone off on?"

"Canoe, dear."

"Godamighty—clear to China?"

Sallie laughed. "He's not China-bound, Rosie, he's paddled downriver to hide out those fellows till the judge can fix things up, that's all."

Rose was close to speechless. "Why that damn Halley Priest, she done tole me he took off plumb to China! Liar, liar, liar!" She whirled and dashed out before she could be stopped.

Sallie shook her head, then continued with her linen changing. After a moment she stopped and laid one of the pillows against her cheek. "You're right, Rosie," she whispered. "He's a blackhearted bastard all right." She plumped the pillow and set it with its twin, smoothed the bedcovers where Rose had rumpled them. She went out, closing and locking the door behind

her and pocketing the key. The room was Dick Grimes's, she'd have no other
guest sleeping in it while he was away.

IT WAS high summer now, and with the onset of the dog days the troubles
assailing Georgiana and her school had not lessened. At the monthly meeting
of the Board of Selectmen—Zion Grimes presiding—Bushrod got up to
demand that "for the good of the children" a town ordinance be passed that
prohibited any Pequot Landing educational institution from teaching pupils
who had arrived there from beyond the town's designated boundaries. The
proschoolers on the Board, including Merrill Ashley and Warren Burdin,
could hardly believe their ears, yet it happened that on this occasion, with
George Ritchie, Newton Gill, and Willy-the-rat Wandsworth in attendance, and several of their opponents absent, the ordinance was voted onto
the Pequot books.

In the face of this petty legal maneuvering Georgiana went on conducting
her classes exactly as before, and the wagonful of Lamentation girls passed
along Greenshadow Road while sullen-faced men stood at the crossways
shaking their fists. But before long Val Morgan was reluctantly knocking
on the seed store door. Georgiana and her pupils were ordered to cease and
desist without ado and to abandon the premises forthwith. Georgiana looked
the order over, then, leaving Val standing on the stoop, and not bothering
with shawl or coat, she flashed across the green to Jack Talcott's office and
placed the document before him. Jack explained to Georgiana that she must
bow to the ordinance or be held in contempt of the court, to be fined or
even jailed. Inside of ten minutes the seed store attic was cleared of its pupils.

Ten minutes more saw her at Helen's house, where, to her surprise, she
found Rod as well. He sat at the kitchen table while his sister applied a
linseed poultice to a carbuncle on the back of his neck. Georgiana made the
most of her opportunity as she described for Helen's benefit what had just
happened at the seed store.

Having heard her outraged words, Rod looked every bit as surprised as
he could manage. He shifted uneasily; altercations with his sister intimidated
him and he didn't relish her sharp tongue. "Honest, I don't know what
you're both talking about."

Georgiana whirled angrily on him. "Rod, don't lie to me. You and your
father are thick as thieves. Your little trick may have worked today, but
if you think you've beaten us, think again."

"What a mean thing to do," Helen said. "And to your own nieces, too!"

Rod got up, using a finger to test the bandage Helen had put on his
carbuncle. "Well, damn it all, how do you think it looks, having those two
kids going to a nigger school? The granddaughters of Zion Grimes—"

"Oh, blast Zion Grimes."

"He's your father!"

"I don't care. I'm ashamed of him—and *you* and your petty machinations. I'm sure you're all very pleased with your handiwork, but believe me, Georgie means what she says—don't you, Georgie?"

Georgiana faced Rod angrily, trying to control her temper. "Tell me, Rod, what do you hope to gain? In the end, what will all this have got you? Personally, I mean?"

Rod hiked up a chair with his toe. "Me personally? Heck, that's easy. One thing, it's getting my name in the papers. And if the folks see it often enough they'll become familiar with it. Don'tcha see, this whole business of the school will put me exactly where I want to be?"

Georgiana studied his face intently. "Where is that, Rod?" she asked quietly.

"First the General Assembly, as you well know, then, well, the governor's seat or the Congress in Washington. You'll see." He straightened and stretched his arms overhead, then turned to Helen. "I'm telling you, Sis, you can't afford to go getting yourself more mixed up in this mess. You'll only be asking for trouble. You've got a family to look out for."

"I'm aware of that. What worries you so much?"

"Because pretty soon things'll start getting real ugly. People are going to get hurt. If you're smart you'll send the girls back to Center School and forget this other business."

The rest of his words were cut off as the kitchen door flew open and Luke Haverstraw appeared, supporting with both arms the sagging weight of the hired man Foote Crowe. Foote's head lolled forward, and from where they stood the women could see the blood as it dripped onto the step.

"What's happened? Bring him in—"

Helen shouldered part of the weight and together she and Luke helped the injured man to a chair. Luke explained that he'd come across Foote lying on the floor of the tackroom, where he'd been attacked and beaten.

Rod observed the scene without comment as Luke fetched a glass of spirits for Foote to down, and Helen poured a basin of hot water from the teakettle. She washed the cuts, one of which was a serious gash that had laid open Foote's scalp behind the ear. A stoic, he never flinched when Luke brought out his cauterizing kit and proceeded to sear the wound and stitch it up.

"Foote, who did this to you?" Georgiana demanded.

"Some mens" was all that could be had from the victim; no amount of cajoling could induce him to name names. When he was bandaged, Helen refused to allow him to return to the shed where he usually slept, but put him to bed in the little anteroom behind the kitchen, covering him and placing a pillow under his head.

When she had closed the door and come back into the kitchen she found a militant Georgiana once again angrily facing Bushrod. "All he did was drive the girls back and forth. And for this they brutalize a good honest man! I want to know who did this thing!"

"What does it matter who did it?" Luke said. "The important thing is that it was done."

"Maybe he was drunk and fell down," Rod suggested with a smirk. "Those redskins do put the stuff away, you know."

"Oh Rod, stop it!" Helen snapped, coming forward. "You're not fooling anybody. We know who's behind this job of work." She quickly filled Luke in on what had happened over at the school.

Luke turned to Rod. "By God, if you weren't my brother-in-law—"

"Whoa there, Doc, where do you get off blaming me? You can't prove a thing. Nobody can. As for the school getting closed down, it was all legal and aboveboard. Board of Selectmen did it."

Ignoring Rod's gloating, Luke went on coldly. "All right then, this is how it is, Rod. If you're Georgiana Ross's enemy then damn it you'd better count yourself mine too, and I believe I can say the same for Helen. So you can just go along now, you're not welcome around here. Not while you stand behind that bunch of bigots and rabblerousers." He opened the door and backed Rod onto the threshold. "One thing more—two of my children are in that school, and if anything ever happens to either of them when it opens again, as it surely will, I promise I'll be coming after you with a gun! Go tell your big tough bullyboys that! Tell that father of yours, too!"

Rod hiked his chin. "Okay, Doc, if that's how you want it." His lips curled in a mean sneer. "But I guess you're all smart enough to figure out the next step, aren't you?"

"Which is?"

"Which is that just about the time your sweet little Chloe gets old enough to start thinking about boys, here'll come along some black buck who'll get her in the barn, he'll be a-tuggin' at her lacy pantalettes and before you know it we'll have us a little Rastus in the family and a fine shiny nigger for a son-in-law. How'll you like that, Doc?"

For an answer Luke doubled his fist and floored Rod with one blow to his chin. Then he picked him up, thrust him outside, and slammed the door on him. Helen had burst into sobs and Luke took her on his lap and held her comfortingly. Presently Chloe and Phoebe came rushing in, followed by the two boys.

"What's happened? Oh, Mama—why are you crying?" Chloe said.

Helen put out her arms and crushed the children into her embrace. "Mama's not crying," she sniffled. "Mama's mad, that's all. You children must learn the difference. And so must some others I could mention."

She shared her frown with Georgiana, who expressed her gratitude for Luke's support, and left to talk some more with Jack Talcott about the injunction.

That night the proslavery faction held a victory parade by torchlight, marching past the seed store, whose door bore the notification of closure. The parade cavorted in front of the Hundred and wound around the Common, passing the Talcott sisters' house, where Matilda and Bettina were hiding three Negroes who had arrived the night before on the way to Canada.

The jubilation over the success of the ordinance did not last, however, for, within a week, at another meeting of the Board at which full attendance was assured, the proschool majority prevailed and the noxious ordinance was summarily revoked. The next day the doors of the Free School were again open to the girls from Lament, who trooped up Burdin's stairs and sat primly at their desks learning that eight goes into sixty-four eight times and that the great Sir Walter Raleigh had been beheaded for treason in the Tower of London.

The taste of victory was like honey in Georgiana's mouth, but she feared it would sour quick enough. Truth to tell, she missed Sinjin Grimes. It was, she told herself, probably a good thing he was gone. Although she regretted their differences and appreciated what he had done and was now doing for the Free School, that same school would have been destroyed if his relationship with Rose had become known to any but Sal, Miss Rachel, Hat, and Georgiana herself. What was it that made him behave as he did—one moment her good, warm friend, the next up to some mischief he must know would put her out of patience with him, that indeed might ruin her?

She recalled him as a boy and youth, as a young man, when he had so handsomely exemplified the virtues of heroes of every time and place. It seemed to her there had been a very real nobility about him then, which, alas, with time had been subverted and corrupted, finally to produce the man he was, to all appearances, today. It was, she thought, as if a brightly gleaming statue had become diseased with time, its shine gradually scaled over with a corrosive patina. Yes, far better that he was gone.

On the other hand, she had to admit, his lectures had been an incontestable boon to her enterprise. By now, the Free School of Pequot Landing was not only well-known in New England, but was becoming known throughout the United States, even in Europe, particularly in the British Isles, where opponents of slavery rallied to its cause; the presence of reporters and dignitaries at Sinjin's lectures had evidently served to inhibit the more violent proclivities of the opposition. Now that these worthies had departed the scene, however, it seemed that a new vein of prejudice and hatred had been tapped—that the antiabolition sentiments that had been more or less suppressed had burst forth anew: the assault on the wagon had turned out to be only the first shot in a salvo of attacks. Not even Stix and Kneebone's fowlers served any longer to intimidate the mischief-making young fry who popped out from behind trees to lob rocks at them, call them dirty names, then run for cover. The girls carried boards to fend off the rocks, but not even this protection always worked. Culla Bryant had her writing hand injured, and a few days later Maria Coleman was struck while bravely attempting to shield some of the younger girls from a hail of flying stones on March Street; Maria herself was hit in the head. Stunned, she lay on the seed store lawn while Helen and Maude tried to revive her, and an outraged Georgiana forewent her customary schoolma'am dignity and chased the offending boys down Greenshadow Road.

Warren Burdin had given up trying to replace broken panes at the seed store, and worse, sacks of seeds had been slit by some undeclared agency, their valuable contents strewn about; one night his horses were taken from the stables and driven clear to Stepney Parish, where they were found wandering about in a farmer's turnip patch. Snug Harbor also fell victim to the haters: rocks were thrown at it, the flower beds were trampled, and obscene remarks were scrawled on the clapboarding. Hat and Georgiana never knew when their sleep would be interrupted by chanting voices—drunken voices—from either of the taverns, calling them vulgar names and ridiculing them. Val deputized two men to stand watch at the cottage, but the fellows weren't much interested in their jobs and fell asleep every chance they got. Disgusted, Georgiana told them to go jump in the river and she herself sat up, guarding Hat's property.

Then, after about two weeks, there came a lull. It brought Georgiana small comfort, for it coincided with Bushrod Grimes's appointment to the Assembly and, more destructive to Georgiana's peace of mind, a campaign in the antiabolitionist press, which now declared outright war, not just on the school, but on Georgiana personally, continually reminding its readers that the radical-minded, trouble-making schoolmistress of Pequot Landing was that same Miss Ross who, a decade earlier, had been the focus of the grisly murders at Grimes Mill. It was further pointed out by certain uncharitable souls that her father had been declared by a medical autopsy to be insane, suggesting to one editorial writer that the daughter might easily be suffering from a similar malady. This scurrilous attack saw an incensed Appleton Talcott boldly storming the newspaper office, threatening to horsewhip the pusillanimous writer, but it was only the first of many: the miller's girl had once more become notorious.

Still, Georgiana was determined to go on. She recalled that sunny spring morning many years ago when she had been gripped by the overwhelming desire to perform some liberating act, to don silver armor, to unfurl white banners and fight glorious battles for more glorious causes. She had been a mere girl then, scarcely comprehending what it was she had felt, baffled by the rush of emotion that had lifted and carried her away on bright white wings. Now it seemed to her that she fully understood, sensibly and unemotionally, exactly what she must do: having taken up her banners at last, she would on no account lay them down again, whatever others said or did. Destiny's wheels were greased, they must turn; the juggernaut must move forward. And so it did, at an increasingly fearful velocity.

Despite Georgiana's determination not to give in, the waves of agitation and violence had their effect, however, fraying her nerves and wearing her thin. With her heavy load of schoolwork, her attendance at various meetings, her days and evenings were kept full—too full. Ever since childhood she had risen at dawn and was bathed by cockcrow, but now it seemed she had only just put out her lamp before it was time to get up again. And, bone tired, she sometimes found herself lashing out at her critics, as when on the street one day, her granite eyes snapping, she told Rod Grimes to go straight to hell. She didn't want to think what her mother, Ruth-Ella, would have said about the use of such language, but somehow she didn't care anymore.

And however dark or bitter her mood might be, she pressed ahead—and saw progress. If, during Sinjin's absence, the first pupil at the Free School had reverted to her former lackadaisical ways, the others were making strides. Moreover, with the girls now weaving ladies' headgear daily, and a ready market for each item produced, there were more coppers than ever in the school fund, while at the same time the enterprise added to the growing legend of the Free School.

And this was a good thing, for with Mab's illness becoming more apparent, the Talcotts, though as devoted to the cause as ever, found themselves considerably distracted. These days Priam kept close to home, visiting daily, and Electra, too, was again expected for an extended visit that must perforce interrupt her schedule of lectures. As for Appleton—losing Mab would be the blow of his life, and sometimes Georgiana wondered if he could long survive.

23

The Revenant

MAB WONDERED TOO. With each passing day it became increasingly difficult to realize her planned stratagem of keeping Appleton in the dark, particularly in the light of her collapse at the town meeting. It had required some clever playacting, which in itself consumed much of her strength. And though her friends and family willingly abetted her scheme, seldom mentioning what they all knew to be true, and then only obliquely, it was unlikely she could go on much longer. Soon she would have to confess the truth to her Jake, but how she was to go about this she could not tell.

It was the major obstacle facing her, along with her reluctance to leave to a chancy future such important matters as her successor. The notion of a second wife for Appleton was one not easily dealt with, yet so practical was her nature and so deep her love for her husband, as well as her knowledge of his character, that she readily perceived how, outrageous as the thought might seem to him today, tomorrow was bound to be another story. She wished she could consult the abbé in the matter, but, alas, this most reliable of her props and supporters had once again been removed, summoned to Boston where His Grace the bishop wished to be informed first hand as to exactly what undertakings were being advanced in the matter of "the priest's folly," that is, the functioning of the Lamentation Mountain settlement. What word had reached His Grace's ears no one could have said, but some speculated that it was personal resentment on the part of Father Rupprecht that had precipitated the matter. Having barred his chapel doors to the Lamenters, he was fiercely jealous of the abbé's success among those unfortunates and had complained to higher authority. In truth nothing had been farther from the abbé's mind than to create any sort of contretemps with his colleague, but to Boston he had gone to toe the mark. Bereft, Mab prayed daily for his return, for now more than ever she had need of him—who else was to shrive her when the time came?

She was pondering these problems when, a few days after Electra's arrival, she had a little visit from Hattie Duckworth. Aunt Hat had come through the blackberry shortcut to join her in the boathouse, where Mab was sitting and talking with her sister-in-law, Susie Talcott, who'd driven over with a basket of fresh peaches.

The day was hottish, but with the broad side shutters bracketed up on hooks, unfolding the interior to the bustling view, there was a bit of breeze. Out on the placid river hung a skiff, in whose stern sat Old Bobby, patiently hunched under a broad-brimmed straw hat, his favorite fishing pole in his gnarled fingers. His line bobbed with the motion of the current, but not a bite had he had all morning.

"The man's indefatigable," Hat observed. "What does he think about, settin' out there for hours, and nary a nibble?"

"I'm sure Granddaddy has a great many things to think about," Mab replied. "Besides, if he was prohibited from fishing, he'd be the most miserable man in the world."

"And Lecky, where's she today?"

"Lunching with Pri, planning strategies. They'll be along, I shouldn't wonder."

Hat again scanned the river scene. "Sakes, if the place ain't near as busy as the High Street," she commented, noting the considerable volume of noonday traffic abroad on the water.

"Positively Venetian," Mab concurred. Today she wore one of her morning caps, pleated and starched, and her fingers industriously plied her tatting.

"I declare, Mabel, if you're not a reg'lar spinnin' jenny. Don't tell me you're startin' another counterpane?"

Mab held up her work. "It's not a counterpane at all, dearie. It's for Caroline. Pina found the sweetest pattern in *Godey's*. Miss Simms has it in work; this is for the trim. I want to surprise Rora with it, I'd like it to get there in time for the child's birthday. Just think—fourteen next year."

"Why, it don't seem but yesterday Rora was runnin' about at Follybrook in her bare feet," Hat declared. "Now she's got a daughter grown. Time passes, it passes."

Mab's needle flashed as she resumed her work. "I had a dream about her the other night—such a peculiar dream."

"Not a bad one, I hope?" said Susie in her sweet, mild voice.

"A strange one, Sue dear, very strange. She appeared to me out of the darkness—in her nightgown, of all things, a plain white nightgown. Her face was pale, and she was carrying a box, a large box, far too heavy for a single person to lift."

"What was in it?"

"I couldn't say. I never saw. She held out the box and said, 'Mama, this is for you, take it from me,' and I could see she wanted to be rid of it, and I tried to take it, but then she refused to give it up. I said, 'Rora, you're playing a naughty game with your mother,' and she said, 'No, Mama, *please* take it,' and I tried again but it was simply no use, her hands clutched it fast. Then, suddenly, she comes skipping into my room, all dressed for a party and she kisses me and says, 'Good night, Mama dearest, sweet dreams,' and when she's gone, there's the same box sitting on the rug. I tried to get the lid off but I couldn't do it."

"What did you do then?" asked Susie.

"I didn't do anything. I just sat down beside the box, then Jake came in. He became quite fussed with me over the thing, he said to just leave it alone and go to bed. So I did, and he took the box away. When he returned I asked him what was in it but he wouldn't say. There—that's all I recall."

Hat clucked over these details. "T-t-t—what a strange dream, indeed," she said. "But you've always had odd dreams; it's the Irish in you, I expect."

Susie stirred and her chair creaked. "But what do you suppose could have been in the box?" she asked. At half a century, Susie had the innocent manner of a ten-year-old girl.

"Haven't a notion, dearie. Nothing good, anyway, depend on that. I wondered if it wasn't a coffin."

"A *coffin?*" She was shocked. "But whose?"

"Who's to say? Mine, for all I know." She held her work out and surveyed it with a critical eye, then spread it in her lap and began measuring with a tape.

"How much more to do?" asked Hat, ignoring Mab's last words.

Mab allowed herself a wan smile. "I hope to finish it soon," she said. Hat's expression sobered; the meaning was clear enough. Mehatibel Duckworth was Mab's oldest Pequot friend, and though Mab might hope to fool members of her own family, fooling Hat was past imagining. It made each day spent in Mab's company more precious, and the old woman snatched every moment she was able in order to keep company with her friend while she was still up to it. Today seemed ideal. It being a Saturday, even Georgiana had taken a respite from her school duties. Having accompanied Hat on her visit, she was now engaged with Appleton in his shed, where he'd been hard at work all morning.

"They're havin' themselves a reg'lar sailor's game," Hat said, noticing Mab's glance toward the laboratory.

"There's the truth," Mab said. Through the open window two heads were visible, her spouse's and Georgiana's, as the pair sat conversing on opposite sides of his workbench. "Jake could always confide in Georgie," she remarked. Doubtless they were talking over some new scheme or other.

"It's books give them this great compatibility of mind," Hat said. "Books, books, books."

It had not escaped Mab's notice that lately Appleton had been spending more and more time sequestered in his workroom, as though by so doing he could avoid the world and its problems, including the cause of abolition. At present he was delving into the possibilities of long-term food storage in sealed cans from which all the air had been drawn.

Mab watched as he passed a hand across his forehead, then with his thumb and finger began his untidy habit of plucking at the bristly hairs of a most unruly set of brows. A moment later, he laughed outright. How good it was to hear that sound, all too rare recently, and not for the first time she wondered if he knew more than he let on after all.

"*Foof!* There's a lovely bit of breeze," Susie commented, making circular motions with her hands, as if to coax the cooler air into the boathouse. With the fresh currents came the pungent scent of tobacco from the fields cross-river.

Susie let the breeze waft her away, for she had dinner to see to for her menfolk and a wash ready to be taken in. She kissed her sister-in-law, said good-bye to Aunt Hat, and drifted off through the meadow with a wave to Appleton and Georgiana in the shed.

"Garden's pretty this year, Mabel, just look at those delphiniums," Hat commented, lifting her chin and squinting through her spectacles. "Such a glory of a blue. They do take a deal o' care, don't they?"

Mab nodded. "They do, they do. Oh, Hattie," she went on sadly, "who's going to look after my garden when I'm gone? My peonies, my irises. My lovely lilies. What's to become of it? It frightens me, to think of it all—all not being kept up, looked after."

" 'Course it'll be looked after," Hat declared. "D'you think a body's goin' to let it go to rack an' ruin? Jake won't let it—he'll take care o' things."

At this Mab closed her eyes and grimaced. "And there's the rub, dearie—who's to take care of Jake, do you suppose?"

Hat searched for some cheering words. "Why, Mabel, he'll catch hold—and he'll have a multitude of happy memories. There's no sense to carryin' on over such matters, they'll take care of themselves in time."

Mab shook her head stubbornly. "I say it won't do. He'll need more than memories, I'm afraid. He's going to need someone here beside him—a helpmeet."

"Helpmeet!" Hat's look was indignant. "Mabel Talcott, I'm ashamed for you to be thinking such a thing! Apple Talcott—a man who's been as faithful to you as my Barn was to me, who's loved you since the day he set eyes on you, who marrit with you against the whole world—to think of his takin' another bride! I say he'll never do it."

Mab's laugh was wry. "That may be, dearie, but I'm sitting here before you to tell you within two years Jake Talcott'll be a man twice wedded and bedded. He's not old, you know, and he's younger than his years, he's still full of spunk and juice. Remember I said it. I know my man. I ought to, I've been married to him long enough. Oh, he's been faithful, I warrant he hasn't strayed—I'd know if he had—but when things are different and he's up there in that big bed all by himself, well . . ." Mab smiled knowingly, more to herself than to Hat; she knew her man, knew human nature as well, knew how the wind blew down the chimney come the cold January nights, when he'd want a warm back to set his shins against.

Hat raised a cautionary hand. "Hush now, Mabel, not another word on the subject. Here's Lecky comin' along." Mab looked to see Electra and her brother making their way down through the garden, Priam carrying a gray stone crock. Electra's dress of palest blue stood out brightly against the meadow and as she stopped now and then to peer down into the tall blades of grass, Priam helloed and waved to Georgiana, who waved back, though Appleton seemed to take no notice.

Electra greeted Aunt Hat as she swept onto the boathouse gallery, then turned to Mab. "Oh, Mother, it's so pleasant down here! How splendid of Father to have built a boathouse. How pretty it is."

"Pull up a chair, Pri," Hat said as he bent and kissed her cheek. "What's in the crock?"

"Halley made you all some lemonade." Priam set down the crock and, taking some cups from his pockets, proceeded to pour.

Hat tasted and smacked her lips. "My, but that's toothsome!" She ran her eye over Electra's face and form and snapped out a pronounced approval. "You're lookin' peart, Lecky. Thought you might be all frazzled from your travels. Did you find much success?"

Electra nodded. Her recent speaking tour through the communities along the Erie Canal in New York State had been worthwhile indeed. Eager to catch every detail, Hat listened attentively while Mab, who had already heard a full account of the trip, talked to her son about his family. Their summers were usually passed at a rustic cottage on a nearby lake, but this summer, due to the exigencies of the school and Priam's schedule, Peggy, who still grieved over the death last winter of her newborn baby, and the children had remained at home.

Priam's eye had been flicking in the direction of Appleton's laboratory. "Will someone kindly tell me what Father and Georgie are up to in the shed?"

"They're just having a chat," his mother answered. "Your father is trying to soothe Georgie—for her own good."

"I gather she's been going hard at it," Electra put in.

"Why-y, th' poor creature's plumb tuckered out!" Hat exclaimed. "Folks hereabouts are gettin' to her, the nasty way they've been treatin' her. Pri, didja hear the latest—what Zeke Archibald done yestiddy? If I thought I'd ever see the day I couldn't buy m'kitchen staples from Zeke—"

"What happened?" Priam asked.

"Why, Georgie went into Archibald's after school to pick up one or two items, and that old curmudgeon up and tells her he can't wait on her. Cheeky fellow! So Georgie asks if her money wasn't any good, and Zeke allows it is, but that he won't sell to her as long as the Free School continues. The very nerve."

An indignant Mab drew up in her chair. "How can he do such a thing?"

"Well, he done it, and he's not the only one," Hattie said. "There's others jest like him who don't want Georgie's custom—no, nor mine either. I've come in for my share of snubs. Why, Flora Ritchie cut me dead at church Sunday." She sniffed and wiped her spectacles on her skirt hem. "I wonder sometimes if maybe Georgie's not asking for extra trouble. I'd as lief see her back workin' for Burdin's as puttin' up with what's come her way lately."

"No, no, Aunt, she mustn't do that!" Priam objected warmly. "She can't give up now, there's too much at stake. Lecky and I agree she's been pushing herself a bit too hard, in fact we've discussed it with Father, but—well, Georgie has become almost a symbol for us."

"A symbol! Whatever do you mean?" their mother asked.

"Just that the things Georgie and her school stand for are what our entire movement stands for," Priam said. "We need her. Why, the other day I received a letter from Bill Garrison. He has persuaded George Cowley to do a portrait of her, to be exhibited in various cities. People will pay to view the work and the money taken in will go toward the advancement of our principles. But if Georgiana stops now, it will all be wasted effort."

"I wouldn't worry 'bout that, Pri," Aunt Hat put in. "'Pears Georgie don't have any intention of closin' down, leastways not now. Maybe your father can persuade her to take things a bit easier though. It's true, she's worn to the nub." She set aside her empty glass and glanced at Mab. "Mabel, you all right?" she asked. Mab nodded. Her hand had gone involuntarily to her breast as a spasm hit her.

"Mother, can we help?" Electra asked, hurrying to her side. Mab shook her head and avoided her proffered hand.

"Sit down, Lecky, I'm all right, I say. A touch of indigestion, no more."

As Electra returned to her place she had a glance for Priam. Neither was taken in by Mab's protestations, but what was there to be done? She refused to stay in bed, and the doctor had said she could be up and doing as much as she felt she could.

WHILE Mab contented herself with the continuing pleasures of the river view, Appleton had been performing yeoman service under what were obviously awkward if not downright impossible circumstances. No one knew better than he how devoted Georgie was to the school, and how willing she was to imperil her own physical person in its furtherance. Second only to the needs of his family were those of Georgiana Ross. Why, she was like one of his own daughters, nearly his own flesh and blood. Could he forget the day, twenty years ago, when he'd first almost literally stumbled across her along Greenshadow Road, after that villainous character, Tom Ross, had beaten her? Appleton's heart warmed to her now as she faced him. Today she looked especially leached out, and, detecting flashes of impatience in her, he maneuvered tactfully into those particulars that required careful voicing. "You know, Georgie, you work so hard you never seem to have time for your own pleasure anymore."

"I'm afraid I don't recognize the word pleasure these days," she replied shortly.

"Everyone should take time for a little recreation," he pointed out. "And Georgie, truly, as much as we all realize its importance in the broader scheme of things, in the end, it's only a school, after all. As I told you, it's been mentioned that—well—maybe you're overdoing a bit. Even Lecky thinks that perhaps you might—"

"Really!" she expostulated. "I do wish Electra wouldn't go about advertising her concern for me. Besides, I can't imagine how a school like this is to function successfully without someone overdoing a little. Look at what we're having to face. But I'm not sick and I'm not done in, and while I'm still standing I plan to do everything in my power to see that nobody harms a hair on one of my girls' heads." Georgiana was boiling, as Appleton had feared, and he squared his shoulders to take the brunt of her ire. "It's easy enough for people to criticize, easy enough for them to turn up to take a quick look at things now and then, but it's quite another thing to be there day after day—"

"My dear, we're only suggesting—"

"I don't require anyone's suggestions," Georgiana interrupted testily. "I appreciate your concern, Lecky's as well, but heaven knows it won't change anything. I imagine it was she who put you up to this little talk, but it's not going to do anyone much good. What may be just a school to other people has become much much more to me. Those girls have been studying hard and they're coming along just fine. Why, Hutta and Easter and most of our older girls would be a credit to any school, and Posie's performing prodigies with the younger ones. In any event, I don't suppose I need to remind you that the whole idea was Lecky's in the first place."

"Ah, my dear Georgie—and if you only knew how sorry she is for the unfortunate turn things have taken. She feels very much responsible for having urged you into this—but all anyone is saying is that there are other things in life as well—or at least should be."

Georgiana sighed. "Until the school is safe I don't suppose anything else matters much to me," she said. "And it *will* be safe. We'll get past all these bad turns, I'm sure of it. We knew they'd come, they were bound to, weren't they? I said so from the start. But we'll win in the end."

Appleton shook his head. "I don't know that you can hope to see it soon. And, Georgie, you've had so much disappointment already, you really don't deserve any more . . . particularly when it's all to be avoided."

Her look was penetrating. "What are you trying to say?"

"I'm trying to say that if the battle continues, as it promises to, if people are so confounded set against the school, has it occurred to you that in the long run the struggle may not be worth the pain it's causing you? I'm simply saying that . . . well, that is to say . . . considering one thing and another, you might just want to think about giving it up—hm? Perhaps only until things settle down a bit. You know, you can't deny you're tired—no, wait now, allow me to finish, please."

He leaned across the bench and affectionately took her hands in his.

"Dear Georgiana, this is a splendid endeavor you've undertaken, and truly, I would not try to dissuade you from it for worlds, but, to be candid, I confess I am fearful. We all are fearful for you. No one ever anticipated such marked resistance, and you do appear to be facing real physical danger now, you and all your scholars. Your friends as well. Naturally, it goes without saying I'm not speaking of myself or Dad or Jack or Pri, we'll stand up with you to the lot of them. But I entreat you—we *all* do—to consider the situation carefully."

He paused while she thought over his words, then she thanked him for his generosity and concern, Electra's as well, and in her gravest manner she explained why she could never consider abandoning the Free School now. She was dedicated heart and soul to its furtherance and no one was going to force her to shut her doors. Appleton responded with equal gravity. "And what if Rod Grimes does get this law he talks of passed in the Assembly?"

He noted how in spite of her weariness her eyes snapped with energy. "I would go on in any case," she said. "And if the school were dealt with by law, I'd just move on to another state."

He stared at her, choked with alarm. "Eh? What's that you say? Leave here? You would just—pack up and go?"

"If I must, of course I would. And if a 'Grimes law' is passed in every state, I'll just go on out to the Reserve and start in again there."

"But this is not to be thought of!" Appleton cried, his face flooding with color. "You mustn't talk of going elsewhere, not now, when I—when we need you so desperately here." His voice grew unsteady and he put an entreating hand out to her. "Whatever happens, Georgiana, I beg you, I implore, you mustn't even consider such a thing, not when Molly—" The look of consternation on his face shocked her and she slipped swiftly around the table to him.

"No, no, you mustn't do this. You *mustn't*," she told him firmly. "You're not even supposed to know."

He roused himself, blinking his eyes as they filled with tears. "Lord, do you all take me for a complete fool? Of course I know—have known for months."

"*She* thinks you don't. She *prays* you don't—"

"Of course, of *course* she does; I've let her think it. I wanted her to think it. But she's—she's—" He reached again for Georgiana's hand and pressed his cheek against it, struggling to hold himself in control. "Georgie, if I must lose her—promise at least *you* will stay. For pity's sake, don't let me lose *you* too into the bargain, that would be more than I could bear. Promise me—"

Seeing how thoroughly alarmed he had become, she hastened to reassure him. "Of course, I promise," she said, touched that her words had affected him so. "I've no wish to leave, in any case. More than anything, I want the school to continue here in Pequot. To continue to succeed. I'll do anything to see it through, if it takes all my strength! Try and put it from your mind, I beg you . . ."

So she did her best to calm him, and in a few minutes he saw her off, watching her wend her way up the path with a wave to the boathouse where

Mab still sat visiting with Priam and Electra, Aunt Hat having already left the scene. Then he drew the shade and sank onto his stool, elbows on his worktable, lost in a maze of dismal thoughts. So profound were his reflections that he failed to notice when Mab slipped in to stand behind him; as she took in his sorrowful attitude; her hand flew to her breast.

"Jake, what on earth can you be doing, sitting here alone like this? Come outside where there's some breeze, won't you?"

"I was just—" He waved a feeble hand and peered at her with apprehensive eyes, then the tears brimmed over.

She was appalled. It struck her then that despite all her pains, he knew what she was trying to keep hidden from him. Yet the truth still seemed unutterable.

"Oh Jake, you *mustn't. Please,* for my sake." Seizing his hand she drew up the other stool and sat beside him at the worktable, laying her cheek tenderly against his shoulder. "Dearest Jake, you've been so brave all these months, you aren't going to disappoint me, are you? I'm depending on you, you know. As I have always depended on you. My Jake, my own dear Jake." Her hand went on patting the fabric of his shirt.

He seemed astonished by her statement and had trouble with his words. "I can't think when *you* have ever had to depend on *me.* Quite—quite the other way round, I'm sure. Can't imagine how I should ever have got so far without you, Molly. Oh, to think—t-to think . . ."

He lowered his head, trying to stem his tears. The room was dim and silent. If some casual viewer had glanced inadvertently in on them they might have taken the pair for courting lovers. Their intimacy went beyond mere physical propinquity, however; it sprang from years of loving each other despite all the setbacks. It was the bliss of habitude. Mab thanked God she had felt better today and that she didn't look as ill as she sometimes did lately. Being with him like this, away from others, sitting close to him, she experienced a vivid flood of memories, bittersweet recollections that blessed and burned. "Dearest Jake, do you remember how you used to ride your horse clear to Guilford, and I'd be waiting by the wellsweep with your laundry case? You'd bring me your soiled shirts and—"

"I remember."

"And that Irishwoman, the poor creature with the wen, said she was a mystic, you told her all Irish were mystics and in your opinion that didn't make her any different than ten other Irishmen, she was still just a spalpeen."

Appleton was forced to chuckle at the memory. "She was not a pretty sight, the widow O'Boyle."

"And do you remember that night you came to the brewery—I let you in at the window and we were kissing on the settle, and Pa came back early—my, wasn't he mad at finding you there?"

"Pat Riley never liked me, before we were wed or after."

"Because you weren't Irish. Because you weren't of the faith."

"Why, that old reprobate, how he could ever call himself a pious man—the way he soaked up his own brew it's a wonder he left you a cent."

She chuckled along with him, her fingers absently tapping his arm, her eyes searching his, hoping he'd stopped weeping. She couldn't bear to see it.

"Jake."

"Molly?" He refused to look at her; he mustn't shed more tears, not before her.

"We still haven't spoken of it, have we? The trouble—*my* trouble."

"No. And I don't want to! Not now, not ever!"

"Ah, dearie, we must. Truly, we must be practical now, you and I. There's much to be done and not much time to do it in. You've known, of course you have. I've known you've known, and you've known *I've* known. I would have said something, but we—Terry and I—we thought it better you shouldn't be told until—until it became absolutely necessary." He made a wretched sound in his throat and fought to master himself as she threaded her way painfully along. "But—now it's time. We must speak of it, no matter how unpleasant, don't you agree? Jake? Dear . . ." He was gazing at her with reddened eyes, but he seemed unable to absorb her words. She groped for his hand again and tugged at it. "Come along, dearie, suppose we just step outside and sit on the terrace. Better yet, let's walk down through the garden, wouldn't you like that? The garden's so pretty, don't you think? Do come, I'd like you to. Won't you, please, just for me—for Molly?"

Unable to deny her, he reluctantly followed her from the room, out into the garden, where they stood for a moment shielding their eyes against the brightness. "Come along, dearie, let's just go this way." She put her arm through his and they went and sat under one of the beech trees in the pair of Hitchcock chairs Sylvester had carried out.

"Look at it—and only two seasons," Mab remarked as she let herself down into the seat. "Oh my, this is nice, isn't it? We've always enjoyed this spot, haven't we, since we came here?" Unconsciously she spoke as if he were a child; mother, son. When he made no reply, she pointed out the family names and dates carved around the twin tree trunks. "What a naughty fellow you were to pull that trick on your Molly," Mab said, laughing. Appleton tugged at his brow and drew his lip in. It had long been a source of gentle mockery between them, how Mab, having innocently asked for a pair of silver birches for her backyard, her Jake had gone out with John Perry to Hubbard's Woods and dug up two saplings which, transplanted to her garden, grew apace, and for seven years she had spoken pridefully of her two birches, only to learn from Maude Ashley that they weren't birches at all, but silver beeches instead.

"And I expect that's not the only clever trick you've played on me, either," she said, smiling fondly at him.

"Don't you like them?" he asked. "Aren't you pleased with them?"

"Yes, dearie, of course," she said. "Think how big they'll be one day. Why, they'll take up the whole yard in another ten years."

It was true; the handsome spreading trees with their pale trunks and bountiful, well-shaped tops were becoming a feature of the place, their shade already making difficult the growing of turf around the trunks that grew thicker every year.

Now that Appleton was more composed Mab once again broached the forbidden subject. "Jake, much as I would like to avoid such talk, there are certain matters we ought to consider in the weeks ahead, and discuss between us, no matter how difficult. There are things that must be seen to, so let's begin, hm?" She paused, but when he failed to respond, she went on, determined to have things out with him.

"It's the children I'm thinking of. You see, dearie—well, look at it this way. If there's anything I can arrange before I go, to ease the burden of their future, I will. I don't want you to worry. Do you hear me, Jake?"

"I hear." He sat listlessly, his look vague and faintly puzzled, making her want to weep for him.

She took his hand again and pressed it over her heart. "Oh my dear, I can't bear to see you this way. Truly. If it must come, why then, that is God's will, and we must submit. Even though you say you don't believe in Him, you must bear it, you must." Again she paused, some unspoken thought coursing through her mind, then she went on. "You really must help me now, Jake. You must help me to be brave. If you don't—I'm so afraid—no, not of *that*—only of being thought a coward. I know you'd want me to be brave. You're such a good brave man yourself."

"You'll be brave, Molly . . . Molly . . ." He used his bandanna again and shuddered horribly. "Will you be waiting for me? Will you be there on the other side?"

Her eyes lit up. "Oh my dear, are you saying you *do* believe?" She was both astonished and gladdened by his question, but he wagged his head dolefully and confessed that he did not.

"It's all right," she said comfortingly. "I'll be waiting anyhow. I'll be there, I promise." She looked at him but his head was still bowed. "See here, Jake—I know you'll miss me, I know how you are, but, listen, my dear, you mustn't mourn me. Mourning's only a waste of time, life goes on, it must be lived, and—Jake—?"

"Molly." He raised his eyes to look at her with the same desperate expression.

"You'll have a good life yet; you must. If you take care of yourself, look after your health, you'll have many wonderful years ahead. You'll have the grandchildren, and, who knows, before too long, great-grandchildren—won't that be nice? And, Jake, I want you to promise me something."

"Yes, of course, anything—anything! You have only to say."

"Marry again."

His mouth dropped open and he stared at her as if she had suddenly gone mad. "Marry again?" he repeated dazedly. "Eh? How's that?" His indignation burst forth like waters through a broken dam. "You dare to suggest I take another—a—" Red-faced and outraged, he sprang from his chair, knocking over a flower pot. "What a preposterous notion! You cannot be serious!"

Calmly Mab assured him she was perfectly serious and in a reasonable tone pointed out to him the advantages that would be his if he sought another mate. What could be more logical, more sound? Surely he could appreciate the practicality of her suggestion. Wounded and aggrieved, he vowed that nothing could be farther from his mind.

"Never!" he cried. "Never in this world!" and rushed up the path, agitatedly flapping his hands about his head as though fending off a swarm of yellow jackets, to shut himself up in his laboratory again. Knowing better than to pursue him, Mab remained where she was, examining the prominent veins in her shrinking hands, but the anguish in her heart at that moment was more than the physical pain she felt, and there was no cure for either that she could think of.

Presently, hearing voices, she lifted her gaze, shading her eyes to peer up at the house where the servants had suddenly begun to gather on the terrace, Halley, Judah, and Trubey, who was excitedly flapping her apron. Mab stiffened in sudden apprehension. What was happening to cause such a dither? Something terrible; she could feel it. Straining in her chair she tried to identify the woman who had just come into view, emerging from the house along with Priam and Electra to stand among the others, a slender figure dressed in black, her long black veil fluttering in the breeze.

"Merciful Mother in heaven!" Mab gasped, crossing herself twice over, as her gaze shifted to the shed, where an astonished Appleton came hurrying outside and almost ran up the path toward the woman, who had descended the terrace steps and was proceeding along the walk with hands outstretched. The two met just at the circle of the sundial, where they threw themselves into each other's arms and hugged passionately. Still watching with her heart in her mouth, Mab grasped the arms of her chair, unable to get to her feet, her mind racing in bewilderment and blind surmise, wondering with a pang of apprehension what strange happenstance it was that had brought her daughter Aurora back from Italy in so astonishing and unexpected a fashion.

PART FOUR

The Swallowtail Summer

24

From the Realm of Death and Darkness

As ROSE MILLS sat turning the pages of a book by the open window in her little room over the carriage house she idly plied a palmetto fan across her perspiring cheeks. Whoever said a Connecticut Valley summer wasn't scorching hot sure didn't know what he was talking about: today, another Sunday, ho–hum, was equal in steamy tedium to anything she'd ever known in Laceyville, South Carolina. Hot and muggy, the summer stretched out before her like that long, seemingly endless road that had carried her here to Pequot Landing in the first place.

Ordinarily, she'd have been sitting up in the hotter'n hell church gallery, listening to that big-mouthed preacher bleat out another of his long, boring sermons, but today Rose had better things to do—as she'd had for the whole week past, ever since Lady Sheffield had so unexpectedly arrived. What a surprise; who'd've thought she'd just turn up at the front door like that, and Rose not knowing who she was or what she wanted. All got up like she was a duchess—she'd had to be let in, even Rose knew that, but Rose had been pushed aside as Trubey flew down the hall, laughing and crying, fit to burst, and then there came Halley, bawlin' like a spring lamb, screechin', "Mah baby! Mah sweet baby done come home!" while the Queen had got so excited she had to be put to bed, and the curious kept coming from all directions to peek in through the gates for a glimpse of the celebrated arrival.

Now almost all the Talcotts were gone off to Sunday service, the women (except for her ladyship) to Mass at New France, Mr. Bob and all the Priests, except Burdy, to First Church. Mr. App was walking by himself along the river. Only Lady Sheffield remained locked in her room, "resting," and thereby giving Rose the opportunity for a few moments' respite over the pages of her book. Nor was this some schoolbook of Georgiana Ross's she had her nose thrust into but something else entirely: a remarkable opus from the pen of Mrs. Olivia Wattrous, *The Romance of Roderick Lightfoot.* The work was contraband, stolen goods. Rose had "just happened across" it squirreled away among an interesting assortment of odds and ends in a battered old hatbox under Miss Agrippina's bed. A quick riffling of its well-thumbed pages had told her that here was reading matter of a sort she had not yet savored, and she had secretly appropriated it for her further elucidation. Since Agrippina seemed not to have missed the volume, Rose planned on retaining it until she was good and done, at which time she would return it to its rightful owner, probably—or maybe keep it for her own. She'd have to see.

"Roderick was not a man for nothing," Rose read now, *"certainly not a cavalier to be taken lightly. More than one woman had good reason to know this, not the least of which was the lovely and virtuous Lady Jeanne, whose heart hammered a tattoo in her bosom. Life with Roderick had been the con—con* '(Jeezus, this was hard!)'—*sum—mation—of a dream, a splendid fantasie to be cherished and adored. Not a lady in the kingdom could hold a candle to the Lady Jeanne, whose feminine grace, winning smiles and elevated deportment were unequaled by any of the other ladies-in-waiting to Her Majesty the Queen. With her sunset-hued hair, her lovelocks curling so daintily about the temples, her slender waist and narrow wrists, her hands of softest alabaster, the famous Leicester pearls her adored father had bequeathed her gleaming at her throat, she was the cynosure of every eye, her name bespoken on every tongue . . ."*

Rose paused to sigh, closing the book on her finger. The Lady Jeanne: the Lady Sheffield—so Rose had come to equate the two. Such a fine grand lady the Lady Sheffield was—so different from all her kin, with her elegant way of talking and her superior manners. But no smile on her lips, poor thing. Rose seldom felt sorry for white folks, but in this case she was willing to make an exception. After all, the death of a husband and a child from pestilence at Naples *was* sad—though Rose had seen worse, much worse.

As a result of Aurora Talcott's unexpected return, however, Rose herself had profited. Before the week was out, her turkey duster had been retired and the former hired girl was elevated to the rank of lady's maid, a promotion that had not so much to do with Rose's suitability for the position as with necessity's parenting of invention. Despite the family's considerable attempts at engaging Aurora's interest, her state of melancholy was both awesome and moving; Electra had discussed the matter with Posie and their mother, and among them they had agreed that what was called for was a steady, loyal, sympathetic companion. However, with Posie seriously occupied with her young pupils at the Free School and Georgiana's visits likewise restricted to after-class, neither of them seemed a likely prospect, while Electra was continually traveling and speaking on behalf of the school, and Agrippina was ruled out as being any sort of "comfort." Of the other servants, Trubey already had far too many duties simply looking after Mab; Burdy was needed to assist Halley and Judah, and she wasn't sharp enough anyway for the requirements of Lady Sheffield. Having eliminated everyone else, then, Electra suggested that Rose, whose company Aurora professed not to mind, be promoted to fill the position. Though it would mean her leaving school, and though Georgiana held serious reservations, especially as concerned Rose's recent relationship with Sinjin Grimes, the girl was not learning much now anyway, and would certainly not suffer in matters of speech and deportment by associating with Aurora. Thus had matters been settled—and Rose for one was delighted: not only was she free at last from the necessity that she attend class (and, as it turned out, church), she was awarded a fresh apron into the bargain.

Her fan halted abruptly while she cocked an ear. Was it that damn Halley screeching for her? She peered down into the garden, then along the terrace, then across the kitchen dooryard. Idiot chile, she told herself; Halley had gone to church. It must have been Burdy; Rose could hear snatches of her slightly off-key singing wafting from the kitchen.

She made a critical assessment of her wrist as she wafted the fan, seeking the appropriate degree of languid grace expected in a well-reared young lady with proper "deportment." Deportment be damned! she thought in a sudden fit of frustration. What good was it anyway when the object of your deportment was who knew where? No good, so far as Rose could see. No, nor Cinnamon's charm, either, that little red cotton bag of magic that still dangled between her legs. Silently she cursed the old Indian woman *and* Sinjin Grimes, damning him for a blackhearted devil for running off and leaving her to nurse a broken heart.

She again took up the copy of *Roderick Lightfoot* and with a sigh cradled it to her bosom, imagining herself to be the pearl-cheeked Lady Jeanne, swept up in the amorous embrace of Lord Geoffrey Willoughby, her rough-tempered master of the hounds, who, while Roderick was in France, had made free with her person under the blasted oak tree in the glen close by the ruined chapel, while a silvery moon rode the scudding clouds. She read for another quarter of an hour, until she heard quick footsteps and Burdy's shrill importuning voice reached her up the stairs. "You, Rose, Grammaw says you're to help me with settin' the table for the dinner. Folks'll be back from worship before we know it. Grammaw'll be mad if it isn't seen to."

Rose slid the book under the pillow and hurried to forestall Burdy's intrusion into her private domain. "Bird-face, what you 'noyin' Rose for all the time anyways?" she demanded, following the older woman into the kitchen. "Like to bust my ears off with your caterwaulin'."

"Grammaw said—"

"I don't give a shit what 'Grammaw' said, you's to leave me alone. I ain't no scullery mop, I is a lady's maid now." She made a nasty face, then, with an insolent switch of her hips, sailed into the back entry and opened the walk-in icebox.

"Now, what're you doin' in there, Rose?" Burdy squeaked, trotting after her. "Oooh, you aren't s'posed to do that! Miss Mab says—"

"Never mind 'bout whut the missus say." Rose had a spoon and was scooping ice cream from the galvanized pail. Ice cream was one of the perquisites that had come with life at Kingdom Come and she adored it. Sometimes she thought that when she died she wanted to go to a heaven where all you did was lie around spooning up ice cream the serabim and cheraphim on high churned up. Then the clock struck and Rose scampered fast to shut the door and wash her spoon.

BEHIND the sheer muslin curtains whose filigree pattern blurred the view from the street, Aurora Sheffield sat alone in her room. From time to time she murmured an indistinguishable word or phrase, or merely shook her head at things unseen. Outside, along Greenshadow, horses and vehicles moved past the house in a continuous stream, and through the branches of the shady elms she could glimpse people strolling by, vague figures of no consequence to her. She relished the knowledge that the house was all but empty, if only for a little while, and that she was free of the anxious importunings of her family, their unending fruitless attempts to cheer her spirits. All too soon they'd be back again for "Sunday in the parlor," just the way it used to be at the farm when she was a girl, and she prayed she wouldn't be invited down to visit with the aunts or other relatives, that between them Lecky and Posie could prevent anyone from coming and knocking on her door "just to say hello . . ."

Leaving her window view and going to her wardrobe, she bent and groped for the small leather case that she kept hidden beneath the skirts of one of her gowns. When unlocked by a little gold key stashed in the toe of a shoe, the smartly tooled carrier revealed a glittering row of square-shaped cut-glass bottles. From among these she selected the one that contained the *Goldenwasser,* and after replacing the case, she brought the bottle to the table where she poured a generous amount into the water glass and drank. By now she had learned to take it neat; no water to dilute the robust flavor.

She resumed her place beside the window. She laid her head back and let her eyes wander about the room—*her* room, as her father had insisted on calling it. How strange to be back here in Pequot Landing, in this big house of Papa's, a bereaved wife and mother. As she sipped the liqueur her glance took in the room's carefully appointed details: its walls of French blue and curtains of deep ultramarine. She was vaguely amused by the fact that the tester bed was that same familiar four-poster of Great-Aunt Susan Lane's, and that, propped upon the pillows, were her two dolls, Melisande and Berengaria. How sweet; how foolish; how like dear Papa. She thought of the night she had climbed out the window of her room at Follybrook into the rainy dark, believing she had left the dolls and everything else behind her. The dolls had waited for her. How long ago that was, a world, a lifetime away. Had she really been that young, foolish, giddy creature?

She laughed out loud, then clapped her hand over her mouth and glanced around. "My dear, you must exercise control," she admonished herself. She swallowed again, watching her image reflected in the dressing table glass across the room, wondering how anyone could possibly believe that *this* person had ever been *that* person. But of course it wasn't true, how could it be! *That* person was long dead, and *this* person nearly so. Holy Mother Mary, help me.

There was a clock somewhere in the room, she could hear its insistent tick-tick-tick; it accentuated her own nervousness. Tick-tick-tick. There it was, half obscured by the vase of dahlias someone had placed on the dressing table. Mama, dearest Mama . . . but something was wrong, terribly wrong. Aurora was not to be fooled, not even by her clever parent. She must ask Posie, Posie would tell her the truth, even if the others went whispering around corners and treating her like a child. She glided to the clock and silenced its pendulum, then closed the glass oval. The whole room felt stuffy. She had trouble breathing. Was she going to faint? She raised the window a trifle higher, the stiff folds of her heavy black skirt drawing against the carpet as she moved, then, reseating herself, she drank some more, as if trying to quench a deep thirst. Happily, the spreading warmth of the *Goldenwasser* dulled her mind, and she felt a languorous wave of relaxation lap over her, and a measure of peace.

A soft knock at the door roused her. "Who is it?" she asked.

"It's me, Rose, mistress. I come to say the folks'll be comin' in from church 'long about now. Do you feel like comin' down?"

Aurora replied quickly. "I don't believe so, Rose, I've a bit of headache." She slipped glass and bottle from sight and went to unlock the door. "Perhaps you'll ask Posie to stop up when she arrives, will you?"

"Yes ma'am, I surely will. Is there anything I can get for you otherwise? Maybe you'd like it if Rose would rub your temples with witch hazel. Halley say she done—did—that fo' you when you was just a little shoot."

"That's all right, Rose, why don't you go along, you needn't trouble . . ."

"Yes'm." Rose started out, then stopped. "I just hates to see you settin' all alone up here, mistress, with noone to talk to. 'Tain't—'tisn't—good for folks t'keep by themselves. You didn't touch your breakfast nary a bit, either. I swear, you is—are—goin' to fade off to a shadow. Won't you let me bring up a cup of tea and a piece of toast to put somethin' in your stomach?"

Unable to hold out against the girl's eager desire to do something for her, Aurora acquiesced in the matter of tea. Gently propelling her across the threshold, she thanked Rose again, and when the door was once more secured, she retrieved glass and bottle from the lower compartment of the commode and returned to her chair. There she continued to sit, a solitary sipper trying to calm the incessant thudding of her heart, a sound that never seemed to leave her.

Cooking odors from Halley's kitchen drifted to her nostrils, presaging the big Sunday family sit-down, though the thought of putting anything in her stomach made her queasy. The doctor had said she must try to eat more—it was true, she was too thin—but the mere thought of food nauseated her. She had much rather take a drink and simply let her mind go blank. Ever since Naples, when she'd said good-bye to Caro—ah, Holy Mother of God—no, no, don't think of it, don't remember. Her hand had begun to tremble, she was in danger of spilling the liquid, and she drank the last drop, then set the glass down before it slipped from her fingers. She squeezed her eyes shut as though to blank out the memory, but it was no use. The horrifying images would not leave her. She crossed herself and muttered appeasement to the angry God who steadfastly refused to hear her prayers. It was her own fault; she had no one to blame but herself. She'd renounced God long before He had renounced her, and if He had any forgiveness in His soul He was withholding it from her. She shuddered at the thought.

She could hear voices coming up the walk, then footsteps in the front hall. "Now. There," she said aloud, "they're home." One by one she recognized the voices' owners; how she'd been dreading their return, and here they were, the lot. Their solicitousness for her health, their gloomy looks because of her bereavement, their tactful little coughs and sudden silences—Pina's well-meant but suffocating attentions—it was all too much for her. If she could only stay by herself, if they would just not bother with her, perhaps she wouldn't feel so apt to jump out of her skin.

Presently she heard a sound along the passageway, and a light tapping at the door. "Sissie, it's me," whispered Posie, "I've brought your tea."

Aurora quickly rinsed the tumbler, rinsed her mouth as well, dabbed on some lilac water, and unlocked the door.

"Dearest Po. How lovely you look," she said. "Why didn't you bring a cup for yourself?"

"I thought perhaps you'd rather be alone."

"Well, I wouldn't," she said, drawing her sister into the room and shutting the door. "I want you here with me. You take the cup and I'll use the glass. No, I insist. How was Mass? Still Father Rupprecht to say it, I suppose." Posie smiled and nodded assent. "And what are they discussing down in the parlor?" Aurora went on. "Is it a council of state? 'What to do about poor Rora'?" She giggled, pressing her lips with her monogrammed handkerchief.

"They're just talking. You know Aunt Blanche."

"Oh yes, I do, Aunt Blanche." She giggled again, causing Posie to marvel at the way she sometimes seemed able to put aside her sorrows and behave normally.

"How old are you, Po?" Aurora asked suddenly.

"Seventeen."

"Seven . . . teen . . ." Aurora repeated thoughtfully. "Why, you're just a bit older than . . . than I was . . . when—goodness, can it be? Truly?" She pondered the matter another moment; the light faded from her eyes, then quickly returned. "Posie," she said, "can you remember at all the night John Quincy Adams came to the farm, to Granddaddy's bean supper? You couldn't have been more than three or four."

"Of course. I remember I gave President Adams a wreath and Pina recited a poem, and you sang, and then—oh, Sissie, I'm so happy to see you again!" She threw herself into Aurora's arms and pressed her cheek against her bosom. Though she caught the odor of spirits, she gave no sign. When she lifted her face she saw the sheen of tears in her sister's eyes.

"Yes, dear, I'm home again. All safe and sound." Aurora's voice was dry and husky and had an odd lilt as she straightened in her chair and touched her hair.

"Sissie?" Posie asked, handing her her cup again.

"Yes, dear?"

"Wouldn't you like to go for a drive this afternoon? It would do you good to get out some. If you like, we might ask Reuben to take us up to Hartford and see the sights."

Aurora pulled a comical face. "Oh dear—Hartford? And the sights? I suppose it's all different. I rather think Hartford might be a bit too lively for me just yet. If you wouldn't mind, perhaps we could drive somewhere else, somewhere less public."

"That's all right, dear, as long as you take some air."

"All right, then, we'll do it. After you've had dinner, shall we?" She put her arm around her sister and fondly kissed the top of her head. "Dear, sweet Posie," she murmured into her hair. "What a joy you are. Darling, you can tell me—truly, tell your Sissie, no one else will—Mama—she's very ill, isn't she?"

Posie nodded. "She didn't want to tell you until you felt better. I'm so glad you've come home so she could see you again."

Aurora crossed herself. "Oh poor Mama. And Papa, whatever will he do?" She cast her eyes to the ceiling. "Oh, dear God, what more? Why must I go on being punished?" She began to sob uncontrollably and Posie held her, comforting her until the flow of tears subsided.

"Sissie, would it help at all if you went with us to Mass? You haven't been—"

Aurora shook her head violently. "No—no, please don't ask—I can't!"

She twisted the handkerchief in her fingers. "Not yet—I hope Mama can be patient with me."

"Don't you want to make confession?"

"Confession?" Aurora laughed. "It's good for the soul, I'm told, but an utter waste where I'm concerned. Darling, please don't be put out with me—I just need a little time, to—to—"

"Of course," Posie replied. "And I couldn't ever be put out with you. I'm just glad you're home. I prayed you'd come—only I didn't want it to be like this. And you're being so brave—"

Aurora's eyes filled with tears. "Oh Posie, I cannot bear it! I've lost my child, my precious baby, and I came home to Mother, thinking—"

"Thinking she'd make everything all right."

"Yes, and now she's dying, she's going to be taken from me as well. And Papa—oh Posie, what will he ever do without her? He'll die, he'll simply curl up and die, too."

"No he won't. People don't die because others do. They go on living. He'll miss Mama, of course he will, but in time he'll get over it, he's bound to."

"He won't, I know he won't. He loves her too much. It's terrible to love someone so much that you'd rather die than live without them—"

She broke off suddenly and put her face in her hands. Posie stroked her arm and patted her comfortingly.

"Oh Posie, dear"—Aurora sobbed—"you're so sweet to care about me, after what I've done."

Posie gave her her handkerchief. "What have you done?"

Aurora shook her head and used the handkerchief. "Nothing—nothing! I—No, nothing—" She leapt up and moved to the window, gazing past the lacework in the curtain down to the street. A wagon trundled by, filled with laughing young people—perhaps they were going on a picnic to Pennywise Island—and as they passed talking and joking they seemed to carry with them the very breath of life, while she—she was like one of those women in India who must fling herself on her dead husband's burning pyre. Out there among the billowing green trees, under the blue Connecticut skies, was life, while she was shrouded in black head to toe, her child dead of plague at Naples. She fell to her knees by the chair and put her forehead on the arm, at the same time fumbling for her rosary.

"Posie, come pray with me, help me!" she cried in anguish. Posie hurried to her, kneeling beside her, and together they bowed their heads and prayed, the murmur of their voices hanging softly in the still room.

They were interrupted as another knock sounded, and without a pause the door opened to reveal Agrippina on the threshold.

"Sissie—darling!" she sang, gliding in. "At prayers, dear? How pale you look. Shall I bring you my salts? She looks about to expire," she added in an aside to Posie. "Perhaps she should lie down."

"She's going to come and have something to eat with us, and this afternoon she's going for a drive."

"Oh, lovely! We'll all come. I must tell Sissie all about Mrs. Sigourney's trip to Ausable Chasm—you'll love hearing—"

Aurora signaled for help from Posie, who tactfully but firmly ushered Agrippina from the room. A quarter of an hour later when Mab came to escort Aurora down she excused herself saying she wasn't hungry after all, and sent her mother away. And after picking at the tray Rose brought up, instead of dressing and going for a drive as she'd promised she pleaded another headache and stayed in her room, begging not to be disturbed. It was assumed by the household that she slept; Rose, however, thought she knew better, for pausing to listen at the door, she could hear the telltale clink of glass against glass.

"Rose!" The voice was Mab's. Rose whirled guiltily.

"What are you doing, spying on your mistress!" Mab was outraged.

"I wasn't spyin', ma'am," Rose explained, "I'm worried about her lady-ship. She's got herself locked up inside and she don't—doesn't—answer me no matter how hard I knock."

Though Mab was impressed by the girl's solicitousness, she brusquely ordered her about her duties, then rapped herself. "Rora dear, it's me. Unlock the door, please. I wish to speak with you." While she waited she felt a spasm in her abdomen and she leaned wearily against the doorjamb. After some moments Aurora opened the door, her eyes glittering with an intensity that gave her mother a start.

"Mama, what is it? Are you all right? I'm sorry to have kept you waiting." She brought Mab into the room and helped her sit down.

Taking Aurora's face in her warm hands, Mab peered anxiously into her daughter's eyes.

"Oh my dear, my child, you are so troubled. I wish—"

"I'm all right, Mama," Aurora said. From the parlor the sounds of Pina's harp caused her to smile wistfully. "She really has quite an accomplished touch, hasn't she?"

"Yes, she plays very well," Mab agreed without much enthusiasm. She loosened the strings of her cap, which were binding under her chin. "Do you miss Henry, dear?" she asked. "I'm sure you do."

Aurora paused before replying, picking a piece of thread from the folds of her skirt. "Yes, Mama, of course. Of course I miss him. He was my husband." Her hands twisted together in the agitated way that now seemed customary with her. "Not like you and Papa, though," she went on.

"Most married people are not so fortunate as your father and I have been," Mab replied.

"You love him so much, Mama—and he loves you, just the same as always. I wonder if you know how lucky you are."

"I hope to tell you I do!" She regarded Aurora a moment, then went on. "I have had my Jake in passion and in sweet contentment, and he has had his Molly. We were well met. And you're right, dearie, I've always believed that those who truly love are the lucky ones, the really blessed beings. The others, alas, have all missed the greatest thing in life."

". . . Greatest thing in life . . ." Aurora's murmuring echo trailed away. The light through the moving leaves beyond the window settled a shimmering golden net across the waxed floor.

"I feel sorry for them," Mab went on. "Everything else diminishes, I think; love alone ennobles."

Aurora's smile was wistful. "Yes, Mama, I think so too. It certainly has ennobled you, and I'm glad you have had Papa—I mean that you *have* Papa." She amended herself hastily.

Mab chose to ignore the slip. "It's all right, dearie, I understand." She could scarcely glance at her daughter without her eyes tearing. "What an awful time for Père Margeaux to have gone off," she complained. "If only he would come—"

"Yes, Mama, if he would—what then?"

"He would put things to right, I'm sure he would. He would comfort you just as he used to."

"Mama, dearest, haven't you guessed why I wouldn't go to Mass with you? I am not—not in a state of grace. I'm sorry to say it, but it's true."

"Yes, I have guessed it. That's what I meant to say—when Père Margeaux comes again he will see you properly shrived."

"When will he come?"

"Soon, I hope." She sighed and closed her eyes.

"Mama, please don't feel sorry for me. I don't want anybody's pity. God has seen fit to punish me this way."

"Punish you? Sweet Mother of Jesus, what on earth could you possibly have done that God should punish you?"

Aurora spun around, her eyes filled with despair. "Oh Mama—Mama! I have done such a terrible thing!" She fell to her knees. "God have mercy on me for the wicked creature I am! God have mercy, God have mercy!" she pleaded, hands clasped fervently before her.

"Rora, stop, you mustn't!" Mab cried. "Don't speak that way. You're overwrought, that's all."

Aurora's laugh was sharp, and her loose hair swung about her face, accentuating its thinness and unhealthy pallor. "Is that what you think, Mama?"

Suddenly Mab was weeping uncontrollably.

"Mama? Mama, please, don't, you mustn't. What if Papa were to come in and see you?"

"Yes, you're right, I mustn't. Only here—with you, like this. Such a relief to cry, you know, but I know I mustn't. It's wrong." She had drawn her handkerchief from her sleeve and was dabbing at her eyes. "Come now, we'll say no more about these matters. When Père Margeaux returns . . . he'll speak to you then, you'll make confession to him, surely you will—"

"Yes, Mama, if you wish."

"Very well then, I shall rest easy, knowing it."

"Yes, Mama—do—rest easy. And so shall I, perhaps—"

"Oh, never say 'perhaps.' Say you will. Make communion with God, accept the wafer and you'll see—the Holy Spirit will be there."

"Yes, Mama, I'm sure He will be. But . . ."

"But not for me" was what she meant but did not say.

WITH Aurora's unexpected return, the village had fallen into a furor of speculation and gossip. Certainly it was an "interesting" situation, worthy of close scrutiny. First Sinjin had come home, after all those years in China, and now his former love had likewise reappeared, *sans* husband or child, and there were those who claimed that this was too much of a coincidence to be accepted as such. Some even guessed that the one-time lovers had been secretly exchanging letters and biding their time, and now, with Lord Henry carried off by plague leaving Aurora free to marry again, one could perhaps expect another wedding before year's end.

But this was the talk of fools, of which Pequot Landing had its full complement. In truth, there was a conspiracy of silence among the Talcott family, who, upon Aurora's reappearance, had closed ranks in a concerted effort to keep from her any news regarding the captain, thus leaving her in the innocent conviction that her former lover was still half a world away in China. And since she remained sequestered from any haphazard intelligence, it was safely assumed that she would not be distressed by random reports until she was ready to hear them. And yet, what was there to fear? After all, she had not set eyes on the man for more than ten years. He had stolen her away once, or tried to, and three years later had run off in pursuit of her, only to have her husband send him on his way. What once might have been was ended by now. Wasn't it? The alarm bell had rung, the fire had been put out, the ashes were cold and black and scattered to the winds, weren't they? Certainly Aurora made no mention of the man, nor, for that matter, did she show the slightest interest in any of the Grimes clan. Indeed, she seldom left the house, except to sit on the rear terrace or wander down through her mother's brimming garden to the boathouse, or, once or twice, to go for an airing with her father or sisters in the Yellow Pumpkin, at such times presenting a figure of deepest bereavement, swathed in black and heavily veiled, and whosoever desired to solace her or offer her sympathy was firmly discouraged; she countenanced neither.

As for Rose, she lightfooted it along the hallways, her eyes sharp, ears alert for every word. Perhaps for the first time in her life she was experiencing some genuinely sympathetic emotions regarding another human being, this one a woman born with white skin. She had become infatuated with Aurora's pale porcelain elegance, the aroma of her toilet water, the grace of her carriage, the melting lilt of her voice, the thickness of her lashes. Being an astute judge of character, Rose had sensed, despite Aurora's erratic behavior, the innate sweetness and warmth that were the keystones of her new mistress's personality, and soon came to regard her with something akin to awe. Privately, she thought that all the Talcott women were elegant, Electra especially; but Aurora, from the little lace-trimmed, beribboned satin hearts filled with lavender sachet that she slipped between the folded layers of her underclothes, to the silky gloves she wore, from the cascade of shining golden hair let down at night to the slender daintiness of her small, shapely feet was the model of grace and femininity and Rose yearned to be exactly like her.

Consequently, as she observed the young widow attempting to fit herself again into the patterns of life in the Talcott household, it was not without a growing sense of change in her own self. She might still play the airy hypocrite with Queen Mab, she might snipe and sass at Agrippina and dare her to do anything about it, she might profess scorn for Halley and ridicule Judah, but with Aurora Rose strove now to disguise her peevish ways, taking special care to speak as properly as she could, to walk erect, never to slouch or sashay, always to be prompt and attentive and neat, and at least pretend to show concern for others. She was becoming, in her own phrase, "a lady of deportment," and she was proving as well of real assistance to Aurora, especially at night. When the bad dreams came, it was Rose, now sleeping on a trundle bed in Lady Sheffield's room, who would hear her ladyship crying out in her sleep. Turning up the lamp, she would find her in the throes of a nightmare, her body broken out in a sweat, her head tossing on the pillow as she moaned and muttered unintelligibly. Rose would soothe her then, whispering to her in the gentle language Knoxie used until she was quiet again.

Then, one night, Rose woke to hear words distinctly spoken: "No, no, please, get them away! Rats! Rats! Caro! *Aiuto! Aiuto!*" She broke into a babble of Italian that Rose could not hope to understand, then half rose up in terror, jerking her feet under her and cowering against the pillows. She flung up her hands before her, her expression a mask of terror as a chilling scream rang out, followed by words that set Rose's hair on end.

"*Sinjin!* Hear me! Merciful God, where are you? *Sinjin!* Help us! The rats are everywhere!" She opened her eyes wide, her screams apparently having awakened her, and stared uncomprehendingly at Rose, sitting in the chair beside the bed.

"It's all right, mistress," Rose told her, trying to reassure her, though her own heart was beating wildly as the name of her lover sounded in her ears. "Nobody's going to hurt you now. Rose is here, you is safe."

"Rose . . . safe . . ."

After another moment the door swung open and a distracted Agrippina appeared. "What is it? Who screamed? Rora—are you all right?"

"She's all right," Rose said. "Just another bad dream is all."

"She never screamed like that before. You'd best leave her to me tonight. You may go along," Agrippina commanded.

But Rose was having none of this. "You go on back to bed, Miss Pina, I'll stay by her."

Agrippina stamped her foot. "Hear the girl, giving me orders! Stay by her indeed!"

Rose rolled her eyes. "It be three o'clock in the mornin' and lookin' after your sister is my re—responsibility." She managed the word with some difficulty. "So you best go along, hear?"

"It's all right, Pina dear, I'm fine, really." Aurora nodded, and with evident misgivings Agrippina withdrew, leaving Rose in charge.

The girl helped her mistress back into bed, covered her, gently stroked her brow and held her hand until she fell into an exhausted sleep. The little clock ticked on the mantel, while Rose clenched and unclenched her fists, staring at the ivory face on the pillow, thinking over what she'd heard. Like the rest of the household, Rose had been convinced that whatever feelings "her" captain might still entertain for his lost love, he no longer meant anything to Aurora. Now she was not so sure. Was it likely that his name would be on her lips when she dreamed if it was not still in her heart? And what did the rats have to do with anything? Around and around spun her thoughts until finally her lids drooped and, closing her eyes, she slumbered upright in the chair.

Faithfully she kept her place until breakfast aromas from the kitchen awakened her and, apparently, her mistress.

"How are you?" Rose inquired.

Aurora smiled wearily. "Did I make a terrible commotion last night?" she asked.

Rose shook her head. "You was just—you *were* just havin' one of your dreams, mistress. Don't you 'member—'bout the rats?"

Aurora's eyes were filled with alarm. "Rats—yes, rats, I remember, but—what did I say?"

"You was—were—powerful scared of the varmints, a ton of rats, sounded like. And you was callin' for help. To—somebody. You said, 'Sinjin—he'p us, Sinjin,' like that, over and over, like you might die of fright."

If she'd hoped to elicit a more illuminating intelligence on the matter she was disappointed, for all Aurora did was to bury her face in her hands, then, sobbing, turn away, curtly dismissing Rose and refusing to touch her breakfast when Burdy brought the tray up. The plates on it sat untouched until Rose returned to help her mistress dress; she found her huddled in the chair, staring through the window at nothing and muttering to herself.

At the sound of Rose's step, she looked up and coughed once or twice, then swallowed with difficulty. "Rose," she said, "I'm glad you're here. My . . . my throat's so very dry, I wonder . . . Do you suppose you could fetch me a bit of brandy from Papa's sideboard? In a glass with water, please?" A sudden plaintive appeal had crept into her voice; Rose hesitated, remembering Mab's stern orders on this important matter.

"I can't, mistress, they locked up the cellarette."

"Whatever for?" Aurora demanded airily. "I only wanted a drop or two to quiet my nerves. I just happen to be fresh out at the moment." She wasn't fooling Rose any, but she went doggedly on. "Do you suppose Halley might have something in the kitchen?"

"Oh, I reckon a drop of something or other. Only, if Rose was to get caught, your momma would fire me on the spot. I'd get my walkin' papers for sure."

"But you'd be terribly careful, wouldn't you?"

"Well—I . . . Rose knows what it is when the human nerves is stretched hard. Let's see what Rose can find."

With a conspiratorial glance she left the room, her feet whispering along the hall runner, while Aurora waited nervously by the window, twisting her fingers in her lap. Finally she heard footsteps, and Rose reappeared with something hidden beneath her apron.

"That fool Burdy was down there floggin' up butter biscuits. Burdy, she don't make—doesn't make good biscuits. She's so stupid, that Burdy," she went on, giggling mischievously. "I told her I heard the missus callin', she run off quick, and see what I snitched for you." She produced a bottle of dark-colored liquid from under her apron. "It ain't—isn't—brandy, but it might do to stifle your nerves."

Aurora took the glass and gingerly tasted. The liquor had a bitter flavor but she sipped it, then sipped again. "Whatever is it?"

"Somethin' Halley puts in her cookin' sometimes. I heard her say it gives punch to vittles. Mistress, Rose knows plenty what it is to hanker after something. I guess if a body wants spirits bad enough she simply got to have 'em. Like a man," she added.

Aurora drained the tumbler, then poured another; the stuff was a far cry from her preferred *Goldenwasser,* but beggars couldn't be choosers.

"A man," she said, and laughed bitterly. "Tell me, Rose, have you got one?"

Rose nodded, fluttering her lashes with unwonted demureness. "Yes, ma'am," she said, "Rose, she already got herself a man." Oh yes, she rushed on with romantic fervor, she had a suitor, a gentleman who was wooing her. "He makes me gifts," she told Aurora with obvious relish. "He gave me this." She displayed a string of green beads Sinjin had presented her with.

"Goodness, Rose," said her mistress in some surprise, "does this mean you'll be leaving us then?"

"Oh *no,* ma'am," Rose protested vigorously. "I ain't—I *isn't*—I—oh, damn, what is it anyways?"

" 'I am *not'* is proper, I believe," Aurora replied.

"I am *not* going to leave you," Rose said. "Anyway, that feller, he wants to marry up with me something awful, but—but—"

"Yes?"

"Well, see, I don't believe he's quite up to it, truth to tell. Seems like he can't keep up with me, quite—'specially now I'm gettin' all my deportment 'n' all."

"You mean you would prefer someone more elevated, a gentleman on a loftier plane?"

"Oh, I don't care none about his plane, mistress. This one, he be plenty good enough for me, I like him very well, only . . . well . . ." Finding herself cast abroad in deep waters, Rose was gingerly oaring her way among selected words and phrases. "Only I'm not ready to marry with him just yet. Lady Sheffield, you can't imagine, he done asked me and asked me, over and over, every time he comes round, and I just tells him, 'Hold on there till I is—*am*—ready.' He'll keep, I expect. Most men will, if you hang 'em up to dry awhile."

Her quaint way of putting things made Aurora smile. "But if you love him, how can you bear to wait?" she asked.

"Oh, I love him with a blue passion!" cried Rose, clutching both hands to her breast. "I declare, mistress, I love him fit to bust. And I'm fixin' to marry him yet. Cinnamon gave me a charm. She sure did, a love charm." She hesitated, wondering if she was on safe ground speaking about Cinnamon.

Aurora was quick upon it. "A love charm? Of what sort?"

Rose thought before answering, then said, "She says I ain't s'posed to tell. Charm won't work if I tell."

"Of course, she's right," Aurora agreed, indulging Rose in her drama. "Don't you tell. Then Cinnamon has read your future, has she?"

"No'm. She just gimme the charm."

"Ah, but you must have her tell your fortune, by all means."

A faint frown appeared between Rose's dark brows. "That Cinnamon, she one greedy cuss; she cost Rose more'n she worth. We got a Geechee woman down home, she don't cost—doesn't cost—like Cinnamon does."

"Oh, I think it would be worth it. She'll tell you if you're truly going to marry your—you didn't say his name."

Rose was ready for that one. "Oh, I'm not s'posed to speak his name either. I just calls him 'the phantom.' Mistress—?"

"Yes?"

"Maybe if you could let Rose have a dollar? Since she stuck her neck out gettin' you potables. Then maybe I could get Cinnamon to tell my fortune."

An infinitesimal pause followed, during which Aurora peered sharply at Rose, then she reached for her bag. "But Cinnamon can't cost more than a quarter," she said, poking among her change.

"Yes'm. But um—there's a pair of gloves in Miz Eales's window, and Rose has been hankering for them. They're vi'let, like the dress you give me, and they're 'zactly seventy-five cents."

Aurora handed over the money and wished her the joy of it, and the next day she was further obliged by an only too willing Rose, who was able to find for her and smuggle into her room a bottle of the *Goldenwasser* she craved—bought for half the sum Rose took from her. The rest went to Cinnamon Comorra: the precise amount needed to purchase a quantity of a certain powder guaranteed to increase the potency of a man's seed.

From the moment she first set eyes on Aurora Sheffield after her return, Georgiana Ross had grieved at the dark spirit lurking within her that drove her this way and that, that made her slender hands work like the nervous wings of caged birds, and caused her so many sleepless nights. Truly, this pathetic, nerve-wracked creature was no longer Aurora Talcott—not at all like the sunny-natured, golden-haired girl Georgiana remembered, or even the young wife and mother of ten years before. The soft ringlets that once had spun a shining aureole about the Dresden head were now severely brushed back from the brow and twisted into thick ropes of burnished yellow of a much deeper shade. The amethyst eyes were dimmed to a pale, indeterminate shade of blue, and their expression alternated between a sharp appraising look and one of unfocused fuzziness. Her rosy, peachlike complexion was dimmed too, faded to the palest shade of ivory, creamy still and unblemished, but unnaturally pallid, and her clear, musical voice had descended in tone generally, but sometimes rose to stridency.

And now, who knew what was to come? Could they simply take up again where they had set down more than a decade before? Would Aurora open up her heart to Georgiana as she had then? Thus far she had not been so inclined with anyone at all. Mab and Appleton had tried and failed, Electra as well, but each time Aurora, like the flower that is too easily bruised and whose petals turn brown at the touch, would wither and retreat at the same time. Now, in desperation Mab turned to Georgiana.

"She must unburden herself to someone—*someone*—until Père Margeaux comes again. She tells us nothing except that they are dead. But something eats at her. I must know what it is." Mab wiped her eyes. "Oh, Georgie, go to her again, try and find out what it can be."

And so Georgiana slipped into the house late one afternoon, and, leaving her satchel of schoolwork in the kitchen, climbed up the back stairs and along the passage to the blue room.

"Dear, you know I wouldn't meddle for worlds," she began after settling in, "but your mother is terribly concerned about you and—well, she thought perhaps it might be easier for you to talk to me." She watched as Aurora's lips drew into a tight line and her brows knit. She shook her head resolutely, then got up and began pacing the rug beside the bed, clasping and unclasping her hands, while Georgiana sat helplessly by, wondering what to do. Perhaps, after all, it was best to wait for the abbé's return.

Still, she decided to try once more, however timidly. "Rora—I'm sure you must miss Henry very much, and—" But before she could finish her thought she drew back abruptly as Aurora's hand flashed out, cutting through the air in a savage gesture.

"Don't say that! You don't know what you're talking about. Miss him? Oh, God—you know I never loved him, not for a single minute. I thought I could be the sort of wife he wanted and needed, that he would be a good father to Caroline, far better than—" She stopped, and turned to face Georgiana squarely. "Georgie, Henry learned the truth, you see. About Caroline. And after that, he hated her and me." The bitter words were pulled from the depths of her, and Georgiana was appalled.

"But your letters—you never told me! Why did you lead us all to believe you were happy?"

Aurora's laugh was sardonic. "Oh my dear, it's so easy, when one is far away, to take a pen and by subterfuge and clever design mislead others into thinking anything you want them to think. But I have paid for my deceit. I have paid! My child is gone, lost—but *he* is gone too, thank God! I would give anything to ransom Caro, but I hope Henry Sheffield burns in hellfire for all eternity!"

"Rora, don't! You can't mean it—"

"I do! Ah, if you only knew how *much* I meant it—" She lurched slightly, then sat abruptly on the vanity bench, her eyes coming to rest on her reflection in the mirror. "Look. Do you see, Georgie—can you see what

I see? That poor thing there? What a sad creature she is, isn't she? I am done now, done and done, and I too shall burn in hellfire for my sins. As my child—*our* child—Sinjin's and mine—has been made to pay. Gone . . . gone . . . that sweet creature . . ."

She sprang up and began pacing again, muttering to herself, then she snatched up the bottle on the nightstand and openly poured herself a drink. She touched the rim of the glass to her lips, tossed her head back, and let it trickle down her throat. "You don't take spirits, do you? No, of course you don't. No lady does, or ought to. I do, but then, I am no lady, despite rumors to that effect." She laughed, holding the bottle up to the light. "It warms. It warms me, Georgie. Do you see, dear? See the little flakes—how they shine? Gold, Georgie, pure gold. 'Golden water,' you see. My secret passion. For many years. Shall I tell you how many? And would you like to know who first introduced me to it? On board his ship? On that pretty dancing brig—" Her hand flew up again. "No—don't say anything. We know what we know, don't we? We know but will not say—cannot say, must not say." She emptied the glass, then dabbed her neck with eau de cologne as Georgiana listened.

"Dear faithful Georgie. There you sit, appalled by these confessions. Don't deny it, you *are* appalled, I know you are. You can't quite believe it's me, can you? Your darling Rora, this intoxicated wraith, this—this nothing. Funny, isn't it? Georgie?" She laughed again, then her voice cracked and she hid her face, drawing her hair across it to shut out her image in the glass.

Georgiana helped her lie down to rest, and when she was tucked under the covers, drew the chair close, trying to assimilate what she had just learned.

"Georgie, where do you suppose he can be?" Aurora asked plaintively. "Now, at this very moment?" It came to Georgiana that she was speaking, not of Henry, but of Sinjin, and her heart was in her throat. "On some ship somewhere? Along the China Coast?" Aurora went on. "Perhaps India? Georgie . . . ?" She looked up with a piteous expression. "Georgie—won't you please tell me about him? Please?"

This was how it came. Just so easily, out of words words words.

Georgiana felt her cheeks warm and hoped it wouldn't be noticed. "Yes, dear, of course," she said. "I hadn't mentioned him only because I thought—" Her mind worked rapidly; she decided to come straight out with it. "He's not in China," she said, "he's here."

Aurora sat up in surprise. "Here? In Pequot?"

"Not exactly." She quickly explained the events that had sent Sinjin downriver to the fishing cabin at Bible Rock.

Aurora listened without comment, absently biting her thumbnail. "Whoever imagined . . ." she said when Georgiana had finished. "That he'd be here, I mean . . ." Her voice trailed off, then she murmured, "I shall speak to him when he comes . . ."

"Rora—"

"No, it's perfectly all right, truly. I just need to—to . . ." Again her voice trailed off. "Why do they call it Bible Rock?" she asked suddenly.

Georgiana was startled. Everyone knew about Bible Rock. "It's because of a rock shaped like a large book," she explained. "It overlooks the river below the Deeping landing. The steamboat passengers are always on the lookout for it. It's quite an attraction."

"Yes, of course, how silly. I remember, Granddaddy showed it to us when we were little. Are they safe there, Ambo and the Malay and—and Sinjin?"

Georgiana replied that no one would think of looking for the fugitives in that place. But she had cause to wonder what might happen if and when Judge Perry's efforts at quashing the indictment made possible Sinjin's return, what would happen when he found Aurora living at Kingdom Come. And Rose, who had an ear pressed to the keyhole, wondered as well.

25

Childhood Scenes Revisited

NO ONE COULD HAVE been more surprised than Georgiana to observe the calm manner in which Aurora received the news that Sinjin Grimes was not twelve thousand miles away on the other side of the world, but a mere twenty-five. Supplied with the details of his surprise return the previous spring, she had simply accepted Georgiana's account of the disastrous voyage of the red junk, casually remarking that he seemed dogged by misfortune, but revealing no inclination to pursue the subject any further.

Relieved yet mystified by this show of indifference, Georgiana had duly reported the conversation to Mab and Appleton, who talked things over between themselves and prudently decided that the safest course was to let sleeping dogs lie, always good advice. Old Bobby, Electra, and Priam concurred, the latter with stringent reservations, having expressed privately to Georgiana the doubts he harbored over what might happen when Sinjin and Aurora encountered each other again, but resolutely shunting these doubts aside for the sake of the cause. Like the rest of the family, he was trusting in Providence Unseen to unravel the threads where his sister and the captain were concerned.

In the days that followed Aurora's talk with Georgiana, there was discernible a general lightening of spirit. The drinking and the nightmares subsided, and Rose returned to her own room. There was a renewed interest in everyday concerns, and now and then Aurora's laugh rang out as it had long ago—at some sally from Priam, who invariably arrived at the house bearing a gift for his adored sister: yesterday a bag of tempting confections, today an embroidered footstool, tomorrow a little bijou from one of the smart shops on Hartford's Central Row. Sometimes on days when Priam had brought along his mandolin, brother and sister would paddle in the old canoe out on the river after supper, just the way they used to do when they were young, and now as then her sweet voice could be heard warbling across the water.

Then, with the arrival of Minerva Peckham of Glens Falls, New York, what had been a slow improvement became a brightness that, if not dispersing all clouds, considerably reduced the pervasive gloom. Upon receiving the news of Sissie's return, Minnie had rushed off to Albany to board the Hartford coach, leaving Lee to sweat over his printing press, and she had brought along her youngest, the darling Sophy. She had come eddying into the house on the bubbly currents of her merry laughter, wearing a bonnet that wouldn't stay straight and a plaid traveling skirt that was a map of colors and far too hot for summertime.

Once installed in the yellow room, Minnie went about doing that which she had made her chief business in life, gladdening hearts and making others laugh. She possessed a magic broom that swept out all the cobwebs and routed the specter of despair. To put it simply, she was a tonic for her ailing mother, as well as for her melancholy sister.

Now, in the velvety evenings after supper, there were occasional musicales in the best parlor for selected guests—Aunt Hat, the Ashleys, the Perrys—with Aunt Betts and Aunt Tilda playing together on the pianoforte that had come from Leipzig, Agrippina at her harp, Priam with his mandolin, Georgiana her flute, and everyone taking turns singing. Peggy and the children would usually accompany Priam on the drive down from Hartford to join in these family get togethers, and even Appleton somehow contrived to rouse himself to a semblance of good cheer. Indeed, it was like old times, Bob said, and if Aurora's gaiety and enthusiasm occasionally seemed a bit spurious, her performance little more than an act to oblige the others' sense of fun and entertainment, no one took any notice, or at least pretended not to. And when she sang the sentimental song "Lavina" not a soul but felt a pang. Even Mab, despite her failing health, managed to take heart, telling herself all might yet be well, and she thanked God for her good fortune. With Aurora returned and Minnie as a bonus, with Appleton restored to some measure of his former sanguine state and Electra visiting as frequently as she could, the house had taken on a new luster; just to see it being put to use and enjoyed as Jake had always dreamed of made those fleeting summer days more precious to the dying woman than any she could remember. Even the gnawing at her vitals seemed lessened because of it, so much so that she was able to reduce the dose of opium she took to dull her pain. Besides, she didn't want her mind clouded, she must keep alert to every precious second, not to miss a single one. Certainly she had more strength these days. Why, she reflected, crossing herself, in another month she might find that she was getting altogether well; that she might live who knew how much longer, after all.

Then, another joyful surprise: shortly before noon one morning, Alabaster Priest came loping up the drive, pumping his long legs, waving his hat, and shouting to beat the band. "They're home! Miss Mab—hear what I'm sayin'? The twins have come!"

And, providentially, so they had. Hector and Achilles strolled up March Street from the steamboat landing looking like two fashionable young rakes out to view the local sights. In their matching military attire, with their gleaming swords and their brass buttons and visored caps, they strode into the house bursting with energy and robustiousness, full of themselves and of life, to be swiftly engulfed by their loving family, drowned in kisses and hugs and the sort of attention they craved but saw blessed little of as soldiers.

"How handsome they are!" Aurora exclaimed to her mother. "And how grown-up. I'd no idea, truly."

And indeed, the boys she hadn't clapped eyes on for more years than she cared to think of were boys no longer, but young men who looked as if they could fight off a full brigade with no outside help. After having been seconded to Colonel Worth's command to fight the Seminole Indians in Florida, they had rejoined their own regiment in Virginia, where, upon learning of Aurora's return, they had requested and been granted an overdue furlough.

For this time, this brief time then, they were all together, and if one didn't think too hard about what lay in store, happiness abounded, proving that even in the midst of death, past, present, or yet to come, there breathes life.

ONE hot afternoon when Helen and Maude had shooed her from the classroom, not even allowing her to take along her satchel of schoolwork, Georgiana let herself be wooed by the beauties of the day. Since her arrival, Minnie had on several occasions come to visit her at the seed store classroom, but Georgiana had hardly spoken with the twins since their return a few days earlier, and so she decided to make the short walk over to Kingdom Come. As it happened the two were off somewhere on a ride, but she arrived in time to catch Minnie on her way out the door, with—surprisingly— Aurora in tow.

"Georgie! How marvelous," Minnie cried, "I've just convinced Sissie to take a walk. Come with us, we're going over to the farm."

Now *there* was a good idea—so typical of Minnie, always cheek to cheek with felicity—and Georgiana happily accompanied them to Follybrook; twenty minutes found the three women in the old kitchen, once Halley Priest's, now Susie Talcott's, where Aunt Sue and her hired girl were putting up peach preserves and spicy watermelon pickles.

"Where is Uncle James?" Minnie inquired.

"Cutting hay," Susie answered. "Where else on such a day as this? Rora, how long has it been since you've been in this house?"

"A long time, Aunt Sue, a very long time."

"Too long, if you ask me. I wish you'd all come over for supper one night. We've hardly seen any of you. We'll have a beef roast."

"Yes, Aunt, of course," Aurora replied. "It's very thoughtful of you."

"Nonsense! We're just so glad to have you back. I told Jim I was afraid I'd go to my grave without ever seeing you again." She kissed her niece warmly, then went to stir the stove pot. "Taste our peaches, they're delicious," she said over her shoulder. "And you mustn't leave without letting me cut some of your mother's roses for her, they're simply gorgeous this year. Georgie, you take some for Hattie, too."

The younger women each tasted the preserves, then slipped out the back door. After refreshing themselves at the pump and looking over Mab's remarkable roses, they strolled past the barn and tackroom, out across the meadow where the men were scything and raking the cut hay. Ten minutes later they were traipsing along the old orchard lane, between the even rows of beehives to that serene and sequestered spot, sweet with lavender clover, where Aurora and Georgiana had sat so long ago, girls in white dresses.

"How wonderful!" breathed Minnie as she deposited her plump form on the lush grass. "It's exactly the same, isn't it? Nothing's changed. Even Granddaddy's beehives. Surely they're not the same ones."

But, yes they were. Georgiana agreed: today everything seemed exactly as it once had been, as if a slate had been wiped clean, and as Aurora arranged her skirts about her ankles, she caught Georgiana's eye on her and saw the sweet, half rueful smile on her lips.

"Are you remembering?" Georgiana asked.

"Oh yes, dear," Aurora replied dreamily. "What a long time ago it seems. We were so young . . . so terribly young . . . We didn't know how lucky we were then. How much we had to learn—how much to suffer."

Minnie reached out and pressed her sister's hand. "But that's all in the past now. It will be a whole new life for you—you'll see." She smiled encouragingly, but a frown creased Aurora's brow.

"I'm not so sure," she murmured.

"What do you mean, Sissie?" asked Minnie.

"I don't know . . . I'm sure it's dreadful of me, but I can't help the feeling that life is over now. For me, anyway. Here I sit in Granddaddy's orchard and regret the day I ever left it. What foolishness—what madness. When I think how different things might have been if—if only I'd never gone, if only—"

"Rora, don't, you mustn't," Georgiana said.

"I know." Aurora sighed and fingered an unruly lock away from her eyes. Today she'd left her hair loose of its confining pins, and Georgiana thought that for the first time since her return she in some measure resembled the girl she had been. And yet her anguish was etched there among her features, the pain she had suffered would never be erased, and Georgiana's heart bled to see her now, and the gallant way she worked to veil her sorrow.

It was Minnie's turn to sigh, and she stretched deliciously, then folded her arms behind her head, leaning back against an apple tree. "Gracious, you can't imagine how pleasant this is, being here again. Truly, I ought to feel guilty, lolling around like this, with Lee slaving away at home—but I don't." Her laughter burst forth, calling up Georgiana's own. Over the years she had become fond of Minnie's husband, who, to the degree that he was able, had done much to publicize the Free School and to champion Georgiana's part in it. While the *Battlecry* was not the *Liberator,* Lee Peckham was nonetheless earning a name for himself in antislavery circles; Georgiana had heard Appleton declare that one day he would be every bit as famous as Mr. Garrison himself.

Certainly they were well matched, Leland and Minnie—in character if not in size, for she was large and fleshy, he spare and wiry—and in Minnie he was convinced he had won a glorious prize, which of course he had—who would deny it? From childhood and the time of dolls, she'd exhibited the maternal nature, the urge for homemaking, the nesting instinct, the desire for children. She loved the sight of wet white sheets drying on a line, she loved neatly folded piles of linens in the cupboards, loved bureau drawers smelling of verbena and balsam sachet, loved neat, glittering rows of jam and preserve pots, shiny brown crocks of pickled watermelon rind, salted swordfish put down for next winter, and well-dusted, cared-for rooms, but with neglected toys half-hidden in corners. Weddings always made her cry, babies made her cry more, and she would drop everything to rush out and pay a call on a new village mother. She was dedicated heart and soul to her family's good, and to watch her bathing her baby was to see a Flemish madonna brought to life, with her pink, dimpled cheeks, her round vivid face, her head of damp curls, her plump, busy hands that were just like her mother's. For Minnie Peckham, life had a whole cornucopia of simple pleasures to offer, and she relished its every benefaction.

Like all the Talcotts, Minnie too was one of the Free School's true believers. "It's exactly what I'd want to do if I weren't married, and with children to look after," she told Georgiana now. Her hand flew to her mouth. "Oh Georgie, I didn't mean—"

Georgiana laughed. "Don't give it a thought, dear, I know what you meant."

"Tell me about Helen Haverstraw," Aurora said, changing the subject. "What is she like? I believe she must be very nice, to have you like her. And Posie adores her."

"Helen's nice as pie. She's been such a good friend to me, I can't think what I'd have done without her. She often asks after you. I'm sure she'd like to see you some time, when Phoebe is better."

For several days Phoebe Haverstraw's health had been at issue. Someone had thrown a dead rat down the Gaunt House well—or perhaps the rodent had merely fallen in—and unaware of the water's being tainted, little Phoebe had drunk from the dipper and been made ill. There had been reason for concern, but Georgiana reported that she was now recovering nicely.

"I think the Haverstraws deserve a lot of credit for enrolling their girls in your school," Aurora said to Georgiana. "If only . . ." She was silent for a moment, and Georgiana thought she must be thinking of Caroline.

"Rora . . ."

"No, it's all right. You mustn't fret, either of you. I was only thinking how different things might be if—"

"Yes? If what?"

"Oh . . . nothing really . . . Georgie, you remember the party—when Cinnamon said that I would marry? I saw afterwards that she meant not Sinjin Grimes but Henry Sheffield." She crossed her breast again and when she looked at Georgiana her eyes were wet, and her voice caught as she spoke. "Oh, Georgie, I believe God keeps us from having the future truly revealed because if we knew the terrible things that lie ahead we wouldn't be able to go on living. No one would have the heart—don't you agree?"

Before Georgiana could reply Minnie made an exclamation.

"Look—here come Heck and Killy!" She pointed across the meadow to the road where the twins ahorse could be seen approaching at a wild canter.

"Mad to ride like that in this heat," Aurora said, opening her parasol. She waved and called, but they were too far away to notice. Then they wheeled into the drive, trotting up to the farmhouse, where Uncle James directed them toward the orchard. They wheeled again and cut out past the paddock, then rode headlong across the fields, whooping like Indians.

"What fine horsemen they are," Aurora said as, exercising a modicum of prudence, the twins reined up and dismounted outside the orchard, knowing better than to urge their horses past the line of hives where the bees swarmed. They came striding through the green grass, switching their crops at the flower heads.

"What are you three wenches doing over here?" Hector demanded. "Stealing Uncle James's peaches, I'll warrant! He'll set the dogs on you."

"Just look at the pair of you," said Aurora. "You're both covered with dust. Where have you been all afternoon? Courting downriver?"

Minnie's merry laugh pealed forth. "I'll bet fathers have locked their doors all along Greenshadow! Did you have any luck at Middletown?"

"We didn't go to Middletown," Achilles said, bussing her cheek. He and Hector were bursting with news about their long trek cross-river, then up to Windsor, and how on the way back they had come across Tyler Gatchell and one of his cronies, Adgie Kroll, at the ferry landing. "Gatchell was boasting about them both stepping up in the world. Seems they're on Zion Grimes's payroll these days—what do you make of that, Georgie?"

"I think it shows that birds of a feather flock together," she replied.

"But see here, Georgie," Hector put in, "if Grimes is actually paying those scoundrels to make mischief, we've got to do something, don't we? What else could it mean but more trouble for you? If we were going to be around longer we'd take care of 'em, by God we would!"

"Heck's right!" Achilles proclaimed. "What they need is a taste of some cold army steel."

"Now, no more of that kind of talk, please, boys, promise me," Georgiana said. "I appreciate the thought, but I'm not concerned about any tricks either of those rascally fellows may have in their sleeves." While she reveled in her two champions, she preferred that they not invite trouble by offering deliberate challenges to her enemies; she had trouble enough.

"All right, Georgie, I promise," Hector said.

Achilles added, "We thought we'd cool ourselves with a swim over at Mirror Pond. Why don't you all come too?"

"We'll ride you over if you like," Hector offered gallantly.

Georgiana's protests were ignored; neither of the twins would take no for an answer, so she gave in, slipping an arm through each of theirs. "Very well, I'll come but I'm not up to going in. You swim, we'll watch."

"Not I, dear," Aurora put in. "Not in this heat. But you and Min go along, please do, I'll enjoy a moment or two alone here; it's so pleasant, you can return for me later. Please."

With sufficient urging, Georgiana and Minnie rode off cruppered behind the twins. A short distance away, at Mirror Pond, while the men stripped among the bushes, the two women conversed as they wandered about in the bright sunshine, picking the blooming mallows. Then they sat down under a buttonwood tree, and presently the twins in their smallclothes sprinted into the pond, animatedly splashing and romping in the water as if they were still boys, while their mounts doggedly nibbled the leaves from the lower branches of a slippery elm.

"I'm so lucky," Minnie said, watching them. "Lucky to have such a family. And you too, Georgie, you've always been part of us. What would we ever do without you?" Her cheerful expression grew somber and she shook her head. "I can't believe it, you know. About Mama. I can't believe that she's dying—" Her eyes blurred and Georgiana comforted her as best she could.

"Your mother's so happy to have you here, and Sophy."

"She wants me to come again at Christmastime. And of course we shall—if she's still here. Oh, Georgie, she will be, won't she?"

"We must believe she will be," Georgiana replied softly, and gave Min's hand a reassuring squeeze.

Presently, leaving Achilles splashing in the middle of the pond, Hector swam to shore where he dried himself off, then jumped into his trousers and sat down for a visit with the women, talking the way he always seemed to take pleasure doing.

"How are you two enjoying army life?" Georgiana asked.

Hector laughed sheepishly. "By gosh, Georgie, I'd never have gone off soldiering if it weren't for Killy. He's the one who enjoys it. Frankly, I don't think I'm cut out for a military man. You'd laugh to see the way I jump out of my skin every time I hear a gun go off."

Georgiana smiled, recalling a conversation she'd once had with Hector in the attic room at Kingdom Come when she'd wondered how he'd fare at soldiering. The truth was that it didn't much matter whether he liked it or not; if Achilles wanted to be in the army, Hector would be in the army too; even in their middle twenties they remained inseparable, each so much the mirror of the other. "What would you be if you had your choice, then?" she asked.

"I might be a sailor, or maybe a Yankee peddler. Or I might go out west and live with the Indians."

"Oh, Hector!" Minnie exclaimed in surprise. "Would you really do that?"

"Sure, why not? They're the real unfortunates of this country, if you ask me, the Indians. We beat the Seminoles, the Cherokees, now we're clearing them wholesale off their ancestral lands—we're robbing them of their property and doing it with impunity, we're herding them like so much cattle—men, women, and children—onto more land that we've stolen from other tribes. And we wonder why they hate and fear us and scalp our children."

"Oh, Hector, must you talk of such things?" Minnie shivered.

"It's true, Min, believe me. In our greed we've persecuted the red men year after year, we've pushed them back from their traditional hunting grounds, we've slaughtered them like animals, we're out to exterminate them to the last man if we can. Indians are like the trees on the land; the first settlers hated them both and were resolved to do away with them all, shoot 'em up or chop 'em down, but wipe them out, exterminate them. What a cruel, greedy people we are."

Georgiana saw how intensely, how profoundly, Hector cared, and it touched her deeply. Two peas in a pod, he and Achilles—yet how different.

"I hated it in Florida," he went on, "shooting at those Seminoles, seeing our boys die in the swamps. I'd be happy if I never saw another army post or barracks."

"But—I thought you liked the army."

"Part of it's fine, but when you spend your days killing innocent men just because they're in someone's way—well, I can think of better ways to spend my time."

Georgiana leaned forward with interest. "Such as? What would you enjoy doing, Heck?"

"I'm pretty good with a pencil and paper. I'd like to draw the Indians, and paint them, if I could. And I've picked up some of their lingo, too. I can talk with them just like you and I are talking now."

"But would you really go out west?" Minnie asked forlornly. "It's so far . . ."

"I might—but only if Killy went with me. I wouldn't want to go without him. He probably won't, though, he's taken a real shine to—to soldiering and—" He broke off, dug his fists into his pockets, crossed his legs. "I don't guess we'll be going very far," he ended up a bit sheepishly.

Minnie and Georgiana were both relieved to hear this, for they knew Achilles was born and bred to Connecticut and Pequot, and like his older brother, Priam, would not be easily uprooted.

Hector's expression sobered. "Georgie, do you think a man can sometimes bend life to his own private needs?"

"I honestly don't know," Georgiana said, equally serious. "I think maybe 'bending' life is a little like bending thunderbolts. You have to have a strong right arm and a steady hammer on the anvil. And not everyone has that, do you think? We all have our weaknesses and foibles."

Hector thought this over and agreed. They broke off their conversation as they were now joined by Achilles, who had splashed his way ashore, but no sooner had he thrown himself down beside his twin than Hector got up and, dragging Minnie to her feet, took her away to search for elderberries. When they'd passed from view Georgiana turned to Achilles, saying, "Dear, you mustn't think I'm prying, but—is anything in particular troubling Heck?"

"Heck? Oh no, he'll be fine once we're back at camp," he said. His speaking tones were stronger, firmer than Hector's, with a slight rasp to them. "It's Mother, of course—he feels these things harder than most. He's going to miss her a lot."

"Of course he is, so will you, so will we all. But he looks to you for support. You have to be in the driver's seat, you know."

"I just wish he were handier. It's no fun knowing he's always pulling against the ropes."

"I see, but—whatever happens you must stand by him. Will you promise me that, darling, please?"

"Sure, I promise. He's my twin, after all. That's the way twins are. But, Georgie, can we talk about *you* for a minute?"

"Me?"

"Yes, you. About your little school, I mean. Can't you see what the proslavery crowd is building up to? With Rod Grimes in the Assembly they might just get that darn law passed. Lots of people don't like what's been going on since you opened your doors to those colored girls."

Georgiana bridled. "I'm not worried," she insisted. "With right on our side, in the end we can't lose. Ask Posie."

"But that's it! It's Posie I'm thinking of—one of these days she's liable to get hurt. You too. We can't have that happening. And then there's this business of that damnable Sinjin Grimes. By God, if that rascal so much as tries to speak to Sissie when he gets back we'll set him hopping, Heck and I! I wish Pri had done him in years ago when he had the chance."

"That's enough, Killy!" Georgiana said sharply. "I won't hear of it. Even Pri doesn't feel the same way anymore. And, dear, your sister is a woman grown, and can't be treated like a girl. No one can tell her what to do or whom she can or can't see. You can understand that, can't you? And for his part, when Sinjin does come back I'm sure he—he will not trouble her further." Here she felt a pang of guilt, for despite all that had happened, Georgiana knew only too well that Sinjin Grimes still dreamed of Aurora, and she feared what he might do when he learned of Caroline's fate.

Not far away, in the orchard, Aurora had not stirred from where Georgiana had left her under the peach trees. With her cheek resting on her drawn-up knee she smelled the old familiar fruity odors that helped to paint so vividly in her mind long-ago scenes from her childhood. Alas, something had been lost; when, she could not say, or even what it was. Nor where it had gone. Something intrinsic, yet not to be identified. She listened to the industrious drone of the bees as they went about their honeyed work. Buzz-buzz, they hummed in unison, a winged corps engaged in their bumbling labors. What was it? What did that deep hum cause her to think of? She was assailed by some strange fugitive longing she didn't recognize and couldn't describe. Buzz-buzz, the multiple vibrations hung in the thick humid air. The familiar tune was like a piece of melancholy music strummed on the heart strings, the nostalgic strains of some half-remembered song that echoed and reechoed. And who was to say if her thoughts were not with the singer of that song, who was not in China at all but less than ten leagues afield, fishing for Connecticut River pickerel?

Loving his Beauty as he did, since her return Appleton Talcott, though grimly anxious about his wife's health, had sought Aurora's happiness in every way he could think of, even going so far as to present her with a handsome butter-yellow curricle to drive around in, as well as a dapper little cob to pull it. But though she accepted these gifts graciously enough she seldom used the pretty carriage, for she still found little reason to go anywhere except to the farm, and most of the time the curricle sat in the carriage house forlornly collecting dust.

One morning, however, having in consultation with his father dreamed up an excursion that he allowed might enliven her spirits, he went after breakfast to visit with her. He found her supine on the chaise, wrapped in an embroidered robe and reading a book.

"My dear, how charming you look!" he exclaimed, coming in. "That Oriental style is most becoming to you." He bent and tenderly kissed her forehead, murmuring, "My dearest Beauty, nothing so lovely as my Beauty."

She closed her book and smiled ruefully at him. "Oh dear, Papa . . . not anymore . . ."

"You are, you are. Grown more beautiful than ever. You've no idea how gratifying it's been for me to see you around this house. If I believed in the Deity, I'd say He sent you to us."

She sat up quickly and crossed herself; the book slid to the floor. "Don't say that, Papa!" she exclaimed. "Don't ever talk that way!"

"Dearest girl, I simply mean to say how happy we all are that you're home, here, where you belong. And you won't go away again, will you? Promise you won't. Don't break your poor old papa's heart . . ."

"No, Papa," she answered softly, "I won't break your heart—I won't go away. Never—never—"

He returned the book to her lap. "There's my darling girl." He used his handkerchief to pat his brow. "See here, my dear," he said. "I had a thought last night. How would it be if we were to venture out on a small excursion, a brief trip in quest of a bit of culture? *Ars gratia artis,* and all that, hm?"

Aurora's Latin had been faulty since school days and she had no idea what her father was referring to.

"To the Hartford picture gallery," he explained, a bit of artistic diversion to provide her a change of scene, if only for an afternoon. To Appleton's surprise, Aurora readily agreed to the proposal. "And Rose shall come as well," she declared.

Though Appleton had hoped to have her to himself, he nonetheless acquiesced, and with good grace, while Rose preened at the prospect of being viewed in public, dressed up in her best finery, showing off her deportment to the white quality. And, indeed, once in the city she managed splendidly at passing; no one would ever have imagined she was anything else but what she seemed to be: a well-brought-up girl out for an afternoon of shopping and recreation, a gay miss of wealth and substance in from the country to see the city sights.

Moving from one lively, crowded shop to another, handling the prettiest and most novel and expensive merchandise, sniffing and smelling, tasting and feeling, all this proved nicely suited to Rose's most ardent yearnings. Soap, scent, ribbons, lace, stockings, gloves with pearl buttons, pretty shoes and prettier bonnets . . . just to pretend she was able to buy such luxuries made her giddy with pleasure, and not to be told to wait outside like a common servant earned Aurora her eternal gratitude.

After two hours of shopping, Appleton shepherded his charges over to the Mansion House, where they took their fill of lobster salad for lunch, then they drove to the gallery. As she climbed the steps, Rose felt more important than ever; only the best sort of people ever visited such places. She scarcely knew what to expect. Mr. Talcott even bowed as he held the door for her to pass inside, where a little old lady in dusty black took change and handed out tickets, then went back to her knitting.

"Ain't—isn't—this somethin'!" Rose exclaimed as she gazed around. Along, the walls were hung rows of paintings in heavy gold frames, and the light streaming in from the window cut into the ceiling—Rose had never heard of such a thing as a skylight—illuminated each scene in turn. Castles, lakes, horsemen coursing with feathered caps, bowls of fruit, pictures of the Lord Jesus nailed painfully on the cross, dogs with gleaming coats of fur beside curved hunting horns, a handsome brace of fowl with red and green plumage and ringed necks carelessly tossed on a table, portraits of solemn, rich ladies with pearls and holding fans, gentlemen in their finest fig, with little puffy-cheeked cherubs winging overhead.

Rose could hardly speak for the depth of her feelings. She thanked her stars over and over that she had got herself enough deportment so that she could fool people into mistaking her for just one more of these elegant white folks so used to viewing such artistic works at every turn, as if "darling Papa" had a whole attic crammed with such pictures at home. This was what the Whitehall Palace must be like, she thought, where Lady Jeanne swept to and fro with feathered fans and hounds on leashes, waiting on the queen in her red ruff and Moroccan shoes.

It was when, having looked their fill, the group was leaving the gallery, that the awful thing happened. They were retracing their steps through the picture room, pausing to glance at one or two works missed earlier, when, inexplicably, Aurora suddenly uttered a little moan of fright. Rose watched as her mistress's face turned pale and she groped for her father's arm.

"Mistress, is you all right?" Rose asked in alarm.

Aurora stared wordlessly at a small picture on the wall. Then she raised her folded parasol and with a sharp cry struck the painting from its hook. It fell to the floor with a clatter, the gilded frame shattering.

"Here, wait!" shouted the little old lady by the door, hurrying over. "What d'you think you're doing?" She bent to examine the fallen picture whose canvas had been ripped where the tip of Aurora's parasol had pierced it, but by the time the woman had turned back to interrogate the perpetrator of the outrage, she, too, lay stretched out on the floor, with her father and her maid trying to revive her.

A doctor was quickly sent for, but when he arrived he found his patient unsteadily on her feet, to some measure restored after her mishap. Rose and her mistress retired to the comfort facilities, where Aurora was further fortified from a flask, and Appleton thanked the doctor for his trouble, then wrote out a check to cover the damage. But before the picture was taken away, Appleton asked if he might examine it more closely, curious as to what there might be about it that could have spurred Aurora to such an unlikely act. Far from a great work of art, it was really quite pedestrian: a small, undistinguished painting entitled *Still Life with Wine and Cheese,* with a straw-covered wine bottle and a glass, and lurking in the background, waiting to nibble the tasty wedge of reddish Stilton lying on a blue china plate, were two gray rats with greedy shoe-button eyes and curling tails.

26

The Purloined Fan

ALMOST BEFORE ANYONE realized it, the family reunion had come to an end. First to leave was Electra: an urgent letter had arrived summoning her home to Georgetown, where Lloyd was reported prostrated by heat, overwork, and a touch of fevernager. The mere mention of that dread word had set his wife to packing and making her way south by coach and train, not before promising her mother that she would return as soon as she could, bringing Lloyd if his schedule and condition permitted. The twins' furlough soon ended too, and brave and smiling until the Yellow Pumpkin carried them away, Mab collapsed and had to be put to bed. They were unlikely to be granted another leave before her death, she knew. She had taken her last farewell of her darlings. And then, within the week Minnie and the baby were gone as well, home to Glens Falls; and the house seemed dismally empty.

No one, either before or after the visitors departed, was able to get a word of explanation from Aurora regarding the baffling episode at the art gallery. Whenever the subject was broached, she flatly refused to discuss it, ascribing it to a "momentary lapse," and with the forlorn emptying out of Kingdom Come and its effect on Mab, most put it from their minds. Rose, however, could not. As puzzled as the others about the reason for her mistress's violent reaction to the little picture, she possessed one clue that they did not, recalling vividly the disturbing dream Aurora had had—recalling as well that she had cried out then for Sinjin Grimes. And so even as Rose longed for the captain's return, she feared what it would augur, for while the Talcott family might believe that Aurora no longer pined for her former lover, Rose knew better.

And when was he to return? Rose had learned by overhearing a conversation between Old Bobby and Priam that Judge Perry and Jack Talcott had solicited the sympathy of a certain person who had the ear of the state's attorney general (namely, the man's wife, an ardent abolitionist), and were hopeful that the safe return of the captain and his two companions could be effected forthwith. As for herself, she prayed only that when the captain did return it would be to her own arms and not Aurora's, that Cinnamon's magic charm would do its work again, long enough at least for her to make use of that other charm now in her possession.

Meanwhile, having paged her way through *The Romance of Roderick Lightfoot,* she decided that it was time to return the book to its original owner, and one day, when Agrippina had gone shopping in the Center, she seized the opportunity to slip into Agrippina's bedroom, leaving the door ajar so she could hear if anyone came along the hall. She moved quickly to the bed, got down on her knees, and stuck her head under it, emerging seconds later with the hatbox. She set it on the counterpane and removed its lid, but before she could replace the book, another object invited her eye. She put in her hand and brought out a lady's fan, a lovely object of ivory and yellow silk, which when unfolded disclosed a painted scene of three rather queer-looking females engaged in some complicated and, to Rose, totally incomprehensible activity.

Still, she thought the fan was a marvelously pretty thing. Ought she to "borrow" it as well? she wondered. Certainly she would like to. Would it be missed? Perhaps; but then perhaps not. Now that things were going so smoothly, she didn't want any unnecessary friction with the irksome Pina. She began wafting the fan, as she imagined Lady Jeanne might, and glancing at her reflection in the mirror opposite the bed, she was pleased. "Oh," she crooned aloud, rewarding her image with a beguiling smile, "that *is* nice." Elegantly swaying and dipping before the glass, the fan fluttering past her face like a yellow bird, she arched her brows and spoke demurely. "You does me—*do* me—great honor, Lord—um—whatchamacallum," she articulated with fastidious care. "Will you pray be so kind—" Then, catching sight of a bit of movement in the glass, she froze.

"There you are, Rose," said Aurora from the doorway. "I've been looking for you." She swung the door wide, entered, and looked around. "What are you doing with Miss Pina's hatbox?"

Covered with confusion, Rose snapped the fan shut and quickly dropped it into the box, clapped on the lid, and was about to shove it from sight when Aurora interrupted her. "Wait, please. Be good enough to let me see that fan."

More puzzled than frightened, Rose set down the hatbox and brought out the fan, which she handed over to her mistress. Aurora opened it and thoughtfully studied the figures of the Three Fates, engaged in their activities of spinning, weaving, and cutting the thread of life. Rose waited for her to say something, but she seemed fascinated by the design. Then, she made an indistinct murmur as something else caught her eye. She moved closer to the bed, took the familiar volume of *Roderick Lightfoot* from the open hatbox, and thumbed the pages. Rose tittered nervously.

"What were you doing with this, Rose?"

"Just tryin' to read it, mistress," she answered innocently. She was relieved when she saw Aurora smile.

"You realize these are Miss Pina's private things, don't you? I'm sure she'd be very upset to learn you've disturbed them. Come now, put them away, quickly, before she returns, and let's say no more about it, shall we? Have you seen my mother? She wasn't in her room."

"Yes, ma'am," Rose said, taking the fan once more, "she's yonder settin' in the summerhouse with Miz Duckworth."

She watched as Aurora went to the window and looked down across the garden. She was about to slide the hatbox back under the bed when she heard a sharp accusatory voice as without warning Agrippina swooped into the room.

"My hatbox! Put it down at once. Who do you think you are, coming in here! Rora, how could you allow this?"

In her wrath Agrippina struck the box from Rose's hands, knocking it to the floor, where the contents spilled out on the rug. With a gasp she dropped to her knees and began hurriedly restoring the things to the box; when Rose bent to assist her she slapped her hand away. "Don't touch anything! This is what comes of your meddling. These are my most precious mementoes in the world!"

She stood again, huffing and red-faced and on the verge of tears, clutching to her bosom a handful of manuscript pages. "And I'll warrant she's been reading my poems, too—I'm certain she has," she declared tearfully.

"Pina," Aurora began, stepping toward her, "I assure you that no one has been reading your poems. It's simply that I was going through my trunk and found a new bonnet that, being in mourning, I cannot wear, but that I thought would suit you, and Rose recalled seeing a hatbox under your bed that I might put it in, that's all. Come along, Rose."

As Aurora moved toward the door, Pina set the box on the bed where she made a quick inventory of its contents. Before Rose could follow her mistress, she heard Pina say, "It's gone."

Aurora stopped on the threshold. "What is gone?"

"Rose, there was a fan in this box—where is it?"

"I didn't see no fan."

Aurora came back into the room, but before she could speak Pina began railing at the girl.

"Don't you lie to me, you wicked creature! I know there was a fan in this box, I put it there myself. If you've decided to take it—"

"Wait, Pina," Aurora said calmly. "Rose, let me have the fan again, please." Rose reluctantly produced the fan from her apron pocket.

"There! Didn't I say it?" Pina cried. "Of all the effrontery!"

"Rose did not steal it," Aurora said. "I gave it to her."

"Sissie, how can you say that? Since when do people go around giving away other people's property?"

Aurora returned Pina's look evenly. "People do not as a rule, but in this case I was merely giving away my own property. Isn't that a fact?"

"Certainly not! I bought that fan in Boston."

"Pina dear, I'm afraid that's quite impossible," Aurora asserted, taking care not to raise her voice. "This fan came from Macao, as you well know. It was painted by an artist there, a friend of—of the person who gave it to *me*."

Pina's face reddened. "That's not true, Sissie! It's mine! You can ask anybody!"

"Perhaps we must ask Georgiana, since it was hers before it was mine."

Agrippina started guiltily. "Georgie? How was it ever hers?"

"It was given to her by the same person who gave it to me. Tom Ross made her return it; it afterwards came into my possession. On the afternoon of John Quincy's party, as a matter of fact. And since it *is* mine to do with as I wish, I have in turn passed it along to Rose. Every girl should have a pretty fan, don't you think?" Aurora turned to go, then lightly added an afterword. "Pina, do come to my room when you have a minute and see the bonnet. I think it will suit you well."

On her way to the door, Rose returned the fan to her pocket, and behind Aurora's back, made a face at Pina.

"Don't you dare put your tongue out at me, you wicked girl!" Pina cried, advancing on her furiously.

Rose giggled. "I didn't put out no tongue. You're just imagining things again, Miss Pina."

"Don't you give me any sass! How can you stand there and lie like that, you despicable thing?"

"Pina, for heaven's sake, don't upset yourself any further," Aurora protested, but Pina would have none of it.

"It's true, Sissie, you never see it, but she's a malicious creature. She sprouts wings whenever you're around, but you don't know the half of what goes on around here."

Smiling, Aurora approached her sister and taking both her hands tried a new tack. "Pina dear, you've been so sweet and kind to me since I've been back, taking such good care, doing so many thoughtful things for me. Surely you can find it in your heart to be kind to Rose, too. She's a good girl, really—aren't you, Rose?"

"Yes ma'am," said Rose, eyes modestly lowered. "Rose is a good girl."

"She is not! She's nothing but a liar and a cheat. *And worse.*"

"What worse?" Rose demanded.

"You're a slut!" Agrippina's pale cheeks had begun to splotch.

"Pina, this will never do," Aurora said. "Stop it, do you hear me?"

"No! I won't stop it!" Agrippina retorted defiantly. "It's true. She's a scandal—"

"Miss Pina, don't—"

"Don't you tell me, you naughty girl."

"Pina, what are you talking about?" Aurora said.

Agrippina turned to Rose. "Tell her. Tell her what disgraceful mischief you've been up to!"

Rose shook her head obstinately, and in her agitation lost control of her speech. "Miss Pina, we's goin' to commence another ruction." She started for the door. "I gots to get down now, 'fore Halley jump on my back agin."

"Never mind about Halley just now, Rose," Aurora said, moving to prevent her leaving. "You have my permission to tell me anything you wish."

"It ain't nothin', mist'ess. Nothin' at all. It just that—the cap'n, he done took a fancy to Rose, that's all, just a fancy. You know how the menfolks is. Cap'n, he got an eye fo' all the ladies." She tried to laugh it away, but Aurora's austere eye held her.

"Go on," Aurora said.

"Ain't—there's not much to tell, mist'ess. Cap'n, he come roun' an' we just—we sort of took up friendly-like. An'—an'—"She was feeling her way inch by inch, word by word, trying to sound plausible, providing at least a few grains of truth while disguising the actual nature of the relationship. "Cap'n Grimes, he just full of all sorts of coaxin' talk, that be all it was, mist'ess, honest." She managed her most guileless look and prayed her story would be accepted. But Agrippina put her foot in it again.

"That's not all!" she exclaimed hotly, facing Rose down. "You're not telling the truth. Halley told me she *saw* you! We kept quiet for Mama's sake."

"Pina, in heaven's name, what *is* the truth?" Aurora demanded with weary exasperation.

"The truth is, dearest sister, that your maid is Sinjin Grimes's whore!"

Rose uttered a shrill cry and fell on her knees, looking up at Aurora and pleading. "Rose ain't nobody's who', mist'ess. I ain't no slut neither. I loves him. Miss Pina got no call to talk like that about me—Miss Rora, is you all right?"

Aurora's face had gone pale, and her hand pressed the fabric over her heart.

"Sissie—*are* you ill?" asked Pina, suddenly frightened.

"No—I'm—all right," Aurora whispered, deathly white. As she turned and headed for the door Rose was tugging desperately at her skirt.

"Don't be mad at Rose, mist'ess," she pleaded, seeing the effect her words had had. "I won't scandalize you no mo'. It's all done with, anyways. Cap'n, he done wash his hands of me. He don't love Rose no mo'. Mist'ess, I know I done bad, but you see, Rose be good from now on, swear to Jesus."

Aurora glanced down at the pathetically weeping girl, then wrenched her skirts free. Two inflamed spots had burned their way into her chalk-white cheeks. "Rose," she said, "though I regret to say it, you may consider yourself relieved of your duties where I am concerned. I shall not be requiring them in future. However, if my mother wishes you to return to your former tasks, that is her affair. As for me, I want nothing more to do with you." She started again toward the door. Now Rose struggled to her feet and blocked her way, clasping her trembling hands before her and starting to cry miserably.

"Name o' God, mist'ess, don't do it! Rose don't want to do no mo' below stairs work. If you tells yo' mama, she gonna kick me out! Then where'll Rose go, what she gonna do? Please, mist'ess, didn't you tell Pina, you say, 'Pina, be kine to Rose, she be a good girl'?—ain't you said so yourself? Don't be mad at Rose. Let's us jes be friends like befo'. Ain't I fetched you the cookin' sherry, ain't I sat by yo' bed when the nightmares was ridin'?"

Aurora made no reply. Fastidiously drawing her skirts aside, she stepped around Rose and left the room.

Rose leaned against the doorjamb, trying to catch her breath, while Pina watched her mutely. "I hope you is satisfied, Miss Pina," she gritted out, scowling at her tormentor. "You is sholy lost me my place now."

"Quite satisfied, thank you," said Pina with ill-disguised satisfaction. "Sacking is exactly what you deserve. I am sorry it was at my sister's expense, but I must say it was worth it. You may as well go and pack now—*wait,*" she cried as Rose started out. "You're not taking that fan with you. It's mine. Give it to me."

"I ain't giving you nothin'," Rose retorted. "If you wants it, then you just come on an' take it from me, Miss Aggappina. Go ahead, just you try, I dares you."

Hearing the threat in Rose's voice, Agrippina evidently thought better of the idea, for she made no move to recapture the fan by force. Instead, she walked over to the bed and removed the copy of *Roderick Lightfoot* from the hatbox. "Really, I wonder that anyone was ever so foolish as to think to improve you," she went on. "What a coarse, ill-bred creature you are."

"If I is, that's how God made me," Rose answered, mustering a tatter-demalion dignity. "At least Rose ain't no dried-up stick of a virgin with no juice, who has to hide books like that under her bed—in a hatbox under her bed—a bed what ain't goin' to get no man in it never!"

"Far too ill-bred for any sea captain, I'm afraid," Pina went on, ignoring Rose's cruel remark, "even a blackguard like Captain Grimes." Her eyes had begun to glitter and there was an odd pitch in her voice. "But, scoundrel that he may be, you shall never have him, Rose, I can promise you that."

"I never did 'speck to have him, so it don't matter much," Rose said with a shrug. "But they wasn't no need to tell *her* 'bout me and the cap'n. 'Cept your own meanness. Pina, you is one spiteful critter—"

Pina reached out and slapped Rose's cheek; just as quickly Rose slapped her back, hard.

Agrippina gave a muted cry of pain and stared in outraged surprise. "You—slapped—me."

"You thank your stars it was just a slap. Next time I'll lay you out like a corpse." She brought out the Chinese painted fan and opened it, then wafted it saucily under Pina's nose. "You don't need this anyhow, Miss Pina. You ain't got yo'self no man to flutter it at, an' you never will."

She went away then, taking the fan with her. Agrippina slammed the door behind her and collapsed in impotent tears. This was not the end of the episode, however. Even before Judah announced dinner, Rose stood on the hearth rug in the study, facing her employer, tearless and defiant.

"A most regrettable incident," she heard Appleton saying. "Most regretta-ble. Striking one of your mistresses. A shocking thing. What have you to say for yourself, Rose?"

"Rose don't say nothin'," she replied, not at all chastened. "Pina done slap Rose, Rose done slap her back, that's all."

Appleton was attempting to be fair. "You must apologize, then. Tell Miss Pina you are sorry and we'll forget the incident."

"Rose ain't done nothin' to be ashamed of, all I done was stick up fo' myself. Miss Pina ought to apologize to me."

Appleton shook his head; he had already known what he was obliged to do, and in this matter his father had concurred. Appleton dismissed the girl with a week's pay and instructions to be gone in the morning.

Surprisingly, Rose seemed to regard her dismissal as a piece of good fortune, for she shed not a tear; nor did she mention her leaving to any of the Priests. There were no sad farewells, no tears and kisses; she went with the clothes on her back and her week's pay, plus the trinkets and geegaws she'd collected. And she went not in the morning but that very night, and by stealth. But first she crept into the room of Lady Sheffield where with Halley's shears she snipped off a lock of the sleeping woman's hair. Then, from the dining room she pocketed the set of Apostle spoons, along with the flannel drawstring bag they were kept in. While the moon rose she slipped from the house, no one the wiser, and was gone from Kingdom Come.

27

In the Green Room

DOWNRIVER AT DEEPING, close by a giant chunk of feldspar and schist structured roughly in the shape of an open tome, Sinjin and his two charges made camp. They had escaped the village without incident, making good their getaway in the canoe Sinjin had borrowed and arriving at their destination below the Deeping landing well before dawn. By some miracle the musty, mildewed old fishing cabin still stood in a small clearing out of sight of the river, and the three exiles were soon settled in, with the cots brought down from the rafters and set up, and the camping gear safely stowed.

Now, hunkered down around a fire, they made plans. Since news traveled fast along the river, and because both Ambo and Mat were instantly recognizable, they must all avoid Deeping village, at least for a while, until they were certain of not being discovered. Ears of corn filched from a farmer's field, some dug-up turnips, a rabbit snared by Ambo would do for a morning repast. Sinjin longed to use the coffeepot—a steaming cup of coffee would go well—but since there was no supply of beans on hand, he must do without. There was, however, sweet water from a woodland spring, wild huckleberries, black and hairy and not at all sour, and fish to be caught in the Connecticut.

Oh, they would do fine as long as they lay low, and Sinjin congratulated himself. His plan had gone off without a hitch; only Georgiana, Hat, and the Jenckeses knew where they were, and while he cursed Ike Bleezer and his confederates for the mischief they'd caused, as long as that trouble had chased him down to Deeping, he intended making the most of it. For as nowhere else in the world, here beside the river Sinjin Grimes felt profoundly and peacefully at home, the way he wished he felt on the deck of a ship at sea; wished, but seldom managed. In this out-of-the-way place he was made safe in a nostalgically recalled world of boyhood and simpler times when all of life had stretched out before him in a long, shining stream, before he had acquired the brooding, saturnine countenance he currently presented to his companions, before the world and everything in it had curdled.

So, day after day, the three men, or one of them at least, played at being boys again. Like the *coureurs de bois* of two centuries before, they would creep along the shadowed paths, their feet all but noiseless on the needle-covered forest floor, winding their way among the mossy tree trunks and boulders, the white man and the yellow rendering up to the red one that which rightfully belonged to him. For it was Ambo Buck, the part-Indian, who picked the trails, observing the signs, pausing to count the rings of a fallen tree, to scrape the blue-green lichens off a piece of bark to mark the path as they moved inland from the river.

As Sinjin had from the first suspected he might, Georgiana's protégé quickly proved his mettle. He was a sterling comrade who knew how to keep silent, yet who could still appreciate a humorous line; a man who knew a thing or two about forest lore, who could slip among the trees with a native grace and cunning that no amount of quill pushing for Warren Burdin had yet divested him of. His tall bulk caught in a shaft of mottled light, he was Rousseau's noble savage come to life, the last breath of a people years dead and gone from all such places, and at his side, his dog, the faithful Mavra, which had been with him on the wagon and could not be left behind. Once Sinjin watched in amazement as he climbed a towering tree trunk limb by limb, there to perch and visit a nesting peregrine, and the bird had not so much as ruffled its feathers. He called to the crows who responded gabbily from overhead; knelt and spoke into an empty hole where presently a woodchuck poked its nose out; stood breast-deep in a brook conversing with an otter conducting business along the muddy bank.

Come evening, Sinjin would lie down by the fire while Mat would produce a brace of wild fowl spitted and roasting, a succulent squirrel or rabbit with tender thighs to pick from the bone with one's teeth. Supper over, the three would laze around watching the fireflies wink among the leaves, the mute Mat Kindu listening while his master and the Indian conversed in a tongue of which the Malay had learned only fragments. Frequently Sinjin would recite from the classics. Fingers laced behind his head, propped against a log, lids lowered, he was able to call forth long, majestic passages committed to memory while at sea, culled from epic poems; entire cantos, even, from *Paradise Lost,* from *The Prisoner of Chillon* and *Childe Harold;* speeches from Shakespeare's plays and sonnets; bits and pieces from Goethe—his old friend, the sorrowful Werther; and all this without a drop of hard spirits or any artificial stimulation.

Though he had grabbed up a few of his personal things, in his haste to flee he had neglected to nab a bottle from Milehigh's bar, but he found it no great lack. Here springwater was more to his palate, and he found he enjoyed watching the night sky without Ursa Major spinning giddily about. One night he took his flute from the canvas bag he had hastily packed when he left Pequot Landing and, wrapped in a blanket, sat with his back against a tree and played. Then the silvery notes floated high above the trees into the darkness, sounds so pure, so bright and perfect as to be marvelous, and he wondered what more a man could ask for than this: a river flowing past, a cozy fire and some grub, and two good fellows for company.

Beyond the flickering flames he could make out the familiar silhouette of Mat Kindu, that slant-eyed Cerberus, and beside him Ambo Buck. Since their return to Pequot Landing Sinjin had been regularly puzzled and amused to observe the odd friendship that had been struck between his manservant and the manager of Burdin's Best Seeds. Villagers declared it a caution to watch the two, to see the primitive hand signs they used to bridge the gulf between them: Matty meager and vulpine, with scarcely any meat on his bones; Ambo large and deliberate; the fox and the bear. On the face of things they seemed the two least likely companions imaginable; yet they appeared to have discovered a number of commonly held interests, not the least of which was a penchant for the outdoor life, this natural existence so like that described in the pages of Rousseau. After the first night at Bible Rock they had left the cabin to Sinjin and moved outdoors to sleep on restful beds of pine boughs, under the stars.

Sinjin watched now as Ambo filled his pipe, then handed over his pouch to Mat, who did likewise. The two bowls glowed in the dark and the dark faces were wreathed in smoke. There was no doubt that Georgiana had done a splendid job with her former pupil; Ambo was a young man anyone could be proud of, more so considering his antecedents. If she could do as well with some of those girls from Lamentation, or even with Rose Mills—but better to forget that one.

"Ambo," he said.

"Yes, Cap'n."

"I was just thinking about Miss Ross and you, about all you've accomplished. Your people must be very proud of you."

Instead of looking pleased by this remark Ambo frowned. "My people are all dead now. Miss Ross, she's my people." He raised his brows. "You're my people too, maybe?"

Sinjin was touched by this obvious petition for friendship. He rolled onto his side. "Ambo," he said, "what would you say to leaving Pequot? Sooner or later I'll be getting another ship, and—I was thinking that I could use a handy fellow like you along."

"Where would we sail?" Ambo asked.

"Havana, maybe, for a start. Maybe even Rio, Montevideo, who knows?"

Ambo listened without moving. For a time he made no response, might even have fallen off to sleep, except that his eyes remained open. "Captain," he said at last, "I am gratified that you wish me to do this thing. It is a great honor."

"Good." Sinjin put out his hand. "Then it's settled."

Without permitting his expression to change, Ambo said, "No, Captain, it is not possible. I am sorry, I cannot."

"But that's foolish. You ought to be thinking about seeing something of the world beyond Burdin's."

"I enjoy working at Burdin's," Ambo returned politely.

"I'll speak with Warren, anyway. He wouldn't want to hold you back."

"That is true. But even if he would permit it, still I could not go."

"Why not?" Sinjin asked.

"It is because of Miss Ross. She has need of friends now. Grave need."

"But if the school is closed—if my damnable brother succeeds in getting himself into the legislature and having that law passed—why then, you should be giving serious thought to your own future."

Ambo's look was dogged. "Miss Ross is my future. If she is injured in any way, if harm should come to her from any quarter whatever, I will be the one to see to punishing her enemies."

As the younger man spoke, Sinjin, regarding him across the fire, saw something in his eyes that was at once laudable and mortally dangerous. "I believe you will at that. Good for you, boy. Yes, you stick with Georgiana. She may have need of you after all. You and I can go voyaging another time."

"Very well, Captain," said Ambo, satisfied that between them they had arrived at a new understanding.

Later that same night, while the others slept, Sinjin stepped from the cabin out into the still darkness. With the glittering, moon-painted river slipping almost noiselessly by, as if to betray its presence were to cause trouble, he stood gazing like some ancient Chaldean soothsayer up at the broad night sky, silently consulting the winking bodies of the heavens, communing with constellations as though they would impart to him his true destiny. They would not, of course. "The fault, dear Brutus, is not in our stars . . ." At this pastime he seemed little better than an eyeless man pouring over the printed page. And if he were able to read his future in the stars, would it have made a difference? Offered him a life a man could take pride in? For, in truth, he thought, excepting a few foolish near misadventures mistaken as acts of heroism, the notoriety disguised as the fame he had courted, a penchant for slogging upstream against convention's flow, he really hadn't much worthwhile to look back on. He shivered, chilled by the night-falling dew, and was startled when Mavra shoved her cold wet muzzle against his palm. He crouched beside the animal, one arm around the heavy furred neck, her head pressing forcefully against his own. Then, suddenly, as he stood away from the dog he glimpsed a flash of blue light, felt the agonizing pain dagger through his head, and the starry sky dissolved in explosions of hideous yellow. With a moan he suddenly clutched his skull, eyes clamped shut, for to open them was unbearable, and tumbled writhing to his knees.

Later, he lay in the same spot; he could smell the piny woods, hear the lapping water. Had he lost consciousness? His head throbbed, he could make out a figure looming over him, a dark shape he slowly came to perceive was Ambo. He could feel the moist warmth of Mavra's breath.

"Good . . . dog . . ." he managed to get out thickly, and Ambo helped him sit up. With his burly but gentle hands the halfbreed began to massage the base of Sinjin's skull, easing the pain, mastering and dissolving it. Then he picked him up as though he were a feather pillow, carried him into the cabin, laid him carefully on his cot, and went out again. When he came back he had a piece of bark that he forced between Sinjin's rigid jaws, and as its bitter taste was absorbed into his saliva he relaxed as though by magic.

The pain having eased at last, he thought about the mighty Julius Caesar and his epilepsy and was determined that, like the great warrior, he would not give in to his own "attacks," these headaches that erupted without warning, occasionally felling him as he had tonight been felled. He never gave in, not to those things outside of himself that threatened to lay him low. It was other things, like the dismal, constant ebb and flow of thoughts he had of Aurora and of Caroline, so far away in Italy, that truly troubled him, and with such thoughts Aurora's face appeared before him, crowned by that aureole of shining hair, and again he heard the piping sound of little Caroline's voice, her laugh, as he had heard it so many years before.

It was to interrupt such musings as these that, the next morning, he resumed his labors on an old piece of work, one that haunted him the same way she did. He had not seen the manuscript of his long poem "Al Qadar" for a dozen years and more, since he had left it with Georgiana after she had criticized it so harshly, and, as he had thought then, so unfairly. But he had not forgotten it, and now, stretched out on Bible Rock, he took up his pen and the paper he always carried in an oilskin pouch in his seabag and rewrote the first stanza. But the lines were not the same as they had been, and reading them now, he liked them very well and thought them a great improvement over the original. Georgiana's opinions had not been wasted, he told himself, and wrote on.

He decided that if he was to continue writing, what he needed was a place in which to write, and at his prodding, Ambo and Mat went about fashioning him a secluded hideaway, a shady, bowerlike structure, which bore a loose resemblance to a leafy pagoda. It was a private aerie, a "green room," from which he could withdraw from the meager society at hand and do what he now desired more than anything to do. Suddenly, his brain was awash with images; indeed, he had only to roll over and a new idea sprang fresh to mind. "Al Qadar," it seemed, had not been dead at all, only waiting for this period of time spent by the river that flowed past his door: Stony Arabia in the green room.

Within days he had a sheaf of new stanzas—pages that were now more precious to him than gold. One aim he had: to finish, finish once and for all, and see it published—if anyone could be persuaded to do so.

ONE evening, when the runaways were devouring an appetizing supper of speckled trout, Mat Kindu, crouched at the fire, suddenly stiffened, his nostrils twitching, slanted eyes sliding left and right. At the same time Ambo began making growling noises deep in his throat, ominous animal sounds of the sort his grandmother was sometimes prone to. Questioning with his eyebrows, Sinjin caught the Malay's frown as he laid a cautioning finger to his lips, then, jerking a nod to Ambo, they each grabbed a weapon and melted into the trees.

What was it? Sinjin wondered. Was someone on their trail after all? Were they to be returned in irons? He stood tiptoe, straining for a look. Moments later he glimpsed Ambo's silhouette bellying Indian-style toward a clump of bushes, where it disappeared. In another moment Mat flashed into view and he too flung himself into the clump of bushes. There followed sounds of a savage encounter, a violent upheaval in the shrubbery accompanied by a fierce caterwauling. What manner of wampus cat had they got hold of? From the sounds Sinjin judged it to be a big beast, maybe a painter. He started off in a low crouch toward the same shrubbery, but before he reached it Mat and Ambo emerged dragging the kicking, screaming form of Rose Mills.

"What in the name of Christ-on-the-cross do you think you're doing!" a furious Sinjin demanded, grabbing her arm and yanking her to her feet. He became angrier when she refused to reply to his questions, volunteering no more than the fact that she'd been discharged from Mr. Talcott's employ, had left Pequot, and swore never to go back.

"By the yellow god," Sinjin muttered, still astonished by her unexpected appearance, "you just don't know when you're well off, do you? Well, what do you want around here?"

"Rose came to pay a visit to you," she said coyly, obviously pleased with herself for having tracked him down, yet afraid to look at him.

"How'd you know where to find us?"

"Heard it." She glared at Ambo and Mat, then dogged Sinjin's heels as he headed back to the cabin.

"You'd better check the trail, Ambo," he growled when they had reached the place. "And you, Mat, feed her up and send her packing."

As Ambo slipped away into the woods, Mat clamped onto Rose's wrist to drag her from the cabin. "Get your hands off me!" she screeched. "God damn it, you lay a hand on me again, I'll kill you!" She yanked free and dashed back to Sinjin. "I come to stay. To take care of you. Please don't send me away," she pleaded.

His voice was gruff. "No one needs taking care of here."

"*He* sure don't." She glared at Ambo, whose bulk suddenly filled the cabin doorway.

"Shut your mouth, woman," Ambo said. "It's all clear, Cap'n. She wasn't trailed."

Sinjin considered. He knew it was wrong, she oughtn't to be there, oughtn't to have come. Rose Mills meant trouble, somehow he could smell it. Nonetheless, the heady aroma of her perfume enticed him. "All right, she can stay the night," he said reluctantly. "But in the morning she leaves. Mat, bring a candle."

Rose smiled to herself. Things were going according to plan. In the light she peered about the cabin. Evidently no other female had been here, everywhere she looked were only men's belongings.

"Uh-uh, no you don't, little lady," Sinjin growled as she eyed the bed. "You bunk outside." He could hear Ambo's hatchet knocking down some pine boughs for her to sleep on. "With Mavra," he added. He enjoyed her howl of outrage. Unless you care to indulge in some feminine companionship for yourself, Ambo, he thought but did not say, still annoyed that she had so brazenly joined them. Suppose she'd been followed?

He bedded down alone and fell quickly asleep, only to be made conscious again by a warm, moist, coaxing sensation that crept through his loins; what a pleasant way to be awakened, he thought, lying back, watching from under an arm flung across his face, luxuriating in her notable performance. The moonlight streamed in through the window, etching her dark, hunched figure with crosshatchings of silver, painting her naked form with clandestine allure.

"Was it good?" Rose asked when she was done.

"Go back outside," he grumbled, but when he tried to evict her she wriggled like a kitten, coming to rest against his bare chest, her legs and arms intimately entwined with his.

"Get out," he muttered again, pushing her, but halfheartedly.

"No." She began to purr like the feline she was.

There was a pause. Well, he decided, it *had* been a long time. Man could not live by bread alone. And so conveniently placed a female presence ought to be made proper use of. He turned her on her back and went to work on her. Later she promised him it was the best ever. Ever.

So Rose Mills joined the party at Bible Rock. Sinjin could fault her neither for her intrepidity at having made her way there on her own nor for her adroitness in fitting herself so slyly into the present scheme of things. She was like a chameleon, darting from one spot to another, changing color for color, picking up the newest hue and making it part of herself or herself part of it. Just as she had fitted herself into the Talcott household, donning her demure alpaca dress and starched cap, as she had even become a begrudgingly serious pupil at Georgiana's school, now she transformed herself into a frontier woman doing for her man. Now there was no mention of "deportment" or of reaching a "lady's estate." Now she thought neither of shoes nor of stockings but went barefoot; she seldom bound up her hair, letting it instead hang loose around her shoulders. It was as though she were playing a role whose dimensions she herself had marked off, having decided what traits of character she would choose to reveal and how, which costume to don, what sort of face paint to wear, which lines to speak. She seemed to sense that it was in this unlikely guise of woodland dryad that she could best reach her lover and most attractively engage his attention.

She thought nothing of slipping out of her clothes in broad daylight and running naked across the clearing down to the riverbank, where with excited cries she would launch herself into the water, splashing and squealing childishly as if all the world were watching her. Eventually subsiding, she became content to paddle aimlessly about, spouting water like a diminutive whale. She was a good swimmer, agile as an otter, as if water, not earth, were her natural element. Sometimes she would make a quick surface dive, cheekily flashing her pale bare bottom as she dove; sometimes, he knew, she showed her backside more than she need have done; sometimes she stretched out and let her tan breasts rise above the surface, the dark nipples glistening in the sun, and he knew that this too she was doing for him.

One day some bearded men came paddling downriver in a canoe low in the water with canvas bales, and they saw her floating thus. Believing her to be alone, they began making crude remarks accompanied by obscene gestures, only to have Sinjin speed to the riverbank where he stood cursing them in a volley of seaman's expletives that set the astonished commuters agape. With their attention thus diverted, Rose cut hastily for shore, whence she returned armed with Ambo's hatchet. Swimming underwater, she hacked a gash of sufficient size to cause the canoe to swamp, and in moments the helpless voyagers found themselves and their goods floating downstream while a dusky nymph pranced about on shore, wagging her fingers in her ears, uttering derisive hoots, and making lewd gestures. Sinjin made her stop swimming, then, except after dark; he, Ambo, and Mat were, after all, still fugitives from the law.

When he would steal away to his green room to write, she pleaded with him to let her sit quietly beside him and watch. Knowing nothing about the act of creation as it touched art, she nonetheless sensed something remarkable in the process and stood in awe of it, remarking to herself his remote expression as he ruminated, and how his thought was immediately preserved as he scribbled furiously. She noticed too how the crow's-foot lines around his eyes relaxed and the muscles in his jaw stopped twitching, and she judged that whatever the ultimate purpose of such works, their creation was not entirely a bad thing.

Sometimes she wondered if the poem might be for *her,* Aurora, and this irritated her. What would happen, she asked herself over and over, what would he do, what would *she* do, when he and her former mistress encountered each other again? Nothing? Let it be nothing, God. How could it be otherwise after all this time, and anyway he loved Rose! Still, she was alarmed and frightened, and sometimes the small hairs at the back of her neck would rise or her stomach would feel carved out from fear, hollow as a rainbarrel.

This was the fear she had brought into the woods with her, the paralyzing anxiety that wouldn't leave her, that gnawed at her vitals. What was to be done? As Princess Cinnamon had decreed, a baby was the best plan, of course, but time—time was the important consideration here, the length of time it ought to take. Her greatest hope lay in preventing him from knowing, keeping him ignorant of what had actually happened back home. If only she could coax him into catching the packet for New York with her before word came that he could safely return to Pequot, then he would see what she could be like, see the lady she could be. She told herself, she swore to God, that if she could only have his love she would give up everything else. She loved him. What did it matter that he didn't love her back yet? She would love him, she would love him and love him until he had no choice but to love her in return. He would love her after she had borne his child—when Cinnamon's magic must finally work. If only she had more time.

She had not come to the green room for dalliance alone. She had affairs to see to, business to conclude, enchantments to perform. Her fingers idly caressed the small leather pouch containing the little vial of powder, purchased at no small cost from the Indian witch and at present attached to a cord around her neck and lodged between her breasts. One or two pinches of the stuff was to be slipped into the captain's food before each meal. "Leetle, leetle," Cinnamon had decreed, and when the charm finally did its work his seed would quicken in her womb, a child would start to grow there, ripening like a melon on a vine. Sinjin, knowing himself a father, would capitulate to the mother. Then he would be hers at last. This time, before handing over payment, Rose had made Cinnamon swear to it. And she took other precautions. Every night she extracted a few strands of yellow hair from the lock she had snipped from Aurora's head and burned them in the candle flame. Quickly, so he wouldn't catch her at it, a flash, a sizzle, a wisp of smoke—most potent sorceries.

"What's that?" he demanded one night, springing up to question her. "What are you muttering about over there?"

"Just sayin' my prayers," she said piously and came naked into bed. In her frenzied lovemaking she became as imaginatively creative as was possible for her, which was saying a lot. She sought to possess him in every way she could think of; she would die if he left her now.

"WILL you fish this afternoon, Captain?" Ambo asked one noontime as they hiked back to the cabin together. "Or do you prefer to write?"

Sinjin replied as he always did, treating Ambo as an equal. "Unfortunately, writers must work when the fit is on them. A Sunday is like any other day if he has words to set down."

"Are you pleased with your work?" Ambo asked with unexpected boldness.

It was Sinjin's turn to be embarrassed. "How can I say?" he said. "See here, what if you were to do a spot of fishing this afternoon and I read a little of it to you?"

A spark flamed in Ambo's black eyes; clearly this was an expression of respect and friendship of the most exalted sort. A man like Captain Grimes was not given to reading his verses to just anybody who chanced along.

So, after a lunch of roasted corn ears, the two sat on the riverbank with their rods and lines. On Sinjin's lap lay his worn leather portfolio, in his hand a sheaf of pages scribbled on and much worked over. And though she had not been invited to be an auditor, Rose, having suddenly got it into her head to wash out some garments, took up a convenient place on a rock just under the overhang where she would have no trouble hearing what was being said.

"Quiet down there!" Sinjin blasted out as she slopped and sloshed her washing on top of the rock, then made a production of the rinsing, the wringing out, the spreading to dry in the sun, and settled down to listen, much to Ambo's annoyance. He had been wary and suspicious of the girl's intentions ever since she'd arrived, even once warning the captain that she was up to no good, that she had been to see his grandmother; she had told him that much herself. Sinjin, however, had refused to take these remarks seriously, holding that Rose was just a simple-minded creature who often needed guidance, but whose instincts were good and will to improve herself laudable. And now, if he had any objections to her presence, he did not register them as he began to read.

"Al Qadar"—the appellation meant "The Fated One"—was the tale of Ibn Abd Rabbu, known as Abdallah, a poor and lowly being (Rose could appreciate this) who had found employment as a camel driver when fate, in the person of a horse trader, intervened. Out among the vast desert wastes, Abdallah heard the trader say, there lived a bedouin chieftain whose prize possession was a magnificent white stallion. Any man desiring to make his fortune had only to secure the animal and bring it to the trader, who would reward him beyond his wildest dreams. Thus, when the caravan set out, as Abdallah plodded along beside the mangy camel entrusted to his care, his mind dwelled on the noble stallion, the desire for it and for the riches it represented crowding out every other thought, until, one night, stealing a goatskin of water and some oat cakes, he abandoned his beast and the safety of the trading route and slipped away across the desert in search of the bedouin camp.

With no compass to guide him nor any reliable indication where this camp might lie, still the boy went on doggedly for some days, until his water was nearly used up and the oat cakes eaten. At last, parched and starving, he fell prostrate on the hot sand, ready to die. But Allah did not wish his death, not yet, and, remarkably, the boy revived in a tent, stretched out on a divan with silken cushions; through the open entrance he could see green date palms and camels drinking beside a pool: an oasis. A stranger, a sheikh, entered the tent with a bowl of honey and wheat. His name was Qasim Ben Ali, a brave desert warrior, chieftain of his tribe, a man revered for his knowledge and wisdom. And behind him, through the entrance, could be seen the wonderful white stallion, East Wind. Even as he mended, Abdallah laid plans to dupe his benefactor and make off with the valuable steed, but then Qasim Ben Ali casually suggested that Abdallah might enjoy taking the stallion for a ride out on the desert, and Abdallah was off, galloping away into the purple dusk. This horse of horses was now his! Oh, now, he thought, he would be a rich and famous man, with many wives, camels, and tents. He would be a great sheikh himself and men would point at him as he rode by in his fine silk and gold robes.

But alas, because he was Al Qadar, the Fated One, it was not written that Abdallah should become rich and famous by virtue of his theft of the fabled white stallion. Rather, having stolen East Wind, by way of repayment he suffered the worst sort of misery, privation, and despair at every turn. bbed of his coveted prize, he was sold into slavery and made to undergo base indignity and cruelty. Little by little, however, weighed down ins and near starvation, Abdallah underwent an astonishing transformation. In the solitude of his prison cell he remembered many of the things Qasim Ben Ali told him, and he was given understanding, and it was this understanding that made it possible for him to endure.

Long years elapsed before Abdallah was at last freed from bondage, and shunning the world he became an anchorite, existing in a cave in the desert. One day an old, white-bearded man came seeking help and comfort, and Abdallah offered him shelter and food. The two became friends, and a pleasurable exchange of ideas began. Imagine Abdallah's surprise when he discovered the old nomad to be none other than his former savior, Qasim Ben Ali! And then—

But Sinjin's reading of his poem could go no further; there was more to be written, and he explained to Ambo that he had long been seeking the proper resolution of his story, but no ending he had yet dreamed up seemed satisfactory. He must look some more. He neatened the pages and slipped them into the oilskin again, then laid the work aside and stretched lazily. Rose had long since dropped off to sleep, whether from fatigue or tedium he could not tell. Her indifference nettled him, though why it should he didn't know, stupid darky girl. As for his other listener, Ambo's face remained as impassive as ever, and Sinjin could not bring himself to solicit his opinion.

THAT night Rose again burned the yellow hair in the flame and repeated Cinnamon's incantation, and afterwards, while Sinjin lay asleep, she remained awake, thinking things over. She had detected no evidence whatever that Cinnamon's costly powder was working; her monthly had arrived on time, and though she would not allow herself to despair, she knew this sojourn at Bible Rock could not last much longer. At breakfast, she decided, she would start putting double the amount of magic into his food and pray that Cinnamon might quickly prove a true witch.

She coughed and Sinjin stirred and rolled over, drawing her to him; at his swift arousal she performed prodigiously, and as the moon rose above the trees and climbed the sky and the river flashed by she lay with him and loved him and talked in his ear like a sea wave talking into the curve of a shell. But did he hear? Did he? Does the shell hear the wave?

Then, discovery, betrayal, and loss, all fell upon her at once, unexpected like most bad things in life, one evil begetting another.

Almost as much as she feared Aurora Sheffield's hold on her lover, Rose feared Ambo Buck. Time after time she caught him silently eyeing her, or, what was worse, them, her and Sinjin together. His brooding countenance angered her and she wanted to destroy it, to obliterate the reproof she found there. Every day she schemed, trying to contrive some plan by which Ambo might be injured as though by accident, but no clever idea came to her.

Then, one night the thought occurred: she would poison his food, and she left Sinjin writing in the pagoda and went to forage in the woods.

At suppertime there was a tasty squirrel pie. Ambo ate heartily of it. After the meal he began to complain of a gripe in his stomach, then it got to be a wicked cramp, and before long he was sprawled on the ground moaning and clutching his belly.

"He's been eatin' green apples maybe," Rose suggested, affecting concern; Sinjin's concern was greater, and though he said nothing she wondered if he suspected. He put Ambo to bed in the cabin and forbade her entering while he and Mat administered an emetic, forcing the patient to vomit up his meal. Later, creeping close to the cabin window, Rose could make out Sinjin's form bending anxiously over the prostrate Indian. *Die, die,* she prayed, kissing and biting her knuckles, but it was not to be.

At first light she could hear Sinjin's voice, then Ambo's reply. He sounded normal, and within minutes he was standing in the doorway, looking out at her. She kept her eyes averted as she went about her chores until she couldn't stand it anymore, and finally she tossed up her head in defiance. He no more than glanced at her contemptuously before turning away, and thus failed to see her as she spat, or the venomous look in her eyes.

Sinjin had already withdrawn with his writing portfolio to the privacy of the green room, and throughout the remainder of the morning she gave the redskin a wide berth, for she felt reasonably sure he must be plotting against her, even as she plotted against him. At suppertime she waited until he had taken Mavra for a walk before she set about "seasoning" Sinjin's food, slipping the little bag from around her neck, and adding a pinch, then a second, then just a tiny bit more. But as she carried the tainted plate across the clearing, she heard a growl. Mavra was blocking her path. No matter how she attempted to get by, the dog forced her back. Finally Ambo reappeared, striding toward her. She turned, only to find Mat Kindu behind her, blocking her retreat. She was hemmed in. Trapped, she uttered a cry as with a murderous look Ambo snatched the plate away from her, then shoved her away and strode off toward the pagoda. She could hear him and Sinjin talking; after a few moments, they came out.

"Is this true?" Sinjin asked. "What the hell are you putting in my food?"

"He's a liar! I didn't put nothin' in it. What for, anyways?"

Ambo pointed at her breast. "She keeps it in that bag around her neck."

Before she could prevent it, Sinjin tore the cord free. He opened the little bag and spilled the gray powder into his palm. "What is it?" he demanded.

"Nothin'. Just somethin' t' make you strong, so as you can make love."

"Aphrodisiac?" He looked at Ambo, at Mat, then turned his palm down. The powder sifted away. When he glanced at her again it was with a withering look that shriveled her up like a dead lizard in the sun.

He reached out and grabbed her by her wrist, nearly jerking her off her feet. "Where'd you get it?"

She began to babble, forgetful of her grammar and diction. "Cinnamon done sold it me. Not to hurt, only to make you love me. Like I love you. She say—we goin' t'be together. She say you is goin' to love me good. We is goin' to be jes' like this." Her two crossed fingers pantomimed intimacy. "Cinnamon say we be linked tight together, a chain what no one can break. She say you give me a baby!"

"Baby!" His eyes raked her scornfully. "Cinnamon's crazy, she doesn't know what she's talking about. Get out of my way." He shoved rudely past her and headed for the cabin, but she rushed after him, dragging on his arm. Then both stopped halfway to the cabin as a small figure appeared unexpectedly at the edge of the clearing.

"Jeff!" Elbowing Rose aside, Sinjin hurried to greet Jeffrey-Amherst, his dark features shaded by a wide-brimmed hat, a knapsack slung across his shoulders.

"Howdy, Cap'n," Jeff said, grinning jauntily as he crossed the clearing.

Sinjin shook his hand heartily. "Am I glad to see you! Did Miss Ross send you?"

"She sure did, Cap'n. I come down on the packet. Miss Ross, she says to tell you it's okay for you to come home, the coast is clear."

"Well, how about that. Here, let me help you with that pack. Ambo, I bet this young fellow's thirsty."

Jeff shrugged the knapsack off his shoulders and Sinjin lowered it to the ground. Ambo brought a canteen with water, while Mat Kindu picked up the knapsack and hung it on a branch. Rose eyed the newcomer fearfully, knowing his appearance betokened no good for her plans.

"What's the news, Jeff?" Sinjin asked, sitting him down on a stump. "All quiet at home?"

"No sir, Cap'n Grimes." Jeff wiped his lips. "There's a heap of goin's-on every day. First off, Mr. Rod got his 'pointment to the 'sembly, and there's been a heap of trouble for the school. And Missus Talcott, she's right poorly, Cap'n. I reckon she's gettin' on to dyin' now." He glared at Rose. "And you didn't help any, runnin' off with her spoons like you did."

"Liar! I never done no such thing!"

"You're a bad woman, stealin' from the folks, and them bein' so kind as to buy you up and free you."

"What spoons were stolen, Jeff?" Sinjin asked.

"Missus Talcott's 'Postle spoons. Rose hooked the lot when she run off. My grammaw was some put out."

Frowning, Sinjin confronted Rose. "Well? What have you got to say?"

"He's one damn liar, that what I got to say! He's just tryin' to make trouble like all them Priests do all the time."

Sinjin nodded to Ambo. "Perhaps we'd better see. Go get her satchel."

"No!" Rose sprang forward. "Don't let that Injun bastard touch my things!"

Ignoring her protest, Ambo strode to the cabin and disappeared inside; reemerging, he gripped the handles of Rose's satchel in his fist.

"God damn you!" The furious Rose scooped up her skirts and dashed headlong at him. Ambo was forced to fend off her attempts to retrieve her property, holding the bag out of reach above her head until Sinjin came to relieve him of it. He carried it to the stoop where he began rifling through the contents, which were quickly seen to embrace several items of interest, among them a flannel roll, which when its ties were undone, produced a glittering set of silver spoons, one for each apostle.

"Struck it rich, first time around. So you did steal them," Sinjin said, sliding one from its sleeve and looking it over.

"They just some ol' spoons the missus didn't need no more. She give 'em to me. Sort of a good-bye present."

"I can imagine," Sinjin said dryly, examining them. "These spoons are worth a pretty penny. Lucky you decided to shake the dust of Pequot from your heels, I think you'd be unwelcome if you were to return." He gave Jeff a look, then rolled up the flannel, adding, "Why don't I just hold onto these, Rosie. Heavy goods for a girl to be toting around, anyway."

An indignant Rose was having none of this. "They's my spoons," she cried. "You give 'em back!"

He disposed of the roll, and said, "Thank you for the tip, Jeff. Mrs. Talcott'll be pleased you helped retrieve her property."

"Yes, Cap'n, thankee. Be good to bring her some cheer. Grammaw, *she* said Missus Talcott, *she* said she don't mind so much to die now that her ladyship is back to stay."

Sinjin's head whipped around. "Her ladyship?" He ignored Rose's stifled gasp of dismay. "Who do you mean?" he asked.

"Lady Sheffield, Cap'n," Jeff explained. "You know—Miss Rora."

Sinjin was staring in disbelief. "You mean she's home? In Pequot?"

"That's right, Cap'n, she's back from It'ly, livin' at Kingdom Come."

Sinjin tried to mask his astonishment. "How long?"

Rose shoved Jeff out of the way and spoke up to Sinjin. "She come home weeks ago."

"And you knew this?"

"Sure, I knew. I was her puss'nol maid. I fetched and carried for her. I sat up nights with her."

Sinjin's face had gone white. "Why didn't you tell me, damn it!"

"Why should I? She don't care nothin' for you anymore. She told me."

Giving him her buzzard look, she hurried on. "She say, 'Rose, that man ain't nothin' but a mizzabul blackhearted bastard, an' I don't want nuthin' t'do with him.' "

Sinjin threw back his head and laughed scornfully. "She never talked that way in her life."

Rose clutched at his arm. "She can't have you! She can't—she don't love you, not like I do! You hear me, damn you, she ain't goin' to see you no more never!"

"She'll see me, by the yellow god she will!" he vowed grimly. "She'll see me if I die for it."

Ambo, who had been rummaging further in Rose's bag, withdrew his hand with a lady's fan in it.

Sinjin took it, slid the vanes open in an arc, then whistled softly. "Well, well, you three charming ladies, fancy meeting you again." He turned to Rose with sardonic humor. "I hope you're not going to tell me this is yours too. How'd you happen to come by this little geegaw, if I'm not prying? Another of Mrs. Talcott's give-aways?"

"It's mine! It's mine, so give it back." She tried to snatch it from him but he was too quick for her.

"I don't think so, sweetheart. This particular fan has a unique history. Remind me to tell you sometime—*Ow!*" With a vicious lunge, Rose had bared her teeth and sunk them into his hand, causing him to drop the fan. While he sucked blood she snatched it up and thrust it from sight between her breasts.

"Didn't I say it was mine? You all the time think Rose is lyin', but she ain't! It's mine, damn you!"

His hand came up and ripped her bodice halfway down her front; the fan fell out and they grappled for possession of it.

"God damn you!" she blazed as male strength prevailed. "It's mine, I tell you. Miss Rora done give it to me herseff! She take it from Pina and she say, 'Rose, you can keep this here fan if you likes it so much!' "

"You can whistle up a pig's ass for this fan. What have you there, Ambo?"

He inspected the lock of hair wrapped in a bit of tissue that Ambo had discovered with Rose's things.

"She's been burning that stuff," Ambo said, scowling at Rose. "She's been incanting."

"Is that true?" Sinjin demanded. "Whose hair is this?"

"Wouldn't you like to know!"

"Damn right." He gave her arm a twist and she spat the name out. Grimly Sinjin pocketed the packet of hair, then turned and spoke to Ambo and Jeff; she caught a mention of the Hartford river steamer and leapt up in fear, her voice rising shrilly. "You don't want to go back there. We is goin' to New York."

He curled his lip. "Go ahead, go to New York, go and be damned. I'm done with you from this day. If you ever come around me again I'll lay you down and shave your head, every last hair. Mat and Jeff," he went on while Rose watched in despair, "you come with me. Ambo, will you pack and see to closing up the place?"

A few more final instructions and the three started off. Rose rushed heedlessly after them, frantically pulling at Sinjin, trying to get ahead of his long strides and prevent his leaving. From where he stood taking in the scene, Ambo barked a crisp order to Mavra, who sprang toward Rose, growling and tugging at her skirt with her teeth, harrying her until she abandoned the pursuit.

"Lady Sheffle is right—you *is* one mizzabul blackhearted bastard!" she shouted after him. Then she gave out all at once. Her arms fell to her sides and she came back along the path and tearfully collapsed on the steps.

Ignoring her, Ambo began moving things from the cabin onto the stoop, along with Sinjin's seabag and his portfolio. He went back inside. He rolled up the mattresses and tied them under oilskins against mildew. He did the same with the pillows. He was hoisting the bed frame to the rafters and securing it when he happened to glimpse Rose through the window. She was bending close to the fire, and a column of white smoke fumed around her shoulders. With an oath Ambo leaped back and the bed frame came crashing to the floor as he let go the rope and sped out the door. Like a ferocious beast, he fell on her and savagely jerked her away from the fire, then stared at the flames, busily consuming the pages of Sinjin's manuscript. The empty portfolio slid from her grasp as his hand slammed her hard and she fell, hitting the side of her face against a rock. He put a foot on her throat and glared down at her. Was he going to kill her? She screamed and he seized her wrist, yanking her upright. Her face was bleeding from a cut on her cheek.

"Are you crazy?" he demanded, pale with rage. "What did you do that for?"

" 'Cause I wanted!" Rose blazed back at him. " 'Cause it's what he deserves. Him and his damn pomes."

"He'll kill you for that."

She spat at his feet. "He'll have to find me first. He ain't never going to see Rose no mo'. I is done. She kin have him, I don't care. He is one lousy polecat all right, and you is one stupid Injun." She started away, then stopped, slid her hand under her skirt and yanked. Her fingers came away clutching the little flannel bag, which she flung in his face. "Give that back to your grammaw, that stupid redskin bitch, she ain't got no magic—no magic at all."

Panting like a tigress, she tossed a contemptuous glance at the fire among whose ashes lay scraps of the unburned manuscript, then she spun and marched off without another word. Ambo watched her disappear among the trees, thinking for a minute that she might be taking the road upriver, but when she continued along the path that followed the bank, he realized that she was heading south. He observed her departure with satisfaction. The captain, and all of Pequot Landing to boot, would be well rid of that one. Brought up to thrift, Ambo retrieved the little red bag and stuffed it from sight. He'd return it to his grandmother; there were other uses to which such items could be put. Afterward, he scattered the fire and peed on it to put it out, then went about completing his duties. When the cabin had been secured, he, too, abandoned the scene, whistling up Mavra and hiking up his gear between his shoulders as he struck out for home. After he'd gone, a small breeze whisked up to scatter about the clearing the scorched and blackened scraps of "Al Qadar," whose end had been written not in printer's ink but in fire.

28

Confessions of a Social Butterfly

MIDMORNING, THREE DAYS after Rose had absconded from Pequot Landing with Mab's spoons in her satchel and the lock of Aurora's hair, Père Margeaux, returning from his travels, chanced to find himself less than thirty miles to the east of Pequot Landing, having within the hour departed the rustic hamlet of Jacob's Ladder, which lay between Providence and Hartford. It was with some fine inner satisfaction that the abbé drove along, for it so happened that, just after dawn, Almighty God had seen fit that a healthy male child should be born to a young farmer of that village, one of the few Catholics in the neighborhood. This infant had no more than been born, bathed, and wrapped in cotton swaddling than the joyful parent, his suspenders flapping at his sides, had dashed from his door into the roadway where he saw the priest passing in his mud-spattered shay. The abbé had reined up, got down, walked in, accepted a fresh bowl of well water, and in a trice the job had been done: the babe was duly anointed James Pollard, with the additional middle name of Léon, the abbé's Christian appellation.

Now, a scant two hours later, the climbing sun was hot, and the sweat oozed from between the priest's brow and the leather band of his wide-brimmed hat, to mix with the yellow dust that had brought such a heavy thirst to his throat. For perhaps a five-mile stretch the road ran through a pine wood, which reduced the sun's heat, until, up ahead, he glimpsed a clearing and a small, dilapidated church. Beside the structure, which sagged quaintly in the shade of a butternut tree, stood a well with a tin dipper hung on a nail, and on this warm sabbath morning it seemed to Père Margeaux the perfect spot to happen upon—if a man may indeed ever "happen upon" such things.

This humble edifice had been haphazardly erected from plain-sawn deal boards, under whose rotted warpings infestations of hungry, swarming insects crawled about, nibbling and gnawing, while in the roof peak hung a paper wasps' nest, too high up to knock down. The abbé noted how precious little glass there was in any of the windows, the steps were nothing more than warped planks, and there was a belfry of sorts over the door, with a squat, lopped-off look. The congregants had got that far in their construction and no farther: obviously there had never been sufficient funds to add a steeple.

While the abbé drank gratefully from the well he listened to the lusty sounds of the voices that pealed through the open windows: "The Lord He loves a cheerful giver," they sang. "From sin and pain He'll us deliver . . ."

Though a Protestant hymn, and hence unknown to him, the song was particularly zestful, and he took his time watering the mare in order to hear the end. As he waited for her to drink he noted the small crudely painted sign nailed up beside the doorway, designating the place as

The Heavenly Church of Kingdom Come

Indeed! Could anything be more propitious than this reminder of that other edifice called Kingdom Come, less than forty miles west as the crow flies, to which he was now returning? He experienced a sudden yearning to be home again, back home in Pequot Landing, back among his people on the Mountain. It had been some time since he'd had word of doings there and he wondered if the silence boded good or ill. There was no way to discover the news unless he went there.

Accordingly, hanging the dipper on its nail and placing some coppers on the church stoop, he climbed back into the rig and proceeded on his way. With luck he'd raise Naubuc Farms by four, five at the latest. As he sped along, soon choking again from the dust, he repeated Bible verses to amuse himself.

The mare, alas, slowed for the last ten miles, however, and it was already evening when he saw the river. Arriving at Naubuc, he paused only to rest his horse and water her again, then proceeded straight to the ferry landing. He drew his buggy up and peered about for the ferryman, who was nowhere in evidence. But a trio of loungers was watching a game of checkers, the board set out on a tobacco bale between the two players, hunched on opposing casks, and Père Margeaux stepped down and dropped the hobble, then approached the group.

"Good evening, friends. Does it happen that one of you is the ferryman today?" he asked in his amiable way.

Heads turned, eyes stared, one man said, "No."

The abbé persevered. "Can you tell me where he is then? I wish to cross."

The men shifted positions and exchanged looks. Père Margeaux quickly sensed an antagonism among them; just as quickly the motive was discovered.

"You the priest?" demanded one in a surly tone.

"I am *a* priest," he was corrected.

"You live yonder? In Pequot?" asked another.

"I do."

"Where they got that damn school?"

"We have several schools in Pequot. To which do you refer, sir?"

"Damn nigger school," said one of the checkers players and spat.

The abbé straightened his spine. "You refer then to the Free School?"

More looks were exchanged and one of the men laughed. Another drank from a jug and passed it on.

"That's it. The Free School. How come they's teachin' niggers over there, anyways? Everybody knows darkies don't go to school."

"I'm afraid that's not true of our village, I am happy to say," returned Père Margeaux agreeably. Across the river the lights of Pequot Landing winked. He spotted the chimneys of Kingdom Come, and, nearer the river, Aunt Hat's kitchen window.

"Reckon they won't much longer," said the same man with a leer.

"Why is that?" inquired the abbé.

" 'Cause they're gonna shut the place down."

"Oh? How do they propose to do that?"

"Bushrod Grimes got seated in the 'Sembly, or maybe you ain't got wind of that."

"Indeed, I had not," said the priest. "I must confess I am sorry to hear of it. Now, where is the ferryman, please?" he asked again. "I desire to cross."

"Eatin' supper, I expect." The fellow jerked the side of his head, indicating a shack where a lamp glowed.

Nodding, the abbé left the men and went to speak with the ferryman, who sat inside the shack, unwilling to have his stew interrupted, even by a member of the clergy. He showed Père Margeaux no more respect than had the checkers players, and the priest returned to his rig where he picked up the hobble again, mounted to his worn buggy seat, and prepared to be patient.

"Papist," one of the men muttered, throwing him a dirty look.

"Dirty papist," muttered another, spitting.

"Damned dirty papist," said a third, not caring if he was heard.

The largest of the men heaved himself up and sauntered over to the rig. "Hey, dad," he said, "when you get over there, you tell them nigger lovers we don't much like 'em teachin' darkies like they was some kinda white folks."

"I doubt they'd listen, sir," the priest retorted, suddenly losing his temper. "In fact, I am certain they would not. The Negroes are poor people, to be sure, but they are as much entitled to an education as yourselves."

Another of the men cracked a laugh. "Whatchou talkin' 'bout, priest, Freddie ain't ben t'school since he was seven. All he kin do is chop tobacco."

By this time the ferryman had deigned to present his person, briskly striding to the slip as if the abbé's speedy crossing were suddenly the most important thing on his mind, and as the ferry swung into the current on its cable, the priest tried to ignore the hoots and catcalls and shaking of fists on the bank behind him. The ferryman offered no comment, Charon midway across the Styx. On the far side the priest paid the toll, with an extra five pence for a gratuity. His reward came in the form of a warning.

"Them boys're tough customers, Father," said the ferryman.

His passenger snorted. "They don't scare me, but thanks for the warning," he said, and shaking his reins, let the mare run the rig up the ramp onto the landing. Almost before he could settle himself in his seat he found himself at the gate of Kingdom Come.

Trubey Priest answered his knock, appearing oddly subdued and fatigued.

"Oh, Father," she breathed in relieved surprise, "I'm so glad you've come. Mrs. Talcott will be too."

She brought him in and shut the door behind him. "Father, Miss Rora's come home," she told him calmly.

The ecstatic expression on the abbé's face was one she never forgot. "The Lord be praised," he breathed, crossing himself. He waited while Trubey supplied a few pertinent details concerning Aurora's unexpected arrival and the loss of her family, then, deciding he would have a word with Mab first, asked Trubey to announce him. Meanwhile, he would go to the kitchen and wash up.

Halley Priest was sitting dejectedly at the kitchen table, and when he appeared she began to weep. "Thank the Lawd, Fathah, you is come. Ol' Halley done prayed an' prayed till she done prayed huhseff out. An' here you is come at las'."

The abbé enfolded her tenderly in his arms, comforting her as one of his flock.

"What has been happening here, Halley?"

"Miz Talca, she ben po'ly, Fathah. She look fo' you to come ever' day. Miss Rora—Trubey done tole you Miss Rora come home? Mah li'l baby; she done suffid so much."

"Yes, yes, Halley, I know."

"She was gettin' some betta fo' a time, but then sumpin' happen. Miss Rora done got huhseff all upset now, not even the doctuh know whut t'do. You gwan up, Fathah, she be wantin' to see you bad."

"Yes, yes, to be sure, in just a moment. Ah—good evening, Judah."

He had not noticed him, tucked away in his corner chair. Judah rose and respectfully shook hands.

"We're glad you're home, Father," he said.

"An' Miss Rora's troubles ain't all," Halley went on, not waiting for her husband to say more. "Them bad folks done kilt dat po li'l cat, Auntie Hat's cat whut she set sech a sto' by. Them mizzabul mens, they come an' they grabbed that critter an' they wrung it neck an' then they slice open that cat stomick lak they was butchahs an' they hangs that po' skinned critter on Miz Duckworth's fence with all the stuffin' hangin' out."

"But why? Who would do such a senseless thing?"

"Some mens fum cross-river—they so fulla meanness an' spite—they wuz laffin' 'bout it affer, too, braggin' they was mo'n one way ter skin a cat. An' that ain't all, neether, wuz it, Judy?" She turned to Judah for corroboration. "Them bad mens, they chunked rocks at Geo'gie. Yessuh—at Geo'gie husseff! She din't get hu't, but afferwuds they comes an' they's chunkin' ho'shit at Auntie Hattie's house an' they done wrote dutty words on the sides an' on the front do'. An' then they done broke the winders an' tear huh fence all up. Po', po' Geo'gie," Halley went on, her tears flowing, "the things whut they done to that chile. Jes case she tryin' t'he'p sum cullid gals with they readin' an' writin'."

Halley's tearful jeremiad was interrupted as the door opened and Trubey appeared. "Father," she said, crooking a finger. "Ready now."

"An' Ah tell you what else, Fathah," Halley called after him, "that no-'count slave gal, that Rosa, she done run off with Miz Talca's 'Postle spoons, evah las' one of 'em!"

With small comfort for the outraged Halley, Père Margeaux followed Trubey from the kitchen. Posie was waiting at the head of the stairs. *"Mon père, mon père . . ."* She put out her arms to him; he embraced her and gently kissed her warm brow and both cheeks.

"Yes, dear girl, I am here."

"Father, after you see Mother, please go straightaway and talk to Sissie. She's been waiting for you."

He nodded. "We must see what we can do to cheer her up, mustn't we?" He smiled encouragingly, kissed her forehead again, and went along to Mab's room, where he found her sitting up in bed.

"Ah, then, you've come at last," she said, trying to sound strong but evidently at some cost. The abbé was shocked to see how sadly altered she was from the day of his departure, how much thinner and worn down. "Jake was ready to send for you directly. You may tell the bishop for me he's kept you at Boston much too long; I wonder you got back at all."

Almost before he could speak, she waved him away.

"Don't waste time with me, Léon, go in to Rora, it's she who needs you. We can talk later. You will not believe me when I tell you she hasn't been to Mass since she came, won't go to confession. Oh, Father—can you find out the trouble?"

"I shall try, *chère madame,*" he hastened to assure her. "Calm yourself. I shall go in at once."

In the hall Trubey and Posie waited anxiously. Their eyes followed him as he knocked on Aurora's door. He turned the knob and entered. Aurora was seated at her vanity; as he came toward her she rose, smiling, her arms outstretched.

"Mon père, mon père," she greeted him, *"vous êtes arrivé, vraiment?"*

"Oui, ma chère, je suis arrivé."

He kissed both her hands and her brow, then reverently made the sign of the cross between them, thinking he had seen few more heartrending sights than the lovely woman who now stood before him. She was steeped in grief, yet something more than grief. Suddenly he felt ill at ease, even fearful, as if he were to be confronted with a problem he could never hope to solve, with the need for solace where he could find none to give.

"My child, would you care to pray with me?" he ventured gently. "As we once used to, you and I?"

Her gaze was piteous as she looked up at him. "Yes, *mon père.* Let us pray. Then you must hear my confession."

"Yes, my dear, to be sure. In the morning, before Mass—"

She clutched his hand and he felt her nails dig sharply into his flesh. "No, Father, please," she implored. "Not tomorrow—now, this very instant! I could not go another night—please, you must!"

"Certainly, certainly, everything shall be as you wish," he said quickly, alarmed by her desperation. "Come, then, kneel beside me and let us seek comfort of the Lord together."

As they knelt side by side at the foot of the bed he felt her body sag against him. He saw a rosary on the bedside table and pressed the beads into her palm, then bowed his head and began praying. When the prayer ended Aurora's long-awaited confession began:

"Forgive me, Father, for I have sinned. It's been many months since my last confession . . ."

The abbé placed the frayed stole across his neck and averted his eyes; the words proceeded haltingly, were forced out with difficulty, one by one from her lips, then became a litany that would not, could not, stop. The dainty chime of the small French clock was heard and still the words continued, unceasingly, as from a stream that could not be damned.

"KATYD-I-I-I-I-I-D—Katy-didn't—Katyd-i-i-i-i-d—no she didn't . . ."

It was the farmers' season, ripe and fecund, with the rankly festering odor of weeds fouling the sultry summer air. Everywhere the sweaty hand of late summer made itself felt, in wilting gardens where the roses turned to rust, in sluggish streams all but dried up in their rocky beds. Ceaselessly the locusts twanged among the curling leaves of the elms arching over Greenshadow Road, where the dust gathered in smoking lees along the shoulders, and in the fields roamed dolorous cows nursing the shade and flicking their tails at green-and-gold flies the size of hazelnuts. Again the farmers' prize swine broke out of Hog Meadow, making a pigline for Fearful Swamp, where they wallowed in the cool, stinking muck. It was also the season of mackerel skies, with their corrugations of gray fishes' scales that since time immemorial New Englanders regarded as the harbinger of storms.

It was, simply, the height of the dog days. Still, not long after the abbé's return, Appleton Talcott roused himself sufficiently from his lethargic dolor to accompany Priam and Old Bobby on a two-day junket to Providence, where both Appleton and Priam were scheduled to address a specially convened council of the local Anti-Slavery Society, and where William Lloyd Garrison himself would be on hand to greet his friends. Georgiana, also invited, chose instead to remain at home, and in her place went Agrippina, always ready to lend her support to the cause.

Père Margeaux, who had stopped by the house to wish the travelers godspeed, kept a careful eye on Aurora, who had come down to see the Yellow Pumpkin off. To look at her, smiling gently as she kissed her father good-bye, who would guess she was so deeply troubled? Since making her confession she had again recovered her spirits sufficiently to manage some trips to New France, where she had begun attending Mass. But so afflicted was his spirit by what he had been told that Père Margeaux had had little beyond prayer to offer for her comfort, and now he must leave her: he was needed at Lamentation, and so, bidding Aurora and Mab good-bye, he too drove away.

In the house, mother and daughter went upstairs again. Aurora returned to her room, where she sat by the window staring out at the tree boughs, tossed by an erratic wind. She failed to reappear the morning long, and her wish for privacy was honored by all. Sometime after lunch she ventured to her mother's room, where they conversed on general topics. Later, when Mab had dropped off into another of her fitful dozes, Aurora returned to her own room, then took a bath and had Burdy wash her hair, and when it was dry Trubey came in to arrange it. Throughout the noon hour the blustering wind had continued to gather force, the sky was darkening by degrees, and Halley predicted a storm: her hip had the miz'ry.

At four, despite all the ominous weather signs, Aurora nonetheless walked into the village to look over the cenotaph she'd ordered engraved with Caroline's name, a memorial that would be erected, not in the Catholic chapel graveyard at New France, but in the Ancient Burying Ground, much closer to home, where the bereaved mother could pay it frequent visits. Back home again, while the wind continued to rise and the servants went about closing the upper-story windows, she sent word to ask Georgiana over for a bite of supper, then sat with her mother once more.

At half past six Georgiana arrived. While Posie took over at Mab's bedside the two women repaired to Appleton's study, where Sylvester had made them a cheery fire. Aurora sat close to the hearth in the wing-back chair, hugging herself as though for protection against the wind that tugged roughly about the north side of the house.

"Georgie, you're an angel to come out in this," she apologized, adding that she hated storms; they frightened her so. Georgiana assured her that providing her with a bit of company was no trouble and said how pleased she was that Aurora looked and sounded so much better. Among her many setbacks, her last decline, at the time of Rose's dismissal, had been the most severe. While Posie remained upstairs with her mother, Aurora and Georgiana supped from trays in the study, talking about Bushrod's appointment to the legislature and what had happened since. They spoke as well of Rose, whose defection continued to be upsetting to her mistress; Aurora still had difficulty believing the rash accusations of Agrippina, even after Rose had confessed to the truth.

"I ought to have been kinder," she said, pushing at her salad with her fork. "I was so angry, I was terribly hard on her, asking Papa to—"

Georgiana interrupted her. "You mustn't blame yourself. I'm sure that whatever happened, Rose brought it on herself." Still, Georgiana had also felt remorse over the abrupt dismissal, blaming herself for not having paid closer attention to the girl. But then, perhaps it was all for the best; who knew what might have happened if she'd stayed on?

Later, when their trays were taken away, another log was laid on the fire and Judah readied the game table for a hand or two of piquet. Georgiana took advantage of the opportunity to slip upstairs for a good-night word to Mab, and when Judah had gone Aurora was left alone in her chair. On the shelves of the corner cabinet the pieces of Amoy china rattled ominously and she got up to lay the plates flat for safety, then sat again in the wing-back, staring concentratedly into the fire. For several moments a face seemed to materialize and hover amid the yellow flames, and she automatically crossed herself, and reverently kissed the cross pendant at her throat.

Her eye traced the outlines of the sailing ship in the hearth rug that her mother had hooked.

She heard the doorbell sound, but waited in vain for someone to answer it. When the bell stopped the knocker started, a loud, urgent pounding. Deciding that none of the servants in the back could hear, she gathered her skirts and rapidly crossed the hall. She could see nothing. When she opened the door the buffeting gale required all her strength to keep it from bursting inward. She peeked through the crack but saw no one. Then she stuck her chin out and called, feeling the full force of the wind now sweeping across the porch and dashing against the face of the house. Puzzled, she peered out for another instant, then withdrew and slammed the door. She had returned to the study and was settling herself again in her chair when she was startled by a brisk metallic rapping on the pane of one of the doors at the side. She drew back in alarm; there was definitely someone out there. She could make out a looming shape behind the spattered glass, and her heartbeat quickened as with a gust of wind two doors burst inward, blowing a man into the room. Before she could react he whirled to shut the doors, then turned again to face her.

Soaked and dripping on the rug, Sinjin stood motionless now, blinking past a disheveled lock of hair as if trying to comprehend her physical existence there in the room, as if such a sight were not possible.

"You—here—" he began and stopped. "Then it's true. You—" he began again, scowling at her and tossing the lock of hair from his eyes. "I couldn't believe it when I heard. You. Here. God. Well, for Christ's sake, can't *you* say something?"

She found her voice. "You startled me. You were not expected. Certainly not—this way." She indicated the doors through which he'd just appeared.

"I rang, I knocked, what's the matter, doesn't anyone answer the front door around here?"

Ignoring this, she summoned a calm she scarcely felt and said, "You have been at Bible Rock. Fishing, I am told."

He stared at her, drawing his sleeve across his lips. "For God's sake, I didn't come here to talk about fishing." His eye fell on the cellarette and he asked if he could have a drink.

"By all means, help yourself to it." She waited while he poured a glass and gulped it down; she nodded at his mute request for another, which he took more slowly. "I am glad you are here, all the same," she told him. "Now that you've come I—"

Something in her controlled attitude irritated him and he spoke again, sharply. "You have something to say, is that it? A couple of well-chosen words? After all these years, some few tidings of general interest? By God, I should hope so."

She realized then that he had not learned of Henry's death, or of Caro's, but she decided to wait for that. Instead, she said, "First you tell me something, please. Why have you come here tonight?"

"To see you. What did you suppose?"

You will find him changed, she recalled Georgiana saying; she found him greatly changed. "And now that you have, how do you find me? Any different?"

He squinted at her again, shifting his weight onto one foot and crossing his arms. His glass tilted perilously but the contents failed to spill. "I fear to answer such a question lest I be misunderstood," he said at last. "Where women are concerned, a man must always worry about being misunderstood, wouldn't you agree?"

Ah, she thought, their conversation was to be a duel then, an exercise in parries and ripostes. His bitterness was evident, yet why so bitter, Captain? she asked him silently. She chose to smile. "If a man may think so, then may not a woman as well?"

He shrugged, sipped his drink. "I suppose, if she wants. She would be wrong to think so, however. Very wrong indeed."

"Wait, please," Aurora said and turned as Georgiana reentered the room, staring at the sight of the man whom she believed still to be at Deeping. "Sinjin—"

"Hullo, George," he said dully. He drilled her with a look, and slapped his thighs with impatience. Then, in the ensuing silence he reached into his pocket and took out a parcel, which he handed to Aurora. "I believe these are the property of your family."

Aurora registered confusion, taken aback by this unexpected gesture. Finally accepting the parcel, she untied the tabs and noted the glint of silver.

"Mama's spoons!" she exclaimed, unrolling the flannel pockets. "But— however did you come by them?"

"What does that matter? You have them back." There was a pause. Aurora looked at Georgiana, then back to Sinjin. "You have seen Rose, then?" she asked.

"We chanced to meet—downriver. She was abjectly remorseful for her—um—lapse. She charged me to return them and pleads to be forgiven." Before Aurora could ask more questions, he posed another of his own, changing the subject. "I was surprised to learn that you had come home again—how long will you be staying?"

"It depends."

"And Caroline? She's here, too?"

"No. No, I am sorry to say, she is not." Ignoring Sinjin's look of puzzlement, she laid the spoons aside and glanced again at Georgiana and back to Sinjin. "Nor Henry, I'm afraid."

Sinjin's disappointment showed. "You mean they stayed in Italy?"

Aurora drew a delicate breath, her gaze lowered to her lap. "Yes. Henry has remained in Italy."

"But Caroline—surely she—isn't she with you?" His expression was more baffled.

"Yes," Aurora murmured, "Caro is always with me . . ." She crossed herself and suppressed a sound in her throat.

"Rora—for pity's sake!" Georgiana exclaimed. *"Tell him!"*

"Tell me what?"

When Aurora refused to speak Georgiana turned to Sinjin. "She has lost both her husband and child. They died in Naples."

"What? No—don't say it. Caroline—dead?"

"I'm afraid it's true," Aurora said. He stared at her wordlessly as he absorbed the awful news. "Oh Christ. Dead," he repeated dully. "Caro is dead? How? How did it happen?"

"She and her father both died of plague. Many did in that city. I'm sorry to have to tell you, but—"

"Dead? She's dead?" He looked at each of their faces, hoping something one of them might say would revise the circumstances. "I had no idea. I'm sorry, truly," he said to Aurora. "I'm intruding upon your mourning. I'd better go—"

Aurora put out a hand. "No! Wait please, I do not wish you to go. Not just yet," she added. "After all, she was your child, too. And there are some things I have to say about—about that and—other matters. Please don't leave yet. I have waited long for this moment, and—"

She looked at him levelly, the faint smile she gave him seeming to derive from somewhere out of their private past. For a moment it was as if the years had been swept away and they were as they once had been, newly met, blinded by their attraction, with only the glorious future lying between them. And now—

At that moment, the study door was thrust open and the sight of Mab Talcott in her nightclothes astonished everyone in the room.

"What is happening here?" she demanded. Her frown took in the group, lingering on Sinjin Grimes. "So you're back, Captain. You do turn up at the oddest times. Will someone be good enough to explain what this man is doing in my house?"

"Mama, Captain Grimes has come to pay his respects," Aurora said quickly. "And look, Mama," she said, proffering the spoons, "he has returned these to you."

"My spoons? But how—? I thought Rose took them. Have you seen her, Captain?"

"Yes, Ma'am, I have. That is how I was able to recover the silver for you."

"But how——?" she repeated.

Aurora went to her side. "It doesn't matter, Mama, I'll explain later. Wasn't it thoughtful of the captain to bring them here straightaway? He knew how much their recovery would mean to you. Now darling, come sit with us for a little. Take Papa's chair, why don't you? I'm glad you've come down because—because there is something I want to say. Something important." She assisted Mab into the chair, where she sat clutching the roll of spoons in her lap. Georgiana made a move to go but Aurora said, "No, don't leave, Georgie, I want you to hear. You too, Posie," she added, drawing Posie, who had followed Mab into the room, to the footstool at her side. "Georgiana, the captain's glass is empty," she added; Mab made a stifled sound.

"It's quite all right, Mama, really." She poured Sinjin another dram of Madeira, then went on speaking.

"When Père Margeaux came back he made me promise that I would do this. And I *did* promise—though I never dreamed that *you* would be here, Captain Grimes. Nevertheless, I am glad you chanced to come tonight. I want to tell you about what happened in Naples and—and the manner of Caro's dying."

"Rora——"

"No, Mama, this is how I wish it. Captain Grimes has a right to know."

"Does he indeed? What right is that?"

Before Aurora could answer Sinjin faced Mab squarely.

"She means I have the right because I am Caroline's father."

Mab's lips formed an O of shock. "What? What's that you say? You— Caro's father? Do not say such a thing to me, sir, I will not hear of it."

"It's true, Mama, the captain speaks the truth."

"And Henry——"

"Henry is not involved in this matter—at least not yet. Please be calm and patient, Mama, I will explain everything, I hope to your satisfaction. And to Captain Grimes's as well. And please remember, this cannot be easy for him. He is undeserving of censure. Or of the pain that is to be inflicted on him." She pressed the corner of her handkerchief to her lips, then moistened them with her tongue. "But I want him to know—and you, too, Mama—what happened—*everything* that happened. It is not a happy story, it is in fact a very sad one, but I have kept it so long to myself, here"— bringing her hand to her breast—"where it hurts, and Père Margeaux said that if I could tell it, perhaps the hurt might somehow be less."

"Rora——" Sinjin's look was anguished and he reached a hand toward her. She drew back from his touch, then, drawing a breath, she began her story.

"As usual in April we had gone to Naples to spend the summer, Caro and I. Henry did not join us—he had chosen instead to visit Capri with friends. Of course we had no idea there was a plague in the city. The first victims began falling ill almost the same week we arrived. Nobody ever imagined such a thing could happen so suddenly, but there it was, it came upon us almost overnight, it seemed to break out everywhere at once. They told us it had been brought by two lascars aboard a tea ship from Madras.

"No one can possibly imagine it, no one who wasn't there. First the tourists began fleeing the city, then the inhabitants joined them in flight, the streets were jammed with traffic, people were being trampled, old people died in the press all the way along the Riviera de Chiaja, on the way out to Mergellina. Every day it got worse, until the dead were being piled in the streets and before long there was no one to cart them away, there were so many. Every place you went you could smell camphor and the odor of burning flesh and clothing. And vinegar. They said to sprinkle our clothes with vinegar and hang a bayleaf on the knocker. We ran out of vinegar soon enough, we never had any bayleaf at all. There were fires everywhere. All day long you could hear the creak of the cart wheels and the voices calling, 'Bring out your dead.' I had no dead—not yet, but I was frightened all the same. Even the men who were carrying away the bodies, many of them fell sick, they began dying too, one after the other. Soon there was no one left to water and feed the horses and mules, so they began dying. Some of the poor beasts went mad and dashed their heads against the pillars of the arches, some even climbed into the fountains to drink. But already the fountains were filled with rats."

"Rats?" Mab repeated.

"Plague is carried by rats," Georgiana explained. "Go on, Rora," she added.

"Yes, yes, I must, mustn't I? By now Caro and I were alone in the house. The servants all had fled, every hour became more dangerous. I saw our peril and knew we must leave quickly and I tried to arrange everything. There was no one to help. I was packing when Caroline sighed and fainted. She was on the far side of the sala at the washbasin and she simply dropped to the floor before my eyes. She had been feverish already and now there was no time to take her away. I put her to bed. I tried to convince myself it was something else, anything but plague, but I knew. Oh yes, I *knew!* I sent word to have her taken to the English hospital, but there was no one to carry her there. The porters had all run off, there were no ambulances or carriages, not even a cart remained. I left Caro and walked to the hospital myself to plead with someone to come and take my child, but all the beds were full at the English hospital and the same at the cholera house, and no doctor would approach the villa with me."

"Jesus God," Sinjin muttered. "What did you do?"

Aurora shrugged. "I returned home, what else could I do? I told myself *I* would nurse Caro, I would do everything, I would see that she survived somehow. God would help me. She would not die. I went out on the terrace balcony." She looked at Sinjin. "You remember, where you climbed up and left the little package."

"I remember. Go on."

"Yes." She thought a moment: Where was I? She sipped her drink, thought another moment. "Yes, of course, the balcony. It fronted the piazza with a marvelous view of the city, and now the city looked as I imagined Sodom or Gomorrah must have looked, with a dark cloud from the fires hanging over it. And the choking smell, that hideous stench. I stood on the balcony calling for someone, anyone, but there was no answer. I was all alone with Caro and I was terribly afraid."

"But I don't understand. Where was Henry?" Mab asked. "Why didn't Henry come?"

"Truthfully, Mama, he had no reason to come. He was staying on Capri at the summer villa of a friend of his. A woman, actually, whose companionship he enjoyed."

"Woman?" Mab repeated. "Henry kept a woman? You never said—"

"That's not important—it's simply that he *didn't* come, that's all—not just then anyway. He *did* come eventually, of course, or he might not have died. In any case, I was trying to remain calm and not panic. I realized I could never get Caro away without help. I went into the streets stopping strangers, trying to persuade someone, anyone, to find a cart and take us out of the city—for money, of course—but no one would."

Pausing in her narrative Aurora sipped from her glass, blotted her lips, and proceeded in a voice that had deadened to a monotone. "Every day it grew worse. There were fires breaking out and no firemen, murders and no carabinieri. Women who could stand were dragged down and assaulted within sight of the churches, no one could do anything to help them. Men turned into beasts, ravening monsters. Since nearly all the food was gone, starving people were roasting dead oxen in the streets—horses, even cats and dogs." She smiled grimly. "They should have saved the cats for the rats. For now began the worst part of all."

"Ohh . . ." Mab groaned and put her hand to her mouth. "Rora, are you sure you want to tell all this now?" She protested weakly. "Shouldn't your father be here—"

"Mama, please let me say it, do."

Georgiana went to stand behind Mab's chair and laid her hands on her shoulders. "Yes, do let her," she said softly. "Go on, Rora."

Aurora nodded and continued. "The authorities were desperate. Now— only *now*—finally they decided at least to attempt to do something about the rats. It was already too late, but they made the attempt. The committee of public safety ordered sulphur bombs to be ignited down in the sewers to suffocate the creatures. But they couldn't possibly kill them all, you see, it was an impossible task, for there were too many, and—" She was laughing now, as if relating a humorous anecdote. "And so they simply drove them out of the sewers and up to us. They came swarming up out of the drains, dripping with filth, out of every subterranean hole in the city, millions of them, *millions,* crazed with pain, mad, mad—why did God ever create such horrid beasts . . . Please may I have something to drink?" she said blankly, as if she had not already been drinking. Sinjin added to her glass and presently she resumed. "Once in the open they went rushing about everywhere, ravening at the smell of flesh. They began with the horses and ended with the babies."

"Babies?" Mab shrieked, while Georgiana pressed her shoulders. Aurora nodded.

"They were eating the little babies in their cradles. They were gnawing on children left in the streets after their mothers had died. Thousands and thousands of rats!"

"It can't be true!" Posie cried out, hiding her head in Aurora's lap.

"I swear it is, I swear by the Holy Virgin." She crossed herself again, took another sip, and plunged on. "There was a woman, she was the laundress for a convent nearby. Eleanora was her name. I had helped her once, some little thing. To show her gratitude she came and stayed with me and did the cooking, what cooking there was to bother with. By that time we were frantically busy doing whatever we could to keep the rats out of the house, but it was no use. They were everywhere, in every room, all the way up to the attic, in the cupboards, the clothespresses, the water closets, everywhere. You can't imagine how it was. No one . . . c-could—"

Her voice faltered, but only for a moment. She went on. "Caroline grew sicker and sicker. By then I was sure she was going to die and I tried to prepare myself for it. It was—hard. I prayed to God and the Virgin to make me strong. I was so terrified I was sick at the stomach and began to vomit. I was so very frightened. I didn't know what to do—I had Eleanora, no one else. It seemed that she and I must be the only ones left alive in the whole district. But then she got sick too, poor woman. They both were going to die and—well, suddenly I decided I must find a priest. Only I didn't dare leave Caro alone, because of the rats. I'd sat by her bed with a stick, trying to keep them away from her, trying to stay awake so they wouldn't . . ." She drank again, and again the glass was empty; no one moved to refill it. "Though she was close to dying, Eleanora, that dear good Christian woman, she said *she* would wave the stick while I went for the priest. She was too weak to go.

"So I went alone, looking for a priest, any priest I could find. But by that time the churches were shut, there were no priests. Think of it, in Naples, where there are so many. Finally, down near the Darsena, I found one. He was old and decrepit. I thought he must be sick too, but he assured me no, he was still well. I had a bit of money. I gave it to him, he said he would come with me. But he was so feeble, he couldn't walk fast. I thought we'd never get there. It took hours to get back to the villa. And in the streets—such sights to be seen! God pity the poor soul who has seen them. People die of such sights—or have dreams . . .

"All the way home I knew . . . even before we came into the courtyard, somehow I knew what we would find. At last we reached Caro's room. Eleanora was there, but the stick lay on the floor, she was dead. And Caro, in the b-bed . . ." Her voice broke and she started to weep, then composed herself as they waited to hear the rest.

"The bed was moving! And she was being eaten—"

"My God!" Sinjin shouted, leaping up.

"—alive! *She was still alive!*" she screamed.

"No! Don't!" Posie cried. Mab moaned and repeatedly made the sign of the cross. Only Georgiana was silent, too horrified to make a sound. Sinjin moved quickly to Aurora and bent over her beseechingly. "Rora—don't, please, in the name of God. You've got to stop now, you can't go on." He entreated her but she was staring at him, her fingers pressing on her long neck as if she were choking.

"*Do—you—understand?*" she shrieked. "*Do you?* No, how could you! Wait—wait—!" She clasped her hands and held them trembling before her, while he stared in horror and an unwillingness to believe. As she collapsed into her chair again he filled a glass and helped her drink. She swallowed gratefully, eagerly, then, blindly clutching his arm, she began anew.

"I was unable to hit the rats, you see, without hitting her. So I had to use my hands. I grabbed at them and they bit me, and there were always more. No matter how many I pulled from her body there were always more. Then I let one bite my hand—I wanted it to. I let my blood drip on them, and they began licking each other. Then I dripped it all across the floor and that was when they left her, to lick up my blood. How greedy they were, how hungry. Vile—vile! And that was how I finally got them off her, but—she was dead—" She shrugged and used her handkerchief again.

"What became of this priest you'd paid?" Sinjin wanted to know.

"The poor man was too frightened to enter the house, but when the rats were gone he performed the rites and helped me cover Caro and together we carried her down to the garden. There was a stone sarcophagus there and between the two of us we managed to move the lid enough to place her inside, and then we slid the cover back so the rats couldn't get at her anymore. By then it was t-too late, anyway. Her face was—oh, Caro— Caro—my child—" She moaned in anguish, then covered her face, and her shoulders shook as she wept.

"In the name of God, won't someone stop her now!" Mab cried, covering her eyes and turning her head away. "Georgie, can't you—?"

By now Sinjin was on his knees before Aurora's chair. She stared at him and her eyes swam in the firelight. She saw him staring at the pale scars along her arm.

"You don't have to go on," he said. "It isn't necessary. No more, no more."

"No, please, let me finish, then it will be all said. Mama, I'm all right now." She sounded calm again and her tears had stopped. "Caro—she was safe at last and I thanked God. Then I thanked the miserable priest and assured him I would be all right alone, although by then I didn't care about myself anymore. I was sure I too would die and I was happy to do that. But I didn't die. And then—then Henry—Henry came back . . ."

"To take you away—"

She drew another breath and swallowed noisily. "No, Mama, Henry wasn't interested in my survival. On the contrary, I believe he came with the idea of murdering me. Not a fresh idea with him. He'd tried it several times before."

Mab was incredulous. "Why should your husband want to murder you?"

"Because he hated me. But instead, *he* died. Poor Henry." She laughed, then blew her nose thoroughly, considered a moment, and went on. "Now you must all listen carefully, and you will understand everything, and then I shall stop. Henry hated me." She looked first at Sinjin, then at Georgiana. "For reasons you both can understand. I have never been sure what his motives were for coming back to Naples just then, but he did and, as I say, I *think*—to kill me. He'd come over from Capri in a caïque. Only no vessels were allowed to dock. Finally he persuaded them to drop him off at a village five kilometers or so below Napoli. He made his way into the city on foot, but when he reached the villa the portal was bolted and he couldn't get in. I was safe inside at the time and I refused to throw the bolt. I could hear him shouting and calling over the wall, threatening, saying he knew I was there and what he would do to me if he could. I hid behind the shutter while he railed against me from down in the street, finally I became so angry I ran out on the balcony and screamed at him to get away, that Caro was dead, that I didn't want to see him." She paused to take a deep breath, then expelled it wearily. "But any words from me only made him angrier."

"So you let him in?" Georgiana asked.

Aurora shook her head. "No, I didn't. He began threatening me with the *municipali,* he said he would go away and bring back the carabinieri. I just laughed at him because I knew there were none about. Finally he went away, but he came back again, he'd got hold of a pistol. He managed to shoot the locks off and open the portal. When he got inside he came looking for me, only I'd hidden and he couldn't find me. Otherwise I suppose he surely would have murdered me. He kept shouting he was going to. I'm sure he wanted to. I know he did."

"Where were you hiding?" Sinjin put in quickly.

"I had found a place in the gardener's cottage at the bottom of the garden. For some reason the rats had avoided the place. I didn't dare show myself, and he never thought of looking for me there, not at first anyway. By then I had begun to feel sick, I thought I would swoon, the way Caro had, and that would be the end, only it never happened just that way. I began laughing again. I remember thinking it was funny that poor Henry had traveled all the way over from Capri to be revenged, and yet by killing me he would only be doing me the greatest favor. How ironic it was. Finally he heard me laughing and that was when he discovered me. I laughed and laughed, then I found I couldn't stop. He stopped me. He began hitting me and calling me the vilest names. Soon he began to cough. He didn't realize at first, but I did. I knew—I knew it the minute he came close to me. He began spitting dark fluid, and he was dreadfully frightened. So he stopped hitting me and after a while he just—"

She shrugged and let her hands fall. "I think one could have blown him over with a breath. He fell down on the flagstones, among all the little pots of chives and fennel."

"And he died?"

"Not right away. It took time. The buboes—that's what they call the lumps—they were the worst imaginable. He was disgusting. I looked at him lying there and I hated him. I hated him for all the terrible things he'd ever done to me, for all the years we'd stayed married. It shocks you, Mama, I can tell, but it's true all the same. I hated him and I wished he would die, there and then, but I couldn't just leave him alone. So I stayed. I found blankets and something for his head. It was too late for nursing, really, I knew he was going to die, so I prayed beside him while he vomited. This was my husband, the man I'd married, who was so eager to win me, and who ended up wanting to kill me. It wasn't his fault, not really. I sat there beside him thinking about all the years we'd been together and all the dreadful things that had happened. Part of the time it was sickening, part of the time I wanted to laugh."

"Rora—"

"Yes, I know, Mama, you never realized. I'm glad you didn't. I tried so hard to keep you from knowing, I didn't want anyone to know." She began hurrying her words, anxious to be finished. "Henry was dead, there was no one to help, so I dragged his body out into the street and left it there. Next I looked it was gone. I suppose they took him away to the lime pit with the rest. Later, his sister made a terrible row—saying he ought to have been sent home for burial—imagine, at such a time. That was when I found out I'd been disinherited. Yes, Mama dear, I'm afraid it's true. Your daughter has come home a pauper. Long before that, Henry had resolved I should never share in his wealth . . . Where was I?" she asked, suddenly gone blank again. "Henry? Something . . . Oh yes, I remember, forgive me, I . . ."

The breath seemed suddenly to leave her, she uttered a moan and her head lolled forward on her chest. Falling, a slight sound issuing from between her lips, eyes closed as though in pacific yearning, falling toward the carpet, she was caught in the arms of Sinjin Grimes, while beyond the glass the rain had stopped and the wind had died to a sudden stillness and in the silent room the clock ticked fast on the mantelpiece.

Minutes later, restored to her senses, she sipped from the brandy glass Sinjin held to her lips, while the others watched in mute astonishment. She was badly spent, her voice was faint, as if having made the effort of the past half hour she had consumed her last residues of strength, but still she went on speaking, now to her mother.

"There is just one bit more, Mama, please. When I found out I was going to have a baby all I could think of was that I must get to Saratoga as quickly as I could because Henry would be there. I did everything I could to make him believe that I was in love with him. I told him I was. I swore it. But I never loved him. Not even later. He was deceived—that was my second sin. And he never would have known if—" She turned again to Sinjin. "I told him the truth after that day when you tried to see me in Naples, when you were beaten by those lackeys. I wanted to get to you then, to speak to you. Henry refused to allow me to see you and we quarreled bitterly. It was then that the truth about Caroline slipped out. Truly, I didn't mean to say it, but when it was said I couldn't deny it. It was the truth; I thought it was better at first that it had been said. But afterwards it was the end for us. Henry had truly loved Caro, had when he believed she was his. But upon learning the truth he became—his feelings toward Caro changed. He became mean and ugly, he treated her scandalously. And of course she had not the least inkling. I couldn't explain, I tried, but it was impossible. It grew worse. Worse and worse month by month. I hoped he would renounce me and let me come back here, but he refused. He wouldn't send me away, but he began to make my life terribly unpleasant. After that we just pretended to be husband and wife." She paused, then went on. "That was the worst part of it—pretending. Ten years is a long time to pretend anything."

"Sweet Jesus . . ." Sinjin's head dropped and when he lifted it again his face wore a look of excruciating pain. He turned away from the chair and went to stand at the window, somberly gazing out at the dark.

"Mama," Aurora went on, "Captain Grimes is not to blame and I won't let it be said that he is. Please don't even think it." Her voice was a hollow whisper. "I know what you're thinking, Mama—you're thinking I did a bad thing. You think I was seduced—"

"You were—you were—and there he stands, your ravisher!"

"No, Mama, no, don't say that. We loved each other so terribly. I had never known such a love could be. We were in the coach alone, the next day we were going to be married. We would have been if Papa—if Priam hadn't stopped us—"

"It's no excuse—"

"But Mama—*we loved each other!* Can you say you didn't love Papa that way? Can you say *you* waited till you were married?"

Mab's eye flicked from Aurora's face to Sinjin's and back again. She swallowed noisily. "It was different," she said begrudingly. "Your father was an honorable man."

"So was Sinjin! Mama, he *was!* And *is,* there is no reason to believe otherwise—"

"I do not care to debate morals tonight. I wish—I wish—" Mab crossed herself, then covered her ears and shook her head as if denying some phantom she had suddenly encountered. "Such things as I have heard this night. What's to be done—what's to be done?"

"Nothing, Mama, nothing," Aurora said. "It's over, it's all over. Caro is at rest. Her monument is close by, where I can visit it any time I want. You may, too," she said, turning to Sinjin, "if you wish."

"If I—? Oh God, oh Jesus!" he cried, looking frantically about, as if trapped and seeking a way out. "Wait—let me go—I want to see it—" He spun round and started for the door.

"No—Sinjin, don't—" Georgiana tried to stop him, but he thrust her aside, moving to snatch up his wet jacket, which he flung on, averting his face from Aurora. "I will go!" he said, his voice cracking. He stopped close to Mab, his grief-stricken face gone white and haggard. "Forgive me. I've disturbed your household enough, ma'am, and for that I again apologize." He nodded dazedly to Georgiana, to Posie, and at the door he turned for a last burning stare at Aurora, then was gone from the room.

"Sinjin—" Georgiana called and hurried after him.

The clock struck; Mab got gingerly to her feet. She seemed suddenly more frail than she had been, leaning heavily on Posie to steady herself.

"Thank you, dearie," she said, having difficulty breathing. Then she looked at Aurora and again shook her head in bewilderment. "I'm sorry, I fear I don't understand matters such as these. In my day we girls did things differently. Men courted us, we preserved our—decorum. I can't imagine what your father will think when he hears."

Aurora sat down again heavily. "Mama, please try to understand. Don't, I beg you, don't say anything to Papa. It's all—all in the past anyway, it doesn't matter anymore. Can't we just—love each other? Oh please, can't we? Won't loving make things easier?"

From the tail of her eye she saw Georgiana reenter and come to slip something into her hand.

"He asked me to return this to you."

Aurora looked down: the yellow Chinese fan she'd given to Rose. Slowly she spread its ribs and gazed once more at the figures of the Three Fates. Spinning, weaving, cutting, those three hags, their bland expressions underscoring their indifference to human want and suffering, went about their allotted tasks. Surely they had managed a fine evening's work this night.

As Aurora stared at the fan, the floodgates burst and she began to weep bitter tears that became wrenching sobs, welling up from uttermost depths, out of all the years of pain and hopelessness too long endured. These were soul-cleansing tears, there was no consoling her, and it was a long time before they ebbed. At last, as the others stood silently watching, she drew a long spent breath and wiped her eyes, then looked around the room, first at her mother, then Posie, then Georgiana.

"Georgie, we never had our game of piquet, did we?" she said regretfully. "See how late it is. Mama, aren't you tired? You ought to be fast asleep; what would Dr. Standish think?"

She saw Georgiana to the door; Posie took her mother's arm, and together they climbed the stairs, wearily, for they had had a busy day, and trailing after them wraithlike, the three fateful ones, Clothos, Atropos, and Lachesis . . .

PART FIVE

Love in Idleness

29

A Yankee Pastorale

WHATEVER THE THREE Fateful Ladies may have thought regarding Aurora's confession, they, like the members of the family whose fortunes they so remorselessly dominated, kept it entirely to themselves, as did all the servants, who through some esoteric process of divination were also aware of what had taken place in the study during the summer storm. But none of the Priests would think of breathing a word of what they were privy to; even the fact of Captain Grimes's unscheduled visit to Kingdom Come would, by tacit agreement, be hindered from reaching the ears of Appleton, Priam, Agrippina, and any others to whom intelligence of the gathering would only have proved distressful.

But as yet the travelers had not returned from Providence, and in the interval Posie, unable to persuade Aurora to speak further with Sinjin, yet making the most of her time, found occasion to meet privately with the captain in the Ancient Burying Ground, where the next noontime but one she smuggled him a piece of Halley's fried chicken wrapped in a napkin.

Having flung himself out of the house, Aurora's sobs ringing in his ears, Sinjin had found himself filled with sorrow for her suffering, yet unable to do anything to help her. Except to love her. Yes, he would go to his grave loving her, and there was no doubt in his mind that now, more than ever, he must strive to win her back and have her for his own.

Since Wednesday night, however, Aurora had been neither seen nor spoken with, and so distraught had he become that not even the desolating report upon Ambo's return that the pages of "Al Qadar" had gone up in the flames of Rose's jealous rage could produce much of a reaction in him. Now, as he savored Halley's tasty chicken, he listened to Posie explaining that Old Bobby Talcott and the others would be coming back late that afternoon and for the meanwhile it was useless to hope for a second interview at Number 17.

"What d'you suppose she's thinking about?" he asked Posie as they sat side by side atop the Fathers' Rise in the shadow of the slender white steeple.

"I expect she's thinking about you," Posie said simply.

"What makes you say that?"

"She certainly seemed happier yesterday. Mama remarked on it, and I believe it was seeing you again that did it."

"What am I to do then?" he asked.

"Nothing—for now. Truthfully, I wonder if this love of yours isn't written in the stars. It's all bound to come right in the end, you'll see. We mortals simply have to overcome the obstacles. It isn't always easy, but it can be done. Even the stars can be vanquished."

Sinjin couldn't contain his smile; Posie had been studying her Shakespeare. "I'm glad you feel that way," he declared, "because I am going to marry her."

"I knew you'd say that," she returned matter-of-factly, "and I hope to be Sissie's bridesmaid, but there *are* obstacles."

"What are they—as you see them?" he asked soberly.

"Well, first"—she began to count them off, crooking her fingers item by item—"first there's Mother—except she can be got round and she'll say yes, positively, I know she will. Second, there's Father—that's going to be a good bit more difficult. But he'll come round in the end, you'll see. Third, there's your current financial position. Sissie's used to the best, you know; it would never do to have her living on pennies in a garret."

"Leave that to me. She'll want for nothing, I promise," Sinjin declared grandly. "But I must see her again, Po, I have to talk to her."

"I wonder . . ." Posie murmured, watching his eyes, in which the pain and frustration came and went. "What if you were simply to chance upon each other, sort of by accident—but not quite, if you catch my drift . . ."

He was forced to grin again. What an endearing ally she was, what a champion of romance. He was more than happy to place his affairs in her hands. "Can you arrange it?"

"Let's say I can 'arrange' to have it 'arranged.' "

So it was that that very evening, after the Yellow Pumpkin had returned and the family had sat down to an early supper, Hermie Light arrived at the door of Kingdom Come with the announcement that Mother Light had "got a hankerin' fer some wild honey." To this end he issued an invitation to a bee hunt. The expedition, he said, was to take place the following day, and he kindly asked Georgiana Ross and the Talcott daughters to join him, thinking, as he told Mab, that a little outing might be just the thing for the ladies. As he had expected—indeed, thanks to word from Posie, he had been sure of it—Agrippina, who had suffered an attack of the megrims as a consequence of her fatigue after her journey back from Providence, felt forced to decline.

And thus early the next morning, proceeding in accordance with a timetable meticulously laid down by Posie, Hermie's wagon pulled up at the gates of Kingdom Come, where his three passengers waited. Halley's hampers and crocks and bottles of stone beer were stowed in the back, along with Hermie's bee box, some fishing gear, and Aurora's old butterfly net, and well before ten o'clock the wagon was rattling clumsily down the western slope of Burning Bush Hill, heading for Two Stone.

At the fork Hermie continued along the Old Two Stone Road, the wagon jolting over bumps and rocks as he deftly navigated the narrow track, which all but disappeared among patches of weeds as they skirted the surrounding woods. Finally, the road dwindled away to nothing and he was forced to pull up and unhitch the horse, which he hobbled and offered hay to; then, loading up their paraphernalia, the little group fared forth on foot, proceeding Indian file along the track through green tunnels of exploding sunshine to the abandoned quarry whose boldly carved ramparts rose awesomely in a wide semicircle among the treetops ahead. As they approached it, Hermie, cupping his hands, gave a hearty yodel whose resonating echo bounced eerily back to them, reverberating against the curved facade of the sandstone outcropping as if they stood in an amphitheater of classical antiquity. Across the worn, uneven brow high above them a pretty waterfall spilled down the face of the reddish stone into the wide pool below, whose crystal-clear water at once reflected the blue sky and revealed in its unsullied depths quarried chunks of stone strewn about the sandy bottom, like the drowned blocks from some pagan temple fallen into ruin. Rising above the pool, also reflected in its mirror, the face of the cliff was pitted with holes and randomly scored with crosscut marks, where the stonecutters' saws and drills had left their inimitable signatures.

No one could recall now why stone was no longer quarried in this place; indeed it was something of a local mystery, since many of the table stones and markers in the Ancient Burying Ground had been extracted here, and stonecutting had once been a thriving local enterprise. For all anyone knew the stonecutters, after working at the quarry over a considerable length of time, had simply decided to pack up and move elsewhere, leaving the place to picnickers, swimmers, and pairs of sweethearts, who came there to be alone.

Surrounding the pool on three sides lay a broad sunny meadow of yellow grass spangled with white daisies and buttercups, and no sooner had the party come upon it than Aurora hiked up her skirts, lofted her net, and commenced the energetic pursuit of a large yellow butterfly that, once caught, she carefully examined, then freed, sending it wafting away across the meadow. In a moment she had swerved in pursuit of another. She made a bewitching sight. Watching her erratic progress across the meadow, Georgiana thought there was something so childlike and innocent in her graceful and delicate movements, it seemed as if she might be twelve or thirteen again as she floated virginally through the grass intent on her chase, her yellow hair loosened and tumbling about her shoulders.

While Aurora frolicked like a girl, and the more practical-minded Posie and Georgiana put the stone beer down to chill in the pond, Hermie proceeded to a nearby patch of white and purple clover where a dozen or so bees hovered. With its lid removed, he extended his precious, intricately constructed catch box before him and clapped it deftly around a bee, trapping the insect with the lid. He then shook the bee into the second chamber of the box and waited patiently until it discovered the aperture and emerged and flew away. Then, shading his eyes to observe its path through the air, he marked where it landed and, calling out to Georgiana and Posie to join him, led them rapidly in that direction. The procedure left Aurora alone in the meadow chasing butterflies, her white net fluttering behind her as she moved fairylike through the tall grass and blossoms.

SOME time later, with her long-handled net drooping over her shoulder, she gratefully sought the shade of a tree beside Two Stone Brook; she lay down on the grass and let the net fall negligently alongside her. Her exertions had brought a light mist to her upper lip and a warm dew glistened on her forehead. Somewhere a woodpecker worked high up in a tree, tapping in a hole, and the occasional lowing of cattle sounded from an upland pasture. Aurora blotted her cheeks with the corner of a scarf and lay back, closing her eyes. Relief, peace, tranquillity she felt; she thanked God for it and then absently crossed herself, a fingertip lingering on the gold cross at her neck.

Presently a shadow fell across her face. Opening her eyes she found Sinjin Grimes standing nearby, silently watching her, with a large dog at his side. He dropped his rod, unslung his wicker creel, and sat down near her, counterfeiting astonishment at "happening" across her thus, and making no allusions to their last encounter. He stretched out close by—but not too close—and after an awkward pause they began to speak of inconsequentials, as if groping to find their footing with each other after being so long apart.

What a treat for the eyes, he thought, what a pleasure to see her like this. The other night in the study she had looked so much the grief-stricken widow in her weeds; today she seemed some other, younger person. His eye took in her pale, slender hand dabbling languidly in the brook, her fingers dripping sparkling droplets as they played with the cool water purling out of the pool and fretting their way across the smooth, tawny pebbles. His studied gaze seemed to make her nervous; she lowered her lids, then glanced up again from under her thick fringe of lashes. In the clear morning light her eyes were pure violet, that hard-to-believe shade he remembered from their first meeting.

Her look was mischievous as she said, "Do tell me, Captain, exactly how did you know to stumble across us here today?"

"Oh, a little bird told me."

She smiled disarmingly. "A little bird named Posie T., I'll wager. It's a conspiracy, isn't it?"

"Anything wrong with that?"

"Not really. It gives you both something to do, you and my little sister; hatching plots." Raising her arm slightly, she beckoned to the dog and it obeyed, lying down close by, its dark expressive eyes moving back and forth between them. "Where did you get her?" she asked.

"Mavra? She belongs to Ambo Buck," he replied. "Ambo let me hunt her today."

Straightening, he lofted a stick, sending it flying across the meadow, while Mavra bounded off in joyful pursuit. Then he lay back on one elbow, reveling in the fact of her being here, so close—yet not close enough. Hungrily his gaze took in the peach-down flesh of her cheeks, the lighted eyes. The years had not changed any of these, though they had mellowed the lustrous gold of her hair, which today she wore carelessly about her shoulders, held back with ivory bars. Tragedy, sickness, sorrow, and death as well as the passage of time had marked her, but only in the way exquisite objects are marked, denoting them rare and of untold value. At sixteen she had been a sparkling diamond; at thirty she was pearls on velvet, luminous and richly glowing.

Still she trailed her hand in the slow-moving stream, lifting it and watching the drops fall from her fingers. A secret smile played about the corners of her lips—her Nile-cat smile.

"What are you thinking of?" he asked, entranced.

"'Upon the rivers of Babylon we hung up our instruments on the willows . . .' That's Psalms."

"Psalm One hundred thirty-six in your Bible."

"Why, Captain, I had no idea. Have you taken to reading the Bible, then?"

"Occasionally."

"Very occasionally, I should think. I *am* impressed however." Her smile broadening, she spread her fan and began cooling herself, blowing tiny iridescent curls about her cheeks. "I'm so pleased to have my fan returned to me," she said, indolently wafting it above her head. "I had counted it lost forever, and it's quite the loveliest one I've ever seen. Do you know," she went on, "that in Venice the *putane* perfume their fans and wave them under the men's noses to entice them to their cribs?"

"*Putane?* Cribs?" He laughed. "How do you come to know of such matters?"

"To live is to experience. Didn't someone say that? Venice is full of all manner of interesting things. The fashionable women dye their hair with henna and sit in their open windows drying it in the sun on large circular frames around their heads."

"I wasn't aware you'd spent so much time in Venice."

"Yes. We did. I enjoyed it." He found her tone odd, as if she wanted to say something else but had thought better of it. Just then Mavra reappeared without her stick; she dropped heavily down in the shade, her tongue hanging out, her brown eyes shining and alert. Aurora watched lazily as Sinjin absently stroked the dog's head, looking up at him through narrowed eyes, attempting to assess the changes in him, for as surely as she herself had altered, so had the years worked on him. Older, certainly; eleven years older than when she had last seen him. He was thirty-four now; yet when his eyes lit on her, she saw how they sprang to life, and the lines of his face were smoothed out. There was even something endearingly innocent and child-like about him. Part of him was still boy, but the adoration in his eyes frightened her even as it attracted her; it was so male and so experienced. She read the desire there, knowing full well what he wanted, and her mind reeled headlong, not forward, but backward, to the first day, the cabin of the *Adele,* the gaily flashing smile, the smoky green eyes that held her in thrall with their hypnotic gaze, the growing urge to surrender herself, there and then. Suddenly she gasped and fought for air. No, please, merciful God—not again, not like that. It was madness to think they could ever be lovers again. There were things in life stamped "never." This was one.

As she lay there she felt the heat of the day rise up out of the grass, descend from the curling tree leaves to envelop her; her cheeks were flushed, her neck and bosom moist, her body languid and complaisant, her lids droopy, insensate. She seemed to float in a dream of remembered passion, remembered pain . . . Then she blinked her lashes several times and changed her position to a more comfortable one.

"Do you know, I still have your letters," she said, "the ones you wrote that summer, the ones Agrippina intercepted. I read them now and again. I think they must have been like Byron's letters to Teresa Guiccioli."

Surprised, Sinjin sat up and swung his legs around. "How do you know about La Guiccioli?"

She smiled sweetly. "I'm not altogether the ninny I once was, Captain. I suppose I may have learned one or two things."

"Unbelievable," he whispered, drawing nearer.

"What is?"

"You. It's not possible, but you're even more beautiful than you were when I wrote those letters." His voice was husky and uncertain. She made no apparent response to his compliment, except with the fan, whose cool breath he could feel. What was to happen now, now that Posie's tender connivance had brought them together like this? He found the mere sight of her impossibly tantalizing, and it was all he could do to keep from sweeping her into his arms and crushing her with kisses. He was starving, but could not eat, thirsty but forbidden to drink; yet the time would come, would come . . .

He was further restrained when, from a good distance off, the sound of Hermie's horn reached their ears. Sinjin held up a finger. "Hark. Honey in the comb. Hermie's found it already." He made her smile again and his expression brightened. "Tell me some things about Caroline," he said. "Did she grow up fair, like you?"

"Actually, her hair went quite dark—more like yours. She was very much like you."

"I've often wondered—why did you name her Caroline?"

"Can't you guess? I was sure you'd have realized."

"No—wait—" His brow furrowed as he thought. "Good God! Not Caroline Lamb? Byron's Caroline?"

She nodded. "I remembered how much you admired him. I let Henry think it was in honor of an elderly aunt of his."

"Caroline . . . Caroline . . ." He repeated the name in amazement and wonder. "I had a little girl named Caroline . . . a daughter . . . and I hardly knew her . . ."

His voice trailed off morosely, and for a moment there was silence between them. Then she said, "Would you like me to tell you a story about Caro? Only you must promise not to think me insane if I do."

He grinned. "I'm sure I won't."

"Very well. On the evening of the day she died, after that pathetic priest had left, I was sitting alone in the garden, trying to—to understand what had happened. It was very hushed and still, almost as if—well, I had this odd feeling that I was actually in church. On the other side of the garden there sat the marble sarcophagus where we'd placed Caro; it had been used to hold gardener's tools—it was carved with a frieze of figures, Roman, I think. As I looked at it I could make out something small tucked in one of the cracks, like a folded piece of paper. Then, as I sat watching, little by little whatever it was began to emerge. Yellow—it was pale yellow, then it grew larger, it was unfolding, spreading, and I realized it was a wing. Then a second wing appeared, and soon there before my eyes was a butterfly. Or at least the wings of one—a just-born butterfly! As I continued to watch, the wings began to move slowly, trying to free the body, which was still caught in the crack. It worked to escape, moving back and forth, until finally it freed itself. It rested, poised for some moments with its wings together, then they parted and fluttered, and it sailed up and over the flagstones straight toward me! It's true, I swear it. It was Caro, you see. She had changed in just that little time, she wasn't in that sarcophagus in the dark, her body disfigured by rats, she was yellow and black with velvet wings, so beautiful . . . so . . . beautiful—no, don't fret, I'm not going to cry, I promise. Then—then she left me, she fluttered off across the garden and up above the wall, up into the sky and out of sight. In my mind she had flown away to heaven and for a moment I believed God had merely wanted my pretty butterfly to come home." She stopped. Her wistful smile faded and she turned to him like a child, with sparkling eyes. "It was only afterward that I began to think she died because of our sin."

"No, but wait—that doesn't make sense. Do you mean that all the others who died in the plague died for our sin, too? And Henry?"

"I don't know. I don't know anything, really. Just that they're all dead and I'm alive and I wonder why. Why couldn't it have been me who died? Why wasn't Caro allowed to live? She never harmed a fly, she was an innocent. But I think that's why God took her, because she was innocent. While I being oh so far from innocent—"

"Hush. Don't say that." He looked into her eyes, his expression somber. "I think perhaps you were delivered from the pestilence so you could come back to me again."

She shivered involuntarily. "Please don't say that. You don't understand how—how afraid I am."

"But it's all past. What is there to be afraid of now?"

"You."

"Me?"

She nodded and spoke in a whisper. "I'm terrified of you. It's true, I am. You're here, I can see you, I hear your voice. And this feeling—I thought it had died with Caro's death. I thought at last I had killed the feeling."

"Why? Why would you want to kill it?"

"So I could live. So I could breathe again. So it should not drive me mad anymore. I thought you were twelve thousand miles away and that I was safe—from you. But now you are here, you are the ghost of my dream returned to haunt me, the ghost of what we lost . . . and I'm afraid it will begin all over again."

"That what will begin?"

"All the pain, the terrible pain—of loving you, of losing you, of not being able to have you." The words flew from her mouth as though they had been too long kept inside her, she must say them now, and to him. "All the lying, the deceit—and you, always you, forever thinking about you, unable to forget."

"Christ, I love you!" he cried. "Don't you know how I love you?"

"I don't want you to. I cannot go through it all again—not for anything in the world!"

"But you wouldn't have to, it's all different now."

"No, it isn't, it's just the same—it's already begun, don't you see? Rose—"

"Oh don't speak of Rose. That's all over and forgotten."

"It doesn't matter, she's suffering somewhere all the same, I know she is."
She was speaking even more rapidly and intensely, as if nothing must stop
her. "All because of *us!* Dear God, I don't want to cause any more pain—for
anyone. It's enough." Her eyes blurred with tears. "Help me, in the name
of God," she cried. "Help me."

He reached out to her. "I'll help you. Oh my darling, let me help you,
let me love you—it will be all right now, I promise you. Don't—don't do
this, I can't bear seeing you upset anymore." His hands gentled and comforted her until she lay quiescent against his shoulder, her sweet warm breath
coming in desperate pants against his neck. Her flesh was warm too, it
exuded a marvelous odor he faintly remembered from before, and he tried
to take her in his arms, to draw her to him, to make her feel the force and
strength of his body, to find some release; but she pulled away.

"I hear them coming back," she muttered. "Listen!" She glanced toward
the trees and began to brush herself off.

"Meet me tonight, won't you? We'll talk some more. Please?"

She made no reply. In another moment he heard Hermie's voice, and
Posie's gay laugh sounded. As Aurora stood up beside him he gripped her
wrist. "Say you will," he muttered urgently.

"Please, you're hurting me," she said, then slipped away and ran to meet
the others at the picnicking spot. Frustrated and disappointed, Sinjin grabbed
his fishing gear and followed, and when he joined them under the trees she
was already helping set out the lunch and refused to look at him.

THE sun began its western descent, casting lengthening shadows; the heat
seemed to draw all the moisture out of the earth, and a breathless hush
descended, humid and ennervating. But by the brook in the shade of the
small oasis of larches and sycamores, it was cooler, and when the picnickers
had depleted the hampers of their ample contents, they lolled about there,
conversing in low, languid tones. Aurora, however, sat a bit removed from
the rest, dreamy and introspective; Sinjin, equally pensive, had dropped his
line in a pool at a bend of the stream and was waiting for a bite. Georgiana,
leaning against a tree trunk, was tatting, her brow faintly frowning, as if
she did not quite approve of the rendezvous Posie had arranged so "accidentally." Her eye flicked from Sinjin to Hermie, who, taciturn as usual, lay
back in the shade, chewing on a straw. The shock of cornsilk hair hung over
his brows in a flat shingle, lending him a schoolboy air; his garments—
trousers, shirt, and even his braces—were impeccably clean and timeworn,
like threadbare church vestments. Would he ever be able to afford better,
Georgiana wondered.

These days she felt sorry for Hermie, so under the domineering thumb
of his mother, who could hardly bear to let him out of her sight. The picture

of Hermie Light stumping along the furrows behind his team was a daunting one. Georgiana was glad he too was taking some time away from the farm he worked and that worked him so hard.

"Rora," Posie said, trying to distract her sister from melancholy thoughts, "Hermie's been telling us that Captain Kidd once came here. Can you imagine?"

"Got as far upriver as Stepney Parish," Hermie affirmed.

"What would provoke pirates to come all that distance from the Spanish Main?" Aurora asked.

"Lots of 'em did. Kidd used to make port at Home Island. Some folks say he even buried treasure hereabouts. Kneebone holds it might have been pirate's silver that Georgie's father was hiding—"

Georgiana snorted in disdain. "Honestly, if that isn't the most ridiculous thing I ever heard!"

"Georgie, did you ever see any of it?" Posie asked.

"Once. And it wasn't pirate silver, it was Chinese. Sycee."

"Whoever got it must be rich as Croesus by now. Who do you suppose did steal it?"

"I haven't the faintest notion. Momma was convinced that the gypsies made off with it. As good a guess as any other." The line of her lips tightened while her practiced fingers continued nimbly working the cotton thread. "Those gypsies were forever coming around the mill then, stealing whatever they could lay their hands on. Maybe they spied on Poppa. I know they loved to bedevil the poor man any chance they got, and he trying to pocket every penny he could save."

Posie showed dismay. "But Georgie, how can you stick up for him after the terrible thing he did?"

"I don't think he meant to do it. He was sick, he ought to have been properly cared for. Anyway, I won't abide Kneebone or anyone else saying mean things about him."

Throughout this exchange Aurora had been leaning listlessly against a tree trunk, letting her eye wander, never once looking at Sinjin, whose own expression was unreadable as he halfheartedly dangled his line. Then his spine suddenly straightened and he held up his hand for silence as he leaned closer to the water.

"What a pair of beauties," he breathed, gazing down into the pool in whose green depths a matched pair of pickerel had appeared, casting incandescent shadows on the pale pebbles below them.

"Can you catch one?" Posie asked, hurrying on her knees to view the fisherman's prize.

"I'll have them both," Sinjin whispered eagerly. "Give me one of those pieces of johnnycake and Aurora's net." He took the buttery square and crumbled it, then cast the bits into the water and raised the net. As the pickerel rose to take the meal that was to be their last, with one sure movement he plunged the net deep into the water and whisked it in a lightning arc to the bank. In a moment both fish were aground, pulsing under the net that had ensnared them.

"I'll drop them by for Grammaw's supper," he said. "She's partial to a good bite of fish."

"More than a bite," Georgiana said admiringly. "They must weigh a pound apiece."

"I reckon." He dropped his line in the water again and once more fell silent, moodily staring off among the trees.

Aurora watched the fish as they lay expiring on the bank, and in a sudden movement she reached out with both hands and flung them back into the water, where they disappeared among the weeds.

"Sissie—why?" Posie wanted to know.

"I cannot stand to see anything dying—even a fish." She glanced at Sinjin to see if he was angry. He had leaned against the butt of a fallen poplar and appeared scarcely to have noticed. She pondered his profile, strong, broken, like the head on an ancient coin, his relaxed torso caught in a net of light and shadow. Then she looked away as she felt Georgiana's glance. Presently she stretched out on the grass, gazing up among the green boughs to the blue sky above. "Oh, how I adore it here," she murmured after a while, breaking the silence. "I'd quite forgotten how lovely it is. It was very nice of you to bring us, Hermie, I can't think of a spot in the whole world I'd rather be today."

"Even with all those splendid foreign places you've been to?" Posie asked.

Aurora laughed. "I'm afraid I never cared for them much, darling. I'd a hundred times rather stay at home. When all's said and done, it's truly the best place." She paused to glance at Sinjin. "I don't think I'd ever care to live in a city again. I don't care to travel anymore, either—I wouldn't mind if I never saw another ship. I even thought the pyramids a bore."

"That's foolish!" Georgiana snapped. "The pyramids were one of the wonders of the ancient world."

Sensing the tension that was suddenly manifesting itself, Posie turned to Sinjin. "Tell us, Captain, where would you live if you had your choice? Where in the whole world?"

"In the whole world?" He frowned. "You know, Po, I've been sailing for more than twenty years and I have yet to find any place where I could live in utter contentment."

"Surely that statement doesn't apply to China, Captain," Aurora said pointedly.

"Why do you say that?"

"Because it's perfectly plain that you relish it—or did. Surely you'll be returning there before too long, won't you?"

He continued to stare at her; she was toying with him, but why?

"Some places aren't everything they're made out to be, you know," he said at last. "China's one." He looked away, his eye directed across the fields to a far slope where a solitary laboring figure toiled behind a team of oxen. "Someday I might just like to take over the old Gracechurch place," he said.

His remark surprised even Georgiana, who had often known him to express a preference for farming instead of sailing, but never in so definite a way. Did this have to do with something he and Aurora had spoken of earlier?

"So many people are leaving these days," she remarked. "Pulling up stakes and going out to the Reserve to start over. What can be harder work for people than farming? Especially when the land's all worked down and the crops fail year after year."

Suddenly everyone was listening; farming and weather and crops were each Pequotter's business in that small agricultural community, where men lived their lives by the well-thumbed pages of their almanacs.

"Georgie, why don't you tell Sinjin your idea about Fearful Swamp," Posie prompted. Georgiana immediately regretted having mentioned it to Posie and Mab one evening in the boathouse. Sinjin was on it quickly. "Fearful Swamp? And what idea might that be?"

"It's of no consequence," Georgiana answered, flushing.

"No, go on, George, let's hear," he insisted.

She folded her hands in her lap and spoke quietly. "Oh, very well, if you insist. I thought that if Fearful Swamp were drained it might provide the best river-bottom growing land in the world—like the Nile delta land in Egypt. Once drained it could be planted and almost anything would grow there."

"Really? And what do you propose to grow?"

"Corn, mainly. For seed. And it's not really my idea, it's Cinnamon's. She saw it once in a dream."

Sinjin's dubious expression changed into one of incredulity. "Cinnamon!" he spat out. "For God's sake, Georgie, having your fortune told is one thing, but—"

"I can give you a list of things that Cinnamon has predicted, any number of which have come true," Georgiana declared, cutting him off. "And I happen to think she's right."

"Well, I'll be damned, Pharaohland on the Connecticut!" Sinjin exclaimed. "Thebes for Yankees, I do declare. George, you come up with some crazy notions, you do indeed, but this one beats all."

Georgiana's voice sharpened appreciably. "Kindly keep your opinions to yourself, Captain Grimes. And I'll thank you not to go blabbing this idea all over town. I promise you it's a good one."

"Don't worry. Mum's the word on that—do you think I want to get myself laughed out of the place?" He rolled over and stuck his face in his arms in an attempt to still his mirth while Georgiana turned away angrily.

Later, when the allotted period for proper digestion had expired; as though it had been discreetly arranged Posie coaxed Hermie away to the quarry pool; Aurora accompanied them, and presently the watery splash and sounds of freewheeling merriment could be heard through the trees. Hermie had unstrapped his leg and left it on the shore; in the water he moved freely and strongly. Back in the grove, from time to time Sinjin would glance Georgiana's way, observing her strong, agile fingers as they worked the needle and thread, rhythmical as engine parts, the same economical motion repeated with minor variations as she drew out an additional length of cotton from the ball or turned her piece to see if it measured up to her exacting specifications.

Sinjin cleared his throat to get her attention. "I'm sorry, George, I shouldn't have laughed. It's just that—well—maybe the stone beer went to my head." Though she had been angry, in moments she seemed suddenly lighter of heart, and something caused him to recall the day when he had first become aware of her as a girl growing into a young woman. It had been that memorable morning when Lafayette had paraded at Hartford and Rachel had taken Sinjin, Helen, and Rod up to the State House to see the "Markey" give Old Bobby a medal. With his crown of chestnut curls and winning smile, the great warrior nobleman had appeared to a tumultuous salute of cheers, but Sinjin had been looking at Georgiana, whom he had caught sight of in the crowd. She had been with the Talcott family, wearing a dress with a bow at her back, and although he'd known her nearly all his life it seemed he had never really looked at her before. Georgie Ross had been a girl worth knowing.

Out of such long-ago memories a warm tide of affection and regard for Georgiana suddenly welled up in him.

"George?" he said softly.

"Yes?"

"How are you really, old friend?"

"I'm doing well," she returned. "What a thing to ask. Your foolishness doesn't bother me a bit."

"I'm glad." He smiled. "What's that you're working on?"

"It's for Hat. A collar. With cuffs to come. If I live long enough." She gave him a narrow look.

"How is Hat?"

"She writes that she's enjoying herself, and I hope it's true. She asks endless questions about Snug Harbor. I think she's homesick. It was very hard on her, losing Murray Hill."

Since that shameful episode, Hattie Duckworth had been paying an extended visit to her sister.

"When does she come back?"

"End of next week. I wish she'd let me find another place to stay. It's not fair, people taking it out on Hat as a way of hurting me. But I know she won't."

"Where would you go if she did?"

"I don't know . . . maybe Sallie would find me a room. Then you and I could really be hammer and tongs."

He reached over to halt the movement of her fingers. "Georgie, I'm sorry, I've been behaving like a bear ever since I came back last spring. Don't ask me why, I don't know, or why I've taken it out on you."

She laid her piecework aside. "I should be the one to apologize," she countered. "I'm the one who's been the crosspatch. A positive shrew; something I've always loathed in other females." Though her impatience with herself was plain, she found herself smiling in spite of it.

"You ought to use your smile more, it's such a nice one," he said. "You haven't much today, you know."

She blushed. "Is it that bad? I hadn't realized." She worked the collar a moment before continuing. "About Rora—"

"Rora?"

"You must give her time, you know. Let her come to you. If she loves you—"

He stiffened. "What do you mean, *if* she loves me? Of course she does!"

"Still, you mustn't rush her. And remember she has a father and three brothers who haven't changed their minds—even though they appreciate your loyalty to the school."

"Has it occurred to her that you too have a brother?"

She was taken aback. Her brothers both lay in the village churchyard, the miller's victims.

Sinjin spread his hands. "I mean, of course, the brother whom you see before you. Who will always be your loving brother, and who cares for you very deeply."

"Don't—please—"

"But it's true, isn't it? I feel like a brother to you, always have. And Helen's so happy to have you for a sister. We make a nice little family, if we leave out Rod and the fact that I'm ex cathedra, so to speak. But George—about the school . . ."

She stiffened. "What about it?"

"Well, you know how Rod and my esteemed stepfather are agitating to have a special session of the Assembly called just to debate that damn law of theirs. They're saying the 'unrest' hereabouts makes it an emergency."

"How well we all know about that." She sat rigid and unyielding, looking suddenly more fatigued than he'd ever seen her, and his heart went out to her. "They don't scare me, my dear," she went on, "not a one of them. Rod is beneath contempt. To say nothing of your stepfather sanctioning the mean doings of low-lifes like Adgie Kroll and Tyler Gatchell and that cross-river bunch that murdered poor Murray Hill. The unrest, as they call it, is all their doing." He saw how hard she was working to make her words convince not only him but herself. "I won't close the school and I won't stop. I'll be darned if I will. And if there's going to be more trouble, well, I *can* shoot a gun, you know."

"Be serious."

"I am." She drew out another length of thread, and this time it was she who changed the subject. "There's something I've been wanting to talk to you about."

"What is it?"

"It's about your lectures in the cemetery."

"What about them?"

"A Mr. Price, from Boston, contacted us while you were away. He read them in the *Courant,* he'd like to talk to you about publishing them as a book. It wouldn't pay much, but—aren't you pleased?"

"Maybe." He turned away from her and gazed off toward the quarry where the others had gone.

She almost regretted having brought up the matter, he was so offhand about it. "What is it?" she asked.

"I don't know. I just get this awful feeling sometimes. As if the sword of Damocles was hanging over my head, just waiting to fall if I make one wrong move, the least mistake."

"Why should you feel that way?"

He sighed. "Perhaps from my vast disappointment in myself, that I'm not the person I used to hope I'd be. These days I'm thinking all kinds of damned foolish thoughts."

"Yes? Is it Aurora?"

He groaned and looked skyward. "I can't lose her again, Georgie, but I'm fearful that's what will happen. I'm afraid I'm going to be punished."

"Punished?"

"By the gods. Don't laugh, it's true—I've dared them to destroy me. I've pulled a lot of mean tricks, rotten tricks. I've stolen, I've cheated, I've hurt people. I know I'm going to pay for it, and the most terrible thing I can think of now is a life without her."

Georgiana looked at him. "Then it's very simple," she said calmly. "You shall have her." He turned back to her, to the gray eyes, so simple and direct and honest. This was the way they were used to talking; touching each other with words.

"How?" he uttered. "What makes you say that?"

"I don't know. But I believe you will. Somehow, in some way we don't even know about yet, the thing you want so much will come about. I pray each night for you that it will. Patience, my dear, patience . . ."

With a gesture he stopped her, and when he responded the words came out in a dry croak. "I don't deserve anyone like you, you know."

His words brought the scarlet to her cheeks. "Nonsense; we all deserve each other. But you must give Rora time. You each must have time. And you mustn't despair—never despair." She smiled at him, a warm token of goodwill, then passingly remarked on the loveliness of the day. "I'll remember this for a long time."

"What will you remember?"

"I'll remember this as the one afternoon of this entire summer when I didn't have to think about long division and the Battle of Hastings."

Sinjin laughed and kissed both her hands and their conversation continued in a humorously intimate vein until the others returned still dripping from the quarry pool. Reluctant to end the day, they all lay around a little longer, speaking of Hermie's trove of honey, the butterflies, and the lost pair of pickerels. Here, in this pastoral setting, among the five there existed an unspoken bond, forged by a mutual appreciation of the fact that Aurora had come home again, and that Sinjin loved her. Here it seemed that all things might yet be mended and made new; here there was solace for pain and balm for badly healed wounds, and the invisible joining of hands.

Though no one made mention of the fact, there was a conspiracy among them, for this they had been at connivance to see, that, first, Sinjin and Aurora were brought into closer propinquity, and, second, that they were vouchsafed periods of time to be alone together, something the conspirators effected by each having pretended to be engrossed in some private interest: Hermie in the pursuit of honey, Georgiana in her cotton-work. Now these activities were done with and a silence that seemed both natural and necessary fell upon them—each of them drowsy, if not altogether content.

When Aurora raised her lids she found Sinjin's eyes fast upon her, those green, hypnotic eyes, and she started visibly.

"What is it, Sissie?" Posie whispered.

Aurora silently shook her head. She had gasped in surprise to see the tears that shone in his eyes. Tears? For her? Suddenly she felt ashamed to think herself the cause. Her heart throbbed in her breast and her look was deep and searching. As she probed him, he turned away; when she saw his eyes again they were dry and filled with bafflement and a certain sheepishness. Yet he had wept. She felt herself coming unraveled, undone by a wave of confused emotions. Against her will she yearned for him; but, she told herself, she must hold back, she *must*. She must not be forward with him now. She knew him, recognized his intentions, but she could no longer afford to make mistakes. Still, a man's tears must be worth something.

When Georgiana and Posie began repacking Halley's hampers, Sinjin moved closer to where Aurora sat. He flopped onto his stomach and propped his chin on his fists, his bare feet crossed behind him, intently studying her face. Presently, she leaned back on her palms, returning his look, her thick, starry eyelashes motionless, like a doll's. His fingers stretched out to graze the tips of hers, and by this tenuous union an unseen but potent current passed between them.

"Rora . . . Rora . . .?" he murmured, tentatively, longingly. The green in his eyes had gone turquoise in the softening light. Suddenly he reached out, took her hand, and touched it to his cheek.

"Tonight?"

"Hush. Hush . . ."

She took her hand away from him and sat with her tilted parasol shading her face, a quivering patch of violet light reflecting on her underchin, her lids drooping now.

"Hush."

Hush . . .

His heart pounded in his chest. He felt excited but apprehensive. The mere sight of her, the sound of her voice worked in him to produce a series of intensely irregular sensations, serene and comforting at one moment, anxious, even furious, the next. To have her so near, yet not to be able to take her in his arms and kiss her and call her his own was torture. He was profoundly grateful to Posie for having so neatly arranged the tryst, to Georgiana for lending her imprimatur to the intrigue, to Hermie as well for providing the modus operandi, but, all other circumstances supposed equal, what was ultimately going to put her in his arms, what would cause her to utter the words he longed to hear? How was it to be accomplished? How was he to meet her again where they could be alone and talk?

Then it was time to go; the day was fast closing, they could no longer keep it to themselves. Georgiana was urging them to their feet, and they obeyed like docile sheep being put to fold. The late afternoon light poured itself like sweet melting honey across the upland slope where the roofs of one or two working farms broke the swell of landscape, their red-sided barns richly glowing; even the treetops were gold-burnished, and to the west the dropping sun threw long blue ribbons of shade over the land. Saying little, the group lazily retraced their morning steps along the grassy track through the woods to the spot where Hermie's wagon had been left. While he and the others were stowing the paraphernalia, Sinjin privately cornered Aurora for a last word.

"You haven't said yes about tonight."

"I can't, I—I'm going to church," she told him. "And after supper I have to spend time with Mama. She needs me."

"I need you. Ride your horse down—please. Meet me at the mill. Around seven. I'll be waiting. Say you'll come."

"I told you, I can't."

He gripped her arms. "Yes you can. You must. I'll be waiting."

Catching Georgiana's look, he released Aurora, and, whistling up Mavra, disappeared into the woods without a good-bye to the others, who were already aboard the wagon. They rode home quietly, each lost in private thoughts, lulled by the trundling of the wheels. The blithe spirit of the day had evaporated like a wish, those all-too-brief hours when their knowledge of the world, its pain and its sins, had been removed from them and they were the children of a more forgiving God, blessed in their innocence and blind to what lay ahead.

30

Connecticut Vespers

AS SHE WAITED FOR the rest of her bathwater to be carried up, Aurora lay stretched full length on the chaise lounge when Old Bobby appeared in her open doorway. "Do I disturb?" he inquired amiably. She welcomed him in and he drew up the bench, his keen blue eyes relishing the sight of her.

"Did you have a pleasant day, my dear? Find some honey?"

She described the trove Hermie had brought home for his mother, prudently neglecting to mention the contrived appearance of Sinjin Grimes but feeling her cheeks flush at the thought of him.

Old Bobby reached into his pocket and brought out a small, flat packet. "Here, Granddaughter, I have something for you," he said, handing it to her. Upon investigation it revealed a pair of matched miniatures hand-painted on ivory and framed in delicate gold beading.

"But who are they?" Aurora asked, mystified.

Bobby chuckled. "Mean to say you don't recognize your old granddad? And that's your grandmother Vicky. I came across it in my drawer today and I thought you might like to have it."

"Oh, Granddaddy, how sweet." She kissed his cheek gratefully. What a dear man he was, how thoughtful and generous. Who in the world had a better, kinder grandfather?

She thanked him profusely, and when, in his bantering way, he suggested that in return she might give him a game of piquet after supper, she declared firmly that she would, with pleasure.

"Mighty glad to have our Rora home again," he told her, his eyes misting as he kissed her cheek and pressed her hand. He slipped from the room as quietly as he'd entered and, admiring her gift, Aurora began pinning her hair up. Ten minutes later she lay back in her bath, letting the warmth of the water ease her mind and body, luxuriating in the quiet of the moment. She could still hear the sound of Sinjin's low, husky voice; it thrilled her, and she worked to make sense of it all. She had felt drawn to him that afternoon, the pull of the nail to the magnet. The very thought made her tremble. No, let him sail away again and leave her untouched; she cared only for rest, peace, a quiet heart, not one to beat as hers had at several points today. He must let her be. If he was so foolish as to go to Two Stone and wait for her when she had already told him no, that was his affair. Grimes Mill would not see her tonight—or any night.

As she reached for the sponge and soap she heard Agrippina's voice advancing along the passageway, then her knock on the door. She had no choice but to invite her in.

"Pina," she said lightly, "wasn't it the loveliest day? Hermie found masses of honey. I hope you are feeling better. Were you able to get out a little?"

"No, as a matter of fact I did not go out at all," Pina replied shortly, "though, as you can see, I am a bit better. I'm glad you enjoyed yourself, however. At least someone's getting the good of this weather. But it seems to me you're being very cavalier about your responsibilities around here. Mama is not well, yet you seem to care nothing about that, only that you should gratify yourself. You do realize she's dying, don't you?"

"Yes, Pina," came the patient reply, "I realize it."

"Then how can you be so selfish? You've been home long enough to know how things are. Anyone can see that I have all the care of this big house, yet today, when I was feeling unwell, you nevertheless insisted on absenting yourself on this frivolous excursion. What will you do after Mama is gone, when Papa's going to need a lot more looking after?"

One thing that had impressed itself on Aurora was Agrippina's infuriating "reasonableness," as if all the world were mad and she alone were sane. "Oh, Pina, don't fret so," she said lightly, "Papa has Halley and Judah and Trubey and Burdy. He has Granddaddy, as well. Surely he doesn't expect you to sacrifice yourself. You have your own life to live. Papa will handle the situation, never fear."

"Surely it will take a very long time for him to come round. In the meantime he will need all our love and support. But if you think that I am going to do it alone you're sadly mistaken. Someone must help me."

Aurora sat up in the tub as if in disbelief at what she was hearing. "Pina, am I to understand that you think I've come back home only to remain a widow, to go about in weeds and to be bereaved for the rest of my days? Do you expect that I'm simply going to take over Mama's keys and cupboards and continue to live with you and Papa in this house?"

Agrippina bridled. "A very nice house, if you are asked. And where else would you go under the circumstances, I'd like to know?"

"That's quite beside the point, isn't it? Don't misunderstand me, I love Papa, and I know how much he'll miss Mama—oh yes, he will for a very long time. But, whether or not you enjoy hearing this, he will get over his grief. People do, you know. It's human nature. And when that day comes he won't need me, or you, or anyone else to look after him because he'll marry again, he'll have another wife, I'm quite sure of it."

Pina's eyes widened. "You are mad to think so! Papa will never marry again, he'll be faithful to Mama's memory as long as there is breath in his body. Do you think after the way he has loved her, so devotedly, so truly, he could even look at another woman? There is constancy in the souls of some if not all!"

Aurora chose to ignore this bit of melodrama. "Whether or not he does will be entirely up to him. But I am warning you, Pina, if and when the time comes, it will be none of your affair. Do with your own life as you see fit, but do not, I repeat, do *not* involve others in it. Most of all, not me. Now hand me that jug, please."

Pina presented the jug, then modestly looked away as Aurora, having laved its contents over her shoulders and torso, reached for a towel and stood to dry herself. She slipped on her wrapper and took up her brush, moving to the window to brush her hair in what rays of sunshine remained. Pina followed her, apparently for the purpose of further complaint, but Aurora anticipated her.

"Pina, I do believe you're deceiving yourself. Papa doesn't want you to do this to yourself, really he doesn't. In point of fact, he would like nothing more than to see you married, settled down somewhere with a husband and family. We all want that for you. Mama, especially, would be so pleased."

"Mama won't be here much longer," Pina returned. "And you needn't try to coach me in how to trap a husband, especially after the shameful way you've behaved today. You really are a wicked creature, aren't you?"

The brush stopped in midstroke. "Pina, what *can* you be saying?"

Pina lowered her voice. "As if you didn't know. Oh, how you love to pretend. How you—"

"Pina, stop it this instant and say what you mean! How am I being wicked?"

"What do you call it when you sneak off for a rendezvous with that scoundrel, who you know is forbidden this house? It would wound Papa terribly to learn how he's been deceived."

"Pina, how is it that you come by such information?" Aurora demanded, stopping her. "Have you followed me today?"

Pina reached into her pocket and drew out a scrap of paper. "I found this," she said with gusto. She handed Aurora the screed Hermie had sent to Posie the previous day about the sub-rosa arrangements for the expedition to the quarry. "It's despicable enough that Georgiana's a party to this, and Hermie Light, but to think that you would draw an innocent such as Posie into your intrigue."

Aurora hesitated for a moment, then went and shut the door. She leaned against it and, with controlled anger in her voice, spoke clearly and evenly. "Pina, let me warn you of something. You must be very careful here, most careful, for you are running on a very short string just now. I have something to say to you, something I probably should have said long before this. I regret the necessity of it, for despite the fact that I find everything you have done to me uncommonly cruel, still I have no wish to offend you. But I must tell you this, and you must hear it once and for all. If it is your choice, your free choice, to live your life without husband or children, why then, that is what you must do. You won't believe me, I know, but I *do* understand you, and I understand your behavior, as unseemly and repellent as I may find it."

"Sissie, you're talking nonsense," Agrippina said, narrowing her shoulders. "Exactly what is it you understand?"

"I understand what it is that makes you so unhappy. And I feel sorry for you."

"Really? And why should you feel sorry for me?"

"Because *you* love him, too. Deny it if you wish, but it's true."

Agrippina drew back in horror. *"Him?* Surely you can't mean who I think you mean! You know how I detest and abominate that scoundrel! The very sight of him disgusts me. I hope you realize how ill you really are, Sissie; obviously any further discussion with you is quite without meaning."

As she turned to go Aurora handed her back the note. "Take this with you, Pina, why don't you? You may want to hide it away in your hatbox as you did the letters Sinjin wrote to me so many years ago, and the fan he gave me then. Did you take the letters out and read them and pretend the things he wrote he wrote to you?"

"That's revolting. It's a lie, I never—! How dare you say such things to me? Your own sister?"

"I dare because it is so. Didn't you ever wonder what had become of those letters? Did Georgie never mention to you that she had discovered them in the hatbox and given them to me when I was last here, when Sinjin—"

Pina's expression was frozen in horror, but Aurora, relentless, marched to the vanity table and unlocked the drawer. "Here they are." She took the packet out and held it up between herself and Pina, who stared fixedly at her. "Why, Pina? Why did you do it? Didn't you know how much they would have meant to me, when I'd been so ill? Wasn't keeping my fan enough? I never hurt you, did I? I never did you harm. How could you deliberately hurt me so?"

Cheeks ablaze, Agrippina dropped her eyes guiltily and knotted her fingers behind her back. "I don't see what you're making such a fuss about," she muttered. "Some old love letters, they can't mean anything now. I really think you're making mountains from molehills."

"*Mountains—molehills!*" Aurora repeated dumbly. "Can it be you are so coldhearted that even now you don't realize the terrible wrong you did?"

Agrippina made a sound of impatience. "Very well, suppose you tell me what terrible thing I did."

"You nearly killed me, that's what you did!" Aurora's voice rose, sliding suddenly out of control, and she clutched her trembling fists before her as the awful realization swept over her once more. "You kept me from marrying the man I loved. The only man I've ever loved, I should say. You intercepted intimate letters that were meant for me, and as a result of your trickery you robbed me of everything that ever meant anything in my life. You have made me unhappier than I ever thought it was possible to be. Yes, you! That is what you did!"

Her accusations seemed to have little effect on Agrippina. "I am shocked to hear you talk this way," she retorted primly. "To think you would have married that terrible man if I hadn't been there to stop it! Yes, I admit it—I *did* withhold the letters, but only to keep you from making the worst mistake in your life! You really ought to thank me. If it weren't for me, you'd doubtless be living in Sailor's Lane now with the tar pots and pitch."

"Had I been obliged to, then Sailor's Lane would have suited me fine," Aurora responded quickly. "I don't see that that's such a terrible place to live with someone you love."

"Poor Sissie, you've always been a foolish creature, you've never shown good sense."

"You're quite right, I never have. If I had, nothing in the world would have kept me from him. Pina—as I am a Christian woman I am trying to forgive you and to understand why you did what you did, but I confess, when I hear you speak so cruelly to me, I am hard pressed—hard pressed!"

Agrippina's eyes glittered with defiance. "I don't care, do you understand? I've done nothing I'm ashamed of. I would do it again, a hundred times over."

"But they were *my* letters, Pina, can't you see that? You had no right to take them or to keep them!"

"Their lines express the most odious thoughts imaginable! No gentleman would ever write such indecent things to a lady. No lady would give cognizance to them. It's obscene!"

"That is no concern of yours whatever!"

Agrippina drew a long breath and rushed on. "I only had your best interests at heart. Heaven knows *you* didn't. You were ill, Rora, do you forget you had tried to do away with yourself? If you have suffered, it is because you have deserved God's punishment, nothing else. God sees, God knows. You called His wrath down on your head by your mortal sin. I only tried to help you, and if anything you owe me a debt of thanks for it."

"Oh noble deed, Agrippina! Listen to me, for this is something I *do* know! There is such a thing as retribution. Such acts do not go unpunished. Yes, God *does* see, He *does* know. He knows what you did and He is sorry for you, as I am. But never say you have done this for me, do not say I owe you. I owe you nothing. I'm sorry for you, I pity you, but you have had all of my life that you are going to get. As for these letters," she said, taking them up again with a trembling hand, "it is plain to me that though you read them, you had no notion what it is to have a man love you. You have no notion now. Don't talk to *me* about the wrath of God, because I warn you, Pina, if you go on as you are that is all you will have in this house for company."

She replaced the letters in the drawer and relocked it, then went and opened the door again. Catching sight of Trubey at the end of the hall, she called to her, "Trubey, be good enough to tell Granddaddy I shan't be able to play cards with him tonight. Perhaps Posie will give him a game. Then come arrange my hair, will you? I'm going to church and I want it to look especially nice. And ask Reuben to hitch up the curricle."

She dug out her breviary and rosary and laid them by, then took from a drawer a pair of silk stockings, interrupting herself to show Agrippina to the door.

"Sissie—wait—"

But the door was shut and Agrippina stared at the knob, then, not knowing what else to do, burst into tears and fled sobbing to her room.

WHILE devout churchgoers passed along the road to New France as the vesper bells rang out across the cooling fields, Sinjin waited alone at Grimes Mill. The day itself seemed to burn out in the trembling bowl of the sky as he watched, and the shadows lengthened. He made fists and raised his arms overhead, gigging first one hip, then the other, and when he had stretched, his body relaxed into a languorous serenity as he awaited the arrival of his beloved. Far off across the fields, a skimming flock of birds wheeled into view, then swooped magically earthward, disappearing within the mantle of tall flower-studded grass, not to appear again that evening. As he squinted across the verge he saw how the glowing heat of the day, which had lingered among the meadow grasses, with the cooling of the sun's rays now rose into the limpid air in palpable waves, making objects waver as in a desert mirage; rose tints against the trees turned them a luminous blue-green above the millpond where the ducks paddled so calmly.

These moments were a welcome pause, a brief transition when the natural rhythm decreed that the day had indeed ended, but it was not yet night. And in this period of quiescence Sinjin Grimes told himself again that he was going to marry Aurora Talcott. He loved her in a way he did not hope to understand, and that, for better or worse, he could do nothing about. If anything, he loved her even more now, for her courage, for her staunchness, her unwillingness to flinch in the face of what must have been the worst kind of horror and loneliness. He loved her for the fragile warmth that hid that strength, he loved her because she was the golden souvenir of his lost youth. He recalled for the thousandth time how bewitching she had looked that first afternoon in the cabin of the *Adele,* how dear and sweet and childlike she had been, and how much he had wanted her, how in what seemed like seconds he had fallen in love with her. And now she had been restored to him.

From across the empty fields the bells tolled again, reminding him of why he had come to this place. Tarrying no longer with his wishful thoughts, he moved quickly about, preparing for the meeting he had envisioned since leaving her at the quarry. He had already set out a bottle of wine under the race where the water was coldest. After feeding his horse, he removed from his saddle the blanket, pillow, and throw he had taken care to bring along, and went inside to have a look around. Thanks to Père Margeaux's flock, the place had been well swept that morning. He had only to find where he and Aurora would be most comfortable. There by the fireplace? Or there, where the breeze would stray through the window? His gaze fell on the cross that blessed the abbé's humble services, and he took it down; best if Aurora didn't see it.

The vespers bell tolled again, as though to summon any latecomers, leaving him to wonder if his wait would be truly rewarded. Would she come? Would she? The truth about him just now was that he too was apprehensive. Like Aurora, he was afraid that the pain and longing might return again to eat at his heart and make him less a man. At the same time he was determined not to let what had happened before happen again. If she came tonight he would take her, for if she did come he would know it was for one reason, to make love with him. But if by some mischance she failed to appear, then he must resort again to Posie's assistance; and more messages and arrangements. For he *would* have her, by the yellow god he would!

After a while, remembering, he climbed to the loft and stared down at the windowsill where yesterday's legend was still visible.

Friendship is Love without his wings.

God! What an eternity it was between the incising of that quotation, for Georgie Ross, the miller's girl, and this moment. He stepped to the west window and peered out along the Two Stone Road. Soon darkness would be on him and with it would come the treasure he had been seeking for so long, and the fire in his blood would be quenched.

The last rays of sun slanted in scarlet oblongs across the bare plaster of one wall, illuminating it like a virgin leaf of paper. He found a pencil in a pocket and began composing. The composition took him only as long as it took to scribble down the words, but before he could complete the last lines he heard the clop of hooves outside. Rushing to the window again, he looked out to see her sitting in the yellow cart.

He all but tumbled down the ladder in his haste to get to her, but she was faster, and by the time he reached the bottom she was standing in the doorway, laughing at him. In three long strides he was at her side and she let him put his arms around her. She was carrying her breviary and her rosary, and he took them from her and kissed each of her fingers, and breathing the scent of her spoke into her ear.

> *"She walks in beauty, like the night*
> *Of cloudless climes and starry skies;*
> *And all that's best of dark and bright*
> *Meet in her aspect and her eyes."*

Smiling, she lightly pressed his hand, then took hers back. "Poetry? How nice."

"Come," he said, leading her to the ladder, "I want to show you something before the light goes. Up there." When she hesitated he urged her to climb. She went first, he following. Beyond the loft window the light was fading. The Mill Woods lay in shadow now, and overhead the first stars were already glimmering through the early dusk. Sinjin stood by the section of wall where he had written out his lines, and taking his pencil again he completed the last words, then with a flourish added a title.

Where Byron Wrote His Name

> *He strode past many another pilgrim 'cross the Attic*
>   *plain*
> *To worship Greece at Zeus's holy shrine,*
> *Sad ruined porch at Soúnion's Cape where once*
>   *white-pleated*
> *Virgins came to celebrate Prometheus' pagan god,*
> *Where vestal smoke did purify the blue Aegean wave,*
>   *There he too had bent his knee in tribute*
> *And on one headless column of broken-footed marble*
>   *With penknife had incised his name into the stone*

And with it carved his legend too, greater than any yet
       there writ.
And who shall say, when at last that seaward-looking
       temple
Falls into the waiting sea and each pillar in its turn
       has turned to dust,
Then who best remember'd shall it be,
Those Greeks who built the place
Or he who carved his name?

She finished reading the lines, her voice trailed away to a murmur and became still. She turned to gaze out the window with her thoughts.

"You don't like it," he said flatly.

She made a half-gesture with her hand and turned back to him. "No, don't say that." Her voice was almost bell-like in its clarity, and her smile was sweetly sad. "Yes, I have seen that pillar at Cape Soúnion, where he wrote his name for all the world to see. And below it—"

"Yes? What?"

Her smile brightened. "You know. *You* were there. You inscribed your name under his."

"Did you find it presumptuous?"

"Oh, too much by far, I think." She laughed. She seemed quite gay, which pleased him enormously. "Georgie's right, though—you *are* a poet."

"Did she say that?"

"Oh, yes, she quite admires your verses."

"I know of some she disdained."

"Which?"

"Never mind, it doesn't matter. Come, let's go down."

"Will you leave your poem there?"

"For posterity, yes. When you and I will come here again, on some other night, like this one . . ." He took her hand and pressed it warmly.

She was shivering when they came down, and the last rays of sun stroked the ancient boards. From the millpond sounded the raucous quacking of ducks, and they went out for a look. He fetched the bottle from the race, and since she seemed reluctant to go back inside the mill, he uncorked the wine, poured it into cups, and they lingered together in the open doorway, toasting the sunset.

No greater happiness for him than to be here, now, like this, with her beside him, watching the dying day, sweet golden day that had brought him such anguish and such pleasure. "Goddess of the dawn, goddess of the sunset," he whispered, setting his glass aside to caress her face and hair, then to toy with the pins that held it. "Do you have any idea how beautiful you are? To me—to any man, I suppose." When he tried to coax her back inside she gave a murmur of resistance and removed her hand from his. "Have you come here only to tease me, as you did this afternoon?" he asked.

He was deadly earnest, she could tell by his expression. Had she? Had she renounced a game of piquet with her grandfather for a love game? He waited for her answer, gazing at her, eager, ardent. Why had she decided to come? Only to spite Agrippina? To cause him more pain? She must decide now. Stay or leave, she must choose.

"This afternoon we were not alone," she replied, staying.

"Tonight we are. I've told you, I love you. You must know I do. I want you," he said simply.

She met his look. "You want other women, too." Her remark had slipped out as though unbidden, but by it she hoped to stave off what she now believed was inevitable.

"What do other women have to do with you and me?" he demanded, taken by surprise.

"I don't know, what do they? These—'wives' one hears about. An exiled noblewoman reputed to be prodigiously rich—a Chinese princess as well? You are steeped in royalty out there, it's no wonder you stayed away so long." Her tone was arch, her eyes sparkled.

"You're toying with me. I have no wife in China—or anywhere, for that matter."

"Oh? But what of this princess—what is she called?"

"Her name is Celeste, sometimes Celestine. She isn't royal. Her mother was French. You would like her, I think."

"Would I?"

"She's a lot like you. Not as beautiful but petite, little ears, a soft voice, pretty laugh."

"Does she speak English?"

"Of course. She's not a flower-and-mist girl."

"What an enchanting expression. What are they, flower-and-mist girls?"

"They are of the same sorority, though hardly so bold as your Venetian ladies with their perfumed fans and henna-dyed hair. Celeste is not one of these, however, but a lady, like yourself."

"I see. And when you leave here will you go back to her?"

He took her by the shoulders. "When I leave here I will not go back to her because I'll have you with me. I'll never go back to China now unless you are at my side. I want you to know that."

"You said that before, as I seem to recall. In truth, I think I shall never see China, China was never meant for me, I'm sure of that now. Such a pretty-sounding name though." She smiled wistfully. "Someday if I have a dog—like Mavra—I shall call it China—for remembrance."

"China for remembrance," he murmured. "China is old, she has been there a long time. She will wait until you come. Until I bring you to her. One day, you will see."

She laughed. "And tell me, what will you do with your Chinese princess when I come?"

"Celeste is wise and understanding."

"You would move her into the back room, while I would be your new concubine. Isn't that how it would be?"

"Don't talk foolishness. *You* would be my wife. My only wife. My adored wife, the sun in my life. We would live in Macao, a marvelous city. One look at you and that whole pack of colonials would fall down before you. They would love you and worship you as I do. You would be my queen."

"There's a pretty thought. First a princess, now a queen." Her smile faded. "Alas, it's not possible, of course."

"Don't say that. It is possible, you have only to say the word. Grammaw's arranged to refit the *Sparrow* for me. We'll sail to China. Together, you and I. Captain and Mrs. Grimes."

The wistful smile returned. "The *Sparrow?* Not the *Adele?* But, no, there could never be another ship like the *Adele,* could there? *Adele,* China, it's all the same. It's too late for them, and us."

He would not listen, didn't want to hear. Tonight he was fired with renewed passion, with the countenancing of every incredible and remote possibility the world had to offer, bursting with plans and ideas, with the thrill of showing himself to best advantage before her, to prove beyond the shadow of a doubt that of all men he was the only one for her. He would be pleased to fling before her all the treasures of the Middle Kingdom, she would be the true princess of all his dreams, pearl among pearls, and no less a personage than the emperor himself would bend his neck to her foot—that little foot!

"And there is a garden there," he added, "one that will please you. The most beautiful garden imaginable."

He could feel her soft breath on his cheek as she spoke. "Tell me . . . what sort of garden?"

"It is called the Garden of the Moon."

"How lovely. What does it mean?"

"It means ah, but you must come there and let me show you. That garden . . . in the moonlight . . . there's an old saying out there—'China Moon, China Madness.' You will see." He spoke into her hair and tried to draw her closer, but she moved to the window and stood looking out. He came after her, turned her head so she was facing him, but she kept her eyes lowered. "No, don't do that," he said huskily. "Look at me." She did so. "I want you to listen to me. It's very important. I've been thinking hard since this afternoon, and I want you to try to understand what I'm going to say."

"Very well," she said. "I shall try."

"Aurora, I find that I have managed after all these years not only to keep myself alive, but to keep my feeling for you alive, too. I had tried to convince myself it was dead, I know now that it's not, it's still alive, as alive as you are, as I am. The heart of it still beats within me. I honestly believe that there's a part of each of us that has nothing to do with our minds or our bodies, a part of us that we have no control over, that exists, whether we will or no. And it is because of this that I think—no, that's wrong—I *know*—I know beyond all doubt that you and I love each other. It's as though our two souls were mated, as if they belonged to each other."

"My soul belongs to God," she whispered.

"Souls belong to humans, not gods."

"Not gods—*God.* There is only one God, Jehovah, Father of Jesus who gave his life on the Cross so men could live."

"And love. A man must love in order to live happily. Please hear me—I'm only trying to tell you how I love you. I love and desire you. Is it wrong to feel desire for something—someone you love and adore? Surely that can't be wrong, not between people like us. Only think how long we have loved, and with what misery, what pain. For me, love is all, I promise it."

"Love," she repeated pensively. "Is this what love does, then, brings us to this? Do you know," she said, shuddering a little as she raised her eyes to the rafters, "do you know that I have not been happy for one single day since I met you? Not once in all that time. Holy Mother of God, what a terrible confession that is. It's true, though. I don't think an entire day ever passed when something or other didn't remind me of you and then I would get this sensation, this dark, dead feeling. I've had to live with it so long it's become a part of me. It pulls me down, it weighs my heart so heavily it makes me wonder if anything in this world is really worthwhile."

"Dearest girl, don't," he pleaded. "Don't you see? We mustn't put each other through this anymore. We can't—it's not fair to either of us. It's not true, what you said this afternoon about the bad things happening all over again. Those things are all behind us now. It's true though that I've loved you so much that I thought at times I'd die of it. I even tried to goad men to kill me, to put me out of my misery and pain. Anything, anything to make it stop! There were times when I thought the memory of you would drive me mad. Once or twice I did go mad, I think. Aurora—?" He stopped and searched her eyes.

"Yes?"

"Do you really love me still?"

"Yes."

She was surprised at her frank admission; it was one she had not expected to make. She was thinking of Pina, of Papa, of empty lives. "Yes, I love you."

He felt a warm tremor of relief. It was so, then. She had said it. He had won. She was his. "It will be all right," he said. "Trust me."

"How will it be?"

"I don't know, but it will be, I promise. Trust me," he said again, and with that sought her lips and kissed her for the first time in how many years?—long and hungrily, drowning in the sublime sweetness of her mouth. Then their lips parted and they fell together, clinging passionately to each other as though to life itself, as if except for them the lamps of the world would go out. Now nothing mattered but that they were alone together. It was not possible that she should go on resisting him any longer, evading him, finding excuses. She had been vulnerable from that startling instant when he'd been blown into the study out of the rainstorm. She had known no other lover, no man had loved her, no man since this one. He held no patent on desire; her own body was trembling with it. She gazed into his eyes, yearning toward him, and his arms tightened around her. They stood holding each other quietly in the room by the door until, leaning over, he drew its top half inward, and their forms fell into shadow. Gently he began unfastening the pins that held her hair and removing them one by one, then let the golden locks fall about her shoulders.

"Yes," he breathed, "like that . . . like that." He began undoing the hooks of her bodice.

"Wait, let me." When she was naked to the waist he took up the candle to look at her.

"Yes. Like that. Oh, God, God . . ."

The light she saw burning in his eyes thrilled her. It gave her a sense of power such as she had not known since that long-ago afternoon in the cabin of the *Adele*. She saw how much he wanted her, and she let him look freely, feeling strangely innocent, as though only with him had she ever known anything of the acts of love and passion that took place between men and women. Then, suddenly overcome with shyness, she tried to cover her naked breasts with her arms, but he took them away, gently but forcibly, then backed off a step to gaze again, silently, with the candlelight gleaming in his eyes.

"Come." He took her hand and led her to the corner by the window, where he had placed the pillow and the throw, along with the red-striped blanket. "Come," he insisted, "lie here beside me."

She let him draw her down and they stretched out alongside each other on the blanket; it smelled faintly of pine pitch and wood smoke. When she attempted a faint protest he drew her close and silenced her with kisses. He felt of her breasts, letting his palms cup their weight, his keen fingers kneading and stroking them, pressing the shining nipples. He thought of the child, their child, who had been suckled at these same breasts. He could cry out with the pain of it—and oh, the joy! He strained fiercely, growing hard against her, and as she felt herself locked together with him, in that instant she knew that she had come here intending all along to surrender, to give herself up to him again as she had so many years before, and she put her lips to his to let him know it. Of their passion on that night had Caroline been born; who knew what this meeting might bring?

What lay ahead for them she could neither say nor cared to think about. Not now, not on this night. Tonight was a thing of soft bright magic, and neither of them would speculate on it; that would have been like poking a finger through a spider's web, and all the hard and clever work that had gone into its creation would have been wasted. Tonight the old mill with its mute wheel lay under a spell in the gauzy moonlight, a wizard's magic by which enchanted lovers awoke from sleep to have their hearts touched as in a storybook. Low in the east over the dark treetops hung the evening star, gleaming steady and bright in the indigo sky. Venus, star of love, brightest of the planets, their private beacon. To Aurora it seemed an insignia, the emblem of their tryst, and in her heart she thanked the Blessed Virgin to whom she prayed,

> *Ave Maris Stella*
> *Dei Mater alma,*
> *Atque semper Virgo,*
> *Felix coeli porta . . .*
>
> *Hail thou star of ocean . . .*

In her soft voice she repeated the words aloud; he listened spellbound, hardly able to believe this was actually happening. He had wanted to create something perfect for her tonight, pristine and joyous, something he could be proud of, that she would remember always. Though she had been married and widowed and was a bereaved mother, he thought of her as a virgin still, as his sweet virgin bride, and such was his fancy that he imagined her to have come here to worship, like the Virgin in the poem. And as he moved with her and in her and kissed her lips he pictured two swans of purest white, two sublime birds together on a moonlit lake, gliding across the argent water toward a splashing cascade. Closer they came and closer to the very rim, but instead of gliding over and falling, they spread their feathered wings and rose up into the starry darkness, up across the dark meadows among the white stars, toward a whiter moon, borne aloft on the wings of the night.

The Course of True Love

AURORA KNELT AT her prie-dieu, hands clasped before her as she prayed for mercy and absolution. It was useless. As with the king in *Hamlet,* her words flew up but her thoughts remained below, and giving over further efforts, she got up and began pacing the rug, one eye on the closet where the liquor case was hidden. Every one of the bottles had been drained, they gathered dust, and with Rose dismissed her chances of getting more were slim.

Among the family that morning, her features had been kept carefully set in a pale mask of composure, but though she might look tranquil, her heart was in turmoil. Over and over she relived in her mind her rendezvous with Sinjin at the mill; over and over she accused herself: she had cast aside everything she thought she had learned, every precept instilled in her by her mother, every promise she had made, not only to Père Margeaux, but to the Holy Virgin, to God Himself! Though she had told herself no, she must not and would not, when it came down to the moment she had been like one possessed. Moreover—and this was worst of all—she had reveled in it. The night had been a rapturous dream. For years, though married to another, she had thirsted to see Sinjin, to hear his voice again, and be with him—and yes, to give herself to him again, as she had that night in the coach. Now it had happened. From the ruins of her disastrous marriage, from the horrors of Naples and of Caro's death, she had been able to extricate herself and return home, never dreaming *he* might be there. But he *had* been there, and she had gone to him. They would marry and he would give her another child in place of the one she had lost, he was love, and she could not live without love. *Ah, he was her lover, then, he was her god.*

Or so it had seemed to her last night. But as she had driven home from the mill her dream had promptly dissolved. She had sinned, she had sinned most grievously, and again, she feared there would be a day of reckoning. "The piper must be paid." How many times had she heard that old adage? If one danced to the piper's tune, in time there must come the sad arithmetic, accounts must be balanced. She required no proof of this; she already had sufficient grounds for belief. As a girl, mired in passion for this same man she had taken a fatal misstep; now, a lifetime later, she felt herself again being drawn into the maelstrom. The same wild feelings assailed her, that giddy desire to surrender herself totally to him, despite whatever it might mean to her family, to dearest Papa, who had troubled to include in his new house this pretty room of blue, with Great-Aunt Susan's bedstead in it and her childhood treasures, as if he had known all along that she would one day come back to reclaim them.

She stared at the note on the table, still sealed in its envelope, for she had refused to open and read it. She knew what it would contain, lines of love and yearning that would bring the blood to her cheeks. She could not bear to read them, must not. There would be no forgiveness for her sins, but there was no need to add to them. She must instruct Posie, who had brought the note, to return it to its author, and instruct him not to write more. Odd; once she had nearly pined away, praying for his letters to come, now she was returning one unopened.

And what would Papa think if he learned that Posie was being used as a go-between, carrying such missives? And if Priam found out, would he come storming into the house, threatening mayhem with sabers or pistols? Why, she wondered impotently, had she allowed herself to fall into this wretched trap? What should she do, whom should she turn to, who was there to help her? No one, she decided, and then, there was only one way: She must give him up. Yes. She must simply stop seeing him. There would be no more private rendezvous. But how could she give him up, now that she had found him again and he had possessed her, she him? She told herself the only answer lay in prayer, in beseeching God and the Holy Mother to give her the strength to renounce him. And so she prayed. Prayed and prayed as hard as she knew how. But even as she prayed she thought of him, longed for him, craved him.

Her doleful ruminations were interrupted as a knock sounded at her door and Posie tripped in to model for Sissie the new frock Miss Simms had been sewing on for two weeks. Aurora's compliments were effusive; the garment was as modish as anything Paris dressmakers had to offer.

"It's just the thing for you, Po!" she exclaimed. "Pina won't approve, but that's all right." She drew her sister close. "Oh, darling, sometimes I think you're the only thing around this place that makes any sense. I hate to think how truly unhappy I'd be if you weren't here."

"Sissie, don't say that. Besides, you're going to be happy now, I know it. You've waited for such a long time, you deserve to be. And he loves you so much," she added, her eyes shining.

Aurora stiffened. "Sinjin? Truly? How do you know?"

"Because he's told me! All these years he's been in love with you. In my belief, it's just a matter of time before you marry him."

"But how can you say that, knowing how Papa feels? And Priam. What would they do if they knew what you were up to, arranging rendezvous and delivering his notes?"

Posie leaned to touch Aurora's lips with her fingers. "Nonsense. Priam is quite pliant about Sinjin these days. And as for Papa, I believe he can be brought around. Certainly he won't do as he did last time. He's always blamed himself for what happened, you know."

"Has he?"

"Yes, he has. Ask Georgie. He won't destroy your chance for happiness."

"Do you believe in second chances, Po?" Aurora asked.

Posie clapped her hands. "Oh *yes!* Yes, I do and you must, too. And I pray for you. I pray all the time—"

"Do you? And does it help?" Her eyes had begun to tear. "Do prayers do any good, really?"

"Of course they do, they must."

"I pray each night and day for Mama, but I know all the prayers in the world cannot save her—nothing will save her, nothing. And I can't bear to think of her leaving us. And Papa—poor Papa."

"Yes, he'll miss her dreadfully." Posie's tone grew somber. "But you mustn't cry." She reached out to take Aurora's hand. "Come, Sissie, pray with me. Let's pray for Papa, and for Mama. We'll pray for all our loved ones—and for Captain Grimes too."

Aurora's smile was wistful. "That will be a waste of prayer, I'm afraid. Captain Grimes doesn't believe in God."

"He *says* he doesn't, but that doesn't prove anything. He has deep convictions—and he's very brave. If he can't find his way to God, perhaps one day God will find the way to him. You could be such a help to him, too."

"How?"

"Show him your own faith. Help him to believe."

Aurora groped but could find no words with which to reply to this. How could she tell Posie of her own doubts—or of her sin?

"I must go away," she muttered to herself, as if she were alone. "I must leave here as quickly as I can."

"Sissie, no!" Posie argued. "You've only just come home. And Papa would miss you dreadfully. He'll need you, too."

"Need me . . . yes . . . that's what Pina said, too," she muttered. "But I'm afraid that if I stay I shall go mad!"

"Darling, you mustn't speak of madness or I shall go mad as well. We must behave sensibly if only for Mama's sake."

"Then *he* must go. Yes, let him take the *Sparrow* and sail off to Havana or wherever he's going."

"He's not ready to leave. And while he's still here perhaps you and he could talk sometimes—"

"No—I refuse to see him. Don't be naughty, Po. He's charmed you, hasn't he?"

"He charms everyone." She laughed gaily and jumped up. "It's so pleasant outdoors, shall we walk in the garden?"

"No, dear, you go. And take this, would you?" She handed Posie the sealed note.

"Won't you at least read it?"

She bit her lip and shook an obstinate head. "It won't help. Tell him—tell him he mustn't write me anymore. And don't you conspire with him, either." She blotted her eyes and tried to smile. "The dress is lovely, truly."

"Thank you. I must find Mama and get her approval. She's bound to say the neck's too low."

"Tell Mama your sister said it's exactly right—after all, we must start thinking of finding you a husband, too, and to do that maidens must show their 'virtues.' At least that's what the girls in Italy like to do."

Posie floated from the room on a trail of laughter and went to find her mother. No sooner had she left than Aurora began to weep again, and to pray.

Posie did not find her mother in her bedroom as expected. Trubey reported that her mistress had gone downstairs, and once down, instead of sitting in her chair on the terrace, as she ought to be doing, she had begun poking about in her garden. Yes, there she was with her gardening apron and clippers, moving about her flower beds, plucking a dead bloom here, clipping back an iris there. She was rummaging in the potting shed for some string with which to tie up her asters when Posie came upon her.

"Mother, are you in there? I've come to show you my new dress!" Posie said, appearing in the doorway.

"Posie Talcott, don't you come in here in that new frock, you'll get it all dirty."

"Yes, Mother dear," Posie said and came in anyway. "Don't you think Miss Simms did a superb job? And there was enough material for a stole." She put out the toe of one diminutive slipper. "Dyed to match. Sissie likes it very much."

Mab gave Posie's outfit her critical eye. "Very pretty, I'm sure," she pronounced. "Miss Simms has done quite nicely. But please tell me, miss, is that your notion of a modest neckline?"

"Goodness, Mama, I hope you don't mean you disapprove. Sissie says absolutely that's the way they're wearing them abroad."

Mab flapped a hand. "Bother abroad."

Posie laughed, that merry, rippling sound that was part Minnie's, part Aurora's. "Mother darling, I'll soon be eighteen and quite grown up. Before you know it I'll have two or three beaux. Besides—please don't scold me today. I need to talk to you about something."

"Very well, what is it?" Mab untied her apron and hung it on the hook.

"It's about Sissie."

Mab was instantly alarmed. "Oh dear, don't tell me, has something else happened?"

"No, no, but—" Posie's face held that combination of gravity and earnestness her mother knew so well. "But what do you suppose she's going to do now?"

"Do? Why I suppose she shall do whatever she cares to do, who shall tell her otherwise? She's a matron, after all, not a mere slip of a girl."

Posie sighed. "Well, that's a big relief, because she truly loves him, you know. She really does. I'm utterly convinced of it."

"Oh you are, are you? And just whom do you mean by 'him,' I wonder?"

" 'Him' is Captain Grimes, Mother."

"*Ahh!* I thought as much."

"Is he really so awful?"

"He'll do for awful until worse comes along. I don't care what noble deeds he has performed or intends performing, the man is still a libertine and a womanizer and a dope smuggler and I hardly know what! Yet here you speak of him as though you and he were intimate, the best of friends."

"But we *are* friends, Mother. Why should it be otherwise? Think of all he has done for the school. And, then, he brought back your silver spoons. You know how upset you were to lose them—"

"Yes, indeed, and I wish someone would please explain to me just how it is that Captain Grimes happened to have those spoons in his possession when it was Rose who took them. He has to have seen her, been in touch with her. She left here—with my Apostle spoons—and fled straight to Bible Rock, to that man's arms, I'm certain of it. And you needn't make any excuses for either of them."

"No, Mama," Posie returned quietly, touching her mother's cheek. It hadn't been easy for Posie to forget Rose Mills. Privately she had wondered what destiny had in store for Rose. Would she fall into the depraved sinks of New York's Five Points or would she somehow triumph over her past? While she could not tell, Posie hoped for the latter. Now she said, "But that was before Sinjin knew Sissie was back. He's turning over a new leaf, Mama, truly. He's promised me."

Mab shook her head despairingly. "A new leaf, is it? Since when? And when, pray tell, did he make you this promise?"

"Two days ago, mother. We met—accidentally, sort of . . ."

Mab drew breath, mentally arming herself. "Persephone Talcott, you had best come along with your mother—take care, don't catch your dress on that nail. If we are going to have this conversation we must go some place where we shan't be overheard."

Taking Posie's hand Mab led her from the shed to the pheasant coop on the far side of the house. "Now, miss, I want you to listen very carefully to what your mother has to say."

"Yes, ma'am."

"You know your father doesn't like you having anything to do with any Grimes. And that's just to start with. Don't interrupt me, please, I have not finished. Secondly, let me say again, I have no personal objection to the captain, if it comes to that. Indeed, he may be the Star in the East for all of me, but he is on the face of it also a reprobate, a drunkard, and certainly no respecter of a lady's virtue. Moreover, he hasn't a farthing to his name, and I doubt he ever will, at least until his grandmother dies—*tt tt tt!* Allow me to finish please before you interrupt—and he is a far cry from a suitable mate for your sister, or indeed for any well-brought-up female of good family. In addition to which, your sister is still in mourning and is not eligible to accept the suit of any man, no matter who he may be—wait please, I am not finished speaking yet. She has many things troubling her, as anyone might expect. She appears to be finding peace of mind through her devotions, though, and I thank God that she has made confession and taken communion. Moreover, she has mentioned nary a word about your precious Captain Grimes since the evening he came to this house uninvited, and I seriously doubt that she has any intention of seeing him again. Now, miss, I see by your expression that you disagree. Why?"

"Because." Posie could not bring herself to mention the fact that Aurora had already secretly encountered Sinjin on the picnic, an arrangement concerning which Posie now felt some guilt.

"Because what?" Mab asked.

"Because he loves her. He's told me so, and she loves him, too, I know she does! Mother, think carefully—he's never married, you realize that, don't you? He couldn't, you see, because he loved Sissie so much, and he just kept hoping that—well, he just kept hoping, like good men with faithful hearts do. It was the feud, you see, but you've said yourself all that business is just foolishness. I've heard you a million times. As for the conventions, you don't give a snap for them and you never have."

"Throw the birds some seed, dearie. Though why your father wants to ornament the place with those screeching creatures—every time I hear one I think someone's been murdered. And please don't speak so declaratively, it shows a lack of form. Now come along, please, we're done here and I need to sit down." She abandoned the pheasants and presently was moving laboriously up the terrace steps. "No, don't help me, I'm quite capable of making my own way." She drew her chair out of the sun and sat down, trying to disguise her breathlessness and fatigue. "Now, dearie, may we dispense with this troubling subject, or have you more to say?"

Posie smiled and caressed the back of her mother's hand. "Mother dearest, do you remember when Father was courting you—down at Stonington?"

"I remember," Mab said tartly. "How should I forget?"

"Of course you haven't forgotten, Mother. But remembering how Granddaddy wouldn't have you, and Grandfather Riley was set against Father—what would you have done if they'd both said no to you? You'd have eloped, wouldn't you? You'd have run off and married Father because that was your heart's desire and you knew no other man would do. Isn't that so?"

"I should hope to tell an Orangeman!" Mab exclaimed fervently. "I wouldn't have listened to Pa or Granddaddy or anyone else. You're right, dearie, I'd have gone anywhere with your father, done anything he asked, lived any way I was forced to. I'd never have given him up, never!"

"Of course you wouldn't!" Posie said triumphantly. "You'd have been miserable for the rest of your life if you hadn't married Papa. Then doesn't it follow that perhaps you could try to sway him to our way of thinking? Then you and I together could help make Sissie happy, far happier than she's been—or is now."

Mab was affronted. "Persephone Talcott, sometimes you surprise me. There is one thing I'm afraid you haven't learned, but you must, and quickly too. Do you know what comes of people meddling in other people's affairs? *Trouble* is what comes of it, and you must stop doing it! Now and in future." She shut her eyes as her fingers palpated the gnawing pain in her abdomen. She opened them again very quickly, then, with a moan, flung her arms around Posie's waist and drew her down beside her.

"My little Po-Peep, my darling child. You are my youngest, my very youngest girl, you will always be my baby. I know you're nearly grown, you are almost a woman, you have your whole beautiful life before you—a splendid and happy life. Only—dearest child, I beg you, be careful. Life is not easy, it is full of peril. We never know, no one does. Things can go so terribly wrong."

"Yes, Mama, as they have for Sissie! She's trying so hard to be gay, it breaks my heart to see her. Doesn't she deserve every chance for happiness? Doesn't she, Mama?"

"Of course she does. I pray every day she may be made happy."

"Then he's the man to do it."

"Oh my sweet child, how young you are, how can you know anything of these matters?"

"I don't know—but I do, Mama, I do. Sinjin could help her."

"Could he? I am far from convinced of that. But—" She hesitated, then went on. "If her heart is set on him, as you insist it is, why then, she shall have him with my blessing."

"And Papa's as well?"

"All things in their own time, dearie. If God desires your father to agree to this union—and please to note I say '*if*'—then God will tell him so. And *that,* my chuck, is all your mother cares to say on the matter. Now, do go and ask Miss Simms to raise your bosom line a trifle; people will take you for a lady of easy virtue, and think what a scandal that would be."

. . .

AT THE same moment Posie had been trying to entice her mother into agreeing to the captain's suitability where Aurora was concerned, the principal subject of their talk lay sprawled in the noonday shade of a leafy tree in the Ancient Burying Ground, attempting the composition of a sonnet. Neither the rhyme scheme nor the sense of his lines was going well, and, exasperated by the failure of his muse, he flung himself back against the tree trunk and plucked at the dandelions gone to seed around the grave site— which, as it happened, was not so very distant from a certain broken table stone. But today Rose Mills was far from his thoughts, as in his distracted gaze Aurora's features continued to replace the clock face on the steeple tower.

Presently he spied Posie Talcott, creeping out of the tangle of honeysuckle beyond the Rise, advancing stealthily, tombstone by tombstone, to come upon him unawares. He closed his eyes and waited, then, when he felt a tickle in his nose he reached out and seized her wrist.

"What d'you mean, disturbing my rest?" he demanded gruffly.

"Oh no, I saw—you weren't asleep."

How like her sister she was, the eyes, lips, hair, voice; entrancing counterfeit. "I was wooing the muse."

"Really." Her look was sly. "Perhaps that may save you wooing elsewhere."

But he was impatient. "Well, did you bring me any message?"

Posie shook her head. "No," she said apologetically, and gave him back his note. "She wouldn't open it."

"What am I to do?" he groaned, tearing it in half.

"I don't think you should take it to heart," Posie advised sensibly, sitting down beside him and daintily arranging her skirts about her ankles.

"If I don't, who will?" he said. "What is she doing?"

The tip of Posie's tongue was caught in the corner of her mouth. "Reading," she said.

"What does she read? Not my verse, surely."

"Oh, no!" The corners of her mouth deliciously curled, just the way her sister's did. "Did you and Sissie make love last night?"

He froze, tried to look amazed; failed; was amazed.

"Good God, I'm sure I don't know what you mean."

"Yes you do. She came home very late from church. And she had straw on her skirts. Please tell me."

"Posie, my very dear young lady, you are still a girl, while your sister and I are adults. You're far too young—"

"I'm not as naive as you think, Captain—and a lot of others, too, Mama included. I know a good bit about . . . things. Rose told me. I know everyone's angry at her, but sometimes people do odd things when they're in love. Love unrequited is a tragedy, even if you're a darky. But, if you did make love to Rora, if you and she got the jitters—"

"Jitters?" He could hardly believe what he was hearing. "Did you pick that up from Rose, too?"

She nodded and artlessly began to share with him the substance if not the sum of her topical discussions with Rose concerning the art of lovemaking as practiced in the purlieus of Laceyville, South Carolina. But talk of Rose made him scowl and he cut her off.

"Very well, we were at the mill last night, we did—get the jitters—your word. Satisfied?"

"I suppose. More or less. But you're not satisfied, are you? Nor Sissie. If you care to know what I think, she's decided it was a wrong thing to have done. She's ashamed. And she's also afraid. But . . ." Her voice trailed off in speculation.

"But what?" he demanded.

"I think she enjoyed herself."

"Did she say so?"

"No-o-o, not in so many words, but I can tell. She has a 'look.' "

"What sort of look?"

"Oh-h—just a look. Sort of dreamy, you know. Sissie needs to be loved."

"Yes, but does she love me?"

"I think she loves you very much, perhaps even more than she realizes. But she has to resolve matters—in her own mind—without help. There are certain flowers, you know, step on them and they're dead. Others you can trample cruelly but they still spring up fresh and new. Sissie's like that, I think. She just needs time. So try to be patient, won't you? Try to. You've gone this long. And—" She paused, thinking, then went on. "If you were to write a poem, I could perhaps slip it into *Emma* in place of Sissie's bookmark. She'd open the page and there'd be your verse."

"What about?"

"Perhaps a flower? Daisies are nice, I think, she's fond of daisies. Or maybe sunflowers, they're humble but they're lighthearted—you might get her to smile a little. Or rosemary. That's for remembrance, you know."

"But Po, if she won't even open my notes and won't see me—"

"She will . . ."

"When?"

"Perhaps when you get back from your next voyage."

"But that's not for months—I can't sail before mid-November."

"So much the better. More time to think."

As she went off down the other side of the Fathers' Rise, Sinjin disposed himself to take her advice in the matter of the verses. But he had not managed even to decide upon his subject when his solitude was again interrupted, this time by a figure of sufficiently intimidating appearance that he instantly sprang to his feet, upsetting his inkpot, to stare speechlessly at Posie's mother.

"Captain Grimes," Mab began, "you'll pardon this intrusion while you're hard at your day's labors, but I wish a word, thank you very much." She gave him a short keen look. "Posie's been with you again."

"Mrs. Talcott—"

She flung up a peremptory hand. "You needn't bother with subterfuge. I wasn't born yesterday—I know what's going on around me, though I probably seem blind as a brick bat to you. Heaven knows what thoughts you have spinning around in that wicked head of yours."

Quelling his injured sense of pride and the desire to be heard out, he bowed his head before the onslaught of her words.

"Indeed, sir, you do well to hang your head," she went on. "The pretty kettle of fish that you've cooked. Oh, you've a winning way to you, I'll grant you that—but what I want to know is, do you intend making mere milkmaid's sport with my girl or are your intentions regarding her honorable? Come, don't stand there twiddling your thumbs."

He was forced to grin at her. "You sound just like my grandmother. She likes chiding me, telling me to keep silent one moment, the next to speak up and be heard."

"It's scarcely enough to chide you, so far as I can see. If you ask me, your grandmother should have taken a switch to you a long time ago, when it might have done some good. You're spoiled, that's your trouble, with your shiny top boots and the swank cut of your coat. Oh, you've fine airs no doubt, but you're still a gypsy by the look of you. Or a highwayman."

"First a gypsy, then a highwayman. I fear I cannot hope to rise in your estimation, ma'am."

"See here, Captain, as you know, I'm not a well woman, I shan't have much longer to arrange matters, and what I wish to know is this: If I withdraw my very well-founded objections, and if I can assure you that my husband will eventually prove no hindrance, will you have the girl? Not as your plaything, but as your legal, rightful wife?"

His heart swelled at her words. "Yes! A thousand times yes! Believe me, she's all I want, she's the breath of life to me, the alpha and omega—"

"Please spare me your Greek alphabet!" she exclaimed. "A good sound promise is what I'm seeking. The point is—can you give it to me?"

"I can, madam, and do, with all my heart!" Impulsively he seized her hand and kissed it, then pressed it against his chest. "And do you promise too?"

She scowled. "You're a scoundrel, Dick Grimes, and frankly I'd rather see the girl married to almost anybody but you. But Posie has sent in a good report on your character, and since I see there's little hope beyond letting you have your way, I've decided to give you leave to pay court—if and when the party in question is so inclined."

"And when will that be, please?"

Mab's laugh sounded through the graveyard. "When, you ask? I've no answer for you there, Captain, sorry. Wait and see." She poked her chin up at him and her eyes danced. "I bid you good day, then." She started to push him away, then whirled with a suddenness that took him aback. "But *love* her, man," she said, gripping his shoulders with her hands. *"Love her!"*

She stepped back breathlessly, her body trembling with emotion. "And for pity's sake get yourself barbered! You look like a Greek," she added as she turned and carefully made her way back the way she'd come.

Like a boy Sinjin jumped and clicked his heels between the table stones of the Fathers' Rise. "By the hairy tail of the yellow god!" he swore. "There's a mother-in-law for a fellow!" and picking up his things he ran down the slope to the cemetery gates. Eighty seconds later he was sitting under a steaming towel, getting his face shaved while composing a tender ode to a daisy.

THE daisy verses were wasted, however, and went unread by their intended recipient. One day passed, then a second, and with its close the alarming news that Aurora had left town.

"Just for a little," Posie told the fretting Sinjin. "She'll be back." Priam, she explained, had been urging his grieving sister to accept an invitation from the Ingolls family to visit them at Nahant—a change might do her good, he had declared, and Asher was due for some time off. He could take her sailing. Posie didn't have to add that Priam was matchmaking—after all, as he had put it to Appleton within Posie's hearing, what could be more "suitable" than "keeping the business in the family?"

Sinjin swallowed the angry curses that rose to his lips. Sailing with Asher Ingolls! He didn't know what to think. Inclined to get drunk and start a brawl with someone, just to keep his oar in, instead he called out Mat Kindu for a sparring session on the side lawn.

By week's end Posie reported that her sister, bored with sailing, had turned her back on Nahant and gone coaching off to Maine, followed by a ubiquitous Mr. Ingolls.

"Will she have him, do you think?" Sinjin asked Posie.

"Oh, I'm sure she means to have you. Asher's so stuffy." Besides, she added, Sissie was in mourning and could not be freely courted. And after all, what did they know of love at Bar Harbor or at Bangor or at Bath?

PART SIX

A Plague on Both Your Houses

32

The Plots Thicken

FOR GEORGIANA, HERMIE'S quest for honey had been no more than the briefest of respites. Whatever had passed between Sinjin and Aurora that day—and Georgiana assured herself *something* had—it was none of her affair. Nor had she caught any hint of their secret meeting at Grimes Mill; still she wished them both well and hoped that things might somehow be happily concluded for them, if that was what they wanted. Aurora's sudden leavetaking and Sinjin's subsequent funk at learning of her defection were indicative of how unpromising the existing situation was, and Georgiana confessed, to herself if not to him, that it would take a good deal more than mere wishing to resolve matters in anything close to a satisfactory way. Meanwhile, her utmost energies and attention continued to be focused on the school.

Two days after Aurora's departure another attack occurred that seemed more fraught with menace than all that had come before. It happened to be Priam's thirty-third birthday, and by way of celebration in the evening all of Appleton's family excepting Mab had gone to supper in Hartford. Since Sinjin's return from his sojourn at Bible Rock and his fateful confrontation in the study with Aurora, Georgiana had had blessed little time to visit with her former mistress, and now she took the opportunity to spend an hour or two alone with her at Kingdom Come. She was just on her way there, passing along March Street, when she noticed three or four men who had exited the Headless Anne sidling down the opposite side of the street as she walked, as if they were keeping track of her movements. The men were still in view when Trubey admitted her at Number 17, though as soon as the door closed Georgiana, peeking through the side lights, saw them scurry off into the dark.

Upstairs, she sat at Mab's bedside talking quietly for a period; Mab found the conversation amusing, particularly Georgiana's anecdote about Georgie Haverstraw and his brother, Darcy, who, rolling tar balls from the tar barrel in the cooper's side yard, had got the stuff stuck in their hair so that Helen had had to take her shears to them. Though she didn't know the Haverstraws at all well, Mab had seen the boys, who sometimes played with Jeffrey-Amherst Priest and Burdy's boy Snowy.

Mab's side annoyed her from lying on it, and Georgiana helped her alter her position and fattened the squashed pillows. Then, in order not to tire her with further conversation, Georgiana opened the book Posie had been reading to her mother and picked up the thread of *Sense and Sensibility*. Before she knew it the clock had struck eight, then the half hour; suddenly Mab straightened against her pillows, cocking an ear.

"Now what's that?" she inquired, cutting Georgiana off in mid-sentence. A low but audible rumble of voices could be heard coming from the street. Georgiana slipped over to the window where she made out a knot of dark figures advancing toward the house. Several appeared to be carrying something among them. The group soon passed beyond her angle of view, but the sound of their voices grew louder and she could hear the front gates being hammered on, then banged open.

"What is it?" Mab fretted. "What's happening down there? Is there going to be trouble?"

In vain, Georgiana tried to calm Mab's fears, then, extracting her promise to remain in bed, hurried downstairs. In the front hall she encountered Judah, Halley, and Trubey, huddled together behind the front door whispering anxiously among themselves. Georgiana dispatched Trubey to stay with her mistress, then joined the others. A noisy crowd had broached the gates and spread out across the front lawn, some trampling the flower beds as others went about erecting on Granddaddy's turf a wooden gibbet, from which dangled a rope whose end formed a noose. In moments this noose was knotted about the neck of a crudely contrived effigy, oddments of women's clothing stuffed with sticks and straw. Skirt, blouse, bonnet, the figure was grotesque; the boisterous crowd cheered and applauded as one of the men produced a lettered placard and hung it around the dummy's neck: CLOSE UP, GEORGIE ROSS! it read, BEFORE WE BURN YOU DOWN!

"Lord!" exclaimed Judah. "It's s'posed to be you, Miss Georgie. They're going to burn you up before our eyes." Scowling, he moved his wife into the corner by the clock, then, before anyone could prevent him, opened the door and stepped outside. Putting up both hands for attention, he called out, "What're all you folks doin', actin' this way? Don't you know we got a sick person inside this house? Take that thing down and scat 'fore I call the constable. You're trespassin' on private property, hear?"

He started down the steps only to be halted by several sullen-looking men, including Ike Bleezer and Tyler Gatchell.

"Get back inside, old man, afore you get yourself in a peck of trouble," said Ike. Turning, he shouted to the others, "Go ahead, light her up, boys!"

"Burn it! Burn it!" chanted the milling crowd, eager for the fun to begin, and as Ike touched a torch to the straw dummy a triumphant shout sprang

up. Georgiana stared as if hypnotized. It was an immolation of the most vivid sort: the flames deliriously limned the form of the effigy, dancing about the head, the shoulders, the bust, the waist like the blue brandy flames thrown off by a plum pudding, the calico fabrics flaring up, then burning away to reveal bunched up straw and twigs, these in turn glowing hotly red, the wires softening and losing shape, expanding in the heat, causing the figure to writhe and dance as if alive, the conflagration going unchecked until it ignited the gibbet, which continued to burn after the effigy, more quickly consumed, sagged to the ground where it smoldered fitfully and died.

In the open doorway Georgiana observed the crowd, making out first one face, then another in the flickering light, almost all men she knew.

"There's a sample of what you'll be gettin' if you don't close down!" cried one whose face she didn't recognize, a cross-river type.

"Crazy Georgie Ross, pack her off to the 'sylum!" shouted another, waving his hat and shaking his fist.

"Up her skirts!" shouted another.

"Judah, come inside, please," was all Georgiana said, but when Judah attempted to extricate himself he was held fast, then roughly manhandled.

"Let him go!" Georgiana cried, marching down the steps.

"Go ahead and make us, teacher!"

"I'll give you a shake, Tyler Gatchell, fresh-mouth!" she cried, but before she could act further, a small, determined figure darted from the open doorway to speed across the lawn and push its way straight into the crowd.

"Take yo' han's offa him!" screeched a frantic Halley Priest, putting her scowling face up to the Bleezer's. "You's swine t'hu't him!"

Seeing what was happening, Georgiana pushed her way forward until she became trapped in the crowd herself. Both Halley and Judah were lost from sight, but she could make out the head and shoulders of one of the intruders at Judah's side. She jammed her way through a solid wall of men, slamming aside the hands reaching out at her, snatching, touching, tugging. One clutched the fabric of her dress and tore at it.

"Lessee whatcha got, teacher!"

Georgiana felt herself being yanked this way and that; her hair had tumbled about her shoulders, and her nose stung where it had been struck. Still she forced her way through to the old man, freed him and Halley from their captors, and shielding them as best she could from further harm, shepherded them toward the safety of the doorway. Halfway there, however, an arm brandishing a heavy stick was raised up among the sea of hands, and before she could warn Judah, it fell with a loud crack across his glistening pate. Halley screamed as she saw him stumble and disappear amid the press of bodies, but Georgiana was unable to reach him. She got Halley to safety, then hurried back. Now Judah's body was being kicked and trampled by those around him, and he lay doubled up, his thin bones jerking from the blows.

"Stop it! Stop it!" Georgiana cried in a blind fury. "Do you want to kill him?" She lashed out on all sides, flailing at the burly forms of her assailants, thrusting them away, and when they had backed off she knelt by Judah's inert form.

"Judah! Judah—can you hear me?"

"Yes, Miss Georgie, I hear you," he muttered weakly. She scowled up at the circle of faces, defying anyone to come near; gingerly, she assisted Judah to his knees, then to his feet, and supporting his frail body, made her way to the doorway and into the house.

Inside, she helped him into the Pilgrim Carver chair. His head was bloody where he'd been struck, and Halley rushed to his side.

"Judy—Judy, honey!" she cried, frantically clutching at him. "Ah b'lieve they done kilt him!"

Now Georgiana, aware that some among the crowd had followed after her, actually daring to cross the threshold and crowd into the hallway, spotted Appleton's fowling piece beside the case clock. In a moment she had snatched it up and was advancing angrily on the intruders, the barrel pointing at their chests. "Get out of this house, all of you!" she shouted. "Before I use this on you!"

"Jesus, woman, don't shoot!" cried one, throwing up his hands and backing off.

"Hey, put the gun down before someone gets hurt," hollered Gatchell.

"Someone has already been hurt." Georgiana's eyes flashed dangerously. "And if there's any more hurting to be done, Tyler Gatchell, I'll be the one to do it unless you and all your crowd make tracks!"

As she spoke the words her look swung to the upper hall where at the head of the stairs she saw Mab Talcott, clutching her wrapper around her shoulders, and beside her Trubey, assisting in helping to support her mistress against the banister. "What do you think you louts are doing in my house?" Mab demanded. "Get out, the lot of you, this instant, before I come down and put you out myself. This is the home of Appleton Talcott, and I won't have the likes of you defiling it, do you hear?" Trembling with outrage, she stood clutching the newel post for dear life.

As further persuasion, Georgiana brandished her weapon in their faces once more. "You heard Mrs. Talcott, now do as she says—"

At her words, the formerly bold invaders commenced to back gingerly through the doorway; with a grim, contemptuous look Georgiana followed. Outside, they tumbled helter-skelter down the steps to mill stupidly about the foot of the still smoldering gibbet.

After the men had gone and the mistress of the house had been returned to bed, Georgiana went down to see how Judah was. She found him patiently submitting while Halley held a towel-wrapped piece of ice on the back of his head. The blow he'd been struck had raised a sizable lump and his eyes were cloudy and vague. To her shame, Georgiana's fingers trembled as she poured some brandy into a glass and held it to his lips.

"Thankee, Georgie honey," he whispered. "You're a good, brave girl. I heard you shouting them down with that gun of Mist' App's, all right." He drank greedily, polishing off the shot, then slumped back in his chair.

Georgiana and Halley sat with him until they heard wheels in the drive. A moment later Posie escorted her father and grandfather into the house, followed by Agrippina.

"What is it? What's that mess out on the lawn?" Appleton demanded as Georgiana stood to greet them. "Why—he's hurt!" he cried. "Judah's been hurt!"

Georgiana explained briefly, then Old Bobby stepped up and leaned close to Judah's ear. "Judah—it's me, Mr. Bob. Can you open your eyes?"

"Yes sir, Mist' Bob, I see you clear." Judah's thin lids fluttered and he smiled sheepishly. "Sorry for all the trouble," he added. "I would have fought 'em off, but they caught me from behind. 'Sides, it was a lot of them varmints, too many for me."

Bob took the wrinkled black hand and pressed it in both of his own. "I know, old friend, I know; you'd have done for the lot of 'em if you could."

"I sure would, Mist' Bob, before God I would. I'm afraid for the Queen, though, them bastards got her mighty riled trampin' inside the house that way!" His speech overtaxed him and his head slumped suddenly.

Bobby knelt beside him, peering anxiously into the gray face, then Appleton bent over and picked Judah up and carried him off to his room.

"Judah goan die?" It was Halley, anxiously peering from Georgiana to Agrippina.

"No," said Georgiana. "No, he's not, I'm sure of it. Now, you go tend him. Pina and I will clean up here and make some tea."

"Never fear, Halleloo," Old Bobby said, "Judah's a tough nut, you know." He laid a comforting arm about her shoulders. "Do you understand me, Halley?"

"Yassuh, Ah unnerstans," she said meekly. "Hit bring to mine the time he done carrit you all bloody up to Miss Vicky's pa's place an' laid you down on the po'ch steps on that battle day."

"That's right, Halley, that's right. It was a long time ago, but we beat 'em that day and we'll beat 'em this day too, the pesky varmints. Now you go on and tend him, as Miss Georgie says. Tonight we'll bring *you* tea, and Miss Mab, too."

. . .

THERE was a sequel to this ugly episode of violence and injury, one enacted by Georgiana Ross with a daring she did not know until then that she possessed. On the following day, shortly before noon, she left the school and strode down March Street to the Town Wharf and into the dusty precincts of Grimes & Co. to beard her tormentor.

"I want to see Mr. Grimes," she informed the first clerk she happened upon. He gave her a suspicious look, then disappeared into the inner sanctum.

"Can't see you," the young man announced smugly, reappearing seconds later. "Busy."

"So am I," came the terse retort. "But not too busy for this call." Brushing past him, she crossed the hallowed threshold to confront the chief executive of Grimes & Co.

"Yes? What is it?" Zion demanded coldly. "If you have come here with the idea of upbraiding me before my employees about the events of last evening, I assure you you are wasting your breath."

"It wouldn't be the first time, then. And I have not come here to upbraid, but to accuse."

Zion drew back in his chair. "Accuse," he repeated. "And of what do you accuse me, pray?"

"I accuse you, Zion Grimes, of instigating that incident, which very nearly ended in a man's life being lost."

Zion presumed to smile, a chilly business. "My dear young woman," he began, unfolding himself from his chair, "truly, I have no time to listen to a pack of unfounded accusations that have nothing to do with me or mine. I suggest you take them elsewhere. I have work to do."

"Do you pretend that the men who burnt an effigy on Appleton Talcott's doorstep were not doing your dirty work?"

Zion bristled. "See here, young woman, if you hope to lay such lamentable acts at my door, you are bound to be disappointed. I know nothing of such matters, I assure you, nor of those who committed them. If you are not careful you will find yourself with a suit for slander on your hands, and I wonder if you'll know what to do with that."

"I'll know well enough. In fact, such a suit would nicely balance the one that will be brought against you, Deacon."

"Yes?" His brows shot up and he spoke as though from Olympian heights. "And what suit might that be?"

"A suit brought in a court of law to establish a matter of paternity."

At the word all traces of Zion's lofty manner vaporized. He covered his brow with one hand and dropped his head. "I don't know what you're talking about."

"I think you know exactly what I'm talking about."

Catching sight of the clerk, eavesdropping outside the door, Zion bellowed at him to be gone, and angrily slammed the open door in his face. Then, turning back to his uninvited guest, he demanded to know what she was insinuating.

"I insinuate nothing; I speak the truth."

"Truth! Bah! Gibberish, it's all gibberish!"

"No it's not. Why won't you admit it? Admit who you are. Say the words. Say them to my face."

Zion's eyes began to bulge and he licked dry lips. "Get out! Get out of here!" He marched angrily to the door and was on the point of flinging it open again when Georgiana's next words froze him.

"Not until I hear it from your own mouth that you are my father."

"This is disgusting! Wherever have you got such a vile and ridiculous notion? Your father was Tom Ross, the miller! Everybody knows that! He died mad, mad! And it now appears that you are every bit as mad as he!"

"Tom Ross was not my father and you know it. You and your father Abednego paid him to marry my mother because—"

"Stop it this instant! I won't have it! Lies, all lies! Who has been filling your head with such things?"

Georgiana's gray eyes snapped and her chin came up stubbornly. "You'll find out fast enough, if you persist in instigating violence in your fight against my school." Strangely, the man no longer terrified her as he once had, and she faced him bravely and contemptuously with the truth spilled between them like dung on a stable floor. "And if you still have any question as to my 'insinuation,'" she added, "there's your own stepmother. Miss Rachel will vouch for the truth if you like. Shall we speak to her? We might tell Bushrod too. And his fiancée—and Isobel's family into the bargain. No doubt now that Rod has gotten himself into the Assembly they'll soon be wed. But will her family permit the banns to be posted if they are apprised of the risk of a scandal?"

Zion was staring gape-mouthed at her, and no sooner did she stop talking than he resumed his sputtering vituperation.

"How dare you threaten me, you vixen! Whatever base falsehoods may clutter your foul mind, there is nothing you or anyone can prove. I am a law-abiding citizen, I am a deacon of the oldest established church in—"

"In the state, yes, I know, but that doesn't give you the right to do the things you're doing, and then—and—and th-then—"

She couldn't go on. Close to tears and detesting the sight of the man beyond all endurance, she raised the dust as she hurried into the street. When she got to Snug Harbor, she sat down at the kitchen table and tried to calm herself. Though she regretted the vast indignation that had impelled her to indulge in such a rash and tasteless scene, she nonetheless felt the better for it. Zion's guilty looks had been more than welcome, an admission she had never dreamed of receiving. As for any lawsuits, however, this had been sheer foolishness on her part; there was nothing to be gained and much to be lost by going to law over such a matter. She could only hope that the threat of exposure might be sufficient to induce him to call off the dogs, and indeed, for a few days it seemed that this might be the case. Though her notoriety increased—the day following her visit to Grimes & Co. a story appeared in the *Hartford Courant* bearing the heading CONTROVERSIAL PEQUOT SCHOOLMISTRESS EXPELLED FROM LOCAL MERCANTILE HOUSE. VENERABLE FIRM BODILY EJECTS MISS ROSS. ABOLITION SAID TO BE BASIS FOR EMBARRASSING EPISODE—there were no immediate further incidents of violence.

It would have been hard to say, however, who was responsible for this welcome lull, Zion Grimes himself or the special session of the Assembly, which saw Bushrod Grimes taking his seat to sponsor the bill that would afterwards bear his name, to wit, that, whereas blacks and Indians were not full, voting citizens of the State of Connecticut, it should henceforth be deemed illegal in the State of Connecticut to assemble more than five of the progeny of such persons for the purpose of educating them; anyone who undertook to teach such an assemblage was to be subject to arrest, and upon conviction, to the payment of a fine of not less than fifty and not more than five hundred dollars.

33

The Tocsin Rings

IT IS NOT OFTEN that men of a given age or period have a deep sense of history being lived day to day. History is a great wave washing over those same men, drowning some, carrying others landward and flinging them onto the shore where they lie exhausted and panting, while the great wave rolls on, carrying all before it. Meanwhile, something has happened, the men are unsure as to what it is. There are deep resonances, echoing reverberations like hollow footsteps along the corridors of time. Something has changed, probably forever—but what, and how? Change is always to be resisted, the best of change seems always to be the worst, and the weight of the age is felt upon a multitude of shoulders. Restless humans scurry about like so many insects on the dunghill, while the mayfly lays its eggs and lives its brief span, and coming events cast their shadows before.

So it was in little Pequot, throbbing like an infected finger, hot and swollen, filled with yellow poisons. Though officially the August dog days had passed, Vulcan, god of furnaces, still held sway. Everywhere nerves were taut, finely drawn like a bowstring, ready to snap. The muggy, airless days followed one after the other, with no relief in sight, and people trudged about the village as though some unseen hand were clutching at them, squeezing them together in a hot, humid mass, trying to suffocate them. The church bell tolled. Old Mrs. Beady, close on ninety, perished of the heat. Horses dragged their hooves in the dust. "Gwine t' be mo' trouble," Halley Priest was heard to declare ominously one morning.

When asked what the trouble was going to be, however, the old woman shook her head. "Bad. Them mens is wukkin' up t'sump'n. Trouble comin' soon," was all she would say. And come it did, and soon.

From the outset it was clear that the abolitionist faction had received a serious setback in the matter of the so-called Grimes Law. While there were few supporters of slavery itself in the Assembly, there were many who were concerned with property values and what it would mean to have their respective towns "inundated by Injuns and darkies," as the new member from Pequot declared his to have been. Such an inundation was bound to lead to violent opposition, as had also happened in Pequot. When it was pointed out that the violence had been perpetrated not by Georgiana's pupils but by her opponents, it was likewise pointed out that without the school there would have been no violence; ergo, the school itself was at fault and must be proscribed.

After several long days of angry debate on these lines, the antiabolition faction sought to bring the question to a vote, certain that a matter so closely connected with the members' pocketbooks would put the majority on their side. The abolitionists, realizing that this was true, decided to prevent the question from being put as long as possible, in the hopes that their eloquence might change the minds of enough of the assembled solons so that, for once, principle would prevail over the value of property. To this end, late in the afternoon of September 28, Cent Dunnoult took the floor, determined to hold it as long as possible and to yield it only to another supporter of the cause; it was further arranged that the gallery be packed with abolitionists. Thus virtually the entire Talcott clan was in attendance—Appleton, Old Bobby, Jack and Priam, even Farmer James and James, Jr., along with aunts Tilda and Bettina; the Burdins were there as well, along with the Ashleys, the Perrys, the Quoiles, the Haverstraws, Hermie Light, and the constable, Val Morgan, who had that afternoon solemnly deputized Stix Bailey and Kneebone Apperbee to look after things in Pequot during his absence. Sinjin Grimes was also present, having taken on the responsibility of driving Georgiana up to Hartford.

That same evening, some of Georgiana's older girls were working late in the schoolroom, finishing up a special order of bonnets for an important New York concern, a hot, tedious and painstaking business that had to be completed in time for the merchandise to make the New York packet the next day. Originally Helen Haverstraw had accepted the necessary onus of monitoring the group, but knowing how badly she wanted to be present in the gallery, Posie had persuaded Helen to attend the meeting while she herself would remain to supervise the completion of the bonnets. Now, at seven o'clock, the eleven girls, who had been working ever since the end of classes except for a brief recess for a cold supper, were still hard at it in the stifling quarters above the seed store. They sat along both sides of the worktables in their clean aprons, their hair neatly brushed or tucked under caps, their fingers busily plaiting the lengths of woven straw as they listened to Posie reading aloud to them from *The Pilgrim's Progress.*

" 'It beareth the name of Vanity Fair because the town where 'tis kept is lighter than vanity,' " she read, then paused for a sip of lemonade, while several of the girls did likewise. Usually placid and uncomplaining, tonight, because of the high temperature, Georgiana's pupils were restive and inclined to fret, apprehensive, Posie thought, about the outcome of the debate in Hartford.

She tried not to think how dreadfully hot it was. There were half a dozen windows along each side and at both ends of the room, and though some were stuck fast and wouldn't open, the sashes of those that would slide were drawn to the middle in even pairs; but as the sun lowered behind the western slope of Avalon there was hardly breeze enough to say so reaching the eaves, and the room was nearly airless. From the ceiling hung a makeshift fan, a local version of the punkah the colonials resorted to in India—Hermie Light had constructed it from bamboo and muslin and suspended it from the overhead beams—but though young Jeffrey-Amherst Priest sat on a stool patiently pulling the cord, the device created hardly a stir. When the sun had set, the Argand lamps Old Bobby had donated to the school added to the oppression.

"Why don't we all stand up and have a good stretch," Posie suggested, and the girls obediently rose from their places and proceeded to do so.

"Awful hot," one of the girls complained. "When can we go home?"

Hutta Teal gave her a sharp look. "When we're done, Loney Bass, that's when."

"Can't we open some more windows?" Loney asked.

"They're open, girl, can't you see? The rest is all stuck."

Posie refilled her cup from the firkin of lemonade that was getting warmer by the minute, then went for a look out the front window. All was quiet except for the sounds of voices coming from over on March Street: tonight the Headless Anne was active. Down on the seed-store loading ramp, she could see Stix and Kneebone seated in the lathe-turned chairs from Alice Burdin's kitchen, an oiled and primed gun across each of their laps. Like the girls, Posie too was weary; she too longed to be at home, having Trubey give her a refreshing witch hazel bath and then visiting quietly with her mother.

The emphatic tread of footsteps ascending the narrow enclosed stairwell startled her, and she turned to see Ambo Buck, lugging on his shoulder a good-sized block of ice which he set into the laundry tub. He nodded a greeting, then went to work chipping bits of ice to cool the lemonade. Posie noted how his dark, reddish skin shone and the alert gleam of his black eyes. His shirt was soaked through, the blue chambray fabric sticking to his broad back in large dark splotches. When he was done, he dropped silently into a corner and began whittling on a chunk of pine as he listened to Posie, who had opened her book again and begun another passage. Posie was relieved to have Ambo for company; she knew he was there because Georgiana had charged him to see that no harm befell either her pupils or her classroom.

Before long the sound of buggy wheels was heard and Posie looked up as she recognized the voice of the Abbé Margeaux greeting Stix and Knee-bone down in the street. The priest had come to conduct Bessie Willotts and her baby home, and Posie closed her book on its marker as he reached the top of the stairs where, glancing around at the warm humid faces, he offered a greeting to all, then smiled at Bessie, whose infant lay calmly on a corn-husk tick in a basket at her side.

"Et voilà, there's our young fellow," he said, giving the baby a chuck under his chin. "So hot, and he's so quiet, so patient. Ready, Bessie?"

As the young woman prepared to leave, Posie offered the abbé a glass of the cold lemonade; he had just taken his first grateful sip when a crescendo of boisterous voices was heard outside, and he and Posie went to a window to investigate; some of the Headless crowd had now spilled out onto the roadway, a dozen or so, staggering from drink. Not so many, Pere Mar-geaux supposed, but sufficient to make a fair amount of mischief, and now they were coming along the middle of the road, passing the church green and proceeding in the direction of the seed store. The abbé's ominous thought was still forming when they reached his chaise parked out front. Silent but aware, the girls began to gather at the windows, watching apprehensively as a couple of rowdies gave the rig a good rattling in an attempt to make the horse skittish. Standing at the priest's side, Posie watched intently, her heart in her mouth.

"What's goin' on, friends?" she heard Kneebone Apperbee ask. Rifle at ease, he had left his place to wander over to the group.

"Well, look who's here—ole Pegleg hisself," said the fellow facing him; Posie recognized Tyler Gatchell.

Stix sauntered to his partner's side, his gunstock deceptively embraced, for he was ready for trouble. "What're you fellows looking for around here?" he asked.

"We come to see that damn papist," came Gatchell's reply. "Seen him drive past a minute ago."

"What business you got with him?" Stix demanded.

"Coupla the fellows here got a bet on. They want to talk it over with the padre."

"What sort of bet?" Kneebone asked.

"Ike, whyn't you come on over here 'n' tell these two boys what it's all about."

Ike Bleezer emerged staggering from the group. "We got a little wager on," he began. "We'd like to know what the priest's wearing under them skirts of his."

Stix glanced up at the faces in the seed store windows. "Fellows, if you'll take a friendly word of advice," he said in a reasonable tone, "you'll hie yourselves back to the tavern and pitch some shoes or something. Now, why don't you go on and do that?"

"Stix is right," said Kneebone. "We don't want no trouble round here."

"That's just fine, splint-shins, *we* don't aim to have no trouble," returned Ike. "Like we said, we just want the papist to settle our wager." He called up to where Posie stood watching. "Hey there, pretty little gal, no sense tryin' to hide that priest back of your skirts. You jest send him down here to us, we got somethin' we want to talk to him about."

"He hasn't time for talking now," Posie replied. "Please go away." She placed herself even more directly in front of the abbé and urged him to remove himself from sight. "Leave us alone," she went on, trying to steady her voice. "We've work to do."

There was jeering and catcalling at this statement, and when their quarry was not forthcoming, the crowd began a chant. "Priest come out—priest come out!" After the abbé still refused to show himself, a stone was thrown. It smashed a windowpane and rolled to a corner of the room. There was a moment's stunned silence, then a second, larger rock crashed through a second pane.

"*Mais c'est imbécile!*" Pere Margeaux exclaimed, and he pushed his way past Posie to thrust his head out the window, placing himself in full view of the crowd. "What is it you men want down there?"

"What ails you, padre, you deef?" Ike Bleezer hollered back. "If you don't come out we'll have to come and drag you away from all those dollies you're entertainin' up there."

This rude sally earned a blast of whistles and more catcalls; the abbé drew back from the window, and despite protests from Posie and the girls he bravely descended the stairs. When he appeared in the street a ragged cheer went up.

"What is it you wish, gentlemen?" the abbé asked.

"Me 'n' Adgie here just want you to settle a bet for us." He pulled his friend to his side.

"Very well. What is your wager?" Père Margeaux asked.

"Adgie here claims you don't wear nothin' under those skirts of yours," Ike said. "He bet me two bits you don't."

"A very interesting speculation," the abbé replied.

"Well, watcha say?" Adgie Kroll demanded.

"As it happens, I don a pair of cotton pantaloons under my outer wear."

At this intimate revelation Ike crowed and clapped Adgie on the back. "Looks like you better pay up, son," he said, putting his hand out.

"Perhaps not, my friend," the abbé went on. "As it happens, the weather being so hot and everyone being inclined somewhat to relax, today I forewent providing myself with pantaloons, hence, I do confess it, this evening under my habit I am wearing only my small clothes. I regret if this fact causes you any inconvenience or puts you out of pocket. Now if you gentlemen will excuse me, I have a pressing errand to attend to." He turned and called up to the window. "Bessie, if you'll come down now, I think we can go along."

"Not so fast, padre," said Bleezer, stepping up again. "How do we know you're tellin' the truth?"

"Because I have said so," replied the abbé simply. "Now I bid you all *adieu* and good night." As he turned again to get into his rig Tyler Gatchell reached out and gave his soutane a rough yank at the nape. The worn fabric parted down the back, and when it was given another jerk the priest suddenly found himself deprived of his garment. A murmur ran through the crowd.

"So you see me," said the abbé philosophically, extending his arms from his nearly unclad form. "You observe, *m'sieu,* I did not lie."

In the upstairs window Posie, at once furious and terrified that some harm might come to the priest, shouted, "Why don't you all go find someone else to play with and let us be!"

"We'd rather have some sport with you, you pretty toy," Tyler shouted back with a laugh. The sound was stopped in his throat as Ambo Buck came bursting from the seed store door and, shouldering his way through the group, strode up to Gatchell, seized him in both arms, lifted him over his head, and tossed him to the ground. With Gatchell sprawling, he turned his attention to Ike Bleezer, treating him in a similar manner, though to more serious effect: Ike's shoulder struck a buggy wheel, and his skull just missed a kick from one of the horses.

These moves signaled the start of a melee, and the snarling pack fell to, each one hot to get in his licks. It was only when five men together piled onto Ambo's back that by sheer weight of numbers they could bear him to the ground, where they began kicking him and raining blows on his head and body, leaving him bloodied and panting from lack of breath.

Now Posie, abandoning her place, hurried down the staircase and to Père

Margeaux's side. *"Mon père,* are you all right?" she asked. "Have they hurt you?"

"No, no, a bit of sport, merely," he replied dazedly. "I'm afraid poor Ambo has caught the worst of it."

"Take your hands off him!" Posie commanded the men sitting on the fallen Ambo. "Let him go!"

"Not a chance, sweetheart," drawled Bleezer, who, having staggered to his feet, was kneeling on Ambo's chest and digging his knuckles into the helpless man's eyes. "I ben waitin' for this chance ever since this redskin 'n' that slant-eyed Chinee knifed my pal in Gypsy Woods." He gave Ambo another cuff, then jumped up and took Gatchell aside, muttering in his ear. As Tyler listened, his face lit up.

"Hooray!" he shouted, clapping Ike on the back. "Come on, boys, we got us a job to do here."

Encouraging his friends to follow, he trotted across the road and disappeared in the darkness. A second group, having disarmed Stix and Kneebone after an uneven struggle, hustled them into the stable and locked them up with the horses.

Posie and the abbé, each held in the grip of two men, stared while Ambo was dragged to his feet. By this time Gatchell and his group had reappeared trundling a sturdy barrow on which rested a sizable barrel—the cooper's tar barrel! "She's all hotted up!" shouted the ringleader, while Adgie Kroll and the others restraining the resistant Ambo finally got his wrists tied behind his back; Posie, tugging against the hands that held her, cried out in protest. "You can't! You mustn't!"

"Oh yes we can!" came the reply and a chant went up. *"Tar and feather, tar and feather!* First the Injun, then the priest!"

"Don't you touch them!" Posie shouted again. "They haven't done anything to any of you. If you harm them you'll be arrested—you'll all go to jail, sure!"

But Bleezer only jerked an insolent thumb under her nose. "Look, missy, your friends is goin' to get what they've got comin', so whyn't you just get on out of the way before we give you a dip too."

Without further ado he seized her around the waist, lifted her feet from the ground, and carried her over to the doorway, then sent her scurrying back up the stairs. From the window she screamed for help, but though a crowd of alarmed and curious passersby had by now gathered along the roadway, no one was inclined to intervene. Some indeed shouted their eager support for what was to come while the rest, after Ike turned Stix's gun on them and informed them that any who didn't care to watch the fun had better be gone, scattered, scampering off in disorderly fashion up the street or taking refuge at the Hundred.

At a signal from Bleezer, Ambo was hustled across the lawn to the Burdins' well, where he was flung to the ground. His ankles were tied and the tip of the wellsweep was inserted between them. With a sudden movement, the sweep was thrust upward, and he dangled in midair; the crowd oh'd as he hung suspended above the mouth of the tar barrel for an instant before being lowered headfirst into it. Obscene remarks were made amid mocking laughter, while Posie stared in horror from the schoolroom above.

"Take him out!" she shouted. "You'll kill him!"

Ambo was at last lifted from the barrel and dumped onto the grass where he lay, a grotesque and pathetic sight, coughing and choking. Then, in series of swift moves the sweep was disengaged, one of the burlap flower-seed sacks that had been dragged over from the seed store ramp was split open, and its entire contents dumped over Ambo's head in such a torrent that in no time it became difficult to believe that under the ignominious coating there existed a human being. While this grotesque being lay writhing and gasping on the grass, his tormentors, proud of their handiwork, cursed and spat on him, then turned to deal with Père Margeaux.

"Okay, boys," Ike Bleezer shouted, "now let's shut this nigger-loving papist's mouth!" In a moment the abbé too had been trussed and dragged across the lawn to the well; in another he too swung upside down, his form ludicrously garbed in only his smallclothes, shoes, and stockings.

By the time they had pulled him out and dumped the second sack of seeds over his head, a stout timber, the traditional rail, had been brought up and a two-wheeled wain rolled onto the lawn. Ambo was thrust into it, followed by Père Margeaux. Both were forced to straddle the rail, which was inserted between their legs and supported on the fore and aft sections of the cart. A pair of the brawniest attackers took hold of the whiffletree while others pushed from the rear, and the cart was trundled out into the roadway; in passing, Stix and Kneebone were freed from their imprisonment in the shed and herded off willy-nilly in the wake of the cart.

While these horrifying events were proceeding, Posie stood at the window, stunned by the sight; only as the cart's iron-bound wheels jolted hard over the stones, the rabble following it jubilantly down the road, did she regain her voice, crying out once more for help.

"Shut your mouth!" one of the rioters bellowed with a shake of his fist. "Before we climb up there and really give you something to holler about."

Suddenly, for the first time, Posie was afraid for herself and her charges; withdrawing from the window, she pressed the others to be silent and as a precautionary measure saw to it that the lamps were lowered. Then, as the cart disappeared around the bend, a small party of men turned back and rushed toward the seed store. Shouting foul oaths at the "nigger girls" and the "nigger lover" upstairs, they circled the building, smashing every window pane they could reach with their sticks, while in the schoolroom Posie silently gripped Hutta's hands. Over in the corner Bessie's baby let out a squall. "He's scared," Bessie whispered apologetically.

"Hush, hush, dear," Posie said, making her way to the infant and trying to calm him. Suddenly she became aware that the shouting had stopped. What deviltry were they up to now? "Please, dear God," she prayed, "don't let them come up here."

For a few more minutes occasional footfalls could be heard along the side porch and up and down the ramp, but in time these alarming sounds died away to nothing. Still they all waited, no one daring to move, to utter a sound. One—two—three minutes elapsed, and no further disturbance was heard from outside. The silence was more ominous than reassuring, however, and Posie strained, waiting for the merest whisper, another footfall, the stealthy opening of the lower door, and with it the violent rush of men up the stairway. At last, when it seemed no intrusion would be forthcoming she set the girls to packing up the bonnets and hastily gathering together the rest of their things.

"Hutta—Easter, you conduct the others to the Hundred. You'll be safe there until the constable gets back and can take charge. Come, hurry now."

Taking Bessie's arm, she directed her toward the stairway, but as they opened the door the girl let out a muffled shriek of terror and drew back, squeezing her baby until it too began to cry. A sinister cloud of smoke came billowing up from below, as the rest of the girls rushed pell-mell toward the stairs to look. The lower hallway was already fully ablaze, blocking their escape. Their exit sealed off, they scurried like frightened animals to the far end of the long room, seeking one another's hands in a desperate attempt to remain calm.

Posie spun and grabbed Jeffrey-Amherst. "Quickly, Jeff, this way!" She pulled him to the window that looked out on the shed roof and urged him over the sill. "Run to the church! Get in some way—ring the bell, hard as you can, get the fire brigade here! Then run to our house, if Sylvester's around, tell him to come. But they're not to say anything to Mrs. T., you understand? Then get yourself a horse and ride to Hartford—find Val Morgan and tell him what's happening—and Miss Ross, tell her too. Can you do that?"

"I better, Miss Posie." His face damp with excitement, the boy scrambled out the window onto the shed roof and clambered down the adjoining tree. Once on the ground he gamely sprinted off toward the church.

"Girls, you mustn't panic!" Posie called calmly as the ominous sounds of crackling wood grew louder. Thinking quickly, she snatched up the corn tick, emptied it, then dipped it in the firkin of lemonade, wrung it out, and laid it against the base of the stairway door. "Come on, everyone," she said, "We'll follow Jeff," and led the way to where Jeffrey-Amherst had made his escape. A rising wind was carrying smoke back into Posie's face, choking her, and she could already feel the heat under her feet. The acrid smell of burning seeds was beginning to fill the air, and hideous snapping sounds marked the end of Burdin's inventory for next spring. Reaching out, she grabbed the arm of the first girl who came to hand and began pushing her to safety. "Hurry, quickly as you can, across the roof and down by the tree," she said.

"Listen!" someone cried. "The *bell!"*

Yes, the bell! High up in the white steeple under the gold cock the old bell pealed its wild tocsin, summoning help, while down below, the villagers, roused at last, were dashing about shouting directives at the terrified girls now huddled together on the shed roof. Lurid shadows leapt across the flame-swept lawn where volunteers were running back and forth to the pump with buckets, doing the best they could to control the flames until the volunteer fire company should arrive with the fire-fighting apparatus.

"Hurry, girls," Posie cried again, and began pushing another of them through the window. "Hutta, Easter, go and get Bessie and Loney Bass over here!" But Bessie, sobbing and clutching her baby to her breast, had retreated into the farthest corner of the room, Loney with her.

"Lord help us! God help us all!" Bessie screamed. Hutta and Easter, unable to budge her or Loney, rushed back to the others and helped Posie drive them out the window, then followed. The room was now rapidly filling with smoke; near the door, telltale tongues of flame had appeared, eating their way upward from below, while more flames licked at the shed roof and at the tree Jeffrey-Amherst had climbed down.

"The tree!" Maria Coleman screamed, pointing. Posie looked. The tree was a mass of flame. "You'll have to jump!" she cried.

By now several men had rushed up with blankets from nearby houses and were stretching them taut. But the lowest edge of the roof was nearly ten feet from the ground, and the girls were terrified. In desperation, Posie herself clambered out the window and without apology pushed Maria Coleman off into the blanket.

"You see?" she cried. "Maria's safe. Hurry, you all do the same!"

And one after the other they did as ordered, while Posie hurried back across the roof for Loney and Bessie and her baby.

"No! No, Miss Posie!" cried Hutta, the last girl to jump. "You'll be burnt alive! Help! Help!" With a wild look she flung herself into the air and was caught in a blanket, then set on her feet.

The walls of the shed had begun to make ominous creaking sounds, and orange tongues of flame licked greedily at its edges as Posie leaned in at the loft window. Through the drifting pall she could make out the forms of Bessie and Loney still crouched together at the far end of the room. She called, once, twice, but there was no response. Then she heard the baby bawling! In a moment she had climbed back over the sill and disappeared into the cloud of smoke that poured through the window. Soon the flames grew thicker and leaped higher, orange and black, black and orange, and the bell clanged without ceasing and there were cries in the night.

34

Up in Smoke

WITH MAT KINDU folded up in the luggage panel behind, Sinjin Grimes's livery rig rattled south along the Hartford-Pequot Road. Beside him, Georgiana tightened her bonnet strings against the hot wind that had arisen from the cross-river fields, carrying the scent of drying tobacco on it. She felt bone-tired, drained—like a rag doll with the sawdust that gave her form and substance all knocked out of her. It was after ten, and the debate was still going on, though it would most likely be suspended before long until tomorrow. Her mind on her girls, Georgiana had insisted on leaving prematurely. She glanced at Sinjin's sharply etched profile as he sat hunched on the seat, the strong lines of his nose and chin cleaving the darkness, his dark brow furrowed in thought. "We mustn't be downcast," she said, slipping a companionable arm through his. "We haven't lost yet."

He slid her a grim look. "You're right, we haven't lost—yet."

"But you think we will, don't you?" He said nothing; she sighed helplessly. "I suppose it's inevitable."

It was true. They hadn't lost—not yet; but tonight had merely been the prelude to the inevitable, and with this certain knowledge there came a wash of despair and futility. Yet she would not give in, would not give up, would not bow her head.

"I'll do it," she muttered stolidly. "I will."

"Do what?" he asked.

"Go away and start again. Start it up all over again, in some other place."

"You're crazy."

"No, I'm not. I'll find some place where people aren't like the ones around here, where they'll rejoice in my school. See if I don't."

These were brave words, but even as Georgiana uttered them she heard their unreasonableness. She couldn't just pull up stakes and go; it wasn't that simple: for one thing, she'd given her promise to Appleton that she wouldn't leave, and she must keep that promise. But for now, not to think about the school, that was the thing; let it go, if only for a little while, just let the whole thing go. She tried to relax the fingers she'd slid along Sinjin's arm, but she was cat-nervous, ready to jump out of her skin. She thought of Posie in that hellishly hot attic with the girls, finishing up the bonnet order, and suddenly she felt a prick of urgency; she had to be there quickly, to reassure herself that all was well.

"Can't we hurry a little?" she pleaded. Sinjin shrugged and nicked the horse with the tip of his whip, causing Mat to hang onto the strap for fear of being dislodged. At that same instant the bell began ringing, and in its wild peal was the sound of peril.

"Listen—!" Georgiana stiffened, her fingers gripping Sinjin's arm. "That's Pequot!" Sinjin shouted, standing up in the box. "That's the church bell!"

Of course it was the church bell! Everyone for miles around knew that sound. But to ring now, at this time of night—it was the tocsin, the alarm bell! Fire! *Fire!*

"Suffering Jesus," Sinjin muttered and gave the horse's rump a healthy crack. The animal leaped forward with a whinny and the buggy raced along, raising a cloud of dust. Georgiana strained forward as the bell ceased for a moment, then began again.

"It's the girls, I know it's the girls," she murmured. "Please God, let them be all right. Don't let anything happen to them!"

"Look!" Sinjin said, pointing ahead.

They stared as, beyond the trees, the sky was painted orange in the distance. But if it was only a fire there were men to put it out, she told herself, trying not to panic. Don't be fearful, don't—

She half rose in her seat as a horseman rounded the bend ahead and Jeffrey-Amherst reined up in front of them. Straining forward from his mount; he gave them the news that Ambo Buck and Père Margeaux had been tarred and taken away and that the seed store had been set fire to.

"You better get there fast, Cap'n," he shouted. "Those girls may be trapped yonder!"

"Good boy, Jeff. Get on to the city, tell them to bring the *Neptune* quick as they can!"

Jeff kicked out his horse, heading north, while Sinjin whipped his buggy and raced south toward the village, Georgie nervously plucking at his arm, Mat hanging on for dear life. As they sped through the darkness they could see nothing on the road ahead, nothing beyond the circle of the carriage lights, but the bell rang ever more wildly, urging them to even greater speed, and Georgiana's heart pounded as the rig leaped forward and the fetid wind rattled the branches overhead.

As the buggy burst onto the north end of Greenshadow Road the sky was a deep yellowish red above the treetops. They raced past the Talcott farm, where the front windows glowed with lamps and dark figures ran agitatedly to and fro out on the lawn. Rolling onto Main Street, they heard the gathering tumult from up the road.

"Lordy!" Georgiana breathed as the horrid sight of flames reached them through the screen of trees. "Oh my God—"

Soon the roadway had become clogged with a maze of vehicles struggling to get past in both directions. As their progress slowed, still Sinjin urged the straining horse on, using whip and reins but never losing patience with the near-foundering beast. They got as far as the middle of the block and could go no farther. Sinjin flung the reins to a bystander, helped Georgiana down, and followed by Mat they ran headlong to where the flames leaped high, Sinjin taking the lead, shoving his way roughly among the spectators, who broke aside to give him a clear path.

It was a scene from Dante that greeted them as they came up to the back of the crowd fanned out in the roadway watching the conflagration. There was no chance whatever of saving the seed store, nothing could quell the flames that were eating up the boarding, the beams and floor and roof. It seemed a hundred people were milling about, trying desperately to help— but none of them from the fire brigade, which had not yet appeared.

"Where's the brigade?" Sinjin roared at Hutta Teal, who stood clutching her elbows and staring wide-eyed at the windows of the schoolroom.

"The firehouse is locked up!" she cried. "The key wasn't on the hook. The men have gone over to break in!"

"Is everyone out?" Sinjin asked.

Before Hutta could reply, Easter Dawn came dashing up, her features smudged with soot. "Miss Ross, Miss Posie's still in there!" she screamed, pointing at the schoolroom. "Bessie too—with her baby! And Loney. Miss Posie went back for them!"

Sinjin did not hesitate. He grabbed Mat Kindu, and Georgiana watched the pair speed off, to be lost in the crowd for a moment, then reappear. Briefly they were surrounded by a busy knot of men, which resolved itself into a human ladder. In seconds, Sinjin, followed by Mat, had been deposited on the smoking roof, and they were making their way up the slope to the window. While Mat stood by, Sinjin took a gulp of air, hoisted himself over the sill, and disappeared inside.

"Oh God, he'll be killed for sure!" Georgiana heard someone say, and a sob escaped her throat. Then, above the hubbub, she heard her name called; she looked anxiously over the heads of the crowd to see Mabel Talcott pushing her way through, along with Trubey and Sylvester Priest, their faces lit up by the flames.

"What are you doing? You shouldn't be here!" Georgiana exclaimed.

"I couldn't stop her!" Trubey cried.

"Come, please." Georgiana took Mab's arm and tried to lead her away and prevent her from learning that her daughter was trapped in the flames. Before she could move, however, a shout went up, and, turning, Georgiana saw Sinjin's head and shoulders reappear amid the smoke. In his arms he clutched a limp form, which he handed to the waiting Mat Kindu. In another second he had tumbled out himself, and together they were on their knees, creeping to the edge of the roof and, stretched flat on their bellies, carefully lowering their burden to the waiting blanket. Then Sinjin, heedless of Matty's attempts to dissuade him, disappeared again into the burning building.

"Posie!" Georgiana heard Mab scream. Yes—Posie!

"Posie—" Georgiana gasped, pushing forward, her progress impeded by Mab, who clung to her arm, while Sylvester ran ahead, clearing a path through the press of onlookers where the men with the blanket had laid it on the ground. A lantern was held up, shining light on the still form upon it. Posie!

Mab fell to her knees beside her. "Posie! Posie, are you all right?" Posie was sobbing weakly, reaching out with both hands.

"Mama—please, Mama—"

"Yes, my darling, yes, my precious girl, your mama's here. You're safe now, my brave, brave girl." She looked around frantically. "Doctor? Where's the doctor? Help her someone . . ."

Then Georgiana, too, knelt, inspecting Posie's face and hands. There were burns, certainly—but how severe? Her hair was singed, her dress scorched. The tears ran down her cheeks, making tracks in the coating of ash.

"Quickly, take her inside," Georgiana said, then felt herself being moved aside as Sylvester bent over Posie and lifted her from the ground. Followed by Mab and Trubey, he carried her across the lawn to the Burdin house.

As Georgiana got unsteadily to her feet, her eyes riveted once more on the seed store window, there was another shout and she saw Sinjin reappear, his mouth and nose now masked against the smoke by a white handkerchief. A second inert form lay in his arms, which as before he and Mat conveyed to the edge of the roof and dropped to the blanket holders below. He had started back yet a third time when Mat Kindu seized his arms, restraining him, and only just in time, for a sudden burst of flame exploded through the window, knocking both men to the roof, where for a moment they lay stunned. Then Matty pushed himself up, grabbed Sinjin under the arms, dragged him to the edge, and dropped him to the men below, after which Mat himself sailed into the air and landed upright, feet on the ground, while the onlookers applauded. No sooner had he touched earth than a violent, eddying cloud of sparks arose from within the seed store, shooting high into the inky sky to be carried through the air by the rising wind.

Georgiana was kneeling beside Loney Bass, who was unconscious, when the cry went up: "Bessie! It's Bessie!"

She turned to see the terrified face of Bessie Willotts in the north window, where the smoke was less dense. Clutching her baby to her breast, half asphyxiated and coughing, she was screaming helplessly. The men with the blanket dashed to a place under the window and shouted to her to jump, but though this was now her only means of escape she made no move.

"Drop the baby down to me!" Sinjin shouted from below. "Bessie, do you hear me, let the baby go!" But the girl remained paralyzed, and only clutched the infant tighter. Someone was carrying a ladder past and Sinjin snatched it and jammed it against the side of the building; he was halfway up when his head was enveloped by a hail of sparks as a portion of the roof fell in and the entire upper story exploded in flames. Bessie and her baby disappeared.

Helpless and defeated, Sinjin descended the ladder. Wearily he planted his feet apart, struggling to remain upright. He was all but unrecognizable now. His hair was singed, his hands and arms black and burned, and Georgiana, having seen that Loney Bass was carried to the safety of the Burdins', hurried to him. Suddenly, Hermie Light emerged from the crowd, followed by the Haverstraws. The rest of the Hartford contingent was returning at last.

"You all right, skipper?" Hermie shouted. Sinjin nodded and drank thirstily from the bucket someone put into his hands. "You're needed at Burdins', Luke," he said to his brother-in-law. "Posie Talcott and Loney Bass are hurt."

As Luke plunged into the crowd, followed by Helen, another feverish shout went up; at last the fire brigade came pelting along the street pulling the village pump, with Milehigh Jenckes, captain of the volunteers, directing the operation. In no time the apparatus was rolled up before the seed store, the hose run out. Then sixteen stalwarts, eight to a side, began laying on the pump cradle, and in moments a stream of water was playing full force into a flaming window. Others set up a water bucket line to refill the tank, which was being quickly emptied. Soon the flames began to die in the main building, but in moments another warning cry went up.

"The stable's going!" The crowd seesawed in several directions as men converged on the adjoining stalls from which the panicky whinnying of the horses could be heard as flames began licking the board siding. Once more it was Sinjin to the rescue, this time with Hermie Light, dashing through the open portal. In a few minutes Hermie came lurching out again, fiercely driving three berserk horses before him. Behind him came Sinjin, flogging on two more crazed beasts, their eyes covered with improvised blindfolds. He freed them, then disappeared back into the yawning hole. Moments elapsed. Georgiana held her breath until, astride the back of a terrified, shrieking mare, he reappeared, his shirt smoldering, along with the horse's mane and tail.

The wind-whipped flames were leaping all around the seed store now, rising above the crowd in a vast curtain of fire, flowing like liquid from roof to roof of the several barns and sheds associated with the Burdin's Best Seeds. The now-empty stable was nearly gutted; other structures would quickly follow.

Sick at her stomach, her face a mask of woe, Georgiana stared at the wreckage, engulfed in smoke and flames, and began to weep. Hats! What did hats matter when lives were being lost? What did her school matter? Was any school worth this?

"Fire's jumped the street!"

She turned to see Milehigh pointing to where the treacherous wind had carried blazing debris clear across Main Street; the roof of the parish house had already caught. Georgiana could make out the figure of Mrs. Weeks on the front lawn, urgently beckoning to the fire fighters as at the same time the flames spread in an easterly direction along March Street, igniting one tree after the other. Georgiana saw at once that the entire street could go; nothing was safe, not even Snug Harbor or the boatyard. Snug Harbor! *Aunt Hat!* She would be asleep, she mightn't have heard anything.

"Milehigh, wait, Aunt Hat's house—!"

But at that moment Milehigh was too busy trying to save both the pastor's house and the church; Georgiana began to run, dodging, side stepping, pushing through the wall of bodies. Catching sight of Sinjin grabbing another drink from a bucket, she dragged him along with her. "Come, I need you!" And the two of them were dashing along the sidewalk as Georgiana explained. Above them they could see the dancing flames through the silhouetted elms; in moments they were at Snug Harbor. Sinjin kicked open the gate, dashed for the door, and burst inside. Georgiana had been right. Fast asleep in her bed, Aunt Hat had heard nothing. Georgiana shook her shoulder, speaking her name gently. There was still enough time and it would do no good to frighten her. When Hat opened her eyes, with one swift move Sinjin snatched back the covers, scooped her out of the bed, and marched with her through the door. Georgiana ran back for Hat's eyeglasses and carpet slippers, then followed.

Outside, the old lady had awakened fully. She sat upright in Sinjin's arms, blinking in the light.

"Put me down!" she cried, pounding his shoulder. "Hear me, you gre't baboon, leave holt of me! What's this all about? Lord, it's the 'pocalypse," she gasped as Sinjin gently set her on her feet. Georgiana helped her with her spectacles, and Hat stared in awe at the flames leaping high at the far end of March Street. Sinjin told Georgiana to escort Hat across the street to the almshouse, then he charged back to the Center, passing a gang of men racing pell-mell in the opposite direction.

"You women, damn it, get out of here!" one shouted. Georgiana recognized Newt Gill, the assistant fire marshal.

"Aren't you a bit late, Newt?" she demanded furiously.

Ignoring her, Newt began ordering the men about. "This house's gotta come down. We gotta save the boatyard."

Georgiana heard the order with horror. "Don't you dare to break one window in that house, Newt Gill!" she shouted, eyes snapping with fury.

"Damn it all, get out of the way—it's got to come down." As he attempted to brush her aside Aunt Hat hurried up to stand beside Georgiana.

"Here, here, enough of this!" she cried. "This here's m'house, Newton Gill, you get those men away from here, all of you."

"Georgie Ross, take this old lady away, will you, before she gets hurt," Newt said.

"Don't you call me 'old lady'!" snapped Aunt Hat. "I birched you in the schoolhouse and I'm not so old I can't do it still!"

"You do that, Auntie, but this house comes down."

"You'll have to do it over my dead body! Not a man jack of you will get me from my own front stoop." She marched over to the doorway where she plunked herself down, arms folded across her breast, daring them to touch either her person or her house. "Now be off, the pack of you, before I have the law on you!"

"Sorry, Auntie, but until Val Morgan shows up we're the law and we're about to lose our boatyard," Newt said. "Now get out of here, both of you." He turned to his men. "Pull that little toy down, fellows," he said. "We got a fire coming this way fast."

Georgiana felt a cold shiver as the truth dawned on her: they were going to tear down Hat's house for revenge! They were doing it on purpose! Because *she,* Georgiana, lived there!

"At least let us get some of our things out!" she called after him.

"No time for that," Newt shouted back, and as his men set about demolishing Snug Harbor, he himself grabbed one of the broadaxes and went to work on the row of fruit trees at the edge of the property. Hattie and Georgiana could only watch in horror as one tree after another fell, and the mauls crashed through the windows and knocked apart the walls of Snug Harbor.

Across the street the aged inhabitants of the almshouse were standing about in clusters muttering among themselves, and now Mrs. Grisby came over and put her arm around Hat's shoulders and hugged her hard. "Come away, Hattie dear. Don't look."

"Got to look, Mary-Martha," Hat said hopelessly.

"Please, Hat. Come inside where you can't see," Mrs. Grisby tried again, only to have Hat pull away.

"Don't you try to take me inside there!" she cried. "I ain't so stove-in I've got to go on the Brick Farm."

"It's just for now, Aunt Hat," Georgiana said. "You'd best do as Mrs.

Grisby says," and leaving the two women, she retraced her steps to the Center. As she hurried along the street she could see that the fire fighters were now massed in front of the church. A second hose had been located, and they were trying to wet down the steeple to keep it from catching fire. Though the fierce intensity of the flames seemed to have slackened somewhat, the blaze was still an inferno.

Georgiana stood at the roadside, raised on tiptoe, peering desperately among the crowd, searching for Appleton, for Old Bobby, for someone of the Talcott party. Where were they? Why hadn't the Yellow Pumpkin arrived? Surely they should have been here by now. Almost everyone else had returned. She could see Warren and Alice Burdin standing as if rooted in the road, staring in stupefaction at the ruins of their seed business, and she was just crossing the road to be with them when her progress was halted by a traffic director who pushed the crowd back to make way for a vehicle rolling down the street from the north. Six flying horses with tossing manes and thundering hooves came pounding straight into the Center.

"It's the *Neptune!*" Georgiana cried joyfully. A jubilant cheer split the air and the seething throng gave way as Hartford's famous force pump, with James Talcott, Jr., up beside the driver, came lurching around the church green. The driver reared up in his seat to pull back on his reins, but even before he had drawn his vehicle to a stop the firemen who had followed in its wake had leaped down and begun running out the long canvas hose.

More than twoscore of volunteers had accompanied the *Neptune,* and they went to work with a will, energetically pumping the cradle for four-minute stretches, then being relieved by alternates as a geyser of water drowned the parson's roof. No sooner had the flames died in that place than, under James's direction, the apparatus was moved on to the church, and thence along March Street, dousing flames as it proceeded.

Right behind the *Neptune* had come the yellow coach, and maneuvering her way through the crowd once more Georgiana hurried to throw open the door and help the occupants down—Appleton, Old Bobby, Agrippina, and the Talcott aunts.

"Posie! Is Posie all right?" Appleton demanded.

Georgiana explained. "She's hurt, I don't know how badly. She and Loney Bass. They've taken them to Burdins'." Without waiting to hear more, the Talcotts hurried across the lawn to the house, while Georgiana responded to questions from Val Morgan, whose rig, with Jeffrey-Amherst beside him on the box, had come in right behind the Yellow Pumpkin. Four deputies, with guns, were quickly dispatched in search of Ambo and Père Margeaux, while thanks to the *Neptune,* the remainder of the fire was at last brought under control and the grisly business of counting the casualties began: Bessie Willotts and her baby dead; Posie Talcott and Loney Bass injured; the seed store and the stable destroyed by fire, the parish house and the church roof badly damaged, and Snug Harbor a shambles—though the fire had come nowhere near it.

Now the crowd once more gave way, opening a path for Appleton Talcott carrying the still form of his daughter in his arms. Posie's appearance was shocking. Her head was heavily bandaged, her hands as well, and she was wrapped in a blanket. Reuben had already sprung inside the coach and was bending down to receive her. Tenderly he took her from Appleton, who was offering his hand to Mab when out of the crowd of onlookers moved Sinjin Grimes.

"Posie? Is she all right?" he asked breathlessly. "I must know."

His appearance seemed to startle Appleton, and as he merely stared, Georgiana spoke up. "He *saved* Posie," she said, by way of explanation. "She went back to get—" Her voice broke. "He went in after her."

"We thank you, Captain," Appleton said simply, as with an audible sob Mab turned her face away and was helped into the coach, followed by Agrippina. Then Reuben mounted the box and the Yellow Pumpkin made a wide circle and rolled off in the direction of Kingdom Come, Appleton and the aunts proceeding after it on foot.

"Well, I reckon that's that," commented a dazed Old Bobby, who had remained behind with Georgiana. "There's an end to our school. Up in smoke. A fair night's work, I reckon. I expect Zion and Rod Grimes will sleep happily in their beds."

"By the yellow god, sir, you're right," Sinjin declared heatedly. "But if that young lady's hurt badly—" Suddenly he swayed and put his hand to his head.

"Captain—" Old Bobby took his arm and steadied him. "Better you should find your bed, sir, let your manservant there put you down for the night. We are beholden to you for the life of my granddaughter. I may add, I am not unaware that this is not the first time I and my family find ourselves in your debt."

Sinjin shook his head, not wanting to acknowledge anyone's thanks. Bobby turned to Georgiana. "My dear, will you come home with us, since it appears you now have no roof of your own?"

Georgiana touched his arm. "No, Granddaddy, you go along, I'll join you shortly."

"As you wish, my dear." Old Bobby kissed her smudged cheek, and turned to Sylvester, who had waited for him. As they made their way along the street Georgiana accepted the shawl someone handed her, and together she and Sinjin stood huddled at the roadside until the last of the flames had sputtered out and with weary shouts of relief the exhausted fire brigades fell to the turf. When the men had revived a bit, refreshed by the food and drink Sallie Jenckes had sent over from the tavern, they began hauling in their hoses, snaking them in circular piles, checking their equipment. Little by little the spectators drifted away. In the distance could be heard the sound of gunfire. Someone was shooting the disabled horses.

As Georgiana turned away in tears, Sinjin took her hand.

"George—I'm sorry—" he said hoarsely.

"It's not your fault."

"Maybe not, but I guess we know damn well whose fault it is." He swung his arm across her shoulder and drew her close and she felt his hot cheek against her brow. A current ran from him to her and for a split second she understood what it was like to have someone to protect her, a man to stand between her and the world, to fight her battles for her. She peered into his eyes, so red and swollen with smoke, his face dark as a coal man's, and as she stared he seemed a stranger to her, yet in another instant it was he, Sinjin Grimes, her dear old friend who once again had come to her aid. Then his body sagged against hers, and with a little cry of surprise she tried to support him until, moving adroitly, Mat Kindu slid a hand between them and, catching Sinjin in the crook of his arm, lifted him as if he were a feather. Carrying his captain seemingly without effort, he made his way toward the tavern, while Georgiana brushed her blackened palms down the front of her skirt and headed for Kingdom Come and the injured Posie Talcott.

35

The Moon and Stars Together

ON A WARM EVENING two days later, comfortably ensconced on the quarterdeck of the *Sparrow,* moored mid-river just below the town at the Stepney line, the Abbé Margeaux had forgone his customary clerical habit, much the worse for wear as a result of the violence recently performed upon it, in favor of a caftan of North African origin resurrected from one of Sinjin's old sea trunks stored at the tavern. An exotic relic, the garment was capacious in size, boasting a once-vivid stripe of Sidonese purple now faded to a muted violet and shot with threads of tarnished silver on a field of creamy cotton. Its hem hung frayed over the priest's feet, whose bare toes showed through a disreputable-looking pair of elephant hide sandals the captain had once come by in the Celebes. Covering the crown of the abbé's shorn pate, in place of his customary biretta, sat one of the brightly woven skullcaps of the Arab nomads.

Still keenly feeling the effects of his ordeal, the priest rested in the chair provided him by the ship's captain, who had gone ashore some time before. Two hours earlier their collective ears had been assailed by a noisy, seemingly impromptu shivaree emanating from the Center, after which Sinjin, Hermie Light, and Billy Albuquerque had boarded the dinghy and rowed upstream to learn what might be happening in the village. Twenty minutes before a cannon had barked several times in succession, to be quickly followed by a vigorous clanging of the church bell, and the sounds of lusty cheering.

A sense of foreboding assailed the abbé, for Pequot Landing no longer seemed the sort of place it had been, a friendly village for the most part, and welcoming. Now, thinking over the tragic events of two days before, he inwardly shuddered, remembering not only his own trial, but that of Ambo Buck, who in addition to the brutal tarring and feathering had seemed destined to be the central figure in a lynching party. Fortunately, Ike Bleezer had been persuaded by saner heads from a hanging, and the two men had merely been carried to a spot below the town where they were unceremoniously dumped in a farmer's field, along with Stix and Kneebone, after which the gang had quickly dispersed. By the time Val Morgan had reached the victims—requiring a search of some two hours—they were being tended by Kneebone, and Val had dispatched Stix to inform Georgiana. She had in turn come back with Sinjin, who had seen to it that the abbé and Ambo were safely sequestered aboard the *Sparrow,* which, just to be on the safe side, had been towed downriver in the middle of the night and moored out of harm's way.

All but immobilized by their ignominious tarring, the sufferers had been turned over to the tender ministrations of Billy Albuquerque. First, their heads had been shaved to the nub, next, their remaining garments had been removed and disposed of; finally, while they huddled in blankets, their naked bodies had been cleansed with turpentine, and they were made as comfortable as possible, Père Margeaux in the captain's stateroom, Ambo in the adjoining cabin. Neither, as each discovered the next day, had slept, for the news of what had happened after they had been taken away from Pequot would not permit of sleep. Poor Bessie and her baby gone, and Loney Bass sustaining serious burns. And Posie. Yesterday they had learned that it was feared the girl was unlikely ever to see again.

Ah, sweet child, thought Père Margeaux, and cursed the weakness that kept him from going to her, and to his dear Maybelle, who had collapsed and was unlikely to rise soon again from her bed. Tomorrow, he thought, I must go back tomorrow, and raising his eyes to heaven he clasped his hands and murmured aloud.

" 'For, though I should walk in the midst of the shadow of death, I will fear no evils, for thou art with me: Thy rod and thy staff, they have comforted me. Thou hast prepared a table before me, against them that afflict me. Thou hast anointed my head with oil . . .' " He paused. How comforting the old words were; yet what infirm solace were mere words when a life—nay, the lives of many—had been so stricken, when so grievous a crime had been committed—and while the guilty went unpunished. It was not to be borne—and yet *must* be borne. All must be borne, until God in His mercy might see fit to render matters otherwise.

" 'And thy mercy will follow me all the days of my life. And that I may dwell in the house of the Lord unto length of days.' " As he finished the psalm Père Margeaux opened his eyes again and started in his chair. A shape hovered nearby, having slipped noiselessly onto the deck: the Yellow Shadow, Mat Kindu. His hands were clasped, and his narrow lips were moving as he silently repeated the final words of the psalm, and as the priest made the sign of the cross for them both he saw a warm flicker in the Malay's eyes, telling him that Mat often comprehended a good deal more than might be casually assumed.

Both men turned as footsteps sounded on deck; the thickset figure of Ambo Buck loomed out of the galley companionway, and the abbé made a welcoming gesture. The young man, who, while no less scorched than the priest, had recovered his strength quickly, doffed his knitted seaman's cap, presented him by Captain Grimes in imitation of his own, which Ambo had admired.

"Good evening, Ambo," the priest said, nodding amiably. "Is there some matter in which I can oblige you?" Ambo ducked his head, crimping his cap in his fingers. "Come, come, no need for humbleness between us. We are brothers, you and I. We have shared calamity. We have been baptized in the same unfriendly font, after all."

Ambo hesitated, regarding the priest from under his dark brows. "May I bring you something from the galley, Father?" he asked.

The abbé declined with thanks and persuaded Ambo to stay and visit with him. The half-breed, who had not altogether grown accustomed to being in such proximity to a man of the cloth, compromised by perching on a convenient keg. From time to time one or both of them scanned the river for the returning dinghy, but there was no sign of it.

"I have been thinking about your people," the abbé said. "Our Lamenters, for whom I have come to care so much. I am going to miss them."

"What do you mean, Father?" Ambo was surprised. "Are you going away?"

The priest nodded soberly. "When Mrs. Talcott is gone," he said. "I have come to the conclusion that my time in this place is at its end."

"But what about your work? Will you just give them up, the Lamenters, after all you've done?"

"I have done far too little, *hélas,*" the abbé returned. "But that is not why I must go. The truth is that without the support of the bishop I cannot continue in the work. I have taken a vow of obedience, you know. And so I have decided that, when Madame Maybelle has departed, I too shall go.

I have long desired to visit my homeland again, and this boon the bishop
will grant me, I think, for it is on the way to Rome. It is very lovely there,
la belle France, where I was born." The priest paused.

"Tell me about it, Father," Ambo said, and so Père Margeaux described
the ancient château at Puy-de-Dôme in the Auvergne, the avenue of Lom-
bardy poplars lining the *allée* to the house where his family had lived for
several centuries; the nearby village, with its stone bridges over clear streams,
and the peasant women on their worn knees at their washing and their
gossip; the wide yellow fields of summer-ripened grain, the green vineyards,
the ancient windmill whose tented vanes had always reminded him of the
headdresses of the nuns of that district, great starched sails buffeted by the
wind. "It is very beautiful," he said again.

From upriver a deep voice hailed the ship. It was twilight, but they could
make out the *Sparrow*'s dinghy a hundred or so yards away, and, as it drew
closer, Hermie's stout back bent to the oars, with Billy athwart the bow and
Sinjin seated in the stern sheets. When they were fast aboard, pleasantries
were quickly dealt with, then the abbé and Ambo were acquainted with the
not unexpected, but nonetheless shocking, news. Numbers of the townspeo-
ple were joyfully celebrating, for the legislators had voted to close the debate
on the Grimes Bill; the question had been moved, the bill passed.

For a while the men gathered on the deck of the *Sparrow* were silent,
each thinking of what this would mean for Georgiana. For despite the fire,
she intended that the school should go on. Then, as Hermie and Billy went
belowdecks with Ambo to see the ship's cook about some chow, Father
Margeaux inquired for news of Posie. Sinjin jammed his fists into his trouser
pockets and clenched his jaw. "She still can't see. Those foul, scheming
bastards. I'd shoot the lot of them—"

"*Mais non, mon capitaine,* what good to talk so? Will it bring back Bessie
and her child? Will it give Posie back her sight?" Sinjin remained silent and
the priest went on. "It was a most courageous thing you did. It tells me that
I have been correct in my opinion of you."

"What does that mean?"

"Do not look so scornful, my friend. It means that I have seen you, the
man that you labor so hard to hide. Not once but two times have I been
obliged to thank you for the life of that same child. I would hope that I
myself would one day be able to show such valor."

Sinjin spun his cigar butt away into the dark, the sparks flying in the
breeze.

"There's a trick to it, padre." He chuckled ironically. "To be a hero in
this world a man has to hold his own life as lightly as I do mine."

"Ah, so that is it?" The abbé smiled and shook his head. "*Mais non, mon
ami,* I do not believe you hold your life for a feather; you esteem life. Your
own especially. You wish to make something of it while it is yours,

something glorious. You simply have not come to terms with it yet—life, I mean."

Sinjin laced his fingers behind his head and leaned back in an attitude of repose, happy to have his dark thoughts diverted by this bit of amiable talk. "You're wrong there, my friend. Rest assured, I have my terms. And my terms are that life should bend itself to me, not I to it. Otherwise it's all over before you even begin. In any case, it's not good to think too much of these things. It starts a man asking all those old asinine metaphysical questions that foolish men always insist upon asking. Where am I going? What is the meaning of life? Is there a God and if so, where and who, and why?"

The abbé smiled. "But these are the riddles of life, my friend. Greater minds than ours have tried to discover the answers for centuries."

Sinjin made a dismissive gesture. "True, but where's the point? Few humans live longer than a few score years, and I don't suppose even the wisest man knows much more at the end than he did at the beginning."

The abbé made a droll moue. "Come, come, *mon ami,* you cannot be that cynical."

Sinjin chuckled. "Don't bet on it, Father," he said.

Further discussion was tabled as the supper bell clanged. After they had eaten the cold but appetizing mess Cookie had prepared, Billy repaired to his locker in the fo'c'sle, while Sinjin and the abbé along with Ambo and Hermie put themselves at ease with glasses of port under the darkening sky, in which an orange moon was rising. Now and then lantern lights winked along the shore as a farm wagon creaked its lopsided way home, and, more occasionally, a river craft passed downstream, and the sound of male voices carried across the water. The abbé eased his back and suppressed a yawn, for he was tired. "It is hard, is it not, for one to conceive of presumably rational men passing a law so implacably medieval in such enlightened times as these."

"But are they?" asked Sinjin quickly. "Certainly Madame La Guillotine and her busy blade put the quietus to any serious enlightenment or gifts of freedom the French may have given birth to. Liberty, Equality, Fraternity? What a joke they made of *those* words. Here in America we watered the Tree of Liberty with the tears of the good Continentals dead at Trenton and Valley Forge; in France zealots and madmen poured the blood of innocents into the roots and grew themselves a dead tree."

Both men agreed that it was both puzzling and disconcerting, the way commonly good, kind people, such as these simple Pequot folk, could turn vengeful and violent when confronted by things they feared and didn't understand, wreaking horror and anguish all in the name of justice and the public good. "Preventive measures," Sinjin observed wryly as he lit another of the aromatic Havana cigars that were so much to his taste.

The abbé nodded. "Alas, it is as the unfortunate Madame Roland declared before mounting the scaffold: 'Ah Liberty, what crimes are committed in thy name!' For the freedom of some, the liberties, the lives of others are lost."

"Were you in Paris in '93, Father?" came Ambo's deep voice. "During the Terror?"

"Assuredly, my son," he replied softly. "I was there."

"But you escaped," Hermie stated.

"I confess it, *mon ami,* I did escape. But only by the hair on my chin, as the goat says." He made a woeful sound. "A terrible time, a most dreadful time for us, for all France. Madness—you know of course it was a madness. They were insane, those fanatical Jacobins—Robespierre, Marat, Saint-Just, he whom they called the Angel of Death. I had scarcely ten years, but I heard the stories, even in the Conciergerie, where I and my family had been imprisoned. Picture if you can an entire convent of nuns guillotined for who knew what imagined crime? Simple pious souls sent to their deaths en masse. You are right, Captain, about the blood. There was so much of it that the gutters literally ran red. Sometimes she did not work fast enough, Our Lady of the Silver Blade—thus that most unhappy affair at Nantes. But perhaps one did not hear of those activities here in America. *Capitaine,* you are familiar with that city, are you not?"

Sinjin nodded. "Pretty place, Nantes, fine old harbor. What happened there?"

The abbé's face had clouded. "So you have not heard, then, of the terrible *noyages?* The 'drownings'?"

"No, Father, I have not." The end of Sinjin's cigar glowed in the darkness, like a small red eye. Ambo said nothing, but sat listening, his broad, pock-marked face cast into shadow as the last twilight glow bled from the sky. Hermie lit a lamp and hung it by the mast.

"What happened was the result of an interesting if grotesque aberration of the human mind, I think you will all agree," the abbé said, including everyone in his remarks. "The revolutionary tyrant of Nantes was a cursed horror by the name of Carrier, a *petit functionnaire* who had been carried into the seat of power by an evil chance. I cannot imagine that God can ever find room for such a monster in heaven, so surely he is burning in hell."

"What did the fellow do?" Hermie asked.

"What did he *not* do? There were so many prisoners condemned to death in that turbulent time that there was constantly a search for new, more convenient modes of dispatching the droves of victims. The guillotine wasn't quick enough for friend Carrier; also it necessitated the added labor of digging the graves. Carrier ordered enormous rafts to be built on the river; they could hold upwards of five hundred at a time. The guilty ones—I say guilty, though none were ever afforded due process of law—were tossed aboard and the platforms were towed to the deepest part of the river where plugs fitted into the bottoms were pulled out. They sank, slowly—helpless women, old men, children, babies even, dragging each other down while on shore the sans-culottes danced. Often Carrier had his victims stripped naked and tied facing one another in pairs, the two sexes, men and women, strangers to each other, terrified but fixed in the most degrading and intimate positions, and in that manner they were thrown into the water. The Jacobins called them 'Republican marriages.' "

"And you were there, *mon père,*" Sinjin asked softly, sensing the priest's need to speak now of these terrible events. There was another pause, then the abbé continued.

"I am afraid I may have given the wrong impression, Captain. I was not there. We only heard of that dreadful business at Paris. As I said, I myself was in prison, at the Conciergerie. My family did not drown in the *noyages,* those were for the 'common people.' My people went to the scaffold like the aristocrats they were. I mean all my family, the entire line, to the last man and woman, except for me. We went back a good way, do you know. We fought at Agincourt and Crécy, there were men of our family in the court of Charlemagne and before. The history of ancient Gaul and the Frankish chiefs could not be fully told without regularly hearing our name. All, all those living lost their heads, I alone survived." He sighed. "So many innocents slaughtered, so many thousands of them, all, as you have pointed out, in the hallowed name of Liberty, Equality, and Fraternity. It is hard for a reasonable man to believe such savagery, yet, as we have every reason to know, it may very easily be encountered here in this small corner as well. The cruel and savage beast lurks in the race."

Sinjin leaned forward in his chair, his cigar gone dead, regarding in the silence the gentle features of Father Margeaux. This solitary priest had proved himself a man of profound thought and prodigious human concerns, of the firmest convictions and beliefs, willing to stand up and be counted, not apart from, but among, his fellow beings. In the two days that he had been Sinjin's guest aboard the *Sparrow,* warmth and trust and mutual regard had been born between the two men.

"But tell us, padre," Sinjin went on, "how did you manage to escape the guillotine? What got you your priestly tabs?"

Père Margeaux made a deprecating gesture. "Ah well, that is quite another story, you know. Interesting to some, perhaps, but, truly, it does not bear retelling here. Let us just say merely that the hand of God intervened. I have since come to realize that He decided then to reserve me for another death—perhaps one even more terrible. But it occurs to me regularly that He has held me aside for some purpose."

"Do you mean you are fated?" Sinjin asked with interest.

"If you like."

Sinjin spun another cigar end away. "You surprise me, Father. I would never have thought to find a Catholic priest who believed in fate."

The abbé laughed. "It is your word, Captain. Such a notion goes quite against the grain of my faith, you understand. I am speaking of the will of God. But you, Captain, the evidence shows that you are a believer in fate—rather a devout believer, may I add?"

"And what evidence would that be, padre?"

Père Margeaux indicated Ambo with a smile. "Your young friend here has spoken to me of the poem you wrote. 'Al Qadar,' is that its name?"

"That *was* its name, yes. 'The Fated One.' " Sinjin likewise shifted his look to Ambo. "And what did our friend here have to say?"

"He was laudatory in the extreme. But perhaps we should let Ambo speak for himself. Repeat what you told me last evening, my son . . ."

Ambo considered his words, then began in his even, measured sentences. "I hope that you do not find it presumptuous of me, Captain. I admired the poem very much. Its story was simple and like all the great stories it spoke from the heart about important things, universal things. It seemed to me it held a mystery, too. To me it asked the great questions."

Sinjin looked at Père Margeaux. "Betrayed—I am betrayed, Father. I must now choke on my jest about those great metaphysical questions. I suppose Ambo mentioned that the poem was incomplete?"

"He did. And why did you not finish it?"

"It was strange, you know. Up to a point I felt I knew just where I was going, then I lost my way, I forgot what I was trying to say—if I ever knew. I couldn't decide what my characters should do next. That was the work's greatest flaw, beyond the fact of its being put in the fire."

"Mais non!" the abbé exclaimed. "That is not a flaw, to lack an ending. Many stories lack endings, as do some men. Their endings must be supplied, that is all. It is a question of time, is it not?"

"But, padre," Sinjin argued, "the problem is that everything that happens to my protagonist must lead to an inevitable destiny. For good or bad, Ibn Abd Rabbu is ruled by fate. It is one's fate that clads him in iron."

"Is that what you believe, Captain?" the abbé asked.

"No. But it is true of Ibn Abd Rabbu."

"Is that the Eastern view?" the priest murmured. "I am afraid I cannot agree with it. To a man such as myself, fate is merely a foolish notion trumped up by men for what they consider to be the inaccuracies and injustices of existence. God the Almighty is life's single great truth. In Him alone lies this thing you call fate—or destiny."

Sinjin stroked his chin like a prophet. "You'll never persuade me to that, Father. This thing you folk call God is merely a figment created by poor tormented souls to account for their dreams. They dreamed and then asked their tribesmen to interpret their dreams. Those who interpreted them most eloquently became their priests, and to remain men of influence they had to create a Deity, which is that thing you call God, and I do not."

The abbé shook his head. "And upon such fallacious thinking is constructed the entire house of cards that is commonly called atheism." He steepled his fingertips together and peered across them to Sinjin. "Atheism aside, one *could* say that the whole notion of fate is now *démodé*. It suited man as he once was, primitive and naive, with few requirements other than to eat and keep warm and procreate and stay alive as best he could. I'm sure you will admit that man is a far more complex creature today, he requires more sophisticated concepts to guide him." He stopped and thought a moment. "Let me understand you perfectly, Captain. Are you saying, in so slavishly subscribing to this 'fate' of yours, that you lack free will, free choice—that you are subject to the whim of fate alone?"

Sinjin grinned and tossed his unruly lock of hair from his brow. "No, padre, I wouldn't say that at all. I'm much more inclined to agree with the Stoics, if it comes to that."

The abbé clapped his hands once. "Ah now, here we have it! Regarding the Stoics I must show my vast ignorance, both to you and before our two friends here. What is it that these ancients of yours said?"

"They held that insofar as he is a rational animal, man need not be controlled by circumstance. It is for him to choose the path of virtue regardless of his so-called fate. Are you by chance familiar with the Persian poet Hafiz? He wrote a line: 'Woe unto him who suffers himself to be betrayed by Fate.' I confess, I'm inclined to agree with him. You see, I have been informed on highly respectable authority that the gods will one day make me food for fish. I mean, I am to die by drowning, but—"

"Not an altogether unlikely end for a mariner," the abbé remarked, interrupting. "If such is the case, however, one might try avoiding the water, thus at least reducing the chances of such a prophecy coming true. But where, Captain," Père Margeaux went on, "was this fate told to you? Was it a fortune-teller?"

"In a manner of speaking. It was that witch, the Princess Suneemon who told me. And, later, a second fortune-teller as well. A seer out in China. She reads the sticks—do you know the joss sticks?"

"I have heard of such, but what are they?"

"Tell him, Hermie."

Hermie, who thus far had remained quiet, spoke up. "Well, sir, for a Chinaman, if somethin' goes athwart, if he has bad luck or a bad fate, then he just shrugs and says it's 'bad joss.'"

"Bad joss for them," Sinjin put in, "is simply the whim of the gods. A Chinese lives by his joss, every event, good or bad. My fortune-telling friend throws the joss sticks, yarrow stalks in a cup, and the pattern they assume signifies a person's fate—his joss."

"It sounds to me like a typically heathen affair," said Père Margeaux. "Joss is merely idle chance, a game of dice."

Sinjin laughed. "But whose dice, padre? Do you appreciate the fact that all Chinese regard every white man, European and Yankee alike, as totally provincial and uncouth? They call us the 'fanquis,' the devil-barbarians, and they laugh at us and ridicule and vilify us. They suffer us to abide in their country only for what profit they may derive. I grant you, that profit is enormous, but they still regard us as odious. They despise us and cheat us and squeeze out the cumshaw from us, but most of all they have profound contempt for us. Their own civilization is five thousand years old, ours less than two thousand—if one can really call ours civilization.

"But, believe me," he went on, "if I go down to the briny deep, like my father before me, as I started to say earlier, it will be through no one's fault but my own—a badly caulked ship or some piece of incompetent seaman-ship. I will not go down among the fishes merely because it was written in the stars. 'The fault, dear Brutus, is not in our stars—' "

" 'But in ourselves'," the abbé finished. "At least I know my bit of the Bard. Then why do you continue to sail?" he asked. "What keeps you from staying here at home or anywhere on dry land?"

"Money. Gelt, lucre, sheckels, specie, the unholy dollar. I need the money."

"The love of which, as we know, is the root of all evil. I shall but trust that Cinnamon and your Oriental soothsayer are both wrong, that you shall not go down to the fishes, but live a long and prosperous life—that you shall marry and have many children." He smiled benignly. "And a wife you love, of course. And . . . carrying your notions of fate somewhat further, do you have it in mind that you and a certain person of our mutual acquaintance are—"

"Fated? By the yellow god I do! Of that I am *absolutely* convinced! We live under a bright star, she and I, that star you men of the cloth call Stella Maris."

"Ave Maris Stella,
Dei atque porta coeli . . ."

the priest quoted softly. "It is a tender verse."

"Father, from that first day when I looked down at her from my quarter-deck, in that one moment that I saw her, I believed she was my fate, my stars, kismet, whatever you choose to call it. I knew absolutely, beyond any doubt, that she was meant for me." He leaned forward intently. "There was nothing else for us but that we had to be what we were and do what we did. I've told her I still feel it, more strongly than ever. I can't believe now that we will ever part again. And I do believe each of us has earned the right to be happy with the other."

"I know how much it means to you to win Aurora," the abbé said. "But . . ."

"But what?" Sinjin asked.

"Though she is at present fleeing reality, she knows full well that true happiness can come only with the repose of her soul. This, however, may require some time and work. She harbors guilt and pain, she suffers from a weighty moral dilemma."

"What dilemma?"

The abbé put up his finger again. "Those that are the secrets of the confessional, my son. Professional secrets. But I can tell you she craves salvation, and I believe she will go to any ends to attain it. This is not to say she does not love you. I am convinced she does, very much. At the moment, however, she loves something else more."

"God?"

The priest smiled. "Peace of mind, let us say. In all candor, I think her conception of God is somewhat muddled. She needs assurance that the salvation of her soul in the next world is secured, else she cannot live in this one. Put another way, she needs the promise of Kingdom Come. But what she does not see is what so many others also fail to see. That while salvation may mean Kingdom Come, salvation is also here and now, today, this very moment. The Kingdom is here on earth as well as in heaven. When Aurora does see it, well, I hope that you should marry her, my son."

"But how?"

The abbé wafted a hand. "In God's own time and in God's own way. And with our own sweet patience. To gain such a precious, I may even say priceless, gift, you must perforce give thanks to something, *n'est-ce pas?* And why not to God?" Before Sinjin could speak he leaned forward and tapped his knee confidentially. "You must excuse me if I grow too intimate, Captain, but I could not help noticing beside your bed—*pardon,* your bunk, as you mariners say—beside your bunk a well-thumbed copy of the *Confessions* of St. Augustine. From the remarkable amount of use it appears to have seen, it has been a close and longtime companion of yours."

"I could easily say I found it in a secondhand shop, padre, just to twit you. But I admit to having owned that volume for many a year. It is a tale I never tire of, how a worldly reprobate and sensualist was transformed into a profoundly spiritual man. As for 'Al Qadar,' perhaps just such a thing crept into my poem. In a way both St. Augustine and Ibn Abd Rabbu exemplify to me the story of the Prodigal Son."

"Is it so?" Père Margeaux seemed surprised. "Then you must read your Bible as well?"

Sinjin was scoffing. "Not *my* Bible; but occasionally I happen upon a stray copy."

"And do you pray, Captain?"

"Yes, indeed, padre—often. Every time I curse I pray. Tonight I'll pray to the lord Buddha, tomorrow to Allah, and Saturday night, who knows, perhaps to Vishnu or Kali, the many-handed."

"But not to Jehovah."

"Oh no, never to Jehovah. At old Yahweh I do draw the line. Or, perhaps I am only praying to the worthy St. Augustine, as one reprobate to another."

"Then I shall pray that he may hear you, one reprobate to another."

Sinjin chuckled. "What fate do you imagine God to have waiting for you, then?"

The abbé's brow furrowed. "I have no notion, Captain. Only He may know His will. I leave all to Him. 'Man proposes, God disposes,' as they say."

"But, what if one day God should just up and leave you, padre?" Sinjin asked. "Even as He revealed Himself to you, what if He suddenly chose to abandon you as He has abandoned so many others? Or what if He never troubled to find you in the first place?"

The priest smiled and folded his fingers in his lap. "My friend, my friend, you are far too intelligent to utter such foolishnesses. God does not abandon *us*—*we* abandon God. I pray that one day you may come to learn that God is always there. Always. It may not be God as *we* have decided He is, as *we* choose to imagine Him. He may even be that 'fate' you so heartily believe in, who knows? But He is there. He simply *is*. Nothing can change that, nothing has or ever will. He is an immutable fact, like the sky, like earth and water, like love itself. There is no room for doubt in any man's heart, not if that heart has been sufficiently illuminated. We cannot see the air we breathe, but without it we would die. So it is with God. Or so I believe it is. A man may deny God, just as he may deny his own belief in God, but I truly think that every person deep down inside has the capacity, nay, the desire, to believe. I think he possesses it at birth. It is part of all that he brings into this vale of tears. Considerations of one sort or another may happen along to prevent him from realizing it, from embracing it, his head may get turned, he may look the other way, he may go lusting after the things he does not really want or need, he may even find other gods to worship, but it doesn't change the fact that the *belief* is there.

"Tell me, *capitaine*, have you ever heard it said, or written even, that 'God writes straight with crooked lines'? Those crooked lines He writes with, they fill the pages of the human heart, they are all there for anyone to read, bent lines that in the end are all made straight and true. *Ma foi*, I love the book God writes, it is unending and it is unendable, it is the Book of all the days of all the years of all the men who ever lived on earth, it is now and it is forever. It is what once was, now is, and what shall ever be, it is the sum of all the books in all the tongues of all the nations upon the earth. And if I may be allowed to say so, there is, *au fond,* one ethical principle at work in all the languages, and you will find it in most of the major religions practiced in the world today."

"What principle is that, Father?" Hermie asked.

"The golden rule, of course."

Hermie nodded. "If only it was more often lived by," he said, and got up to lean by the rail, stretching his leg, which had begun to throb. Now the quiet night had stolen on them and only the lapping of the water and the lackadaisical strumming of Billy's guitar sounded from the fo'c'sle. Above decks the men talked on for a while longer, then Père Margeaux rose, saying, "Thank you, *mes amis.* Thank you, one and all. I cannot say how much I have enjoyed talking with you tonight. It has meant a great deal to me. I hope one day to be told that you have gone back to your poem, Captain. I long to hear the end of the story." He slipped his hands into the pockets of his caftan. "Truly, I shall be most reluctant to surrender this very comfortable garment, I have become so fond of it."

"Then you must have it for your own, padre," said Sinjin, touching his shoulder. "Say Mass in it if you like."

He would hear no protestations, but insisted on making a gift of the robe. When Père Margeaux had thanked him and Ambo had lighted his way below, Sinjin called Billy up to hold parley with Hermie concerning the reberthing of the *Sparrow* at the Old Town Wharf, after which, his two lieutenants also having gone below, Sinjin remained alone on deck, smoking the day's last cigar. Tomorrow, he thought, tomorrow. What would it bring? He could hear the gentle creak and give of the *Sparrow*'s timbers as she rode her anchor, and the fibrous stretch of her shrouds, those familiar nautical sounds he had been listening to since his boyhood, when he was only a cabin boy aboard the doomed *Nonpareil.* As he sat thinking and smoking he heard voices floating over the dark water and the faint thrum of several stringed instruments along with the notes of a concertina. Presently a flotilla of canoes came gliding by—a group of young people who had paddled down from Hartford to Hermitage Island and now were homeward bound. The paddles dripped silver drops from their edges and, with the music, soft, laughing voices reached his ears, voices holding attractive, otherworldly consonance that human speech sometimes manifests when passing across the water's surface. The young women's faces lay in shadow, but Sinjin felt sure they were pretty; some of them lightly trailed their fingers in the water. In another few moments, the canoes had slipped into darkness again and the disembodied voices mixed with the lilting mandolin notes floated back to him. He put his head back and listened to the familiar song:

"I sing your song, Lavina,
Sing it the long day through . . ."

The plaintive melody the musicians had played that night at supper, when he'd first held Aurora Talcott in his arms, and they danced close together in the summerhouse at Follybrook Farm. A sentimental, overly romantic ballad, whose memory now caused him a bitter wrench he would have confessed to no one. A sword, cold and sharp-edged, struck his heart dead center and he stood at the rail staring bleakly back down the years with a wound that was exquisite in its agony. Where had they gone, the years, why had he not used them better, why had they not used him better? Why the waste, the pointless meandering, the emptiness, the sense of loss and failure, the solitude that had become grinding loneliness, the gnawing belief that he would never find his own measure, never his true happiness? So intense was this feeling of futility and remorse that it brought him to the brink of tears, hot tears that stung his eyes even as he fought them.

He had been about to go below but now he lingered for another three-quarters of an hour with a dead cigar, his thoughts dwelling with Aurora, and when he at last retired to his bunk he was no closer to any acceptable answer than he had ever been.

"Give me the night," he prayed to his unnamed god, "give me the long dark night to cloak my sins and comfort my soul." He lay waiting, as though for an answer, while the ship strained at its lines. "Are you there?" he whispered; he waited, but no answer came back to him.

36

Elegiac

THE DOCTOR'S CHAISE sat in the driveway of Kingdom Come, where Sylvester Priest was watering the horse from a dripping bucket. Additional vehicles stood in the street, drawn up in a row, for in its accustomed manner the Talcott family was once more gathering in the best parlor, prepared for the worst, and word was being quietly passed through the village that Mabel Talcott would not last the week. By ones or twos or threes or fours, people browsed from the Center along Main Street, to loiter in front of the gates, waiting in hushed knots for any news. Mabel Riley, up from Stonington— of course you knew she was a brewer's daughter, didn't you?—and look how far she came—all the way to Kingdom Come.

Twice a day, Judah Priest would proceed solemnly down the walk to stand inside the gate and supply the latest bulletin of the dying woman's condition. Things altered little from day to day; she ate less, slept little, suffered pain, resorting at last to morphia. At any time now would come the final announcement: The Queen is dead, long live—who? What queen was there to succeed the great Queen Mab? Her friends, the folk she'd known for nearly forty years, came and went; came in the hope she might today be better, went knowing she was weaker and nearer to her end. Aunt Hat, Maud Ashley, Erna Quoile, Bettina and Matilda Talcott, Great-Aunt Blanche, the Griswolds, the Demings and the Wellses, most of the town's Old Guard, all passed through the gates and in at the door, to be received by Agrippina in the parlor and await their turn to be conducted upstairs to the dying woman's bedchamber and take their farewell.

The children had been sent for: Electra and Lloyd in Washington, Minnie and Lee in Glens Falls, the twins in Virginia on maneuvers, and Aurora. Until they arrived, however, the main responsibility for the care of Posie had fallen to Agrippina, whose quixotic character had always thrived on domestic disaster. In such extremities she seemed to change before the family's eyes, so meltingly concerned and diligent was she, so zealously intent on the patient's welfare. It was as though, faced with the misfortunes of others she more readily expressed the better side of her own nature than was normally possible for her.

She could not, however, contain herself where Georgiana was concerned. It had been surmised that with the destruction of Snug Harbor Georgiana would naturally take up her abode at Kingdom Come, instead of which she'd gone to stay with the Haverstraws, into whose barn the Free School had been moved. Agrippina had never approved of Georgiana's intimate relationship with the daughter of Zion Grimes, and she took this change in the status quo as a personal affront. To show her displeasure she contrived to be on hand every minute of the little time Georgiana could find to spend with Mab or Posie.

One afternoon, however, when Georgiana arrived, Posie asked her sister to leave the room so she and Georgiana could speak privately. Agrippina darted the visitor a reproachful look and fingered her collar brooch. She had taken to wearing subdued colors these past weeks, as if to be ready for what was to come, and her skirts of indigo swung as she left the room without a word, pointedly shutting the door after her. Posie stirred under the light coverlet, her face pale. The blinds were drawn and only a single lamp burned dimly in the corner.

"How did you find Mama?" she asked.

Georgiana said that Mab was resting.

"Is she in pain?"

Georgiana confessed that it had not been a comfortable day for Mab, who had in fact been forced to double the dose of laudanum she took to ease her affliction. This depressing report dampened any show of spirit in Posie, who fell silent for a few moments, then said, "There's something I want to ask you."

Georgiana drew her chair closer. "Very well. I'm listening. How are you today?"

"I'm all right. I'd like to get up, though—I'm awfully tired of staying in bed. And I wish they'd take this bandage off my eyes. Is it really necessary?"

"I'm sure the doctors must think so. It's better not to touch it, don't you think? They'll remove it soon, I'm sure."

"I guess so. I hate having to be here, not being able to see anything. It's like being in the dark all the time. Like the man in Poe, remember? How is school? Georgie? Are my little girls behaving? Are they paying attention to their assignments? Do they miss me?"

Georgiana replied in the affirmative; Posie was indeed missed. But Helen and Erna Quoile between them were dividing the time required to teach the younger girls, so classes went on.

"You must tell Helen and Mrs. Quoile I'm grateful. Tell them I'll be back as soon as I can. Will you let the girls come see me, to visit?"

"Yes, of course. As soon as you're up to it."

Posie remained silent and unmoving a while, thinking, Georgiana supposed.

"Po—?"

"Yes. I haven't gone anywhere. It's just that—Georgie—do you love me?"

"Of *course* I love you! Why do you ask such a thing?"

"I need to put a question to you, and if you really love me, you'll answer me truthfully."

Georgiana drew a breath. She knew what was coming. It didn't seem fair that, of all the family, she should be the one to tell Posie the truth. Yet, what could she do? "Yes, dear," she said. She leaned closer to Posie. "Ask your question."

"I want to know—when they take the bandage away, will I be able to see?"

Georgiana folded her hands on her lap and looked out the window, where the flowers that had bloomed brightly along the brick garden walks were withered now.

"Georgie? Did you hear me?"

"Yes, Po, I heard." And then she spoke the words that no one had wanted to say to Posie. "No, my dear. The doctor says there is small likelihood of that."

"Oh." There was another, longer pause. "I thought it would be something of the sort," she said. "Will I see again ever?"

"It's hard to say. These things take time, often a lot of time. But it's something to hope for, isn't it? That you *will* see again? We won't give up hope, will we? Posie? Will we? Not ever?"

"Yes, of course, we won't ever give up hope. Does everybody know? Does Mama?"

"Everybody knows, and everybody is praying for you to get well. As well as it is possible for you to be. Do you understand?"

"Yes. I understand. Well, I have to think about it, then. And . . ."

"Yes?"

Posie's smile was wistful. "Homer was blind, they say—he told his stories and they lived on. Maybe I'll just . . . go on telling stories, as he did."

Georgiana was impressed by this admirable show of positive intent. "That's a good thought, Posie dear. All the girls, even the older ones, love your wonderful stories."

"I'm glad. And Georgie—"

"Yes?"

"Thank you. For telling me the truth. I couldn't have stood it much longer. And—hadn't you better say something to them, that we talked and that I know? It might make things easier for everybody."

"I'm sure they'll be relieved. They've been so worried—about how to tell you. You're a very brave girl, Po. I doubt I'd be so brave if I were you."

"Yes, you would. You're much, much the braver. I think I'm able to be brave because of you. Because of what happened when your father—when those terrible things happened to your family, you just went on."

"That's all there is to do, sometimes—just go on. It comes to most of us, one time or another."

"I'll just go on, then."

"Oh, I *know* you will, of course you will! Posie—I would give you my eyes if it would help you."

"Don't say that. You need them more than I do. You have the school to worry about. You mustn't let anything happen to that, you know. Else it won't have meant anything, all our hard work will have been in vain, everything. You'll continue it, somehow, won't you?"

"I'll try, dear. We'll speak of the school another time."

They were quiet for a while, then Georgiana moved to get up. "Perhaps I'd better go down again so you can rest, all right?"

Posie shook her head. "Please don't go just yet. I want you to do something for me. Will you? Do you think you could? Without letting anyone know?"

"What is it, dear?"

"I want you to bring Sinjin Grimes here to see me. There's something I want to tell him."

Georgiana was not at all sanguine about this request. "Don't you think it's a little too soon for such a visitor? Perhaps you could talk to him when you're up and around again. With your mama not well and all—"

"I need to see him now, Georgiana," Posie said quietly. "They needn't know. I've worked it all out. Tomorrow evening Pina and Granddaddy will be going to the abolition meeting at the Academy. They'll be gone at least two hours, probably longer. And Papa will be with Mother, as he is every evening. You can sneak Sinjin in through the side door and up the back way. Will you do it?"

Georgiana was at a loss to reply. Past Halley and Judah, past Trubey, who never missed a trick? How could she manage it? And to admit Sinjin Grimes to Posie's room behind Appleton's back? The thing was unthinkable.

"Is there something I can tell him for you?" she ventured.

"No. I have to tell him myself."

"You could dictate a note to me, he'd understand—"

"Georgie, no, that won't do at all, really. I must speak with him privately, please bring him. It's the only thing I'll ask of you, ever."

Georgiana went away deeply distressed, hardly knowing what to think or do. She talked it over with Helen, searching for some way out of the difficulty, but Helen was inclined to side with Posie, and in the end it was Georgiana's own deeply felt sense of guilt that became the deciding factor. "If it weren't for me and the school, Posie wouldn't be blind," she told herself, over and over, and when she discussed the matter with Sinjin, who quickly seized on the opportunity of visiting Posie, he became impatient with her.

"Good God, if she wants to talk to me, where's the harm? Come on, George, be a stalwart. Smuggle me into the sanctum sanctorum. I love to look at those white plaster ceilings and crystal chandeliers. Maybe I'll have a chance to see the famous Stuart, hm?"

His flippancy irked her, but against her better judgment she allowed herself to be persuaded to do that which she knew was both unethical and fraught with serious consequences.

Thus it was that the next evening Sinjin placed himself within view of the front gate of Kingdom Come to wait for Georgiana's signal. The clocks were striking seven when it came, a lowering and raising of the window shade in the parlor. Sinjin headed for the side door at a lope to find Georgiana waiting. Admitting him quickly, she led him up the stairs and guided him along the hallway to Posie's room, where the door was ajar, then motioned him inside.

"Here he is, Po," she said, slipping in behind him. "And remember, not too long, please?" Giving Sinjin a severe look, she went out and shut the door.

Sinjin looked over at the bed where Posie lay with the bandage covering her eyes. A heavily shaded lamp burned steadily on the table by the window.

Above it hung a palm cross, and over the bed a hand-colored engraving of the Holy Virgin.

"Posie? Are you awake?"

"Would I be asleep when you were coming to visit me? Won't you come closer, sit in the chair?"

Sinjin sat and reached out to take her hand. There was a lump in his throat as he looked down at the still, neat form under the sheet. A faint beading of perspiration lay on her upper lip, but behind the bandage her features seemed tranquil and composed.

"Don't pay any attention to the wrapping," she said. "It must look outlandish. Like an Egyptian mummy."

"Not at all," he replied. "I'm sorry to see it, though. How are you? Georgie said you wanted to talk to me about something."

"Yes. I do. First of all, I want to thank you. It's the second time you've been on hand to save my life. You must know I'm terribly grateful. I'm sure I'm embarrassing you, but these things should be said." Her free hand groped toward him. Her sister's hand; she had her sister's crystalline laugh, too.

"What is it, Po?"

"Do you think if we hadn't been making bonnets that night, if it hadn't been so hot and those men looking for trouble, that all this would have happened? The schoolroom burned down, Bessie and her baby dead, me— like this—"

Her voice caught and her shoulders shook. He moved quickly to the edge of the bed where he cradled her in his arms and stroked her head. "Don't— don't, you mustn't cry. You've been a good brave girl, Georgie says. If you cry they'll think you're beaten. And you're not."

"But I am! I am!" She made fists to pound the air with; he held them until they relaxed and became hands again, limp and fatigued. "What must I do?" she asked wearily. "Whatever shall I do now?"

"Hush, Po, you don't have to decide anything today. There's plenty for you to do, up ahead. Be patient. And don't let the bastards get you. If you do, if you let them know it, they'll never stop. Thumb your nose at them, that's what you've got to do."

She managed the trace of a smile. "Is that what you do?"

"That's right. Though it isn't always my nose."

He got a little laugh for that. "I'm sorry, I didn't mean to behave like this, truly."

"Don't apologize; you may behave with me any way you wish." He settled her again on the pillow. "And to answer your question, would it have happened regardless, I'd say *something* was bound to happen some time or other. But none of us would have driven off to Hartford that night if we'd had the least inkling. And don't forget, Ike Bleezer had it in for Ambo for shooting at him that time. So it wasn't *just* the school. An unfortunate confluence of circumstances, you might call it."

Posie's dainty fingers soothed the counterpane as she soberly considered his words. She sighed, as if dismissing the matter, and abruptly changed the subject.

"Do you think we could talk a little about you and Rora?"

"Certainly. What's on your mind?"

"A great deal. It's the real reason I wanted to see you—but you know that, don't you?"

He smiled. "I suspected."

"When do you sail?"

"That depends on how soon she returns," he said, and his brow furrowed.

"You're still worried, aren't you? But you mustn't be, it's going to be all right, truly it is. That's what I wanted to tell you. The other day Mama said"—she paused for a moment, a catch in her throat—"Mama said, 'All things in their time, dearie,' and I know she has spoken with Papa. In the end it'll be up to Rora, you'll see. And Sissie will surely come round."

"You sound pretty definite about that."

"I intend to make sure of it this time—what else do I have to occupy me these days, anyway? And it's the least I can do for someone who's saved my life twice now." Below the bandaged eyes the pale lips wore the hint of a satisfied smile. "Do you know, Captain, I consider myself fortunate in knowing you. I regard you as a most remarkable individual. Even unique. Quite misunderstood, too."

"Really? Do *you* understand me?"

"I like to think I do. At least I don't find you the Greek mystery everyone else seems to. Mama says you're nobody's enemy but your own."

Sinjin's look was droll. "Tell your mama I have worse ones." He paused. "Did she say why?"

"One reason is that you go to Bolivia so often." She giggled. "Gracious, I wish I could see your face. I know you don't have any notion what that means." She explained about "going to Bolivia," causing him to chuckle.

"I expect you're right, Miss Po; I seem to go to Bolivia fairly often."

"Maybe if you married Sissie you wouldn't. Maybe you'd renounce demon rum and tread the straight and narrow."

"Perhaps," he replied with a grin, leaning over to blot her brow with his handkerchief. "Now why don't you just lie there quietly and think good thoughts for all of us, and I'll just slip out quiet as a mouse. Someone's liable to catch me here, and then Georgie would really be put out with me."

"Yes, all right." Posie lay quietly breathing against the pillows and he saw how the color had come into her cheeks.

"Good night, sweet girl," he said, bending to brush her cheek with his lips.

"You kissed me."

"My privilege. After all, if you're right, I'm to be your brother."

"Then I'm well forever," she said, and smiled again. He gave her a last lingering look, and went to the door.

The hallway was empty. He glanced around, wondering where Georgiana had disappeared to. Did she mean him to go down of his own accord? Idly he speculated on which room might be Aurora's—in the front, he'd heard her say. He felt a sudden reckless desire to investigate it, a passion to see the bed she slept in. He followed his nose, peering into one room after the other. No, he told himself, none of these.

At last he came to a partly open door. He stopped at the threshold, swung the door back a foot, then slipped inside. Hers, no doubt of it. For some moments he stood looking at her neatly made-up bed, then he approached it and allowed his fingers to browse across the quilted coverlet to the spot where he imagined her head would rest. He found himself suddenly filled with a feeling of overwhelming tenderness. He glanced about the shadowy room, picturing her just there, sitting in that chair, watching out the window for him. As he bent closer to the pillow a heavenly aroma reached him, the room seemed pervaded with her sweet, feminine essence. He had the uncontrollable impulse to stretch out on the bed, to bury his face in her pillow . . . he closed his eyes . . . imagining he held her there, close in his arms . . . Aurora . . .

"What in the name of heaven—!"

He was half aware of Georgiana's sharp tone, her silhouette appeared in the lighted doorway. As he roused himself from his reverie she flew across the carpet and gave him an angry shake. "Are you completely mad?" she hissed, tugging him from the bed. "What if someone should come along?"

"It's all right, I was just leaving."

"I should hope so!" Motioning him to follow, she started out, then darted back into the shadows. "Oh lordy," she breathed, "Pina's just come in." She pushed him behind the partly open door. "Stay here, don't move," she whispered. "After she passes, use the back stairs and be quick about it—go down through the garden and take the shortcut over to the Burying Ground."

But before she could make another move Agrippina came into view, her thin, angular figure accentuated by the flickering flame of the candle she carried before her. While Georgiana and Sinjin pressed back against the door, she approached, her face a waxen mask, hair pulled severely back, eyes gazing straight ahead, wavering in light and shadow. Then, almost as if she had somehow known from the beginning that an undesirable presence lurked in the house, and that she was being surreptitiously observed, she stopped and whirled suddenly around, her skirts belling outward. Her face paled under the layer of powder, and an ugly line drew down between her brows.

"*You!* How dare you!"

"It's all right, Pina," Georgiana said, stepping forward. "Posie sent for Captain Grimes. To thank him. He's just leaving. Go along, Sinjin."

As Georgiana made a desperate gesture, urging Sinjin to hurry, Pina's glittery eyes impaled her, sharp with accusation, saying plainly, "So *this* is how you behave when no one is looking, *this* is how you betray us." Compressing the tight line of her lips, her brows arching as though to emphasize the severity of her expression, she blinked her lids rapidly and whirled again, retracing her steps back along the hall, to disappear downstairs, no doubt to report to Old Bobby, who would, Georgiana hoped, calm her and induce her to keep silent. At the same time, hurrying down the back way, Sinjin accounted himself lucky to have escaped with his life, for Pina's was the Medusa's look, that turns men to stone.

LATER that same evening, while the little clock ticked away on the night table beside Mab's collection of apothecary bottles, Appleton sat in the chair, leaning as close to her as he was able, stroking her shrunken hand and feigning a cheerful mien. Though he had sought to dredge up one or two amusing remarks, he was aware of her agitated state. Something was preying sharply on her mind. He thought he knew what it was, and though the last thing he wanted was a discussion of Aurora and Sinjin, he encouraged her to tell him what troubled her. He quickly regretted having prompted her words.

"Jake, listen to me—it's something we've not spoken of. May we talk about it now?"

"Yes, my dear, whatever you wish," he returned reluctantly.

"I mean, the continuing link 'twixt Rora and a certain party. You know who I mean, of course."

He put up a hand. "Oh Molly, are we to speak of such things now? What can they matter to us?"

"We may not get another chance, dearie, and the happiness of our children must be seen to if I am to have any peace. It matters greatly, dearie, I promise you."

"What does, my dear?"

"Why—that thing called love, I expect. *Love* matters. And you won't part them with swords or pistols and you won't make them forget. Never, never, never. I tell you—"

Appleton grew anxious. "You're upsetting yourself. Don't, I beg you."

Mab waved an impatient hand. "Would you like to know what Posie said to me? You recall how upset Pa got when he found you were sneaking around at the brewery, how he threatened to take his shillelagh to you, set the dogs on your heels if you came skulking around again and I would never see a dime of his money? And do you remember how Granddaddy threatened to disinherit you if you married me because I was an Irish, bogtrotting papist? Do you remember what you said—about both of them? You said 'I'll see them to the Devil's table before I'll give up my Molly.' Do you remember?"

"Something like, I suppose," Appleton replied, absently plucking at his brow.

"Would you have done it then, as you said you would?"

"By Zeus I would! I'd have done it a hundred, a thousand times over if they'd gainsaid us, either your pa or mine."

"Well, then, dear, *my* advice is—lift that gate on Captain Grimes. Try to forget that he bears that odious name—through neither his fault nor his blood—and let him have Rora if she'll have him. Otherwise he'll spirit her off to China when you're not looking and you'll lose her. You're going to be in need of all your daughters, and I'm sure you won't want to be deprived of your Beauty a second time."

Appleton threw up his hands. "Then what, for pity's sake, would you have me do?"

She reached out her hand and laid it lovingly against his cheek. "Jake, just try and make it right, that's all. Promise me."

"Anything, I'll promise anything." He sighed and tugged again at his scraggly brow.

"Jake," Mab said, scolding him, "don't do that, you're pulling them all out, you'll have bald eyebrows before you're done." She used her handkerchief, then picked up the thread again. "You know that Posie has given this—romance, if such it can be termed—her full blessing. But that isn't enough, is it, Jake, not by a long shot."

"What is, Molly?" He shrugged hopelessly.

"It's up to Rora to say if she will have him or no. Lord knows *he's* willing, but she's another story. But *we* must not—*must not*—be the reason for their further separation. Oh, let them be happy if they can, let them try to be happy as *we* have been. We *have* been happy, Jake, haven't we, you and I?"

Again his eyes filled with tears and brimmed over. "Yes," he managed, "alas, far too happy, for now the thought will surely kill me dead. Never fear, I shan't be far behind you when you go, they'll bury me beside you in the orchard—"

"Stop it! Jake, you'll do nothing of the kind. And I've told you the thing that I want—that I wish to be assured of before I die. You know what we talked about—"

Appleton's look was desperate. "Good lord, woman, you're not going to mention that madness again? I won't listen—I shall not! Leave Rora to her sailor, I'll interfere no more in that matter—but not another word of this remarrying business!"

He leaped up, covering his face with his handkerchief, and stumbled from the room, leaving Mab pushing at the gripe that had started again in her stomach. Soon, merciful God, soon, she prayed.

Next evening, determined to see this important matter through to a satisfactory conclusion, she sent for Georgiana, who, fearing the worst, arrived as promptly as she could. She found Agrippina waiting for her in the front hall. "Go up, quickly—she's asking for you."

"But what is it? She's not—"

Agrippina firmed her lips and smoothed the part in her hair. "No, but please remember, she is a dying woman. I won't have you saying anything to upset her. Really—letting that dreadful scoundrel in to see Posie—"

"Pina, please, this is hardly the time."

"I just want it understood, that's all." Georgiana followed Agrippina's stiff back up the staircase. Leaving her in the hall outside, she slipped into the bedroom where she found Mab in bed, wearing her good cap and a knitted fichu pinned across her round shoulders.

"There you are, Georgie, come in, come in, I've been waiting for you. Come and kiss me, there's a good girl. Sit there, take Jake's chair—poor man, he's so weary and no wonder. I sent him off to his club. We can have a little talk, you and I. Will that be all right?"

Georgiana drew up the chair and sat. "Yes, of course," she said.

Mab reached for her hand and held it tightly. "Now, Georgie . . ."

"Yes, ma'am?"

"I am dearly in need of your gentle and, I hope, wise assistance."

"Of course, anything."

"Hush, now, don't promise so hastily, dearie, you don't know what it is I intend asking."

Georgiana smiled. "Still, I say, anything."

"Very well; if I later hold you to that, then please to reflect back to this moment." She considered for a little while before continuing. "I am dying. Yes, I know you know it. It is not to be thought of; what happens to me now is of no consequence. I've come to the end of my life sooner than I had expected to, that is all. I have lived my time and it is done." She sighed. "You can get used to it, you know, the idea. And God provides the strength that enables us to bear that which we must. He always does, somehow. So we shan't concern ourselves now with me or my condition."

"Yes, of course. Was it about Posie that you wanted to see me?"

"No. She does not enter into this. I pray she will recover her sight, but if her eyes are not restored, she will still survive. I know my Posie. May the good Lord love and protect her sweet spirit." She blew her nose and went on. "I am troubled about something else, and it's the one thing that makes it all so very hard. It's Jake, of course, my Jake."

Georgiana nodded. "I know."

Mab gave her an entreating look. "Do you, dearie? I mean to say, that while it's hard enough leaving him, certainly, it's harder still to leave him lurching about in this big house on his own. We have loved each other for such a long time and he will miss me. Too much, I fear. Fine upstanding man that he is, he's still a child in many ways and—well, we have become used to each other, Jake and I. Couples do, after over thirty-five years. Even so—Georgie, I tell you this as a fact, though he himself doesn't know it—not so long after I'm gone he will want another wife. Come, don't look so surprised, it's true. One fine spring morning he'll wake up and he'll suddenly say to himself that he must take another wife—and he'll be right. Just now he thinks me a paragon, but he'll soon be wanting another paragon. He'll go sniffing about hither and yon, here in town or up in Hartford, where there are plenty of marriageable widows or young girls lurking about who would think they're just the one to take my place, but I mean to have none of them."

"I see."

"Ah, do you, then? Oh, dearest Georgiana, I pray you do."

"You're asking me to help find him another wife. Someone to look after him—and Posie."

Mab clapped her hands to her face and laughed over her pink fingertips. "Mercy, dearie, nothing of the sort. What good to look when I have found what I seek? I wish you to *be* his wife."

Georgiana stared dumbstruck. Not a word came to her lips.

"There's no need to act so surprised, dearie," Mab went on. "I promise you, I've given the matter a good deal of thought and I know without fail that the time will come—"

Georgiana stopped her before she could continue. "But ma'am, I implore, think what you are saying, please do!"

"I know very well what I'm saying, Georgie Ross. I am telling you that I wish you to marry my husband. I wish you to live in my house and continue to give the love you have always given to me and mine. Give it to them, Georgie, and I shall die safe and happy. I know, I know, you're going to say, What of Jake, isn't he to be consulted? That is not yet necessary; we will deal with that in due time. But the time *will* come and I want you to be prepared and ready to oblige me in this. And then I hope that I may look down from heaven and see you and him proper wed and I will wish that you could see me too, and then you and I could smile and say together that I was right. For you shall see; I am right. And in the meantime I shall have died a happy woman, don't you see?"

During this speech Georgiana had sat, mouth agape, shaking her head uncomprehendingly, and now she burst forth with, "But it's impossible. You can't mean all this."

Mab drew back. "Do you think I would joke about anything so serious? I say again that you, Georgiana, should marry Appleton Talcott when I am gone."

"But I can't, ma'am, it's inconceivable. Never in this world—"

"Because you don't love him?"

"I would do anything to bring about his happiness, but not this. Never this! It cannot be."

"Why do you say so?"

Tearfully Georgiana shook her head and bit her lips. "Please, ma'am, you must not ask such a thing of me."

"Is it because you believe him too highly placed and yourself too low?"

Georgiana hesitated. "Partly—yes. Yes, that's it, the difference in our stations . . ."

Mab was not to be fooled. "Oh no, my dear that may be some of it, but there's more, I can see there is. It's in your eyes. Tell me. Out with it."

Georgiana folded her hands in her lap and studied her knuckles before answering. "I cannot," she said. "That's all. I can't, oh dear ma'am, I entreat you, you mustn't ask it of me. It would be a terrible wrong. I cannot," she repeated stubbornly; and again, "I cannot."

"Cannot or will not?"

"Goodness, what does it matter, ma'am? Cannot or will not, it's all the same. I tell you I am no fit wife for your husband. He will not want me. Will never have me. I am sure of this."

Mab's fist trembled. "I say he will. I say it and you must believe me. Georgiana, see here, you have trusted me always, since we've known each other. Do you mean to say you cannot trust me in so important a matter as your future—and Jake's as well?" She sagged against the pillow. "If that is so, I am sorely disappointed in you. You will never know how disappointed."

"I'm sorry. Forgive me, do." Georgiana stood. "Without offense, may I leave now, please?"

Mab sighed and said shortly, "Yes. By all means, go along. But, Georgie, don't put this all out of your head. Give consideration to my proposal. After you've thought it over quite seriously, I believe you'll come to another conclusion. The right one. You'll see! Kiss me before you go."

Georgiana did as she was bid and went out. On the other side of the door she found Agrippina. Had she had her ear to the keyhole?

"Is she all right—Mama?" Pina asked with a display of innocent curiosity. Georgiana nodded shortly and fled the house, scarcely knowing how she got out the door. Mab's proposal had, literally, stunned her; that Appleton should take as his second wife the bastard daughter of his detested enemy

Zion Grimes. For that was what it came down to, and it was simply not possible. If the truth were ever to come out Appleton would be made a laughingstock. But how was she to explain it all? How make Mab see— understand the matter without revealing the shameful truth? To tell her, on her deathbed, that the woman she had chosen for her beloved husband was the daughter of the master of Burning Bush—no, a hundred times over, her answer must be no.

A day passed, and another. Georgiana fretted and worried, but in utter loneliness, was no nearer a satisfactory solution when word came that the Queen desired her presence again. It was with the deepest reluctance that she retraced her steps. When she arrived, Terry Standish was just leaving Mab's room.

"She's badly troubled today," the doctor warned. "Have a care what you say to her."

Georgiana nodded. Dreading the moment, she went in and the door closed behind her. Mab was propped against several pillows, looking thinner and weaker than even two days before. Her hair was done up in a meager braid, the end caught with a piece of red wool from Trubey's workbasket, and it lay beside her head, lank on the pillow, like something that did not belong to her. Obviously tired before she'd even begun, once again she beckoned Georgiana to the chair that Appleton usually occupied, drawn up as close to the bedside as might be done, where he could hold her hand and smooth the covers and touch her cheek.

"Well, Georgie, here you are again," she began, summoning reserves that must have been among her last. Even those few words helped Georgiana gain a measure of composure. "What have you come to tell me, then? Are you going to make me happy or sad? I love you with all my heart and being . . ."

"Dearest ma'am, I hope never to make you sad."

Mab gave her a feeble smile. "Well, then, I'm pleased for that. And you'll do as I ask?"

Georgiana shook her head. "Please, ma'am, I cannot."

"You cannot." By way of reproof, Mab took away the hand Georgiana had been holding and slid it under the hem of the sheet. "Very well. I understand. There's no more to be said, then." She closed her eyes as a curt form of dismissal. Georgiana felt shattered, unable to do anything. Yet how could she let Mab die without explaining?

"No, you don't understand," she said tentatively. "Please, dear, dearest ma'am, will you listen to me?"

"There's nothing further I care to hear." Mab's shoulders rose as she drew in a tired, sickly breath, then drooped. "There is nothing for me to do now but to die," she went on, "since I cannot see to the happiness of my beloved husband. I had hoped . . . Georgie, Georgie . . . can't you grant an old woman her dying wish? I have not been unkind to you. I have always kept your welfare uppermost in my mind—"

"Please don't talk that way," Georgiana pleaded. "There is nothing I can say to make you know how much I am in your debt. You see"—Mab had made an impatient gesture—"you won't hear of it."

"I see that I must speak plainly to you, Georgiana." Mab tried to push herself up against the pillow but only weakened herself by the effort. "I am convinced that my husband's future happiness lies entirely in your hands."

"Please," Georgiana whispered in desperation, "I would do anything in the world for you, but this one thing, it is impossible, even if he asked me, which I can't believe he would ever do; but even if he did, I still couldn't."

"Then say no more." Mab's eyes flicked over the ceiling, down the wall, then came to rest at last on Georgiana's face. Something of the old, elfin Mab dimly gleamed in her eyes and Georgiana saw, or thought she did, what she must have been as a young girl, the bride of Appleton Talcott.

"Say no more," she said again, touching the corners of her mouth with her lace-edged handkerchief. The swansdown trim of her wrapper was badly flattened and two or three of the feathers had escaped their threads and sailed upward on a current of air. With a desperate pang Georgiana realized this was the last time they would ever be together, that they would sit and talk and feel the closeness that had existed between them, mistress and servant, woman and girl, for more than twenty years.

"It's all right," she heard Mab saying, "we cannot have everything we want in life, can we? I have been lucky, I got almost everything. Except—" Her voice broke and she turned her face to the wall. Georgiana reached out a commiserating hand.

"Tell me. Say it."

"I only wanted to eke things out until he died, you know, not a day longer, but not to leave him alone. He mustn't be alone. Loneliness will wither him. Then, when I knew I was going to die, I thought, No, I can't be in two places at the same time, I can't be lying there in the orchard with my babies and busy here at home, too. If only Georgie will help me, I said to myself. She will live out the life I had hoped to live, she will take my place in this house he has built. She will love him as he deserves to be loved. I held such hopes."

"And I have disappointed you so dreadfully."

"Dreadfully." Her hand flew up in an abrupt, ireful gesture and she clenched her fist, almost bringing it down hard on Georgiana's hand, then it was arrested, and when it fell it merely touched, gently patting her arm. Georgiana hoped it was a sign of forgiveness. Then Mab seemed to doze off, her lids closed again, her breath came in light drafts.

After a while, however, she roused herself again. "But why?" she whispered plaintively, her brow wrinkled with anxiety and yearning. "I must know. Don't let me die this way, not knowing. Please tell me. I will listen. I will try to understand."

There was a long pause while Georgiana wrestled with her deepest feelings. Should she? Ought she to? Tell it now, just this side of death? Then she leaned close and her lips began to move at Mab's ear. Names, dates, events—money, greed, theft, madness, horror . . . Ross the miller who had murdered all of Georgiana's family was *not* her father; Zion . . . Zion Grimes, and it made her sick to utter the name, was in fact her parent.

Mab listened to the words, her gaze fixed on the ceiling. The words continued for some time; then, when Georgiana straightened in her chair, Mab's eyes remained shut. Had she died? Georgiana spoke her name; the eyes opened again.

"I'm still here," Mab said. She groped for Georgiana's hand and stroked it. "Ah, poor girl. My poor, dear sweet Georgie. What a thing—oh, what a terrible thing for you. You have not deserved this. You of all people." She crossed herself and her eyes rolled in her head. "Ah, the pity of it. A hard life . . . you've a hard life . . . ahead . . . you were my best . . . girl . . . God be good to you now, God protect you . . . Jake, I want Jake."

"No—you mustn't tell him!"

"No, I shall not. That is for you to do, if you can—and you shall. I know it. Marry him, Georgie . . . he will understand . . . none of this will matter a whit to him, I promise . . ." She sighed deeply, hoarsely. Then her body stiffened under the coverlet. Suddenly she sat bolt upright with staring eyes as a terrible shriek sprang from her lips. So penetrating was the scream that the door burst open and Agrippina came rushing in, just in time to see her mother fall back onto the pillow, senseless.

"Mama!" she cried. "Mama! Speak to me! Speak, Mama!"

Georgiana moved to her side. "She can't hear you, Pina. She's gone."

"Dead? Mama's dead?"

"Yes, she's dead."

"Why did she scream like that?"

"She was—distressed."

"Why? What did you say to her? Tell me—I want to know!"

"I said nothing."

"Don't lie to me!" Pina cried. "What were you talking about?" She gripped Georgiana's arm fiercely. At that moment Appleton appeared in the doorway, followed by Père Margeaux and Old Bobby.

"Mama's gone, Papa," Agrippina said and began to weep copiously. Père Margeaux fell to his knees at the bedside and began to pray as Appleton took Mab's hand as if to ascertain for himself that she had, indeed, died, and he, too, wept. Georgiana went to Old Bobby's side, their hands sought each other's.

"Well," he murmured, as a tear rolled down his cheek. "She was a grand creature, wasn't she?" From the foot of the bed he looked at the still form, then, holding tight to Georgiana's hand, he, too, began to pray.

"Our Father which art in Heaven, Hallowed by thy name, Thy kingdom come, Thy will be done . . ."

37

The Death of Love

THE PASSING OF Mabel Talcott was profoundly felt in Pequot Landing, for she had been dearly loved, and people were dazed by the loss of that gentle person who had meant so much to so many. It was all over; Queen Mab was no more; Mab Reilly, that little nobody who'd come upriver from the Stonington brewery, to rise to a position of eminence in the village, the bearer of twelve children into this vale of tears, wife for thirty-six years to one of the town's leading citizens.

The funeral was noteworthy. The requiem mass was sung, not in New France, but at the Church of the Most Holy Trinity in Hartford, for even Père Margeaux realized that the village chapel would never have accommodated all the mourners, especially with Bishop Fenwick of Boston presiding. The governor and his lady attended, as well as many other notables and dignitaries, important friends of Old Bobby's and Appleton's, and the local stock of funeral wreaths was depleted in the desire of friends wanting to remember the deceased.

The burial in the little plot, among the apple trees in the Follybrook orchard, was a family affair. Like large families everywhere, the Talcotts drew together in moments of great joy and of great sorrow, and they drew together now, sons and daughters, brothers and sisters, aunts, uncles, cousins—Talcotts, Lanes, Demings, Poindexters, anyone who could lay the slenderest claim to a connection with the venerable Talcott line, and not forgetting the Priests, who had shown such devotion to their deceased mistress.

The sole family member not attending the orchard service was Posie. The day was cold, a bitter wind blew among the trees, and it was doctor's orders that she remain at home, which she had done, with Trubey for company. The other mourners wound through the lane where Bobby's beehives stood in rows; chairs had been brought for the older women who sat with folded hands while Père Margeaux committed the earthly remains of Mabel Reilly Talcott to their eternal rest. And afterwards they came processionally to the farmhouse where they paid their respects to the children and to the grieving widower, Appleton, whose lugubrious task it was to greet each one of them, to embrace, kiss, and shake hands, when he would far rather he himself were dead.

It was Georgiana who had persuaded Aurora to sing that afternoon, and like an angel she did give voice, a pale, thin figure standing at the piano, her blondness accentuated by her black mourning garb. And there were some among her listeners who reflected sadly, sentimentally, on the last time they had heard her sing, at John Quincy's bean supper so long ago, and all that had happened since that fateful night when she had tossed up all for love, and was betrayed.

THERE was one mourner present at Mab's burial who was not of the Talcott clan; an unexpected, and to some an unwelcome, guest: Sinjin Grimes. Resolved not to make himself conspicuous, he had stood apart from the other mourners, watching the coffin being put down into the ground. He had not gone unnoticed, however. Agrippina's eyes had flashed with indignation, while Aurora, standing at Priam's side, had refused in any way to acknowledge his probing look, keeping her eyes stubbornly averted from his. She continued to ignore his presence as she left the orchard, only to be accosted by him in the lane.

"I must see you," he muttered. "Tell me where and when."

She bit her lip and shook her head, murmuring that she could not. When she tried to catch up with the others he held her back.

"You must. I can't go on like this. The *Sparrow* sails soon, we have to talk—"

She murmured something unintelligible, and because others were watching he had no alternative but to let her go. Her coldness devastated him; how quickly—and greatly—she had changed.

He returned to his rooms in despair, growling at the hired girl and deliberately picking a quarrel with the glove man in the next bedchamber. Fretting and stewing, he forced himself to set about the final preparations for his embarkation for Cuba. In the meantime, he continued earnestly to solicit Georgiana to arrange a private meeting in the hope that before the *Sparrow* sailed he and Aurora would arrive at some understanding, but as the days passed it became increasingly evident that such was not to be.

Aurora's perverse and infuriating behavior left him in a quandary. He burned with the merest thought of her, longed impatiently to see and touch her, to crush her in his arms, feel her lips on his, hear her voice again. After the night at the mill he'd truly believed he'd won her back, that at long last all would come right, but she was more elusive than ever, and he did not know how to reach her and tell her what was in his heart. Always a man of action, yet now having no plan of attack, he believed he had no choice but to do nothing and see what might develop. Then, at almost the eleventh hour Georgiana appeared at the ship's gangway where the *Sparrow* was lading the last of its cargo at Town Wharf. She had been sent to summon Captain Grimes to Kingdom Come, and at Aurora's behest.

"You needn't worry," she assured him, "no one will interfere."

Leaving Billy to oversee final disposition of the cargo, Sinjin grabbed his jacket and cap and hurried along at Georgiana's side. Full golden autumn had touched the elms either side of the roadway, a westering sun cast dolorous shadows aslant his right shoulder, and along the roadside a crew was raking leaves and burning them in smoking windrows; the pungent odor carried him back to a boyhood he seldom enjoyed remembering. The solemn tolling of the church bell behind him was like a death knell as he stepped through the gates of Kingdom Come, and Georgiana hurried ahead to open the door.

"Yes sir, Cap'n," said Burdy Tando, coming into the hall to take his coat and cap as if she had been told to expect him. She bobbed a curtsy and hurried away. He stood there, feeling awkward and unwelcome, and fearful of encountering Aurora. Yet, she *had* sent for him, she must want to see him, he reasoned. In the parlor the fire burned cheerfully and Trubey could be seen laying out the tea things. Georgiana pressed his hand and wished him luck. "I'll go upstairs and read to Posie for a bit," she said, and left him.

Burdy returned. "This way, please, Cap'n." She led him through the parlor to the terrace doors, one of which she opened to let him outside again. Aurora was standing by the railing, gazing out across the garden to the river. She wore a dark cloak with a wide collar of curly reddish fur, and her hair was trapped by a crocheted scarf of some soft material, dotted with little cotton tufts. How assured she looked, how mature and in control of herself. Who could ever have imagined that she had been hounded and encircled by death for months. She turned when Burdy announced him, and held out her hand as he walked across the terrace to her.

"Hello, Rora," he said, trying vainly to smile.

It was she who smiled, however, so that he felt inclined to hope again; his heart raced and his knees grew weak. "I'm happy to see you," he added, and waited for her to reply in similar fashion; she did not, and his small glimmer of hope faded.

In aspect she was grave, in tone maddeningly matter of fact. "You sail tomorrow, I understand. How long will you be gone?"

"Ten or twelve weeks is all."

"Then you'll be returning to Pequot?"

"I believe so, yes." Did that thought please her? He couldn't tell.

"And China?" she asked lightly. "What of China?"

"Nothing of China. I told you I'd go only if—well, you know what I said."

She glanced away. When she looked at him again her eyes were clear and level. "I'm glad you've come. There was—is—something I wanted to tell you."

"Very well. I'm listening."

Her cheeks flushed with warmth.

"I wanted you to know—that night—at the mill—you remember, of course—?"

"Of *course!* How could I forget?"

"Nor I. It was one of the, well, actually the loveliest evening of my life."

"It was?" He was enormously elated.

"Oh yes. Truly, it meant so much to me. And the wonderful afternoon we spent, you can't imagine how I needed them both. I shall treasure the memory always."

He waited for her to go on, but she did not. Her smile lingered, wilted, disappeared. He spoke, his heart in his mouth. "But there'll be more—hundreds of them. We'll have many afternoons like that. And nights . . . Oh, Rora, dearest, I was afraid you'd—that perhaps you'd forgot. I thought maybe you were just toying with me, that it didn't mean anything—"

"No, that's not true."

"But afterwards you—you—wouldn't see me, you went away and never wrote—"

"I know. I'm so sorry, truly. You must forgive me, I haven't been myself, you see—"

"I *do* forgive you, it's all right. Only now—we'll be together, won't we? Won't we, darling? Always together—never parted?"

He made a desperate, even awkward, move to take her in his arms but she stepped away, gently but firmly brushing his hands aside. Beyond the garden, past the meadow, the wind riffled the clear blue surface of the river. He noticed that the boathouse had been boarded up. "I'm sorry," she said. "It's not going to happen that way."

"No?"

"No. You see, I too am going away."

"You're going away." He repeated her words dully. "Where?"

"To Baltimore."

He stared at her, feeling rising panic. "Why Baltimore?" he asked. "What attracts you there?"

"The convent," she replied. "You remember. The one I was sent to school in as a girl." He continued to stare at her, taking her in, the pale cameo face, the delicate features, the tiny wire springs of gold blowing at her temples. "I'm sorry. Truly sorry. You've every right to be angry with me, as angry as anyone could be, but I couldn't let you go away thinking I'd be here when you got back. It occurs to me from some of the things you've written to me, as well as your words now, that you have it in mind that we should be married. Am I mistaken in that belief?"

"No. I mean—yes, of course; married. The two of us—" He waited. She moistened her lips, lifting the axe; the axe fell.

"Oh my dear, I don't know how to say this except to come right out with it. Forgive me if I am brutal-sounding but—I cannot marry you. It isn't possible. I'm sorry. At present I intend to marry no one. No one at all."

He grabbed her wrists and pulled her toward him. "What are you talking about? This is mad! You have to marry me! You know you do! It's all been arranged, Posie—"

"Yes, I know, Posie talked to Mama and Mama talked to Papa, but it's useless to imagine now that—"

He put his fingers to her lips as he wrenched out a cry. "No! Don't say it. Don't even think it. You're upset, that's all, it's only natural—your mother dying—I have told you—how sorry I am she's gone—she was a fine, good woman—we talked, you know, or maybe you didn't know—in the churchyard—she said—said it was all right to marry, she would sanction it. Rora, do you hear me?"

"Yes, I hear you. Mama was impressed—by your sincerity. But it is wasted, you see, since—since the whole idea of marriage between us is now out of the question. I must leave for Baltimore as soon as my passage can be arranged."

His hands fell limply to his sides; his mind was reeling. "I don't understand. Baltimore . . . the convent . . . I remember how you hated it. What do you propose to do there now?"

"I want to begin a search."

"A search for what?"

"I'm not sure. I must discover what God wants of me. I have made Him wait too long."

He cursed, and the expletive lay between them. She did not appear offended. "You must try to understand. None of this is easy for me to say."

"Isn't it?" His tone sharpened. "It doesn't seem to me you've found it so hard. Just a few well-chosen words and off goes sailor boy across the sea while lady fair mews herself up in a nunnery playing at being a saint. Good God, Aurora, after all the waiting I've done, do you think I'm just going to bow my head and accept the harebrained notion of you ending up as a nun?"

She spoke steadily and calmly, with no sign of heat or upset. "I have not said I would be a nun, I merely said I wished to examine my feelings. I do have them, you know—if you do not. Have you forgot? Have you no feeling for what has happened, no sentiment at all?"

"If you mean do I have any *genuine* sentiment, any real, deep feeling, yes, by the withering blue Jesus, I do! I feel right down to the soles of my boots and I'll bet those boots that they're as honest a set of feelings as you're likely to come across in that damn convent! But it seems that you do not." He shook his head contemptuously and all hell was in his eyes. "By God, if you're not the most dishonest, the most calculating female I've ever come across! Your mother hasn't been dead a week but I'll bet she's spinning in her grave to know what a fraud you are." His voice had grown louder and she glanced nervously toward the house. The mournful face of Halley could be briefly glimpsed at the kitchen window. Sinjin groped for words. "This—this whole crazy idea is just something you've concocted because for the moment it happens to suit you—suit your—your notions of proper, pious behavior. Because you just happen to be feeling guilty this week. Isn't that it? Admit it."

"It's true, I *do* feel guilty. I *am* guilty, and this is the only way I know to atone."

He cocked his dark brow. "Oh Christ . . . so that's it, eh? You want to atone." He stepped toward her and she put her hand up as though to deflect a blow. "Damn it, Rora, if you think this atonement nonsense is going to impress anyone after everything that's happened, you're wrong."

"I'm sorry—I can't—you—" There was a look of desperation on her face; all her aplomb had disappeared, she was the child again; he wanted to hit her, he wanted to grab and kiss her and hold her. Close to tears, she drew back against the railing. Then she turned her collar up, shivering. "May we go inside? It's getting cold. No—come this way." She crossed the terrace to the door, which she held open for him to precede her. "It's all right, only Papa and Posie are at home. Pina is out with Granddaddy." Closing the outside door after him, she quickly crossed the room to slide shut the mahogany pocket doors. When she turned toward him again he was standing hunched over at the mantel, head down, staring into the fire.

"Would you care for something to drink? Sherry, something stronger?" He shook his head and watched her as she took off her cloak, which she laid over the arm of the three-cornered chair. Her yellow hair was drawn back in a style unusually severe for her, and she wore a dress of burgundy wool with a prim collar and no jewelry; for a moment she reminded him of her sister Agrippina.

"Rora, I'm sorry," he began anew, "I didn't come here to quarrel with you. I love you and—and I want—I want desperately to understand what you're trying to tell me but . . ." He drew a baffled breath and expelled it. He was about to go on when he suddenly felt washed by a wave of fatigue, a bone-deep weariness, even dizziness, that unsteadied him. His mouth was cotton-dry, his tongue tasted sour, his eyes felt scratchy and swollen.

She moved to the mantel and straightened the candle in the pressed glass stick. The firelight outlined the fall of her dress, the curve of her back under her arm. For a moment her self-possession seemed to desert her, her serene demeanor fled before an incipient collapse into tears and nervous futility, yet in another moment she had rallied again, expressing in her hands and the little half-smile an infuriating calm.

"Do I mean nothing to you, then?" he asked. "Nothing at all? You said you loved me. What of that?"

"I did. I do. I shall love you every day of my life . . ."

He flung his arms out in blind appeal. "Then why? If you love me— Is it my family? *Me?* My unchurched soul, my vile, unshrived body? If that's your concern, let me assure you, I am close to taking orders among the Buddhists."

"Please, must you joke at such a time? Simply because you don't believe is no reason to mock my faith—as if to be an atheist were such a fashionable thing. When humans sin, they must do penance for those sins. This is what I've been brought up to believe. I cannot unlearn those lessons now."

"Oh my God . . ." He stared at her, mouth half-open. "I knew it, God damn it, I *knew* it. This is all because of—because you let me make love to you. Isn't it?"

"Yes, it's true. I let you. That's the worst part, the shameful part—that I gave myself so willingly to you. I even lied to get to you, at the mill, saying I'd gone to church, when church was the farthest thing from my mind that night. I couldn't help myself, I wanted you too much. I'd never known a feeling like that, never. I was filled with desire for you. Everything about you I hungered for, I worshiped and adored. My sin is the greater for that. I am not an idolator. And if I hadn't gone to you, Posie might be able to see today. First Caroline dead, then Posie blinded, and now Mama gone. It's all our doing, don't you see? Yours and mine."

"By Jesus!" He swung away from her, making a fist and pounding it on the back of a chair. "Who has been filling your head with this sanctimonious foolishness?"

"I've prayed and prayed for an answer," she went on, ignoring his question. "I think God has finally answered me, He has told me what I must do. And I cannot go against Him again," she whispered. "At the peril of my mortal soul I cannot."

"So you're choosing to set God ahead of everything else. Your whole life?"

"Yes. That is the way it is. He must be placed ahead of everything now. It is time. In Naples he heard my prayers and He saved me with His love, I know He did. I can still feel it, it pulls at me all the time. Then I wanted you so much I forced myself to stop feeling it." She placed her palms together under her chin and her eyes were filled with entreaty. "But I can't run away and I can't be torn apart anymore. I believe I need Him more than anything else now. Most of all I want peace of mind. And until

I have it I am useless to anyone—to you, to myself, even to God. I am—nothing . . ."

Her look of anguish only bewildered him more, and he felt the hot rage rising in him like leavening. When he spoke again it was with a conscious effort at control and reasonableness.

"Rora, I see that in a time of deepest extremity, when you had nothing or no one to help you, you turned to God and prayed. It's a natural thing to do. You've suffered, you've suffered terribly, God knows you have. But that's all in the past now, surely God doesn't want you to suffer any more. He wants you to be happy. Everyone wants you to be happy. When Posie had her accident, all she could think of was you and me, she made me promise not to be angry with you, to be patient—and I'm *trying,* Jesus!—she thought only of us. I promised her. Now you want that promise to be in vain. Worse, you're trying to blame yourself, and blame me. But you're wrong. Posie's blindness, your mother's death, these aren't punishment for anything *we* did. They both tried to make everything right for us." He grew desperate. "Damn it, Rora, listen to me! *Don't do this thing!*"

She looked at him with a smile that was wistful and profoundly sad. He sagged for a moment, trying to marshal his thoughts. He heard no clocks ticking, no tolling chimes, yet he was grimly aware of time sliding by and he unable to help or hinder it. What a fool he had been to allow her to elude him again after that night at the mill! Suddenly she seemed to him like some true and perfect object that had somehow become corrupted, a priceless treasure fallen into crafty, traitorous hands and now debased. Those cunning, shell-like ears had been listening to other voices than his, alluring poison had been dropping amidst the honey. It must have been the priest, he thought; his "friend," Père Margeaux.

"Tell me . . ." he asked cautiously, "has all this been discussed with the good abbé?"

"He is my confessor, of course."

"And he endorses what you're doing?"

She nodded.

He jammed his fists into his pockets and marched to the window. Outside, scarlet maple leaves were blowing across the terrace and in the flower beds the iris plants wore little straw bonnets against the frost. He consulted with himself for a moment or two, then stared coldly at her.

"I see," he said at last. "Of course. Now I understand." He stood nodding his head at her, his hands still in his pockets, one of them jingling coins. "It's he who's talked you into this damnable decision, hasn't he? 'Do it for God.' 'Absolution.' 'Retribution.' 'Sin.' And he's convinced you in his damned confessional, that little booth of expiation and penances, he's told you you sinned with me, he's convinced you of it, and you believe him, and now to save your immortal soul you're just going to throw away any happiness we might have together, isn't that right?"

She was toying with some flowers in a silver vase, a few late blooms, with faded petals whose faint aroma still lingered about them. Her hands, shapely and ringless, seemed to regret the flowers' decay.

"Why don't you say the truth?" he shouted. "This is all *his* doing, isn't it?"

"Père Margeaux does care about me. He always has, ever since I was little. He's trying to help me now. He does want to save my immortal soul! I must let him try!"

"Because you sinned by making love to the same man twice in your life?"

"Oh, God help us, can't you see there are *other* sins!" Her voice rose sharply. "Père Margeaux has not played you a trick. Never, never—he admires you, he's told you so, he's told me too. He said . . ."

"What did he say?"

"He said if he had . . . a son . . . he would wish him to be like you. He said God would find a way . . ."

"A way for what?"

She sighed. "To reach your soul and make you understand. But you don't understand. You can't." She sat down abruptly, as if her strength had suddenly left her, and laid her arms along the arms of the chair, her fingers gripping the curved ends so the blood left her knuckles. He stared down at her, watching as the tears welled in her eyes and ran down her cheeks.

"I can't," she whispered hollowly. "Forgive me, my dearest, but I cannot."

He knelt at her side and took her hand. "Don't—don't, my sweet love," he said. He spoke tenderly, stroking her hair. "You mustn't do this to yourself. All this will pass—it will—you'll see—"

"No! It will never pass." She sprang up with such force her skirts knocked over a footstool with its needlepoint cover. Sobbing, she bent to right it; she felt his hands on her and with a cry she tore them away and fled to the mantel where she cowered like a trapped animal.

"Mea culpa, mea culpa, mea maxima culpa," she muttered, crossing herself repeatedly and pressing her gold pendant to her white lips. It was as if she were suddenly demented.

"Stop it! I won't have it!" He raised his voice as he strode toward her. "You're *not* guilty! You have done nothing!"

"I have done murder!"

He stopped where he was, staring at her as she clung to the mantel.

"What? What are you saying?"

She nodded and nodded.

"It's true. Murder, I have done murder." Still she nodded.

"Murder? I don't believe you." His voice had dropped to an urgent whisper. "What are you saying? Tell me."

She moved, putting a chair between them, grasping its back for support. Her eyes sparked with a strange light, her voice was hoarse. The cords in her neck strained. "It's true," she said. "I killed Henry. *I killed him!*"

"But, you said—he died of plague . . . didn't he?"

"No. He did not." She was looking at him now with that sweet sad smile he had come to know, new and familiar both. "He was ill, certainly, but he was still alive. Until he came into the garden that afternoon. That was the end of him. I shot him."

"You *shot* him?" He was thunderstruck.

"With his own gun. He fell, just as I said, by the fountain, but with a hole in his head. There wasn't much blood." Still the smile. "I shot him," he heard her say again. "I killed him and I was glad. I was glad he was dead, finally. I felt so free. I don't regret what I did. Don't imagine that I shall ever regret it. But you see—that is one more sin added to so many others."

"Who knows this?"

"No one"—she looked toward the door—"only Père Margeaux. And you. I'm sorry, but I couldn't let you say all those things or even think them. That I would throw away any of our love simply because—of caprice— that would be an abomination."

"I'm sorry, I didn't mean—I thought—Christ, what difference does it make what I thought. Rora—name of God . . . no wonder."

She rose to him at last and laid her hand gently along his arm. "Now perhaps you understand?" Some slight movement of her body against the table jarred the vase of flowers, their petals fell, several at one time; later he swore he had heard them strike the tabletop.

"It doesn't matter," he said. "It wouldn't matter to me if you'd killed a hundred men. I don't care, I love you. Believe me, I love you."

Her hands were folded now before her, and in her dark dress with its collar of demurest white, she looked uncorruptible, invulnerable, already halfway lost to piety and sisterhood. "Yes, dear, I believe you. And remember that I love you. But please—you will forget me. You must. Put me out of your mind now. Otherwise it will be too painful for you."

"Painful? Oh, God! *This* is *painful!* Listening to all this—this *nonsense!* Shooting Henry has nothing to do with us, nothing does, only that your father will let us marry. Marry me, Rora, now, tomorrow, before I said— before we must wait another ten or twenty years to love each other—"

"No."

"No, what?"

"*No,* we may not love each other. Not anymore. Not in this lifetime. That is our forfeit, our debt to be paid. I'm sorry that you must pay as well as I, but . . ." She shrugged, a tiny shrug, and folded her hands, then rose and faced him. "I'm sorry, I must go," she said coolly, unequivocally. "Thank you for coming to see me—I wish you . . . bon voyage . . ."

She crossed the room; he came quickly after her, but not quickly enough to forestall her exit. As the doors slid open, she was momentarily framed in the entrance; beyond her stood the black-clad figure of Père Margeaux.

"Rora—wait!" Sinjin called out as she stepped into the hall. She paused on the bottom stair, her back to him, her bent elbows held close to her stiffened body. With a baffled, reproachful glance at the priest, Sinjin began speaking in a low, forceful voice. "Aurora, none of what you have told me matters a damn. I love you. I will always love you. That's the only important thing. And I know it is the same for you, too. I *know* it, beyond any question or doubt, Rora, so listen to me. If you let me walk through that door without you this time, I promise we'll both regret it for as long as we live."

She shook her head, a series of minute vibrations, then lifted the folds of her skirts and without a backward glance proceeded up the stairs. When he started after her the abbé intercepted him, taking his arm and forcibly leading him back into the parlor.

"I regret, my son," he began when he had drawn the doors shut. "I ask you to believe me—she has no wish to hurt you, this I know. But you see how it is. She is laden with guilt, burdened, heavily burdened."

His look was wild. "I don't give a damn if she killed him, can't she see that?"

"To be sure, but it makes no difference, you know, she is convinced she has committed murder. That is what we have to contend with."

"What are you saying?"

"Assuredly she shot the man, but it was self-defense, he would have killed her for certain. You can imagine her state of mind at that point. She is not culpable, certainly not under any law, and she has paid many times over for taking that life. But—*but,* the point is she *believes* herself guilty. It was her sin after all that drove Henry mad, or so she is convinced. Truly she is to be pitied."

Sinjin was scornful. "*You* pity her, padre, I'll love her."

The abbé shook his head. "I am sorry for you, my son. God give you strength."

"Damn your God!"

Somewhere a door opened and closed. Moments later the sound of wheels was heard as a carriage pulled out of the drive. Sinjin rushed to the window and yanked aside the curtains. He saw the carriage, a gloved hand holding the seat strap, no more.

Sinjin cursed again, then turned to face the priest. "I thought you were my friend. You said you wanted to see us happy."

"I am your friend, and I have told you I wish to see you both happy. It is my fondest wish in all the world."

"Then get her to change her mind! Tell her the mistake she's making! What is she going to do, become a nun?"

"I cannot answer that. We must wait and see."

"Have you no hope to give me then?"

The priest shook his head. "My son, under the circumstances, none. Your solace must lie in the knowledge that the heavier your burden, the lighter hers will be. If by your pain she can be made whole again, if your understanding—"

"There's that damn word again. I don't want to hear it!"

"Then, please, hear this. As you love her, let her go. Yes—release her to God. It is to Him that she must look now. Your plans are made. Sail and God go with you. By the time you have returned from your voyage, she may have found that her hope of heaven lies here on earth—as we spoke of it. I need not remind you, Captain, she is a woman and women have been known to change their minds, have they not? It is said to be their prerogative."

Sinjin swung round again. "Listen to me, padre—you're right. She *is* a woman, she's flesh and blood, she's like every other ordinary flesh-and-blood woman, she wants a lover, a man, she wants to make love. She wants children, a home, she wants me for a husband, Father, she is *passionate*—I can't tell you."

"You can, but there is no need."

"She'll never make a nun, I promise you. I know how it'll work out. A few months in that place will change her mind, she'll say to hell with it and come running home to papa again. But she can shout 'come back' from the church steeple and I won't hear it. You tell her that, padre. Tell her! I was a fool . . . a fool . . . She didn't murder Henry Sheffield—she has murdered me . . ."

"Wait—"

But he had started for the door. Catching his heel in the rug fringe, he stumbled awkwardly, his fore-arm striking the doors, which he threw back, barely saving himself from knocking against Agrippina Talcott, who stood outside. The look of triumph on her pallid features was unmistakable.

He did not stop, but yanked open the heavy front door and rushed out. "Père Margeaux, will you stay for tea?" he heard Agrippina say as he flung himself headlong down the steps and through the gate.

There was no sun and he cast no shadow as he walked along the street, and though the distance from the house to his waiting ship was not so great, it seemed very great, and the blue supper smoke rose up from the chimneys of houses along the way where he let himself believe love and life abounded and there were no mysteries, no betrayals, nothing uncomprehended, only a mutton roast on the table, simple blessings to be said, tender kisses on a cheek, and the bedside prayers of innocent babes.

Lost, all was lost. Nothing remained but to go. He hastened about his business. He had one thing left to do. It necessitated a quick trip to Grimes Mill to accomplish it and took very little time. On the way back to town he stopped to say good-bye to Rachel Grimes, then he hurried on and boarded the *Sparrow*. When her anchor was hoisted he turned his nose to the smell of salt water and sailed away, down the river to Saybrook, across the Sound, and out through Plum Gut, carrying nuts and bolts, and last winter's ice, to the hidalgos in Havana.

PART SEVEN

The Winter of Her Discontent

38

Locking Up the Miller's Girl

TUESDAY THE FIFTEENTH day of November 1842 was a noteworthy one in village history, for that day saw the demise of the Free School of Pequot Landing, and, shockingly, the incarceration of its mistress, Georgiana Ross, in the same jail cell where a hanged murderer had formerly been lodged. Classes at Burdin's seed store and in the Haverstraw barn had lasted not quite a year. A noble experiment, some judged; good riddance, claimed the rest, whistling on their fingers. The upstart miller's girl had at last got what was coming to her.

In the aftermath of the fire, even though the effort seemed doomed, Georgiana had marshaled her last resources to see that her school should continue. Ever an early riser, while breakfasting she would assiduously go over her schoolwork, discuss in detail the day's lessons with Helen, and then be ready for the girls when they arrived promptly on the morning wagon from Lamentation. But all during the lagging month of October, she could do little more than limp along, for her presence was sorely needed at Kingdom Come. It was left to Judge Perry and Merrill Ashley to pursue the case against Ike Bleezer and Tyler Gatchell and their gang of weasels for having set the blaze, at the same time strongly refuting the contention of the proslavery faction that Georgiana herself had plotted to have the fire set so she could claim legal injury at the hands of the known enemies of the school. And, indeed, a grand jury had been impaneled to consider charges of arson and assault as well as dereliction of duty on the part of Newt Gill and his men. But despite the condemnatory testimony of numerous witnesses, in the end Newt Gill was merely handed a perfunctory reprimand, after which he continued to enjoy the boastful leadership of the fire brigade, while Bleezer and Gatchell escaped unindicted "for lack of evidence," even in the appalling tarring of the abbé and Ambo Buck.

Nor did Georgiana participate—in person, at any rate—in the campaign that was initiated by the abolitionists as soon as the Grimes Law was passed to alert supporters of the Free School worldwide to what was to come. Not that the mistress of the school went unrepresented at the hundreds of rallies and meetings held throughout New England, for as Priam Talcott or Mr.

Garrison spoke from the rostrum, at his side would be exhibited a copy of the already well-known oil portrait of Georgiana Ross, commissioned by the Anti-Slavery Society. The artist had chosen to depict her seated next to a window inside the parlor of Gaunt House, posed in a stiff ladder-back chair whose turned ends poked up behind her shoulders, and since it was her own desire, he had presented her in the austere style she currently professed, her dun-colored hair severely drawn back in a bun, the firm, almost stern line of the mouth, the earnest gray eyes that gazed out at the world with no hint of guile or affectation; a decorous Puritan spinster if ever there was one, but unmistakably Georgiana Ross, the Pequot Landing schoolma'am. The finishing touch had been the inclusion in the background of two of the Tando girls as representatives of all those peoples of color the cause was meant to serve. In later years, Georgiana, in a considerably different set of circumstances, was heard to declare, "If I'd known, I certainly never would have worn that awful-looking dress." But brown dress or gray, the portrait had quickly declared its value in focusing attention on both the school and its mistress.

Meanwhile, for Georgiana, there was the slowly lessening grief of Mab Talcott's dying, and following her burial the wrenching exodus of old friends. First to leave, and without even saying good-bye, had been Sinjin Grimes. He had scribbled some hasty lines, bitter in tone, and posted them at Saybrook, saying that as far as he was concerned he'd run to the end of his rope. Aurora could rot in her convent for all he cared and he wished her the joy of it. Georgiana was appalled by the vehemence of his words and quickly destroyed the letter for fear of its falling into the wrong hands.

Aurora herself had embarked for Baltimore a few days later, and with Père Margeaux, who, good as his word, was departing Pequot Landing forever. With his adored "Madame Maybelle" in her grave, and forbidden by His Grace to continue with his "indigents" at Lamentation Mountain, he had offered to accompany Aurora south, where he would see her installed at the convent, after which he would continue his voyage to the homeland he had not seen in so many years. In a farewell interview with Georgiana Père Marqeaux confessed how deeply he regretted having angered Sinjin, and hoped that they might meet again in some other time and place. When Georgiana confessed to him Mab's final request regarding her marriage to Appleton, the abbé said he was aware of it and suggested she should consider honoring the proposal, if it was within her capacity to do so. Georgiana became more agitated, and pushed the notion from her mind.

Last to leave was Posie. Her departure had come as the most anguishing, for it had been assumed that, with her handicap, she would of course remain at home with her family, who would look after her as was fitting and needful. But it was precisely this situation that Posie had found intolerable, and it had dispatched her north to Boston, to the Massachusetts

Institute for the Blind at Watertown, where she had undertaken to learn the skills and techniques that would in time make possible for her a measure of independence.

During this period of deep sorrows, however, as Georgiana doggedly went on with her teaching she thought much of what she would do when the moment came, as she knew it must, that the school would be closed down. And so, on that fateful Tuesday morning when her pupils arrived at the Haverstraws' barn to find a guard posted at the door, she was ready, and it was with studied calm that she admitted Val Morgan to Gaunt House and acknowledged the writ he had in hand.

"Doggone, but I'm sorry to have to do this, Georgie," he apologized.

"It's all right," she assured him, "the law must be served. Do your duty and think no more about it," and at his request meekly accompanied him to John Perry's house, where she was formally arraigned and a bond of twenty-five dollars was set. There followed a considerable shuffling of papers and feet and an embarrassed clearing of numerous throats as officialdom awaited the posting of this sum, and it was then that Georgiana Ross, schoolmistress, showed her truest mettle.

"I do not wish to post a bond," she stated to the amazement of all.

"But you'll have to go to jail," the astonished Judge Perry pointed out.

"Precisely. Such is my intention. I shall be grateful if you will see to the matter directly," she answered, calm but determined.

The judge was shocked. "But Georgiana," he pushed on, to be sure she fully understood the circumstances, "there's no need for your being held in jail. There are many who would be happy to post your bond. I myself will gladly do it."

"Thank you, Your Honor, but I don't want anyone to do so," she replied. "I intend to go to jail and I intend to stay in jail until I am taken to trial."

"But I don't see the sense," the judge protested.

"Judge Perry, I have never sought publicity, but if I am locked up, every newspaper in New England, even in the United States, is bound to write about it. A person lodged in jail because of this disgraceful, hypocritical law is going to make people wonder about it, and those who wonder will start to talk, and if they talk enough maybe someone will do something, and that's what we want, isn't it?"

John Perry could not refute Georgiana's logic, and she went back to Helen's house to pack her bag in readiness for what should next befall.

The word quickly spread through the town and beyond, that as a result of the piece of legislation known as the Grimes Law, Georgiana Ross was going to jail; quickly Zion and Bushrod Grimes realized what this kind of personal martyrdom could mean for the cause they opposed. In consequence, the next morning, upon leaving his office on the way to Gaunt House, Jack Talcott, in company with his nephew Priam, was accosted by an agitated

Willie Wandsworth, who came scurrying out from Archibald's, saying he wished a word.

"Sir," the deacon breathlessly demanded, "is it possible that you intend to let that sadly misguided female be lodged in the county jail?"

"Highly possible, sir," replied Gentleman Jack.

Willie-the-rat fluttered his hands. "I certainly hope you do not think I or my friends are in favor of her incarceration," he exclaimed. "In fact, I stand here to say to you that as a Christian gentleman, I will post the necessary bond out of my own pocket. What d'you say to that?"

He stood back proudly, allowing his words to sink in and waiting for the two Talcotts to accept his magnanimous offer. Then he darted forward to add confidentially, "That is, of course, providing she would not decamp."

"I assure you, Deacon," said Jack, "my client has not the slightest intention of decamping."

Willie jerked a nod. "Then my offer stands." He cracked his knuckles, producing a thoroughly affirmative sound.

Neither Jack nor Priam was having any of it. "Miss Ross does not care to avail herself of any such offer, Deacon," said Priam. "Nor do we wish it for her. To jail she will go and in jail she will remain until her date of trial. Good day, sir."

"Then she may rot there for all of me!" snapped the deacon, quickly casting aside the guise of benefactor. "The creature's a mischief-maker, she'll come to no good end, and haven't I always said so?"

He would have started away but Priam caught him by his coat collar and spun him into place again. "Yes, Willie, you have indeed said so," he said, jerking the deacon's face up close. "Too often, I should think. You are the lowest sort of rodent, you live in a hole with a baited trap, and one of these days you're going to catch that hairy tail of yours."

"Why—what! Here! Let me go, sir, I beseech you let me go—!"

"I'll let you go when I'm ready to let you go. And when I do I want you to trot along to Grimes & Co. and tell that pompous villain whose creature you are that he may think he's won, but he hasn't. Tell Zion Grimes that Priam Talcott sends him this message: we know him for what he is, and we know how to deal with him. He has been at the bottom of all the trouble Georgiana's suffered, not to mention the reprehensible law under which she is now about to be locked up. But he will not win. Tell him that for us!"

He gave the deacon a shake for good measure and thrust him aside. Willie stumbled backwards, outrage inscribed across his pinched features, then hurriedly took himself off in the direction of Grimes & Co. while Priam and Jack proceeded to Gaunt House to be on hand when the mistress of the Free School was carted off to jail.

The church bell was tolling as the high sheriff arrived at the Haverstraws' with a horse and pillion to escort Georgiana to the county jail in Hartford. A sizable crowd had gathered to see her mounted; the sheriff himself led the horse by the reins, conducting her with all the grave ceremony of a medieval seneschal. On this day there were no signs of violence, no catcalls were heard, no jeers; the people looked on in a state of silent awe as the schoolmistress rode slowly off toward Hartford on the sheriff's brindle mare: Georgiana Ross, the miller's girl, being locked up for her beliefs. There were even those among that sober gathering witnessing her departure who had been her opponents in the matter of the school, and who, reflecting on all the terrible things that had happened and were about to happen, were ashamed, suspicioning that though they might have won, their victory would prove a Pyrrhic one.

Pearl Street, in Hartford, where the county jail stood, was jammed with a myriad of conveyances when the small cavalcade from Pequot Landing arrived. Every idler in the city, it seemed, had congregated to learn what was up, so many that in the congested alley behind the jail one of the dalliers got himself trampled for the sake of his curiosity. Grisly tales of the Miller Murders of more than a decade ago were once again dusted off and recirculated, so that within a cat's wink every child present knew that this felonious Miss Ross was the daughter of an axe murderer, and, it was strongly suspected by those who opposed her, her rash course was now merely proving that blood will tell, that she was as lunatic as her father. The hubbub was to continue throughout the night, nor did the authorities seem overly inclined to clear the street and see to the proper restoration of civil order.

And what of the "mad woman" herself? While a thicket of reporters attempting to force entry inside the stone walls to interview the prisoner was fended off by a brace of husky deputies who couldn't grasp why anyone, particularly a genteel type such as this Quakerish schoolteacher, would deliberately choose to stay in their jail, Georgiana sat calmly in her cell in her good gray dress waiting until a bed, a chair and table, and a tallow candle could be provided her. The authorities had been liberal in offering to permit her a female companion, but she had spurned the gesture, and meticulously prepared to pass her first night's vigil alone, merely requesting that paper and ink be procured as well so she could pass part of the evening writing letters.

No sooner were these essentials produced, however, than the turnkey officially presented himself to inform her she had a visitor. This turned out to be Priam Talcott, come with mail and to inform her that no less a personage than Cent Dunnoult, in response to an appeal of Old Bobby's, had agreed to take the case for the defense, assisted by Jack Talcott. Georgiana Ross would have the best lawyers to be found.

"So you're sure to win," Priam assured her. "By the time we're finished,

Zion Grimes and his pack of curs will be heading down the pike with their tails between their legs."

No sooner had Priam left than the jailer appeared at the open doorway to announce another visitor. This time it was Helen Haverstraw who entered the dimly lighted room, carrying a small traveling bag with her. She had driven up to town with her grandmother; Rachel had been delayed at the bank and would be along presently. "I've brought you some things," Helen announced, and, having removed her bonnet and gloves and laid aside her shawl, began extracting from her bag an array of items that she set out on the table: some of Aunt Hat's blackberry jelly, thick buttered slices of brown bread, and tea-brewing paraphernalia, including a small spirit lamp for boiling water. In addition there was a comforting note from Luke, and another from Maude Ashley, as well as an amusing drawing Chloe had made "to cheer Aunt Georgie up." At this Georgiana, sitting on the edge of the hard steel bed, suddenly put her hands to her face and her shoulders began to tremble.

"Georgie! What is it?"

"It's nothing—nothing, really, I'm all right." Helen lifted Georgiana's hands away and saw her tear-stained face. "Everyone's being so good to me. I'm sure I don't deserve it."

"But of course you do. Darling, don't, please, I beg you. You mustn't give way now. Besides, we can have you out of this place in a minute if you've changed your mind. Just say the word."

Georgiana shook her head. "It isn't that; it's Bessie and her baby and Posie, and the school being closed. Dear God, I don't understand—was it so wrong to try to help those girls?"

"It *wasn't* wrong!"

"It must have been. It was wrong to too many people. I'm such a fool, I've got exactly what I deserved! But why? Why is it? I know it's wrong and still I can't do anything. Nothing in my life—nothing, Helen—has worked out as I'd hoped. I don't know how much more I can bear."

"Oh, darling, you can bear it all, and you will. You're strong, you're the strongest person I know."

"I'm not!" Georgiana cried out resentfully. "I'm not! Everyone just thinks I am."

"Nonsense!" came a voice. "I'm one of those, Georgie Ross!" A bristling Rachel Grimes stood in the passageway, her lips working as she gazed at the two young women in the cell. She rustled in and the jailer tactfully closed the door at her back. She gave Georgie's hand a squeeze, undid her bonnet strings, set aside her muff and reticule, and began drawing off her gloves finger by finger. "Well, if this isn't a pretty pass!" she exclaimed, pointing to her withered cheek, demanding it be kissed, and when this formality was seen to she plunked herself down in a straight-backed chair and fell to closely scrutinizing Georgiana's face.

"Thin. You're thin. And you've been crying. This dreadful nonsense—whoever heard of such a thing, going to prison when there's no need. Stubborn, you're a stubborn woman, Georgie Ross." She worked her lips some more then went on: "Georgiana, I want you to know how mortified I am that it's some of my family who are responsible for this pretty pass. Oh, no, no shame to you, my girl. *You* can hold your head up, it's not you who've done wrong, no, indeed—it's *him. That* one! *He'll* pay, one way or t'other he'll pay through that long nose of his for his wicked mixings in all this. God will see to it, and if God won't, by Old Nick, *I* shall. There's what I've come to say to you, though it's not much, I warrant. Wait, now, I'm not done."

Her eyes still could flash sparks, and her lips were like iron. She talked on as though she were sitting at home in her own parlor with her own tea tray spread before her, instead of here in the county jail. "Dear girl, I'm spent with worry. I must know what you plan to do now."

"I'm going to wait for my trial."

"Oh yes, oh yes! Those fidgeting fools couldn't make up their minds if they were trying to decide to hang a hog east of west or north of south. Never mind, never mind." She slipped an envelope from her muff and held it before her. "Now Georgie, look here, here's a little tuck for you. Yes, it's money, a check drawn on Hartford Riverside Bank. They'll tell you it's good, all right. For the school, Georgie." She attempted to press the envelope into Georgiana's hand. "No, no, take it, don't vex me, there's a dear, take it, do."

"But there isn't any school anymore," Georgiana protested, "it's been closed. I've failed."

"Failed!" Rachel jerked her chin. "*Faugh!* Why, if your mother was alive today, how proud she'd be of you, to know what you've done in *our* town! Yes, right there in our own Pequot Landing!" She deposited the envelope on the table and delicately mopped her eyes with the corner of a handkerchief. "Let *me* go your bail, then, Georgie. There's no need to stay here any longer." She peered around reproachfully at the cheerless room with its rank air, dirty walls, and verminous floor.

"No, Grammaw, Georgie's going to stay right here," Helen declared loyally. "It's what she wants to do and I agree. We'll stand behind her, everyone will. We'll come again tomorrow. And every day after that. And Georgie, when you leave here, people will be with you, so many people, I know it. You have so many friends. People who believe in the right, as you do!"

"What if it's Judge Palfrey who hears the case?"

Miss Rachel bridled and her nostrils flared. "Why, that Louis Palfrey oughtn't to be let out in daylight, he needs a keeper with a lock and key. Georgie, you're not going to be frightened of Judge Palfrey!"

"It won't make any difference anyway," Helen added staunchly. "We're going to fight."

Georgiana put her hands over her face and shuddered. "It doesn't matter anymore. Lordy, how little of it matters now." She drew in a long breath and expelled it, sagging back against the stone wall. "I'm just so tired," she murmured. "I want to go away somewhere, when all this is over, I shall, I must—oh dear—" She broke off suddenly.

"What are you thinking?" Rachel asked.

Georgiana's laugh was bitter. "Of Appleton Talcott. I made him a promise."

"What promise?"

"That I wouldn't leave . . . that I would stay no matter what . . ." She shook a weary, puzzled head and absently ran her fingers through her hair. "I promised him I wouldn't leave him when Mab died. He begged me . . . and now here I am in this place. And Mab. I haven't told you—before she died she told me she wanted me to marry him."

The two women stared as if they had indeed been confronted by a madwoman, as Georgiana described her last meeting with Queen Mab and its unhappy conclusion. "Of course I couldn't promise. And at the end I told her everything. It was shameful, I despised myself, it was dreadfully difficult. But I couldn't let her die without knowing the truth from my own lips."

"And if Apple Talcott were to ask you now to marry him, would you reconsider?" Rachel asked.

Georgiana stood up from the cot and looked through the bars at the window. "I'd sooner die. Please stop, I beg you. I don't know why I brought it up, I don't want to hear any more."

"Darling, of course not. We won't speak of it." Helen was afraid Georgiana would break into sobs again.

Instead, Georgiana drew a shuddery breath and looked at her friend with exhausted gratitude. "How kind of you both to care so much."

"Of course we care! After all, we're kin!" Rachel said indignantly.

"We all care, Georgie," Helen said, "and we're so proud of you; you mustn't ever doubt it."

These words left Georgiana on the verge of weeping again, and she clasped Helen in her arms.

The chief jailer himself now put in an appearance, saying he regretted the necessity, but he must close and lock the cell door for the night. Georgiana steeled herself to say good-bye, but when her friends had gone, she did weep a little, and prayed more. Then she sat at the table with her lighted candle and went through the mail Priam had left. One was a letter from a sympathetic woman out in Indiana, offering encouragement, another in Pennsylvania, a little town called Gettysburg, a third came from a Reverend Lukather of Duxbury, Massachusetts, containing intimations of a forthcoming proposal of marriage to their mutual benefit. Another from an antislavery society in New York requesting the loan of the portrait in oils to serve as inspiration at a lecture, and still another from a Catholic nun at Portuguese Macao, at the edge of China. This Sister Mary Omnia was a member of a charity order called the Sisters of Mercy. Even as far away as these nuns were, they had nonetheless heard of Georgiana Ross and the Free School of Pequot Landing. Sister Mary Omnia hailed from Aberdeen, Scotland and had joined her order soon after its founding, some ten years before. She warmly congratulated Georgiana on her school (she was as yet unaware of its demise), and as a friendly memento she sent a sample of linen drawnwork, executed by her own hand. As one Scot to another she urged Georgiana to keep up the good work, and if Georgiana could find the time, the sister would be pleased to hear from her. Not tonight, however, she told herself, suppressing a yawn. Eventually she would read all the letters, answer them, thank the writers; tonight, however, she was too tired.

Tomorrow the reporters would want to hear what she had to say about the school, and she would be obliged to state her case for the record. Some of those reporters would be hostile toward her and would print lies, no matter what truths she endeavored to set forth. She would have to try to explain her feelings in an orderly fashion. Just now they were deeply confused and disordered. Sleep she craved, longed for, sleep. Wrapping herself in the warm shawl Helen had left, she lay down on the narrow cot where, alas, she remained awake, listening to a host of unfamiliar noises, while all manner of unsavory odors assailed her nostrils.

While she could not sleep willy-nilly her mind ran back and forth over the past months, searching for the flaw, the place where she had erred, where all might have been saved, had only the correct steps been taken. Presently her thoughts strayed from the cell where she presently lay far across the miles to Macao, where on one of that city's several hills a simple pious nun went about her humble chores. A Scotswoman from Aberdeen, the sister had written; a woman who had devoted her life to the service of God and who had taken the time to pen a letter to a stranger.

Georgiana sat up suddenly and struck a light, then, seating herself at the table with a page of paper, she dipped her pen into the inkwell and began to write a note to Sister Mary Omnia. The note required another page, then another. Soon she became oblivious of the time; the candle had begun to gutter and still she wrote on, her neat, legible script traversing page after page as she poured out her heart to a Catholic nun in China whom she had never met and was not likely to. A place like Macao was such a long way to go to make a friend.

39

Damsel in Distress

LEAVES RED AND gold tumbled across Main Street to gather by the horse troughs outside the tavern, across the road among the legs of the tilted-back chairs where the whittlers ritually gathered with their knives and butts of soft pine, to drift about the feet of the tall elms. A melancholy season, surely, somewhere betwixt and between, tinged with remorse for things past as well as apprehension of other things yet to come. The pungent, smoky odor of burning leaves hung in the gray damp air (English air, for New England had inherited its weather too). A deep cordovan shade had bled into the melancholy landscape along with the more banal browns and dun shades, and at teatime the thickening mist crept up from the river, blurring everything, working its way into creaky bones, and errand goers turned up their collars against the deepening chill.

Passing Number 17, a stranger might suppose that it had been shut up for the season, as if with the falling of the autumn leaves, the house had drawn in upon itself, huddling against the long dreary winter to come. All commonplace functions and normal social intercourse had been suspended, and those few who were still tenanted under the slate roofs moved among the rooms in a kind of dumbshow, enacting the mournful pantomime of bereavement. Having presided over Mab's funeral, and staunchly blessed Aurora's and Posie's departures, the master of Kingdom Come had withdrawn from life, doing precisely what he had promised his dying wife he would not do. Day after day he wandered like a lost soul through the near empty house, while his father and Agrippina kept a watchful eye on him and the servants whispered in the kitchen, fretting for Mist' App but knowing there was nothing to be done.

Every morning Alabaster serviced him as usual, trying by hook or crook to coax him into a bit of discussion on various current topics, but receiving in return only monosyllabic replies. Nothing Halley might produce from her cook stove could tempt his palate, and even the *Courant,* whose perusal had for years been habitual, lay untouched beside the silver spoon monogrammed with Mab's initials. Through each of the long, bleak days he seemed eager for the approach of darkness, as if the dimming of the light could somehow dim his melancholy.

Alone of all the household, Trubey Priest remained hopeful. "Momma, he's going to get over it," she told Halley, who fanned herself and shook her head.

"Ah doan think so, baby. That po' man plumb tuckidd. Ah doan think he goan evah get ovah losin' the Queen." The catastrophes of the preceding months had taken their toll on Hallelujah as well, and though her quiet strength remained undiminished, though she retained the unwavering spirit, unquenchable, unassailable, indomitable, she had brought with her from the Deep South so many years ago, for how long this would last no one could say; Halley's life, too, lay in God's hands, as whose did not?

Not even the current travails of Georgiana Ross had in any way roused Appleton from his lassitude. There he sat slumped in the Chippendale wing-back chair whose graceful curves were matched by its fellow, imposing, but alas, unoccupied, on the opposite side of the fireplace. That chair, this room, this house, this life; it had come at last to this. His gray hair, which he would not suffer anyone to trim, stuck out in unruly tufts that he exerted no effort to neaten. His eyebrows were like twin gardens of disorder, filled with whorls and brambles and twisted matter. What lay ahead for himself he neither knew nor cared: All he could do now was gaze yearningly backward in time across his full thirty-six years of happy marriage; all that really mattered to him was that Jake's Molly was no more. She was dead and lying under apple trees where the bees sang.

No, he told himself, no, a thousand times no, she was not dead. Women like Mabel Talcott didn't die. They went on forever strong and vital and life-giving. They did not leave you so cruelly alone, adrift in a world that had gone dark, they did not go away and abandon you, they did not turn to dust. One part of him wept as another part raged. It wasn't fair. It wasn't right. Why couldn't he have been the one to go? How much more prepared she would have been to face the loss, to accept and cope with it. He, not she. In such moments of introspection and unbridled grief, all his enlightened theories and stoical philosophies of life deserted him, and he was rendered cowardly, even womanish, by unnerving and overwhelming emotion. And he raged at this as well, for he had prided himself on his reason, and now reason too had deserted him.

He was sitting thus on the frosty Monday morning on the first day of Georgiana's trial. He could hide here in the study, he thought, for a time at least, but *they* would not leave him alone for long: his dad and his son and his son's wife and his grandchildren and his daughter Electra, who had returned to Pequot for the trial, and far from the least of them, the Priests. Soon, *they* would be coming for him, blast them! Yes, yes, they would cosset him and nurse him and indulge him, they would be gentle and respectful of his grief, and fry him kippers for breakfast, but in the end they would have him back again, dragged back to the world he detested, to the life he loathed, back to cold reality. Bit by bit, day by day, they would urge him back, when he desired only to be left alone. Surely a man was better off dead.

He had vowed he would join her; since her death he had dreamed of it. No man was meant to suffer as he suffered. What need had *they* of him?

Had he not done enough, by God? Yes, indeed, he had exerted himself in behalf of each and every one. Why weren't they content then, to leave him be? Why couldn't he simply follow the path she had taken before him? He knew that she must be waiting for him on the Other Side. Hadn't she told him she would be? How long must he go on making the poor darling wait? His darling Molly?

He stared at the pocket pistol lying on the tabletop. It carried its required charge; he himself had loaded the weapon. He had not discharged any sort of firearm in many years; this particular pistol had been Old Bobby's, a present from his old friend Judge Perry; it had hung there under the mantel since Kingdom Come had been built, waiting. Waiting to perform this present service.

He observed himself as he reached for the gun, saw his fingers close around the burled handle and take it up. There was an alien quality to the simple act, yet something oddly familiar about it, too. Yes. He remembered: Ross the miller; the base fellow had shot himself, hadn't he. Two pistols, two bullets, two transverse balls through the cranium. One was sufficient to make a job of such a business, surely. But not here. Not in the house. His sense of fastidiousness told him that this would be wrong; he must choose another site. The boathouse? Perhaps. It wouldn't matter so much there, down at the river, where the willows wept in the spring. Someone was bound to hear the shot; they would find him soon enough.

He lifted his tired head, shielding his eyes, as a light knock sounded at the door and he heard the familiar sound of his father discreetly clearing his throat to identify himself. Appleton hastily slid the pistol down between the chair arm and the cushion, at the same time blotting his moist eyes and blowing his nose.

"Come in, Dad," he said when he had arranged his posture and mastered his emotions.

"Do I intrude, son?" Old Bobby stepped decorously into the room.

"No, no, not at all, come in, do. I was just . . ." He sighed and made a feeble gesture that did not fool his father. "Sit down, Dad."

Old Bobby drew up the side chair, with typical sensitivity avoiding the one that had been "Mab's chair," and for a while father and son merely sat together, their eyes meeting without words.

Then Appleton roused himself. "Well, Dad, what are you about this morning?" he asked with some show of spirit. "Have you had your walk? Been downstreet?"

"To tell the truth, I've not. As a matter of fact I walked over to the farm. It's been a spell now."

"How are they? James and Susie?"

"Well enough. Weather's a bit crisp. Cider's tangy, too."

"Good. Good. Glad to hear it."

They looked at one another again. Appleton smiled and reached to tap his father's knee, a gentle touch, filled with every dolorous thought that lay between them.

"Son," said Bobby, "I would not for worlds intrude on your grief. I only thought I should be the one to remind you—it's Monday, you know."

"Oh? Yes? Monday, you say?" Appleton looked blank and made a business of polishing his spectacles, which lay on the cherrywood candlestand at his elbow, wondering what "Monday" could mean. He could feel the firearm against his thigh.

"Ayuh. A matter of no small importance . . ."

"Yes, Dad?" Appleton put on his glasses, hooking their temples over each ear. His eyes blinked behind the shiny lenses. "How so? Of what sort?"

"The trial." Old Bobby almost whispered the word, as if to apologize for mentioning it.

"How's that? Trial, you say?"

"Georgie's," Bobby reminded him gently. "Opening arguments are scheduled for today. Last night you mentioned you might care to be present. 'Twould please her, I daresay. Our girl can use all the support we can give her, hey?"

Oh. The trial. Stupid of him. How could he have forgotten? "Yes. To be sure. Of course she can. She has good counsel, has she?"

Bobby tried not to show his shock; this was old, familiar territory by now, Georgiana's defense. "Jack's seeing to it, App. And Cent Dunnoult."

"Yes. Yes, of course. I remember. Cent'll give 'em a good show, won't he? He'll paste 'em, won't he?"

"We certainly hope so. We do indeed. Look here, son, Reuben's just bringing out the coach. Electra and I, we didn't know but what you might care to go along with us, what say? There'll be no end of folk showing support for Georgie. You can bet Aunt Hat will be on hand, too."

"Ah, will she? How is Aunt Hat? Keeps to Snug Harbor, cozy as a cricket, I'll warrant."

Bobby could do no more than nod; what use to remind Jake that Hat's cottage had been pulled down or that she was now sheltered on the Brick Farm?

Appleton peered around him, absently plucking at the hairs of one brow until not a few of them lay on the carpet. "Tell me, Dad—how is this whole business faring, anyway? I haven't seen the paper."

"Well enough, except that as sponsor of the law, Bushrod Grimes has been invited to join the prosecution. It'll make things harder on Georgie, I'm afraid." He took Appleton's hand. "If we went on up to Hartford, you could have a personal word or two with her, that would be a help, I'm sure."

"Yes—but I'd have to listen to that horned demon, Palfrey. By Zeus, how he ever got to sit on a bench in a decent American court of law—the law is mocked, I say!"

Appleton was not the only man to frown at hearing the name of Judge Louis Palfrey, who was a notable member of the proslavery faction, with heavy investments in some cotton mills along the Quinnebaug River in the eastern section of the state. Outspoken in his contempt for Negroes and Indians, and an indefatigable warrior against the least hint of liberalism, he could be counted on to permit any outrage in his courtroom so long as it advanced his cause.

"Yes, yes, to be sure," said Bobby, pleased at Appleton's sudden show of awareness. "The man's a thoroughly bad customer, as we know." He turned as Electra glided in with a smile, and went over to kiss her father's cheek and straighten his stock.

"Good morning, Father, dear. Aren't you ready? The coach is at the door." Her feigned indifference to his heavy sorrows hurt Appleton and he firmly told her that he would not be going, but he reckoned without his Lecky's wiles, and she soon had him on his feet, saying obligingly, "Yes, I see, this sounds most serious. Had no idea. Never. Why then, certainly I'll go along. You're right, Lecky, Lecky's always right. We must render Georgie all the support we can." He considered for an extended moment, a look of confusion playing across his features. "Georgie Ross on trial. Our Georgie. What a world, what a world." He shook his head and blew his nose vociferously, then got up and stood blankly peering about the room as if it were totally unfamiliar to him. "Where's my coat, my stick?" he asked, then sat down again.

But presently *they* returned with coat and stick and led him away, got him dressed and groomed and hatted, stuck him in the yellow coach, and he went riding off to Hartford, only half aware of the trial and all it meant, to Georgiana Ross, to the village of Pequot Landing, to the hopeful everywhere. Later, Trubey came in and, plumping up the chair cushion, found the pistol, which she took to Halley, who removed the ball and hid the gun in the back of a drawer.

IN THE county courtroom, filled to overflowing, the sun streamed in in long, golden pencils, exposing the layers of dust along the mullions and sills and bringing a certain liveliness to what were otherwise sober proceedings. The potbellied stoves had been lighted on either side of the room; and spittoons had been strategically located at each post to encourage their use, though everyone knew perfectly well the floor would do far better.

The dramatic appearance of the defendant stationed between two uniformed guards caused just the sort of stir the newsmongers were all looking for, and the general hubbub continued for some minutes as Georgiana accepted the chair that Jack Talcott was holding for her at the defense table. Here she sat, prim and proper, seemingly unaware of everything that was going on around her. The long days in jail had so refined her mental processes that with little trouble she could isolate her thoughts, inducing vocal sounds and visual impressions to recede into the ether while she forced her mind to concentrate on matters she regarded as of greater import, a primary consideration being the unlooked-for presence of Appleton Talcott, seated amid the attendant Talcott faction, Old Bobby on one side of him, Electra on the other, as well as Priam and Agrippina, and a host of others who had come to give her confidence. There sat Aunt Hat, her ancient bonnet clapped on her head, the strings hanging loose. Catching Georgiana's eye, she responded with a smile and a cheery wave. At her side was Ambo Buck, regarding her earnestly, even hopefully, as he waited with the other spectators for the arrival of the judge. Nearby, ready to take down every scrap of testimony in shorthand was Helen Haverstraw, who had been enlisted by William Lloyd Garrison to record the details of the trial, since Judge Palfrey had been heard to declare along Central Row that the editor of the *Liberator* was nothing but a rabble-rouser and a printer of lies and scurrilities, and as such was not welcome in his courtroom.

Georgiana's glance shifted to Appleton again; how tired he looked, she thought, how thin and worn down. So little like the vivid, robust man she'd known all her life. Her heart went out to him. She felt guilty that her own woes had kept her from his side, where she knew he needed her to be, and to this extent she allowed herself to feel remorse for the stiff-backed position she had insisted on maintaining. She longed to be able to comfort him, as Mab would have wanted, but even in the face of his need the school and the things it stood for came first; and must. Mab would understand; Appleton would, too, she felt sure.

Suddenly the bailiff was intoning "All rise," and in a moment the judge was seated and the courtroom called to order.

There was nothing abstruse in Georgiana's case, only a simple, straightforward—and heavily disputed—matter of modern American jurisprudence. In the most basic terms, and irrespective of what shadings the prosecution might wish to paint upon the matter, the fact remained that Georgiana Ross had deliberately conspired with as yet unnamed confederates to call forth and assemble in a school a number of "colored misses" from outside the boundaries of the village wherein that school was located and, indeed, from outside the boundaries of the state, for the purpose of instructing them. She had moreover continued to teach them after the Assembly of the State of Connecticut had passed a law expressly forbidding such activities. As a consequence of these unlawful gatherings, and the unrelenting social and political agitation on the part of interfering abolitionists, the village and its environs had been subjected to increasing "strife and fractious discord," as well as "serious danger to life and limb."

From the beginning it had been the strategy of the defense in no wise to seek to prove Georgiana innocent of the charges lodged against her, but to challenge the law itself: to persuade the jury that the Grimes Law was unjust, and that therefore the defendant should be acquitted. Just so, one hundred years before, had Alexander Hamilton won an acquittal for the printer John Peter Zenger, who had dared to write the truth about the colonial government of New York, though writing it was "against the law."

The prosecutor, one Harry Fletcher, was called "Fortify 'Em Fletcher" because he liked to fortify the spirits of his witnesses with smiles and then proceed to knock them down. Thus he began in this case by inviting Georgiana's pupils to occupy the witness chair, one after the other, gaining each one's confidence with humorous remarks and using his winning smile to distract them, then attempting to draw from them an admission of what was really on his mind: that Georgiana Ross had conspired with Chief Waikoit to get the girls to fill the desks in her classroom by duplicity and false promises, thus establishing the existence of the Free School on the one hand, and on the other duping the girls into the belief that they would be promoted to a better way of life when in reality they were innocent pawns in a carefully devised plot to inflame the community at large.

So, one by one Hutta Teal, Easter Dawn, Loney Bass, Maria Coleman, and the other girls were questioned concerning the means by which their tuition had been paid, via public subscription or through the generous contribution of funds at abolition meetings; where they lived or boarded; what subjects they had studied and who had taught them. But though Fletcher tried his best to elicit testimony as to the conspiracy and thereby impress the gentlemen of the jury, the witnesses did little to advance his argument, since despite his tactics none would admit to anything other than an honest and sincere enrollment in a school dedicated to the educational advancement of colored misses.

The prosecution's case certainly suffered in the matter of the conspiracy from the absence of its principal witness—from the prosecution's point of view the witness who could no doubt provide the most detailed evidence on the conspiracy, namely the school's first and possibly foremost pupil, Miss Rose Mills. But though diligently sought by a team of detectives in the City of New York (where it was widely rumored she had gone) she had not been located.

The prosecutor next called Warren Burdin to the stand and together they looked over the books of the school, which Burdin had so carefully kept for Georgiana, and from which it was learned, to the shock of some, the dismay of others, and assuredly the personal embarrassment of Deacon

Grimes and his sympathizers, that no less estimable a party than the Deacon's own stepmother, Rachel Grimes, had been a generous contributor, while Zion's daughter, Helen Haverstraw, had served the school as a teacher.

A sometime instructress herself, Maude Ashley, was then called upon to describe her classes in "deportment," and, nettled by the prosecution's overbearing tactics, Maude declared she would not respond to the questions as they were being put to her. She had shown the girls how to pour tea and to sit properly in a chair, and was that against the law? She subsequently addressed some highly inflammatory remarks toward the bench, from which Judge Palfrey threatened her with contempt, then cited her, and the witness was summarily dismissed and required by the court to pay a fifteen-dollar fine.

Next to take the stand for the prosecution was Georgiana's enemy Flora Ritchie, who, her parrot's profile cleaving the air around her, settled back in the chair and proceeded to describe the schoolroom visit made by her and other members of the Fairness Committee, and the verbal exchange that had taken place. Georgiana's response to the committee's "attempting to reason" with her was quoted more or less verbatim, while Flora sniffed through her beak and editorialized on the schoolteacher's "intransigence" and "uncooperative spirit" in rejecting out of hand the attempts at "peacemaking" that would have seen the streets of Pequot Landing rendered tranquil once more, places where little children might safely play at dolls and ball.

But the "recreational hours of the village young fry," as Bushrod Grimes now smugly pointed out, had been seriously jeopardized by the outbreak of violence occasioned by the school's being called into existence as a result of nefarious and underhanded plottings by the abolitionist forces headed by Miss Ross's confederates at Number 17 Main Street, the house known as Kingdom Come. To illustrate his point, Rod now called Tyler Gatchell to the stand to testify that he, an innocent party out beating Gypsy Woods for a fox gone to earth, had been set upon by a pair of ruffians, namely Ambo Buck and Mat Kindu, an incident that had seen Tyler impaled by the Malay's knife and Ike Bleezer shot at by "that scowling redskin." Gatchell's testimony was quickly corroborated by that of his crony, Bleezer, who, with as innocent a face as he could muster, lied in his teeth, heaping all blame on the wrongdoers who had merely been trying to protect the girls placed in their charge.

Foxy Dunnoult had a field day in his cross-examination. With a few well-crafted questions he demonstrated that both the prosecution's witnesses had perjured themselves. But the canny Cent's moment of glory was filched from him when the bench characterized the witnesses as "men of probity and honor whose original testimony the jury could accept as gospel."

These witnesses were followed by Val Morgan, who was forced to admit that a series of violent acts had occurred in the village after the founding of the school, and even John Perry—a hostile witness if ever there was—was forced to give evidence of the sentences he had meted out to various disturbers of the peace during the time the Free School was in operation.

Last to testify for the prosecution was the United States marshal who told of how he had found the Free School still in operation in the Haverstraw barn after the passage of the Grimes Law, and that when he had informed its proprietress that the school was now illegal, she simply defied him, inducing her girls to sing hymns and then, while he stood there, denouncing the Grimes Law as unconstitutional and worthy of breaking. The next day, upon a warrant from Judge Perry, the school had been closed and the schoolmarm arrested.

Having made the prosecution's point by fair means and foul, Bushrod Grimes then began to harangue the jury, eulogizing the efforts of the antiabolitionist forces to promote peace in the village, shining a light on Zion Grimes as a kind of benign benefactor who had been at considerable pains to calm the villagers; were it not for such upstanding citizens as he, Rod said, anarchy would have reigned. So long and drawn out were these remarks of Zion's son that Jack Talcott rose to object that the prosecution was giving its summation during the examination of witnesses, and this time not even the judge could allow Rod to continue. So, reserving its further planned perorations, the prosecution rested its case and the defense began its own by presenting its one and only witness, the defendant herself, who took the stand on a Tuesday afternoon and was still in the witness chair answering questions a full nine days later.

ON HER third day of cross-examination, Georgiana had been awake since the first speck of light. Wearing the same familiar dress of navy blue wool that had been Electra's, with the lace collar and cuffs that she had worked for herself and the millefiori pin Mab had given her and that was so becoming to her, her hair dressed "à la Quaker," she prepared to face her inquisitors once again. Two days of badgering by Rod Grimes had left her spent, nor did her lack of sleep or appetite help matters any. When the jailer came with the same sort of breakfast tray she had seen produced every day, a meticulously laid-out arrangement, but composed of pallid, monotonous food, she ate a slice of buttered bread, then, with her coffee at her elbow she set out her writing materials on the table. Since yesterday, she had at intervals been composing a letter to Posie at Boston, apprising her of the trial's conduct and her personal views of the highly biased proceedings, and now she took up her quill again.

If the handwriting of human beings can be considered as revealing of inner character, Georgiana's certainly was: bold, assertive, forthright, with the proper execution of each letter, the whole bearing a slight bias to the right, and unlike Sinjin's, perfectly legible. She crossed her *t*'s and the stems of her *f*'s, she dotted her *i*'s with exactitude, a sturdy, handsome script, like its author.

"Oh, Po," she wrote, "if only you were here, to listen to some of the silly things that are being spouted like whale steam in that courtroom, you surely would laugh, as I would like to but dare not, for this judge is a very ogre and would have my head on a platter if only he could. Dear suds, how that diabolical visage haunts my dreams.

"I was so pleased, touched, too, by your dearest papa's appearance on opening day—his first in public in so many weeks. Though he tried to look attentive I fear all this courtroom nonsense only bores and confuses him. Aunt Hat comes every day as well, bringing a bit of tatting, for you know how she believes idle hands are the devil's instrument. She did not make her mincemeat this year; said she hadn't the heart, with her kitchen things all scattered."

This report saddened Georgiana and she rested her feather, her elbows on the oilcloth covering the table, splaying her overworked fingers against cramp. She sat there absently noting the sounds of the neighborhood as it had come gradually alive and caught up with her early start. The crooked alley behind the jail was already active with creaking wagons and clopping hooves; she could hear the call of the draymen as they passed, and presently she noted the familiar-sounding, welcome voices of the "Georgiana Talcott Freedom Supporters," who as was their daily habit had come to present themselves under her cell window, where they delivered themselves of such sentiments as they deemed fitting to buoy her spirits up.

When that faithful group had dispersed—court was about to open and they rushed off to grab the best seats—Georgiana spent another twenty minutes reading from the Bible, then the turnkey appeared, announcing that her lawyers were just on their way from the courthouse. Each morning her two "stalwarts," as she had dubbed them, insisted on presenting themselves before her, to greet her and take counsel with her: Uncle Jack and the redoubtable Cent Dunnoult. Calm and unshakable in the face of the shifty, underhanded tactics employed by the prosecution and the hypocritical calumnies that daily spewed forth from the bench, loyal and hardworking, the two defense lawyers were knights in armor when it came to protecting a damsel in distress; while Georgiana Ross was in their safekeeping, they would see their graves before letting any harm befall her.

"Going to law must agree with you, Georgie," Jack Talcott said, coming in with an amicable eagerness that gave her pleasure. "Every time I see you, you're that much prettier."

She colored, for she could never gracefully accept or even believe a compliment, but the gallantry touched her and she thanked Jack sincerely.

"I'm sorry you have to go through another day of this," he went on. "Grimes is playing to the gallery, and effectively, too."

"Do you think we have lost, then?" she asked.

"Certainly not!" declared Cent. "But in the unlikely event we do not prevail, well, there's not so much lost, is there? A fine to be paid, a negligible amount, I should think, and there's an end to it."

"Yes, of course," she responded meekly, knowing he was only trying to reassure her, that he knew as well as she did that what was at stake was not merely the payment of a petty fine, but the future course of the whole movement of abolition. In this courtroom—Judge Louis Palfrey's courtroom—would be decided the fate of thousands of beings whose "crime" was that their skins were darker than the judge's.

When the guard appeared, the defense group proceeded from the cell to the courtroom, where as usual Georgiana was turned over to the bailiff. And just as usual, the schoolteacher's appearance caused a commotion, though by now the crowd was used to being admonished from the bench for its outbursts, invariably unfavorable to the defendant. Georgiana's "claque" was far better behaved, and by their seemingly calm, unflagging presence they made themselves more profoundly felt than the vulgar antiabolition rowdies with whom the prosecution endeavored to pack the place.

There was the same interminable shuffling of feet and papers, the dry coughs and sniffs, the insistent mutter of bored voices while the court awaited the entrance of Judge Palfrey, an appearance that Georgiana anticipated with the greatest distaste: while she had no personal fear of the man, his detestable look and manner often reminded her of Zion Grimes.

In due course, His Honor made his usual brisk, scowling entrance, loudly coughing, and staring balefully at the defendant from under his furrowed brow.

"Proceed! Proceed!" he barked, startling the bailiff who shot from his chair and called the courtroom to order. The judge sat back, idly toying with a quill while the state's attorney recalled Georgiana to the stand.

Once again Bushrod Grimes, representing the prosecution, began his vociferous barrage of questioning as though there were before the court not a mere village schoolteacher, but some infamous murderess who had perhaps poisoned her lover or taken tongs to the iceman. By now Georgiana was more or less prepared for this browbeating, but her attorneys were plainly fed up, and each time their client was assailed Cent Dunnoult was quick upon Bushrod, objecting to the line of questioning. Rod, younger by far, had many aces up his sleeve, and plainly relished annoying his much senior colleague, while Judge Palfrey employed voice and gavel in a blatantly prejudicial denial of every one of Cent's objections.

"Mr. Dunnoult!" he thundered, banging on his benchtop, "I demand you restrain your objections, lest the jury be given no evidence whatever on which it may judge this case. I would like to think we may be done with the whole business before Christmas, so that this woman may receive her just deserts and we may enjoy our plum puddings."

"Your Honor!" Cent was aghast at this tirade. "I demand you retract your words! The Bench is being deliberately provocative—trying to sway the jury!"

"Sit down and be silent!" the judge thundered. "Let the jury be swayed, they need the exercise, heh-heh. By God, if *someone* doesn't sway the jury we'll be here till doomsday. Mr. Prosecutor, continue, pray. The defendant will answer the last question and be quick about it."

Shaking with indignation, Cent was persuaded by his associate to subside, while Rod pressed his line of questioning.

"To continue, Miss Ross," he went on, adopting the formal mode he had rehearsed to a fare-thee-well, "I would learn from you if in formulating the idea of your school you did not from the outset have in mind to deliberately sow the seeds of dissension, to foment trouble and discord among your neighbors—if indeed you did not plan to use your school from the outset as a divisive scheme?"

"Such was never my intention."

"What then, if I may make so bold, *was* your intention?"

"My intention was to offer a place where young misses of color—"

"Yes, yes, we all know well enough about these so-called misses of color of yours. You planned to school such low types, the shade of their skins not being merely incidental to your plan but being completely necessary to it, is that not so? Ordinary *white* misses would have done you little or no good whatever."

Georgiana's eyes snapped. "If you mean that I planned my school to embrace pupils of color, it is true. I did. And will do it again, if it please the court."

"It does *not* please the court!" thundered the judge, whose face purpled even as Georgiana regarded him from the witness chair. "It pleases the court not a whit, and for you to sit there and say that it does is a mockery, do you hear me—a mockery!" He shook his dewlapped bulldog's face at her, the eyes starting from his head. "Mr. Grimes, get on with it. Stop all this shillyshallying and round off your point!"

"Good Your Honor, I shall, if I can but persuade the witness to answer other than by indirection." Rod paused, aiming a long, steely look at Georgiana, then opened his mouth again and spoke with that brand of biting sarcasm for which he was becoming distinguished.

"Miss Ross, if I may make so bold, what exactly *did* you hope to gain by this revolutionary idea?"

"I'm glad you recognize that it was 'revolutionary,'" Georgiana replied with asperity. "I hoped it would make people sit up and take notice, I believed it would make them stop and think——"

"Stop and think? I do believe it has done exactly that—made people stop and think! But was such a ploy not actually designed as a slap at your neighbors, those good, kind folk living all about you, was it not to bring them up short and say, 'Here's a nasty thing for you good people, here's a dirty stain on your escutcheon, here's a blot on the village,' while you proceeded to parade wagons full of darkies from out of town and even from other states and half-breeds off Lamentation Mountain before their eyes twice a day, permitting these woolly-headed dregs of humanity to loll about in public places, picnicking in the village cemetery—*yes!* gentlemen of the jury, if you can believe your ears, *there* in the hallowed precincts of the Ancient Burying Ground of Pequot Landing! Our much vaunted misses of color casually disporting themselves amid the gravestones, lunching, if you please, on chicken sandwiches and stuffed eggs, whilst a renegade sea captain regaled the lot with wicked and lustful tales of dancing hulas on the beach at Lahaina and smoking the evil poppy in the cribs of Canton! There's education for a pack of darky misses, there's a fine thing to be bringing into the homes of good and decent folk! What have you to say to that, school-teacher Ross?"

"It wasn't that way at all, Rod Grimes, and you know it! You're deliberately mixing this all up."

Cent rose. "Your Honor, I must object to the prosecution's continued badgering of the defendant!"

"Silence. There is no badgering allowed in my court, sir. Sit down before I strap a muzzle on you. Mr. Grimes can get no more than four words out before you're on your feet objecting. Sit *down,* I say!"

"Rule then, Your Honor. I have objected—you will rule."

"I *overrule!* Sirrah, if you object one time more this morning I shall hold you in contempt of court! Grimes, continue."

Rod bowed to the bench. "Very good, Your Honor. Now, Miss Ross, I ask you again if this school of yours, this notorious forgathering of flotsam, was not designed to foment discontent and disorder among the village landowners and those listed on the rolls?"

"No, it was not so designed."

"Well, then, perhaps you can tell us for what purpose—and whose—it *was* designed."

"I can."

"Then pray do."

"Mr. Talcott—Mr. Robert Talcott, sitting there—came to me on a Sunday morning last year with the idea. He was accompanied by his granddaughters, Posie Talcott and Mrs. Electra Warburton, it was their joint suggestion and——"

"Wait! Stop there, if you please, go no further. You say Mrs. Electra Warburton—the granddaughter of Mr. Robert Talcott?"

"That is correct."

"*The* Mrs. Electra Talcott Warburton, that notorious advocate of abolition, whose every public utterance invites the breaking of the law—?"

"Sir, I object!" Once more Cent Dunnoult had sprung to his feet, shaking with rage.

The judge pounded his gavel and again his features began to darken. "Sir, I told you that if you objected one more time in my court—"

"I heard what you said, Your Honor, but by Jove I'll stand here and object till the cows come home when such talk is permitted to be entered in the record."

"Withhold your profanity from our ears, sir, and *sit down!* Now I've warned you, and I find you in contempt of this court, and fine you the sum of ten dollars. Bailiff, see that you collect the entire consideration. Court's recessed for twenty minutes."

He rapped again, then thrust out his arms, precisely evening the barrels of his cuffs, and abruptly left the bench. The courtroom broke into tumult as the spectators leaped noisily up, starting for the doors, which sprang open while they burst into the cold sunlight outside.

Relieved to be free of the confines of the courtroom, Georgiana welcomed the short recess when they conducted her back to her cell. She ate and drank a little, another slice of buttered bread, a cup of cider, and was punching up stray crumbs when Bobby appeared in the doorway. Behind him came Appleton, with Uncle Jack and Electra. Georgiana was not prepared for the anguishing sight of Appleton: clearly it all was wearing hard on him, if she was any judge.

"My dear, my dear, what a thing," he moaned, pressing her palms against his chest and searching her eyes. "Who ever thought the business would come to this? And you, lodged in this place—I'm glad Molly isn't here to see it."

"Nonsense, Father," Electra put in, "Mother would be every bit as proud as we are. Georgie, you were superb this morning—wasn't she, Granddaddy?"

Old Bobby stepped forward and clasped Georgiana's hand. "Indeed she was, and why should she not be? She's our Georgie. She makes me proud to know her."

They spoke quietly and to some effect, Old Bobby indicating by his encouraging nods that Jake had got a firm handle on things today, and by the time they had to leave Appleton was behaving normally.

"Georgie, my dear, you are a brave, gallant girl to endure this outrageous situation. All decent folk must take pride in the devotion to principle you are demonstrating."

The bell rang, people shuffled their feet and started for the door. Electra took her father's arm and prepared to lead him out. "Kiss Georgie for luck, Father."

Appleton obliged, giving Georgiana a smile as well, but at the moment of parting he sagged again, his eyes tearing, his voice faltering.

"It's all right, you mustn't worry," she tried to assure him.

"That man! That monstrous caviler, Palfrey! Why, he should be driven from the bench, he's so plainly prejudiced. Ought to be flogged!"

There was no time for more. "All ready, please, gentlemen," called the bailiff, and Georgiana was hurried away again, for it did not do to rouse the judge's ire by the sin of tardiness. Back in her seat, she forced herself to relax, closing her eyes and sneaking deep, surreptitious breaths, but the handkerchief in her clenched hand was matted into a thousand messy wrinkles. She lowered her gaze and silently began instructing herself in proper demeanor, absently pressing out the linen square on one knee, while the bailiff rose and reconvened the court. The judge bustled in, spectacles atop his head, and sat down, and though she didn't look at him Georgiana could feel that glittering basilisk's eye battened on her.

"Recall the defendant to the stand," came that sepulchral voice. Georgiana rose from her place and was about to approach the chair when a man, one she had never seen, a stranger, appeared in her path, urgently brushing past to approach the prosecution's table. A hasty colloquy took place, with the men darting meaningful looks toward the doors and at the judge, then Harry Fletcher rose, and with Rod Grimes asked to approach the bench. Another whispered conversation occurred, after which His Honor reset his spectacles and cleared his throat to make an announcement.

"The prosecution has temporarily waived further cross-examination of the defendant in order that we may hear the testimony of yet another witness. We shall proceed accordingly."

Arranging his sleeves again, Palfrey sat back with that grim death's-head look, content for the moment to attend and observe what would next take place. All heads had turned to the rear of the room where just inside the doors several latecomers milled about. Georgiana recognized the face of Val Morgan among them, and the mystery was heightened when, following a slight rearrangement of the group, a vividly dressed female was presented to view. Tossing her head so the feathers on her bonnet danced, her skirts swelling, she tripped to the center of the aisle; then, as she turned more full face, Georgiana's surprise at the disturbance turned to shock. The woman was Rose Mills! Moreover, that gaudy, overdone outfit—the taffeta was plaid, red and yellow with a bright green windowpane overcheck, her bonnet feathers were dyed emerald, and her silk reticule pleated and gathered on a tasseled closure. Clothes such as these were costly; who was footing the bill?

Georgiana stared as, glancing neither right nor left, Rose proceeded to slip into one of the empty seats, whence she smiled coquettishly at Bushrod Grimes, who hovered about her with a show of solicitude and concern, then she began ostentatiously slipping off her gloves. As in a dream, Georgiana heard the judge's gavel rapping for silence, the bailiff calling the court to order, saw the roomful of spectators by degree settling down, watched as her counsel conferred, and Rod Grimes, having spoken again to Judge Palfrey, marched down the aisle until he reached the place where Rose sat. Turning to the bench, he loudly announced:

"The prosecution calls Miss Rose Mills to the stand."

Bending, he assisted her to her feet and conducted her to the witness stand. Her wide hoops swayed and bounced as, head high, she marched to the indicated chair, where she ensconced herself with artful coquetry, then demurely folded her hands and waited for the bailiff to approach her with the Bible. Laying the four fingers of her right hand on the gilt-embossed cover, she held her left palm beside her face, stretching her pale, thin neck as the bailiff gave her the oath.

"Do you swear that the testimony you are about to give here shall be the truth, the whole truth, and nothing but the truth, so help you God?"

"I do," replied Rose.

"State your name."

"My name is Rose Mary Mills——"

"State your address."

"The Old Hundred Tavern."

"Where?"

"I told you, the Old Hundred, at Pequot. My name is Rose Mary——"

"You said that," carped the judge, showing impatience.

"He never let me finish!" she returned resentfully, shooting an accusing look at the erring bailiff.

"Finish, then," the judge demanded. "We haven't all day."

"The fact is," said the witness, "I'm no longer Rose Mary Mills."

"Be good enough to state your full name, then."

"I'm Rose Mary Mills Grimes." She held her hand higher, displaying the gold ring encircling her finger. "I'm the wife of Captain Richard Grimes. Sinjin, to folks hereabouts."

There was a violent stir among the spectators as she sat smugly back in her chair, arranging taffeta folds while a noisy clamor arose and the judge pounded unavailingly with his gavel. The uproar had shown no signs of subsiding when the doors banged open again and all heads turned as Sinjin Grimes himself entered the room to stand looking about him, legs spread, hands on hips, his expression unreadable. Staring, Georgiana fought down the impulse to rush to him. As their eyes met, a familiar current leapt between them. He was sending a message to her alone, she thought, as he laid the palm of one hand over his heart.

For fully five minutes the judge strove to call the courtroom back to order as the rising tide of shocked surprise swept over the proceedings.

"Quiet! Quiet in the courtroom!" shouted the bailiff.

"Clear the room if they won't be silent!" cried the judge, furiously banging his gavel on the bench. At this threat the racket subsided. No one wanted to miss what would happen next. When calm was at last restored, the judge turned once more to Rose.

40

A *Surprise* Witness *Testifies*

IT REQUIRED NO little time for those present in the courtroom to get over the shock of the unscheduled appearance of Rose Grimes, née Mills, before the bar of justice. If her sensational entrance had been staged, an admirable job had been done of it; and if people continued to gulp at what they had learned from the lips of this surprise witness, it was understandable, even pardonable, given the circumstances. And it might even have been forgiven if the witness preened a bit on the stand, for, honestly, what woman wouldn't being the newly declared wife of the dashing Dick Grimes?

In the past Rose had harbored an acute fear of courts and such proceedings as went on in them. Courts were meant to enforce the Law; to her the law was a pack of howling hounds with slavering jaws and sharp claws; was men with badges and loaded guns; was chains and balls and floggings and brandings, starvings and even killings, was families separated at whim, babies torn from their mothers' breasts, husbands stolen from their wives and sold downriver. Rose spat on the law and all its minions. But what, after all, had she to fear from the law now? She was no runaway slave in a red-sprigged dress of yellow calico, with a brand on her shoulder; she was decked out in trappings fit for a queen, and she had a legal spouse, a white man of respectable antecedents, to protect her. What had she to fear from the likes of Louis J. Palfrey? He was not the first bigot she'd ever met, and despite his evil look he wielded no whip, carried no smoking brand.

So Rose faced her interlocutor—her brother-in-law!—with aplomb, while Bushrod, plainly unnerved by her disconcerting announcement, nevertheless took up the questioning, realizing that whatever the embarrassment, Rose's interjection into the proceedings as a prima facie example of the numerous interracial marriages that could be expected as a consequence of such enterprises as the Free School of Pequot Landing could not but aid the prosecution's case, whatever the substance of her testimony. Indeed, on the same grounds, Rod determined to call his brother to the stand as well, and the judge, when the matter was explained to him, agreed, overruling once again the objections of Cent Dunnoult and Jack Talcott, who saw as clearly as their opposite numbers the way in which the testimony of this unlikely pair must play among the jury.

Bushrod cleared his throat ostentatiously. "Now Miss Mills, if you please—" he began.

"Mrs. Grimes, if *you* please. Honest, I don't understand how you keep forgettin' when you 'n' me are brother and sister."

Again there was a hubbub in the court. "Quiet!" charged the judge. "And you"—he was speaking to Rose now— "keep silent on that matter. Your relation to the prosecutor is of no interest to anyone in this place!"

Rose bobbed her head toward the bench. "It's of interest to me, Judge, being as how I've married as far up as Knoxie could ever've hoped for with this little rice picker. I bear the name of Grimes and I am bound to say so."

"*Silence, you—you—!*" He couldn't think of anything odious enough to call her. "One more word out of you, woman, and I'll have you gagged. I'll come down there and gag you myself!"

"But—"

"*Hup!*"

Rose subsided; her "brother" put the question. A silent witness, Rose demurely drew out the silken fingers of her gloves and eschewed reply.

"Answer the question, confound your black hide!" shouted the judge. Still the witness kept mum. Palfrey flung back his sleeves and leaned across his ink-stained blotter.

"Young woman, did you hear me? Answer the question or you'll be jailed for contempt of court."

Rose tossed her head at Rod. "Judge told me not to talk. He told me to shut up. Now I've shut up and he wants me to open again. Why'n't you tell him to make up his mind?"

Palfrey's face turned a dangerous shade of indigo. "By thunder I'll—I'll—" He sputtered and wiped his lips with his sleeve. "Counselor, don't put the bit in that woman's teeth, she'll run with it. Rein her in, rein her in. Squeeze out your answers and then get rid of her."

"Yes, Your Honor. Now—Mrs. Grimes—"

"Yes, brother dear."

This flip rejoinder caused some levity and the judge again had recourse to his gavel.

Rod leaned forward in a confidential manner. "It's easy for us to see, you enjoy scenes, don't you, Mrs. Grimes?"

Rose shrugged. "Not 'specially," she returned laconically.

"Is it not a fact that upon one occasion you went to church and sat downstairs—"

"All kinds of folks sit downstairs at church," Rose retorted.

"But you seated yourself in the pew assigned to one of the deacons of the First Church of Christ Congregational. An act of deliberate malice and provocation designed to give affront to persons of established authority."

Rose wagged her fingers. "If you mean your paw, a man like him takes affront if you no more than sniff at him."

"He has eyes to see with."

"Yes sir, to look down the front of a dress with. A man like that'll about pop his eyeballs to get a good look at a girl's titties."

"That's enough of that kind of talk in my court!" the judge vociferated, banging his gavel again. "Mr. Grimes, will you please attempt to control your witness."

Regarding the bench, Rose spoke solicitously. "Judge, you don't want to get so worked up. You'll bust a gusset. I saw a cast-iron boiler once—"

"Silence!" The roar was leonine.

"I was only saying—"

"Madam—" Rod interrupted her. "What we wish is for you to tell the court what happened on your first night in Pequot Landing."

"I ate roast beef for dinner and I slept in a featherbed. First time, too."

"Hooray for the nigger!" someone shouted. "Hear the coon!" Cheers and catcalls were heard, but this time the judge did nothing to silence the outburst. When the courtroom subsided of its own volition the examination of the witness continued.

"But wasn't there a meeting that very night? And as far as you were able to ascertain—"

Rose tossed her head, setting her feathers dancing. "See here, brother, if you'd stop using all those big words we'd get on some faster. There's other folks want to get to sit in this here chair."

A desperate Bushrod rolled his eyes and rephrased his query. "Is it not a fact that the so-called Free School of Pequot Landing came into being because of you and your sudden advent in the village?"

"Well-l," Rose said with a coyly modest bob of her head, "it's true, I *was* the first pupil. I guess you could say it was Rose gave the teacher there the idea."

"You of course refer to the defendant, Georgiana Ross. Exactly how did you give Miss Ross the idea for the school?"

"I was tellin' all the folks 'bout Miz Frain. She's the preacher's wife that first taught me readin' and writin'."

"And tell us, Rose, isn't it a fact that the Talcotts drove to New York in mid-October of last year with the express purpose of bringing you back to the village of Pequot Landing where Appleton Talcott had arranged with the local constabulary to create a public debacle?"

"No, that is not a fact. The fact is what everyone knows. I ran off from

Laceyville, like my grammaw Knoxie told me to. I came north with Becker and Donald, we got to New Haven, we were headin' for the border, Becker and Donald were taken, but I got plumb away. Being thirsty, I stepped into some woods lookin' for water and the birds came—"

"What birds would those be?"

"Well, all them damn pigeons!" Rose exclaimed indignantly. "Millions and millions of 'em, they like to of scairt me outta my skin, I came runnin' outta the woods, the Talcotts were just passing in the yellow coach, they were kindly folks and they took me along home. Then the slave-catchers caught me, the Talcotts bought me my freedom. That's how I came to be in Pequot Landing."

"Yes, I see. Most interesting." Rod's tone was smoothly suggestive. "And once you had been insinuated into the Talcott household you no doubt heard certain things, didn't you?"

Rose shrugged indifferently. "I heard plenty. What kind of things?"

"Things about the school?"

"I guess. Everyone was always talking 'bout the school."

Rod sucked his teeth and pursed his fleshy lips. "I'm sure they were. Now, please, tell the court, what sort of talk did you hear?"

"They were sayin' the school was going to make people sit up and take notice. They were sayin' it would make a big stir hereabouts." She glanced at Georgiana. "And it did, for sure."

"And you were the first pupil at the school?"

"That's right. Miss Ross said I was in the vanguard."

"And what else did Miss Ross say to you?"

"She said we was—*were*—livin' in troubled times, and things were bound to get worse before they got better. But if I and the other girls would be model students, then people would get the idea that all us colored folks should have schoolin'. *I* says, 'I ain't colored folks'—that is, I *said,* 'I'm *not* a colored lady.' And she said—"

"Yes? What did she say?"

"That's all right." Rose was suddenly subdued. "Never mind."

"But we do mind. Go on, by all means."

Rose pressed her fingers to her lips. "I disremember."

Rod leaned close in a confidential manner. "That's all right, Mrs. Grimes, try and remember; we have plenty of time."

"I just don't recollect." She shifted uneasily in the chair.

Judge Palfrey's eyes snapped and he jabbed his finger at the witness. "You had *better* recollect, missy, and quick or I will know the reason why."

"I can tell you the reason why, Judge, it's 'cause my brain's got flustered, that's why."

"That's to say if you have a brain, or the tenth part of one. Proceed."

"I forgot the question," said Rose, licking a fingertip.

Her words evoked further hilarity. Again the judge threatened to clear the courtroom. Then, as the pale winter light filtering through the grimy windows began turning blue in the cold, Bushrod Grimes resumed his questioning, eliciting from the witness all she knew about the "conspiracy" by which was founded the Free School of Pequot Landing.

"Is it not a fact that Georgiana Ross entered into deliberate acts of collusion with such people as Robert Talcott and his granddaughter, Electra Talcott Warburton, with the full knowledge and approval and financial encouragement of others in the village of Pequot Landing to deliberately cause friction and incite civil unrest, no matter the cost to law-abiding folk?"

Rose blinked. "My, brother, how your words do run on!"

The gavel sounded its warning tattoo. "Answer the question!"

"No! No! And no, again! When you've lived the life I have," she went on, "you're never sure of anything—'ceptin' to know there's mean and cruel men 'round every corner, behind every tree 'n' bush, waitin' to do you a bad turn if they can. All Miss Georgiana Ross tried to do was to start up a little school to teach folks like me how to get on in life so's they wouldn't lie around at the bottom of the barrel." All trace of raillery had disappeared from Rose's voice, her features were composed and set, and her large dark eyes flicked from face to face as she talked, as if she had traveled a long distance to speak these words.

"Miss Ross didn't do anything wrong. What she done—did—was good, and she did it from the goodness of her heart, 'cause she's a good person. And she got back a lot worse than she gave. But that's what happens in the world, you do something nice for folks and you get back a slap in the chops. But if you think you folks dragged us back to Pequot to get Rose to say Georgie Ross did somethin' wrong, you's—you are—sadly mistaken—'cause she never did. Georgie, you was—were—true blue."

She looked past Bushrod at Georgiana, who flushed, then lowered her head.

Reddening, Rod abruptly dismissed the witness, giving up hope of eliciting any damaging testimony, and, after the defense, deciding to let Rose's telling words stand, declined cross-examination, Sinjin Grimes was called.

The moment he got to his feet among the spectators and strolled to the witness chair, boot heels clicking smartly on the planks, he became as much the center of the proceedings as his wife had been before him.

He seated himself calmly enough, however, and having stated his name, occupation, and place of residence, he smiled agreeably at his stepbrother and awaited his first question.

"You are the legal spouse of the previous witness?"

"So it would seem."

"How long have you been married?"

"Some few weeks, no more. We got spliced at New York City."

"Arrrgghhhh—!" The judge leaned aside and spat into the spittoon by his chair leg. Wiping his lips on his sleeve he glared at Sinjin. "Mean to tell this court you married that wench without a muzzle at your ear?"

"That's correct, Your Honor, the pretty creature's mine and I love her dearly."

"Arrrggghhh!" Palfrey's features contorted into those of a gargoyle. "This is the *most* disgusting—the most *reprehensible*—the most *disgraceful* thing I have ever been forced to look upon while seated on this bench. The state would indeed do well to look to its laws when such travesties are perpetrated among decent, God-fearing people."

Sinjin crossed his legs. "Are you speaking to me, Your Honor?"

"Yes, Captain Grimes, it is to you that I speak." The judge's voice shook with acrimony. "I regard this—this *liaison*—as an affront not only to myself and this court, but to all decent-minded citizens of this fine state. What civilized white man of good family and standing in the community would debase himself so wantonly as to join in wedlock with a member of an inferior race? Why, indeed, would a supposedly intelligent man of property so degrade himself—"

Cent stood and interrupted. "Your Honor, I strenuously object to these offensive remarks. My client has nothing to do with the private affairs of Rose Mills and Captain Grimes."

"Does she not? What was that school but the occasion for making niggers forget their place? And here we see the results. The next thing you know, having bedded her, he'll have seeded her, too, and then there'll be a little nigger baby in the cradle."

"Your Honor, I *do* protest!"

"Sit down, sir, and be silent till I've finished speaking." The judge turned again to Sinjin. "By God, sir, if I live to be a hundred, I'll never understand what can have possessed a man like yourself to have done as you have done. Have you given no thought to the offspring of such a union?"

Sinjin smiled easily. "I have, your Honor. Indeed, I am pleased to say that as a result of just such a congress Mrs. Grimes is enceinte, and in due course is going to make me the father I have always yearned to be." Having divested himself of this surprising statement, he went on to insert his tongue squarely in his cheek. "In which happy event," he continued, "and should fate be disposed to provide me with a male heir, we shall mayhap christen him Louis, in order to suitably memorialize these historic proceedings."

The judge ran a palm over his brow and tugged at his hair. "Do you make sport of me, sir? Do you joke with me?"

"Not I, Your Honor. As I am sure you are aware, the name Louis is an honorable one, a venerable appellation, is it not?"

Palfrey pushed back and pinched his earlobe. "I hope to say it is!"

"Indeed," the captain went on in his smoothest tone, "were not eighteen of the reigning monarchs in one of the world's great nations of that same name?"

The judge bridled with pleasure. "Well, yes, to be sure. Louis the Sun King, for one."

"To say nothing of the fat doltish one, I mean the poor booby whose head the mob lopped off, as well as the one currently squatting on his big rump in the Tuileries. The Citizen King, they call him, you know. But a Louis all the same. According to the published cartoons he is shaped like a pear and carries an umbrella. So much for all the Louis's, what say, Your Honor?"

He waggled the shiny toe of one boot so it caught the light and waited for a response that was not immediately forthcoming. His mockery had produced a reaction from the judge so violent as to be nearly apoplectic. Palfrey's eyes started in their sockets, he spat cottony flecks of white, and though his lips moved no words were audible. It was some moments before he found his tongue.

"How dare you, sir! How dare you address me thus and use me for an object of ridicule!"

The witness was innocence personified. "Alas, I fear your Honor misinterprets my remarks."

"Do I? Prosecutor, you have ten minutes to conclude your questioning of this witness. When you're done he'll pay his fine and vacate."

"Am I fined, then, Judge? You haven't said, you know."

"You'll be fined and generously, before we're done this day," growled Palfrey.

"Thank you, I was only asking." Sinjin turned to Bushrod, who, his cheeks red with embarrassment, nevertheless resumed his questioning, for a glance at the jury had assured him that, however amusing to the courtroom at large, Sinjin's antics in offending the dignity of the Court had offended their own dignity as well.

"Let us pass on, Captain, to your association with the defendant, Miss Ross, mistress of the Free School. You are long acquainted, I believe."

"Oh yes, as you should well remember, Brother Rod, since it was directly because of you that she and I first met. In case the incident has slipped your mind, this occurred one afternoon after school when you'd chased Georgie into the woods and were trying to toss up her skirts for a loutish peek. I gave you a good clout, a thing I have always found it agreeable to do. You ran home and squealed to His Nibs there. I got a good flogging; I can still feel it. But on that day my fortunes turned, for that was when Miss Ross and I first became acquainted with each other. We have been friends ever since."

Rod, who had been unable to squelch this outpouring, attempted to redirect his line of questions. "What can you tell us of the Free School?"

"That it's a fine school, a reputable and worthwhile institution, that the pupils studying with Miss Ross are receiving valuable learning."

"In what way?"

Though formerly his levity and irony had been evident with his every word, now he spoke earnestly, explaining that he had on numerous occasions visited the schoolroom over the seed store, that he had talked to Georgiana's pupils both there and in the cemetery. He readily enumerated the topics of his talks and stated what enlightening effects he hoped his words had had on the girls. He confessed that he'd enjoyed himself thoroughly and would be happy to do it again should the occasion arise.

"It won't, I promise you!" snapped the judge.

"But Your Honor, how can we know these things?" Sinjin mildly remonstrated.

"As we know the sun shall rise tomorrow. Prosecutor, finish up and be quick about it!"

Rod did his best to comply. "Is it not a fact, Captain, that at the behest of Miss Ross you used this opportunity to address to a pack of ignorant darkies inflammatory remarks, designed to stir in the breasts of each and every one of them resentments and longings never to be realized, to inculcate in innocent, one might even say, retarded, minds, revolutionary ideas unfitting for their stations in life?"

"It's true, I did attempt to stir them to higher hopes. After all, 'Hope, like the gleaming taper's light, adorns and cheers our way; And still, as darker grows the night, emits a brighter ray.' "

"Come, come, witness, omit the verse, this is not a classroom but a courtroom!"

"Thank you for explaining the distinction, Your Honor," returned Sinjin politely. "I did wonder."

This response provoked another fit of mirth among the spectators, which the judge again rapped his gavel to quell.

"That's enough!" he shouted. "Leave the stand, go on, get down!"

"Yes, Your Honor. If I may have but one word more . . ."

"Well? What is it? Make it brief."

"Thank you, Your Honor." He looked across the spectators' heads to where the representatives of the press were jotting notes on the tops of their hats, then went on. "In one of those little schoolroom talks the eminent prosecutor has made such pointed reference to, I described for Miss Ross's pupils some of the events surrounding a shipwreck I was involved in, the luckless but gallant *Nonpareil* that went down off the coast of Africa. Some of us aboard were that lucky to be washed ashore and rescued from drowning, but we were captured by Arabs who sold us into slavery. It's true. We were nineteen white men, and Americans to boot, yet they riveted iron rings around our necks and put fetters on our legs and made us walk barefoot over the burning sands to a fortress where we were locked up in stone cells."

"Doubtless you deserved the locking up," grumbled the still choleric Palfrey.

At his words Sinjin bristled visibly. "No sir, we did *not* deserve it! We were free men, but we were made slaves, and I will tell this court as I told Georgiana's pupils, slavery is a very bad thing. It stinks to high heaven, and I say to any man who would enslave his fellow—no matter the color of his skin—I say be damned to him. Be damned to your blasted cotton kings who grow their crops by the sweat of a bonded man's toil and be damned to these northern hypocrites who condone it."

The judge strained forward and his voice rasped. "It's the law that condones it, sir! As do I, as an upholder of the law."

"Then the law must be changed. As for yourself, Judge, you know better than I just what *you* are."

"What am I then?"

"Since you so kindly ask, I shall try to tell you. Just to look at you makes me want to puke. But I guess you're not the only long-earred jackass to sit at a courtroom bench. You are bought and sold like Dickon, you can be had for a handful of silver, no man in these parts is a greater hypocrite or owns a more scurrilous or lying tongue. You are, in short, a despicable excuse for a judge, or a human being for that matter."

Palfrey was on his feet gesticulating at the bailiff. "Call in the sergeant-at-arms. I want this man put in irons! I want him hanged!"

Shoving the bailiff away, Sinjin sprang onto the witness chair, shouting as he pointed at the judge.

"Go stick your own scrawny neck in irons, you piss-ant. If you're a judge I'm a five-toed sloth, and if this is a court of law I'll kiss your fat ass on Central Row at high noon." He shook his fist while the spectators roared their own opinions on one side or the other and the bailiff came rushing at him and tried to pull him from his perch.

"Is he mad?" the judge screamed above the din. "Has he completely taken leave of his senses? This is a court of law!"

"No it isn't!" Sinjin shouted back through cupped hands. "It isn't anything like a court of law. It isn't a court of justice, either. This is a roman cloaca. If this proceeding is what passes for legal justice in this world I'd as lief seek another."

"As you soon shall, when I'm done with you!"

Hearing these words, Rachel Grimes was on her feet, pushing her way through the crowd. "Oh no, Judge, he doesn't mean it, he's not himself."

"Be silent!" thundered the judge. "Get that harpy out of here. Haven't I enough trouble trying to bring order to this bedlam?"

Rachel drew back in affront. "Don't you tell me to be silent, sir!"

"Shut your trap, old woman."

"Your Honor, this is my grandmother, Rachel Grimes!" exclaimed Bushrod.

No sooner had the name been spoken than the judge was obsequiously bowing across his bench. "Oh, madam, I offer you my sincere apologies, I did not know you. Please ignore my outburst."

"Don't do it, Grammaw," Sinjin urged. "A minute ago he was ready to curse you, but when he found out your name was Grimes—"

"Sit down! Sit down, I say!"

Sinjin stopped his prancing in the chair and sat again. "Very well, Your Honor. Now what?"

"Now what? *Now what?* I'll tell you what? You have finished yourself here. I might have known the minute you sat down in that chair what mischief you were up to. You are a poltroon, a shabby man without morals or scruples. You have connived with the defendant in this shabby school affair, you are in league with the Antichrist, you are a blight upon the whole community, and you are offensive to all decent people everywhere. Now, sir, what have you got to say to that?"

Sinjin smiled thinly. "Fuck you, Your Honor."

Palfrey froze, his eyes popping under his beetling brow. *"What—did—you—say?"*

"You heard me, Looie. Fuck you and fuck all your kind, fuck you from the tops of the tall mountains to the bottoms of the lowest hell of hells. Fuck you now and evermore."

"And that's where I'll see you gone to, to the lowest of hell, you and your filthy mouth."

Sinjin's laugh rang out, while the spectators gaped, silenced at last.

"That's where we'll meet, I am sure of that, in hell."

"Oh, Sinjin, don't," wailed his grandmother, "the man'll get the upper hand of you."

"I *have* the upper hand of him, madam," said the judge ominously. "As he quickly will see."

"It's all right, Grammaw, the big bad man's not going to hurt me."

"Not much he's not! Let's start with a hundred dollar fine or thirty days for contempt of court. How do you like that?"

"Fine, Judge." He reached into a pocket and produced a purse fat as a Polish sausage. Extracting a handful of coins, he tossed them onto the bench. "Don't spend it all in one place, Louis," he said. "Oh, and get yourself a shave while you're at it." He spun a shiny quarter through the air and it landed in the judge's lap.

"Come on, Grammaw," he said, putting Rachel's arm through his, "let's get some lunch, I'm starved. And I want to introduce you to my wife . . . Rose, come and meet your new grammaw—"

41

The Ides of March Street

ROSE HAD TO LAUGH. Honest, who would've thought things would ever turn out like this? That she'd sweep into a courtroom and be able to announce her married name in such a public way and knock the whole place upside down? More, that she could sit there in the chair, with one and all hanging on her every word, and make sport of Bushrod Grimes. And the judge with that hound-dog face of his gone the color of an eggplant and him spitting like an adder. Humph! She'd shown him not to call her a nigger.

Rose's triumph notwithstanding, exactly as predicted, a day and a half later Georgiana Ross lost her case. She was convicted by a jury of her peers, and for her offense was fined the sum of five hundred dollars, the full amount allowed by law, which Palfrey had taken to the extreme. Refusing all offers of financial assistance from friends and well-wishers, she had insisted on paying the fine out of her own meagre savings, and with this payment the most notorious and unjust of cases came to a close, except for the appeal to the Court of Errors, which was filed the next day.

Thus, when Georgiana Ross regained her freedom it was not at the hands of judge, jury, or justice. The first had denounced her, the second repudiated her, and the third had shown it was—well, blind. For her counsel had been proved right, as indeed had been Bushrod Grimes, concerning the effect of the testimony provided by the captain and his spouse. Moreover, not only had Georgiana lost the case, the cause had suffered grievously as well, for the antiabolitionist press had a field day on the subject of Sinjin Grimes and his "colored wife." Few who had known of it had forgotten, and all were eager to report that not too long ago this same Mrs. Grimes had made off with Mab Talcott's silver spoons or that little more than twelve months ago she had been advertised in the papers as a runaway, pursued by slave catchers, thereafter manumitted and put into paid service with a cap and feather duster, or that she was, no matter how "white," at bottom, of tainted blood! The headlines alone were sufficient to make any decent person cringe (an outraged Old Bobby Talcott decreed that the *Courant* no longer be delivered to the doorstep of Kingdom Come), and it was thus with heavy heart that Georgiana returned to Pequot Landing.

There, while she waited for the appeals to run their course she took up her life again, though without the teaching it seemed empty. Still, there were frequent visits to Aunt Hat at the almshouse, semi-weekly excursions to Lamentation, where Hutta, Easter, and the rest of the girls continued to weave hats, and regular attendance at Abolition meetings, for she had in no way deserted the cause. And, because no matter what he had done she could not bring herself to abandon her old friend, there were calls to be made upon those newly wed village folk, Sinjin and Rose Grimes.

As described in the newspapers, the pair were the focus of attention for man, woman, and child, their names on everybody's lips, their frequent sartorial innovations the cynosure of every envious eye. Rose's colorful ensembles especially seemed calculated to attract the admiring or curious glance; if Georgiana Ross had sought to shun the spotlight, Rose was as a flame to the moths. She and Sinjin were, in fact, living the good life, for while he had never arrived at Havana, Sinjin's voyage had nonetheless proved a success. Though, thanks to his hasty departure, his ice cargo had all but melted even before he made Savannah and the resulting residue of liquid had to be pumped out of the bilge, at the gaming tables of that city his luck had been good, and he had traded his winnings for a cargo of indigo and rice, which he had in turn carried to Key West and exchanged for the Havana cigars he had just sold at a handsome profit in New York.

Within a week of their sensational return to Pequot Landing, while Sinjin oversaw the refitting of the *Sparrow,* Rose was busy setting up housekeeping in a small two-bedroom house at the end of March Street—at the unfashionable end of March Street to be sure, where the wooden sidewalk became sand and weeds, adjoining an indifferently harrowed field in which in summertime a quit-rent farmer raised onion sets and sugar beets, and ragged lines of scrubby trees ran away into a thick tract of gloomy firs extending nearly to the river at the ferry slip—but March Street nevertheless. While Sinjin despised the place—he had bought it only because no one in town would sell him any better—Rose was pleased enough, and soon made it known that she was "at home." What she really expected, Georgiana did not know, but the fact was that, except for Georgiana and Helen and Rachel Grimes, who no more than Georgiana could abandon their adored Sinjin, none of the town's ladies ever came to visit, and even while Georgiana marveled at Rose's new estate, she could not help feeling sorry for her. There was something so pathetic in her attempts to appear "genteel," to show off her new clothes and furbelows, whose tawdriness in turn made her look cheap and overdressed. She wanted so desperately to be accepted, to be taken for what she hoped she might be as much as what she actually was. But no matter how luxurious her plumage, the fact remained that her husband had, in the view of all the village, committed a cardinal sin by marrying Aurora Sheffield's lady's maid, who, though she might look as white as the driven snow, could still be pointed at and called a nigger.

Why he should have done so, even given the fact of Rose's pregnancy, remained a mystery, one that Georgiana's first private conversation with him since his return did little to dispel, though it proved otherwise enlightening. One evening when she had rounded off an especially dramatic address before the Anti-Slavery Society, she was surprised to find Sinjin waiting for her outside the Academy Hall. He had his natty hired chaise, and asked if he might drive her home.

"Take me for a little ride, won't you?" Georgiana asked, climbing in beside him. "I haven't had any fresh air all day."

They drove to the ferry and went across to Naubuc Farms, then rolled and bumped along the dirt paths that passed for roads on that side of the river, among the dead tobacco fields, forlorn in the evening mists. Sinjin complimented Georgiana on her speech, which she was pleased to learn he had made an effort to come and hear, and was admiring of the manner in which she, always shy in public, had handled herself before an audience. She thanked him, but when she added nothing more, he glanced sideways at her, curious and, for him, unsure of himself.

"I guess you're probably angry with me," he said.

"Why should I be angry with you?"

"For marrying Rose."

" 'Of all people,' do you mean? It's hardly any of my affair, or anyone else's, I should think. If you love each other—"

He snorted contemptuously, bringing her up sharp.

"Love," he said under his breath, as if the word were a curse. "That's a good one."

"Oh dear," she murmured. "I'm sorry, truly."

The look he gave her was filled with self-loathing. "Don't pity me, George, I couldn't stand it. Not from you."

"Don't you love her?"

He stared at her. "Do you think I've completely taken leave of my senses?"

"Then why?"

"That's the tinker's tale, it'll catch a crowd at any crossroads."

"You are jocular this evening. I thought perhaps you waited for me because you wanted to talk—seriously I mean."

"Oh, it's all *quite* serious, if truth be told. I just don't know where to begin."

"Perhaps the beginning might be a good place. For instance, how did you and Rose meet again, after . . ."

"After Bible Rock, you mean. Well, that was as neat a piece of bad luck as ever man has seen." He chuckled mirthlessly. "She was right there, waiting for me, like Miss Muffet and the spider. I was Miss Muffet, she was the spider, black and leggy and with a powerful bite. There she was—"

"Where?"

"We'd put in at New York, Billy and I had a bite of supper and were looking to take in a show."

"Lordy, don't tell me Rose was in it."

"Not our Rose. But there she was, the belle of Castle Garden. She was all dandied up and she had a farmer from Elmira in tow. You'd have hardly recognized her. She gave her flatfooted companion the gate and joined us for supper. We renewed our acquaintance."

"After she'd burned your manuscript?"

"She said she was sorry for that. Ambo made her lose her head. In any event, Billy and I invited her along. She said yes."

"Billy and you. When will you learn?"

He made no response to this, merely going on with his story. "I was planning to kiss friend Rosie good-bye when we got back from our little cruise, only . . ." His haphazard remarks wobbled to a halt.

"You found you couldn't live without her," Georgiana suggested.

"Um, something like that."

"So you married her and brought her home to your grandmother and the whole town, where as anyone can see she's been welcomed with open arms."

Sinjin ran his fingers through his hair; his tone was self-deprecating.

"I had to marry her, George. Because of the baby. I didn't want to, God knows, only I couldn't just, well, slip her a few bucks and then leave her." Georgiana was silent. "Well, you tell me—could I?"

She stared at him, his grim profile sharp against the river light, his cheeks in need of a shave. A thousand others, perhaps, would have paid Rose off and abandoned her, but not Sinjin Grimes; she sorrowed for him. "I don't suppose you'd have been the first man to have avoided a wedding in such a situation," she said, by way of answering his question.

"I know it, don't think I don't. But I got to thinking. There was Caroline, you see. She was raised by some other man for a father, not me. Then, before I could see her again, get to know her a little, she was taken from me. Dead, and in such a way." He cleared his throat and went on. "I decided that here was another child and I was its father and I wanted to make things right. And maybe when she does come, this baby—"

Georgiana smiled. "Why are you so sure it will be a 'she'?"

"I'm not, of course; maybe it'll be a boy, but—I still think of Caro, I suppose. Truly, I hope it's a girl."

"Of course you do! I'm glad. And I'm glad that Rose can make you happy."

His bleak expression reflected the unlikelihood of this. Still, he was game, he would try. He had brought her home a bride, they would settle down and raise their child—there might be others, and one day they'd be the Darby and Joan of Pequot Landing.

"But why here?" she asked.

"Hm?"

"Why did you bring her here?"

"I live here, don't I?"

"Only occasionally. Have you thought about what it will be like for Rose, married to you, living among these people who've been so unfriendly to her?"

"She'll get used to them."

"I'm not so sure they'll get used to her."

He shrugged and wiped his lips. "She looks white enough, I guess."

"But she's *not* white and everybody knows it. The same people who burned down my school."

"Spilt milk, George," he said roughly. "No sense crying over it, and when Aurora—never mind, forget it."

"No. Say it. Right out." But he wouldn't. She turned sideways to him. "Sinjin, if you meant when Rora comes back, I don't think you can count on that."

"Why not?"

"She intends to take orders."

"You mean she's going to go through with it?" Georgiana nodded. "Well, that tears it, I do believe. Lady Sheffield in a wimple, with a solitary couch? Little prayers tucked away in nooks and crannies. She'll go into spectacles, too, no doubt. Why, I wonder, are there so many nearsighted nuns! Perhaps religion is bad for the eyes." He slid her a sidelong look. "How is the worthy padre, by the way? I've never had the opportunity to thank him for helping me out of Rora."

Regarding his sarcasm as unworthy of response, she merely said that he was well. When they got to Siam below Naubuc Farms Sinjin turned his rig around and they came back the same way they'd gone; by the time they reached Pequot again Georgiana had promised him to do what she could to assist Rose in finding her footing in the village, though she thought the task would prove impossible. One thing she did manage was to find Rose kitchen help, something she was in need of. The tavern slavey, Annie Skaats, came in three or four times a week to char and neaten up, and to prepare meals. No great cook, the girl could nevertheless put together simple fare without scorching it, so that Sinjin didn't fall to complaining about the vittles he was being served at home. But that didn't keep him from eating out of Sallie's kitchen every chance he got.

AND what of Rose herself? It would seem that in a relatively short time she had got everything she'd ever wanted. Casting her mind back to those longing-filled spring evenings when she'd shed tears over the beauty of the blossoms in Mab Talcott's garden, the waxy lustrousness of a single moon-drenched magnolia flower, the heady fragrance of honeysuckle, the ineffably sweet nights that anguished her because she was so lonesome; back to her deep yearning to become someone of consequence, and, heading the list, her passion for Sinjin Grimes—why, in almost the blink of an eye, all had become hers. The lowly slave–turned–hired girl was now the wife of the most famous, handsomest captain along the river, a village matron with her own house (it had a picket fence into the bargain), a bay horse and a chaise, a variety of clothes and hats and shoes, everything a girl like Rose could possibly want. Time and time again she took stock; time and time again it all totted up like the neat columns of figures in a bank ledger. Time and time again she told herself how lucky she was. No matter how humble her abode, as Captain Grimes's wedded wife she owned a rightful place in the world. The name of Grimes, readily recognizable among the descendants of the old River God aristocracy of Hartford, gave her cachet on several levels, and while as a female with African blood flowing in her veins, formerly the bound property of another, she knew she would never be admitted to the parlors of Pequot Landing's first families, this realization did not overly trouble her. Though it irked her to be deliberately snubbed along Main Street or on Hartford's Central Row; if, having learned how to play whist, she found herself excluded from a fashionable card party (and admittedly, she would have relished an invitation, if only to show off her newly acquired skills), she was certain in the core of her being that somehow, sometime, in some way, the day would arrive when such snubs wouldn't matter a hill of beans to Rose Grimes. For by that time she would have thought of a way to make these turnip–heads eat their dish of crow, herself to proceed along to more important matters.

Meanwhile, she was resolved to bend with the wind, at least for now; she must bide her time and keep a sharp eye out for inadvertencies. She knew this as if by some arcane agency, and would hold herself in patience until things took a happy turn or the right opportunity arose. She had sharp ears, she would hear that knock when it came.

Moreover, if not "smart" in the scholastic sense, Rose was both shrewd and enterprising, intrepid as a fox, or the vixen of that clever species, and she was possessed of a keen awareness of which side her bread was buttered on—as well as of who happened to be holding the butter knife. It didn't take a genius to see that her surprise appearance on the witness stand and the way she'd managed to hold both Bushrod and Zion Grimes up to public ridicule had earned her enemies. But what cared she, when her shocking marriage to Zion's stepson doubtless would have accomplished the same thing? And with Sinjin her champion—wasn't she his "to have and to hold, from this day forth"? That's what Captain Goodnaught had read out in their wedding ceremony aboard the *Grace & Favour*—and surely she had nothing to fear from any Grimes living, whoever he might be. It even occurred to her that the time might come when it would amuse her to toy with one or the other, old Grimes or young Grimes, or perhaps even both together. Given the chance, she would work her wiles; she'd seen how the elder

Grimes's lecherous eyes had looked her over every chance they got, lingering on her figure, and the way his toad's tongue ran around his cracked lips as he tried to wet them. She wanted to laugh, the old goat, she knew why she made him quiver, and what he wanted to do about it. It would suit her just fine to make him her own creature.

And Zion's son offered even better; as far as Rose was concerned Bushrod was nothing to fear. Despite the fact that he was a blowhard and frequently full of hot air, she had also decided he would get ahead, maybe even in a big way; she had an eye for these things. Properly handled, a man like that could prove useful—if not right now, perhaps at a later time. She thought back to that cold, snowy day he'd taken her for a sleigh ride and she'd had to fight off his burly advances. One snap of her fingers and couldn't she just get him to sit up and bark for her! He might even run and fetch; she might stick a ruff on him and a pointed hat with a pom-pom, like a trick dog in a show. Yes, she would like to make him sit up and beg. She had learned that a little planning ahead never hurt a girl, especially where the opposite sex was concerned, and when Sinjin was off on one of his voyages, a friend like Bushrod Grimes could easily prove useful, and who knew, maybe even diverting. Of course it all depended on what he would be looking for when that day came in return for favors offered or services rendered. At present he remained incensed over the way she'd provoked him in court, and it was going to take a while for him to cool down before she could speak to him privately.

Still, so far, according to her own estimate, Rose reckoned to have improved her lot about five hundred percent. She was no Cinnamon, she couldn't foretell what tomorrow might hold for her, but one thing she did know: her future was certain to be rosy. Marvelous things lay in store, and when they came she would make the most of them. And why not? Only a fool would let her chances slip by, and Rose was no fool.

42

The Forge

As THE OLD YEAR came to an end and the new one began, Appleton Talcott's mood continued one of deepest despondency despite all the efforts to draw him out—efforts that included a more or less regular schedule of amusing, absorbing, or otherwise distracting activities instituted by the various family members, with a routine of games, readings, picture puzzles, cryptograms, reports of new inventions, and the like. To round things out, a formal tea was served each afternoon at five sharp, in front of the parlor fire where agreeable talk would be exchanged, and Priam would regularly stop by with news of the city. Together his family and friends worked matters out so that Appleton was seldom left to his own devices, except at night, when his solitariness did not admit of sleep, so that he lay spent and exhausted even at first cock's crow.

One hope, or the tiniest glimmer thereof, was his reaching out to Georgiana, as if she alone was able to help raise the millstone of grief that hung so heavily about his neck. However she was able, she did her best to fill in the abyss created by Mab's untimely passing; mornings when Luke Haverstraw's buggy deposited her at the house, she would read articles to him from the newspaper, and they spent long hours with his old favorites by Sir Walter Scott, as well as with such recent works as Thackeray's *Comic Tales and Sketches,* which made him laugh aloud. Any talk of Mab, however, proved fruitless; the merest mention of her name invariably occasioned tears, some lachrymose reminiscence that only lowered his spirits again, and sometimes Georgiana feared he might never be persuaded back from the melancholy road he had chosen for himself. Then, on the second day of the new year, when they were "second-day-ing" on the New Year's ham, when the family visitors had left—Posie to Boston, Minnie and her family back to Glens Falls, Electra and Lloyd to Philadelphia, where she was to give an address at Independence Hall in the shadow of the bell the abolitionists had begun calling the Liberty Bell—when at last Number 17 lay quiet, empty, and austere, on that morning, while Appleton was taking his morning coffee in the breakfast room, while Old Bobby worked on his history of Pequot Landing and Trubey waxed the Pilgrim Carver chair, the knocker sounded and the door opened. Aurora Sheffield stood on the stoop.

Looking thinner by far than when she left, and of a decidedly nervous disposition, she swept into the house asking Alabaster to help her driver with the luggage, then greeting first Trubey, then Burdy, then Halley and Judah, then her father, whose eyes streamed with tears at the sight of her, and finally Granddaddy, who'd appeared quill in hand to see what all the noise was about.

Her things were carried up to the blue room where she was soon reinstalled, while Agrippina fluttered about, chattering ten to the dozen, and Trubey opened her trunk and sent Burdy off with articles to be pressed. The minute Pina went down to see about Appleton's lunch, Aurora instructed Trubey to send Jeffrey-Amherst to Gaunt House and tell Georgiana to come immediately.

Georgiana was not at Gaunt House; Jeff learned from George and Darcy that she and Helen had taken the girls skating on the Cove, so it was a good hour before she appeared in Aurora's doorway.

"Georgie, darling, you look like a schoolgirl, you have apples in your cheeks!"

Aurora rushed to greet her friend, pressing her lips to Georgiana's cold, rosy face and hugging her hard. Georgiana, who could not have been more taken aback, allowed herself to be seated in the window chair, while Aurora, after closing the door, pulled up a chair and, holding tightly to Georgiana's hands, divulged the sequence of events that had brought her back to Pequot Landing once again.

"I'm sure Mama would be very disappointed in me," she confessed humbly, that sweet, meek innocence returning to displace the more worldly creature who had only an hour before untied her veil and removed her feathered bonnet.

"But what happened?" Georgiana asked. "You're not ill, are you?"

"No, I'm perfectly fine. I *was* sick—for a little—"

She proceeded to a series of revelations that Georgiana listened to with suppressed surprise, even shock. Aurora declared that she had entered the convent with the sincerest profession of faith and the fervent desire to bring herself closer to God, but try as she might she could not forget the past, that recent and most distressing past whose linchpin was and remained Sinjin Grimes. For the truth was—she realized it now—she had been using her faith like a magic wand, to her own warped ends. She had been fleeing from a man's hot hands in the misguided belief that merely to be removed from a bitter world would wipe out all memory of him and provide her the peace she so desperately sought.

Divining this, Mother Veronica had sent for her former charge and minced no words. "When you come here," she had told the would-be postulant, "you come here vouchsafed to God, to serve Him and love Him all your days, you do not come to hide from the world. You do not run away, you run *to*. Now, Aurora, I demand to know, which are you doing?" And in the end she had been obliged to confess that it was the desire to hide from people, more particularly her lover, that had lured her there, to shut out the pain and guilt simply by removing herself from the path of danger. Mother Veronica had been at pains to impress upon her the fact that this sort of thinking would not do. Hiding was no cure for anything. Trouble and sorrow must be met head-on. Moreover, the way of the nun was far too rigorous and demanding, she could not possibly hope to answer its requirements, no matter her professed devotion and love of God.

Aurora had begged for time, which was duly granted, but had fared no better as a result. She took an oath of fasting, but failed to honor it. Made an oath of silence, couldn't keep it. Overslept, so she had to be awakened. Was late for chapel, late for meals, prayers. Was exposed in the wicked act of smuggling hard spirits into the convent. The sisters were scandalized!

Riddled with sin, she had begged forgiveness from God, from the sisters, from Mother Superior, from herself as well. Her knees had become callused from being put to the stones, and she had taken to wearing in private a sinister undergarment of her own devising, a plain cotton chemise into whose fabric she had inserted pins that mortified her flesh as a constant reminder of what she had done. But the wounds had become infected, making her ill and forcing out her secret. Mother Veronica had been outraged.

"We need no fanatics here," she declared. "You are of the flesh, even though you pretend otherwise. You cannot chastise yourself on the one hand and revel in the profane memory of this man on the other."

At last Aurora had been forced to own that everything she stood accused of was true: she took false pride in her suffering, she was not humble, but vainglorious, she did not believe deep down that she could ever be a good nun, however much she claimed she wished to be. And at the bottom of it all lay her inchoate feelings for the man she had given herself to, the memory of which colored her every breathing minute, the mere thought of whom had continued to drive her to distraction. Her passion was both undeniable and unconquerable.

So she had failed, failed miserably in her sincere intent, but from that failure was now born the realization that although a miscalculation had been made, it was one that upon her return to the world could be easily corrected.

"How corrected?" Georgiana asked, finally getting in a word. "What do you plan to do now?"

Aurora sprang to her feet and twirled away to the pier glass where she stopped and flung her hand up.

"Do? Darling, what do you *think* I'm going to do? I've come home to marry Sinjin Grimes."

Georgiana stared openmouthed as Aurora twirled again and regarded herself in the glass.

"I do look thin, don't I? I must tell Halley to fatten me up. And I'm so pale—I simply have to use some rouge, that's all—"

"Rora, stop it."

"Oh, I know, Pina will have a fit, but that's all right. Why do you look so schoolma'amish, Georgie, lots of women wear paint—"

"I don't care about that. It's—"

"Yes? What? What is it, Georgie?"

Georgiana bit her lip, looking for words.

"Georgie! What is it? He's not dead, is he? *He's not drowned?* I haven't lost him?"

"He is not drowned; but, yes, you *have* lost him . . ."

"No! Don't say such a thing, Georgie! What are you talking about? Do you mean to say he's not coming back? Is he gone to China again?"

Georgiana shook her head sorrowfully. "No, dear, he *is* back. He came home for my trial."

"Oh, the good man. He knew you would have need of him—he's so fond of you, Georgie, he's often said so."

She flew to the wardrobe where her cloak had been hung.

"Where are you going?"

"To find him. To tell him—"

Georgiana spoke sharply. "Rora, sit down."

Obediently Aurora sat down at the dresser. "I must see him, Georgie," she said, "tell him how wrong I've been. How could I have been so stupid? I'm sure I hurt him, but he'll forgive me, I pray he shall." She crossed herself and breathed a quick prayer. She began prattling of wedding dresses, of a bridal trip, a fanciful plan to go and live in China with him. He'd have a ship there, they would stay aboard and sail the waterways; she babbled of music, flowers, birds singing in cages, spoke of embroidered silk, goldfishes in blue pools, of moonlit gardens, and visits to Peking where the Emperor himself awaited their coming in the Forbidden City.

"And, Georgie," she went on, taking up her scissors to trim her nails, "you're to be my bridesmaid, you know, just as we always planned. I want you to help me with my trousseau, too. What do you think? Or would it be better if we just slipped away somewhere quietly? Mightn't that be best under the circumstances? Of course, I intend that we should wait through Papa's mourning period. We mustn't be precipitate. Oh, how I miss Mama. She'd like to see me married again and know she didn't have to worry, don't you think—? Georgie, what's the matter?"

Georgiana knew no gentle way to tell her; she stated the obstacle flatly: "Sinjin is married."

Aurora halted the movement of her scissors to listen, but if Georgiana had looked for an explosion over this piece of news it was not forthcoming. Aurora nodded slightly, considering. Married. Yes. Very well. "What else?"

"He's married to Rose. Rose Mills. They have a house on March Street."

She looked up. "Yes, of course." She proceeded again calmly with her nail care. "Well, it's too bad, but it can't be helped," she went on matter-of-factly. "For Rose, I mean. Do you know, Georgie, I truthfully expected something of the sort. He did it to spite me. But all can be remedied."

"How?"

"Rose will simply have to—"

"Have to what, dear?"

Aurora flung down the scissors. "Give him up, what do you think? He only married her because he couldn't have me, surely you realize that, don't you?" She looked up, her blue eyes earnest and bright. "Certainly he doesn't love her. He loves me. Always has, always will."

Realizing all too well the truth of that statement, Georgiana preferred to keep her own counsel.

"What do you plan to do?"

"Don't be a ninny, dear, what do you think I'll do? I'll simply go to him, that's all, I'll explain exactly what's happened, how I couldn't remain in the convent and why, and that I've come back to him to be his wife."

"And what do you think he'll do?"

She held out her hand and inspected her nails. "Oh Georgie, must you be obtuse? He'll tell Rose the truth, that's all, and he'll—she'll—we'll—" Her brave expression suddenly crumpled and Georgie's heart went out to her.

"Rora," she began cautiously, but saw that it was no use.

"It's perfectly clear, really," Aurora prattled on. "He can get a divorce. Or an annulment, whatever is required."

"But Rora—"

The blue eyes narrowed. "But what?"

"She's going to have his child. You've got to give him up."

"Never!" Aurora pushed aside her nail-care paraphernalia and leaped to her feet. *"Never never never!* Don't you dare talk to me like that, Georgie Ross! He loves me—I love him! We belong together. We will not be parted. Not this time!"

"Rora, be reasonable. You told him you wouldn't marry him, you said you didn't want him. Obviously he took you at your word. How can you expect him to throw Rose over and get a divorce? She loves him."

"But does he love her?"

Georgiana was compelled to say that in her opinion he did not.

"There you are then! I told you it was simple. Anyway, that's all in the past. Mama wanted us to be married, she promised me that Papa would give his consent. And he will, as soon as he- -he—"

A frantic look had sprung into her face and she burst into a flood of tears. A moment later the door opened and Pina hurried in, evidently having heard. "Georgie, do something before she hurts herself!"

Aurora was now careering about the room in a near-hysterical state, flinging things helter-skelter, sweeping the glass and silver objects from her vanity table, tearing the counterpane from the bed, and nothing Georgiana or Agrippina could do would calm her. Not daring to leave her, Georgiana hurried Agrippina downstairs to fetch the doctor. Terry Standish came and gave Aurora a sedative, and left orders that she was to stay in bed.

But Aurora had no intention of remaining in bed or even obeying the doctor. At the first opportunity she dispatched Burdy on a bogus errand, then hurried into her things, flinging on her cloak against the cold, and before anyone could stop her was out of the house, hurrying her step to the Center. With little thought of what she was going to say to Sinjin, and none whatever if she should unexpectedly run into his wife, she hurried along Main Street and was about to turn down March when she saw him exiting the tavern, in company with Mat Kindu.

Aurora stood huddled in her cloak, the wind blowing strands of hair across her eyes, trying to get him to look her way and recognize her. He did not, however, and when the ostler passed, Sinjin hailed him and they went off together toward the smithy under the elm trees at the edge of the property. Catching up her skirts, Aurora hurried after; as she passed the Malay, she noticed his slitted eyes widen in surprise at seeing her here when he obviously imagined her to be elsewhere. She hastened her step, eager to surprise his master as well.

The blacksmith's forge, situated behind the former livery stable which had been converted into the jail, was the bailiwick of Sid Smyth, the giant, taciturn African who had held down this trade for more than fifteen years and whose muscular brown arm pulled the bellows and wielded the hammer with fervor and industry. On cold days such as this the warmth of his fire was welcome, and usually a handful of men or boys could be found lingering in the shed, roasting chestnuts and talking things over. Not so today, however. As Aurora lifted up the flap of canvas serving to keep out the cold, she found Sid heating up a shoe on the fire, at the same time engaged in conversation with Sinjin, who stood with his back to the doorway. Feeling the draft that blew in behind her, both men turned to look. Aurora let the flap drop and stood gazing into Sinjin's face. He showed no surprise. Without noticeably altering his expression, he left the black-smith's side and approached her as though he'd seen her only yesterday.

"Hullo, Rora," he began, hands stuffed casually in his pockets, his eyes bleared with drink. "I heard you were back. What brings you here?"

His nonchalance caught her off guard and she groped helplessly for a way to begin. "I must talk to you," she said with a nervous glance at the smith. It was all so different than she'd imagined. Of all places, this freezing, filthy shed, this black giant listening.

There was a sputtering sizzle as the blacksmith drowned his red-hot shoe in the tub of water, then he put some nails between his teeth and crossed to the stall where Sinjin's horse waited. He began expertly hammering home the new shoe. Trying to keep herself from shivering, Aurora was determined to act as if the man didn't exist. Sinjin, however, had other ideas. Moving her closer to the fire, he lowered his voice, commenting that he didn't think this was an advisable place for them to talk. Still he showed no emotion; certainly he didn't seem glad to see her.

"What does it matter?" Aurora said. "We're here, aren't we?"

He glanced toward the stall; then, when the smith had finished nailing the shoe, he handed him fifty cents and asked him to return the horse to the tavern stable.

"What do you want to talk about?" he asked when they were alone.

"Why did you do it?" she demanded, her eyes bright with the tears she could not help.

"Do what?"

"Marry that creature!"

He folded his arms across his chest. "Why shouldn't I? Every man needs a wife—sometime or other."

"You don't love her. Georgie told me you didn't."

He all but laughed in her face. "You've no proof of that, my dear, Georgie notwithstanding. And even if I don't, what then? After all, you didn't want me, you sent me packing."

"You oughtn't ever to have gone!"

"Oughtn't I? That statement might require further evolution, don't you think?" His voice, easy and soft until now, became cutting and sardonic. "After the things you said to me, it's hardly likely I'd hang around hoping, is it?"

She was trying to think, but thoughts seemed to come only with difficulty. The lock of hair fell over his eye just the way she remembered it.

"I forget. What did I say?"

"Do you, really? I remember quite well. I have warmed my hands at those words over many a long night. You told me some infernal nonsense about your being guilty and you had to be absolved of your sins, that you had a duty to God, a debt to repay." He coughed into his hand and yanked out his handkerchief. "I trust you and He are now square, no outstanding debts and so on." He blew his nose loudly and returned the handkerchief to his pocket.

"Please don't be so—" She stared at him, agony in the lines around her eyes. "Never mind. You must see—I was confused that day, I didn't really understand the matter. I tried, truly I did, only—" She broke off again, sniffling, and in her own turn began rummaging for her handkerchief. To him she looked pitiful, miserable, with her red nose, her pale pinched face, rather like Agrippina, he thought, and not nearly so pretty as when he'd left her.

Desperately she said, "Has it come to this, then? You actually married Rose? It isn't some kind of joke?" She had to hear him say the words.

He stood regarding her with his infuriatingly illegible expression. "I'm very much afraid that's just what it has come to: I married her. We two are made one. I'm sorry, Aurora."

"But—if you don't love her, then why? Who are you punishing?"

Sinjin shrugged. "Myself, among others. I'm punishing myself. That's my right, isn't it? One may punish oneself if one is moved to do so. For all one's many sins? You, I gather, have sought out the Almighty to pay for yours, while I simply have gone to the devil. Which is only what you predicted, isn't it? I trust your own efforts at salvation have been more amply rewarded. I have sometimes wondered—did the Great God Hoo-hah manage to forgive you your so-terrible sins? That little murder, for example: I confess it,

I supposed the next time we chanced to meet I'd find you all wimpled and kirtled, a regular little penguin of a nun. Or was your sin so colossal the good sisters refused to have you?"

"I'm not going to be a nun."

"Ah. Well, that is undoubtedly the sisters' loss." He blinked, taking her in. "What now? What lies ahead for Lady Sheffield?"

"I've come home. I've come back." She spread her hands in a feeble attempt to demonstrate her corporeal self. "Here I am."

"Yes. Indeed, there you are. So I see."

"To humble myself."

"A little humbling never hurts one, so they say."

She gulped a breath and spattered him with eager, childish words.

"But it's all so funny, truly—I was wrong, that's all. I was wrong. Oh darling, I have come home to tell you, to tell you that I was wrong, that I love you—I've never stopped loving you, not for a minute, not a single moment."

"Rora—please—"

"No, wait—let me say it! Say that I love you and that I'm ready to become your wife. You did propose marriage, didn't you?"

He pushed his fur cap back. "I seem to have had a run of such proposals. But as you may have heard, I am already possessed of a spouse. Let me add that she bids fair to be all the wife I need just at present. Two would run contrary to law—unless I were a Mohammedan, which I am not."

"Don't make bad jokes."

"Why not, when it's all such a bad joke? Really, it's a little late for this conversation, isn't it?"

"You haven't answered my question."

"Which was?"

"*Why* did you marry her? *Her,* of all people?"

"Why? Well, to my vast surprise, I found that upon our meeting once again—quite by accident, as things fell out—Rose presented before me a person so drastically altered in mind and spirit, a being so humbled and contrite as to be very nearly the personification of maidenly virtue, that quite to my surprise I was emboldened to ask for her hand in marriage. One might say I fell beneath her spell. Such are the twists of fate. Interesting, don't you think?"

Her anger flared. "Don't be ridiculous! Need I remind you who she is, where she came from, or that only last year she was my own maid!"

"Then we are obliged to live in the hope that with my uxorial help she may in time rise above such obvious drawbacks. I do not draw the line where others like to do. I did draw it at your mother's silver spoons, but happily those have been restored and now safely repose in the drawer of your sideboard, while my bride has herself expressed suitably remorseful senti-

ments for her lapse of trust. Perhaps"—he slid her his most devilish look—
"perhaps you could take her back, you may be in need of a well-trained
maid just now."

"Are you utterly mad?" she cried at him.

"North by northwest, perhaps. I still know a hawk from a handsaw,
however. Hawk—feathers; saw—teeth; isn't that the way of those two?"

His saturnine expression and sardonic turn of phrase irritated her beyond
control and she burst out at him.

"Oh, you *are* mad! The way you go on with your nasty little jokes as
if—as if—oh, this is a wicked thing you've done. Now we shall all be
punished! You and me *and her! She* may deserve it, but I don't! You loved
me, you said so, I know you did! Now you've thrown it all away, everything, gone—and I despise you for it!" Her eyes narrowed like a cat's, and
her voice came in harsh little pants. "You have done this vile thing to pay
us all back! Me and my father and your father and your family and my
family and everyone who's ever hurt you or angered you. You did it
deliberately, maliciously; and now you've settled down right here under
everybody's eyes, keeping house with that creature, while I—I—" He
laughed outright and the sound stung her to greater fury. "Don't you dare
laugh at me!"

"My dear, I was not laughing at you. It is not my ambition to mock you
or—or anything. I was merely emphasizing how far you stand from the
truth when you say I mean to settle down here. Alas, I have no such
intention, especially under anyone's eyes, even your own sweet violet ones.
The fact of the matter is, I'm soon away."

"You're leaving?"

"I am."

"To China?"

"No. Philadelphia, first. The *Sparrow*'s already laded, down at Saybrook."

"And taking her with you, I've no doubt!"

"By no means. Mrs. Grimes will reside here in Pequot, as is only fitting."

She shook her fist in his face. "Oh, you beast! You are a terror! That
poor woman, she loves you! And now you'll leave her by herself." She flung
herself angrily away from him, then whirled on him, wild with reproach.
"What kind of man are you? Don't you know what love costs? Don't you
know what it is to be alone, to be lonely, to love only one person so much
that you could die? To *want*—yes, actually want to die? Don't you *know?*"

She faced him furiously and the anguished look that came over him
reminded her of that look he'd had in the cabin of the *Adele,* on that
long-ago afternoon of their first meeting, when they'd spoken of loneliness.
His voice cast a spell as he spoke, compelling, vibrating, a soft, light tone,
but with a core of steel.

"Ah, yes, my dear, I think I do. I do think I know what love costs. Believe me, I have counted every penny. I know what it is to be lonely, too. And I know what it is to love one person so much that I wanted to die. I did die—for love. It's true—dead, for love. But I have lived to learn that love's not really all that important in the grander scheme of things. Don't look so pained. Those are the lessons of life, bitter as they may be to swallow, and I have been well taught, believe me. My teacher birched me most thoroughly, bent and birched me. Yes, yes, my little golden-haired instructress, 'tis you who have put me to book and slate and rapped my poor boy's knuckles, and taught me things to break my heart. Yes, it's true, my heart is broken—you have done that."

"Then I will mend it—oh, let me mend it, can't you, won't you? I beg you, I beg—" She faltered before his accusing eyes whose terrible truth she read in the blacksmith's glowing fire. Too late, the flames said, and as her tears came, the fire went cold.

Between chattering teeth she appealed some more, holding her small hand out to him, inviting him to her; but he would not come, would never come now.

"If you had only met me halfway, Rora—no, not even halfway, only a little way, a few steps, if you could have been more forgiving, more understanding. Only a little—then I could have borne all, submitted to all. But you did not—or could not, and now, here we are—in a blacksmith's shop—a very cold blacksmith's shop." He stepped to the bellows and gave the coals a blow or two. Aurora was quick after him, her hands raised as if to clutch him to her.

"You mustn't talk like that!" she cried. "It wasn't a case of understanding or not. Don't *you* understand? It was a case of guilt. What we were doing was wrong, terribly wrong. And you wanted me to go on doing it. You can't imagine the revulsion I had!"

"Alas, I do know—revulsion, disgust, contempt, and all because I loved you, I tried to be the lover I thought you wanted me to be."

"I did! Oh, I *did* want you to be! But we were sinning. Can't you feel that we were? In the eyes of God and of the world as well we were committing the worst of sins. All I could think was how terribly much we'd been forced to pay after that first time. Poor Caro, she died that ghastly death because we'd sinned, that sweet innocent child, because you and I—" She burst into sobs but he ignored her tears and spoke bitterly.

"And now we're paying again, it seems. Expensive things, love and passion. But we've had an even trade in the marketplace, I dare say. You have your God, I have my Rose. You've nothing to complain about, you know. Stop wailing. You've made your bargain with life, now keep it."

"I'm trying!"

"Trying is not succeeding. If you want marks for trying, fine, I give them to you. For the rest, what's done is done and I'm very much afraid it can't be undone. Not anymore. It's over and finished now, we're last month's news. No one cares anyway. People don't want us to be happy, they don't want us to be together. People like us never are, you know."

"Never what?"

"Allowed to be happy. We're like the shoemaker's children, always the last to get shod."

Just then the blacksmith came in with a pail of beer, for which he signaled thanks to Sinjin. He used his bellows on the fire, then, taking his pint into the adjoining lean-to, tactfully withdrew. Sinjin tossed the hair from his eyes and when he looked at her again his lowering expression had lightened and he smiled ruefully, penitently. "Rora—Rora," he said softly, and the sound of his voice thrilled her. "I had hoped above all things that together you and I would be the exception that proved the rule. I thought we were truly meant for each other, I believed we were both clinging so hard to some— ideal, some grand shining love that only you and I were lucky enough to have experienced. That we were linked together by a glorious golden cord, together against all the rest of them. I believed that you'd been restored to me because I'd had true repentance and someone somewhere had finally decided I'd lived in hell long enough and I didn't need to be punished any more. I didn't *want* to be punished any more. Posie once said to me . . ."

She felt an unbelievable spasm of pain and remorse at his mention of her sister. "What did she say?" she asked, grasping at straws.

"I once told you, but obviously you've forgotten. She said you needed to hear that you were loved for you to really believe it. Jesus—she wanted it almost as much as I did. But not you—*not you! You* didn't want it, you tossed it over the moon in a basket."

"But I *do* want it—I *do*. Believe me, I was wrong, I've learned, it's all different now! Don't you see? Things change—people change. *I* changed. Can't you believe me?"

His smile was complaisant. "If you say you've changed, very well, I believe you. And I'm happy for you. But it won't do either of us any good because *it's too late now!* Nothing's going to change anything important, nothing's going to do either of us any good anymore, not me, not you." He stared at her as if taking her in for the first time. His voice came in hoarse beats. "D'you want me to say it? D'you want to hear the words again? All right—I love you. I've loved you since that first moment aboard the *Adele,* that dear little shepherdess face under that ridiculous comic bonnet. It was as if the sun had suddenly come out from behind all the clouds of my life. And I've loved you every day since—loved and loved—and loved. Only it wasn't enough for you. *I* wasn't enough, my body and my mind weren't enough, my loving you wasn't enough, my dying of pain wasn't enough for you. *Nothing* was enough! You wanted the sun and the moon and the stars. But you had to have your precious God too. You had to punish yourself with guilt and remorse and punish me too. You couldn't just be happy with what we had, and let me be happy too. You had to throw any chance of that away again, grind it all into the dirt."

"I didn't—I—"

"By Christ, you did, you poor little fool! You see, you don't really love me because—"

"I do! I do!"

"—because you know I don't believe in your God. That stupid God of yours. And you think that's wrong, you think I so richly deserve punishment, as though I hadn't had enough already. You want me to feel every bit as guilty as you do."

"But I don't!"

"Yes you do. You wouldn't be happy until you had me down on my knees crossing myself and muttering Paternosters and eating Christ's flesh in luncheon biscuits."

"Stop! I can't bear to hear it, you break my heart!" she cried, putting out her hand to silence him.

"Your heart be damned!" he swore fiercely. "You have broken *my* heart, yes, broken it forever with your damned God and Jesus, and I hate you for it as I hate your God! God damn you both! You and your false priest who coaxes you to your knees and whispers in your ear, lures you into the confessional with his lies and mumbo-jumbo. It's all shit and I shit on him and on them all—*all!* Don't ever talk to me again about your damnable God! By Jesus, I won't hear it! No more. And now you'll pay and I'll pay and, yes, Rose will pay, by the horny cloven feet of the yellow god she will, for ever daring to think for one Godamned single instant that she—that you—oh, Christ, what's the use—" He made a desperate move to go, but she thrust out her hand to stop him.

"If you go off now, I'll never see you again."

"No great loss there," he tossed off. "Anyway, I'll no doubt be back ere long."

She sprang on this, dog on a bone. "When? *When?*"

"Who knows? Maybe in time to see the baby."

"The baby—" Her voice became a tremor.

"Oh—didn't Georgie mention that? Perhaps she forgot. I'm about to become a proud papa. Yes, it seems that, villain as I am, I've rather put my little bride in the family way, as you proper ladies prefer to couch such delicate matters. She will soon be couched herself."

"The baby," she said again, and hugged herself, shuddering, her eyes coruscating with bright tears. He raised the tattered canvas flap and stood in the doorway, a dark silhouette against the bleak winter light, his body held in an unconsciously graceful posture; statuary.

"Good-bye, Rora."

"Wait!" she cried. "Don't go! Take me with you!"

He stepped a pace or two back into the room, staring at her. "What are you talking about?"

"I say take me with you."

"The woman's lost her mind," he told the rafters.

"I haven't! I'll go!" She seized each of his arms, reaching on tiptoe to his face. "I want to go! Take me, take me with you. I'll do it, if you'll only let me!"

His smile was sad and painfully mocking. "Truly, you do me exceeding honor, Lady Sheffield, but unhappily I must demur. Can you have forgot so soon, I am a married man? You cannot trifle with my affections this way, it is not meet. *Au revoir.*"

He turned on his heel and was surprised to find Rose standing just beyond the flap, along with Sid Smyth. "Ah, and here she is, just on cue, Mrs. Grimes herself. Rose, you remember Lady Sheffield. She and I have just been talking over old times. And I have kept you waiting because of it. For the which, forgive. Now I believe I'll have a drink. Coming, Rosie?"

Wordless, Aurora stared at the sight of this "Mrs. Grimes." She wore an outrageous bonnet with plumes and flowers and ribbons. The feathers in her hat, dyed ultramarine, trembled in the chilly wind, chilly like her half-smile. She said nothing. Her face looked whiter than Aurora's own. She slipped her hand through Sinjin's arm and held on to it as if it were a possession. Her cheeks were thin, her neck was long, arching, proud. She was whiter than white and she had her husband, the one who belonged to her. She took him away like a parcel, turning wordlessly from her former mistress while her outrageous feathers shivered in the wind.

The flap fell, Aurora stared at the holes in it, then, heedless of the smith, she tore it savagely from the nails and fastened her eyes on Sinjin's departing back every step of the way until he and Rose disappeared from sight, and it was a long time before she set eyes on him again. He was wrong and she was wrong and life was wrong, they were not saved and their sin lay on their heads like an axe blade. What he'd said was true: happiness was not for them, nor forgiveness, but the awful truth was that she loved him and would love no other man but him, and the prayer on her lips was murderous as she thought of Rose Mills, who had presumed to come between them. No, no, she thought, not Rose Mills, Rose *Grimes*, who lived in the little gray house at the far end of March Street.

The blacksmith had kept his back to her, studiously avoiding her eyes, yet she sensed that he had half guessed what had taken place in his forge during the last ten minutes. When he did look, his gaze told her nothing. On a little hopeless breath she ran outside into the chilly gray. She hated leaving the cheeriness of the smithy's fire, to walk the short distance back to Kingdom Come, but she did it nonetheless, ashamed and desperately empty.

At home again, she refused to tell anyone where she'd gone. She went upstairs to her room where she took the pins out of her hair and let it fall about her shoulders and she sat by the window drinking rum toddy, reviewing what had passed between herself and the husband of Rose Grimes in the blacksmith's shop. Thereafter, as days passed, she often sat by that same window, gazing glumly out, watching the snow fall. She so often sat there that people began habitually glancing up at her face behind the pane, so she drew the shade and looked at nothing. She told herself it was her own fault, there was no one else to blame. Rose Mills, her onetime maid, had stolen a march on her, stolen the man she loved to boot. In summer Rose's first child would be born, and after that there would no doubt be a passel of bouncing babes filling the small rooms of the little house on the wrong end of March Street. She recalled Sinjin's saying he wanted a large family; there was a chore Rose could doubtless manage very well. One morning she heard Trubey telling her mother that Sinjin Grimes had left town.

Not long after, Miss Simms came in and cut several new patterns for Aurora, and Agrippina helped pick out fabrics, pretty things for spring. There were three new bonnets as well, though where she'd ever wear them she hadn't a notion. She was surprised one morning, glancing at the paper, to find out it was the fourteenth of April. Was it possible? *"Tempus fugit,"* Pina told her. No it doesn't, Aurora thought, but didn't say so.

When she finally pulled back the curtains she was surprised to find the weeping willows in bud. Spring was sad; nothing to look forward to. April was the time for heartbreak. She began to drink a little more than usual. Secretly; no one must know. Rum had become tiresome; she switched to rye. Sometimes she drank a little eau-de-vie; or maybe some schnapps for her sore throat. And she'd always liked the taste of *Goldenwasser*.

43

The Swan Bride

GRAY GULLS, WHITE against the bright heavens, swooped above the soughing waves as a lone lobsterman trawled the sandbar, pulling up his traps. When he had heaved the last of them aboard, he turned his dory and rowed for shore. A neatly curled breaker caught the keel, lifting and slipping her bottom buoyantly through the ragged band of tide kelp that turned the blue water brown, then, amid the churning foam, the prow slid onto the sand with a grating rasp, the wave receded, the lobsterman jumped nimbly out, settled his vessel on firmer ground, and began unloading his dripping traps.

Beyond him, on the far dune, he could make out the figure of Georgiana Ross, shading her eyes against the sunlight, watching him as he worked. When Nate Finn straightened, she waved and he waved back. Georgie Ross was a good person, a rare female, if it came to that, one a smart man would appreciate admiring. Nate's mother, wise hen, had been at him and at him to pop the question, but Nate declared himself a confirmed bachelor. Besides, he knew Hermie Light was sweet on Georgie, always had been. Nate Finn's code of honor would never allow him to poach on another man's romantic preserves.

Nate went home to his mother having trapped a handsome suppertime catch, and as the sun began to set Georgiana came off the high dune, walking toward the point, where she stood gazing off at the hull of the *Adele* still clinched in the teeth of the infamous Nag's Head. She could never look upon that sight without sorrowing, it was such a dismal end for so noble a vessel; nor could she ever view it without reflecting on the *Adele*'s former master, Sinjin Grimes, whose courageous efforts to save his luckless ship had failed. There was something base and grotesque about the melancholy vision of that naked, dismasted hull perched among the dark rocks, with the ocean spray dashing up across her fantail as the surf crashed, and Georgiana sometimes wondered how long it would take nature and her destructive elements to obliterate the last earthly signs of the gallant brig.

"Brave little ship," she said aloud. And where was her master now? Sometimes she thought the *Adele* had been held prisoner among those rocky molars to remind her of the plunging descent of Sinjin Grimes. It never did much good to wonder about the captain, to sorrow over him as Miss Rachel and Helen did, or to wish things might be otherwise. Georgiana told herself she could save her tears, weeping would not help any of them. Life's bitterest lesson; she had learned it long ago, on Christmas morning of 1829 at Grimes Mill.

With an inward, hopeless sigh she retraced her solitary steps down the beach. She passed along the marshy path between the dunes and the brackish pond where the swans still made their abode, one pair to a lagoon, gliding about with such stately hauteur, lovely in the evening light, serene and placid in the way of swans, a warming sight to reflect on. Pairs . . . pairs . . . these swans came only in pairs, as did so many of God's creatures, couples, mates, maritally intentioned, two by two they had furnished the ark of Noah and had replenished the earth, while she—no pair, she, alas. It was just as she had suspected, Georgie Ross was cut out for a solitary maiden lady, a virgin spinster, violated by no male, pristine. Suddenly she felt ashamed, ashamed of her condition, her arid, unfulfilled estate. What had Cinnamon said? "Chilluns, many chilluns"? Well, Georgiana decided, it would not be the first time Cinnamon had been wrong, and she forced herself to march on. She was hungry; that was good. The salt air and outdoors gave her the appetite of a trencherman.

Back at Blue Shutters she found a four-pound lobster sitting on her steps, its fat, lumpy claws pegged, its whiskers wriggling. With it lay four ears of fresh corn in their husks. Manna from heaven; she supped like Belshazzar that evening, thanks to Nate Finn and his ma.

The month was July, and Georgiana had been at Home Island for close to three months. Mab's cottage—*her* cottage now, for Mab had left her Blue Shutters outright—had served her comfortably and well. Once more the shutters had their coat of fresh blue paint; in the windows boxes geraniums flourished; the shingles had been oiled, all leaks caulked; the portulaca still ran riot; and gray gulls waddled sideways along the roof peak. Across the way in Sandy Lane the Widow Finn kept her house neat as a pin and proved the best of neighbors, if curious-minded as ever. Cap'n Joss, older and hoarier, came by now and then for a game of checkers; the minister, Pastor Leete, was always welcome, and the children in the vicinity regularly managed to sniff out the gingerbread baking in Georgiana's oven. It was good to be back among her old island friends, where she had sought shelter thirteen years ago, after the miller had slain her family and she had lost her powers of speech. To Home Island she had come, to live in the old smock mill, to try and restore her distraught mind and recapture her voice again.

The idea that she owned a piece of property, no matter the size, pleased her immensely, and she had put in many hours fixing up the gray shingled cottage just the way she wanted it. She had painted her bedroom white, the pine bedstead yellow, and there were white curtains of Baptist cloth at all the windows; seashells were set out everywhere, on the tops of the furniture, along the beams, their pleasing shapes filling glass jars, lining the steps, and every one of them she had collected herself. In her spare time she embroidered pillow covers, filling them with tickings of balsam needles and bayberries, an aromatic mixture pleasant to rest the head upon, pillows that island visitors sometimes came to buy from her. Every day she sought serenity, and every day she came a little closer, though the final prize still eluded her. No; it had not been an easy time for Georgiana, but to her credit she kept her head when to have lost it altogether would have not been surprising. Impossible to divine what lay ahead for her, though she often found herself pondering it. What should she do, now that the appeals had failed and her school was forced into nonexistence? In May the Supreme Court in Washington had refused to hear their appeal, which had been denied by the Court of Errors—thus confirming the infamous Grimes Law in all its particulars. The decision had been a blow to all the supporters of abolition, but to Georgiana most of all, for she felt somehow that the failure was her fault.

And so she had come to Home Island, as she had come once before, for healing.

After supper she went and sat on her porch and enjoyed the view that she had become so fond of. Beyond the strand lay the sea, the vast and ceaselessly moving, now bright, now dark, impervious sea that was so much a part of her life these days, emblematic of the constancy and unchanging quality of the greater universe, and of change as well. In more rational moments she reminded herself that changes were inevitable, that change was really what life was all about. Curry favor with the status quo and the world would slow in its turnings and civilization, robbed of gravity, would slip into the abyss. God and His glories alone were unchangeable, and the world entire would wear away before He and they were dust.

The months since her trial had seen Pequot Landing once again governed by that peaceful state that for a long time before the episode of the Free School and for a long time after it would be the village's most obvious trait, despite the occasional eruption of the smoldering quarrel between Talcott and Grimes. Tranquillity, amity, staidness—these were Pequot's prime virtues, and just as they had been for two hundred years, so they were likely to be for yet another two hundred. Connecticut was still the Land of Steady Habits; so had it been, so let it continue.

The long, wearying winter had brought alterations of a regulated, natural order, betokening little more than those daily progressions, fast or slow, that dictate the lives of ordinary folk everywhere, obliged to live by the pages of the Farmer's Almanac and rapid shifts of weather. Came births, deaths, weddings, and funerals, enough to keep Dr. Haverstraw, Dr. Standish, Pastor Weeks, Father Rupprecht, and the new Methodist minister, Reverend Coe, laboring on with a will, while the lives of so many connected with Georgiana Ross and her school or Aurora and the tenants of Kingdom Come seemed to falter, to fall listlessly off, simply to peter out altogether, as if this were life's one true and natural course. One heavy snowstorm after the other had kept the shovelers busy and the snow rollers in active service; the blue drifts climbed to the eaves to meet crystal fringes of icicles.

Then, in late spring, with hardly any warning, Aurora had gone away again from Pequot. Georgiana thought that it was probably better that she leave, and there seemed little sense in attempting to persuade her to stay, even for her father's sake. Asher Ingolls was still eager, but there was little evidence that she either loved him or would ever make him a good wife, and truthfully Pequot was not for her, not anymore, though she made no explanation of her reasons for leaving, save her own ennui and craving for amusement. Her father, who had at last begun to creep out of his shell, lamented her absence but did not stand in the way of her going. There were tearful farewells and promises to write faithfully, promises seldom to be kept, at least by her.

Once on her way, she had first paid a visit to Electra and Lloyd in Georgetown, attending parties in Washington that were reported in the papers. Later, with friends, she had traveled south, to New Orleans, where she had spent the balance of the spring and where currently she still was. The money due her from Mab's estate was being sent by Uncle Jack Talcott to the Bank of New Orleans for deposit, so she had no pressing financial problems, and reports of her doings and whereabouts became sparse; what news there was came via friends of Lloyd's, who had connections in the Crescent City.

And what of Rose, the third corner in that unhappy triangle? Georgiana's heart went out to Sinjin's wife. For not long after he left Pequot Landing in the *Sparrow,* Rose had suffered a fall, and in consequence had miscarried. Georgiana knew few details. Annie Skaats had gone over with a jar of soup left over from a large dinner Sal had put on. Some of the soup had spilled on the floor and Rose had slipped in the grease and fallen down the stairs, the narrow, crooked wood staircase of the little house on March Street. Helen had tried to convey the sorrowful news to Sinjin, but no one knew whether he had received it, for he had been trading up and down the Eastern seaboard and the Caribbean, making money certainly, for he sent sums home regularly, but had not yet returned to Pequot, though he was expected before the baby should be born. Only, now there was to be no baby.

ONE splendid cool morning she took her empty market basket and set off for Saltaire. Proceeding along Sandy Lane, she passed Mary Finn hanging out a modest wash.

"Someone's coming," Georgiana called over the pickets.

"Whatsay?" Mary Finn cupped her ear against the offshore wind. "Folks comin'?" She peered around as though the awaited one would at just that instant magically appear. Georgiana laughed.

"Not yet, but they will. It's in my bones—isn't that the expression?"

"I expect so, if you're a swamp Yankee." Mary encountered difficulty talking around the trio of clothespins clenched between her teeth. With a wave and an encouraging nod, she watched Georgiana continue around the bend and so out of sight. The good woman spent another hour performing her yard chores, and shortly before lunchtime the breeze carried to her ears the sound of a deep baritone voice and Georgiana's responding laughter. Presently Mary's bright eyes viewed her neighbor coming back along the same path between the fences, this time in company with a gentleman, his arm tucked companionably through hers, his head lowered under a tall hat. The couple was engrossed in an animated conversation and passed without noticing her; Mary felt inclined to be miffed at having been overlooked. She would have liked to meet Georgiana's friend, whoever he might be. It was only as they were climbing the wooden steps up the dune that she recognized him as none other than Mr. Appleton Talcott himself.

Georgiana's bones had told her true. Her visitor had appeared without warning, stepping off the ferry onto the landing. His greeting was as warm as it was affectionate, and she was impressed with the evident change in him, her former employer. He had put on a dozen pounds and looked keen and almost robust. His suit and hat both were new and his collar and stock were of the latest mode.

"You look spanking!" she cried, overjoyed to see him.

"It's you who are spanking, my dear," he said, kissing her cheek. "How glad I am to see you again," he added.

As they climbed the steps, he noted the blooming geraniums and portulaca, the touches of fresh paint, and declared that the sight of the old place greatly lifted his spirits.

"Well now, Georgie," he continued as they stepped through the front door, "here we are, just like old times." He glanced around the room, deriving evident satisfaction from the fact that the place continued to exist unchanged in a changing world, unchanged except for certain small, but to his eye quite apparent, evidences of Georgiana's tenancy, such as the shell collection on the windowsill. "Here, let us have a look at you," he said, setting down his bag and parcels. He took her hands and spread her arms out and took his fill, pronouncing her hale and healthy-looking. "You like it here, don't you? It was always one of Molly's favorite spots," he added, a bit sadly.

She nodded. "I'm so grateful to her for it. There's nothing like the sun and the sea to cure one's wounds."

Appleton was quick to agree. "I hope the sun and the sea will return you to us soon." He blinked at her, raising and lowering his bristly eyebrows, now shot with white. His cheeks were of their usual high ruddiness, and his eye had regained more than a hint of its former liveliness.

Georgiana suggested they sit on the porch and enjoy the sea view while he told her the news, but before they went outside Appleton presented her with a parcel he had brought with him. It had come aboard Captain Goodnaught's ship, the *Grace & Favour,* and was dropped off by the river packet. Georgiana laid the package by, saying she preferred to open it later, after which they sat facing the sea, rocking side by side while a full hour's worth of news was exchanged. Aunt Hat was "ischiatical" and consequently feeling lame, but Old Bobby was fine, he had left for Saratoga declaring that Appleton wasn't to return to Pequot without Georgie. Pina also was well, and looking forward to Posie's return to them at Kingdom Come this autumn. There was good report to be made of Posie. She wrote—yes— actually wrote in her own hand, using a steel ruler as a guide—about her new life and the school where she was being taught—so many things. And she was learning how to groom herself, how to feel safe on the outside and to move without trepidation from place to place. Her decision to leave home had been a harrowing thing for her father, but a necessary one, he now realized.

When she inquired after Rose, Appleton frowned and shook his head. "The girl's of an unfortunate character," he declared. "I think the loss of her child has affected her. She's drinking, one learns."

"I am sorry," Georgiana said simply. "I wish——" But she left the thought unexpressed, and soon Appleton had turned the conversational eddy into another stream altogether.

"And you, Georgie," he went on, "when you return—have you given any thought to what you might do?"

"I'll have to look for something, I expect. I've one or two ideas."

"Pray tell me."

"Well, I was wondering if I mightn't perhaps go into the seed business again with Warren Burdin." She explained that she felt the burning of Burdin's Best Seeds had been her responsibility and that she would like to help restore Warren's fortunes. But in view of the fact that Warren had carried no fire insurance, Appleton was not especially sanguine about the seedman's current prospects.

"He'll need capital, won't he?" he asked.

Georgiana agreed. "But surely a loan might be arranged. I have been wondering if Priam——"

"Now that's a thought, Georgie. It was in the cause that the store was lost, after all."

"Yes, it was." For a minute she was silent. Then she went on. "I have this weird notion, you know, about Fearful Swamp."

"I know nothing of any such idea." He laughed. "All I know is that in the springtime the place lies under five feet of water."

"So does the Nile, and just look at it," Georgiana replied. "If that land could be bought cheap enough and properly drained, with all that good rich muck and mud, I think it could be some of the best seed-raising land around. Mab thought so too."

"Did she indeed?" Appleton's brows shot up in surprise, and he began to pay closer attention.

"She said she thought anyone who put money into such a scheme would be doing a wise and prudent thing."

"If Molly said it, then we must investigate. She was very clever, you know, in fiscal matters . . ." Appleton stopped abruptly; nonetheless Georgiana had heard something in his tone that made her take note, apprehensive that the awkward moment she dreaded had come. But the moment passed and he spoke lovingly and with sublime resignation about his dead wife.

"I'm sure you still miss her greatly," Georgiana remarked.

He confessed he did. "But she is always with me."

"She said she would be."

"Did she?" He smiled at the thought. "What else did she say?"

"Nothing, really." To avoid further pursuit of a topic she wished to avoid discussing, she suggested they go for a little walk. Along Sandy Lane they paused for a few words with Mrs. Finn, who instantly melted under the warmth of Appleton's considerable charm. He even offered to show her his "new" house, providing she would pay Pequot Landing the favor of a visit.

"You'd best be careful," Georgiana told him, laughing, as they walked along the shore, "you're liable to have company. Mary Finn's dying to visit 'upriver,' as she calls it."

They sat on a shelf of sand, talking. Georgiana bared her face to the sun, which had already tanned it and brought out her freckles, while her hair had lightened to that tawny blond shade that was so becoming to her. She mentioned the *Adele,* and when she described the condition of the wreck, Appleton listened with a musing expression. "She was indeed a gallant vessel," he agreed. "Too bad she came to such an unlucky end."

Georgiana observed his face closely, wondering if his words applied to the ship's master as well; was he implying that Sinjin would likewise come to an unlucky end? But no frown creased that serene brow, he seemed quite jovial, as if he had now put the past behind him and was looking forward to happier times again.

"It's hard for me to believe you actually lived in that old smock mill," Appleton remarked, lying back on his elbows, heedless of his clothes, his shoes stuck straight up in front of him.

"It was like living in one of those little houses set on stilts," she said, "the way they do in the tropic islands. I know everyone thought I was mad; I suppose I must have been." She laughed and he laughed with her. "Anyway," she said, "I can imagine worse places in which to live."

"I'm sure you could. I'm sure you could be happy anywhere you chose to. Molly never really was happy once she left the farm, you know."

"I loved Follybrook too. Ah, but I do love Kingdom Come. In a different way. A charming house, that—a lovely home."

He was elated by her words. "I'm very glad to hear you say that. Molly always found the place too big." He looked sidelong at her over his spectacles. "Truthfully, my dear, I've begun to think perhaps she was right."

"Have you?" Absently but affectionately she touched his arm. "She told me you would be lonely there."

"And so I am. Georgie . . ." He reached and gently took her hand in his. "I am fifty-seven years old now, I'm not the man I was nor the man I hoped to be—"

"But you're more, much more," she replied.

She looked at her hand in his, powerless to take it away, yet fearful of what he might say next.

"I was married for over thirty years to an extraordinary woman. So extraordinary that she even urged me to remarry someday—or perhaps you were aware of that fact?"

Georgiana's free hand fingered the curves of a crab shell she had picked up. "I believe she did mention something about it."

"And do you know whom she thought I ought to wed?" She did not respond and he saw her acute discomfort. "You do not wish to discuss such a subject, is that it?"

"Yes," she murmured, her voice almost lost in the sound of the waves.

"Do you know at all why I have come here today? Can you think what has brought me so impulsively to your doorstep?"

She was modesty itself, her eyes were lowered, her cheeks flamed as the blood rushed to them. "No. Only—I hope you won't—that is, I don't believe—oh lordy . . ."

Appleton laughed, and it seemed to her it had been years since she'd heard that sound. "Dear Georgiana, do me the kindness to raise your eyes so I can see them. You have lovely eyes, you know. They are quite one of your best features. They say Athena had gray eyes. A very wise old goddess, Athena. She was fair and wise and full of cares. My dear, my very dear dear, you are a prize, a glorious prize for any man, and—come, out with it, Jacob!—I have ventured here today to set before you a most serious proposal. A bona fide proposition." She saw him digging first into one pocket, then another, and in a moment he had taken her hand and awkwardly slipped a ring onto her finger. "My dear," he said with touching gravity, and not without some humor too, "I have come all this distance and at such an hour in the fervent hope that you will deign to wear this ring, and that in return you will soon give me this same hand I am holding. Georgiana, I wish you to be my wife, and I have come to ask if such a thought is at all agreeable to you?"

Daring not even to glance at him, she stared at the ring that sparkled on her finger, feeling embarrassment and not a little fearful. "I think—it is not possible," she told him, unable to return his gaze.

"What do you say?"

"I said—I do not think it is—possible."

"But it is possible, I'm telling you it is. I've made up my mind, it is time." He thought for a moment, still holding her hand, which she made no effort to retrieve. "I pray you, come home with me to Kingdom Come and be its mistress. Live in it as my honored wife, as Molly wished you to. Yes, she did. She said so. She told me. You would be a fine lady, Georgiana, the finest in the town. I would take care of you and give you everything you wanted, all your heart's desire, everything; I promise I would be a loving husband to you. I would cherish you, I would value you very highly."

She felt herself wilting like a flower in the sun. The moment she had feared for so long was upon her, and she was helpless before it. "Sir, you do me such honor. It is so great an honor that I truly don't know what to say."

"What to say? Why, say yes, of course!" he cried. "That is the only thing to be said, nothing more."

"I fear I am not fitted to such a place in life. It wouldn't do, it simply wouldn't do at all."

"Still the miller's girl, is that it?"

She colored again and was overcome with shame, for he had gone right to the heart of the matter. "Something like that, yes. I think Mab was right, you certainly ought to marry again. But I fear that you have not come to the proper place in search of a wife."

His voice grew grave. "Georgiana, I will have you know that I have allowed myself to set my heart on you. I have known for some time that I would make this proposal, that it was you I wanted." He laughed at himself. "But perhaps I must learn to be content with what I have had. Certainly I am not young any longer. And after all, I have had the love of one good woman. Perhaps it is too much to ask that I should win a second. I do have my fireside and my slippers, my port and pictures, my books, but—" He paused, some unspoken thought passing through his mind, reflected in his keen eyes. "Georgiana," he ventured after a moment, "had you considered that if you should possibly change your mind, we might travel abroad? Visit all the places you've always wanted to see?"

"That would be delightful, certainly. But I feel sure I won't change my mind, truly I shall not."

"Is it simply that you will not have me?"

"*Cannot.* I *cannot* have you."

"Because you love elsewhere?"

"No, no," she protested, "it isn't that at all. I love nowhere."

"Then it must be that you cannot love *me.*" He looked at the light coming and going in her eyes, making them more luminous than he remembered. Suddenly she seemed to stand out to him in all her quiet strength and resolute character. "I could love you dearly, Georgiana. It would take nothing from my love for Molly. We could have our own family, our own children—you love children so. And the house is large, plenty of room, now that so many are gone from it."

She saw the hint of moisture that had seeped back into his eyes, betraying his deeply felt emotions, and her heart went out to him. Her mind was racing, hoping he would not attempt to press her further, ask her for more reasons.

He coughed and cleared his throat, his mood seemed to change. "Well, well," he went on in his philosophical way, "who knows, perhaps you are right. Perhaps I ask for too much."

"No, no, it's not that at all. You will find what you're looking for, I'm sure of it."

"I do not want anyone else, Georgiana, I want you. But I suppose it was not meant to be. I'm sorry that you should find me so lacking," he apologized.

"No," she cried passionately, "please, you mustn't say such things. You have no lack—none! It is I. I am honored that you want me for your wife, but—"

"Then why?"

"Please don't ask me, I beg you. I would never want to be a disappointment to you. And I know I would be. I am bound to be. It is inevitable I should be."

"But that's not possible, Georgiana. You've done great things, fine things. You must feel proud. I am. Lecky and Dad are, Molly was. Everyone is proud of what you have done."

"Thank you," she whispered, getting up, "that's kind of you to say." Averting her face, she took the ring from her finger and handed it to him.

Silently he took it and restored it to his pocket. Then, abruptly, he got up and held out his hand to her. "I'm so sorry to have alarmed you," he said. "Join me in a bit more walk? Clear the head."

"Are you all right?"

"Yes, perfectly." He stopped and shook his shoulders, then took her arm. They walked along in silence for a while until the chimneys along Sandy Lane appeared behind the dunes. As they came into the lane they found Mrs. Finn pruning her ramblers. They exchanged a wave, no more, and went to sit on the porch again. Georgiana felt constrained and inclined herself to silence. Appleton too fell mute, and she could see how deeply she had confounded him, this dear, kind man whose happiness meant so much to her. In such a short space of time his appearance had altered drastically. When he arrived he had looked so fresh and spruce, now he looked tired, and sadly defeated. At last he said, "Forgive me, my dear, I'm just an old man, I have these ridiculous outbursts. They mean nothing, as you well know. Forgotten, all forgotten. Now. When *may* I tell Dad you will be coming back?"

"I can't be sure. Perhaps the end of the summer. September? You're welcome to visit here any time you like, you know. After all, it's always been your house too."

"Yes, dear, as mine is yours, of course."

He so wanted to exhort her one last time to reconsider his proposal, but instead he prepared to flee; he would spend the night at the inn. He embraced her in his customary avuncular fashion, lightly brushing her cheek with his lips, then fearful of saying any more he all but ran away.

She felt a dry sob rise in her throat as she watched him making his way doggedly along Sandy Lane, attempting a jaunty wave for Mary Finn, as if his visit had been of an utterly perfect sort. She fought a rush of tears, thinking, There it is, so much for that. So much for Appleton Talcott's proposal, so much for whatever Mab had promised would happen, so much for Georgiana Talcott, mistress of Kingdom Come, so much for the future, so much for hopes and dreams.

She felt the urge to extricate herself from the cottage where the air was still redolent of the words that had been spoken under its roof. She slipped off her shoes and went barefoot down to the beach, heading up toward the Nag's Head. But instead of going out to the point she veered inland, among the bayberry bushes, where, inevitably, she came again to the brackish lagoon. Here she saw her friends the two swans; again she took in the majestic sight. How beautifully they complemented each other, how perfectly matched they were. She continued to observe them as they moved calmly across the water, and it struck her how much greater was the whole of them than the mere sum of their parts. Separated, they were just two birds; together, they created between them another entity entirely, which was their principal reason for existence; they seemed in such tandem state to be fulfilling their destiny on earth in exactly the way God and nature had required them to do. Would that all couples, human and otherwise, could manifest so serene and tranquil a joint existence. One, the swan bride, was gorgeously bedecked in her gleaming white plumage, as if she were just on her way to the altar. Georgiana pictured herself in ivory satin, coming down the aisle of some church, with Appleton waiting beside the altar to claim her as his bride.

But no. She would not be his swan bride, she would never pair or mate with him, good man, gentle and generous man as he was. She turned her back on the birds in their domain and headed for home. Inside Blue Shutters again she took the time now to open the package Appleton had brought to her off Captain Goodnaught's ship. It was a beautiful gift from that same nun in Macao whose letter she had had while in jail, Sister Mary Omnia, a chemise with exquisite needlework, banded in eyelet lace through which narrow blue ribbon had been pulled and tied in a tiny bow. Far too fine for the spinster Georgiana ever to wear. She would put it safely away until a more useful idea occurred. With the chemise was another letter from the sister.

". . . think of you, I and my sisters-in-God and we bless you and your work. You and I, though of different faiths, we too are sisters, for our faith is of the same nature and we believe in the glory of the good . . . I pray for you, brave friend, that God will help you and succor you and reward you for all you have done . . ."

The letter went on to thank Georgiana for the various items she had sent out to Macao for the sisters. After her release from jail she had collected from village families a batch of secondhand clothing that might be useful for the little girls at the orphanage administered by the order. A sudden thought came to her; she would embroider one of her balsam pillows for Sister Omnia. She must think of an appropriate design. That evening, however, as she sat alone on the porch listening to the sound of the waves a suitable idea eluded her. She imagined Sister Mary Omnia at her convent on the hill in Macao, as it had been described to her by the nun. In her mind she also pictured a line of ships hull-down along the horizon, their sails set square and dark against the night sky. It was Homer's wine-dark sea; breathing more quietly now, it spilled onto the wet strand in deep, hollow-sounding plunges. Flashing birds swooped out over the water; others pecked along amid the wrack, fastidious with their dainty pittering steps, while the tide drew out with a heavy sucking noise and the stony clatter of rocks and pebbles as they turned over on one another. Out there beyond the gray twilit horizon, over the earth's curve, lay Lisbon. Lisbon and all those other fine cities her fancy sometimes took her to. Tonight she felt alone, alone with a bleak, ponderous hopelessness that both perplexed her and moved her nearly to tears. It was Appleton's visit, of course. Mab had been right after all—as she had so often been right about so many things. He had come seeking a wife, just as Mab had foretold he would, to bid for Georgiana's hand. Bad hunting at Home Island, she thought. And thought, for the long hours as the evening turned to darkest night and she remained where she was, her mind lingering over the words he had spoken, the promises he'd made.

With the oncoming night her fingers automatically reached to undo the laces of the disreputable looking shoes she wore, and she slipped her feet out, gratefully wriggling her liberated toes. The tired old chair creaked comfortably, and in its sound she thought she heard the whisper of Mab's voice. The brewer's daughter was dead and gone, leaving behind the miller's girl—who wasn't the miller's girl at all. Was—who? Georgiana—Grimes? How unnaturally that unfamiliar name fell on her ear. Once upon a time she had considered almost anything to be better than to have been born the daughter of the miller; but this other, more sinister knowledge of herself—to have lived with that for the past thirteen years had certainly been far worse. It was because of this single fatal defect in her person that she must say no to Appleton and forfeit all that his proposal might have meant. Her mother had been seduced by a lecher, and in that fact had lain her own "fatal defect." On such fatal defects had Georgiana's entire life hung. It was like a red strawberry mark or some other blemish that a person is born with and carries all his life. The grave alone would erase such defects for her, as the grave must do for all.

And now . . . what? What ought she to do? she asked herself again. She had no more idea than anyone else of why she was here. Not on this island, merely, but here on earth. What was the purpose in it? What was she meant to do? Should she stay on at Blue Shutters? she wondered. Should she go back? Take up her old life, such as it was? Live with Helen and Luke at Gaunt House, continue being the universal aunt to children who weren't hers? There was something in her character she didn't understand, had never understood, something in her being that drew her to these extremities, that shut out all the world in her greatest times of need. Then it came to her how small and insignificant she was, and how infinitesimal were all her desires, how inconsequential her plans, inconsequential even her failures. She was a gnat, nothing more.

Still, she realized that Père Margeaux had been right about one thing. She may not have gone far in educating her girls, not altogether, not satisfactorily so, but she had educated Pequot Landing. She had taught the village things it needed to learn, things it had not perceived before, and in its brief moment of existence the Free School had become one small indication of what lay ahead. The dull minds of people or their stupid acts of cruelty and violence could not halt the idea that all men had been created equal. So stated the Declaration of Independence, and if the Declaration said so, then this must be so, else that document was a lie and America was a lie. And because that could not be, whatever it might be called and in whatever place, another school like Georgiana's Free School was bound someday to spring into being. She firmly believed this to be inevitable. Some enterprising young man or woman would come along and recall these events, would stand up and say, "This thing I shall do." Perhaps even some Negro would rise up and be recognized, not as a colored man, but simply as a man like all other men, who would say "Give to me what is rightfully mine, do not keep me from it," and it would be given, not for any reason other than because it was fitting and proper, because it was his human due and that was the way of the world. By whatever means the colored people might in future time win their freedom, whatever wars might be fought to win it, they would somehow be taught. The stars were theirs to reach for, too.

Tonight she was alone. No one was near her, save Mary Finn and the fishes in the sea, that was all. Whimsically she thought she might keep to Mab's chair for the rest of her life, an old lady rocking herself off the planet. Here all was pleasantly serene, here she felt at rest. Then, some unperceivable portion of her being seemed drawn out and away from her, it rose up and was borne upward and lifted away in the ghostly darkness above the ocean. Her spirit seemed to hover somewhere out across the vast dark tableland of water that stretched from the edge of the beach to the horizon and beyond, and in her mind she journeyed in the wake of all the hundreds of ships that had sailed from these New England waters to all the ports of the world. Her chance ever to see them was lying close by, she had only to say the word and Genoa would be hers, and Venice and Capri, Leghorn and Athens; Constantinople, even Macao and Canton, Bombay and Madras and Cairo could all be hers as well. Wherever she chose she could go, for she knew well the man who had proposed marriage to her. Whatever she wished for would be made hers through his generous heart; she had only to ask. With Appleton Talcott for a husband, life would be a cornucopia.

Still, she didn't think so. It was too much to expect of him, too much to ask, not only that he should marry "the miller's girl," but that he should marry her who was not the miller's girl, but the deacon's girl, a Grimes. Impossible. Not to be thought of. Then why was she thinking?

Presently, yawning, she took up her tired shoes and went inside, where she readied herself for bed in the little white room. She missed Murray Hill, cat of cats. She missed that deep thunderous purring, the lazy curling waft of that bushy tail, the tickle of his whiskers. The cat was part of the past too, although not the part she must try to forget, the dark, haunting past filled with melancholy phantoms and moaning spirits. There was the future, the consoling, brightly shining optimistic future, the future that was built on hope, Pandora's saving grace.

She got into bed and leaned back against the two down pillows that had been among Mab's personal treasures. Feeling now that she had made a grievous error she told herself to sleep on it; things always looked different in the morning. She turned down the light and slipped beneath the coverlet, her mind aswirl with thoughts, a mental turbulence she could neither understand nor hope to quell. So agitated was she that it was a full five minutes before she remembered her prayers. She said them staring up at the flickering shadows dancing among the overhead beams—a dance that annoyed her, so that she shut her eyes. What a strange pass she had come to. What girl in her right mind would presume to turn down so sincere a proposal from such a man? Who did she think she was, saying no to Appleton Talcott? And so strange that it had all come about exactly as Mab Talcott had promised it would; why, her prognostications were on a par with Cinnamon's. But Georgiana had felt compelled to say no. No to the love of a good man, no to a life of comfort and ease, no to the finest house in town, no to the children she might have had—Appleton had said he'd enjoy starting another family—no to a coach-and-pair and a voyage to Europe, to travels through foreign lands, no to a visit to Aurora at New Orleans, to Sister Omnia at Macao.

But what other answer could she have given him? How could she say, Yes, Appleton, I, the daughter of your great enemy, I will be your wife. I, not the miller's girl but the flesh of Zion Grimes, I will come and live with you and be your wedded spouse to love and to cherish forever and ever. I will be the mother to your children, though my own dear murdered mother was the toy of the Grimeses. Do but take out the ring again, put it on my finger, and I am yours.

Or, alternatively, she could have said only yes, and kept all else secret. The dread name could lie unspoken on her tongue, she could keep her terrible secret from him, never speaking the truth and trusting to providence that it would never come out. This some other person might do, but not Georgiana. To lie—for it would be a great lie—to Appleton, the man she most admired, for whom she cared as for no other, to deceive him would make life intolerable. Every breath she took, every word she spoke, every act she performed, it would all be a lie. Just the thought made her sick at her stomach and she lay in her bed abhoring any such prospect.

Then she calmed herself and remembered that her decision had been the only one she could have made, the real and right one, even while seeing again that dear face so stricken with embarrassment, remembering the haste with which he had removed himself from her sight. He would get over his disappointment. Time would heal his wound and he would forget, would have another look around and find himself another, a better, wife. And so, she told herself again, all was for the best.

And yet . . .

What of Mab, the woman on her deathbed beseeching Georgiana to give her promise. Mab, a wise and sensible woman and a good one, surely she had the sense to see the situation clearly. Why had she urged it on Georgiana, especially when she'd been told the truth?

At last, listening to the distant boom of the surf, she drifted off, but had not been long asleep—at least this was how it seemed to her—when she heard a voice she knew well.

"Georgie, Georgie," Mabel Talcott said. Georgiana was sure she was awake in that moment and that she could see the stocky, robust figure of her dead mistress standing in the corner by the window. She had on a white gown whose folds caught the outdoor light as they fell about her knees.

"Can you hear me?"

"Yes."

"Good. You really must listen to me now. There is no more time. You're right, he's bound to take a wife, and if it is not you it will be another, I know it."

"But what am I to do? There isn't any other choice."

"Yes there is. The right choice."

"But I *made* the right choice."

"You *think* you did. But think again. I will not, *cannot,* mislead you in this, it is too important. Can you love him? Georgie, *can* you?"

"Yes. Yes, I think I can."

Mab smiled then. "I'm sure you can, dearie, if you'll only let yourself."

"But I don't know what to do."

"Certainly you do. You don't *think* you do, but it's no matter. Here is what you must do. Are you listening carefully?"

"Yes ma'am."

"Tut, no 'ma'ams,' we agreed. Now attend me carefully, do exactly as I say and all will be well. Jake will make you happy and you will make Jake happy. You have listened to him, now he must listen to you. You must tell him the truth. Let him know the facts, let the decision be his. But unless I'm sadly mistaken in him, he will not hold you to account for what you are innocent of."

"What I am innocent of . . ."

It was true. No child chooses its parents, they are given to it. Zion's guilt, or even Ruth-Ella's, was not Georgiana's guilt. Heaven's angels have no guilt.

She looked again toward the window. The space was empty. But Georgiana had heard Mab aright, and she knew what she must now do. For all their sakes, Appleton's, Georgiana's, and Mab's; for how often is it given to a human to make happy both the dead in the other world and the quick in this one?

She would see to it on the morrow. After all, wasn't it a woman's prerogative to change her mind? She turned her face toward her balsam-and-bayberry pillow. She slept long and well, and the next day's dawn was full of promise.

PART EIGHT

In Which Fate Takes a Hand

44

The Bells of Pequot Landing

LOUD AND CLEAR the bells rang out on a bright autumn day at the end of October, 1843. The village was agog: the banns had been put up announcing the betrothal of one of the town's leading citizens. Appleton Talcott and his bride of choice, Georgiana Ross, were to be joined in holy wedlock in much the same way Electra and Lloyd had been, on Christmas Day. This time, however, the nuptials would be celebrated, not in a house parlor, but at First Church, and a wedding gathering held at Number 17 Main. For the first time ever, Kingdom Come was to welcome a new bride under its roof.

What had happened to Georgiana Ross, Pequotters asked themselves? Exactly what had taken place at Home Island to change her so much? She had gone away not a patch of her former self, a kind of wraith, pallid and underweight, nervous as a tick, and now she had come back—on Appleton Talcott's arm, mind you, stepping off the morning packet as nice as you please—quite another Georgiana, thank you. You could see it at a glance, everyone could. She'd filled out, of course; the salt air always gave a person a healthy appetite; her cheeks were ruddy, her skin tanned, and when she smiled—she smiled a great deal these days—the gleam of those strong white teeth flashed right out at you. But that wasn't all. There was more, much more, things that didn't happen to a person simply because she'd had a holiday at the seashore.

For nearly a year they'd been asking one another if the Widower Talcott would go seeking a second wife after his deep attachment to his first, and while one and all heartily approved of such a notion, they were surprised, even shocked, to learn that Appleton's eye had fallen on Georgiana Ross. With so many other young, attractive girls of good family in the neighborhood, why would such a man have chosen Mab's former hired girl, the daughter of the mad miller, Tom Ross?

The family stood divided, however unevenly, not only on this matter at hand but with old resentments that if they had lain buried now arose again. When Mab had named Georgiana as one of her legatees, leaving her a sum of money along with the property known as Blue Shutters, that alone had been a shock, and Agrippina in particular had been vocal in her displeasure

that her mother had made so free with her legacy. Now to have Georgiana
brought into the family in this surprising way, made mistress of the finest
house in town, this was a bitter pill even for some besides Pina to swallow.
Great-Aunt Blanche was known to have gagged on the news, had in fact
engaged in charged words with her nephew, asking that he take more
thought of what he was about. The miller's girl at Kingdom Come, mistress
where Mabel Talcott had been mistress? Tut! And tut! again.

Appleton, however, had stood firm, swift to suggest in the strictest of
terms that his aunt tend to her knitting, leaving him to his. Blanche had gone
home to Pennywise with her nose badly out of joint, declaring that she
would not be returning to Number 17 Main. But she was back again soon
enough. She couldn't help herself. As it happened, Old Bobby had invited
fifty or so "close friends" in for afternoon tea, to congratulate the happy
couple and welcome the bride-to-be, and people said that once ensconced
Blanche acted as if the festive gathering had been all her own idea. Playing
hostess in the front parlor, she had insisted that Georgiana be seated at her
elbow while she poured. Appleton was amused to see how quickly his
fiancée had Blanche tittering across Miss Vicky's Paul Revere silver service,
and how Georgie's infectious spirits captivated everyone present.

As for the other family members, Electra had written promptly from
Washington wholeheartedly endorsing the engagement; over at Glens Falls
Minnie-Minerva was ecstatic at the happy news; and Posie had sent her
father and Georgie much happiness—of course she would be present for the
ceremony. The Priam Talcotts, however, were divided in their sentiments,
Peggy warmly in favor (she and Georgiana had always enjoyed a friendly
relationship), her husband perched on the fence, not really for the match but
not inclined to oppose it either.

Georgiana herself floated about in the seventh transport. Never had she
known such light-headedness, swept away as she was by all that had happened since that fateful morning on Home Island when she'd made up her
mind after experiencing Mab's midnight "visitation." As dawn streaked the
eastern sky she had arisen from her bed, made the fire and put the kettle
on, then stepped out onto the porch of Blue Shutters to investigate the
weather. Not promising; there were no auguries of a Homeric sunrise. It
was, in fact, quite foggy and chilly. She'd made coffee, carrying the hot mug
down to the beach where she'd walked barefoot, as she so often liked to do,
along the strand, and, lost in thought, was startled when she heard the
ferryboat whistle. Lordy—sailing time already! Almost without thinking
she had snatched up the hem of her skirts and gone flying barefoot over the
dunes, down into the gulley, puffing hard as she hit the end of Sandy Lane
and glimpsed the shingled roofs of Saltaire beyond the scrub oaks.

Mercifully, the ferryboat still lay in its slip, and few New London passengers had as yet been boarded, none of them Appleton Talcott so far as she could make out.

She hurried her step until she reached the inn, where she saw him sitting on a porch rocker, calmly drinking from a cup and reading a newspaper. As if he'd been waiting for her, he looked up with an expression of hope, mixed with puzzlement. The moment she reached the bottom porch step, where she pulled up short, gazing breathlessly at him, the sun suddenly broke through the overcast and the whole world changed, brightened, became alive—and with it, her life.

Coming to greet her, smiling the while, he tucked her arm through his, and as the boat whistle gave another blast and more passengers tripped up the gangway, together they wandered to the end of the dock, where they sat down on an overturned dory and she began to talk. Quietly and candidly she bared her heart to him just as Mab had told her she must. He listened right down to her last word, taking it all in, this remarkable confession, the astonishing revelation, but in the end it made no difference. Mab had been right on every score. He would have her no matter the cost, devil take the hindmost. He didn't give a hang who her real father was. He wasn't marrying the father but the daughter!

And now, with the first snowfall already behind them and Thanksgiving just ahead, Georgiana went busily about her marriage preparations. There was much to be seen to, for Appleton had decreed that their union was to be observed with the utmost pomp and circumstance. Only Aurora and the twins would not be home for the occasion. At the end of October Hector and Achilles had regretfully communicated that their application for leave had been denied: a family marriage ceremony was of no consequence to the army. As a token of love, however, they were sending a special gift to Georgiana, to be opened on her wedding morning, but not a moment before. As for Aurora, a formal announcement had been sent to her along with several letters, but there had been no word in return, a lack Georgiana felt keenly.

In the meantime she had again taken up her abode at Gaunt House. Here she and Helen thrilled together over all the details of her engagement, exclaiming over the ring Appleton had given her and enjoying future prospects. But what would happen when Georgiana was mistress of Kingdom Come? Would Zion Grimes's daughter be welcome there? What about Pina? Georgiana brushed away Helen's apprehensions, saying simply that any friend of hers, no matter who, would naturally be welcome at Number 17. Georgiana and Helen were sisters, after all, no matter how privately, and nothing or no one would ever come between them. Mercifully, Appleton understood. Together he and his bride-to-be had gone for a quiet tea on the Common, where he had captured the heart of all the Haverstraws, and in turn pronounced them a fine family, a credit to the town.

In general everyone experienced a deep satisfaction witnessing the profound change in Appleton. From the moment he returned after his visit to
Home Island he had looked and acted twenty-five years younger. His red
cheeks were ruddier—apple: "Apple"—his blue eyes shone, and he was
groomed and buffed to a high gloss. He was gay, humorous, courtly; he and
Georgiana spent long hours together, recarpentering the relationship of
many years, which while intimate must soon become more intimate yet, and
everywhere he went he enjoyed describing his plans for the honeymoon,
laying out the itinerary he had decided upon, talking about the cities they
planned to visit. He also enjoyed mentioning the "new" family, "to fill up
the house," as he put it, now that his first brood, with the exception of Pina,
had left the nest and no one had provided him with grandchildren nearer
to hand than Hartford.

A complete physical examination had been undergone; Appleton wanted
to be as certain of his health as he was of his wealth. Nothing came to light.
An annoying cyst was located and removed, his hearing was improved by
an irrigating of his ear canals, and the wire frames of his spectacles were
fitted with tighter lenses—the quantity of his reading tired his eyesight.
Other than these minor considerations, Terry Standish reported his patient
in A-one condition, though he privately mentioned to Georgiana and
Electra that Appleton had a slight flutter of the heart and care must be taken
that he didn't overdo. It would be hard to avoid excitement at such a time,
and a word to the wise would not be amiss.

But Appleton had thrown himself into the fray like a Don Quixote with
lance lowered against a score of windmills. Up early and late abed, it was
as if some hidden spring in him had been released, or a liberally inflated
balloon had been set free of its moorings. He could say no to no one, he
must know all, be a part of all, no scrap of information might be kept from
him, and the doors to his house were thrown wide, the gates of Kingdom
Come. The afternoons and after-dinner evenings were crammed with the
happy visits of well-wishers. The drive was filled, the roadway glutted with
conveyances, and while everyone partook of libations in the parlors their
coachmen, postilions, and linkboys enjoyed the warmth of the kitchen
anteroom, the domain of the Priests, all of whom were delighted with what
had happened to the fortunes of Mab Talcott's "best" hired girl.

One glowing encomium came from Halley Priest herself. Chancing upon
her in the kitchen soon after her return from Home Island, Georgiana had
drawn her to the big worktable where they sat down and had tea together.
"Well, Halley, and what do *you* think of everything that's happened?" she
asked, looking with some apprehension at that old brown face, a face it
seemed never could have belonged to a young girl.

Halley's ancient eyes shone with happy tears. "Miss Geo'gie, hit all come
true. Hit all done wukked out jes lak me 'n' Judy hoped. Ah 'members when

you come t'us, that scrawny you was, Mist' App carryin' you on his horse, an' Ah sez to Judy then an' there, *this* chile she gwine t' be part an' parcel of this house. An' so you was. An' now, jes lak the queen you is. An' you can take a passel of pride in it too! Some things is fine-fittin', an' this be the finess-fittin'ess thing Ah could ever hope fer."

"You're kind to say so, Halley, but remember: there will be only one Queen in this house ever."

"Doan Ah know it, honey, but she gone now, Miz Talca, bless her good kinely heart. Ah prays fo' her with every breath in mah body, an' Ah axes the good Lawd to love huh in heaven. But this yo' house now, Kingdom Come hit b'long t' you. You brings joy to it."

Georgiana held her hands in her lap, while Halley's praise washed over her, filling her with a mixture of embarrassment and self-esteem. Halley, she felt, was right about one thing: The house Appleton had built to shelter his brood, and that recently had been so bereft of human congress and social intercourse, would soon echo to merry bursts of laughter.

Assured of Halley Priest's support, there remained only the matter of "Mab's chair" to cause Georgiana some discomfort. In the evenings before supper Appleton liked for the two of them to be together in the study, always so cheery and cozy, occupying the matching Chippendale wing-back armchairs that had been Royall Talcott's. For many years one of these chairs had been known as Appleton's, the other as Mab's, and while Mabel Talcott was alive few others ever sat there. Yet now, as Appleton made providentially clear, he intended that "Mab's chair" should become "Georgiana's chair." At first she managed to avoid using it by perching on the stool beside him, but this arrangement could not go on indefinitely. The chair was so palpably, so eloquently unoccupied, yet was there obviously to be used, and Appleton's insistence was so urgent that she was at length persuaded, if only to save him from dwelling on the fact that for the better part of a year Mab's chair had been so unspeakably empty. This, Georgiana finally realized, was part of the marriage bargain she had undertaken; it was now required of her to fill all the empty places needful of attention: chair, and bed, and breakfast table, garden, linen cupboards, attic and cellars. She must assume her expected place in the new, yet often disquieting, scheme of things and with as much grace, ease, and housewifely know-how as she could muster. This was what was expected of her, this was how Mab had wanted it, and this was what the new mistress of Kingdom Come would do or know the reason why.

FOR Georgiana it was also a matter of considerable importance to discover what fresh tack Rachel Grimes might sail on in view of the impending event, but for some time the opportunity did not present itself. With anyone else she would merely have pressed a call at home, but Georgiana still shunned Burning Bush Farm, and Rachel's visits to town provided no chance for them to be alone.

Finally, the two women encountered each other at the Center. Oddly, Rachel was making her way down the walk from Jack Talcott's office. In her shiniest green bombazine, her "farthingale" with its spangling of jet beads, her wide-porched bonnet bristling with its ebony cock feathers, her form mummified in a fur-lined pelisse of antique mode, and employing, like a beadle's staff, the gold-headed cane that had been Abednego's, formal and ceremonial, she fastened her keen eye on Georgiana, then stopped and waited for her to approach.

Georgiana smiled warmly as she closed the gap. Whoever would have imagined that the gorgon of that fateful morning when she had stopped at Burning Bush to return the yellow fan, that so stony and flint-eyed a countenance should have become so dear, so precious to her. How was it that she had once been terrified of this woman who, however forbidding her appearance, had become almost like a mother to her—a grandmother, at any rate. Yet now it was with some trepidation that she greeted her.

"So, Georgie Ross, it's true, then?" Rachel began. "Come Christmas Day you'll be a Talcott?"

Try as she might, Georgiana couldn't refrain from coloring. "Yes ma'am."

"Well, it's nothing to be ashamed of!" the old lady declared. "I only hope Apple Talcott appreciates what a jewel he's getting! Yes, I expect he does, if he's got the sense God gave a chicken. And you're to be the lady of the house into the bargain!"

Georgiana hardly knew how to reply, but a response became unnecessary as Rachel plunged on. "Still, you're not going into this thing blind, are you, Georgie? Nor leaving your husband-to-be in the dark about matters, hm?"

"No. He is in the dark about nothing."

"Ah! He knows, then! That's as it should be. And he'll have you all the same. He *is* a sensible man. I always gave Jake Talcott credit; I'm glad to know I wasn't in error. And he—will *he* keep mum? On this same matter?"

Georgiana hastened to assure her that the secret regarding her birth lay locked in Appleton's bosom. Rachel seemed satisfied.

"What has—what has Deacon Grimes said regarding this matter, if anything?" Georgiana asked.

"Nary a word, Georgie, not a syllable. That doesn't mean he hasn't brooded on it, though. After all, at its very best it's still peculiar doings."

"Will he—"

"What? Say anything? *Faugh!* I'll dare him to do it. One word from his false lips and he'll catch it from me. Besides, the man'd be a fool to admit the truth of such a tale. He'd be publicly branded for the womanizing knave he is. You've nothing to fear from him, I warrant it. So rest your mind, Georgie, and be happy. There's the thing. I told you, didn't I? I said the day would arrive, and it has, praise be!"

"Will you come?"

"To the wedding, you mean?" She rolled her lip in speculation. "Georgie, nothing would afford these old eyes of mine greater pleasure than to see you made a bride. You'll be the loveliest creature in six counties. But it's a Talcott you're marrying, while I, God rest me, was wed to a Grimes. I'm stuck with the name and it wouldn't do for me to come traipsing into church like a favored guest. You and I cause enough talk as 'tis, folks wondering why we're thick as thieves. *We* know, and it's no one else's business. But if the widow of Abednego Grimes dared to show her face at your wedding, it would cause a sensation, and you don't want that. *You* be the sensation, and one day soon after we'll meet quietly at Helen's and you'll tell me all about it, what it's like being a Talcott. Watch out for Blanche Poindexter, though, she'd as soon sit on you like a brood hen and see if she can't hatch out just her kind of chick."

Georgiana laughed; the image of that old pea-hen, Great-Aunt Blanche, hatching chickens was highly amusing.

"I expect this will come as a surprise to a certain sea captain of our acquaintance." Rachel's coyness came as a shock; it was as if she felt compelled to bring Sinjin into the conversation, however awkwardly.

"I'm sure it won't matter to Sinjin one way or the other," Georgiana returned, her cheeks reddening.

"Now, no need to get all stirred up. I was only remarking. He'll be glad for you, I warrant it."

"Will he?"

"Certain he will," she retorted. "He ought! I won't have him playing dog-in-the-manger where you're concerned."

"He won't get the chance if he doesn't come home soon," Georgiana said sadly. There had been no word of Sinjin Grimes for many months, nor had any funds arrived to help Rose out, and she had been forced to seek employment. In this, in fact, Georgiana had been of some assistance. With the exception of Georgiana and Helen, among the locals, only Liza Eales had expressed to Rose any genuine sort of amicability, and through Georgiana's friendly offices Liza hired Rose to work in her shop. That clever needle of Rose's, her knack for getting the most out of little money, helped her along in her new undertaking. Rose was a devotee of *Godey's Lady's Book,* and with a little research and page thumbing she soon became an authority on madame's millinery. And there she sat, in the window corner, where every passerby could lay eyes on her and whisper maliciously that the wife of Sinjin Grimes was being paid the wages of sin.

Rachel shook her head. "For one whose heart used to be set on being a writer he seldom bothers putting pen to paper. I always hope to have him with me at Christmastime. I haven't so many Christmases left now. Let me go, there's a good girl, or I'm bound to catch an ague."

Suddenly, as she prepared to embark in her waiting coach, she leaned over and pressed sere lips to Georgiana's cheek. "Be happy, my dear," she said. "Please try to be happy . . ."

"I will be," Georgiana replied simply. "Good-bye." Then she continued on her way to the almshouse to spend some time with Aunt Hat.

GEORGIANA thought often of Sinjin during the weeks preceding her marriage, trying—and invariably failing—to plumb his reaction to her new circumstances. Never having been one to care much what others thought or said about her, she was forced to confess that she wanted Sinjin's approval for the step she was about to take, and while she did not think that he would disavow her, yet she feared his mocking brow, his caustic tongue.

It became a case, if not of "Talk of the devil and he will appear," then surely one of "Think of the devil" and so forth. For on a snowy, gusty afternoon, just ten days before Christmas, when Georgiana and Appleton, who had been shopping up in Hartford, were heading for the Snuggery at the Mansion House to rest their tired feet over a cup of chocolate she heard his voice, addressing the clerk behind the counter of the cigar stand.

"See here, my man," he said. "Anyone knows a good Manila's a far better cigar than a Havana any day. You'd better stock up. I'll bring them in for you, if you like. And I won't charge the sun and moon either."

Georgiana froze at the sound, and tried to slip past without being noticed. Much as she wanted to see him, she did not want to meet him so publicly before she had a chance to break the news, and certainly not on Appleton's arm. Her efforts were for naught, however, as the cigar buyer turned and saw her.

"Georgie!" he called out, his dark features lighting up. Georgiana clung to Appleton's arm as Sinjin approached them, half a dozen cigars clutched in his right hand.

She evinced surprise. "Sinjin! I didn't know you were back."

"You've caught me just off the packet. I came upriver last night."

Georgiana turned to Appleton with some apprehension. But Appleton, at his most cordial, was already putting out his hand; Sinjin did likewise, transferring the fistful of cigars to his left. "How are you, Captain Grimes?" Appleton said.

"I'm well, sir, thank you. As you are too, for I see it written plainly on your face."

Appleton beamed. "I am happy to say that such is the case, but thank you for pointing it out. I owe it all to this young lady, who is soon to do me the great honor of becoming Mrs. Appleton Talcott."

"Yes, I've heard the news," Sinjin said affably. "Congratulations to you both."

"I trust you approve of my choice, sir," said Appleton.

"I do indeed, sir. Nothing could bring me greater pleasure than to know that Georgiana's happiness is assured, as I know it must be when she is delivered into the hands of a gentleman such as yourself." Sinjin's face was suffused with such ill-disguised pleasure as he spoke, the light in his eyes was so warm, his manner so sincere, that Georgiana was deeply touched. Nothing among all the heady joys of the past weeks had afforded her more pleasure than these wholehearted words of his.

"Georgie and I were just slipping into the Snuggery for a cup of chocolate," Appleton said now. "If you are free, Captain, we would be most pleased if you'd join us."

Georgiana was surprised; while she knew Appleton as the most generous of men, she had not expected he would put aside so readily not only the long history of enmity and ill feeling, but Sinjin's more recent behavior as well, in the intimate matter of Rose Mills and the demise of the Free School.

Sinjin also seemed surprised, but responded with his usual aplomb. "I'd be glad to," he declared, "on the condition that I am permitted to propose a toast and then to take the bill."

"No, no, it is my invitation," said Appleton, reddening.

"But I insist."

Georgiana spoke up gaily. "Very well, then, Captain, we accept your gracious offer, do we not, Appleton?"

Her smile was engaging, and they proceeded into the small room. The Snuggery was just that: very intimate and snug, and at this time of day convivial. Its cozy glow exuded the pungent fragrance of pine and the spice of cinnamon and nutmeg, a perfect spot to get warm on such a gray, chilly afternoon. Several branches of holly lay on the mantel, a generous fire blazed in the grate, throwing its warmth into every corner. From where they sat they could look out the window onto Central Row and watch the holiday makers, hurrying past with their parcels, and the sleighs, horses all a-jingle with bells.

The talk in the room was animated but subdued. People were mannerly here. Gentility was the mode in the Snuggery, gentility and a good stiff toddy against the weather. A waiter in eighteenth-century dress, with a curled peruke and buckled shoes, came to take their order. Appleton asked what sort of drink Sinjin would like. "We can't order a Sallie's Flip here, but they serve a comforting mulled wine with spices."

He waggled his eyebrows in that characteristically amiable way of his, awaiting Sinjin's reply.

"Mulled wine goes down nicely, sir," the captain said, taking off his cap and tossing back a lock of his hair, and when their order had arrived, raising his cup, he made his toast:

"Sir and miss, allow me this happy moment to propose both your healths. May your joys be great, your troubles small. My homecomings have not always been felicitous, but on this occasion to discover Georgie being made happy consoles me for—" Here he broke off, and Georgiana thought, He knows then, about the baby, but before she could say anything, he had resumed his speech. "Sir," he said, addressing Appleton, "I wish to apologize to you and all your family for any grief or anguish I may have brought you and yours in the past. It is true, I have loved your daughter. True I wished to make her my wife. I assure you, sir—and I believe Georgie will back me in this—I wished and longed for Aurora to be mine every bit as much as you perhaps may have longed for Georgie to be yours. Alas, fate has decreed otherwise. Some things are not meant to be. One might even say they are not—destined. I cannot speak for the rest of the family whose name I bear, but for myself I would wish for all strife to be put behind, and I live in the hope that your kin may be as forgiving."

"Well spoken, Captain," returned Appleton. "These are welcome words indeed, and they warm my heart. For my part, I assure you such is the case, and I concur in your sentiments."

Georgiana was imbued with a sense of warmth and security she had not thought possible. There had been a considerable change in her seafaring friend, she thought. Not so cocky and full of himself as he had been, he seemed to have cloaked himself in the mantle of meekness and simple gentility. He was friendly without being overreaching, engaging without contrivance, modest and guileless in a way she had never seen before. Was it possible that Sinjin Grimes had learned *humility?* God knew he had been knocked down enough times, had suffered greatly. This was there in those dark eyes for anyone to see. But, withal, there was an enviable ingenuousness, a boyish earnestness that Georgiana found most becoming, while Appleton seemed completely won over. How strange, that it must come *now,* when Rose—when Aurora—

"Will all the members of your family be gathering for the happy day?" Sinjin asked now, relighting his cigar.

"Most, I trust," Appleton returned. "The twins could not get leave. And Aurora's absence will disappoint us." Sinjin's cigar ash fell on his lapel; he brushed it away and fingered the spot fastidiously.

"No? Not coming then?"

"She's still in New Orleans," Georgiana explained. "It would be an arduous trip for her to undertake. We'll miss her, of course—"

"You will miss her, I'm sure." Was there a trace of irony in his words? They sounded sincere, yet—

"Do you intend staying with us a while this time?" asked Appleton, changing the subject.

"No, not long," Sinjin replied. "Fact is, I sold the *Sparrow* in New York and bought a new ship. She's a beauty. A bark, built at Newburyport, the *Grace B. Coppard.* I'm going to call her the *Hattie D.,* though."

"Tweaking fate's nose, aren't you, Captain?" said Appleton. "Isn't changing the name of a ship bad luck?"

Sinjin shrugged. "Plenty have done it," he said. "I went to see Aunt Hat this morning, that's when I got the idea. I figured to make it up to her for having lost her the original. And she was pleased. I'll make my own luck." He paused, then went on. "I'll take command in the new year."

Appleton beamed expansively as he rolled the conversational ball. "And where away, Captain, if one may ask?"

"We'll ship for Macao and then get up the Pearl to Canton. After that I'll most likely be running her between there and Goa."

"I see." Appleton frowned. "And your cargo, Captain?"

"The usual mix, I should think, calico, India tea, shawls, spices. Grammaw's backing the voyage. It's what brought me to Hartford this afternoon—the insurance."

Appleton leaned over and clapped him on the shoulder. "And I hope you prosper. We both do so, don't we, Georgie, dear?"

Georgiana nodded, but she was thinking of Rose. Sinjin had only just come home, and now he was to be off again. And he hadn't once made mention of his wife.

Sinjin emptied his cup again. "Well, it's getting on," he said, making a move to get up. "I still have some things to see to." He stood, again expressing his pleasure over the nuptials, shook hands warmly with Appleton, took his farewell of Georgiana, grabbed his hat and left, neglecting to pay the check he had earlier claimed.

"I'm sure it was an oversight," said the loyal Georgiana.

"To be sure, my dear. Here, waiter—"

Appleton laid a dollar on the table, and for a time they watched Sinjin through the snow-flecked windowpanes, a dark figure in a bright swirl of sleet, hands jammed into the pockets of his coat, leaning a bit forward in that aggressive posture so much his own. Grimly he jammed his cap down over his brow and turned as he was approached by another man. Georgiana recognized the Oriental eyes and prominent cheekbones of Mat Kindu. No bare feet in this weather, he was bundled up like an Eskimo. He followed obediently as his master turned the corner and was gone.

"Appleton?" Georgiana began.

"Yes, my dear?" He leaned toward her, smiling. "I believe I know what you're going to say."

"You *do?*"

"You'd like to invite Captain Grimes to the ceremony. Isn't that it?"

Leave it to Appleton to read her thought. "Yes. Yes, I would. Do you think—?"

"That it could be arranged?" He nodded. "I believe it can. We have only to address to him one of our fancy invitations. And the captain to reply in the affirmative if he is of a mind to do so. We might ask Reuben to stop by March Street."

"Yes. I think that would be nice. Will the family disapprove?"

Appleton's look was fondly indulgent. "My dear, this is to be our life together, and as such we cannot—and *shall* not—waste time worrying about or fearing what others may think or say. Shall we agree to that, do you think?"

Georgiana was grateful; he was giving her the utmost support and understanding. "I wonder, how do you think the invitation should be addressed?" she asked tentatively.

Appleton sipped his drink. "What do *you* think, my dear?"

"I think it ought to be addressed to 'Captain and Mrs.,' don't you?"

"My thought exactly. I know that two of my children won't like it, nor Aunt Blanche, for that matter, but they'll just have to get along, I suppose. It's only for a few hours, anyway." He chuckled wickedly. "Shall we lock up the spoons? Matthew, Mark, Luke, et al.?"

"Appleton, really! As if—"

"As if indeed!" His eyes sparkled in the firelight. "Georgie, do you have any idea of the immense and abiding joy it gives me to hear you call me 'Appleton' at last?"

He reached out and took her hand, warm and soft in his own. She smiled at him, her eyes radiating warmth and affection. The man who had been a father to her for so long was soon to be her husband, she hoped for that many more years. Her gratitude was inexpressible. They would have plenty of evenings together at Kingdom Come, a lifetime of evenings. That was how Queen Mab had decreed the matter; and that was the way of the world. The dead had spoken, the living would be content, the flames in the family hearth would be kept brightly burning.

45

Chats

ARRIVING BACK AT Kingdom Come following their shopping excursion, Appleton and Georgiana found a letter waiting for them, a surprise communication from Aurora, mailed from New York, informing them that she would be arriving in Pequot Landing in time for the wedding. But amidst the general rejoicing, there were several who gave uneasy thought to the fact that by hook or crook and willy-nilly, fate had decreed that Sinjin Grimes and Aurora Talcott were to be together again.

"Don't be foolish," Georgiana told herself. "Nothing will come of it. You'll have your two friends here for your wedding, what more could you ask?"

She could ask for a tranquil heart, for her misgivings were tiny flashes of worry that nibbled away at her like pantry mice at a cheese in the night.

And so, once again Aurora Talcott came back to Pequot Landing. Like both Georgiana and Sinjin, she too had changed, though in her case the alterations were subtle, not easily discernible. She wore about her a peculiar muteness, as if some portion of her had passed out of the bright light into the shade, and the keen observer might discern in her pale face a delicate tracery, not of lines or wrinkles, but signs of aging nonetheless. Her smile, formerly often wistful, was now either plaintive or fugitive, and in the winter light her eyes were often less gentian than cornflower. She spoke more slowly and with greater deliberation, and was slower, too, in her movements, methodical and somehow joyless, a strange thing indeed in such a woman. She was thirty-one this year, and no longer Goddess of the Dawn.

It was inevitable, with Sinjin's house on March Street only a stone's throw from where Aurora was temporarily installed at Kingdom Come, that an encounter should take place. It happened the day after Aurora's return, the eve of Christmas Eve, just at dusk. All around the Center the lamps were being lit, candles winked in the shop windows, and a light snow had begun falling. A supernal, crystalline blue in the frosty air greeted Georgiana and Aurora as they opened the door of the variety store and stepped out onto the walk. Shoppers were everywhere hurrying to and fro, clutching parcels and other wrapped objects. Some boys had built a little fire at the edge of the roadway, its flames lighting up their ruddy features; they were waiting for two potatoes to roast before partaking of them, and they shouted and called out to the passing sleighs. Outside the Old Hundred a handful of carolers were offering yuletide selections and sending round the hat. Georgiana slipped her arm through Aurora's and hugged her close as they stepped away from the shop, only to draw back in alarm as without warning a dark,

phantomlike figure wrapped in a cloak appeared before them, nearly collid-
ing head-on. She was about to remonstrate with the careless passerby when
she realized who he was. Like a specter in a supernatural haunting, he seemed
to materialize out of nowhere, looming before them with gaunt cheeks and
wildly staring eyes as he took in the sight of Aurora. It was an eerie moment,
as if two ghosts from the past had suddenly met again. Then he was gone,
swallowed up in the dark, or in the spell of the invisible necromancer who
had conjured his earthly spirit.

Aurora stared at the empty space where he had stood a moment ago. "Was
it—? Was it *he?*"

"Yes. It was Sinjin," Georgiana replied, urging her along. What a thing
to do, popping up out of Archibald's that impetuous way, startling them
half dead, then rushing off into the dark without so much as a word.

"He could at least have said hello," murmured Aurora, glancing back
over her shoulder as if he might be following them.

They continued on through the ultramarine twilight, so icy that they
were both chilled before they reached the front walk of Kingdom Come.
Inside, at the master's orders, the house had been done up as though for a
hundred Christmas celebrations. The pungent fragrance of the pine boughs
was everywhere—their needles and cones festooned the lintels, garlanded the
banisters and newel posts, canopied the doorways, and graced the ta-
bletops—and everything mingled with the more subtle smell of bayberry
from the Cape Cod candles burning in the sconces.

A welcome fire greeted them in the cozy back parlor where they found
Trubey setting out the tea service and some of the family gathered. This
evening the aunts were absent—Aunt Tilda and Aunt Bettina had "things"
to see to, which meant a load of "hay" had been delivered to their barn,
cold-weather work for the old but determined ladies. Colored folk still
needed warming and feeding before continuing on their way to Canada.
Lloyd Warburton and Lee Peckham were pitted in a game of cribbage,
while Minnie tried to deal with her spirited progeny, who were making the
most of visiting Grandpa's house, playing with their cousins, Priam's and
Peggy's offspring, and the room was noisy to boisterousness. One after the
other the children jumped up to troop across the rug and greet their Aunt
Aurora and Georgiana, whom they would continue to call Aunt Georgie
when she became their stepgrandmother the day after tomorrow.

Their entrance had interrupted Old Bobby, "Great-Granddaddy Bob,"
who was just then engaged in telling his traditional and justly celebrated
story of "Dobblegotz's Turkey," a good deal more than a twice-told tale,
and a family favorite, which not only amused his auditors but invariably
brought tears of mirth to the storyteller's own eyes.

"But you must begin again, Granddaddy darling," cried Aurora, describing a graceful arc as she swirled free of her caped pelisse. Georgiana, moving

quickly to Appleton's side to enjoy the feeling of closeness that had grown between them, seconded this request, and Granddaddy, in his best jacket and gleaming stock, began anew the story of the celebrated fowl, won in a raffle by a man called Dobblegotz, who, never having cooked a turkey, had plucked it of its feathers while it was still alive, then, taking pity on it, had sat down and knitted a woolen sweater to keep it warm and never roasted the bird at all.

The effusion of warmth and humor the story drew forth among those who had heard it countless times before was astonishing—it always provoked Priam's hearty baritone laughter and made even Peggy giggle, while the raconteur, ever cognizant of his cue to slip offstage, modestly subsided into the background (not an easy feat in Bob's case) and prompted a few remarks of general interest from the lips of his son.

Responsive to each quirk of mood and temperament among the family members gathered in the room, Georgiana, on the footstool beside her husband-to-be, her skirts drooping across the polished toes of his boots, was warmed in the almost palpable glow of the family's—*her* family's—happiness.

"Where's Posie?" Aurora asked, her cheeks still pink as roses from the cold, when the expressions of admiration for Granddaddy's story had subsided.

"She's been resting, but she'll be down shortly," Minnie answered, catching hold of the toddling Sophy and straightening the green sash that had been sat upon and wrinkled. The moment "Aunt Posie's" name was spoken the children hushed themselves, and hopeful eyes were raised to the ceiling. The presence of Persephone Talcott in the house was a profound source of pleasure and excitement, for she told the best stories of all, better even than Granddaddy's.

As she sipped her tea from her cup of Mab's set of Amoy china, Georgiana stole glances at Aurora. Had the surprise encounter with Sinjin upset her? Georgiana thought she seemed a bit nervous; her eyes flitted from one face to another, and when she spoke her voice had a forced gaiety.

"Sissie, have you completed all your shopping?" Agrippina asked. She had taken a chair near the fire, and the light softened her features, making them especially attractive this evening.

"Indeed I have," Aurora replied. "Really, darling, you can't imagine how hard it is to get served. The stores are simply jammed."

"That's good for business," Bobby pointed out. Uncle James concurred, though he hadn't seen the inside of a commercial office for many years.

The sound of singing was heard from the street. "Oh, the carolers!" exclaimed Aunt Susie. "How nice."

"Hadn't we better give them some coppers?" said James.

"Let's make it silver, Jimmy." Old Bobby reached into his pockets and dropped a handful of coins into Alabaster's palm. "Spread that around, 'Baster," he said, and watched him go to the front door.

"Hello, everyone." All of the women jumped up, the men rose too, as Posie appeared on the parlor threshold.

"Posie darling," said Agrippina, hurrying toward her. "We wondered. I was just about to come and see if you wanted anything."

"Thank you, Pina dear, but there was no need. I'm perfectly capable of taking care of myself, you know."

"Of course you are," said Electra, moving Agrippina a little aside as, employing the tip of her cane, Posie made her way across the carpet to occupy the chair reserved for her. She settled herself and, having hung the cane on the chair arm, smoothed out the folds of her dress and gave the room her warm smile. It was not that Posie of old whom the family regarded now. Everything of the happy-go-lucky, winsome child had fled, leaving in its place a sweet-faced but somewhat austere-looking young woman with a firm set to her mouth, a simple coiffure, dressed in a plain, neat dress, and wearing the pair of smoked glasses that marked her as blind.

As she had several times since Posie's arrival, Georgiana remarked the quiet authority herein evidenced, the fuller, richer flowering of that character that had promised so much at such an early age. Had her life been blighted by her blindness? Had her handicap overwhelmed her? To some extent, yes, for she would be forever locked in a dark world. But her infirmity was not impairment; not one acknowledged by Posie, at any rate. She refused to honor her affliction or allow others to express undue sympathy or show those special marks of concern that the able-bodied often exhibit to the disabled. But now, the fact that she had been returned to the family bosom sounded resonances that harkened back to that fall day when the gay, dimply child she had been, the object of everyone's adoration, the apple of her father's eye had lost her sight.

"Georgie, what about our school?" she asked suddenly, as if the matter had been weighing on her mind.

"I don't know—what about it, dear?"

"It was such a fine idea, our little school. I truly loved it. I'm so sorry it came to an end. It could have been the start of something wonderful, and—it could have stood as an example."

"But it does," Appleton said, getting up and going to the side table. "The Free School is known far and wide, and so are you, Posie, for having helped teach those children."

"Your father's right. No one must think our school is over and done with," Georgiana said. "As I was writing to Sister Omnia at Macao just last night, it is *not* the end."

"It's not?" Priam was as surprised as the others.

Georgiana looked first at Appleton, then at Old Bobby. "Never. We are resolved."

"But, do you have a plan?" asked Posie. "Are you going to go on with the school after you marry Papa?"

"Your father and Granddaddy and I have talked about it. Maude Ashley, too. We all feel the same way: the school shouldn't be allowed to die."

"But what about the law?" Lee Peckham asked. "I'm as much in favor of the school as anyone, you know that. But you'll have to get rid of the Grimes Law first."

"And so we shall," Georgiana said. "It's only a matter of time." She stopped by Posie's chair to kiss the top of her head. "Chloe and Phoebe Haverstraw have been asking for you. I said you'd visit them soon."

Posie smiled. "Oh, I shall. Perhaps tomorrow. Have they grown? I'm sure they have. And they'll want a story, won't they? I haven't told you all, but I have a new occupation. I'm writing down all of those little stories I used to tell the children."

"You mean you're writing a book?" crowed Minnie. "How wonderful! Now we'll have two authoresses in the family."

"And perhaps three," said Pina significantly. She was putting together a slender volume of verse she looked forward to seeing into print.

"I'm hungry," said little Sophy suddenly. "Me too, me too," came the chorus.

Appleton turned to Georgiana. "Why don't you go and ask Halley to hurry things along?"

Agrippina was out of her chair like a shot. "Stay where you are, Georgie, I'll see to it. Posie, we're having baked ham and sweet potato pie, your favorite."

"Did you remember to speak to Sallie about the ovens?" Appleton asked Georgiana. He was always anxious about the welter of detail relating to the wedding and the party afterward. Rather than burdening the Priests with the mountains of victuals to be prepared, caterers had been called in, and the Jenckeses had been enlisted to roast the braces of fowl, the pigs, and the whole ox that had been ordered up, while Izz and Erna at the Sunshine Bakery would see to the baking of hundreds of loaves of bread, rolls and twists, cookies, pies and cakes. The baking of the wedding cake, however, Halley had reserved for herself, an honor she refused to relinquish to any white folks.

Suddenly, Minnie, who had been looking through the cards accepting invitations to the wedding exclaimed, "Dear suds, here's one from Captain and Mrs. Grimes." There was a silence. Georgiana looked to Appleton.

"Yes," he said calmly. "We—that is, Georgiana and I—decided that they should be invited, Min. Captain Grimes is an old friend of Georgie's, and—and we found him a considerably changed character when we bumped into him in Hartford the other day. It would appear that life has humbled him a good deal."

"Not an entirely bad thing in his case, hey?" said Old Bobby.

"It's just a sham," Priam snorted; Pina, who had gone to the kitchen and returned, felt compelled to agree. "Pri's right. He'll never change. He's still the same egotistical dandy he always was."

"That isn't true, Pina," Georgiana said mildly. "Your father's right, he *has* changed."

But Pina was having none of it, and the bright glow of family love and general bonhomie was thus dimmed by the same old difference of opinion. Agrippina couldn't bear to hear anyone stand up for the man she professed to despise, while, since the debacle in Judge Palfrey's court had destroyed any chance of winning the case for the Free School, the mere mention of Sinjin's name had produced in Priam the iciest of glares and muttered threats. As she invariably did, Georgiana attempted to spread oil on troubled waters.

"Pri, dear, don't you think we could put old quarrels behind us? Especially now, when there's to be a wedding?"

"Georgie's right," said Old Bobby, coming to her side and taking her hand. "I for one think it would be a fine idea if we all tried more often to remember that we owe the captain a debt of gratitude—several of them in fact. And whatever his past misdeeds, he is an old and valued friend of Georgiana's. Jake was perfectly right to invite him to the wedding, and, as his wife, Rose must be included, and I would like to suppose we all will act as the sort of liberal thinking, decent folk we've been brought up to be."

"Bravo, Granddaddy," said Electra, clapping her hands lightly for emphasis.

But Priam's brow knit. "Don't applaud, Lecky. We owe that villain nothing. Except a knock on his head any time we get the chance."

"Recollect yourself, Pri," said Old Bobby sternly.

Priam extended well-muscled legs to the fire; the barely scratched soles of his boots said they were new. "I wonder the dirty bugger dares show his face around here."

"Priam, please don't talk like that," Georgiana said. "Poor Rose . . ."

Priam's laugh was harsh. " 'Poor Rose' is right; I wager he'll lead her a merry chase. Not that she doesn't deserve it, the thieving baggage."

Old Bobby spoke up again. "Pri, must we remind you, it's Christmas? A little charity, a little love."

Priam rose and went to the mantel for a spill to light his cigar. "Charity, Granddad? Love? It'd be wasted on that pair. What do you think, Sissie?" He went to Aurora's side and stroked her hair. "He's a bounder and she's no better than she should be."

Aurora took his hand away. "I'm sure I wish Rose every happiness.

Captain Grimes, too. Granddaddy's right, it's Christmastime; everyone should be happy now."

"Well, I won't be satisfied until that blackhearted bastard's six feet under and planted with sod and his wife's whipped out of town like the slut she is!"

"That's quite enough!" said Old Bobby, getting to his feet. His face had paled and his voice trembled with anger. "I will listen to no more, Priam."

"I guess I can speak my mind if I like. Why not? We're family here."

"It doesn't matter. If you unbosom yourself of such callous remarks, they will surely come back to haunt you."

" 'As we sow, so we reap,' eh, Granddad? Then let others take note."

"Pri, you are not to say another word on this subject." This time it was his father who was speaking. Having remained silent until now, but sensing Georgiana's discomfort, Appleton was compelled to try to clear the air. But even at the command Priam was not to be squelched.

"My God, has everyone gone soft around here? Granddad doesn't want me to speak the truth, and Dad and Georgie have made sure we'll be up to our necks in Grimeses for the wedding. By God, I've half a mind not to attend!"

"Priam!" Georgiana leapt up and went to Appleton's side. "You really must end this. Can't you see how you're upsetting your father? Really, I won't have it."

"Save it, Georgie, you're not running things here—not yet, you're not. Maybe we'd better leave, Peg—"

"No!" Appleton shouted. "You leave this house and it will be a long time before you're invited back. And when Captain Grimes and his wife are under this roof I expect them to be shown every courtesy. I will not have any guest of mine spoken ill of. Pina, I require to know that you also have heeded my words."

"Yes, Papa," said the dutiful Agrippina, even though her sentiments were clearly on the side of Priam, who sat sulking in his chair. Then Judah appeared to announce the meal and they all went in to table, and over the steaming platters the wrathful talk was forgotten, as was generally the way with the Talcotts.

It was still early when Great-Aunt Blanche ordered her coach around and prepared to depart Kingdom Come. James's family also took themselves off early—the farmer spoke—leaving only the occupants of the house, Georgiana, and Priam and Peggy and their children, who had been temporarily put to bed with Minnie's brood. Then Appleton and Old Bobby having slipped off to the study for brandy and a pipe as they often did, taking Priam, Lee, and Lloyd with them, the ladies were left to themselves. Stays were loosened—blessedly—and literally and figuratively their hair was taken down. In earlier years, the elder Talcott sisters had welcomed their mother's hired girl among themselves with sisterly love. Now that same hired girl was soon to wed their father, but if they found that circumstance peculiar there was no sign of it as they chattered away like so many schoolgirls.

An antique chest of drawers sitting between the two front windows bore an oval framed portrait of Mab Talcott in her youth. "Wasn't Mother lovely?" Electra said, taking up the picture to look at it. "The eyes . . ."

Yes, they agreed, Mab's eyes had been her best feature, honest and forthright, frank eyes that gazed out at you solemnly but that you knew at any moment would sparkle with laughter.

Georgiana included each of the women with her smile. "While we're all together, there is something I would like to say to you, and perhaps this is a good time to say it. I love you all very much. I love your father very much. I'm proud and happy that he has asked me to be his wife. I shall be the best wife I can be, I promise. But I can never replace your mother. I can only be Georgiana. Your mother was a remarkable woman, the most remarkable I've ever known. I can never hope to take her place. But I shall do everything I can to see to your father's happiness."

"It's all right, Georgie," said Posie, "you don't have to say it. We know what you mean."

Electra echoed these sentiments. "You are no happier at being in the family than we are to have you."

"Oh, I'm so glad we're all here together," Minnie sighed. "Aren't you glad to be home again, Sissie? In this lovely house. How safe you must feel. Everything's going to be all right now, I know it is. And to see Papa so happy. It's all your doing, Georgie dear."

"Min's right," said Electra. "But Georgie—"she smiled at her friend—"how do *you* feel about it all? Are you happy too?"

"Deliriously. Ecstatically. Though how I am to be a mother to all of you I can't think. You're going to have to be very patient with me, I'm afraid."

"But you don't have to try to be our mother—just be our darling Georgie and take care of Father."

"Yes, Georgiana, our father is your responsibility now."

"Thank you, Pina, I shall do my best."

Minnie leaned toward her. "And try to forgive Pri, he doesn't mean half of what he says. It's only Sinjin Grimes that sets him off that way."

"I know it," Georgiana said. "But isn't that the problem? And Rose, of course."

"Rose can look out for herself," said Pina meanly. "She's the dog that bites the hand that feeds her."

"She's never got over losing her baby, has she?" said Electra.

"She might have kept it if she hadn't been careless."

Pina seized the chance to unburden herself of further uncharitable senti-ments. "Women like that are never fit mothers, they deserve to lose their young. The children are the better for it. And I'm sure that Captain Grimes is greatly relieved not to have to bring up a child by *that* wicked creature."

"Really, Pina, why must you say such things?" Georgiana remonstrated as gently as she could. "Sinjin is still deeply distressed by the loss."

"Yes," Minnie said. "And, really, what sort of life must *she* have, with her husband gone all the while? It can't be an easy thing."

Agrippina shook out her sleeves. "Well, I'm sure I don't care. The very idea, to abscond with Mama's good silver spoons."

"Pina," Georgiana said gently, "your mother's spoons were returned some time ago. They are safely stowed in their drawer. Have you forgotten we have Captain Grimes to thank for that?"

Pina stroked the arch of her neck. "Georgie, you are the soul of loyalty, but I vow, he'll come to a bad end yet, see if he doesn't."

"I pray you're mistaken, Pina dear," said Posie, speaking up. "And since it is Papa who has professed goodwill toward Captain Grimes, I think the least we all can do is to follow that example."

"Maybe, but you won't catch Pri making up to the scoundrel again, I promise you that," Pina retorted.

"So much the worse for Pri, then. If he *were* to make up he might just find an interesting fellow behind all the braggadocio. And a friend to boot."

Pina bridled. "Not likely. If I know our brother, and I think I do, he'll make a pig pie of Sinjin Grimes yet. And I for one will be perfectly glad to see it happen."

"Well, I won't," Posie declared staunchly. "Have you forgotten he saved my life—two times?"

"No, but another thing I haven't forgotten is the vulgar spectacle he and that wife put on at Georgie's trial last year either. Or many other things," she added.

"But we should let bygones be bygones. He's Georgie's friend and she and Papa have invited him to their wedding. It's up to us to make him welcome, him *and* Rose."

"Bravo, Po," said Minnie. "Now let's change the subject. Rora, tell us about New Orleans."

Aurora, who had been thoughtfully biting her thumbnail, looked up, startled out of the reverie into which she had sunk.

"What? Oh—yes, yes, of course," she said. "New Orleans." She seemed exceedingly abstracted, as if something in all the talk of Sinjin Grimes troubled her deeply.

"Sissie, are you all right?"

"Yes, of course. Just a trifle tired. I think I'll go along."

She kissed each one in turn and passed through the doorway. In the hall they could hear her speaking to Burdy, who happened to be passing.

"Ask my brother to come to my room, please, Burdy. Right away, if he can. I wish to speak with him." Then she was gone, leaving behind her a silence of some duration.

"Poor Sissie. What's she to do?"

"Well, she can't just go on, can she? Being a butterfly, I mean, flitting from place to place. She's got to think of settling down, of putting her life in order."

"I agree," Peggy said. "We ought to persuade her to stay at home."

"No, Peg, Aurora must do whatever she feels she must," Electra argued. "One day things will come right for her."

"But when?" Minnie said.

"In God's time, dear. As is true for all of us."

"I think perhaps our talk of Captain Grimes upset her," Posie said.

Pina was shaking her head in dismay. "Every time that man comes around here something happens. Something bad. You and Papa really ought to have thought twice before inviting him, Georgie. Especially now that Rora's home. Think of the trouble it might cause if—"

She was denied the chance of completing her foreboding thought. "Pina, stop it," Electra said. "He's invited and that's that. Now mayn't we pass on from this provoking matter? It's distressing Georgie, and besides, he's not going to hurt Rora."

"How can anyone be sure? I'd say he has every excuse, at least in that dark perverted mind of his. She threw him over, you know, sent him packing—as he deserved."

Georgiana, who knew differently, bit her tongue.

Pina continued to worry her bone. "He may try to take revenge on her—on all of us. Priam's right—the man's not to be trusted. We must all beware—especially Sissie."

"That's nonsense."

"Go on, then, stick up for him, you always do. But you had better be warned—"

"Pina dear," said Electra, interrupting tactfully. "Won't you show me some of your watercolors before bedtime? I'm always so envious of your clever work."

"Very well, Lecky, come along and see my pine boughs." Pina seemed happy to be leaving the room. She stopped in the doorway and turned. "Georgie, I warn you, if Sinjin Grimes comes to your wedding and drags that common creature with him, there's bound to be trouble of some kind. You just see if I'm not right!" She settled back with a triumphant gleam in her darting eyes.

"Thank you for confiding your sentiments to me, Pina," Georgiana returned evenly. "Forewarned is forearmed."

When Electra had taken Pina away Minnie spoke up. "Georgie, you mustn't pay any attention to what Pina says. You're going to have a simply heavenly wedding, the loveliest imaginable, I just know it."

"Indeed you are, Georgie," said Priam, who had entered the room in time to hear this. "It's time to go, Peg. I'll come up with you and Min to get the children."

Peggy and Minnie both rose. "Yes, of course, Pri," Peggy said. "Come on, Minnie. You'll have to untangle ours from yours, you know."

When they had left, Posie got to her feet. "You know, Georgie," she said, "I'm a bit tired myself. Will you come along with me, see me to my room?" It was a rare request—Posie didn't like being "helped"—and Georgiana was touched. Quickly she moved to Posie's side and arm in arm they made their way down the hall, stopping for a moment at the study doorway to say good night before going upstairs. When they got to her room Posie drew Georgiana inside for a private word.

"Georgie, I want to apologize for Pina. She loves our father so. It's her saving grace, don't you think?"

"Yes, dear, I'm sure it is," said Georgiana warmly. "She adores your father—as do I."

"You *do,* don't you, Georgie? And you and Papa will be happy, won't you? I do so pray you shall."

"And so we shall. You need have no fears on that score. If I am pledged to his happiness and in this am successful, how can I possibly fail in my own, since the two are inextricably linked?" She kissed Posie's cheek and pressed her hand confidently.

Just then, the door opened and Trubey came in bearing a tray with the warm, meadlike posset laced with port that had become Posie's nightly potion. When she had gone out again, Posie completed her thought. "And yours with mine, Georgie. Nothing has ever made me happier than knowing that Papa's welfare has been entrusted to you. I know it was Mama's wish, her dying wish, but I never thought—"

"No, dear, why should you? Why should anyone?"

"That's why I'm so happy—and pleased. And proud. I think we're very lucky to have you in the family. It's like having a mother and a sister and a best friend all rolled up together. As for Captain Grimes, you and I know what an extraordinary man he is. I think of us as his muses—"

Georgiana was touched. "Do you really?"

"Yes. A little. As if we are needed to be around him, to inspire him."

"I'm sure he can use all the inspiration he can get."

Posie turned her lip thoughtfully under her front teeth. "Is he happy, Georgie?"

"I don't think so. Though he does seem determined to make the best of things. The new ship will help. Your father and I have promised to go aboard and look her over. The *Hattie D.,* imagine, in its reincarnation."

"You're stony, Georgie, you're a rock."

"No, darling, *you* are the rock. And you're my sweet, brave girl and I love you. Always have, always will. If only—"

"Yes?"

"Nothing."

"If only I would come back home to live, is that what you meant to say?"

"Oh, darling, if only you would. It would mean so much to your father. *And* to me. To all of us."

"But you all have each other. You don't need me. And Georgie, *I* need—"

"Yes, dear, what do you need?"

"I need to be *there.* I must stand up by myself. I must earn a living and be independent. It's most important, really. I'm just not the kind to, well— it's nice to be loved and wanted by others, but I'm not going to let life pass me by merely because I can't see. I'm going to do something of consequence. You'll see."

"Of course you are, darling. I *know* you are. And your book, too. What a grand thing that will be, to see your stories published." Georgiana bent to kiss her one more time. "Good night, Posie dear, sleep well. I'll come to breakfast with all of you at nine."

Posie returned her kiss, smiling. Then Georgiana crossed the braided rug, intending to slip away, only to be met at the door by the four elder Talcott sisters, whispering among themselves.

"We have news," said Electra. "Or rather, Rora does."

"Yes, Pri told me I must make it known to you before tomorrow." Aurora smiled, rather sadly, Georgiana thought. "The truth is," she said, "I too am soon to be wed."

46

Adeste Fideles

AGAIN THE STEEPLE bell pealed out across the village, this time on Christmas Day. Giles Corry was giving them their very best ring. At eleven of the clock on that tingling winter's morn Georgiana Ross would be joined in holy wedlock with Appleton Jacob Talcott of Kingdom Come. It was an event of no small pomp, even for those folk not privy to the deeper, perhaps more obscure resonances of the occasion in which a Talcott wedding ring would be slid upon the finger of a Grimes.

Georgiana, the recipient of said ring, had been awake since before dawn. She'd heard one of the village cocks crowing, recalling to mind that spring morning when she'd awakened at Grimes Mill on the day that John Quincy was coming to town, and as she lay in her snug bed she thought of the girl she had been, and of all the events that had happened since that day. Good and bad alike, they presented themselves for her review, and it seemed that that long ago morning had signaled the real beginning of her life. The President of the United States of America had passed aboard the *John Paul Jones,* Posie Talcott had fallen into the river and Sinjin had tried to fetch her out and nearly drowned in the bargain, and with that fateful splash the world had been jolted on its axis and nothing had ever been the same again. Nor ever would be, and it was useless to hope or even pretend it might. Still, her mind would not let it go. She, who had the blood of Zion Grimes in her veins, was this day to be joined to a Talcott—son of the preeminent Talcott, mind you—yet she had begun as the miller's girl, and that was in her, too, and Ruth-Ella Deane, poor creature.

"Oh, dearest Momma," she whispered, "I hope you can see me today. I hope you'll see how pretty I look in my bride's dress. I've tried, Momma, I really have, to be the person you wanted me to be. And now—"

For a moment she wept, sentimental tears, wishing that Momma could be there today, but then the cock crowed again and she dashed away the tears and rose from her bed. She began with a prayer at the window. The sky was clear, it would be a beautiful day, this Christmas Day, her wedding day, and she asked God's blessing on it.

AT PRECISELY a quarter before eleven she came down the stairs of Kingdom Come dressed in her ivory silk gown. Priam and Jack Talcott had prudently spirited the bridegroom away to the tavern taproom where Milehigh was nailing him together with a good bracer, while his daughters clustered happily about the bride. Trubey sped in with a package: Ah—of course, the gift the twins had sent Georgiana, to be opened now, before the wedding. Electra helped her with the wrapping, and, looking into the box, Georgiana discovered another box. It was of tortoiseshell, inset with bands of some black material, and the initial "G" was set into the lid.

"A musical box!" proclaimed Agrippina as Georgiana raised the lid. And so it was. What was its song? they asked. She tripped the little wire and the metal spool turned, plinking out the familiar melody.

" 'Lavina'! It's 'Lavina'!" they chorused. Touched, Georgiana smiled.

How wonderful that the boys had remembered. No, not both, she felt quite sure that the idea must have originated with Hector, Achilles wasn't sentimental; but she blessed them both for their thoughtfulness.

No one whose gaze then fell upon Georgie Ross would ever again think of her as plain. Her lustrous gray eyes mirrored a deep happiness and womanly satisfaction, as if by becoming the bride of Appleton Talcott she had found her own self at last, had discovered her niche in life. And though thirty-three on her last birthday, on this December morning she was the child of spring, flushed with youth and glowing health. Her radiance brimmed over—what cup could contain it?—yet none was wasted, for there were too many about her eager to take up the overflow, down to the last drop.

The musical box was still playing its sentimental ditty as, amid this veritable crush of grace and femininity, Old Bobby Talcott appeared. In another moment the Yellow Pumpkin had rolled up to the house, with both Alabaster and Reuben on the box. When the doors were opened Bobby offered Georgiana his arm (he was to give the bride away), and in what seemed only a minute, she stood trembling at the church entrance, wrapped in Electra's long fur cape, waiting for the wedding music to begin.

"Granddaddy—?"

Old Bobby blinked at her. "Yes, my dear. What are your last words as an oceangoing passenger embarking on the seas of matrimony?"

She plucked nervously at his sleeve buttons. "You're not angry with me? You don't think I'm marrying above my—that is, you don't mind that Appleton asked?"

"Silence, my girl, I won't hear of such a thing. 'Marrying above your station,' is that what you were going to say? Well, let me assure you that you are, and why should you not? When my boy Jake married his Molly I took shameful umbrage, she had married above herself, or so it seemed to this foolish fool. But how happy I was to have her, how she enriched my life. It is a debt I can never repay. And now we have you, my dear, every one of us, and no man luckier than our Jake. I welcome you among us with all my heart!"

He embraced her warmly and tearfully, and drew her out of the draft. Giles Corry was there and presented her with a lovely white floweret, which she tucked into her bouquet. "For luck and happiness, Georgie Ross," he whispered. "God rest the souls of the dear departed."

Giles had known her when she was only a babe-in-arms and Ruth-Ella carried her in for baptism, and Georgiana was touched by this display of sentiment.

Inside, the church filled to its capacity as Mehatibel Duckworth played a hymn and the Reverend Bushnell entered by the side door, nodding and smiling at faces he recognized. Then, heads turned to watch as Georgiana appeared on Bobby's arm at the head of the center aisle, and, as the music swelled, they proceeded toward the altar.

The ceremony was short and sweet, the way Appleton had wanted it, and at the end he took her hands and affectionately pressed their palms against his chest, then leaned forward and gently kissed his new wife on the lips. In that moment of simple purity and chasteness, as Georgiana gazed into Appleton's eyes her features became suffused with an inner radiance, the luminous gray eyes regarded the man to whom she was now joined in matrimony with such adoring trust, that to those who saw her, including Sinjin Grimes, seated in the Grimes pew between Rose and his sister Helen, she seemed the personification of all of womanhood, the embodiment of all the goodness and sweetness in the world. For a moment, Sinjin's heart swelled and choked him, and he swallowed hard; the sight was one he would never forget, particularly a single infinitesimal but telling detail: Georgiana's hand lying lightly along the dark fabric of Appleton's sleeve, so confidential and trusting. The warm, complaisant intimacy caused Sinjin a surprising pang of jealousy, as if, by noticing, he had seen his beloved delivered into the hands of some hated rival. And this was an odd thing indeed.

In another moment his eyes were directed away from the bridal couple up to the choir loft, where Aurora had risen and approached the loft rail. Backed by the choir, with Hat's accompaniment, she sang *"Adeste Fideles,"* her father's favorite Christmas carol, and her clear, melodious voice filled the church with song.

As she sang, her porcelain face caught in sunlight seemed to Sinjin like that of some ethereal seraph floated down from on high to grace the solemnities. At his arm Rose darted glances all about, avidly remarking to herself what the various ladies were wearing and feeling as nervous as she had the first time she'd ever come into the church and outraged the congregation by sitting down in the Grimeses' pew. In a moment, not comprehending exactly what was happening, but feeling the evident agitation of Sinjin's frame, she gave his arm an impatient jerk, and as they joined the others going up the aisle she clung to him with a kind of wifely desperation, as if to be separated from him meant disaster of a kind she was not prepared to deal with.

EVERYONE who was at the wedding party that day at Kingdom Come agreed that it was indeed a splendid occasion, one to be joyfully savored and remembered. If Appleton Talcott's first wedding had been a simple affair, as befitted a recent graduate of Yale with ample prospects but little means, his second, nearly forty years later, was quite another matter. As a wealthy property owner, residing in one of the finest houses in Hartford County, he had ordered up the greatest gala within memory in those parts. It was as if he felt some inner need to be expansive, brimming over, even a trifle ostentatious (and there were those who accused him of deliberately violating those sumptuary laws still on the books since the days of the Ten Adventurers). He had won himself a rare prize and he aspired to show her off for everyone to see. She had nearly slipped away from him, eluded his grasp, but she had at last consented—something to do with swans, it seemed—and in the end all had turned out exactly as the dear departed Mab had so fervently prayed it would: Georgiana Ross was to be the mistress of Number 17 Main Street, the handsome house that was emblematic of the best the whole country had to offer, American to its foundations, created of the finest materials by the finest craftsmen, the house that had been built, as John Quincy Adams had so felicitously put it, "to last till Kingdom Come."

In every room that day there was ample evidence of the traditional values the house embodied: the warmth of many stoves, dark bubbling bottles that had lost their corks, glasses raised and good healths drunk to both bride and groom and blessings called upon their heads. From doorway to doorway, along the halls and passageways, up the staircases and down, from room to room to room thronged convivial groups of guests, happy to share in such an uncommonly happy occasion. Of food and drink there was aplenty. Viands to whet any sort of palate, trays full of tasties set out on sterling silver salvers that white-gloved waiters in scarlet jackets, hired from Hartford for the day, passed with meticulous care over the heads of the bobbing guests. In came the quartered ox, with Milehigh himself to carve it up, the rare roast of beef Appleton doted on, the done-to-a-turn guinea fowl, the game pies and savories, with Erna Quoile's biscuits and bread.

Even the former First Executive John Quincy Adams was on hand, standing alongside his crony Old Bobby Talcott. Though, fifteen years after the end of his term as president, he had been lodged for nearly as many in the House of Representatives in Washington, John Quincy did not allow himself to be lionized by the village bon ton at the expense of Appleton's and Georgiana's moment of glory, but kept himself well in the background, taking his every cue from his old friend Bob. "I congratulate you," he said to the groom, "on your choice of a helpmeet. One look at your bride tells me that your happiness is assured." He bowed over his salutation and turned to Georgiana. "And you, Mrs. Talcott, I remember watching you dance the night the gypsies came. Danced with Bob here, and looked a gypsy yourself, with colored ribbons in your hair. And by crackee wasn't that a storm we had that night?"

No one saw fit to mention the alarming high point of that evening, when a certain member of the Grimes clan had stolen upon the property, only to be knocked to the ground by Old Bobby's grandson. Though the entire cast of that domestic drama were here present, it was only the elderly coachmen who in hushed tones recounted the event again, then passed along to more pleasant topics.

But many agreed: perhaps the most remarkable sight among so many others was that of Captain Grimes and his wife. With Rose glued to his side, her arm unrelentingly locked in his, they moved about, he in his best blues, looking smart and spanking, she dressed to the nines in a burgundy and red shot-silk combination, a handsome bonnet atop her hair, gloves, fan, and reticule with a silk tassel that swayed and bobbed with her every move. She was exceedingly animated, brightly flashing like a piece of chrysolite, and determined that no one should miss the fact that another former serving girl at Kingdom Come had returned to the village in a markedly elevated state.

Rose continued to cling possessively to Sinjin's arm, and as they passed along the greeting line, she chattering like a mute who had just discovered his tongue, adopting a fruity social tone she believed she had heard in others of a genteel complexion, while Sinjin could do nothing but cringe in embarrassment. She fell silent, however as they came abreast of Agrippina, and allowed her spouse to speak for them both. Having been privately advised that neither Priam nor his sister, no matter how fervently they might wish that Captain Grimes and his wife had declined Georgiana's invitation, would do anything to humiliate her or their father on this occasion, Sinjin greeted her evenly.

"Hullo, Miss Talcott. You remember Rose."

"Indeed I do, who could forget Rose Mills? Beg pardon, I ought to have said Mrs. Grimes, oughtn't I?" Agrippina smiled but withheld her hand from Rose. Turning to her brother, she said, "Priam dear, pay attention—here are the Grimeses."

Priam, polished and buffed, turned with flushed countenance, and bowed stiffly. "Captain, for Georgie's sake, you are welcome here," he said.

"Thank you, sir," replied Sinjin.

"She makes a lovely bride, does she not?" Priam went on. Sinjin agreed, saying no man had ever had a lovelier. Briefly he took in the handsome face before him, a trifle florid, rosy as a baby's behind, with those two large blue Talcott eyes, the long patrician nose down which Priam was frequently so adept at looking, the hint of matching dimples beside the curly lips. Obviously both brother and sister had been placed on their best behavior.

Agrippina opened her lips for another word. "I wonder if we might tell Captain Grimes and his wife Sissie's news. Quite a surprise, I must say." She smiled like a cat. "We're simply all agog in this family. Imagine, not a word about it until last evening, and then quite privately. Pri dear, perhaps you should be the one to speak out."

"Sir and madam," said Priam, "what Agrippina intends me to say is that our sister Aurora has confided to us the happy news of her recent engagement to be married. Though she chose to make a secret of it, she has been officially betrothed since before Thanksgiving."

"Isn't it quite the most exciting thing?" Agrippina pressed a palm to her breast, stilling the fervor that abounded there. "I do declare, if Sissie hasn't stolen a march—"

Stunned to silence, Sinjin was compelled to listen, while Rose clutched his arm and Pina's words flowed on. ". . . met at New Orleans, of all places . . . fiancé a successful merchant from the Brabant . . . Swiss-Belgian . . . a man of infinite taste and wealth . . . Rora simply mad about him . . . too too wonderful."

Just ahead, Sinjin glimpsed the crown of Georgiana's head and Appleton's beaming countenance as he stood proudly at her side. Then she was smiling and putting out her hand, first to Rose, then to Sinjin. The very soul of her was in her eyes, warm and luminous, filled with an inner joy that words could not describe.

"Georgie," he said huskily, bending to peck her cheek in dutiful admiration. "I wish you much happiness."

She gazed at him with a smile of ineffable sweetness that went straight to his heart.

"Thank you, Captain. Appleton, here are Rose and Captain Grimes."

Appleton turned to greet them. "Ah, yes, here they are indeed." He shook Rose's hand, then Sinjin's, more robustly, his face red and wreathed with a great happiness. He actually seemed to shed light, so aglow was he with health and happiness.

The line was crowding behind them and they were forced to move on.

"Well!" Rose exclaimed as they broke free of the gathering. "What do you think of that?"

What was there to say? What sane comment was to be made? Covering his shock and dismay however he could, Sinjin allowed himself to be maneuvered among the laughing, excited guests as the news raced about the rooms. To the congratulations made to the bridal couple now there were additional hugs, kisses, and expressions of felicitation being offered to the groom's daughter as well, and before long even the coachmen parked in the back kitchen were proposing toasts in cider to the newly announced fiancée of the Brussels merchant.

"Damn him for a clockwork man!" Sinjin thundered inside his head, accepting the proffered cup of Fish House Punch. His first reaction was to doubt the whole story, to cast it from his thoughts as an unlikely thing, nay, an impossibility. Yet even as he rejected the idea he somehow knew it must be so. People didn't invent Belgian merchants from the Brabant.

In a daze he cruised from room to room, Rose always close at his side, familiar faces popping up before him—Hermie and Mother Light; Melody

Morgan and Talley Welles, both née Griswold; Helen and Luke and all their brood clamoring for Uncle Sinjin's attention; Aunt Hat under a new "bunnit," looking tinier and more fragile than ever, her expression one of concealed anxiety for her former pupil who was so gallantly rechristening his vessel in her honor; Maude Ashley, who, with her husband Merrill, went out of the way to extend Rose a friendly word; Judge Perry and Cent Dunnoult, Old Bobby's cronies of over six decades, with thatches whiter than Arctic snow, but ever in the pink; Stix Bailey and Kneebone Apperbee in the best bibs and tuckers they could assemble; a smiling Izz and Erna Quoile, who had done all the baking for the party except for the wedding cake; Cap'n Joss and Cap Oysterbanks, Reverend Leete and his wife, Nate Finn and his mother, the lot of them from Home Island; Ambo Buck and the Burdins; and on and on.

At last he escaped Rose, leaving her with Helen—blessed Helen, who *knew;* Helen understood what her brother must be feeling—and made his way toward that golden head: Aurora was smiling as she listened to a remark of Posie's, who sat beside her sister on a striped sofa—his ally, his congenial little go-between.

"Who is it?" asked Posie, sensing his presence.

"It's your old friend Captain Grimes," said Aurora. "My, how distinguished he looks." Her laugh was gay, her manner even coquettish as she smiled up at him, but he was on to her. Tonight Number 17 Main was her stage and she was prepared to make the most of it.

Posie manipulated her cane to one side and made room on the sofa, crushing her skirts close about her knees.

"Hello, Posie," Sinjin said, accepting the place between her and Aurora. "Hello, Rora." His heart was beating wildly—surely she could hear it—yet she gave no sign, was cool and self-possessed.

"Yes, hello," she returned crisply; avoiding use of his name. "Wasn't it a lovely wedding? Doesn't Georgiana look superb?"

"Yes, yes, she does—that's the word! And your father looks as happy as a man can."

"And *is!* I've never seen him so light-headed, he's positively giddy."

She laughed, not a happy sound, not Aurora-like at all, then something caught her eye and she moved quickly to rise.

"There's Melody," she said, giving her skirt a shake. "I'll just go and thank her for her Christmas present. And while I'm gone, Posie, you shall amuse the captain."

She cocked her head at him, a pert, birdlike gesture filled with such intimations that it infuriated him, and was gone, leaving him with Posie. He was gratified to find that behind the smoked glasses and slight pallor Persephone Talcott was much the same person he'd become so fond of two summers ago. Obviously she'd matured in the space of a year, and was every bit the grown-up young lady. They spoke together like old friends. Sensible, humorous, and lacking in pretension, Posie made an enviable conversational partner, describing her new life at Boston, commenting on her studies and saying how greatly she was enjoying Mr. Emerson's lectures, which friends had taken her to hear at Faneuil Hall.

Yet, even as he listened, Sinjin's eye kept straying to where Aurora stood talking animatedly with Melody, Talley, and some other females, none of whom profited by even the most cursory comparison to her. She was still the town beauty, still the belle of Pequot Landing, the latest word, and who could deny it?

"You needn't worry," Posie said with an indulgent laugh, "She won't run away." Sinjin was dumbfounded. How had she known? How could she tell? It was true of the blind that they did find the four remaining senses becoming more acute, but he had the distinct impression he was being read like a book under a magnification glass.

He moved closer; her skirts rustled.

"Po—" he began in a low voice.

"Yes?"

"We're still friends, aren't we? You and I?"

"Of course. How could you imagine we're not?"

"It's all different now. *I'm* different. I just thought—with my having married Rose and all—"

"Captain, do you actually imagine that I would disavow you? I never would. How could I ever forget your astonishing bravery on my behalf? I want you to be happy, we all do, but you must never suppose I could ever think badly of you or reproach you. You have a new vessel, Georgie tells me, and I pray it may one day make all your dreams come true."

"It can't. Not without her."

"But it must. You must not be unhappy. It's wrong to want what we cannot have; we must try to make the best of things."

That was what she had done of course; and for a moment he was ashamed. Then his eye fell again on Aurora. "But, Po, what of this—this—engagement?" he asked.

"Oh, it *was* a shock, truly. I had no idea, no one had. Rora had locked the secret in her bosom—I really don't know why."

"Who is he, this man?"

"His name is Martin. Evidently well-known in international circles."

"Where will they live?"

"At Brussels, I expect." She sighed. "It takes away some of today's happiness, to know she will be so far away again."

"But, Po, do you think she really means to marry him?"

Posie sighed. "Unless she can be persuaded otherwise." Did he detect a hopeful note in her reply? He couldn't be sure, and yet . . .

She was smiling and nodding agreeably. "You have always had exceptionally persuasive powers over her," he heard her saying. "Perhaps if you were to make one last effort—"

"But how? I can't get near her. You see how she fled—"

She slipped her small warm hand into his and gave an encouraging squeeze. "We must find an opportunity for the two of you to meet and speak in private. I'm sure she'd like that—even though she pretends otherwise. I always know when she's pretending. Perhaps if you were able to casually maneuver her into the back parlor . . . you know, just slip her away before she realizes it—there might be fewer people there—"

Absorbing each of Posie's well-intentioned words, he found himself already plotting. If he could just talk with Aurora, convince her of the terrible mistake she was making. If he could but be alone with her, draw her into his arms, kiss her and caress her, ah, then—

He was certain of his powers as a man, he knew that the things he'd done to her, mind and body, were not the sort to be easily dismissed; he even permitted himself the male conceit that behind that cold, bored facade she still burned for him as he did for her. The thought gave him a glimmer of hope. And why not? Hope was always better than despair, the kind of grinding desperation that had weighed him down for the past year and bent him so out of shape. He recalled how cleverly Posie had finagled that oh-so-gratifying rendezvous at Grimes Mill, on that gorgeous, starlit night, whose memory even now shed its faint, warm glow about him. Two times only had he made love to her in fifteen years. Would there ever come a third time, or was he asking for too much? He always demanded, of course, he was greedy. He had crammed his years with every sort of sensation of self-gratification, and he harbored few regrets. One only, really—but that one would grieve him forever, all down the long road to dusty death.

His blood began to race heatedly, shamefully, as he thought back over his great folly. If only he hadn't met up with Rose again, if only he hadn't slept with her, got her with child, if only he'd been smart enough to settle a sum on her, a generous sum, for he could never be stingy in such matters, and then have washed his hands of her. Only a fool would feel duty-bound to make her honest in the eyes of the world. And in the end the child had been lost. A boy, she'd said; perhaps it was better he'd died, that black-and-white child whose chances in the world would have been sadly diminished.

"Where is Sissie?" Posie was asking, craning her head as if she were looking. "Do you see her?"

"She's talking with Asher and your brother."

"Ah, Asher." Posie giggled. "He's still smitten with her. Sissie's ever the enchantress, isn't she?"

"Now she's moving—"

"Quick, then, after her," Posie urged. "Catch her and take her into the other room, it will be quieter. Tell me later what she says!"

Gazing at Aurora across the packed room, he felt the delicious lick of old flames, and the old hunger rose in him anew. It was almost as if she'd been waiting for him, as if she had glided into view at precisely that moment with the express purpose of exciting his attention or admiration. He had that feeling. Rising, he went straight to her and taking her arm wordlessly escorted her out of the best parlor, into the adjoining room, where couples were dancing to the music of the orchestra Appleton had hired for the occasion.

A clump of potted plants partially screened them from the looks of others, and he gazed breathlessly upon her loveliness. Her eye was bright—a hint too bright?—her smile charming as she indulged in the sort of clever badinage he had no wish to listen to. The bride, the groom, the house, the music, his health, *Rose's* health— He listened to her, silently cursing her with every syllable as her shallow scarlet words flew up about them like so many brightly dyed birds.

"Come, Captain, no thunderclouds on so happy a day. You mustn't let people think you are downcast when there is no reason to be so."

"Why didn't you tell me?" he muttered in her ear.

"Tell you?" She turned dazzling to him. "Do you mean of my engagement? And when, pray, should I have done that? When you appeared to Georgiana and me as that ghostly figment the other evening on Main Street? In any case, I wished no one to know of my plans until Georgiana and my father had had their day. The news—slipped out, unfortunately. Pina's doing; you know how Pina is."

"Very altruistic of you. But—will you be happy?"

"When?"

"*When?* When you're married, of course."

"Oh, I certainly hope so, else it shall all have gone for naught. Even as you and I have done."

"Don't—"

She crinkled her brows. " 'Don't'? Oh, please don't say 'don't' to me." Her voice was both weary and bitter. "I have had ample time and then some to reflect upon our last conversation—you will doubtless recall it—in the blacksmith's forge? You were at considerable pains to tell me how you had washed your hands of me. Soap and water and a towel, was that not the recipe? Did you not advise me to—stop being silly and to get on with my life? I believe that was how you phrased it."

"My words were ill advised, I admit it."

"That's handsome of you. But, as you see, I have taken them to heart. I *am* getting on with my life. And you? How is *your* life these days, Captain?"

"Never mind about that. When?"

"When am I to be married, do you mean? In the spring. I have a yearning to be a bride at least once more in my life."

"Stop it, name of Christ." His eyes were genuinely pained, his voice trembled. "Rora, don't behave this way."

"Which way is that, pray?"

"So arch. So—" He was about to say "so like Agrippina," but checked the impulse. "You don't love him. You know you don't, you're only doing this because—you know."

She fiddled with a bracelet.

"Truly, Captain, I haven't the least idea what you're talking about."

"Because of Rose and me. Because I married *her,* not you."

Her sarcasm was superb. "Yes, that's right, you did, didn't you? Marry Rose. One sometimes tends to forget these things, spending so much time away. You and Rose—married . . . It *is* a *tiny* bit hard for the mind to—to grasp, isn't it?"

"No matter, no matter," he muttered darkly. Suddenly he seized her by both arms and gave her a little shake. "See here, God damn it—I want you to stop this right now, do you understand? Right now. We'll have no more of it."

She was having trouble checking her temper.

"Let me go! You're hurting me! Oh, but then I forget—you enjoy hurting people, don't you? You relish that sort of physical mauling. I only hope poor Rose manages to fare better at your hands."

He held them before her eyes. "See them? My hands? I'll use them all right, try me, test me, go ahead."

She returned his look flatly.

"You will murder me? Is that it? You want to choke the breath from me, here, before all our guests?"

"Stop it, God damn you. We aren't playing games now."

"I had not thought we were, believe me. But you do make me wonder, Captain, you really make me wonder. I truly fear I don't know you at all, not the least bit."

"Can't we talk?" he pleaded, changing his tack. "Rora, don't let it—it mustn't be—"

"Mustn't be like this? Please, I detest a man who begs. Come, you're so big and strong, you cut such a manly figure, don't abase yourself."

"Very well, I won't. Only—"

"Only?"

"Only you don't love him!"

"Do I not? How can you know where and whether I love? We are done, you and I. You'll do well to remember that. Our song ended in a forge on a very cold and windy day, and I caught a dreadful cold, I took to my bed, and when I got up again—*poof!* Birdie had flown the coop. And with you went—" Her expression grew touchingly sad, her voice as well. "Ah, we now speak of things best forgot. It's true; forget. It is over. Ended. You are wed, while I shall be shortly. Think of this moment as merely a—an interlude. One terribly sad moment of parting. And we both know the truth. You said it yourself: we were never meant—"

His hand flew up to stop her words. "Don't say that! It's a lie! You *know* we were, meant for each other, you believed it with all your heart, we both did. Something happened—"

"A good deal happened, alas. We missed our chance, that's all."

"Christ, don't say that—!"

"Why not, when it's true? It must be as plain to you as it is to me. If you think about it, you'll realize it never could have possibly succeeded. There were so many reasons."

"What do they matter now?"

She shook her head regretfully. "They do, oh, they do. Believe me, I have thought much about these things and I know." Her voice had changed; no longer brittle, it was filled with remorse and pain. She spoke intimately, almost invitingly. It was as if they were still lovers. "You talked of fate; you said you believed we were fated. But we weren't, were we? Surely you can see that, for if it were so, if we *had* been fated, then things would be far different."

She spread her fan, reminding them both of that other fan of yellow silk. "Perhaps there *was* a thread," she went on, "perhaps we *were* woven together for a little, but the lady with the shears cut that thread, and that was the end of us. *That* is what it was all meant to be, nothing else. But it really doesn't do to think about such things; they have a way of working out for the best, don't you agree?"

"Don't, in the name of God—!"

"The God you don't believe in, do you mean?"

"Jesus, stop it! Stop it—why must you be so cruel?"

She laughed, a little, rueful sort of laugh. "I'm not being cruel, my dear, I'm only facing the truth. Though, believe me, if I wished, I could be terribly cruel." She tapped his sleeve with her fan and her look was chary. "Remember that. Would you like it, I wonder, if I were? We have been cruel, each to the other. I hated you—when you went rushing off the last time, and left me."

"I didn't rush off, damn it, I *had* to go—"

"Yes, I know. But I hated you so much I could have killed you, just as I killed Henry. I still hate you. I hate you with every speck of my being. But I shall let you live. I *want* you to live. I do. Live in all the misery and despair the world has to offer. It will give me some pleasure to think how unhappy you are."

Her face had become a grimace; he had never seen her look so unattractive as in that instant. He saw lines there and a hard pinched look.

"Liar!" As from a gun he shot the word at her.

Her features again assumed their normal lines and planes. She regarded him equably. "Why 'liar,' pray?"

"Because you don't hate me. You love me. You do. You don't love him, you couldn't!"

"But I never said I did. Did I?"

"You're marrying him, it's all the same."

"Oh no, it is not. People do not always marry for love, in fact it's my growing impression that very few do. My mother and father did, and, I am happy to say, my father and Georgiana have. As for me, I am not so foolish as ever to look for love where I cannot hope to find it. But he will make me a good husband, he will give me what I want and need." ·

"What is that, if one may ask?"

"Peace, security, a home, friends, standing, new places to see and enjoy. I am weary, Sinjin, so weary, truly, so terribly tired. I don't suppose you can understand that."

"Yes, yes I can, of course I can. And I'm weary, too. God, Rora, can't we forget the past, can't we just—"

"Hush. Please stop now. No more, I beg you. Such words are painful, to both of us, and we must try to rid ourselves of pain. Let us make a truce, shall we? You and I. For the little time that is left to us, let's pretend we are friends. I would like to be your friend."

"Friends be damned!" he blazed. "I'm not looking for a friend. I want *you!*"

"And may not have me, Captain. Must I remind you that both you and I are already spoken for?"

"But you don't love him! By your own confession! You can't love him, because you love me. Admit it! Say it!"

She lowered her lashes a moment, then raised them and gazed at him with misty eyes. "Very well," she said, slowly nodding. "It is true, I admit it. I love you. I have loved you from the first, and would have loved you unto the last. Until the final cock crow. But the last has come and I must stop loving you, it's too great a price."

She glanced past his shoulder as the orchestra began to play again. "Come," she said, taking his hand. "Here's a waltz and you shall dance it with me. Then you must promise to go back to Rose, for I mustn't earn another of those black looks of hers."

Almost before he knew what was happening she had moved them away from the screen of leaves, out onto the floor. He held her right hand in his left, his other encircled her waist, that narrow alluring waist. He was in a kind of daze as they spun around the room. She was in his arms, and the notes rang in his ears, and with every beat of the music he took heart, drawing her closer, loving her . . . loving . . . He glimpsed Rose among the guests watching them, many faces watching, but what did he care for that? With her so close, her scent in his nostrils, everything seemed to have been put to rights and his heart lay serene within him. They moved as one with that sureness and intimacy that had marked their first meeting in the cabin of the *Adele,* that first, swift awareness of each other. And as settled in his mind as he had once been, he was now swept up and away by an electrifying current whose source rested utterly in her and communicated itself simply and readily to him—that golden silken cord that bound them together. Again he felt it tightening, tightening . . .

All the rest was words, mere chaff, and he had a heightened sense, not of what had been, the sorrows and the pain, the tears and the parting, the bitter loneliness that had weighed him down like chains, nor even a sense of the present, which was merely the shadow of the past; but only of the future. Yes, the future! Something divinely wonderful began to bubble up inside him, a rich, juicy froth, a feeling that, trapped at the brink and about to tumble over, he might still be pulled back from it, that even in the face of the cold facts *something* might be done, some way out might be found. Oh God. God—hear me. Suddenly he hoped where he had not dared hope, scarcely dared to breathe, nor even to look at her for fear she would evaporate before his eyes.

The expression on his face told nothing, however. His inner joy and ecstasy were prudently disguised by a grave demeanor, serious as a school-boy's, and when next he looked at her there were tears in her eyes! Real human tears! They glistened on her starry lashes. He was appalled and overjoyed at once. It was more than he had dared to hope for—yet he had hoped. It was a miracle! Suddenly he felt as if he had won a great victory. But no, not yet. He dared not press her too hard, or all at once; he must move cautiously to recapture her, his lovely swallowtail. But he would win her back before she ran away to her rich man with all his diamonds.

Just so long it lasted, their dance. Then the violins threaded their way through the closing bars and stopped. Before he knew it she had slipped out of his arms again.

"Wait—!"

"No. We must part now or we may cause a scene. Go. Back to Rose as you promised." She led him across the room and transferred his arm to Rose's. "The next dance must be with your wife." Then she was carried away on a little laugh, without a backward glance. He stared after her until she disappeared, then felt Rose's elbow insistent in his side.

"Well, aren't you going to dance with me?"

"Not now. Later, perhaps."

"Let's eat, then, I'm starved."

"Why don't you join the line, I'll be with you in a moment. I have something to say to Georgie."

Rose was smartly coy. "Secrets, always these little secrets. Well, go on, then, mind you don't forget me. I'm your wife, remember."

He ducked away before she could say more and went to seek out Georgiana, who, catching his eye, excused herself and joined him.

"Here you are. I was hoping for a word," she said, "but it's been impossible. Was it—did you like the wedding?"

"Oh yes, George, it was fine, just fine. I'm glad I was here, I would have hated having to read about it in a letter." Her happiness added to his own desperation. "I talked with Aurora," he said.

"And you danced, didn't you? I'm pleased to see that you and she are—"

"Yes? What? Getting on?"

"Well, it has been some time since you and she have spoken. I'm glad that seeing her again hasn't made you unhappy."

"Christ, George, I'm as wretched a man as anyone could hope to see. Do you *realize* what's she's gone and done? *Do* you?"

"Oh my dear, please don't, I beg you. Don't be unhappy, not on my wedding day."

"But she's mad to do this thing! Don't you think she is? She doesn't love him! She loves me!"

"Has she said so?"

"She admitted it! I knew it! I always know with her. She's done it only to spite me. Yes! To spite and hurt me. It's nonsense, it's crazy. Some Belgian clockwork fellow—"

Georgiana would not permit this sort of self-indulgence. "You know nothing of him. None of us does. It isn't fair to judge. And it's wrong to say she doesn't love him, when—"

"I hate the bastard! And I love her. Oh, Christ, I love her so much. Help me, you must help me—"

"How? How can I help you?"

"Go to her, tell her. You're her friend, make her understand. She mustn't do this thing, it could be irrevocable."

"And your marriage is not? Oh, my dear, I don't want to see you hurt, but you must be sensible. Aurora is a grown woman, I'm sure she knows her own mind."

"But she doesn't! Her feelings are all mixed up. I know it's partly my fault, that day at Sid's forge I wasn't very understanding. Or kind."

"But that's all water over the dam. If you're as wise as I believe you to be—"

"I don't want to be wise! I want to love her. She mustn't escape me again. If she does I swear I'll—I'll—"

"Don't say it, please do *not* say it. That sort of talk helps nothing. Be good to Rose, be kind, dear. She loves you, truly she does. She wants to make you a good wife."

"But I don't want her. After the baby—"

"Hush—"

"No, I'll say it. When Helen wrote that the baby was gone, something broke for me. Maybe it was my heart. I just didn't care. I'd never even have come back except that Grammaw—"

"Yes! Think of your good luck. And count your blessings. When we return from our honeymoon next summer, will you have returned from China?"

"Not if I can help it I won't. I don't care if I never come back," he said, and then he looked at her and broke into a rueful grin. "I'm sorry, George, you're right. I'm spoiling your wedding and that's not fair. You're my good and handsome girl, and I meant everything I said that day uptown. I wish you joy and happiness, all the rest of your life, you and Appleton. I won't forget you."

"Nor I you. You're my—my champion."

"Am I?"

"Oh, yes you are! In so many ways, and for so long." She spoke earnestly and gravely. "I pray—we *both* pray—that you may have a safe voyage and that we shall meet again—here, right here in this house, you and Rose. And perhaps, if things go aright, when you next come home she will have given you another child, a living child."

"No, damn it, I don't want *another* one. I had the harebrained idea that because of Caro—Caro—"

"Yes. I know."

"Do you? Then you must know it's not with Rose that I want a child, but with *her*—oh, God, look at her. Look at her, Georgie!"

Georgiana's eye followed his, across the room to where Aurora had become the centerpiece of a group of old friends, including Maude and Merrill Ashley, Judge Perry and his wife, Asher Ingolls, Talley and Harold Welles. Laughing and smiling, her golden head nodding like a summer flower, Aurora seemed in her element. Georgiana knew that for her sake Rora was doing everything she could to tone down her vivaciousness, almost to stay in the background—something Aurora Talcott had never been adept at. She sympathized with Sinjin's plight, but what was there to say? And if she could have found a comforting word there would have been no time to speak it, for she saw Old Bobby Talcott making his way through the crowd, smiling at her.

"Georgie, I hope Captain Grimes won't mind, but I have come to claim a dance before they're all used up."

He bowed politely and Sinjin watched him escort Georgiana onto the floor. The musicians had been alerted: the song was "Lavina."

Swift go the years, Lavina,
The dim stars slide down the sky,
Come dry my tears, Lavina,
Kiss me before I die.
Gone is the face that cheers me,
Sadly the music must end.
I wait for the shade that wings o'er me,
And the peace only heaven shall send.
Lavina . . . Lavina . . . Lavina . . .

Again the music ended. With a courtly air Old Bobby returned his partner to her husband, his son. At Appleton's side, John Quincy bestowed his approval with a formal kiss on Georgiana's brow and began his round of farewells. It was time for him to leave; he would not be caught by darkness. With his going a concerted movement was initiated toward the front of the house. Sinjin was suddenly left alone in the room. The notes of the sentimental melody rang in his head and his mind was on one thing, one thing alone . . .

Turning, he drew a sharp breath, for he saw her standing in the doorway—watching him! She made a slight movement; he could not interpret it. What was he to do? What did she expect of him? It was but a moment out of the thousands they'd spent together, but something told him no more meaningful or important moment of communication had ever been between them, not even in their lovemaking. He, his future, everything hung in the balance; his fate lay in her hands.

"Did Posie—" he began as they met in the center of the room. Again she did that little trick of cocking her head, pert, yet with veiled intention. Why was he unable to read her today?

"Posie is a darling," she said, "very wise for her age, that young lady."

"But did she—"

"Hush, not here, someone may be listening."

"Where, then? *When?* Say!" He moved closer, wanting to sweep her into his arms again, dance her away forever. "It's not—it won't—" Why did he stumble over his words like a dolt, an oaf! Yet it seemed not to matter to her; her look was understanding, appreciative, even.

"You mean there are things still to be said, is that it?" she asked.

"Yes. *Yes!* We must meet. Quickly, before—"

"Before the world ends, do you mean?"

"I meant, before you go away. Before—"

"Yes. I knew that was what you meant. You've been trying to say it all along. I wondered why you had not. Had you thought *where* we might meet?"

"You mean—"

"I mean *nothing,*" she said mysteriously, "I merely asked."

"Will you? *Will you?*"

"Whoever knows about these things?" she said, lightly tapping his sleeve with her fan.

What was she saying? Was she trying to tell him something without committing herself?

"You—*you* must know," he said, passionate and eager as any schoolboy.

"Must I? Does anyone? Perhaps—"

"Yes? Perhaps . . .?"

"We must see. Another time. Be patient."

We must see! Another time! Be patient!

Those veiled words held all the hope in the world. The door had opened, not wide, only a crack, but it *had* opened. Oh God, let him pass, let him come to her . . .

Then they were calling her. Georgiana was coming down. Everyone trooped eagerly into the hallway, and there she was, dressed for traveling, leaning over the railing and waving to her friend Aurora. And was her friend to be the next lucky bride? No, it must not be! Sinjin's blood ran cold at the thought. Then, as he stood at the foot of the stairs, he closed his eyes and told himself a thing. He told himself that if, when he opened his eyes again, she was standing somewhere within his range of vision, all would be well. If he was able to look upon her in that moment, she would be his, unequivocally and everlastingly. And he swore that if—no, when— *when* she became his, he would believe in her God. He would no longer deny Him, but would render honorable and fervent service in His name.

"Give her to me, let her be mine again and I will be faithful to You," he muttered, careless of who might be looking or listening. "God, until the death, I will believe in You. This I do here swear and promise. If I fail, kill me dead, let me die and send me to hell for all eternity."

Upon opening his eyes his gaze fell straight upon her. She was there, unmistakably. He took it as his sign, and whispered thanksgiving.

As he stared, hard and full of fervency, she gave evidence of awareness, for she turned her head toward him, so their looks met again, and in that moment he comprehended beyond a doubt what was to come. He knew her, read her like the words on a page, and he congratulated himself for his good fortune. She was good and kind. She was forgiving of everything, even of himself. Blessed creature.

Her lips bowed prettily in a smile that was both intimate and knowing, as if in turn she could read him, knew everything he was thinking, knew the pledge he had made to her God. Then she turned altogether away, to be swallowed up amid the gathering.

There ensued a delirious whirl of romantically inclined friends craning to view Georgiana and Appleton as they were escorted out to the yellow coach waiting in the drive. One more kiss thrown, then the coach door was shut and away they went, while the cold air blew into the hall to ruffle the fringes of the Turkey carpets.

47

"Her Just Deserts"

SINJIN SAT STARING into the fire that thanks to Mat Kindu he had come home to. In the lamplight sleet sizzled with a chemical blueness against the glass and the panes sang, rattling in percussive monotony. At the "wet end" of March Street, where his house was, a man might as well be on the moon, so remote did it seem from the village center. The small room had often reminded him of a prison cell; tonight it was more Bastille-like than ever. He chafed at its drabness. Rose's pathetic efforts to add dabs of Christmas cheer made him ill to look on them. After the grand splendor of Kingdom Come, with all its brilliance and color, to come back to this shabby room was more than he could bear. Though he had fled it within the hour, in his mind he was still inside that other house, with its large, bright rooms filled with animated people wearing happy smiles, with banks of flowers and candles and choice wines, good food, and delightful music.

The notes of "Lavina" still filtered through his head, while the lyrics echoed ironically about the corners of his mind. But he *had* danced with her, that much was true. Thanks to Posie he had held her in his arms and claimed his waltz. He showered that dear girl with blessings, even as mentally he showered Aurora with a thousand kisses. Then he was overcome with desperation as it came home to him that in leaving the party so abruptly he had renounced her forever. This had been their last waltz, the final words had been said between them, and no farewell had been taken of her. He had relinquished her to a shadow, a phantom, that awful faceless name that had laid claim to her.

Married in the spring! To a clockwork man in Brussels!

Though he sat still, his heart raged inside him. Alone; he was alone now, and when Rose came home he would be just as solitary, only more so. He was prepared for an unpleasant scene. She was bound to berate him for having abandoned her, but he couldn't think about that now. Someone would take pity on her and see that she got back safely. Meanwhile, he considered his present lot. Was this what he had come to in his thirty-five years, this dreary little room in this dreary little house, with a nagging, intractable wife he couldn't bear to look at?

He opened his eyes at a sound. Mat Kindu had slipped into the room with a tray, a steaming bowl of soup, crackers on the side; it would make a satisfactory light repast. If Rose was hungry she could look after herself; but how could any woman have an appetite after the amounts of food she'd consumed at the reception? She was already popping out of her dresses. He insisted that Mat take a chair while he spooned up the broth, so spicy it made his tongue curl. The Malay's nut-black eyes glinted as he observed Sinjin's satisfaction with his efforts, and, leaning back in the chair, he listened to his master talk. They had sailed the world round in just such fashion; there was something to be said for a man, Sinjin thought, even a bloodthirsty marauder, who would harken endlessly to him ramble on without uttering one syllable of criticism or comment.

As he talked on, Sinjin could hear the drone of his own complaining words, the litany of woes and injustice. It was nothing new. Over the years Mat had followed the myriad convolutions of the captain's sometime relation with the Talcott woman, had been privy to its remarkable vicissitudes, ever since that first afternoon when she came aboard the *Adele* at Town Wharf. It was captious saga, but one filled with tragedy, too, and not even a Stoic could have shown less emotion while feeling more than that skinny yellow-skinned heathen, Mat Kindu.

When the bowl was empty, one or two crackers broken and nibbled, he carried the tray to the kitchen; the floorboards squeaked as he moved about, otherwise making scarcely any sound. Sinjin continued to stare moodily into the flickering tongues of flame, listening to the moan of the wind gusting about the eaves and chimney, whining down the stove throat and blowing ashes across the hearth. He used the tongs to toss back stray coals, then sank deeper into his mood of reflection. In South China there would be flowers now, and the first rice crop would be planted. He could picture the verdant, manicured terraces, the peasants under hats of pointed straw, working knee-deep in paddy water, the smell of blossoms on the vernal breeze. He hated these icebound New England winters that chilled the very marrow of a man, the heavy snowstorms that made traveling difficult. By the yellow god, he would be glad to be away from here, damn it, he would!

He sat up suddenly, alert. From the street came the throaty sound of singing, a husky contralto. "Lavina" again. The notes continued, and added to them was the sound of horses' hooves. Sinjin got up and leaned on the windowsill. A cutter was in the drive. Hermie held the reins, while a struggling Ambo Buck tried to hand an obstreperous Rose down from the seat. She evaded his grasp, wobbling about and scrabbling at the air with her fists.

"Get away from me, you dirty redskin, don't you touch me!" she cried, with no thought to the place or the hour.

"Come down and stop your caterwauling before you wake the neighborhood," Sinjin heard Ambo growl. Good for him. Old Man Johnson across the road was always complaining about the noise.

Hermie had checked his reins and got down to help the tipsy Rose. Between him and Ambo they wrestled her to the ground where she staggered and fell against Hermie's chest, knocking him off balance. His wooden peg skidded, his foot went up, and they landed together in the snow. Rose cried out, then lay back in a snow bank and cackled uproariously.

Sinjin threw open the door and strode out in his shirtsleeves to lend assistance. Ambo was helping Hermie up; Sinjin hauled Rose to her feet. What a disgrace. Her hair was mussed, her bonnet had slipped askew, half of her was covered with snow and ice.

"Go on, get inside," he barked, motioning to Ambo to take her in the house.

"I said get your damn hands off me, you redskin bastard!" She was beating her fists at him and stumbling up the walk.

"You all right?" Sinjin was concerned for Hermie who was rubbing his back.

"That I am, skipper," came the easy reply. He glanced at Rose, picking her way toward the door. Mat, on the threshold, stood aside to admit her.

"Too much of the spiritives," Hermie commented to Sinjin, trying to rid his voice of a disapproving note.

"Come on in and get warm."

"No thanks, skipper, Ma'll be waiting up."

Ma; always Ma. Sinjin waited while Hermie planted his peg on the runner and swung onto the cutter's seat, then hurried inside and slammed the door.

Rose was all in a heap by the fire, her hair hanging down as she clutched a glass in one hand. An open whiskey bottle sat eloquently on the table. Both Mat and Ambo had tactfully withdrawn from the scene, leaving them alone.

"Well, well, here he is," Rose started in, "my lord and master. Where the hell'd you go to, anyway? I looked around and you'd left. Without a single word. Honest. What way's that for a man to treat his wife? Leaving her to be looked after by others?"

Sinjin had the grace to be embarrassed. "I'm sorry. I got an urge to leave," he said. "I was sure you'd get home on your own hook."

"Oh, you were, were you? Last time I saw you you were tripping the light fantastic with my fair lady. Before that you had managed to disappear, the two of you. You were gone the longest time. And what did folks suppose you were doing all that time with her?"

"We were merely talking, that's all. It's been some time since we've seen each other."

Rose took a snort of whiskey and choked it down. "I expect it'll be a longer time pretty quick," she rasped.

"Why do you say that?"

"She's gettin' married, isn't she? Going to live in Europe, too. You don't get over that way much, so I expect you won't be seeing her."

Sinjin started across the room. "Rose, I'm really tired. I'm going to bed."

She moved quickly after him. "You don't even see what you did, do you?"

"No, but I bet you'll tell me."

"I saw you, your eyes sliding all over her like they was fingers to grope her with. Everyone saw. They were all watching the show you two put on. Laughs, too, plenty of laughs. You were licking her up like cream."

"Aren't you exaggerating the littlest bit? Maybe you'd better put that bottle back and come to bed."

"I'll come to bed when I'm good and ready, not before. Where's the point, anyway? I might as well be sleeping alone for all the attention you paid me since you come back." The whites of her eyes had turned a yellowish-red, her face was the very image of rage. He stared at her, repelled by what he saw.

"You hate me, don't you," she said thickly. "You really do, don't you. Answer me! Say it, go on. I disgust you."

"Rose, for Christ's sake, please don't. I've got a headache."

"Well, I have one too, so what do you think of that?"

"I'm sorry. Take some Glauber's salts, that should help."

"I d–don't want any s–salts." She had begun to weep into her handkerchief. "I hate her and I hate you, I hate you both!" She hissed; her small triangular head stuck out on her slender neck like a snake's.

But tonight he was resolved not to be drawn into another of their interminable quarrels. He wanted to be let alone, to think over the things that troubled him. He stared at his sorry companion a while longer, but this time seeing not her dark eyes and hair, the dusky tints of her flesh, her thin face, not these, but golden curls, bright blue eyes, red laughing lips, the skin of a milkmaid. His ears heard not mean grumbling but a merry laugh, a bubbling stream flowing over pebbles into a clear crystal pool whose waters tasted like the waters of the moon. The sight, dream that it was, lifted his spirits.

"We shall see . . ." she had said.

The memory of those words made him happier than he had been since that evening when he'd left Kingdom Come fourteen months ago, his hopes of marrying Aurora all dashed.

"I'm going to bed," he asserted dully.

"No you're not. You're going to stay right here and pay some attention to *me!*" she returned in a pet. "I'm your wife, aren't I?"

"Yes you are, Rose, you surely are, my legally wedded spouse. My paragon, my helpmeet, my virtuous mattress-mate."

She tossed her head at him. "Say, you making fun of me again?"

His patient smile infuriated her. "No, my dear, I leave that for all the others to do."

Ignoring this, she went on. "You know what she's doing, don't you?"

Sinjin whistled lightly. "No, but I feel reasonably sure you'll tell me."

"She's just playing games. She's just turnin' you around her finger. She don't care, not really."

"Why are you so sure?"

"I'm a woman, ain't—*aren't*—I? I can always tell." She drank from her glass, spilling some. "You don't love her, anyways."

"Hm. Can you tell that, too? Cinnamon Comorra lives in Rose Mills."

"*Grimes,* damn it, my name's *Grimes!* And I don't have to be no witch to see which way you're heading."

"Do tell. And that way is—?"

"That way's straight down to hell. I'm telling you, you don't love her. You love *me!* At least y'ought to, being's how I'm your wife."

"I could hardly forget, Rose, since you are at such frequent pains to remind me of the fact."

"Listen, you don't have to look so ashamed about it. Lots of men wanted to marry with me. Wanted to keep me in a nice house, buy me fancy things, have a fam'ly."

"Try to recall, Rose, there was a reason why you became my wife. A reason that unfortunately no longer holds true, which doesn't leave us with much of a marriage. In fact it doesn't leave us with much of anything."

"I don't want to hear about that again. It's her that makes all the trouble. She went away but she couldn't stay away. Now she's come back and bewitched you again! Don't think I don't know what's going on. You plan to go sailing off to China again, you got those women over there and—and don't give me that innocent look of yours. Everybody knows you got all kinds of women over there. Con—con—*damn!*"

" 'Concubines,' I expect you mean. No, Rose, you have been listening to idle gossip again. It's what happens when you give ear to the ladies' wicked tongues. The life I lead in China is really very circumspect. Very— dull . . . You wouldn't like China much, anyway. And I'm afraid that they—"

"—wouldn't like me!"

"I didn't say that."

"It's what you meant, though."

"I was going to say they wouldn't understand you."

"What is there to understand? I'm Rose Grimes, that's all. Captain Grimes's wife. China would be—well, different, like."

"It would be that, all right. *Too* different. You'd never adapt to their ways. They're a strange people, the Chinese. I've been going there for twenty years and *I* don't understand them most of the time. It wouldn't be at all the way you imagine it to be."

"Well." She muttered into her glass, then tossed back the dregs. "You'd take *her* quick enough—if she'd go."

He felt a sharp pain. How had she read his thoughts so clearly?

"Not much chance of that. As you say, she's leaving. She's going to marry again."

"And good riddance, I say!" She stared at him over the rim of her glass. "You men are all alike. You take a wife and in two minutes you're bored and looking to screw something else."

"I don't like to hear you talk that way."

"Oh, you're such a gentleman, aren't you! You don't fool me, you're always looking for something to screw, you've always got a bone in your drawers. But you never give me any of it. Oh no, Rose comes at the end of the line! *Now* you want to screw *her!* And then you'll go sailing off. *And you're leaving me here alone!* I won't stand for it!"

"Of course I'm leaving, but I'll come back."

"Sure, and I'll be an old hag when you do. If you cared anything about me you'd take me with you. Like you did the first time, on the *Sparrow.*"

"Rose—"

"Oh yes, I know, '*Ro-o-o-ose.*'" She mimicked him spitefully. "You don't have to explain. You can't afford to take me along. You don't want me to see those slant-eyed bitches you've got hidden away over there. *No!* that's not it. You don't want *them* to see *me.* You don't want folks out there knowin' you're married to a nigger."

"Damn it, Rose, that's not fair! I never said—"

"Yeah, but you think it all the same. You want to keep me hidden away right here in this house. What do you care that I'm alone. I never go anywhere, never have any fun. I hate it! I *hate it!*"

She began to sob desperately. Her little balled fists beat at the air, and her eyes bulged with rage. Hands hanging between his knees, he sat back, unable to stop the flow of words that came burbling from her lips. "It was disgusting, the way you was lookin' at her, makin' up to her! Holdin' her like that when you danced. You never asked *me* to dance!"

He shrugged helplessly. "We danced only for a little."

"Oh sure, a little. You're not foolin' me." She pointed to the ceiling. "When I go up there to bed you'll sneak out and meet the pretty Miss Aurora, then you'll dance a *lot!* All over the bed. I never saw anyone I hate as much as her! Hate her—hate her—" Her words were lost in a kind of witchy incantation as she muttered her rage.

"Don't, Rose, you've got to stop this."

"I don't got to stop anything! I'll kill her, Rora Talcott, I swear to God I will!"

He had run to the end of his rope. "Rose, that's enough now," he said sternly, but she rattled on.

"I know what you're thinking. You hate being here with me. You'd like to be over there with her. You want to be married to her, living in that big house 'stead of here! You'd give anything if you wasn't hitched to me, wouldn't you? Come on, tell the truth, you'd like to see me dead so you can marry her!"

"Rose, I swear to Christ, if you speak her name again I'll—"

Rose jutted her pointed chin and her eyes blazed. "Oh, I'm not to speak Her Majesty's name, is that it? You is just one big blackhearted sucker, Sinjin Grimes."

He sighed, his shoulders drooped. "Yes, you're right, I am that. A sucker." His laugh did not hide the deep tide of fury rising inside him. In a minute he would paste her. "But understand one thing, Rose. That person to whom you refer so slightingly cast her spell on me long ere this day." He grabbed hold of her arm, pulling her to him, and his voice sank to a hollow whisper. "Bewitched me, she did, and it's not you who'll be the death of me, but her. She's my life, her heart beats here inside me." He pressed her hand to his chest. "Ten thousand miles away and I still think of her. No word of her for months at a time and still I think of her. Shall I tell you something else, Rose?"

"Go ahead, no one's stopping you."

"We were married in that moment."

"Married!" She spat the word back at him. "That's crazy. You never had no preacher. You ain't got no paper to make it legal."

"We don't need a paper, it's all recorded here, in our hearts." He let her go and turned away again, and again she was after him. As he reached the stairs she pivoted around the newel post, stumbled, and fell against the wall. She sprawled, gaping up at him with a dazed look. "By God, you're a mess," he muttered, yanking her to her feet. "Look at you. Drunk as a fiddler's bitch. I can't stand a woman who can't hold her liquor—watch out, you'll fall again."

He tried to guide her up the stairs but she pulled free, stumbling again. It was just here that she'd fallen that night when—

"Were you drunk then?" he demanded, picturing the incident as he suddenly imagined it to have occurred. "Is that why it happened?"

"What?"

"I said, were you—drunk then? That night you slipped and fell, when you lost the baby?"

"No! Wasn't drunk!" She shrank back.

He seized her arm. "By God, I do believe you were drunk. You couldn't even safeguard your baby, you sodden—"

"Go on, hit me! You'd like to, wouldn't you—"

"You killed our baby! Damn it!"

"No!"

"You did! You were drunk, you fell down—you lost it."

"You're a damn liar! I wasn't drunk, I didn't fall!" Her scornful laugh rang out, striking him full in the face. "Fer Chrissakes, there wasn't no baby to begin with!"

Her words stopped him dead in his tracks. "What?" he said. "What's that you say?"

She snarled. "You heard me. There wasn't ever any baby." She flung the words and they hung in the air between them. His brow was furrowed in an attempt to take in her meaning.

"Say that again," he said softly. The levelness of his voice bore a threat that alarmed her, but she faced him defiantly.

"You heard what I said all right."

"Repeat it, please."

"*I said there wasn't any baby!*"

"Are you telling me you lied? Why? To get me to marry you?"

"So what if I did?"

He shook his head. "I don't believe you. You're lying, you're just trying to sink your teeth in me."

"If you don't believe me, go ask Annie Skaats. See what she says! Go on, I dare you." She gave him a fleering look, than backed away.

That's right, he thought, Annie—Georgie had said the girl had been with Rose that night of the accident. He left the stairs and went back into the front room. She lurched after him.

"Well, say something!" she demanded. "Damn it, talk to me!"

"Wasn't . . . a baby . . .?" he repeated blankly. "But you told me—"

"I don't care what I told you, I just made it up, that's all. I was funnin' you. Wanted to see what you'd do. See how far I could lead you out. See if I could get you to propose. And you *did!*"

He glared at her. "By God, I'll kill you—!"

With a scream of terror she ran from him, he charged after her, flinging furniture aside helter-skelter until he reached her. He seized her by her hair and savagely yanked her to him.

"Help! Murder—!" she cried, struggling to free herself. She caught him a good knock in the shins but though he howled he held her fast. She screamed louder and he shoved her away. She fell back against the bookcase, which struck the wall with a bang. Books tumbled out and fell in piles on the floor. She scrambled sideways into a chair in the corner, covering her face and sobbing in fright.

Sinjin was panting and staring down at the fire, a faint frown on his brow, one corner of his lips moving spasmodically. The hawklike profile was thrown into deep relief, the crooked nose caught a fiery tracing along its chiseled length. His shoulders lifted and his head sank between them. He ran his fingers through his hair and spoke softly and evenly.

"I hope you're satisfied, Rose. Between you and Pina Talcott you've about done away with me, you two. You and your damnable tricks and lies."

"You oughtn't to blame me," Rose protested. "I did it because I loved you! I loved you so hard. I like to died of love for you. But that's something *you* can't *ever* understand! 'Cause there's no love in you. You don't know what love is!" She wept passionately. "An' I'd do it again if it meant the difference between keeping or losing you. I'd lie or cheat or steal—or kill if it meant the difference."

"You've killed me for fair, my girl," he said. "When I look at you what I see disgusts me. You say I don't know what love is, but that's wrong and you know it. You know sure as gun's iron that I love every bit as deep and strong as you. The difference is, *you* can't have what you love."

"Neither can you!"

"Oh, yes I can!" He turned to face her. "Or by the yellow god I can try. And I'm going to. Make no mistake about that." He spoke with deadly earnestness. There was a glint in his eyes, a trace of irony curled up in the corners of those lips she adored.

"What do you mean?" she cried frantically. "You're married to *me!*"

"That will make no difference in the end. One of these days you'll see that, Rose, all your rotten tricks won't mean a tinker's dam. And why?"

"Why? Go on, tell me!"

"Because my being married to you has nothing to do with it. No one cares about you, not any of my kin, not my grandmother, or Georgiana or Helen or anyone else who has ever tried to help you. No one cares a whit about you, Rose, that's the truth of it, least of all me, your husband. You pay back people's kindness with wickedness and spite. You're an ingrate. Now you're going to get your just deserts. If you're smart you'll just move along. You're all finished around here. But don't worry, Rosie my pet, after a while you'll forget. You'll forget you ever married me, just as I'll forget I ever married you."

"No! I won't forget! I won't ever forget!"

"You had better." His words were like a death sentence; she could catch an ague from their iciness.

He threw her another look, then moved to the peg and took down his hat and cloak.

"Where are you going?" she demanded, struggling to get up.

"Why should that concern you?"

"No!" With difficulty she wrestled herself out of the chair and stood, feet planted apart, staring at him. "If you go, what'm I to do?"

"What do I care? You haven't an ounce of decency in you, no shred of goodness."

"You're going with her! You're running off with her! Like you did before. You're leaving me for her!"

"If I am, it's not an even trade, believe me, Rose." He called for Mat. When the Malay appeared he told him to pack their gear and meet him at the taproom.

He shrugged on his cloak, set his hat, then moved toward the door, but not without a final protest from Rose.

"You'll pay!" The words were ripped from her throat and her face was the mask of fury. "You'll pay good for gettin' rid of me, I promise! It's gonna cost you and cost you. She'll be the most expensive thing you own. You haven't got enough money for what I'll be wantin'! Go ahead, go 'way to Grammaw and tell her she'd better be hotfootin' it to the vault and take out some of that gold she's got hid away, the old miser! She'll part with every penny before I'm done."

"Good-bye, Rose. I wish you the joy of this humble abode, but you won't see me under its roof again."

"Oh, go then and be done, I won't be sorry!" She rushed at him, panting, her eyes like coals. "But you'd best beware or *you'll* end up sorry. I'm warnin' you. She'll fix you. She will. She'll do you bad. You'll regret the day!"

"And if I do it won't be half of how much I regret you." He opened the door to a blast of wind that rushed through the room, sending papers flying. Pages of a fallen volume fluttered in the gust as he went out.

The door shut between them. She flung herself at it and yanked it open again, rushed out onto the stoop and began screaming imprecations at him. Her words were lost in the wind and he paid no attention as he hunched his shoulders and disappeared into the darkness of March Street.

48

The Cry of Love

WITH SIGNS OF another snowfall in the air, the afternoon lay still and quiet, and at Burning Bush Farm little was doing of a domestic nature. Shutters in a few upper story windows were closed; smoke issued from two chimneys, east and west. The gloomy old house beside the great tree atop the hill was battened down for the three remaining months of winter. Nuthatches and scarlet-capped vireos, like sober little prelates perking about on thin legs, all but impervious to northern climes, doggedly pecked up the scattering of breadcrumbs put out each morning by Rachel Grimes for the well-being of her feathered friends.

For an hour past, that same lady had been seated in her customary place beside the front parlor window, keeping a weather eye out for signs of traffic from town. There had been blessed little activity of any kind, vehicular or pedestrian, and not even a glimpse of any of the Two Stone sledders who could usually be counted on to reap the greatest profit from a good hill in snowtime. Down at Grimes Mill the pond had been partially cleared for skaters, but even that merry crowd was nowhere in evidence this afternoon. The world might have slipped entirely away, for all that Rachel could tell.

She was sure it was making to snow; she recognized the signs. The light had gone silvery, soft and limpid, with a peach-tinted cast, and the shadows lay about in a deep ultramarine tinged with violet. The least bit of wind stirred the branches of the trees, and she'd already noted one or two flurries, promising more to come.

Rachel was keeping this windowside vigil because she knew that sooner or later someone would be arriving at her door: her grandson, who had consented to a visit to the farm because his detested stepfather would be absent just at that time. Rachel awaited his coming for what might be a final meeting—final in this world, at any rate. What God had in mind thereafter remained to be discovered. In the meantime, farewell and good-bye. Each parting she took from him sorrowed her more than the last, for provoked as she could get at him, irksome as only he could be, she loved him, yes she did! He was precious goods to her, and as the hour approached for him to go voyaging again her heart always softened toward him. And if, when he returned this time she should be in her grave, she had seen to it in her last will and testament, on file with Jack Talcott, that he would have sufficient resources of his own to make his own luck and owe no more to Grimes & Co.

The clock struck the half hour. Joseph appeared and added to the fire, for the room had begun to grow chilly. It was pleasant, thought Rachel, being in the house this way, without the prospect of having to endure another evening in the company of her stepson. Truth to tell, it had been an acute relief for her to have Abednego gone to his reward (if such reward there should be for the likes of him, that flinty, hardfisted, covetous misanthrope), and the conclusion of her own natural span could bring no greater boon than never having to look upon the face of his son Zion again, never to hear that cold implacable voice. The man had been a thorn in her side for too long.

She sighed and stirred in her chair while the wind rattled the shutter. Its insistent creak and bang made her impatient for the time to pass, and she thought again of Sinjin. She had been profoundly saddened—and savagely angry—to learn how that vile creature he'd wed had made such wicked sport of him, had deceived him into marrying her! *Faugh!* Why, it was the oldest deception in the world, an Eve's trick. And then to have blurted it out that way. Strong drink loosened many a tongue, and Rose wasn't as smart as she thought, the black vixen. No—not black, not so's you'd notice, but with a black heart all the same. And now, what was to be done? What indeed? Learning of the situation, Rachel had gone to Helen and discussed the matter with her and Luke, but they had come up empty-handed as to a solution. The best Sinjin could do was get quickly aboard his new ship and sail for China. Forget, just forget. It was, she thought, astonishing, the terrible jolts the human heart could suffer, yet how with a measure of forbearance the spirit could prevail. She knew it; this was something that old women knew, like the cross-stitch and a good recipe for soda biscuits.

Had the clock struck again? Goodness, the little hand was fast on four. Rachel had a care to the out-of-doors. As she had sat lost in thought the sky had further grayed and snow was beginning to fall in earnest. Soon the snow roller would be trundling along Greenshadow. Her present vigilance was rewarded by the sight of a bit of traffic, one vehicle only. A single cutter was coming up the hill from the village. She wiped the mist from the window pane. Sinjin at last, she thought, though the driver was not wearing Sinjin's Russian karakul hat, but merely an old cap. Across his knees lay a buffalo robe, with more robes piled on the seat beside him. By the time the cutter reached the drive she was certain it was he, and prepared to welcome him, when, with a nonchalant wave over his shoulder, he passed her by! Mercy! Rachel pursed her lips and produced a sound of affront. What now? And she'd waited nearly the whole day for him. How odd.

She took up Abednego's telescope and trained it on his back as he negotiated the hill down toward Two Stone. At the bottom he pulled onto the branch road, his runners slicing through a four-inch fall of snow, where could be seen the crisscrossing tracks of hunters coming and going across the mill property, into and out of the woods. He guided his sleigh across the mill bridge over the frozen race, and reined up. He hopped down, and made his way to the pond, where he took a run on the ice. The run became a slide and he skidded along like a schoolboy, right up to the mill doorway. For a moment Rachel thought he might go in; he didn't, though, but turned and skidded back the other way. He had a third slide, then he stopped. She saw him hurry over to his horse and cutter, spring aboard, and drive around the corner of the mill house, as if anxious not to be seen. With the cutter hidden among the birches, he led his horse out of the shafts and hobbled it. He tossed a plaid blanket over the animal's back and dragged the armload of heavy fur robes from the cutter and entered the mill house by the side door.

Shortly thereafter, a thin spire of smoke began rising from the chimney, making its way in a steady line into the snowy, windless sky.

"Now what's he up to?" Miss Rachel asked herself as she accepted the cup of tea Joseph had brought her on her favorite tole painted tray. The smoke had disappeared; the fire must be going well. What mischief was he up to? She knew he was prone to all sorts of sly antics and arrant nonsense, but this was a new wrinkle. She would keep the glass handy to see what transpired. The tea was hot and sweet the way she liked it. She felt her lids droop and she caught herself twice as her chin touched her chest and sat upright again, eagle in her aerie.

It was not too long before her sometime vigilance was rewarded by the sight of a small sleigh coming along the road from New France. Its driver was a female, holding in gloved hands the reins to a dappled cob whose nostrils smoked with steamy plumes, its hoof falls muffled by the hard-packed snow. In its turn the little sleigh also gained the Mill Road where it too made its way among the trees, to pull up to the mill house door.

"*Aah!*" Rachel cackled, it was a rendezvous then; she observed with sharpened interest as the woman got down from the sleigh and, skirts flapping, moved to the doorway. Well, thought the old lady, who had good reason to know, these wouldn't be the first ones to tryst at the mill. Indeed, the place had its corner in her own heart; in summer . . . in good green summertime before the flax harvest . . .

She fell to musing until her grandson appeared in the doorway and, stepping out, claimed the horse's bridle and coaxed the sleigh around the corner, putting it out of sight along with the cutter. In seconds he and his lady love had disappeared inside the keeping room and the door was closed.

Telling herself that she was unlikely to see anything more of interest, at least for a while, Rachel set aside her telescope and stirred her tea as she stared down at the bleak landscape, wintery and Dutch, and the frozen pond. In the golden frame of her mind the picture was verdant, the trees were full-leafed, the flax was yellow; the water spilled over the dam while in the bright sky-reflecting pond a handsome youth swam, his pale form sparkling in the water . . .

She fell into a reverie for how long she could not tell. She dreamed a bit too, of love, foolish as that notion was. When she touched the rim of her cup to her lips again it was cold. She emptied the contents into a nearby potted plant, then poured hot aromatic tea from the pot. Yes, that was some better. She settled back in her chair and waited to see what Dame Fortune might next present to view.

. . .

IN THE keeping room of the mill Sinjin Grimes passionately gathered Aurora in his arms and cocooned with her in a glistening fur robe. Holding her tight against his chest, he raised her to the sill so she could look out at the silvery world, enchanting, he thought, in the soft gray light. The warm flesh of her cheek lay tenderly against his, her eager little heart beat warmly and rhythmically against his naked flesh. Yes, it was lovely, she said. Her bare legs sticking out from the robe were cold. He allowed her one last look, for it was a sight neither was likely to look upon again, surely not this way, not together, and he returned her to the coziness of the fireside.

In a drowsy, rapturous state they clung together under the warm furs. "Good," she murmured. He pressed her closer. Oh God, yes—yes, it *had* been good. They had been afloat on the waters of remembered passion; with what ease they had negotiated its eddying currents and recaptured the same elusive white-feathered bird whose strong wings had carried them aloft on that sweet summer's night. Such ecstasy was not easily felt, yet for them it had been. They said they were blessed. They were properly thankful.

She breathed in even rhythm with him, a little sigh of pleasure escaped her lips, and he cuddled her more closely, his rosy porcelain princess. And when her rising sighs again became the cry of love he performed for her, creative in his amorousness, the way he liked to do. Later, they lay wrapped in each other, limbs plaited together; his cheek, stubbled now, rubbed against her breast, so warm and soft, the naked breast that fed him, the hungry child, and without seeing each other's faces they began softly to talk and plan. How delicious, how wonderful. They had come together once more as though in the throes of first love, and they were resolved not to surrender their happiness again to laws of man or God. So he said, and she eagerly seconded his sentiments, vowing that it must be so. There had been nothing sweet in the bitter sorrow of their many partings, and each cruel good-bye must now be made up for. They were resolved: Now one, they would never be parted again.

Meanwhile, there was much to be seen to. She must quickly return to Kingdom Come for her family farewells. Old Bobby had offered her the use of his coach to New York, where she was expected to join Appleton and Georgiana at their hotel, and with them meet Aurora's fiancé. Instead of this plan, however, Sinjin would be with her. He would go up to Burning Bush and have supper with his grandmother; Rachel would be informed of their plan, and some way out of his desperate entanglement with Rose would be found. Then, together, they would coach to New York to board the *Hattie D.* and hoist anchor for the East. China waited, as it had been waiting over the years.

At last they were going to undertake the adventure he had promised her so long ago, and as he had done before, he called up the Flowery Kingdom for her again, the strange mystery of it, the palaces and pleasures and delights to be found there. He described the villa where they would live at Macao, with its flock of white doves and moon-drenched garden. He would take and show her, his fair prize, to the emperor himself at Peking. Chinese women would stare and wonder at her beauty, the men would have to avert their eyes for fear of being blinded.

His words inspired her, as they had on that first day in the master cabin of the *Adele*, and she clung tightly to him, as if, even now, she could not believe it would really be so. Would he make it happen? she asked plaintively. Would he? He promised and promised again. He vowed it on his life's blood. This time all would turn out well, nothing could go wrong. Her heart was beating fast in her breast, and her eyes shone with the excitement he had kindled in her. Would she go? Ah, would she not? To the ends of the earth would she travel if he would but take her.

And so, with their troth thus plighted, their plans laid, and darkness fast upon them, they left the mill, she to Kingdom Come to say good-bye to her family, he to Burning Bush to take farewell of his, with no further word or thought of her luckless fiancé at New York, awaiting the arrival of his promised bride.

49

The Snows of Yesteryear

THE SNOW WAS FALLING thick and fast as Sinjin drove his cutter in at the farm. Tossing the reins aside, he bawled for the hired man to look after his horse, then trudged toward the house, grateful for the signs of warmth emanating from inside. He came into the front hallway beating his palms together and stamping his feet on the carpet runner, then tugged off his fur-lined gloves with his teeth and remarked to Mary, hovering in the hallway, that a brandy would well suit his current needs.

Crossing the parlor threshold he found Rachel seated by the fire. The game table was set up near the hearth, the window shade was drawn to the sill, she had some mending in her lap. Setting her work aside, she put her cheek up for a kiss and directed him into the other chair. His cheeks were red and healthy looking and he had a decided gleam in his eyes, a flushed, lively look that betokened the significant uses to which the livery stable's fur robes had been put.

"Hullo, Grammaw," he said, a model of filial geniality. "How are you? How nice you look. Is that a new brooch?"

"*This?* You've seen it a thousand times, it's a *cammy*-oh."

"So it is. Where'd you get it?"

She bridled a little and rubbed her thumb across the intaglio face. "It was a present."

"From an admirer?"

"Oh, hear the boy! Ardent—he wants everything ardent. Now you just sit right there and tell your old granny how you've been faring."

He took the indicated chair and began to talk, telling her things he thought might amuse her, his eye flicking nervously about the room. He always felt wary here, never at home, though his mother had died right up there, in the room directly above, and by this very window his grandmother had read to him as a child.

Rachel clicked her teeth. "Now tell me, what on earth were you doing down there on that millpond?"

Sinjin's eye flicked to Rachel's spyglass. "So I was, Grammaw, so I was. Trying to figure out a way to keep ice from melting on a months-long sea voyage. If I could do that, then I could ship it clear to China and make another fortune."

"So you could, Sonny," she said. "But it looked more to me that you were sliding about on the ice like a truant. And I think I know why, too."

"Do you?" He eyed the spy glass again.

"Yes," she said with a touch of tartness. "You were anticipating the arrival of your doxy."

"Grammaw, that was Aurora Sheffield and she's no doxy."

"Don't try to tell me what she is, Sonny. I *know,* so there. I guess you and she were engaged in philosophical discussion, eh? Leaving your poor old granny to pine for you up here on the hill."

He jumped up and gave her a big smack on the cheek. "There's a kiss for Grammaw, so she won't have to pine away anymore."

"That's what you were doing, giving her kisses; come, confess it. Why, there's no harm in it, it's perfectly natural. Though it strikes me as peculiar conduct for a woman who claims to be about to embark on the perilous seas of matrimony once again."

"Not necessarily . . ."

"How's that? What d'you mean, 'Not necess—' Yes, and what's that sly look about?"

Sinjin drew his chair closer. "Grammaw, we're going away together tonight," he began.

"What's that? Who's going away?"

"Aurora and I." He spoke lightly and rapidly as he described their plan. They would go to New York and obtain the blessings of Appleton and Georgiana. Rora would sail with him on the *Hattie D.* "Just as we intended when we were young," he said. "What do you think of that?"

Rachel stared at him in disbelief. "Apple Talcott will flay the living hide from your bones, is what I think."

"No he won't. He'll like having me for a son-in-law. I'll be a darn sight better than that Lloyd Warburton, poor droop."

"That 'poor droop,' as you call him, has done well enough for himself. And if you think Apple Talcott'll approve his daughter being a party to bigamy, think again."

"Bigamy?"

"That was my word, sir. Unless I miss my guess, this little plan of yours is not going to sit very well with your present mate. What do you intend to do about Rose?"

Sinjin got up and began pacing the rug. "Damn her to hell, what do I care how anything sits with *her* anymore? She can go hang for all I care."

"It's true, the woman's used you badly. Ought to be scalped. But her trickery doesn't change the fact that you and she are still married."

"What's that to me?" he cried. "If it weren't for her damnable schemes we wouldn't *be* married!"

"She's done you a fierce wrong, there's no doubt of that, but two wrongs never make a right."

"Are you saying it's wrong for Rora and me to want to be happy together?"

Rachel shook her head. "Dearest boy, I pray with all my heart that you shall be happy. But I ask you to take careful thought of this situation. You could be trading misery for more misery, and that's a fact."

"Don't say that," he implored. "It's not like that at all."

"Last time we talked, you and I, you said she wouldn't cock a snoot at you, and now, how great a change is here, I do declare! Are you some Merlin, then, who's put a spell on her? Some Puck squeezing magic flower juice in her eye to make her love you?"

"I said it's not like that. We just love each other, that's all. I'm going to divorce Rose and then Rora and I can be married. It'll be all legal and neat, just the way you want."

"The way *I* want?" she echoed. "Good heavens, man, have you forgot the last time you proposed to the creature and she sent you off to sea with your anchor rope dragging? Was going to be a nun, that was the thing. And this time—" She flung her hands at the ceiling. "Mad! The man's mad!"

"Don't say that."

"It must be true, else how could you be behaving like such a zany? Besides, I ask you, do you imagine for a minute that that sweet wife of yours is just going to up and give you what you ask? Do you think she'll take warmly to your claims to happiness, that, being Rose, she'll put up with your running off and leaving her in the lurch?"

"She'll have to, damn it! She'll just have to."

"No she won't, Dick. She doesn't have to do anything but sit tight and let you go to the dogs. *Divorce?* Why, she'd let herself be branded and shot before she'd do it. There's one thing in all this to remember: your wife is a *Grimes* now. You made her that when you married her. A woman's not worth a heifer in the eyes of most men, but in the eyes of the law she does have some rights. Even if she's of darky blood, she hitched herself to a white man."

"But she lied! She tricked me!"

"A court won't take that into account. She's got a certificate of marriage. Don't matter how she came by it, it's all legal, and I promise you, Dick Grimes, she won't let go till doomsday. Now chew on that for your supper!"

"But *something* must be done! I'll pay her off."

Rachel barked a disheartening laugh. "With what? Your every penny's tied up in the *Hattie D.*"

He flung himself on his knees beside her chair, pleading passionately. "But you could do it, Grammaw. *You* could! You've enough to—to—"

"Oh, listen to him. Make her take the bait and swallow the hook, is that what you're saying? I'm to dangle *my* cash under her nose? Go a-wheedling and a-begging of her?"

"Damn it, Grammaw, she cheated me! She's put a knife through my heart, and all because I tried to do the decent thing. Christ, why am I such a fool?"

"Why is the air blue?" she muttered to no one, turning the rings on her finger. Her forehead wrinkled with thought. "Ah, Dick . . ." She sighed deeply. "I'm an old woman, and I've loved you strong and true. You weren't really my kin, not one iota, but I cared for you like you were my own flesh. It's not easy loving a fellow like you, Dick, and many's the time I wished I could put quietus to it, it was so painful. There's a raging devil in you that'll be your death some day." She took his face in her withered hands and looked anxiously into his eyes. "You've done wicked things in your life, Dick. You've done things to curl a body's hair. Even done murder, they say, and if it's so you'll have a deal to answer to at the day of judgment." He kept silent, answering neither aye nor nay as she went on. "But there's something shining in you, Dick, a little light deep down in the dark soul of you, and I pray that one day it will flame up. I've never been very observant in my relations with the Deity, not formally, but I keep Him here"—she tapped her flattened breast. "God's in you somewhere too, Dick, if you'd only listen to His voice."

"I do listen, Grammaw, but I don't hear any god, just my own voice, telling me how to get on. Listen, if Georgie were here, she'd tell you—"

"Yes, Georgie . . ." she said. "She's worth a hundred weight of the other, you know. Sets a goodly store by you, too, always has."

"Migosh, Grammaw, she's just married and you talk as if—as if—"

"Let it pass." She glanced at the clock, the constant watcher and warder of her days, and pondered matters yet a while. "See here, Dick," she said finally, "I'm not so rigid as all that. And your old granny's of a mind to bargain with you, if you'll but bargain a little with her."

He was instantly all hope, all eagerness, and imprudently missing the change in tone and tack. "All right, that's what I want to hear. Anything, Grammaw, just say. I'll do whatever you want, if you'll just do this one thing for me."

He got a smile out of her. "There's my Dick, my lamb," she said, gentle and sweet again. "I shall do just as you ask. I'll use the money that would have gone to you when I'm dead. Then I can at least know you're made happy from it. But—"

"Oh, thank you, Grammaw, thank you!" he cried, cutting her off. "You'll never regret it!"

"*But.* Did you hear me, Dick, I said 'But.' You'll not get off so easy. A bargain, I said, remember?"

He nodded eagerly. "Yes, I do. Go on, then, what is it? Something about the ship, I wonder?"

"That vessel is yours, free and clear. There'll be no disputing over her helm when I'm gone. No, Sonny, it's not her I'm thinking of, but another 'her.' You know of whom I speak. And if I agree to do as you ask and draw Rose's teeth, then you must do as *I* ask and show the Talcott woman a fleet pair of heels. You must wait a piece before you put any more of these 'plans' into motion."

He sat frozen in his chair. *"What? Wait?"*

"That was my word. You must promise to wait until you return from China before—"

"No!" he burst out. "I won't. I can't! I'm taking her with me. It's all planned. When I get the divorce we'll be married."

"Then, my dear, you shall never get your divorce, because I shan't go to Rose on your behalf. So let's forget everything."

"No-o!" he roared like a wounded ox. "You can't mean it!"

"I do. I won't get you out of the frying pan only to see you leap into the fire. And I won't be made party to a farce. I have my dignity."

"Why do you call it a farce?"

"Because that's what it is, or soon will be. She'll make a fool of you, again, that hoity-toity enchantress, mark my words. Only this time it won't be the Holy Virgin and a wimple, either, it will be something else just as diabolical. But she'll lead you by your nose, she will."

He pulled away, blazing with resentment. "You've always hated her, haven't you? Right from the start! You never wanted us to be together, never wanted us to be happy. All you care about is making me do whatever you want. Be at your beck and jump the minute you snap your fingers. But not this time! No ma'am, not this time! I won't do it and you can't make me!"

Rachel folded her dessicated fingers in her lap. "Sonny, I have no intention of making you do anything," she said, choosing her words. "I have merely proposed a bargain—a business proposition, if you will—that is all. And since you give me to understand that my suggestion is not to your liking, let's end our discussion. It's very simple, really, I shall keep my money and you shall keep your wife. Perhaps that will be best in the end." She used her cane to get to her feet. "Now go along, Sonny. I want my bed before I take a chill. *Joseph!* Forget supper. Captain's leaving!" She gave him a push. "Hustle now. There's an end to our affairs."

He stared, disbelieving. Was it indeed to end like this? Was she going to dispatch him like a naughty schoolboy? No! No, by God, not like this! He knew what to do. He'd make her sorry, she'd rue the day she tried to read the riot act to him. She'd come crawling to him, she'd beg him to come back, she'd—

Oh God!

He flung himself at her again, clutching her hand and pressing it to his cheek. "Please, Grammaw, try to understand. I love her!"

He pleaded with all the passion in him; these might be the most important words he would ever say to her, for she could be his savior, *must be!* Here in the musty room with the lamplight on the carpet and the blue snowflakes beyond the window, time was so short; he must convince her or it would be too late. He couldn't leave without her solemn promise to handle the situation with Rose, for without that all was lost, their plans would all be knocked into a cocked hat.

His voice cracked, and the violence of his tone made her draw back. Her hooded eyes searched the blazing light in his, seeking truth. She sank back into her chair, leaving him her hand to hold.

"Is it true, then?" she asked in a pained voice. "You truly love her? Do you, Dick?"

"Yes, Grammaw! I do! I love her so much! Much more than anyone knows. She is the other half of me. She is all my dreams, all my hopes, everything. The first time I ever saw her she stirred my heart, and I have never once drawn a happy or a calm breath out of her sight or hearing." He moved closer to her. "Grammaw, listen—she is the source of my greatest—my *only* joy, and of my deepest despair. For I do despair—to lose her. I can't! Not again! I mustn't!" In the uncontrollable sweep of his passion he began to weep, and his tears fell on her hand. "She is everything to me! She is all of heaven I shall ever know, and all of hell as well."

She winced and shook her head. "Oh, Dick, please, I don't like to hear you talk so. It can't be good, to love someone with such a wildness—"

"But I must! Don't you see? I *have* to!" He rushed on, hot and heedless, choking on his words. "You've got to understand, Grammaw. Listen to me now." The index finger he put up before her trembled. "I want you to answer me one question, but you must promise to answer it truthfully."

"Yes?" She dropped her gaze, feeling some embarrassment. "And what is it, this question you wish to ask?"

He knelt and lifted his blotched eyes to hers, clutching her hand as if to let it go were to end his life. "Grammaw—you once loved someone. You loved a man—very much. Isn't that true?"

She looked away. "What have old dead loves to do with this matter?"

"They do, believe me. Say, please say."

She drew a breath and expelled it wearily. "Yes. It's true."

"Yes, of course. Now—wasn't this man—a Talcott?"

Her voice was utterly weary. "Yes. He was."

"And *is*. Bob Talcott. Isn't it so? You were in love with Old Bobby Talcott."

She tried to wave him off. "Please, Dick, don't—not now. I'm very tired. Leave me in peace, won't you?"

"I want you to answer. I need you to. You did love him."

"Yes, I loved him."

"But you didn't marry him."

"No," she said shortly.

"But why, Grammaw? Why, if you loved him?"

"People do not always marry for love."

"Yes, but tell me, please—I want to know all about it, you and Bobby."

"It was such a long time ago."

"But not so long ago that you don't remember."

"No, not that long ago." She stroked her chin and her voice was dry and papery. He could smell the familiar odor of the sachet she put among her clothes, that "grandmother" scent.

She had sworn to go to her grave with the secret of her shame, but despite that vow she now found herself telling him of things that had lain buried deep inside her. She unlocked her heart of its sorrows and laid them all before him.

"Odd . . . It was down there," she said, glancing out the window, making a halfhearted gesture toward the glass, and her voice climbed in wonder and amazement. "Down there at Grimes Mill. Fancy that."

"What was? That you and he met?"

She nodded and told him her story.

"In those days my father used to come here to Two Stone every few summers—he had business with Cyprian, Abednego's father. One year I came with him. We put up at the old Cumberland Inn at Stepney Parish, I remember. It was early summer, and General Washington had just arrived, he and the Count of Rochambeau. Oh, what a time that was!" Her ancient eyes sprang to life as she recalled the event, the whole village done up for a fete, flags and banners and ribbons everywhere, people thronging the streets as during holiday time, the flash of musketry, the uniformed soldiers with their crossed straps and white leggings and tricorne hats, the rattle of sabers, the roll of drums, the fifes and flutes, the trumpets and horns. What luck to have arrived just at that time.

Then had come the French, she said, marching over from Newport where their frigates lay at anchor. It was like one great party, but because my father had important business I was left on my own a good deal of the time.

"Unchaperoned, too," she pointed out with a wry touch of humor.

And in that time of gaiety and fun, with dancing in the streets and hugs and kisses behind the coop, while she had been a modest maiden, there came the time of love and she gave her heart away.

"Flung it away, I ought to say," she went on, nodding at the memory. "It fell out that with my father busy I had myself a look about the countryside. There was the mill, I knew of it, but I'd never investigated it; now I did.

"At that time it was not in operation; the old miller had died of an injury and a new one hadn't been found, so there was no one on the place. I had a pony cart and I drove over the branch road and pulled up just there where you were this evening. What a pretty spot it was in those days, and what hard times have fallen upon it. Tom Ross." She shivered, then went on.

"I was charmed by the millpond and went for a closer look. I heard some splashing, and as I neared the mill I saw someone in the water, thrashing about. I crept closer but didn't reveal myself. Presently the swimmer made his way to the dam and hauled himself up and stretched out along the stones to dry in the sun."

"Naked, was he?"

"What young men go clothed swimming in millponds?" She smiled. "He didn't know he was being watched. When the sun had dried him he put on his clothes and went over to the bank where he lay down in some shade and took up a book. Something possessed me, and I crept closer, watching him through the bullrushes. He was reading, his mind was occupied, but then he looked up suddenly and saw me spying."

"Did you run away?"

"I'm ashamed to say I did not. No, I am *not* ashamed to say it. I stood there while he ran around the pond and came up to me. I looked into his eyes, eyes of such a blue, so warm and sparkling and I saw—"

"—Old Bobby Talcott."

"Yes. But *young,* remember. He was reading *La Nouvelle Héloïse.* Such a sad story, but very beautiful, and we fancied ourselves Julie and Saint-Preux, though with a very different ending."

She was a good storyteller, a good romancer, and why not, since it was her own romance she was telling? The summer was at its zenith. Ceres and her sickle roamed languidly amid the golden sheaves. The very sultriness of the weather, the buzz of the honeybees in the yellow sunlight, the lap of the water in the millpond where the green ducks paddled among the rushes, the plash of the spill over the dam, and overhead the broad blue Connecticut sky—such was the country world when you were in love and a man would have his way with a maid.

"Why didn't you and he marry, Grammaw?" he asked.

"We did talk of it. And one evening, Bob drove to the tavern and picked me up. We went in his trap to the Middletown Fair, for the harvest was in there. It was a wonderful fair. I never had so good a time. He bought me this—" Her swollen fingers touched the brooch at her throat. "That night he spoke to me of marriage. He was eager, he wanted it, he begged me to run away—"

"Run away?"

She nodded. "Yes, to elope. It seemed—precipitous, to me. No matter how we felt, how could I so flagrantly defy my father? Nor would his family be pleased. I was eighteen, of marriageable age, but he was two years younger, a stripling really, though fully grown. I couldn't say yes, but I couldn't say no, either. It was a dilemma. The worst of my life. We returned to Stepney, feeling we'd pulled a smooth trick enjoying the fair and being seen by no one. But we were wrong. We'd been noticed by some of the Two Stone harvesters. The cat was out of the bag, and there was talk. Father flew into a rage, as did old Cyprian Grimes, who wanted to have Bob killed for 'trifling' with the daughter of a friend of his. It was far from trifling, I promise you."

"Sounds like me and Priam."

"Very much, I should think."

"What happened then?"

"Bob went off to war, while I was sent home in disgrace. But I had pledged my love to Bob, and vowed that when he returned we would be wed. Meanwhile, there would be no other, not for me—" She stopped, then resumed. "But when he came back, he was betrothed to Miss Vicky— Victoria Fairfax, you see. And when I returned to Pequot Landing it was in middle age, and married after all to Abednego Grimes, who was by then widowed. And not a day has passed when I haven't thought of Bob. He brought Abednego's body home to me, you know. He's a great gentleman, a great, great gentleman, Bobby Talcott. And of course he picked the right bride—Victoria Fairfax, *she* was the girl for him."

She sighed. Her eyes were tired and red. They filled and overflowed, glistening in the light.

"Oh dear!" she exclaimed. "My eyes—my eyes—"

"Grammaw, what is it?" He searched everywhere for the source of her discomfort.

"I mustn't weep. It hurts. The tears—they burn me, blind me. Oh—oh—"

He became alarmed; she was suffering acute pain. Her eyes were flooded, the fluid leaked down her cheeks.

He pulled out his handkerchief. "Take this."

"Oh, Dick, thank you. I fear I'm a terrible trial to you."

"No. No, you're not. Honestly, you're *not.*"

She dabbed at her eyes, delicately, meticulously. The candle burning in the pewter holder deep-etched her lines and wrinkles. Presently she returned his handkerchief. "I'm beholden," she said primly.

"It's all right. But Grammaw—listen," he rushed on, forgetting her sore eyes. "If you loved Old Bobby—God bless his soul—then surely you must have some idea—can't you understand? About Rora and me?"

"Of course I understand, Dick."

"Then you mustn't ask me to give her up. You can't deny me!" He drew closer to her, speaking urgently. "Grammaw, help me, in the name of God, help me. I love her. I'll go mad without her. But you can save us, save us both! Don't ask me to leave her behind—not again. If I lose her this time there won't be another, I know it. It doesn't matter what it costs. You can fix it, I know you can."

She sighed again, and her eyelids fluttered delicately. "Ah, Dick, hear me. I'm not a conjuror, I'm only your old lady grammaw. But my heart aches for you, to see you so unhappy."

"Then make me happy! Please? Please!"

She pushed back against her chair and stretched the cords of her neck. Her smile was faint and wistful. "Ah well . . . I cannot deny you. You know that. You've always known it."

"Then you'll do it?"

"I don't like it, but for your sake I'll do it. I'll try, that is."

He sank back on his heels with relief. "Oh Grammaw, thank you—thank you!" He was covering her hand with kisses, stretching to reach her cheek and neck.

"Careful, I'm an old lady, you'll break me in two," she said.

He jumped up and righted his jacket. "You'll never be sorry, Grammaw, I promise. You'll be proud of me yet, you'll see. You'll never have cause for regret."

"I pray you may be right," she said, almost to herself. "And, Dick, let *you* not have cause for regret. Let you not find that you have made another mistake among so many."

"I won't, Grammaw. I won't! You'll see." He was sighing with pleasure and relief. He had won! Had *won!* "Everything's going to be all right," he said. "I knew you'd do it. I told Rora—" He caught himself. "That is, I said—I hoped you would."

"Rose won't come cheap, I promise you that."

"It doesn't matter. Not to me."

"No, of course not, since it's not *your* money I'll be spending, but my own."

"But you've always said you were going to leave it to me, didn't you say that?"

"So I did, I suppose."

"You will go to her, talk to her, make her sign a paper, won't you? It's terribly important, you know—"

"Yes, I can see how important it is. Never fear, I'll disembarrass you of this wife, even though I fear you'll be greatly embarrassed by the taking of this other one. But all's well that ends well, I say. Come, then, give me a last kiss and go along. You've much to do, I've no doubt. Help me up."

He assisted her to her feet and braced her in his arms, kissing her forehead, cheeks, the withered lips. How frail she was.

"All right, let me go," she said. "I'm not your play poppet. You've another one for that sort of thing."

"Grammaw—I believe you're jealous!"

She bristled and batted at his hands. " 'Course I am! Do you think I want to see another hussy get her hooks into you? And now, since our humble fare has failed to please your palate and since I have lost my appetite for food altogether, you must excuse me. Joseph, move smartly! The captain's leaving."

Joseph hurried through the kitchen door to order Sinjin's cutter brought round, while Mary helped him on with his things. His parting from his grandmother was tender and affectionate. He was the dutiful grandson. He had come to plead for her help and understanding, and she had not failed him. Tomorrow—she would settle matters.

"You promise?"

"I had better. I may not be here when you come back."

"You will, of course you will."

"Yes, of course." She spoke softly, a breath of sound. "Just know my heart goes with you, and that in the end . . ." She trailed off, her head nodding.

"Yes, Grammaw? In the end?"

She perked up. "In the end all will come right for you. It will. It must. I'm certain of it."

He looked into her eyes. "Why so certain, Granny?"

"Because you're not a man to go down in defeat. I know you're not. When you're felled, you rise up again. You've a hard head. That's the trick in life, at all costs one must survive. Georgie Ross—no, we must say Talcott now, Georgie Talcott—"

"What about her, Grammaw?"

"She's a survivor. She'll do well as Apple's wife. Though in time past I had hoped otherwise for her."

"Hoped how?"

"Hoped that you and she—Georgie and *you*—You take my meaning."

He was flabbergasted. "But Grammaw, that's crazy. What are you saying? Georgiana Talcott and I—we're—we're friends, that's all. Just friends. She *understands.*"

"Oh, certainly." She laughed. "I know she does. *She* understands you better than anyone. It was Georgie who said it best . . ."

"What did she say?"

"She said, 'Sinjin Grimes can set any ship to his desire, set any helm to his course, and bend any wind to his will.' And so you can, so you will. Believe it, Sonny, won't you?"

"I do, Grammaw. I believe in myself. With *her* by my side. I know who I am and what I want and how to get it. I really do. You'll see."

One last kiss and he was out the door, hurrying through the flurries to his cutter. She shut the door against the cold and watched through the window as he drove away.

SHORTLY after ten the yellow coach of Old Bobby Talcott traveled that way, toiling ponderously up one side of Burning Bush Hill and down the other, brakes groaning, chains biting, rolling past the branch road and the ruined mill, the team stretching out along the straightaway of the Old Two Stone Road, rounding the foot of Lamentation Mountain, where Abednego Grimes had breathed his last, on to Still, and from Still to Southing, then to Meriden, New Haven, and points south. For the coach's two occupants, lapped in the intimacies of love, it was much the same as that night of happy memory, when another coach had carried them off into a dark night on a similar adventure. Then they had been young and love's flame had burned bright, and as they had on that night they did on this, made love among the cushions and the furry pelts as the great wheels' iron-rimmed fellies turned back the miles and the smoking horses forged ahead.

With the passing of the coach, the wheel tracks along Greenshadow Road began to fill with snow, for no other traffic was to be seen along the way that night, and in the still and silent dark the snowfall grew heavier, sifting white and downy out of the sky, forming ice blue caps atop the village chimneys, along the window sills and across the wooden porch railings, silting up the crotches of tree branches and crowning the dark spires of the hemlocks.

The snow continued falling until well after midnight. Rachel Grimes was fast asleep by then, but beyond her windowpane, all around and about, the world lay hushed and still. Presently the clouds parted and the moon came out, shedding its silvery beams over the snowy fields and rooftops, and with it, the stars in their infinite multitudes twinkled away in the frosty sky, diamonds flung on velvet. And among all the stars, one in particular gleaming more brightly than all the rest shone on the lovers as it had those many years before, Stella Maris, the Ocean Star, illuminating the village sheltered among the frozen hills, emphasizing how truly small a place like Pequot Landing was and how vast the universe, and how little the plots and plans of humans mattered in the face of God's more vast and purer plans for His children. It really was a lovely sight; except who was there to see it when all the world slumbered so peacefully?

A NOTE ABOUT THE AUTHOR

After a notable career as an actor on the stage, in television, and in films, climaxed by his award-winning performance in *The Cardinal,* Thomas Tryon retired from acting to concentrate on writing. His first novel, *The Other,* published in 1971, became a huge best-seller (and a movie), and is now taught in high schools and colleges across the country. Six other books followed: *Harvest Home, Lady, Crowned Heads, All That Glitters, The Night of the Moonbow,* and *The Wings of the Morning.* His novel for children, *The Adventures of Opal and Cupid,* will be published in 1992 by Viking.

Thomas Tryon died in September 1991.

In the Fire of Spring
is the second in a sequence of historical novels called *Kingdom Come.*

A NOTE ON THE TYPE

The text of this book was set in a digitized version of Bembo, a well-known Monotype face. Named for Pietro Bembo, the celebrated Renaissance writer and humanist scholar who was made a cardinal and served as secretary to Pope Leo X, the original cutting of Bembo was made by Francesco Griffo of Bologna only a few years after Columbus discovered America.

Sturdy, well balanced, and finely proportioned, Bembo is a face of rare beauty, extremely legible in all of its sizes.

Composed by ComCom, a division of The Haddon Craftsmen, Inc.,
Allentown, Pennsylvania
Printed and bound by R. R. Donnelley & Sons,
Harrisonburg, Virginia
Typography and binding design by Virginia Tan